THE YEAR'S BEST SCIENCE FICTION & FANTASY

2018 EDITION

OTHER BOOKS BY

RICH HORTON

THE YEAR'S BEST SCIENCE FICTION & FANTASY

2018 EDITION

EDITED BY

RICH HORTON

PRIME BOOKS

THE YEAR'S BEST SCIENCE FICTION
& FANTASY, 2018 EDITION

Prime Books
www.prime-books.com

ISBN: 978-1-60701-526-0

In memoriam
Gardner Dozois.

CONTENTS

CONTENTS

THE WORLD AND WORLDS OF SCIENCE FICTION & FANTASY, 2017

RICH HORTON

The State of the Art

It's trite to say it these days, but it's still very true: the world of science fiction (emphasis on "world") is more diverse than ever in terms of nationality, ethnicity, and gender, reflected not just in the authors but in the characters they write about. Of course, none of that really matters if the stories aren't excellent as well, and that's what we see here. Sometimes this diversity is presented as important in that it means a wide variety of voice are given the opportunity to be heard—and that's important of course. But that's not the key, I think. The key point is that we readers have the opportunity to hear a wide variety of voices. Isn't that central to science fiction anyway? Aren't science fiction and fantasy centrally about difference—a celebration of change, of color, of difference? Of course, even those words are othering—what is different to me is familiar to you. Science fiction and fantasy remind us, then, that the world—the worlds!—are gloriously different.

One source of originality is new voices, and thus I am excited every to see new writers producing excellent work. This year, to see people like SL Huang, Madeline Ray, Ryan Row, Jamie Wahls, J.R. Dawson, Giovanni De Feo, Hanuš Seiner, and Vina Jie-Min Prasad represented with truly original, and profoundly varied, stories is really cool. I hadn't heard of any of those folks until I read their stories. (They're not the only writers new to the book here—it's exciting as well to welcome the great Samuel R. Delany to these pages, and likewise Kathleen Ann Goonan and Nina Kiriki Hoffman, as well as writers whose careers fit somewhere in between those examples: Minsoo Kang, Lettie Prell, and Matthew Kressel.

But one of the reasons I choose stories by some writers over and over again is that they are always fresh. What story this year is stranger than C.S.E. Cooney's "Though She Be But Little"? Likewise, Robert Reed has appeared in these books more often than any writer, but every story is challenging and thoughtful. I was thrilled to publish exceptional story after exceptional story by Yoon Ha Lee before he produced a novel—and his novels are as exotic and different as his stories, so to be able to feature a remarkable story about one of the main character in Lee's first two novels is a delight. And so with all the repeat authors this year.

In this space I usually try to sum up the state of the field by looking at changes at the major short fiction outlets, but this year I don't feel there's a whole lot of real interest to say—the state of short fiction in both print and online venues stayed pretty stable in 2017. As for novels, we did see a similar mix of new writers and established writers producing excellent work. Annalee Newitz, who has appeared in these pages, published an exceptional first science fiction novel, **Autonomous**; and Theodora Goss, who has appeared here several times, published a wonderful first fantasy novel, **The Strange Case of the Alchemist's Daughter**. Besides those, I'll mention three more truly exceptional novels: **Spoonbenders**, by Daryl Gregory, **The Moon and the Other**, by John Kessel, and **Ka: Dar Oakley in the Land of Ymir**, by the great John Crowley.

Finally, in speaking of the state of the field, I must proceed to sadder news. Earlier this year we lost two titans, Ursula K. Le Guin and Gardner Dozois. Le Guin was one of the very greatest writers of our time, in or out of the field. (She was regularly mentioned as a potential Nobel Prize winner.) We were fortunate to be able to reprint her story "Elementals" a few years ago in this series. Gardner Dozois was a first-rate writer as well, particularly at short lengths, and a magnificent editor, best known for his time at *Asimov's Science Fiction*, and for the thirty-five volumes of his **Year's Best Science Fiction**, a major point of inspiration for me in editing these books.

As I wrote about Le Guin at the time of her death: I can still easily call up in my mind the cover of **The Dispossessed**, in front of me on the cafeteria table at Naperville Central High School some time in 1975, as I read it during lunch hour. **Malafrena** was a gift from a friend—I read it eagerly, and loved it—it's a young person's book, I think, an ardent book—I understand it was her earliest written novel to see publication, and that shows, but it is still one of my favorites. And her last novel, **Lavinia**, from 2008, is also one of my favorites, a beautifully written and moving and involving story of the wife of Aeneas.

Her prose was truly elegant, truly lovely. Her speculation was rigorous and honest and fruitful in itself. Even from the earliest she was striking—the story "Semley's Necklace" (the opening segment of **Rocannon's World**, her first published novel) is heartbreaking and powerful. And her first story in an science fiction magazine, "April in Paris", is sweet and lovely and romantic . . . I don't know how it was received at the time but to me in retrospect it seems an announcement: "This is special. This is a Writer."

So many of her short stories are special to me . . . "Winter's King", "Nine Lives", "The Stars Below", "Another Story", "Imaginary Countries", the Yeowe/Werel stories, all the fables of **Changing Planes**.

I am an emotional reader at times (aren't most of us?), and one thing Le Guin could do, repeatedly, was bring me to tears—tears of awe and wonder, tears of sadness, tears of love. I leave with some of my favorite quotes:

"Kaph looked at him and saw the thing he had never seen before, saw him: Owen Pugh, the other, the stranger who held his hand out in the dark." (I tear up just typing this.)

"Stars and gatherings of stars, depth below depth without end, the light."

"But all this happened a long time ago, nearly forty years ago; I do not know if it happens now, even in imaginary countries."

And, of course, from **The Dispossessed**: "True journey is return."

As for Gardner Dozois, who was closer to me in a personal sense—I was really shaken by the news of his passing. He was one of the greatest editors in the field's history (an argument can be made—and I've made it—that he ranks at the top); and he was also a very significant science fiction writer. His writing should not be forgotten—stories like "Strangers", "A Special Kind of Morning", "A Dream at Noonday", "The Visible Man", "Horse of Air", "A Kingdom by the Sea", "Chains of the Sea", his Nebula winners "The Peacemaker" and "Morning Child", his excellent later story "A Knight of Ghosts and Shadows" and many others are exceptionally written, imaginatively powerful, very moving—truly an oeuvre, at shorter lengths, to stand with the best writers of his generation.

In a more personal sense, he was an important influence on me, and indeed something of a mentor. He was generous in treating me as an equal (I was not), and in happily discussing the state of the field with me at the drop of a hat. He was wonderful company, a true *bon vivant*, as somebody said always ready raise the spirit of a gathering and to lower its tone. He was one of those in the field I could call a friend, and I'm proud to have known him.

We who produce these similar books, the best of the year volumes, never regarded ourselves as rivals. Our books are paragraphs in a long conversation about science fiction. I talked with Gardner about science fiction for years, in different ways—face to face; or on message boards, discussing our different ideas about who should have won the Hugo in 1973 or whenever; month by month in our columns in *Locus*; or in the tables of contents of these books, each of us proposing lists of the best stories each year. I always looked eagerly for Gardner's "list", and his stories for me represented a different and completely interesting angle on what really mattered each year.

I already miss that voice.

PUBLISHER'S NOTE: Due to space considerations in the print edition the following sections: "About the Authors" and "Recommended Reading" have been posted to the Prime Books website. Both are included in the ebook edition, however.

EXTRACURRICULAR ACTIVITIES

YOON HA LEE

—◆—

For Sonya Taaffe

When Shuos Jedao walked into his temporary quarters on Station Muru 5 and spotted the box, he assumed someone was attempting to assassinate him. It had happened before. Considering his first career, there was even a certain justice to it.

He ducked back around the doorway, although even with his reflexes, he would have been too late if it'd been a proper bomb. The air currents in the room would have wafted his biochemical signature to the box and caused it to trigger. Or someone could have set up the bomb to go off as soon as the door opened, regardless of who stepped in. Or something even less sophisticated.

Jedao retreated back down the hallway and waited one minute. Two. Nothing.

It could just be a package, he thought—paperwork that he had forgotten?— but old habits died hard.

He entered again and approached the desk, light-footed. The box, made of eye-searing green plastic, stood out against the bland earth tones of the walls and desk. It measured approximately half a meter in all directions. Its nearest face prominently displayed the gold seal that indicated that station security had cleared it. He didn't trust it for a moment. Spoofing a seal wasn't that difficult. He'd done it himself.

He inspected the box's other visible sides without touching it, then spotted a letter pouch affixed to one side and froze. He recognized the handwriting. The address was written in spidery high language, while the name of the recipient—one Garach Jedao Shkan—was written both in the high language and his birth tongue, Shparoi, for good measure.

Oh, Mom, Jedao thought. No one else called him by that name anymore, not even the rest of his family. More important, how had his mother gotten his address? He'd just received his transfer orders last week, and he hadn't written home about it because his mission was classified. He had no idea what his new general wanted him to do; she would tell him tomorrow morning when he reported in.

Jedao opened the box, which released a puff of cold air. Inside rested a tub labeled KEEP REFRIGERATED in both the high language and Shparoi. The tub itself contained a pale, waxy-looking solid substance. *Is this what I think it is?*

Time for the letter:

> *Hello, Jedao!*
> *Congratulations on your promotion. I hope you enjoy your new command moth and that it has a more pronounceable name than the last one.*

One: What promotion? Did she know something he didn't? (Scratch that question. She always knew something he didn't.) Two: Trust his mother to rate warmoths not by their armaments or the efficacy of their stardrives but by their *names*. Then again, she'd made no secret that she'd hoped he'd wind up a musician like his sire. It had not helped when he pointed out that when he attempted to sing in academy, his fellow cadets had threatened to dump grapefruit soup over his head.

> *Since I expect your eating options will be dismal, I have sent you goose fat rendered from the great-great-great-etc.-grandgosling of your pet goose when you were a child. (She was delicious, by the way.) Let me know if you run out and I'll send more.*
>
> *Love,*
> *Mom*

So the tub contained goose fat, after all. Jedao had never figured out why his mother sent food items when her idea of cooking was to gussy up instant noodles with an egg and some chopped green onions. All the cooking Jedao knew, he had learned either from his older brother or, on occasion, those of his mother's research assistants who took pity on her kids.

What am I supposed to do with this? he wondered. As a cadet he could have based a prank around it. But as a warmoth commander he had standards to uphold.

More importantly, how could he compose a suitably filial letter of appreciation without, foxes forbid, encouraging her to escalate? (Baked goods: fine. Goose fat: less fine.) Especially when she wasn't supposed to know he was here in the first place? Some people's families sent them care packages of useful things, like liquor, pornography, or really nice cosmetics. Just his luck.

At least the mission gave him an excuse to delay writing back until his location was unclassified, even if she knew it anyway.

Jedao had heard a number of rumors about his new commanding officer, Brigadier General Kel Essier. Some of them, like the ones about her junior wife's lovers, were none of his business. Others, like Essier's taste in plum wine, weren't relevant, but could come in handy if he needed to scare up a bribe someday. What had really caught his notice was her service record. She had fewer decorations than anyone else who'd served at her rank for a comparable period of time.

Either Essier was a political appointee—the Kel military denied the practice, but everyone knew better—or she was sitting on a cache of classified medals. Jedao had a number of those himself. (Did his mother know about those too?) Although Station Muru 5 was a secondary military base, Jedao had his suspicions about any "secondary" base that had a general in residence, even temporarily. That, or Essier was disgraced and Kel Command couldn't think of anywhere else to dump her.

Jedao had a standard method for dealing with new commanders, which was to research them as if he planned to assassinate them. Needless to say, he never expressed it in those terms to his comrades.

He'd come up with two promising ways to get rid of Essier. First, she collected meditation foci made of staggeringly luxurious materials. One of her officers had let slip that her latest obsession was antique lacquerware. Planting a bomb or toxin in a collector-grade item wouldn't be risky so much as *expensive*. He'd spent a couple hours last night brainstorming ways to steal one, just for the hell of it; lucky that he didn't have to follow through.

The other method took advantage of the poorly planned location of the firing range on this level relative to the general's office, and involved shooting her through several walls and a door with a high-powered rifle and burrower ammunition. Jedao hated burrower ammunition, not because it didn't work but because it did. He had a lot of ugly scars on his torso from the time a burrower had almost killed him. That being said, he also believed in using the appropriate tool for the job.

No one had upgraded Muru 5 for the past few decades. Its computer grid ran on outdated hardware, making it easy for him to pull copies of all the maps he pleased. He'd also hacked into the security cameras long enough to check the layout of the general's office. The setup made him despair of the architects who had designed the whole wretched thing. On top of that, Essier had set up her desk so a visitor would see it framed beautifully by the doorway, with her chair perfectly centered. Great for impressing visitors, less great for making yourself a difficult target. Then again, attending to Essier's safety wasn't his job.

Jedao showed up at Essier's office seven minutes before the appointed time. "Whiskey?" said her aide.

If only, Jedao thought; he recognized it as one he couldn't afford. "No, thank you," he said with the appropriate amount of regret. He didn't trust special treatment.

"Your loss," said the aide. After another two minutes, she checked her slate. "Go on in. The general is waiting for you."

As Jedao had predicted, General Essier sat dead center behind her desk, framed by the doorway and two statuettes on either side of the desk, gilded ash-hawks carved from onyx. Essier had dark skin and close-shaven hair, and the height and fine-spun bones of someone who had grown up in low gravity. The black-and-gold Kel uniform suited her. Her gloved hands rested on the desk in perfect symmetry. Jedao bet she looked great in propaganda videos.

Jedao saluted, fist to shoulder. "Commander Shuos Jedao reporting as ordered, sir."

"Have a seat," Essier said. He did. "You're wondering why you don't have a warmoth assignment yet."

"The thought had crossed my mind, yes."

Essier smiled. The smile was like the rest of her: beautiful and calculated and not a little deadly. "I have good news and bad news for you, Commander. The good news is that you're due a promotion."

Jedao's first reaction was not gratitude or pride, but *How did my mother—?* Fortunately, a lifetime of *How did my mother—?* enabled him to keep his expression smooth and instead say, "And the bad news?"

"Is it true what they say about your battle record?"

This always came up. "You have my profile."

"You're good at winning."

"I wasn't under the impression that the Kel military found this objectionable, sir."

"Quite right," she said. "The situation is this. I have a mission in mind for you, but it will take advantage of your unique background."

"Unique background" was a euphemism for *We don't have many commanders who can double as emergency special forces.* Most Kel with training in special ops stayed in the infantry instead of seeking command in the space forces. Jedao made an inquiring noise.

"Perform well, and you'll be given the fangmoth *Sieve of Glass*, which heads my third tactical group."

A bribe, albeit one that might cause trouble. Essier had six tactical groups.

A newly minted group tactical commander being assigned third instead of sixth? Had she had a problem with her former third-position commander?

"My former third took early retirement," Essier said in answer to his unspoken question. "They were caught with a small collection of trophies."

"Let me guess," Jedao said. "Trophies taken from heretics."

"Just so. Third tactical is badly shaken. Fourth has excellent rapport with her group and I don't want to promote her out of it. But it's an opportunity for you."

"And the mission?"

Essier leaned back. "You attended Shuos Academy with Shuos Meng."

"I did," Jedao said. They'd gone by Zhei Meng as a cadet. "We've been in touch on and off." Meng had joined a marriage some years back. Jedao had commissioned a painting of five foxes, one for each person in the marriage, and sent it along with his best wishes. Meng wrote regularly about their kids—they couldn't be made to shut up about them—and Jedao sent gifts on cue, everything from hand-bound volumes of Kel jokes to fancy gardening tools. (At least they'd been sold to him as gardening tools. They looked suspiciously like they could double for heavy-duty surgical work.) "Why, what has Meng been up to?"

"Under the name Ahun Gerav, they've been in command of the merchanter *Moonsweet Blossom*."

Jedao cocked an eyebrow at Essier. "That's not a Shuos vessel." It did, however, sound like an Andan one. The Andan faction liked naming their trademoths after flowers. "By 'merchanter' do you mean 'spy'?"

"Yes," Essier said with charming directness. "Twenty-six days ago, one of the *Blossom*'s crew sent a code red to Shuos Intelligence. This is all she was able to tell us."

Essier retrieved a slate from within the desk and tilted it to show him a video. She needn't have bothered with the visuals; the combination of poor lighting, camera jitter, and static made them impossible to interpret. The audio was little better: " . . . *Blossom*, code red to Overwatch . . . Gerav's in . . . " Frustratingly, the static made the next few words unintelligible. "Du Station. You'd better—" The report of a gun, then another, then silence.

"Your task is to investigate the situation at Du Station in the Gwa Reality, and see if the crew and any of the intelligence they've gathered can be recovered. The Shuos heptarch suggested that you would be an ideal candidate for the mission. Kel Command was amenable."

I just bet, Jedao thought. He had once worked directly under his heptarch, and while he'd been one of her better assassins, he didn't miss those days. "Is this the only incident with the Gwa Reality that has taken place recently, or are there others?"

"The Gwa-an are approaching one of their regularly scheduled regime upheavals," Essier said. "According to the diplomats, there's a good chance that the next elected government will be less amenable to heptarchate interests. We want to go in, uncover what happened, and get out before things turn topsy-turvy."

"All right," Jedao said, "so taking a warmoth in would be inflammatory. What resources will I have instead?"

"Well, that's the bad news," Essier said, entirely too cheerfully. "Tell me, Commander, have you ever wanted to own a merchant troop?"

The troop consisted of eight trademoths, named *Carp 1* to *Carp 4*, then *Carp 7* to *Carp 10*. They occupied one of the station's docking bays. Someone had painted each vessel with distended carp-figures in orange and white. It did not improve their appearance.

The usual commander of the troop introduced herself as Churioi Haval, not her real name. She was portly, had a squint, and wore gaudy gilt jewelry, all excellent ways to convince people that she was an ordinary merchant and not, say, Kel special ops. It hadn't escaped his attention that she frowned ever so slightly when she spotted his sidearm, a Patterner 52, which wasn't standard Kel issue. "You're not bringing that, are you?" she said.

"No, I'd hate to lose it on the other side of the border," Jedao said. "Besides, I don't have a plausible explanation for why a boring communications tech is running around with a Shuos handgun."

"I could always hold on to it for you."

Jedao wondered if he'd ever get the Patterner back if he took her up on the offer. It hadn't come cheap. "That's kind of you, but I'll have the station store it for me. By the way, what happened to *Carp 5* and *6*?"

"Beats me," Haval said. "Before my time. The Gwa-an authorities have never hassled us about it. They're already used to, paraphrase, 'odd heptarchate numerological superstitions.'" She eyed Jedao critically, which made her look squintier. "Begging your pardon, but do you *have* undercover experience?"

What a refreshing question. Everyone knew the Shuos for their spies, saboteurs, and assassins, even though the analysts, administrators, and cryptologists did most of the real work. (One of his instructors had explained that "You will spend hours in front of a terminal developing posture problems" was far less effective at recruiting potential cadets than "Join the Shuos for an exciting future as a secret agent, assuming your classmates don't kill you before you graduate.") Most people who met Jedao assumed he'd killed an improbable number of people as Shuos infantry. Never mind that he'd been responsible for far more deaths since joining the regular military.

"You'd be surprised at the things I know how to do," Jedao said.

"Well, I hope you're good with cover identities," Haval said. "No offense, but you have a distinctive name."

That was a tactful way of saying that the Kel didn't tolerate many Shuos line officers; most Shuos seconded to the Kel worked in Intelligence. Jedao had a reputation for, as one of his former aides had put it, being expendable enough to send into no-win situations but too stubborn to die. Jedao smiled at Haval and said, "I have a good memory."

The rest of his crew also had civilian cover names. A tall, muscular man strolled up to them. Jedao surreptitiously admired him. The gold-mesh tattoo over the right side of his face contrasted handsomely with his dark skin. Too bad he was almost certainly Kel and therefore off-limits.

"This is Rhi Teshet," Haval said. "When he isn't watching horrible melodramas—"

"You have no sense of culture," Teshet said.

"—he's the lieutenant colonel in charge of our infantry."

Damn. Definitely Kel, then, and in his chain of command, at that. "A pleasure, Colonel," Jedao said.

Teshet's returning smile was slow and wicked and completely unprofessional. "Get out of the habit of using ranks," he said. "Just Teshet, please. I hear you like whiskey?"

Off-limits, Jedao reminded himself, despite the quickening of his pulse. Best to be direct. "I'd rather not get you in trouble."

Haval was looking to the side with a where-have-I-seen-this-dance-before expression. Teshet laughed. "The fastest way to get us caught is to behave like you have the Kel code of conduct tattooed across your forehead. Whereas *no one* will suspect you of being a hotshot commander if you're sleeping with one of your crew."

"I don't fuck people deadlier than I am, sorry," Jedao said demurely.

"Wrong answer," Haval said, still not looking at either of them. "Now he's going to think of you as a challenge."

"Also, I know your reputation," Teshet said to Jedao. "Your kill count has got to be higher than mine by an order of magnitude."

Jedao ignored that. "How often do you make trade runs into the Gwa Reality?"

"Two or three times a year," Haval said. "The majority of the runs are to maintain the fiction. The question is, do you have a plan?"

He didn't blame her for her skepticism. "Tell me again how much cargo space we have."

Haval told him.

"We sometimes take approved cultural goods," Teshet said, "in a data storage format negotiated during the Second Treaty of—"

"Don't bore him," Haval said. "The 'trade' is our job. He's just here for the explode-y bits."

"No, I'm interested," Jedao said. "The Second Treaty of Mwe Enh, am I right?"

Haval blinked. "You have remarkably good pronunciation. Most people can't manage the tones. Do you speak Tlen Gwa?"

"Regrettably not. I'm only fluent in four languages, and that's not one of them." Of the four, Shparoi was only spoken on his birth planet, making it useless for career purposes.

"If you have some Shuos notion of sneaking in a virus amid all the lectures on flower-arranging and the dueling tournament videos and the plays, forget it," Teshet said. "Their operating systems are so different from ours that you'd have better luck getting a magpie and a turnip to have a baby."

"Oh, not at all," Jedao said. "How odd would it look if you brought in a shipment of goose fat?"

Haval's mouth opened, closed.

Teshet said, "Excuse me?"

"Not literally goose fat," Jedao conceded. "I don't have enough for that and I don't imagine the novelty would enable you to run a sufficient profit. I assume you have to at least appear to be trying to make a profit."

"They like real profits even better," Haval said.

Diverted, Teshet said, "You have goose fat? Whatever for?"

"Long story," Jedao said. "But instead of goose fat, I'd like to run some of that variable-coefficient lubricant."

Haval rubbed her chin. "I don't think you could get approval to trade the formula or the associated manufacturing processes."

"Not that," Jedao said. "Actual canisters of lubricant. Is there someone in the Gwa Reality on the way to our luckless Shuos friend who might be willing to pay for it?"

Haval and Teshet exchanged baffled glances. Jedao could tell what they were thinking: *Are we the victims of some weird bet our commander has going on the side?* "There's no need to get creative," Haval said in a commendably diplomatic voice. "Cultural goods are quite reliable."

You think this *is creativity*, Jedao thought. "It's not that. Two battles ago, my fangmoth was almost blown in two because our antimissile defenses glitched. If we hadn't used the lubricant as a stopgap sealant, we wouldn't have made it." That much was even true. "If you can't offload all of it, I'll find another use for it."

"You do know you can't cook with lubricant?" Teshet said. "Although I wonder if it's good for—"

Haval stomped on his toe. "You already have plenty of the medically approved stuff," she said crushingly, "no need to risk getting your private parts cemented into place."

"Hey," Teshet said, "you never know when you'll need to improvise."

Jedao was getting the impression that Essier had not assigned him the best of her undercover teams. Certainly they were the least disciplined Kel he'd run into in a while, but he supposed long periods undercover had made them more casual about regulations. No matter, he'd been dealt worse hands. "I've let you know what I want done, and I've already checked that the station has enough lubricant to supply us. Make it happen."

"If you insist," Haval said. "Meanwhile, don't forget to get your immunizations."

"Will do," Jedao said, and strode off to Medical.

Jedao spent the first part of the voyage alternately learning basic Tlen Gwa, memorizing his cover identity, and studying up on the Gwa Reality. The Tlen Gwa course suffered some oddities. He couldn't see the use of some of the vocabulary items, like the one for "navel." But he couldn't manage to *un*learn it, either, so there it was, taking up space in his brain.

As for the cover identity, he'd had better ones, but he supposed the Kel could only do so much on short notice. He was now Arioi Sren, one of Haval's distant cousins by marriage. He had three spouses, with whom he had quarreled recently over a point of interior decoration. "I don't know anything about interior decoration," Jedao had said, to which Haval retorted, "That's probably what caused the argument."

The documents had included loving photographs of the home in question, an apartment in a dome city floating in the upper reaches of a very pretty gas giant. Jedao had memorized the details before destroying them. While he couldn't say how well the decor coordinated, he was good at layouts and kill zones. In any case, Sren was on "vacation" to escape the squabbling. Teshet had suggested that a guilt-inducing affair would round out the cover identity. Jedao said he'd think about it.

Jedao was using spray-on temporary skin, plus a high-collared shirt, to conceal multiple scars, including the wide one at the base of his neck. The temporary skin itched, which couldn't be helped. He hoped no one would strip-search him, but in case someone did, he didn't want to have to explain his old gunshot wounds. Teshet had also suggested that he stop shaving—the Kel disliked beards—but Jedao could only deal with so much itching.

The hardest part was not the daily skinseal regimen, but getting used to wearing civilian clothes. The Kel uniform included gloves, and Jedao felt exposed going around with naked hands. But keeping his gloves would have been a dead giveaway, so he'd just have to live with it.

The Gwa-an fascinated him most of all. Heptarchate diplomats called their realm the Gwa Reality. Linguists differed on just what the word rendered as

"Reality" meant. The majority agreed that it referred to the Gwa-an belief that all dreams took place in the same noosphere, connecting the dreamers, and that even inanimate objects dreamed.

Gwa-an protocols permitted traders to dock at designated stations. Haval quizzed Jedao endlessly on the relevant etiquette. Most of it consisted of keeping his mouth shut and letting Haval talk, which suited him fine. While the Gwa-an provided interpreters, Haval said cultural differences were the real problem. "Above all," she added, "if anyone challenges you to a duel, don't. Just don't. Look blank and plead ignorance."

"Duel?" Jedao said, interested.

"I knew we were going to have to have this conversation," Haval said glumly. "They don't use swords, so get that idea out of your head."

"I didn't bring my dueling sword anyway, and Sren wouldn't know how," Jedao said. "Guns?"

"Oh no," she said. "They use *pathogens*. Designer pathogens. Besides the fact that their duels can go on for years, I've never heard that you had a clue about genetic engineering."

"No," Jedao said, "that would be my mother." Maybe next time he could suggest to Essier that his mother be sent in his place. His mother would adore the chance to talk shop. Of course, then he'd be out of a job. "Besides, I'd rather avoid bringing a plague back home."

"They *claim* they have an excellent safety record."

Of course they would. "How fast can they culture the things?"

"That was one of the things we were trying to gather data on."

"If they're good at diseasing up humans, they may be just as good at manufacturing critters that like to eat synthetics."

"While true of their tech base in general," Haval said, "they won't have top-grade labs at Du Station."

"Good to know," Jedao said.

Jedao and Teshet also went over the intelligence on Du Station. "It's nice that you're taking a personal interest," Teshet said, "but if you think we're taking the place by storm, you've been watching too many dramas."

"If Kel special forces aren't up for it," Jedao said, very dryly, "you could always send me. One of me won't do much good, though."

"Don't be absurd," Teshet said. "Essier would have my head if you got hurt. How many people *have* you assassinated?"

"Classified," Jedao said.

Teshet gave a can't-blame-me-for-trying shrug. "Not to say I wouldn't love to see you in action, but it isn't your job to run around doing the boring infantry work. How do you mean to get the crew out? Assuming they survived, which is a big if."

Jedao tapped his slate and brought up the schematics for one of their cargo shuttles. "Five per trader," he said musingly.

"Du Station won't let us land the shuttles however we please."

"Did I say anything about landing them?" Before Teshet could say anything further, Jedao added, "You might have to cross the hard way, with suits and webcord. How often have your people drilled that?"

"We've done plenty of extravehicular," Teshet said, "but we're going to need *some* form of cover."

"I'm aware of that," Jedao said. He brought up a calculator and did some figures. "That will do nicely."

"Sren?"

Jedao grinned at Teshet. "I want those shuttles emptied out, everything but propulsion and navigation. Get rid of suits, seats, all of it."

"Even life support?"

"Everything. And it'll have to be done in the next seventeen days, so the Gwa-an can't catch us at it."

"What do we do with the innards?"

"Dump them. I'll take full responsibility."

Teshet's eyes crinkled. "I knew I was going to like you."

Uh-oh, Jedao thought, but he kept that to himself.

"What are *you* going to be doing?" Teshet asked.

"Going over the dossiers before we have to wipe them," Jedao said. Meng's in particular. He'd believed in Meng's fundamental competence even back in academy, before they'd learned confidence in themselves. What had gone wrong?

Jedao had first met Shuos Meng (Zhei Meng, then) during an exercise at Shuos Academy. The instructor had assigned them to work together. Meng was chubby and had a vine-and-compass tattoo on the back of their left hand, identifying them as coming from a merchanter lineage.

That day, the class of twenty-nine cadets met not in the usual classroom but a windowless space with a metal table in the front and rows of two-person desks with benches that looked like they'd been scrubbed clean of graffiti multiple times. ("Wars come and go, but graffiti is forever," as one of Jedao's lovers liked to say.) Besides the door leading out into the hall, there were two other doors, neither of which had a sign indicating where they led. Tangles of pipes led up the walls and storage bins were piled beside them. Jedao had the impression that the room had been pressed into service at short notice.

Jedao and Meng sat at their assigned seats and hurriedly whispered introductions to each other while the instructor read off the rest of the pairs.

"Zhei Meng," Jedao's partner said. "I should warn you I barely passed the weapons qualifications. But I'm good with languages." Then a quick grin: "And hacking. I figured you'd make a good partner."

"Garach Jedao," he said. "I can handle guns." Understatement; he was third in the class in Weapons. And if Meng had, as they implied, shuffled the assignments, that meant they were one of the better hackers. "Why did you join up?"

"I want to have kids," Meng said.

"Come again?"

"I want to marry into a rich lineage," Meng said. "That means making myself more respectable. When the recruiters showed up, I said what the hell."

The instructor smiled coolly at the two of them, and they shut up. She said, "If you're here, it's because you've indicated an interest in fieldwork. Like you, we want to find out if it's something you have any aptitude for, and if not, what better use we can make of your skills." *You'd better have* some *skills* went unsaid. "You may expect to be dropped off in the woods or some such nonsense. We don't try to weed out first-years quite that early. No; this initial exercise will take place right here."

The instructor's smile widened. "There's a photobomb in this room. It won't cause any permanent damage, but if you don't disarm it, you're all going to be walking around wearing ridiculous dark lenses for a week. At least one cadet knows where the bomb is. If they keep its location a secret from the rest of you, they win. Of course, they'll also go around with ridiculous dark lenses, but you can't have everything. On the other hand, if someone can persuade that person to give up the secret, everyone wins. So to speak."

The rows of cadets stared at her. Jedao leaned back in his chair and considered the situation. Like several others in the class, he had a riflery exam in three days and preferred to take it with undamaged vision.

"You have four hours," the instructor said. "There's one restroom." She pointed to one of the doors. "I expect it to be in impeccable condition at the end of the four hours." She put her slate down on the table at the head of the room. "Call me with this if you figure it out. Good luck." With that, she walked out. The door whooshed shut behind her.

"We're screwed," Meng said. "Just because I'm in the top twenty on the leaderboard in *Elite Thundersnake 900* doesn't mean I could disarm real bombs if you yanked out my toenails."

"Don't give people ideas," Jedao said. Meng didn't appear to find the joke funny. "This is about people, not explosives."

Two pairs of cadets had gotten up and were beginning a search of the room. A few were talking to each other in hushed, tense voices. Still others were looking around at their fellows with hard, suspicious eyes.

Meng said in Shparoi, "Do *you* know where the bomb is?"

Jedao blinked. He hadn't expected anyone at the Academy to know his birth tongue. Of course, by speaking in an obscure low language, Meng was drawing attention to them. Jedao shook his head.

Meng looked around, hands bunching the fabric of their pants. "What do you recommend we do?"

In the high language, Jedao said, "You can do whatever you want." He retrieved a deck of jeng-zai cards—he always had one in his pocket—and shuffled it. "Do you play?"

"You realize we're being graded on this, right? Hell, they've got cameras on us. They're watching the whole thing."

"Exactly," Jedao said. "I don't see any point in panicking."

"You're out of your mind," Meng said. They stood up, met the other cadets' appraising stares, then sat down again. "Too bad hacking the instructor's slate won't get us anywhere. I doubt she left the answer key in an unencrypted file on it."

Jedao gave Meng a quizzical look, wondering if there was anything more behind the remark—but no, Meng had put their chin in their hands and was brooding. *If only you knew,* Jedao thought, and dealt out a game of solitaire. It was going to be a very dull game, because he had stacked the deck, but he needed to focus on the people around him, not the game. The cards were just to give his hands something to do. He had considered taking up crochet, but thanks to an incident earlier in the term, crochet hooks, knitting needles, and fountain pens were no longer permitted in class. While this was a stupid restriction, considering that most of the cadets were learning unarmed combat, he wasn't responsible for the administration's foibles.

"Jedao," Meng said, "maybe you've got high enough marks that you can blow off this exercise, but—"

Since *I'm not blowing it off* was unlikely to be believed, Jedao flipped over a card—three of Doors, just as he'd arranged—and smiled at Meng. So Meng had had their pick of partners and had chosen him? Well, he might as well do something to justify the other cadet's faith in him. After all, despite their earlier remark, weapons weren't the only things that Jedao was good at. "Do me a favor and we can get this sorted," he said. "You want to win? I'll show you winning."

Now Jedao was attracting some of the hostile stares as well. Good. It took the heat off Meng, who didn't seem to have a great tolerance for pressure. *Stay out of wet work,* he thought; but they could have that chat later. Or one of the instructors would.

Meng fidgeted; caught themselves. "Yeah?"

"Get me the slate."

"You mean the instructor's slate? You can't possibly have figured it out already. Unless—" Meng's eyes narrowed.

"Less thinking, more acting," Jedao said, and got up to retrieve the slate himself.

A pair of cadets, a girl and a boy, blocked his way. "You know something," said the girl. "Spill." Jedao knew them from Analysis; the two were often paired there, too. The girl's name was Noe Irin. The boy had five names and went by Veller. Jedao wondered if Veller wanted to join a faction so he could trim things down to a nice, compact, two-part name. Shuos Veller: much less of a mouthful. Then again, Jedao had a three-part name, also unusual, if less unwieldy, so he shouldn't criticize.

"Just a hunch," Jedao said.

Irin bared her teeth. "He *always* says it's a hunch," she said to no one in particular. "I *hate* that."

"It was only twice," Jedao said, which didn't help his case. He backed away from the instructor's desk and sat down, careful not to jostle the solitaire spread. "Take the slate apart. The photobomb's there."

Irin's lip curled. "If this is one of your fucking clever *tricks*, Jay—"

Meng blinked at the nickname. "You two sleeping together, Jedao?" they asked, sotto voce.

Not sotto enough. "*No*," Jedao and Irin said at the same time.

Veller ignored the byplay and went straight for the tablet, which he bent to without touching it. Jedao respected that. Veller had the physique of a tiger-wrestler (now *there* was someone he wouldn't mind being caught in bed with), a broad face, and a habitually bland, dreamy expression. Jedao wasn't fooled. Veller was almost as smart as Irin, had already been tracked into bomb disposal, and was less prone to flights of temper.

"Is there a tool closet in here?" Veller said. "I need a screwdriver."

"You don't carry your own anymore?" Jedao said.

"I told him he should," Irin said, "but he said they were too similar to knitting needles. As if anyone in their right mind would knit with a pair of screwdrivers."

"I think he meant that they're stabby things that can be driven into people's eyes," Jedao said.

"I didn't ask for your opinion, Jay."

Jedao put his hands up in a conciliatory gesture and shut his mouth. He liked Irin and didn't want to antagonize her any more than necessary. The last time they'd been paired together, they'd done quite well. She would come around; she just needed time to work through the implications of what the instructor had said. She was one of those people who preferred to think about things without being interrupted.

One of the other cadets wordlessly handed Veller a set of screwdrivers. Veller mumbled his thanks and got to work. The class watched, breathless.

"There," Veller said at last. "See that there, all hooked in? Don't know what the timer is, but there it is."

"I find it very suspicious that you forfeited your chance to show up everyone else in this exercise," Irin said to Jedao. "Is there anyone else who knew?"

"Irin," Jedao said, "I don't think the instructor told *anyone* where she'd left the photobomb. She just stuck it in the slate because that was the last place we'd look. The test was meant to reveal which of us would backstab the others, but honestly, that's so counterproductive. I say we disarm the damn thing and skip to the end."

Irin's eyes crossed and her lips moved as she recited the instructor's words under her breath. That was another thing Jedao liked about her. Irin had a *great* memory. Admittedly, that made it difficult to cheat her at cards, as he'd found out the hard way. He'd spent three hours doing her kitchen duties for her the one time he'd tried. He *liked* people who could beat him at cards. "It's possible," she said grudgingly after she'd reviewed the assignment's instructions.

"Disarmed," Veller said shortly after that. He pulled out the photobomb and left it on the desk, then set about reassembling the slate.

Jedao glanced over at Meng. For a moment, his partner's expression had no anxiety in it, but a raptor's intent focus. Interesting: What were they watching for?

"I hope I get a quiet posting at a desk somewhere," Meng said.

"Then why'd you join up?" Irin said.

Jedao put his hand over Meng's, even though he was sure that they had just lied. "Don't mind her," he said. "You'll do fine."

Meng nodded and smiled up at him.

Why do I have the feeling that I'm not remotely the most dangerous person in the room? Jedao thought. But he returned Meng's smile, all the same. It never hurt to have allies.

A Gwa patrol ship greeted them as they neared Du Station. Haval had assured Jedao that this was standard practice and obligingly matched velocities.

Jedao listened in on Haval speaking with the Gwa authority, who spoke flawless high language. "They don't call it 'high language,' of course," Haval had explained to Jedao earlier. "They call it 'mongrel language.' " Jedao had expressed that he didn't care what they called it.

Haval didn't trust Jedao to keep his mouth shut, so she'd stashed him in the business office with Teshet to keep an eye on him. Teshet had brought a wooden box that opened up to reveal an astonishing collection of jewelry. Jedao watched out of the corner of his eye as Teshet made himself comfortable in the largest chair, dumped the box's contents on the desk, and began sorting it according to criteria known only to him.

Jedao was watching videos of the command center and the communications channel, and tried to concentrate on reading the authority's body language, made difficult by her heavy zigzag cosmetics and the layers of robes that cloaked her figure. Meanwhile, Teshet put earrings, bracelets, and mysterious hooked and jeweled items in piles, and alternated helpful glosses of Gwa-an gestures with borderline insubordinate, not to say lewd, suggestions for things he could do with Jedao. Jedao was grateful that his ability to blush, like his ability to be tickled, had been burned out of him in Academy. *Note to self: Suggest to General Essier that Teshet is wasted in special ops. Maybe reassign him to Recreation?*

Jedao mentioned this to Teshet while Haval was discussing the cargo manifest with the authority. Teshet lowered his lashes and looked sideways at Jedao. "You don't think I'm good at my job?" he asked.

"You have an excellent record," Jedao said.

Teshet sighed, and his face became serious. "You're used to regular Kel, I see."

Jedao waited.

"I end up in a lot of situations where if people get the notion that I'm a Kel officer, I may end up locked up and tortured. While that could be fun in its own right, it makes career advancement difficult."

"You could get a medal out of it."

"Oh, is *that* how you got promoted so—"

Jedao held up his hand, and Teshet stopped. On the monitor, Haval was saying, in a greasy voice, "I'm glad to hear of your interest, madam. We would have been happy to start hauling the lubricant earlier, except we had to persuade our people that—"

The authority's face grew even more imperturbable. "You had to figure out whom to bribe."

"We understand there are fees—"

Jedao listened to Haval negotiating her bribe to the authority with half an ear. "Don't tell me all that jewelry's genuine?"

"The gems are mostly synthetics," Teshet said. He held up a long earring with a rose quartz at the end. "No, this won't do. I bought it for myself, but you're too light-skinned for it to look good on you."

"I'm wearing jewelry?"

"Unless you brought your own—scratch that, I bet everything you own is in red and gold."

"Yes." Red and gold were the Shuos faction colors.

Teshet tossed the rose quartz earring aside and selected a vivid emerald ear stud. "This will look nice on you."

"I don't get a say?"

"How much do you know about merchanter fashion trends out in this march?"

Jedao conceded the point.

The private line crackled to life. "You two still in there?" said Haval's voice.

"Yes, what's the issue?" Teshet said.

"They're boarding us to check for contraband. You haven't messed with the drugs cabinet, have you?"

Teshet made an affronted sound. "You thought I was going to get Sren high?"

"I don't make assumptions when it comes to you, Teshet. Get the hell out of there."

Teshet thrust the emerald ear stud and two bracelets at Jedao. "Put those on," he said. "If anyone asks you where the third bracelet is, say you had to pawn it to make good on a gambling debt."

Under other circumstances, Jedao would have found this offensive—he was *good* at gambling—but presumably Sren had different talents. As he put on the earring, he said, "What do I need to know about these drugs?"

Teshet was stuffing the rest of the jewelry back in the box. "Don't look at me like that. They're illegal both in the heptarchate and the Gwa Reality, but people run them anyway. They make useful cover. The Gwa-an search us for contraband, they find the contraband, they confiscate the contraband, we pay them a bribe to keep quiet about it, they go away happy."

Impatient with Jedao fumbling with the clasp of the second bracelet, Teshet fastened it for him, then turned Jedao's hand over and studied the scar at the base of his palm. "You should have skinsealed that one too, but never mind."

"I'm bad at peeling vegetables?" Jedao suggested. Close enough to "knife fight," right? And much easier to explain away than bullet scars.

"Are you two *done*?" Haval's voice demanded.

"We're coming, we're coming," Teshet said.

Jedao took up his post in the command center. Teshet himself disappeared in the direction of the airlock. Jedao wasn't aware that anything had gone wrong until Haval returned to the command center, flanked by two personages in bright orange space suits. Both personages wielded guns of a type Jedao had never seen before, which made him irrationally happy. While most of his collection was at home with his mother, he relished adding new items. Teshet was nowhere in sight.

Haval's pilot spoke before the intruders had a chance to say anything. "Commander, what's going on?"

The broader of the two personages spoke in Tlen Gwa, then kicked Haval in the shin. "Guess what," Haval said with a macabre grin. "Those aren't the real authorities we ran into. They're pirates."

Oh, for the love of fox and hound, Jedao thought. In truth, he wasn't surprised, just resigned. He never trusted it when an operation went too smoothly.

The broader personage spoke again. Haval sighed deeply, then said, "Hand over all weapons or they start shooting."

Where's Teshet? Jedao wondered. As if in answer, he heard a gunshot, then the ricochet. More gunshots. He was sure at least one of the shooters was Teshet or one of Teshet's operatives: They carried Stinger 40s and he recognized the characteristic whine of the reports.

Presumably Teshet was occupied, which left matters here up to him. Some of Haval's crew went armed. Jedao did not—they had agreed that Sren wouldn't know how to use a gun—but that didn't mean he wasn't dangerous. While the other members of the crew set down their guns, Jedao flung himself at the narrower personage's feet.

The pirates did not like this. But Jedao had always been blessed, or perhaps cursed, with extraordinarily quick reflexes. He dropped his weight on one arm and leg and kicked the narrow pirate's feet from under them with the other leg. The narrow pirate discharged their gun. The bullet passed over Jedao and banged into one of the status displays, causing it to spark and sputter out. Haval yelped.

Jedao had already sprung back to his feet—damn the twinge in his knees, he should have that looked into—and twisted the gun out of the narrow pirate's grip. The narrow pirate had the stunned expression that Jedao was used to seeing on people who did not deal with professionals very often. He shot them, but thanks to their loose-limbed flailing, the first bullet took them in the shoulder. The second one made an ugly hole in their forehead, and they dropped.

The broad pirate had more presence of mind, but chose the wrong target. Jedao smashed her wrist aside with the knife-edge of his hand just as she fired at Haval five times in rapid succession. Her hands trembled visibly. Four of the shots went wide. Haval had had the sense to duck, but Jedao smelled blood and suspected she'd been hit. Hopefully nowhere fatal.

Jedao shot the broad pirate in the side of the head just as she pivoted to target him next. Her pistol clattered to the floor as she dropped. By reflex he flung himself to the side in case it discharged, but it didn't.

Once he had assured himself that both pirates were dead, he knelt at Haval's side and checked the wound. She had been very lucky. The single bullet had gone through her side, missing the major organs. She started shouting at him for going up unarmed against people with guns.

"I'm getting the medical kit," Jedao said, too loudly, to get her to shut up. His hands were utterly steady as he opened the cabinet containing the medical kit and brought it back to Haval, who at least had the good sense not to try to stand up.

Haval scowled, but accepted the painkiller tabs he handed her. She held still while he cut away her shirt and inspected the entry and exit wounds. At least the bullet wasn't a burrower, or she wouldn't have a lung anymore. He got to work with the sterilizer.

By the time Teshet and two other soldiers entered the command center, Jedao had sterilized and sealed the wounds. Teshet crossed the threshold with rapid strides. When Haval's head came up, Teshet signed sharply for her to be quiet. Curious, Jedao also kept silent.

Teshet drew his combat knife, then knelt next to the larger corpse. With a deft stroke, he cut into the pirate's neck, then yanked out a device and its wires. Blood dripped down and obscured the metal. He repeated the operation for the other corpse, then crushed both devices under his heel. "All right," he said. "It should be safe to talk now."

Jedao raised his eyebrows, inviting explanation.

"Not pirates," Teshet said. "Those were Gwa-an special ops."

Hmm. "Then odds are they were waiting for someone to show up to rescue the *Moonsweet Blossom*," Jedao said.

"I don't disagree." Teshet glanced at Haval, then back at the corpses. "That wasn't you, was it?"

Haval's eyes were glazed, a side effect of the painkiller, but she wasn't entirely out of it. "Idiot here risked his life. We could have handled it."

"I wasn't the one in danger," Jedao said, remembering the pirates' guns pointed at her. Haval might not be particularly respectful, as subordinates went, cover identity or not, but she *was* his subordinate, and he was responsible for her. To Teshet: "Your people?"

"Two down," Teshet said grimly, and gave him the names. "They died bravely."

"I'm sorry," Jedao said; two more names to add to the long litany of those he'd lost. He was thinking about how to proceed, though. "The real Gwa-an patrols won't be likely to know about this. It's how I'd run the op—the fewer people who are aware of the truth, the better. I bet *their* orders are to take in any surviving 'pirates' for processing, and then the authorities will release and debrief the operatives from there. What do you normally do in case of actual pirates?"

"Report the incident," Haval said. Her voice sounded thready. "Formal complaint if we're feeling particularly annoying."

"All right." Jedao calmly began taking off the jewelry and his clothes. "That one's about my size," he said, nodding at the smaller of the two corpses. The suit would be tight across the shoulders, but that couldn't be helped. "Congratulations, not two but three of your crew died heroically, but you captured a pirate in the process."

Teshet made a wistful sound. "That temporary skin stuff obscures your musculature, you know." But he helpfully began stripping the indicated corpse, then grabbed wipes to get rid of the blood on the suit.

"I'll make it up to you some other time," Jedao said recklessly. "Haval, make that formal complaint and demand that you want your captive tried appropriately. Since the nearest station is Du, that'll get me inserted so I can investigate."

"You're just lucky some of the Gwa-an are as sallow as you are," Haval said as Jedao changed clothes.

"I will be disappointed in you if you don't have restraints," Jedao said to Teshet.

Teshet's eyes lit.

Jedao rummaged in the medical kit until he found the eye drops he was looking for. They were meant to counteract tear gas, but they had a side effect of pupil dilation, which was what interested him. It would help him feign concussion.

"We're running short on time, so listen closely," Jedao said. "Turn me over to the Gwa-an. Don't worry about me; I can handle myself."

"Je—Sren, I don't care how much you've studied the station's schematics, you'll be outnumbered thousands to one *on foreign territory.*"

"Sometime over drinks I'll tell you about the time I infiltrated a ring-city where I didn't speak any of the local languages," Jedao said. "Turn me in. I'll locate the crew, spring them, and signal when I'm ready. You won't be able to mistake it."

Haval's brow creased. Jedao kept speaking. "After you've done that, load all the shuttles full of lubricant canisters. Program the lubricant to go from zero-coefficient flow to harden completely in response to the radio signal. You're going to put the shuttles on autopilot. When you see my signal, launch the shuttles' contents toward the station's turret levels. That should gum them up and buy us cover."

"*All* our shuttles?" Haval said faintly.

"Haval," Jedao said, "stop thinking about profit margins and repeat my orders back to me."

She did.

"Splendid," Jedao said. "Don't disappoint me."

The Gwa-an took Jedao into custody without comment. Jedao feigned concussion, saving him from having to sound coherent in a language he barely spoke. The Gwa-an official responsible for him looked concerned, which was considerate of him. Jedao hoped to avoid killing him or the guard. Only one guard, thankfully; they assumed he was too injured to be a threat.

The first thing Jedao noticed about the Gwa-an shuttle was how roomy it was, with wastefully widely spaced seats. He hadn't noticed that the Gwa-an were, on average, that much larger than the heptarchate's citizens. (Not that this said much. Both nations contained a staggering variety of ethnic groups and their associated phenotypes. Jedao himself was on the short side of average for a heptarchate manform.) At least being "concussed" meant he didn't have to figure out how the hell the safety restraints worked, because while he could figure it out with enough fumbling, it would look damned suspicious that he didn't already know. Instead, the official strapped him in while saying things in a soothing voice. The guard limited themselves to a scowl.

Instead of the smell of disinfectant that Jedao associated with shuttles, the Gwa-an shuttle was pervaded by a light, almost effervescent fragrance. He hoped it wasn't intoxicating. Or rather, part of him hoped it was, because he didn't often have good excuses to screw around with new and exciting recreational drugs, but it would impede his effectiveness. Maybe all Gwa-an disinfectants smelled this good? He should steal the formula. Voidmoth crews everywhere would thank him.

Even more unnervingly, the shuttle played music on the way to the station. At least, while it didn't resemble any music he'd heard before, it had a recognizable beat and some sort of flute in it. From the others' reactions, this was normal and possibly even boring. Too bad he was about as musical as a pair of boots.

The shuttle docked smoothly. Jedao affected not to know what was going on and allowed the official to chirp at him. Eventually a stretcher arrived and they put him on it. They emerged into the lights of the shuttle bay. Jedao's temples twinged with the beginning of a headache. At least it meant the eye drops were still doing their job.

The journey to Du Station's version of Medical took forever. Jedao was especially eager to escape based on what he'd learned of Gwa-an medical therapies, which involved too many genetically engineered critters for his comfort. (He had read up on the topic after Haval told him about the dueling.) He did consider that he could make his mother happy by stealing some pretty little microbes for her, but with his luck they'd turn his testicles inside out.

When the medic took him into an examination room, Jedao whipped up and felled her with a blow to the side of the neck. The guard was slow to react. Jedao grasped their throat and grappled with them, waiting the interminable seconds until they slumped, unconscious. He had a bad moment when he heard footsteps passing by. Luckily, the guard's wheeze didn't attract attention. Jedao wasn't modest about his combat skills, but they wouldn't save him if he was sufficiently outnumbered.

Too bad he couldn't steal the guard's uniform, but it wouldn't fit him. So it would have to be the medic's clothes. Good: the medic's clothes were robes instead of something more form-fitting. Bad: even though the garments would fit him, more or less, they were in the style for women.

I will just have to improvise, Jedao thought. At least he'd kept up the habit of shaving, and the Gwa-an appeared to permit a variety of haircuts in all genders, so his short hair and bangs wouldn't be too much of a problem. As long as he moved quickly and didn't get stopped for conversation—

Jedao changed, then slipped out and took a few moments to observe how people walked and interacted so he could fit in more easily. The Gwa-an were terrible about eye contact and, interestingly for station-dwellers, preferred to keep each other at a distance. He could work with that.

His eyes still ached, since Du Station had abominably bright lighting, but he'd just have to prevent people from looking too closely at him. It helped that he had dark brown eyes to begin with, so the dilated pupils wouldn't be obvious from a distance. He was walking briskly toward the lifts when he heard a raised voice. He kept walking. The voice called again, more insistently.

Damn. He turned around, hoping that someone hadn't recognized his outfit from behind. A woman in extravagant layers of green, lilac, and pink spoke to him in strident tones. Jedao approached her rapidly, wincing at her voice, and hooked her into an embrace. Maybe he could take advantage of this yet.

"You're not—" she began to say.

"I'm too busy," he said over her, guessing at how best to deploy the Tlen Gwa phrases he knew. "I'll see you for tea at thirteen. I like your coat."

The woman's face turned an ugly mottled red. "You like my *what*?" At least he thought he'd said "coat." She stepped back from him, pulling what looked like a small perfume bottle from among her layers of clothes.

He tensed, not wanting to fight her in full view of passersby. She spritzed him with a moist vapor, then smiled coolly at him before spinning on her heel and walking away.

Shit. Just how fast-acting were Gwa-an duels, anyway? He missed the sensible kind with swords; his chances would have been much better. He hoped the symptoms wouldn't be disabling, but then, the woman couldn't possibly have had a chance to tailor the infectious agent to his system, and maybe the immunizations would keep him from falling over sick until he had found Meng and their crew.

How had he offended her, anyway? Had he gotten the word for "coat" wrong? Now that he thought about it, the word for "coat" differed from the word for "navel" only by its tones, and—hells and foxes, he'd messed up the tone sandhi, hadn't he? He kept walking, hoping that she'd be content with getting him sick and wouldn't call security on him.

At last he made it to the lifts. While stealing the medic's uniform had also involved stealing their keycard, he preferred not to use it. Rather, he'd swapped the medic's keycard for the loud woman's. She had carried hers on a braided lanyard with a clip. It would do nicely if he had to garrote anyone in a hurry. The garrote wasn't one of his specialties, but as his girlfriend the first year of Shuos Academy had always been telling him, it paid to keep your options open.

At least the lift's controls were less perilous than figuring out how to correctly pronounce items of clothing. Jedao had by no means achieved reading fluency in Tlen Gwa, but the language had a wonderfully tidy writing system, with symbols representing syllables and odd little curlicue diacritics that changed what vowel you used. He had also theoretically memorized the numbers from 1 to 9,999. Fortunately, Du Station had fewer than 9,999 levels.

Two of the other people on the lift stared openly at Jedao. He fussed with his hair on the grounds that it would look like ordinary embarrassment and not *Hello! I am a cross-dressing enemy agent, pleased to make your acquaintance.* Come to that, Gwa-an women's clothes were comfortable, and all the layers meant that he could, in principle, hide useful items like garrotes in them. He wondered if he could keep them as a souvenir. Start a fashion back home. He bet his mother would approve.

Intelligence had given him a good idea of where Meng and their crew might be held. At least, Jedao hoped that Du Station's higher-ups hadn't faked him out by stowing them in the lower-security cells as opposed to the top-security ones. He was betting a lot on the guess that the Gwa-an were still in the process of interrogating the group rather than executing them out of hand.

The layout wasn't the hard part, but Jedao reflected on the mysteries of the Gwa Reality's penal code. For example, prostitution was a major offense. They didn't even fine the offenders, but sent them to remedial counseling, which surely *cost* the state money. In the heptarchate, they did the sensible thing by enforcing licenses for health and safety reasons and taxing the whole enterprise. On the other hand, the Gwa-an had a refreshingly casual attitude toward heresy. They believed that public debate about Poetics (their version of Doctrine) strengthened the polity. If you put forth that idea anywhere in the heptarchate, you could expect to get arrested.

So it was that Jedao headed for the cellblocks where one might find unlucky prostitutes and not the ones where overly enthusiastic heretics might be locked up overnight to cool off. He kept attracting horrified looks and wondered if he'd done something offensive with his hair. Was it wrong to part it on the left, and if so, why hadn't Haval warned him? How many ways could you get hair wrong anyway?

The Gwa-an also had peculiarly humanitarian ideas about the surroundings that offenders should be kept in. Level 37, where he expected to find Meng, abounded with fountains. Not cursory fountains, but glorious cascading arches of silvery water interspersed with elongated humanoid statues in various uncomfortable-looking poses. Teshet had mentioned that this had to do with Gwa-an notions of ritual purity.

While "security" was one of the words that Jedao had memorized, he did not read Tlen Gwa especially quickly, which made figuring out the signs a chore. At least the Gwa-an believed in signs, a boon to foreign infiltrators everywhere. Fortunately, the Gwa-an hadn't made a secret of the Security office's location, even if getting to it was complicated by the fact that the fountains had been rearranged since the last available intel and he preferred not to show up soaking wet. The fountains themselves formed a labyrinth and, upon inspection, it appeared that different portions could be turned on or off to change the labyrinth's twisty little passages.

Unfortunately, the water's splashing also made it difficult to hear people coming, and he had decided that creeping about would not only slow him down, but make him look more conspicuous, especially with the issue of his hair (or whatever it was that made people stare at him with such affront). He rounded a corner and almost crashed into a sentinel, recognizable by Security's spear-and-shield badge.

In retrospect, a simple collision might have worked out better. Instead, Jedao dropped immediately into a fighting stance, and the sentinel's eyes narrowed. *Dammit*, Jedao thought, exasperated with himself. *This is why my handlers preferred me doing the sniper bits rather than the infiltration bits.* Since he'd blown the opportunity to bluff his way past the sentinel, he swept the man's feet from under him and knocked him out. After the man was unconscious, Jedao stashed him behind one of the statues, taking care so the spray from the fountains wouldn't interfere too much with his breathing. He had the distinct impression that "dead body" was much worse from a ritual purity standpoint than "merely unconscious," if he had to negotiate with someone later.

He ran into no other sentinels on the way to the office, but as it so happened, a sentinel was leaving just as he got there. Jedao put on an expression he had learned from the scariest battlefield medic of his acquaintance back when he'd been a lowly infantry captain and marched straight up to Security. He didn't need to be convincing for long, he just needed a moment's hesitation.

By the time the sentinel figured out that the "medic" was anything but, Jedao had taken her gun and broken both her arms. "I want to talk to your leader," he said, another of those useful canned phrases.

The sentinel left off swearing (he was sure it was swearing) and repeated the word for "leader" in an incredulous voice.

Whoops. Was he missing some connotational nuance? He tried the word for "superior officer," to which the response was even more incredulous. *Hey Mom*, Jedao thought, *you know how you always said I should join the diplomatic corps on account of my always talking my way out of trouble as a kid? Were you ever wrong. I am the worst diplomat ever.* Admittedly, maybe starting off by breaking the woman's arms was where he'd gone wrong, but the sentinel didn't sound upset about *that*. The Gwa-an were very confusing people.

After a crescendo of agitation (hers) and desperate rummaging about for people nouns (his), it emerged that the term he wanted was the one for "head priest." Which was something the language lessons ought to have noted. He planned on dropping in on whoever had written the course and having a spirited talk with them.

Just as well that the word for "why" was more straightforward. The sentinel wanted to know why he wanted to talk to the head priest. He wanted to know why someone who'd had both her arms broken was more concerned with propriety (his best guess) than alerting the rest of the station that they had an intruder. He had other matters to attend to, though. Too bad he couldn't recruit her for her sangfroid, but that was outside his purview.

What convinced the sentinel to comply, in the end, was not the threat of more violence, which he imagined would have been futile. Instead, he mentioned that he'd left one of her comrades unconscious amid the fountains and the man would need medical care. He liked the woman's concern for her fellow sentinel.

Jedao and the sentinel walked together to the head priest's office. The head priest came out. She had an extremely elaborate coiffure, held in place by multiple hairpins featuring elongated figures like the statues. She froze when Jedao pointed the gun at her, then said several phrases in what sounded like different languages.

"Mongrel language," Jedao said in Tlen Gwa, remembering what Haval had told him.

"What do you want?" the high priest said in awkward but comprehensible high language.

Jedao explained that he was here for Ahun Gerav, in case the priest only knew Meng by their cover name. "Release them and their crew, and this can end with minimal bloodshed."

The priest wheezed. Jedao wondered if she was allergic to assassins. He'd never heard of such a thing, but he wasn't under any illusions that he knew everything about Gwa-an immune systems. Then he realized she was laughing.

"Feel free to share," Jedao said, very pleasantly. The sentinel was sweating.

The priest stopped laughing. "You're too late," she said. "You're too late by thirteen years."

Jedao did the math: eight years since he and Meng had graduated from Shuos Academy. Of course, the two of them had attended for the usual five years. "They've been a double agent since they were a cadet?"

The priest's smile was just this side of smug.

Jedao knocked the sentinel unconscious and let her spill to the floor. The priest's smile didn't falter, which made him think less of her. Didn't she care about her subordinate? If nothing else, he'd had a few concussions in his time (real ones), and they were no joke.

"The crew," Jedao said.

"Gerav attempted to persuade them to turn coat as well," the priest said. "When they were less than amenable, well—" She shrugged. "We had no further use for them."

"I will not forgive this," Jedao said. "Take me to Gerav."

She shrugged. "Unfortunate for them," she said. "But to be frank, I don't value their life over my own."

"How very pragmatic of you," Jedao said.

She shut up and led the way.

Du Station had provided Meng with a luxurious suite by heptarchate standards. The head priest bowed with an ironic smile as she opened the door for Jedao. He shoved her in and scanned the room.

The first thing he noticed was the overwhelming smell of—what *was* that smell? Jedao had thought he had reasonably cosmopolitan tastes, but the platters with their stacks of thin-sliced meat drowned in rich gravies and sauces almost made him gag. Who needed that much meat in their diet? The suite's occupant seemed to agree, judging by how little the meat had been touched. And why wasn't the meat cut into decently small pieces so as to make for easy eating? The bowls of succulent fruit were either for show or the suite's occupant disliked fruit, too. The flatbreads, on the other hand, had been torn into. One, not entirely eaten, rested on a meat platter and was dissolving into the gravy. Several different-sized bottles were partly empty, and once he adjusted to all the meat, he could also detect the sweet reek of wine.

Most fascinatingly, instead of chopsticks and spoons, the various plates and platters sported two-tined forks (Haval had explained to him about forks) and knives. Maybe this was how they trained assassins. Jedao liked knives, although not as much as he liked guns. He wondered if he could persuade the Kel to import the custom. It would make for some lively high tables.

Meng glided out, resplendent in brocade Gwa-an robes, then gaped. Jedao wasn't making any attempt to hide his gun.

"Foxfucking hounds," Meng slurred as they sat down heavily, "*you*. Is that really you, Jedao?"

"You know each other?" the priest said.

Jedao ignored her question, although he kept her in his peripheral vision in case he needed to kill her or knock her out. "You graduated from Shuos Academy with high marks," Jedao said. "You even married rich the way you always talked about. Four beautiful kids. Why, Meng? Was it nothing more than a story?"

Meng reached for a fork. Jedao's trigger finger shifted. Meng withdrew their hand.

"The Gwa-an paid stupendously well," Meng said quietly. "It mattered a lot more, once. Of course, hiding the money was getting harder and harder. What good is money if you can't spend it? And the Shuos were about to catch on anyway. So I had to run."

"And your crew?"

Meng's mouth twisted, but they met Jedao's eyes steadfastly. "I didn't want things to end the way they did."

"Cold comfort to their families."

"It's done now," Meng said, resigned. They looked at the largest platter of meat with sudden loathing. Jedao tensed, wondering if it was going to be flung at him, but all Meng did was shove it away from them. Some gravy slopped over the side.

Jedao smiled sardonically. "If you come home, you might at least get a decent bowl of rice instead of this weird bread stuff."

"Jedao, if I come home they'll *torture me for high treason*, unless our heptarch's policies have changed drastically. You can't stop me from killing myself."

"Rather than going home?" Jedao shrugged. Meng probably did have a suicide fail-safe, although if they were serious they'd have used it already. He couldn't imagine the Gwa-an would have neglected to provide them with one if the Shuos hadn't.

Still, he wasn't done. "If you do something so crass, I'm going to visit each one of your children *personally*. I'm going to take them out to a nice dinner with actual food that you eat with actual chopsticks and spoons. And I'm going to explain to them in exquisite detail how their Shuos parent is a traitor."

Meng bit their lip.

More softly, Jedao said, "When did the happy family stop being a cover story and start being real?"

"I don't know," Meng said, wretched. "I can't—do you know how my spouses would look at me if they found out that I'd been lying to them all this time? I wasn't even particularly interested in other people's kids when this all began. But watching them grow up—" They fell silent.

"I have to bring you back," Jedao said. He remembered the staticky voice of the unnamed woman playing in Essier's office, Meng's *crew*, who'd tried and failed to get a warning out. She and her comrades deserved justice. But he also remembered all the gifts he'd sent to Meng's children over the years, the occasional awkwardly written thank-you note. It wasn't as if any good would be achieved by telling them the awful truth. "But I can pull a few strings. Make sure your family never finds out."

Meng hesitated for a long moment. Then they nodded. "It's fair. Better than fair."

To the priest, Jedao said, "You'd better take us to the *Moonsweet Blossom*, assuming you haven't disassembled it already."

The priest's mouth twisted. "You're in luck," she said.

Du Station had ensconced the *Moonsweet Blossom* in a bay on Level 62. The Gwa-an passed gawped at them. The priest sailed past without giving any explanations. Jedao wondered whether the issue was his hair or some other inexplicable Gwa-an cultural foible.

"I hope you can pilot while drunk," Jedao said to Meng.

Meng drew themselves up to their full height. "I didn't drink *that* much."

Jedao had his doubts, but he would take his chances. "Get in."

The priest's sudden tension alerted him that she was about to try something. Jedao shoved Meng toward the trademoth, then grabbed the priest in an arm. What was the point of putting a priest in charge of security if the priest couldn't *fight*?

Jedao said to her, "You're going to instruct your underlings to get the hell out of our way and open the airlock so we can leave."

"And why would I do that?" the priest said.

He reached up and snatched out half her hairpins. Too bad he didn't have a third hand; his grip on the gun was precarious enough as it was. She growled, which he interpreted as *Fuck you and all your little foxes.* "I could get creative," Jedao said.

"I was warned that the heptarchate was full of barbarians," the priest said.

At least the incomprehensible Gwa-an fixation on hairstyles meant that he didn't have to resort to more disagreeable threats, like shooting her subordinates in front of her. Given her reaction when he had knocked out the sentinel, he wasn't convinced that would faze her anyway. He adjusted his grip on her and forced her to the floor.

"Give the order," he said. "If you don't play any tricks, you'll even get the hairpins back without my shoving them through your eardrums." They were very nice hairpins, despite the creepiness of the elongated humanoid figures, and he bet they were real gold.

Since he had her facing the floor, the priest couldn't glare at him. The frustration in her voice was unmistakable, however. "As you require." She started speaking in Tlen Gwa.

The workers in the area hurried to comply. Jedao had familiarized himself with the control systems of the airlock and was satisfied they weren't doing anything underhanded. "Thank you," he said, to which the priest hissed something venomous. He flung the hairpins away and let her go. She cried out at the sound of their clattering and scrambled after them with a devotion he reserved for weapons. Perhaps, to a Gwa-an priest, they were equivalent.

One of the workers, braver or more foolish than the others, reached for her own gun. Jedao shot her in the hand on the way up the hatch to the *Moonsweet Blossom*. It bought him enough time to get the rest of the way up the ramp and slam the hatch shut after him. Surely Meng couldn't accuse him of showing off if they hadn't seen the feat of marksmanship; and he hoped the worker would appreciate that he could just as easily have put a hole in her head.

The telltale rumble of the *Blossom*'s maneuver drive assured him that Meng, at least, was following directions. This boded well for Meng's health. Jedao hurried forward, wondering how many more rounds the Gwa-an handgun contained, and started webbing himself into the gunner's seat.

"You wouldn't consider putting that thing away, would you?" Meng said. "It's hard for me to think when I'm ready to piss myself."

"If you think *I'm* the scariest person in your future, Meng, you haven't been paying attention."

"One, I don't think you know yourself very well, and two, I liked you much better when we were on the same side."

"I'm going to let you meditate on that second bit some other time. In the meantime, let's get out of here."

Meng swallowed. "They'll shoot us down the moment we get clear of the doors, you know."

"Just *go*, Meng. I've got friends. Or did you think I teleported onto this station?"

"At this point I wouldn't put anything past you. Okay, you're webbed in, I'm webbed in, here goes nothing."

The maneuver drive grumbled as the *Moonsweet Blossom* blasted its way out of the bay. No one attempted to close the first set of doors on them. Jedao wondered if the priest was still scrabbling after her hairpins, or if it had to do with the more pragmatic desire to avoid costly repairs to the station.

The *Moonsweet Blossom* had few armaments, mostly intended for dealing with high-velocity debris, which was more of a danger than pirates if one kept to the better-policed trade routes. They wouldn't do any good against Du Station's defenses. As *signals*, on the other hand—

Using the lasers, Jedao flashed HERE WE COME in the merchanter signal code. With any luck, Haval was paying attention.

At this point, several things happened.

Haval kicked Teshet in the shin to get him to stop watching a mildly pornographic and not-very-well-acted drama about a famous courtesan from 192 years ago. ("It's historical so it's educational!" he protested. "One, we've got our signal, and two, I wish you would take care of your *urgent needs* in your own quarters," Haval said.)

Carp 1 through *Carp 4* and *7* through *10* launched all their shuttles. Said shuttles were, as Jedao had instructed, full of variable-coefficient lubricant programmed to its liquid form. The shuttles flew toward Du Station, then opened their holds and burned their retro thrusters for all they were worth. The lubricant, carried forward by momentum, continued toward Du Station's turret levels.

Du Station recognized an attack when it saw one. However, its defenses consisted of a combination of high-powered lasers, which could only vaporize small portions of the lubricant and were useless for altering the momentum of quantities of the stuff, and railguns, whose projectiles punched through the mass without much effect. Once the lubricant had clogged up the defensive emplacements, *Carp 1* transmitted an encrypted radio signal with the command that caused the lubricant to harden in place.

The *Moonsweet Blossom* linked up with Haval's merchant troop. At this point, the *Blossom* only contained two people, trivial compared to the amount of mass it had been designed to haul. The merchant troop, of course, had just divested itself of its cargo. The nine heptarchate vessels proceeded to hightail it out of there at highly non-freighter accelerations.

Jedao and Meng swept the *Moonsweet Blossom* for bugs and other unwelcome devices, an exhausting but necessary task. Then, at what Jedao judged to be a safe distance from Du Station, he ordered Meng to slave it to *Carp 1*.

The *Carp 1* and *Moonsweet Blossom* matched velocities, and Jedao and Meng made the crossing to the former. There was a bad moment when Jedao thought Meng was going to unhook their tether and drift off into the smothering dark rather than face their fate. But whatever temptations were running through their head, Meng resisted them.

Haval and Teshet greeted them on the *Carp 1*. After Jedao and Meng had shed the suits and checked them for needed repairs, Haval ushered them all into the business office. "I didn't expect you to spring the trademoth as well as our Shuos friend," Haval said.

Meng wouldn't meet her eyes.

"What about the rest of the crew?" Teshet said.

"They didn't make it," Jedao said, and sneezed. He explained about Meng's extracurricular activities over the past thirteen years. Then he sneezed again.

Haval grumbled under her breath. "Whatever the hell you did on Du, Sren, did it involve duels?"

" 'Sren'?" Meng said.

"You don't think I came into the Gwa Reality under my own"—sneeze—"name, did you?" Jedao said. "Anyway, there might have been an incident . . . "

Meng groaned. "Just how good is your Tlen Gwa?"

"Sort of not, apparently," Jedao said. "I *really* need to have a word with whoever wrote the Tlen Gwa course. I thought I was all right with languages at the basic phrase level, but was the proofreader asleep the day they approved it?"

Meng had the grace to look embarrassed. "I may have hacked it."

"You what?"

"If I'd realized *you'd* be using it, I wouldn't have bothered. Botching the language doesn't seem to have slowed you down any."

Wordlessly, Teshet handed Jedao a handkerchief. Jedao promptly sneezed into it. Maybe he'd be able to give his mother a gift of a petri dish with a lovely culture of Gwa-an germs, after all. He'd have to ask the medic about it later.

Teshet then produced a set of restraints from his pockets and gestured at Meng. Meng sighed deeply and submitted to being trussed up.

"Don't look so disappointed," Teshet said into Jedao's ear. "I've another set just for you." Then he and Meng marched off to the brig.

Haval cleared her throat. "Off to the medic with you," she said to Jedao. "We'd better figure out why your vaccinations aren't working and if everyone's going to need to be quarantined."

"Not arguing," Jedao said meekly.

Some days later, Jedao was rewatching one of Teshet's pornography dramas while in bed. At least, he thought it was pornography. The costuming made it difficult to tell, and the dialogue had made *more* sense when he was still running a fever.

The medic had kept him in isolation until they declared him no longer contagious. Whether due to this precaution or pure luck, no one else came down with the duel disease. They'd given him a clean bill of health this morning, but Haval had insisted that he rest a little longer.

The door opened. Jedao looked up in surprise.

Teshet entered with a fresh supply of handkerchiefs. "Well, Jedao, we'll reenter heptarchate space in two days, high calendar. Any particular orders you want me to relay to Haval?" He obligingly handed over a slate so Jedao could look over Haval's painstaking, not to say excruciatingly detailed, reports on their current status.

"Haval's doing a fine job," Jedao said, glad that his voice no longer came out as a croak. "I won't get in her way." He returned the slate to Teshet.

"Sounds good." Teshet turned his back and departed. Jedao admired the view, wishing in spite of himself that the other man would linger.

Teshet returned half an hour later with two clear vials full of unidentified substances. "First or second?" he said, holding them up to the light one by one.

"I'm sorry," Jedao said, "first or second what?"

"You look like you need cheering up," Teshet said hopefully. "You want on top? You want me on top? I'm flexible."

Jedao blinked, trying to parse this. "On top of wh—" *Oh.* "What's *in* those vials?"

"You have your choice of variable-coefficient lubricant or goose fat," Teshet said. "Assuming you were telling the truth when you said it was goose fat. And don't yell at Haval for letting me into your refrigerator; I did it all on my own. I admit, I can't tell the difference. As Haval will attest, I'm a *dreadful* cook, so I didn't want to fry up some scallion pancakes just to taste the goose fat."

Jedao's mouth went dry, which had less to do with Teshet's eccentric choice of lubricants than the fact that he had sat down on the edge of Jedao's bed. "You don't have anything more, ah, conventional?" He realized that was a mistake as soon as the words left his mouth; he'd essentially accepted Teshet's proposition.

For the first time, Jedao glimpsed uncertainty in Teshet's eyes. "We don't have a lot of time before we're back in heptarchate space and you have to go back to being a commander and I have to go back to being responsible," he said softly. "Or as responsible as I ever get, anyway. Want to make the most of it? Because I get the impression that you don't allow yourself much of a personal life."

"Use the goose fat," Jedao said, because as much as he liked Teshet, he did not relish the thought of being *cemented* to Teshet: It would distract Teshet from continuing to analyze his psyche, and, yes, the man was damnably attractive. What the hell, with any luck his mother was never, ever, *ever* hearing of this. (He could imagine the conversation now: "Garach Jedao Shkan, are you meaning to tell me you finally found a nice young man and you're *still* not planning on settling down and providing me extra grandchildren?" And then she would send him *more goose fat.*)

Teshet brightened. "You won't regret this," he purred, and proceeded to help Jedao undress.

EMERGENCY PROTOCOL

LETTIE PRELL

In case of an emergency occurring in your immediate vicinity, you may be activated.

Should you be activated, you will hear a tone in your ear signaling remote operation is about to begin. Remain calm. A controller will be with you shortly.

It is common while being operated remotely by a controller for your sympathetic nervous system to trigger the fight or flight response.

It is common for the controller to use your fight or flight response for the first of these options. Do not resist.

Should the fight or flight response be triggered, your heart rate will increase to as much as two hundred beats per minute.

You may notice yourself focusing on a single person in your immediate vicinity to the exclusion of everything else. This phenomenon is known as perceptual narrowing.

Be assured the controller has made positive identification prior to taking action.

During remote operation by a controller, your body may execute tasks you have not been trained to perform. Remain confident the controller possesses the required expertise.

The controller will use the least amount of force necessary in order to handle the situation. Such force may include deadly force. You will incur no liability as a result of actions taken by a controller during remote operation.

You may notice your inability to close your eyes. This is for your own safety, as the controller must have an uninterrupted view of the situation. Be assured resolution of the emergency is at hand.

During the resolution phase, you may experience events happening in slow motion. Alternatively, events may appear to occur so quickly that the situation is over before you can fully comprehend what has occurred.

Should circumstances indicate, additional persons in your vicinity may also be activated. Be assured all controllers are in direct communication with each other at all times. Please keep in mind we highly value your safety, and the safety of those around you.

Most emergency situations are resolved within ten minutes. Fifteen percent of situations take longer to resolve.

Should a situation take longer than thirty minutes to resolve, remote operation of your body may cease, as fresh bodies are activated and directed to respond.

In the event you are deactivated in the middle of a situation, please move away from the epicenter of the emergency as soon as possible. It is likely your body's flight response will engage at this time. Keep your upper torso low in the event projectiles are being used. In some situations, crawling on all fours may be advised.

Following resolution and deactivation, it is common to experience a parasympathetic nervous system, or PNS, response.

The symptoms associated with PNS are those of faint or freeze and include: dizziness and light-headedness, fatigue, and difficulty thinking. You may become aware of injuries at this time. Cuts that seemed inconsequential at the time may bleed more.

Should you require medical attention or psychological counseling, you will not be billed for these services.

Regulations require compliance with the protocol at all times. Tampering with, disabling, or destroying the device that enables your remote activation will constitute an emergency situation.

This concludes our presentation on this protocol. If you would like this instruction repeated, you may review it at any time, as it is one of your primary stored procedures.

Thank you for your attention.

WINTER TIMESHARE

RAY NAYLER

—◆—

What are "I" and "You"?
Just lattices
In the niches of a lamp
Through which the One Light radiates.
                              —Rumi

Dead Stay Dead

The words were scrawled in scarlet, hurried script on a concrete flower box. In the spring, the flower box would be full of tulips. For those who could afford the spring, there would be sunny days and crowds. Right now there was nothing in the concrete box but wet earth.

A city worker in a jumpsuit a few shades darker than the drizzling sky wiped the letters away with a quick swipe of chemcloth, leaving no trace of their message, and moved on.

Whoever wrote those had probably already been caught by the police. Why bother? The risk of a fine, of a notch against you—for what? A pointless protest against a world that would stay just as it was, ugly words or no.

Across a cobblestone street and defoliated winter gardens, the minarets of the Blue Mosque rose, soft-edged in the drizzle, their tips blurring into the mist. It was chilly in the open-air café, even under the heater. It was a familiar chill, bringing immediately to Regina's mind years of Istanbul in winter— memories of snow hissing onto the surface of the Bosporus, snow melting on the wings of seagulls. Mornings wrapped close in a blanket, watching the rain on the windowpanes distort the shipping in the strait. The icy, age-smoothed marble of mosque courtyards. And ten thousand cups of black tea in pear-shaped glasses, sign and substance of the city: hot to the touch, bitter on the tongue, a cube of sugar dissolving in their depths, identical to and yet different from one another. This, and so many other deeply pleasant repetitions, comforted her. They were in her past and, now, ahead of her again.

She flexed her tanned, muscular hand. She had spilled her first cup of tea with this clumsy hand. So eager to get to the café, not waiting even to get settled in, still pins-and-needles and misfires, but wanting that first taste of Istanbul, of its black tea against its chill. The old waiter had shrugged and brought her another. "Do not worry, *beyfendi*," he had said, wiping the tea from the table with a rag. "No charge." Now she lifted the second glass, carefully, to her lips. Yes, that was it. Now another year's Istanbul had begun.

And now Regina saw Ilkay, walking toward the café with that uneven step that said she had just woken. Ilkay was scanning the seats for her. Ilkay was blonde, this year. Beautiful—an oval face, this year, eyes set wide over high cheekbones, long-limbed. But Regina would know her anywhere. And Ilkay knew her as well, scanning the seats in confusion and concern for a moment and then catching her eye, and smiling.

"Well," Ilkay said, when they had embraced, and embraced again, kissed cheeks, held one another at arms' length and examined one another's faces. "This is a new wrinkle in things."

"Is it bad?" Regina asked, keeping her voice light and unconcerned, but feeling underneath an eating away, suddenly, at the pure joy of seeing Ilkay again. *All things fall forever, worn by change / And given time, even the stones will flow . . .*, a piece of a poem she had read once. The poet's name, like much else, gone to time.

Ilkay grinned. Even, smallish teeth, a line of pink gums at the top. A different smile from the year before, but underneath, a constancy. "No. It isn't bad at all. It will be something new, for us." The waiter had approached, stood quietly to one side. Ilkay turned to him. "Two coffees for me. Bring both together." She settled into her cane-bottom chair. "I never feel, this first day, as if I can wake up all the way."

All was well, Regina told herself. Despite her heavy, clumsy hands. Despite her nervousness.

"Tell me," Ilkay said. "Tell me everything. What is your highrise working on?"

"You would not believe it, but it is a contract piece for the UN Commission on Historical Conflict Analysis, and what they are focusing on is conducting the most detailed possible analysis of the Peloponnesian War. All year we've been focused on the Battle of Pylos—refining equipment models, nutrition and weather patterns, existing in these simulations for twelve-hour shifts and feeding data to other teams of analysts. No idea what they're looking for—they're concealing that to keep from biasing the simulation—but the level of detail is granular. I've been fighting and refighting a simulation of the battle of Sphacteria. Half-starved, trying to keep the phalanx together. I've been taken hostage and shipped to Athens so many times as a Spartan hoplite, I should get danger pay. It was supposed to be a six-month research project, but it's already run all year and looks set to run another year."

"You actually look like you could handle yourself pretty well in a battle, right now. That's a heavy blank you're sheathed in."

Regina felt a flush of shame. "When they pulled me over to my new Istanbul distro, someone had walked off in the factory blank I ordered for this timeshare. It was this ugly thing, or wait another week. I was furious."

She looked down at the hairy back of the hand. "It's terrible, isn't it? My highrise had to take a ten percent pay cut across the board this year. I couldn't afford my old distro. The new distro is dreadful. I woke up with pins and needles all over, felt like I had a clubfoot, and could barely move my fingers for two hours. At first I thought they had installed the receptors wrong in the lab and were foisting a defective blank off on me. You've heard the scams. I staggered here like a zombie—everybody who passed me on the street staring at me. And nobody at the distro even apologized about the mix-up."

"It isn't terrible." Ilkay had been too impatient in drinking her Turkish coffee, and a thin line of grounds marred her perfect lip. She wiped them delicately away with a napkin. "Fortunes change, and we're all reliant on our highrises. I'm just so thankful that you were here when I walked up. I had a fear, crossing the hippodrome, that you would be gone. That there was a recall, or a delay, or you had been waitlisted, or that you had . . . reconsidered."

Ilkay was always so fragile, this first day. Always certain there had been some disaster between them. Ilkay could afford a better timeshare—something in the spring, when the tulips came, or something in San Francisco Protectorate—but she came at this cut-rate time each year to meet Regina, slumming it in the off-season. In the end, it was Ilkay who was the most uncertain of them, most sure she would one year lose Regina. Money, Regina had to remind herself, was not everything—although it seemed like it was to those who did not have it. Ilkay worked in a classified highrise, cut off from the rest of the world, plugging away at security problems only the fine-tangled mesh of reason and intuition, "gut" feeling and logical leaps of a highly trained and experienced mind could untangle. For Ilkay, cut off from any contact for the rest of the year, and restricted to the Western Protectorates for her timeshare because of international security reasons, it was not about money at all. She was afraid of losing Regina, even more than Regina was of losing her.

Ilkay took her hand. "Don't worry about the mix-up. It will be . . . interesting. Something new. Okay—not exactly *new*, but something I have not done for a long time. And I'm just so glad that you came, despite everything."

"What do you mean?"

Ilkay's eyes widened a bit, and Regina saw she had slipped, had revealed something not to be known outside the silos of the classified highrises that crunched the world's ugliest layers of data. No wonder they didn't let her out much: she may have been one of the world's greatest security analysts, but she was a clumsy liar.

Ilkay recovered and continued. "You know, this really is going to be fun. This guy even looks a little dangerous. God only knows what he's been put up to while we weren't around." Ilkay grinned wickedly, and ran a nail along the inside of Regina's ropy wrist. "I can pretend you've traveled through time all this way from Pylos to be with me. . . . "

"I guess that, in a sense, I have."

At that moment the muezzin's voice called from atop one of the minarets. Cutting clearly through the rain, the muezzin's trained voice, a rich contralto, carried so commandingly through the air that it almost seemed to come from speakers, despite the laws in Istanbul forbidding any amplification of the human voice. Both Ilkay and Regina paused until she had finished her call, staring at each other, cow-eyed as a couple of teenagers on a first date. Like it was every year, and just as exciting and good. When the muezzin had finished her song, Ilkay caught the eye of a waiter and made a sign in the air for the check. The young man nodded, unsmiling. The bent, friendly old man who had been serving their table was nowhere to be seen.

When the check came, Regina saw she had been charged for two teas.

"Sorry," she said to the young man. "The other waiter said that I would only be charged for one of these. . . . "

The young man shook his head. "You spilled the first one. You're responsible. You pay."

Regina began her protest. "Look, I'm happy to pay, but . . . "

"No, you look." The young man spat back at her. "I don't care what he said. You blanks think you can do anything you want. Spill a tea with your clumsy hands and not pay, forget to tip us because we won't even recognize you next time. You pay for what you took, like anyone else. Like the real people here."

Ilkay interrupted. "It's no problem. We'll pay. You can save the speech."

Stunned by the young waiter's hostility, Regina felt the pure, chemical haze of rage rising in her body. This was new—a feedback of violence that seemed embedded directly in the muscle and bone, a sudden awareness of her physical power, and a desire to use it so strong that it distorted thought. She wanted to smash a fist into the young waiter's face. Or a chair.

Grasping Regina's knee under the table to restrain her, Ilkay waved her palm over the check. "It's done, and a regulation tip for you, as well."

The young man shrugged. "I deserve more, putting up with you people every day." He muttered something else as they got up to leave. Regina did not catch it, but Ilkay's cheeks flushed.

As they were walking away, Regina turned and looked back at the terrace of the little café where they had met for countless years. The young waiter stood, arms crossed, watching them. As Regina caught his eye he turned his head and, keeping his eyes locked on hers, spat on the sidewalk.

Ilkay squeezed her hand. "Come on. We've got . . . "

Regina interrupted her. "What did he say, that last thing?"

"It's not important."

"Tell me."

Ilkay smiled gently. "You're going to have to get used to that male blank. You've never been in one before, have you?"

Regina shook her head. "No."

"You need to ride on top of it, the way you would a horse. Don't let its adrenaline surges and hormones get the better of you, or the feedback will distort your decision making. Cloud your thinking."

Regina shook her head, as if to clear it. "Yeah, I can feel that. But what did he say?"

Ilkay tugged at her hand, and they walked in the direction of the Hagia Sophia. In this early hour, there was almost no one on the sidewalks and the squares. The figures that they saw, all locals going about their own business, drifted in a clinging mist that did not quite turn to rain. "I'll tell you," Ilkay said, "but only if you promise, then, to concentrate on me. On us, and our time here."

Regina stopped walking, gathered herself. "Yes, of course. I'm sorry. I got carried away. It's embarrassing."

Ilkay punched her arm, playfully. "Well, don't forget to add this to your simulation. You can bet those men on Sphacteria were feeling exactly the same adrenaline surges, and it was having the same distorting effect on their decision making."

Regina grinned. "I was thinking the same thing. Always the analysts, the two of us."

Ilkay pulled them along toward the Hagia Sophia's entrance. Its heavily buttressed mass loomed. "He said, 'why don't you dead just stay dead?' "

Regina felt her teeth *actually grit themselves*. "I earned this. We both did. We've worked hard, both of us. We spent lifetimes sharpening our skill-sets, making ourselves valuable, making real contributions to science. I'm not some trust-fund postmortem cruising around in a speedboat off Corsica. We competed fairly for our places in the highrises. We worked for this. And . . . who do they think keeps them safe? And who spends all their money here, pays for the maintenance of these places, keeps their restaurants open? And . . . " She trailed off helplessly.

"I know, I know," said Ilkay. "Now forget about it, and let's go visit a church that has stood for over two thousand years, and let the temporary things be temporary."

The house Ilkay had rented for them, one of the ancient wooden homes along the Bosporus, was like a wedding cake fresh from a refrigerator—all white paint thick as frosting, china-fine detail, silken folds, and chilled from top to bottom. The heating system was apologetic but insufficient. They built a fire in the master bedroom's fireplace, found wool blankets in a trunk, ordered a very late lunch, and clumsily explored the possibilities of their new configurations. Then, increasingly less clumsily.

By the time lunch was delivered, they were exhausted and starving. In near silence, wearing their blankets like woolen superhero capes, they spread fig jam on fresh bread and watched sleet spin down over the Bosporus and spatter slush against the windowpanes. Out on the roiling chop of the strait, a fisherman in a small rusty boat and black rubber raingear determinedly attempted to extract some protein from the water. His huge black beard, run through with gray streaks, jutted from under his sou'wester, with seemingly only the axe blade of his nose between.

Regina dabbed at her mouth with a napkin. "It's amazing to think that these people have lived in a nearly identical way for centuries. Technology changes some things, like maybe fish-locating sonar systems and nearly perfect weather forecasting—but for the fisherman who actually has to get the fish on the hook, in any weather that comes, not much has changed."

"The physical things—the actual moving of matter around—are immutable," agreed Ilkay. "As we have been experimenting with all morning." She grinned, carefully applying fig jam. "And that's why, I think, these weeks are so important. They remind us of the base—the essentials, the substance of life and the world. Not that what we do isn't important. Not that who we are usually isn't real . . . "

Regina finished the thought: "But it's just so abstract. Immaterial. Not without consequence, but . . . "

"But without immediacy." Ilkay interjected. Then, after a long pause . . . "Regina, I miss you terribly. All year. And I cram everything I can into these short few weeks. And every year, I am afraid."

"Of what?"

"Afraid that next year, you will not be waiting for me at the café. These few weeks, always in winter . . . they are everything to me. They aren't a vacation . . . they are the sum and total of everything of meaning in my life. It's not that . . . it's not that I don't value my work, or think it saves lives. I haven't lost faith in the project. We watch over a troubled world, in my highrise . . . a world cruel people are constantly trying to tear to pieces . . .

but none of that work seems to matter nearly as much as the moment I see you again. Sometimes, I feel my work is eating away at who I am. It's like watching a shadow underwater: you know it is just seaweed, this shadow, a harmless mass writhing in the current, nothing to worry about. But what if it is a shark? A shadow with teeth and volition? The more you stare at the shadow, straining to make out its outline, the more certain you become that it is a shark—until you convince even yourself. This constant watching—it eats away at your feeling of security. It eats away, I think, at your sanity. And I've been afraid to tell you, because I feel as if once it's said, it will shatter all this . . . this causal sort of . . . easy feeling between us."

Regina put an arm around her. Her thicker arms were increasingly feeling as if they were her own. She pulled Ilkay toward her. "This was never casual or easy for me, Ilkay. And I'll always be at the café. Every single year."

The weather did not improve after lunch. The Bosporus swelled and churned, and the rain came down in columns. There was time to sit and talk, and to lie under the heavy covers of the four-poster and talk. Dinner was brought in a dripping container, and they tipped the young woman who brought it, soaked to the skin, double for her efforts. The sun set, and on the strait the lights of small boats bobbed in the dark between the chop of the water and the sky. Just after eight, the door buzzer jangled. They had been having cups of tea in front of the fire. Regina saw Ilkay immediately tense, like a cat hearing a dog bark in the distance.

The man on the doorstep was in a long, gray raincoat, black rubber boots, rain pants. Under his sou'wester an abglanz turned his face into a shadowy swirl of flickering abstract patterns. In a tech-limited city, the effect of the identity-shielding device was particularly jarring.

"Good evening," the composite voice said to Regina. "I apologize for the interruption of your timeshare. I hope to take up as little of your time as possible. I must speak to Ilkay Avci. This is, unfortunately, a matter of urgency." His credentials drifted across the shimmer of the abglanz. Istanbul Protectorate Security High Commission.

Standing in the corridor behind Regina, Ilkay said, "Come in, Inspector. Hang up those wet things."

As he did so, Regina noticed a port wine birthmark on the back of his hand. It was large, spreading across his wrist and up to the first knuckles of his fingers in a curious, complicated pattern, like a map of unknown continents. They should have given him an abglanz to cover that, she thought. I would know him again anywhere. They went into the living room.

"I apologize," the inspector said to Regina, "but due to the classified nature of this conversation, I will have to ask you to wear this momentarily. Once you are seated comfortably." He produced the slender metal cord of the scrambler from the pocket of his shirt. No matter what they did to that thing (this one was a cheerful yellow) it still looked like a garrote. Regina settled into a chair and let him place it around her neck. He clipped it into place gently, like a man fastening the clasp of his wife's necklace.

She was in Gulhane Park, at the peak of the Tulip Festival. The flowers—so large and perfectly formed they seemed almost plastic—were everywhere, arranged in brightly colored plots, swirling patterns of red, white, orange, maroon, violet, and cream. A few other tourists roamed the paths of Gulhane, but the park was, for the most part, empty. It was a cool spring day, smelling of turned earth. It was an Istanbul she had not seen—had not been able to afford to see—since the austerity, so many years ago now, had reduced her highrise's benefit levels. But, she thought, bending to cup the bloom of a Chinese orange tulip with a cream star at its center, what I gained when I lost this season was Ilkay. And that is enough to replace all of this. Though—just for a moment—it was good to feel the warm edge of summer hiding in the air, to close her eyes and let the sun bleed through her eyelids.

She wondered how wide the extent of the simulation was. Did it extend beyond the walls of Gulhane? The face of a passing tourist was glitchy, poorly captured, the woman's features wavered. No, it would be only the park, a tiny island of flowers, green paths, and good weather. But did it extend as far as the Column of the Goths? She would like to see that ancient object, surrounded by flowers in the spring. She began to walk further into the park. A crow glitched from one branch to another in a tree just beginning to leaf, its caw jagged with digital distortion.

She was back in the chair. The inspector stood over her, putting the scrambler back into his pocket. "Give it a moment before trying to stand. Just in case. And again, my apologies for any inconvenience. The Istanbul Protectorate Security High Commission thanks you, and will apply a small amount in contemporary lira to your accounts for the inconvenience. It isn't much, I am afraid—but enough for a good meal on the Galata Bridge for the two of you."

Ilkay was standing at the fire, warming her hands. "The courtesy is much appreciated, Inspector. At a later date I will review this interaction and give it the full five-star rating."

Once the inspector was gone, they both found they were too exhausted even to watch the fire burn down to its embers. They went to bed early, sliding into sheets as cold as the skin of ice on a river. Regina asked nothing about Ilkay's conversation with the inspector. It was one of the rules of their relationship, unspoken between them. Sometimes things about Ilkay's work were offered up, but Regina never inquired about them.

"Perhaps next year," Ilkay whispered in the dark, "we should meet somewhere else. Maybe it is time for a change."

"What happened?" And now Regina felt the rise of anger in her. Somewhere else? Where? It was not enough that she had no contact with Ilkay during the year, only these few weeks when they could see one another—now they had to intrude on this as well, eroding this small island of peace, as if it were too much to ask to have even this one thing. The face of the young waiter at the café rose up in her mind, spitting on the pavement.

"Nothing," Ilkay said. "Nothing at all. Tensions, or rumors of tensions. That's all it ever is, it seems. Like the shadow in the water. It's almost always seaweed. It's almost never a shark. But my job is to watch the shadows. And I'm tired, Regina. So very tired of being afraid. Why can't they let me at least have this? These few weeks. Haven't I earned a little peace in my life?"

The morning of the fifth day was bright and cold. The sky was opalescent. The mist that had clung to everything had risen to become a single, thin sheet of gauze, shrouding sun from earth. Under the Galata Tower, huddled beneath the glowing hood of a terrace heater, they drank black tea and coffee and had breakfast—honey and butter, warm bread and white cheese, tomatoes and hard-boiled eggs—and lingered over the meal. There were other blanks at the café, together and alone, smiling and laughing or quietly reading newspapers. Real newspapers, on real paper: one of the great joys of Istanbul.

The blanks sat on the terrace, oblivious to the cold, with only the heaters preserving them from the chill. The café's waiter, on the other hand, stood inside the café, watching his patrons from behind glass, continually rubbing his hands together for warmth. He was a middle-aged man moving toward old age, his thin hair combed straight back on his scalp. The cold, thought Regina, was different for him—lasting months out of the year, coming too soon and leaving far too late. For the blanks on his terrace, it was a joy to experience it, after their highrised, simulated year. Who were they all? Number-crunchers, of course, of one kind or another, moving data around. There were pure mathematicians among them, financial analysts, scientists and astronomers, astrophysicists, and qualitative historical analysts. And those, like Ilkay and herself, working in more esoteric fields.

Regina had never thought deeply about the difference between the blanks and Istanbul's permanent residents, the "locals," as they were called by some—but not by Regina, who liked to think of herself as a local, liked to think of this city as her city. Hadn't she earned that, by returning here every year for so long? Over the last few days she and Ilkay had "made their rounds," as they called it—despite the bad weather, they had visited all their old places—eating fresh fish on the Galata Bridge (subsidized by the Istanbul Protectorate

Security High Commission), walking the land wall that had protected, for a thousand years, an empire that had been destroyed well over a thousand years ago. On the third evening, from an open-topped ferry crossing the strait to the Asian side, they had watched the interstellar array on one of Istanbul's distant hills fire the consciousness of another brave, doomed volunteer into the stars, riding a laser into failure and certain death. The blanks on the ferry had applauded. The locals had hardly seemed to notice.

But it was different for them. The waiter blew into his hands and watched his patrons with no expression on his face at all as they laughed and spread honey on their bread. He simply wanted to be warm, wanted the spring to come. Time moved along—and the faster, the better. The blanks were his economy, providing him with a living. In winter, the tables were half empty. In the summer, they would be full. All the tables would be full. The blanks would take the city over, ferreting out even the most local of the cafés, the most "authentic" places to eat. Raising prices, elbowing out the city's residents, who would retreat deeper into the alleys and back streets. And the interstellar program ground on, engaging the imaginations of thousands, employing a hundred highrises, but without any news or result or breakthroughs for generations. Its promise was now ignored by the majority of the five billion, whose main task was just to live, here and now, not to worry about homes beyond the stars.

On the other side of the terrace, one of the breakfasters, a young woman with dark hair in a braid, seated alone, was having a conversation with a local teenage boy on a bicycle. The boy had drawn out a map, and was pointing to something on it. He handed the map to the blank, who began examining it, her easy smile displaying a row of white teeth. And then, the boy reached into his pocket and drew out a small, red canister with a nozzle at the top. He aimed it at the young woman's face and depressed the button, firing a spray into her eyes, nose, and mouth.

Without thinking, Regina was on her feet, across the terrace, then on top of the boy, slamming his hand again and again into the pavement until the canister fell from it and rolled bumpily away across the cobblestones, wrestling with him as he tried to twist away from her. The boy struck her in the face, hard, his hand impacting with a strangely sharp pain. But then others joined her, from the street and from the terrace. Whistles blew. The boy disappeared behind a mass of struggling backs and legs. Ilkay was on the terrace, pouring water from a bottle over the young woman's face. The woman's eyes were red and swollen closed, coughing and gagging. Near her, others were wiping at their eyes, trying to clear them of the irritant spray. Another man offered Regina a cloth, a napkin from the terrace, and now she noticed that her face was bleeding. She pressed the napkin to her cheek, feeling the warm pulse of blood from the deep cut there. Only then did she notice the policeman, carefully placing a small, bloody folding knife into an isolation bag. The café's proprietor stood in the center of his terrace, all tipped over tables and shattered tea cups, wringing his hands.

At the medical clinic, the nurse who applied the seal was a young man, ex-military, his silver-sheathed prosthesis of a right arm, twelve-fingered and nimble, deftly working the seal into place as he cheerfully bantered with Regina.

"Luckily, your insurance covers this damage. They can be picky about what you put the blanks through, you know. There are all sorts of clauses and sub-clauses. That knife just touched the zygomatic bone, but there are no fractures, no bruising. A lot of people don't read the fine print, and go paragliding or something, break a leg and find themselves footing a huge bill for repairs later, or a scrap and replace that they can't afford. But you made the right choice, bought comprehensive. You must have gotten into the program early—those rates are astronomical these days. Nobody can afford them but the highest ranking minister councilors and, of course, the postmortems. There we go. This guy's face will be good as new in a few days." He patted Regina's cheek affectionately, flexed the smoothly clacking many-fingered hand. "Just try not to smile too much." He admired his hand. "God, I love this thing. If anything good can be said to have come out of the Fall of Beirut, it's this hand. A masterpiece."

Ilkay was giving a deposition in another room. Looking up, Regina saw the inspector from the IPSHC standing in the doorway in a casual polo shirt and slacks, abglanz glittering weirdly under the medical-grade lights. She recognized him by the pomegranate-colored birthmark on his hand.

"I hope you are well," he said. "After your adventure."

Regina nodded slightly.

"Hold still one second," the young nurse said. "I have to fix the seal along the edge here."

"We are going to have to take a bit more of your time, I am afraid. Of Ilkay's time, to be more precise. Will you be able to get back to your residence all right? If not, I can send someone to accompany you. We will return her at the soonest moment we can, but I am afraid . . . " His digital smear of a face turned to the nurse. "If you are finished, can you leave her for a moment?"

The nurse shrugged and left the room.

"I am afraid," continued the inspector, "That we will need her particular skill set over the next few days. We have encountered . . . a rather fluid situation. It needs further analysis. Normally we would not . . . well, to be honest, the austerities have left us a bit short staffed. Ilkay's presence here, with her particular skill set, is an opportunity we literally can't afford to pass up."

Ilkay was in the doorway. "Inspector, can I have a moment alone with her?"

Once the inspector had departed, Ilkay crossed the room to Regina. She ran a finger lightly along the seal. "They've done a good job. It's the best work I've ever seen." She blinked back tears. "God, you are an idiot. You've spent too long in that simulation, or maybe that body is getting to you."

"I don't know what came over me," Regina said seriously. "It's something in the air, I suppose. I just reacted."

"Well," Ilkay said, "Stop reacting. I'll be back with you in a day. Two at the most. In the meantime, try not to play the hero too much. And I expect a full report of your adventures. But . . . " And now she seemed uncertain, lowered her voice. "Play it safe a little, will you? For me? It might be better . . . " she leaned in and whispered in Regina's ear. "It might be better to stay away from the touristy areas for a while. Can you do that for me?"

She pulled away. Regina nodded.

"Oh," Ilkay said, running her finger along Regina's razor-stubbled chin. "And by the way—you really need to shave more often. You're a beast, and it's not that I don't like it, but it's giving me a bit of a rash."

They had met here, so many years ago. It had been a different Istanbul, then—a city dominated by a feeling of optimism, Regina thought. No, not dominated—optimism could never dominate the city's underlying feeling of melancholy, of nostalgia for what was always lost. But the city had been brightened, somehow, by optimism. For years, there had been a feeling, ephemeral, like a bright coat of whitewash over stone. The relays were in place on a hundred possible new worlds, the massive arrays on Istanbul's distant hills were firing the consciousnesses of the first explorers into interstellar space. It was in that time that they had met. They had met on a Sunday, at the Church of St. George. Regina, who was not religious, had gone to a service. She had been trying things out then—meditation, chanting, prayer—all of it a failure. Where does one go when one has lost everything, risen back from nothing? But she found the drone of the priest's voice and the smell of incense—a thousand years and more of incense soaked into the gold leaf and granite—comforting. The flat and meaningfully staring icons, the quietude. In those first years of adjustment, it had been all she had.

Ilkay had found her outside in the courtyard. She had been doing the same—wandering from temple to mosque to church, searching. They fell in together, naturally, talking of the most private feelings immediately, walking up the hill through neighborhoods that had been crumbling for as long as they had been standing, where the burned shells of houses mixed with those restored, and all of them leaned on one another, the whole leaning on the broken for support, the broken leaning on the whole. They ate a meal together in a little family restaurant whose courtyard was the ivy-covered walls of a shattered house, long ago consumed by fire, open to the sky. The meal felt, for Regina, like a communion. Someone had found her and had made her whole. And there had been no struggle, no doubt, no sacrifice. They had spent every moment together afterward, never parted, and agreed to meet the next year. That was all. They had never questioned it.

Regina did not question it now. If Ilkay was gone tomorrow, she would not think it was because she had abandoned her. This was not possible. It would be because she was gone completely.

Regina lasted three days, waiting in the icy house and keeping to the city's Asian side. She found some comfort in a book she dug up in a bookstore there, a long-forgotten treatise on insect architecture. The book came complete with color plate illustrations of the complex constructions of bugs. It was a labor of love written by some Englishman, obscurely obsessed in the best possible way. She pored over the book's slightly mildewed pages, rich with the vanilla scent of their paper's chemical decay, for hours. Ilkay sent her reassuring messages, full of her bright sarcasm, hoping every day for their reunion. And the time slipped away. Would Istanbul Protectorate pay for their separation? Reimburse them for what they were taking? Unlikely.

On the fourth day, Regina decided to return to the European side. She would avoid the popular places, as she had promised Ilkay. But most people went to the hippodrome and Hagia Sophia, the Blue Mosque, and sometimes strolled up to the Grand Bazaar. She would avoid those places.

The Church of St. George itself was surprisingly small, suited now to the dwindling number of pilgrims and tourists it received, though once it must have swelled full of the faithful on holy days. Pilgrims would have filled the small courtyard that, now, was nearly empty. The gray stone of the simple façade was more like a house than a church, though inside it was filled with gold leaf and light.

But Regina stayed in the courtyard. A group of blanks was there in a cluster around a local guide who Regina could not see, but whose voice carried in the air. Pigeons walked around the feet of the tourists.

"The church's most precious objects, saved from each successive fire that consumed parts of it, are the patriarchal throne, which is believed to date from the fifth century, rare icons made of mosaic, and the relics of two saints: Saints Gregory the Theologian and John Chrysostom."

Regina walked toward the group to hear more clearly. A message was coming in from Ilkay.

"Regina, where are you?"

"Some of the bones of these two saints, which were looted from Constantinople by the Fourth Crusade in 1204, were returned by Pope John Paul II in 2004. Today the Church of St. George serves mostly as a museum . . . "

Regina could see the guide now, standing in the semicircle of faces. The faces of the blanks were pale, lips and noses red with cold. Most of them bored. Some carried on quiet conversations with one another as the guide spoke. Why did they come to these place if they did not care?

"I am at the place we met," Regina sent. "Still laying low, waiting for you."

The guide wore a heavier coat, and a warm hat. As Regina approached, he saw her and looked up, continuing his speech. "Though there are still pilgrims."

It was the young waiter from the café on her first day. Recognizing her, he smiled sarcastically. "They return here every year . . . "

Another message came in from Ilkay. "GET OUT!!!"

The guide raised his hands. "And they will keep coming until we stop them."

There was a flash of blinding light.

The trireme lurched free of its anchorage and began a slow rotation to starboard, oars churning in the gray-blue water. Regina was crouched on the deck, the sun white-hot on her exposed neck. Her hands were bound behind her. Blood was spattered on the wood, small droplets from a wound she had received across her cheek in the final moments of the battle.

There had been chaos, and many had thrown down their shields, but for some reason she had kept fighting until finally one of the Athenian hoplites had struck her on the side of the head with the flat of a sword, and she had fallen, dazed, struggling to get to her feet. Then they had moved in, knocking her sword from her hand, wrestling her to the ground, finally subduing her and binding her wrists with a leather thong.

Her head still throbbed from the blow from the sword, and a hundred other bruises and scrapes ached. Behind them, Sphacteria's flat, narrow expanse, fought for so hard and at such cost, began to fade as the simulation's boundaries drifted into opalescent tatters. Finally there was only the trireme, and the lingering sound of its oars in water that was no longer there.

An Athenian hoplite approached and handed her water, but she did not bother to take it. Sensation was already fading, the materiality ending. The water would be nothing in a mouth that had ceased to feel it. The wound had stopped throbbing, was gone. Blood remained on the deck, and the sun's warm color, but not the warmth of the sun.

"Do you really think they would have kept fighting like that? After it was impossible to win?" The Athenian cut her hands free with a small bronze knife.

Regina lay down on the deck. Moments ago there had been the physical feeling of exhaustion, heat. Now there was none of that, though there was a faint sensation of the deck beneath her. She laced her fingers behind her head and looked up into the glaucous simulation edge that was the sky.

"I do," Regina said. "Some would have given up. But others were beyond reason, beyond caring about consequence. They would have carried on when it was impossible. Hatred, fear, and anger would have ruled them. I was missing it in my reports last year. The stubbornness, the things beyond strategy."

Astrid, who had played the Athenian but was now becoming Astrid again, was silent for a moment, then tossed her helmet to the deck where it landed without a sound and was gone. She sat down with a sigh. "You're probably right. Anyway, it seems to come closer to the truth. But I'm so tired of doing this every day. I wish I knew what they were looking for. What's the key to all of this? Anyway . . . another year almost gone, and no end in sight. Is your timeshare still in Istanbul? Will you really go back there, after everything that happened there last year? After almost getting killed, and totaling your blank? You barely made it out of that place alive."

That morning, before the start of the day's simulation, Regina had received a message from Ilkay: "Here a day early, already waiting for your arrival. Tell me you are coming, though I won't stop worrying until I see your face."

Regina grinned into the blank swirl of false sky, seeing black tea there, and cobblestones, incense aged into stone, the hiss of snow along a seagull's wing, and Ilkay's face—the many faces Ilkay's being had illuminated, her smile each year both different, and the same.

"Of course I'm going back. Now, and every year. It is my home."

THE HERMIT OF HOUSTON

SAMUEL R. DELANY

⊷⊶

"First off," I remember the Hermit's assistant told us, "you can't tell the entire story." She was perhaps ten years older than I was and had that pigment thing some black people get where blotches on their skin are missing the melanin. She had a large one on her left cheek. I was a child and that was weeks after I'd been brought to the door and turned loose to see if I'd enter or run away. Immediately I'd gone inside, though it wasn't natural curiosity. "Like me trying to tell you everything you're going to learn here," she told the group of us, in our high-ceilinged classroom. "Or why you're going to learn it, whether from me or on your own, or from each other. I couldn't do it," she repeated in the hallway when I went up to say I didn't understand.

("You better go in there with the rest," my older sister had said, looking at the shrubbery and the rocks beside the door, "or you'll be killed—")

I remember leaving by those same doors—twenty feet tall they were, of patinaed bronze, practically black, around panes of scratched glass. On wet days raindrops blew jaggedly down and across. Sometimes clouds reflected in them, during the glorious weather that obtained for ten-and-a-half months of the year. We children would gather in front of the building for our trips and wanderings, for wherever, in those years, we thought to go off to. We could explore anywhere on the Yucatán coast, in sight of the squat pyramid, down the shore, above the neat city between.)

The Hermit of Tolmec herself we saw far less frequently. She was rich, old, and a woman I'm pretty sure had been born that way on all fronts—though a decade later Cellibrex, once we met and learned to talk to each other, told me you really can't tell about gender. People change it all the time—though he never had.

Neither had I. But by then he and I both had known people who'd done so. I'd never knowingly been to bed with any, though he said he had several times. He preferred what he was used to, however—which apparently, at least he said so, was me.

And by that time we were used to each other.

In my very unclear memory of childhood (lucid about some things and nonexistent about others), the Hermit of Tolmec wore blue rags one week, and red ones the next. She had old boots and a supply of different colored laces, which she changed every morning to receive the visitors who came while she sat in a big wooden chair in her part of the building. The chair—an ecclesiastical throne—had knife scars on its frame that spoke of age and a history I didn't know anything about. I didn't know if the Hermit did, either. Once I whispered to the assistant, "What are they . . . ?" and she put her hand—which also had some white patches—on my shoulder:

"I don't know. And I don't want to. But we're slated to get a replacement by the end of the month: something simple. Then we can all forget such atrocities."

The Hermit's laces beneath her torn skirts that day, at the foot of her chair's carved wooden legs, above a small fur rug, glimmered black.

Her assistant liked her: me, the Hermit frightened.

For most of the time, those of us in the hermitage lived pretty much alone, in the shell of what her assistant explained had been a suburban supermarket, though she said that even earlier it had been an urban cathedral, when this had briefly been the site of the city of Tulum on the eastern Yucatán coast, before the Texans came. (I think they were Texans, but I don't know for certain.) Then it was a village again. They had invaded before I was born, but later drifted away. No, I hadn't been born there either. Though I'm not sure where I'd came from, or if I ever knew. I remember the assistant also telling our group that there was once a movement to tell stories that focused on how you got food, how the technology worked, how you related to something called "Mean Production," how some of it was really dangerous, and some of it was actually helpful. But you couldn't accept all of it without serious thought, which was the notion of an ancient religious leader named Marx, who at one time you could learn about in various threads on the greatest of the old religions, Facebook, but that an older—or was it newer—religion called Handbook had gone back to the idea that everyone could live naturally and not have any mean production at all, though she used to laugh and say it didn't seem any more natural to her than any other kind.

"Listen to me, Smart Girl (you know that *still* sounds strange to me, because you are a male), I am delighted you are not terrified to come see me," said the Hermit in our own conversation, having been called in to discipline me. "I've killed so many children—babies they were, little female babies that we called boys, to make it easier—and for a while many people knew it. I hope that's something you never wake up one morning and realize you've done, no matter how inadvertently. But at that time it seemed the only way to bring down the population. As followers of Facebook go, we were fairly deluded;

almost as deluded as the followers of Handbook who tried to replace them." She sorted. "And just ended up mingling with them . . . I suppose we are lucky that Facebook has such a short memory. Or, who knows, maybe some other little girl like you told a tale . . . " and I was startled, because I thought she might have known about my sister giving up her own place to get me in there. "Be glad you're a boy." But that's just a name, and I am not sure what you would call me if you actually met me this week, though most probably it would be different from next week. These categories change much too quickly for anyone to keep up, though I feel as if I've been sexually stable since I came back to the area after my traumatic childhood wanderings.

But then I had my coming-of-age forgetting process, as did all those in the hermitage and all those in any government education system I was told; and while all of us worried about it beforehand, since it wasn't a complete memory erasure but highly selective, certainly it made me and all of the rest of us feel better, even a bit superior, if not privileged. And there was the shared paradox of thousands and thousands of children, I just assumed, not remembering what it was we'd forgotten . . .

Today, more than thirty-years later, the Tolmec Hermit must be dead. I know my sister is. I wonder about the other children who were there with us. (Though I still know where Ara lives, who was in my group back then.) I like to think we were there, all those years ago, because we were smart. Or was it because someone thought we needed to be taught certain things and might learn them more easily there, which is not quite the same . . .

The story I put together for myself about my very confused adolescent travels is that I must have gone more than two thousand kilometers by bicycle, helicopter, horse, barge and boat. After that I lived (I learned I ended up there almost by accident.) between thirty and fifty kilometers from the old supermarket-once-cathedral in Tolmec, though it might as well have been on the other side of what people around here still argue could be a globe turning in space or an endless plane that stretches to infinity in all directions. I didn't intend to tell you that much about *my* childhood, or how I got my food, or which of the vegetables I ate, or which I gave to my companions or which were stolen by my enemies (I don't think I could bear it: too many people died in that process to make it the kind of story acceptable on Facebook *or* Handbook), and the Handbook priests used to come through with their guns, to police the tales we told at the seasonal gatherings, where we got to make music and those who wanted to be Great Writers themselves told tales in keeping with the Algorithm Transparency Act and that for a while was all the news with the people who were concerned with what was and what wasn't Acceptable to the Tribe.

I wonder if, on that trip that's so unclear in my memory, I went all the way around—or only described a small circle.

It's interesting listening to stories in a closed arena while priests stand in the aisles with guns. Twice I saw them shoot a Writer. As soon as it happened, people began to check on their pocket phones for what was acceptable to say and what was not, while the blood ran to the platform edge and down the front of the stage.

(Cellibrex says that during his childhood he never heard any official tales told, but lived in among gangs of hundreds of children, mostly underground, and you could watch all the porn you wanted. But nobody did. Cellibrex said he too had gone traveling in his youth, though almost instantly he had been set upon, captured, dragged away through trees and rocks, imprisoned, and held as part of another gang from which he did not really get loose until his mid thirties. He said it was very much like the first one, only the children in it looked more like he did. All memory of where he'd started was now gone. Though in his gang sex among the kids boys was constant, there was what I assumed must haven been age-mate guidance, but nothing like adult supervision; as he said, there *were* no adults.)

Everyone knows straight men and women and gay men and women do lots of different things. But the only act you can talk about in a public telling, either in a local gymnasium or a great auditorium with murals hanging on the cinderblock walls, is a penetrative one that's supposed to be common to all. Especially once they are married. You can describe that act for anyone in as much detail as you wish. Because it is Universal, as is Marriage itself. But the mentioning of anything else outside of Marriage could get you shot. I knew even before I went traveling that many things called safe sex that were part of what men did together, most of what went on between men and the men who were called women, you could not mention in Public. (It's what got the second Great Writer who I saw shot and wounded in his—she was a woman—performance.) But it meant that I grew up thinking "safe sex" and "oral sex" were the ultimate evils for all.

It certainly cured me of wanting to be any sort of Writer, Great or otherwise.

I've lived with so many Round Earthers; most of my life it never occurred to me to take Flat Earthers seriously. Someone once told me a story about a famous old detective who didn't know that the Earth was round because he didn't need such information to do his detective work. He had a friend who was a doctor who lived on Baker Street—or was he a Baker who lived with a doctor?

That part I *didn't* remember.

I do remember public demonstrations and big arguments—shooting ones, with stun guns—among critics over whether they had a heterosexual relationship or a homosexual one. You could find old DVDs of versions in which Watson was played by a woman, which was supposed to clinch the argument. Then someone cited an earlier written text which was supposed to clinch it the other way. Then a third voice upheld that we should take each version for exactly what it said, and not get lost in decoding, which finally drew the biggest guffaws.

That got the commune of a friend of mine smashed up.

But I may sneak in a few accounts of such forbidden topics about Cellibrex— not his real name: my nickname for him, because years before, I read in some library it had been a kind of recording tape, and so many of the things he did say were things he repeated. But we were together for a long time. I learned quickly that he had grown up with many more children than I had. Neither he—nor any of the boys he'd grown up with—ever learned to read. He didn't even know his family. "Clone" was the worst insult you could call someone, he told me. And if anyone one in any group looked too much like anyone else in the clique, often that person was driven out to seek people who were physically different—for friendship, sex, or other social bondings. But we are broaching the kinds of differences that, were this an official tale, I would not be able to tell.

Cellibrex says the world is flat—there is no argument, as far as he is concerned, and saying otherwise is silly. To me that sounds so absurd, I never thought to argue. In his childhood, he saw men and adults kill people who held contrary opinions. He says he grew up in a commune—which I always assumed meant an artificial environment, the way it's used here—but I can't be sure since I wasn't there—with an apple in it, which was like a big pocket phone or a pad with a screen on it, which I never encountered. It's not a popular opinion, but it's not one that would get you killed at a public tale telling, either. (Those are the parts of the story I'm *not* allowed to tell.) Though he never was taught how to use it, Cellibrex knew we were ruled by the Internet, which was not a book but a group of men and very shortly he found himself rounded up and shipped to a sprawling penal combine, where he spent a dozen years of his life. (I assume dozen meant twelve, but I can't be sure of that either: he says he learned to use the word for an approximate general number from us. What he and the boys he was captured with were incarcerated for, he does not know or refuses to say. He says he didn't learn the word "dozen" meant a specific number until after he'd escaped from the military.

That's when I began to wonder if "flat" to the Flat Earthers meant curved so slightly that it might as *well* be flat in all directions . . . and just gave up because they didn't need to know anything else to do their work. Like the famous detective (who was probably gay, since his best friend was an Asian woman).

From the time he was eleven until he was twenty-two or so, Cellibrex has told me, he does not know where he was either; but it was far away. He killed people while he was there, and he does not believe he can go back, which at first made me wonder if he had been a Hermit or a Hermit's assistant. But later I realized he'd been in a gang called a family, or a family called a gang: It had lots of people in it, of all ages. His gang-family had no parents in it that he was aware of. There was a lot about age mates, which were important. It was all male and the sex was pretty ritualized and possessive. He remembered standing on some rocks, either in the morning or the evening, seeing fields full of his gang moving below, in groups of what he was sure had to be hundreds.

Then, somehow, he spent some years in a military unit, which he said entailed thousands of men—again, no men who were even called women had survived among the gangs of his childhood.

But the sex and the work were so different that he thought for the first six months it would drive him crazy, learning to understand them. But somehow he found, once he stopped resisting, it was actually both inter- esting and easier. And he'd traveled around enough to make him believe in the world's flatness.

I remember a childhood of living in units with people who were respon- sible for me. He remembers sleeping in piles of brothers in which anything might happen.

But I didn't find out he believed all these things about the world and had seen so much to make him sure of them—unless he was just bat-shit crazy, which now and then I have considered, though he was pretty quiet most of the time—until after we had known each other almost a year.

He was a very expressive man, but not a communicative one.

He knew his real name—which I don't think there's any reason to tell—but not where he came from, though he had an ID number. But it began with QX4, which makes me think it was from a long, long way away.

You want to know how we met?

It was during my recurring two days off from my job that—like I say— good literary form stipulates I not specify as to time and place, though I'll be vulgar and mention it entailed baskets and boxes and keeping track of the food and electronics they contained. But I don't want to get myself in trouble, telling whether I worked indoors or out, or if it was mostly physical labor or information tracking that I did, whether I was paid in copper notes or material certificates, etc. Distinctions of that sort are not literary. Today what is valued in a tale is the universal, not the specific, what is common to all men and women, whatever their sex; how we are all alike.

You get in the habit of not talking about things like that with others, and soon you don't think about such things yourself.

It's that forbidden mean production again.

At any rate, I was walking up through the recreation area between the major living hoods and the farming areas, through trees and by ponds, where the wild animals are kept with their tracking collars and the tame ones walled away on the Farms (another kind of institution entirely) that smelled so incredibly when you rode by them on a bicycle or glided over them in a glider. I'd taken my blue shirt off and tied the sleeves around my neck and was wondering about taking off my sandals and going barefoot, when a very large, unshaven brown-skinned fellow wandered from behind some trees.

He was already barefooted. He had lots of rough tattoos on his chest, arms, shoulders, thighs, buttocks and face—he's was practically naked. That is not common in this part of the world. He had on a belt under a furry belly that looked full, fed, and strong, and a kind of—I guess you'd call it—groin cloth. (I was eighteen. I kept a neat beard back then in which a lot of folks said they recognized my Asian ancestors, which is not rare at all in this part of the Yucatan.) He was at least thirty or thirty-five, and his broad bones were heavy with muscle and that looked kind of threatening. I've seen pictures of the natives who were supposed to have lived in this area a few generations ago, in the local library, with its forty books that anyone can go in and look through (though I gather I am one of about a hundred people in the neighborhood's three thousand who does), and he looked like one of them, though physically a lot larger. He had a beard and was starting to go bald, and a broad, brown nose. He had bright, oddly blue eyes for such dark skin and rough, straight hair.

We are a small enough settlement that we don't get a lot of strangers, but I guess we are on the sort of routes where the ones we get can be pretty varied from one another in this odd world we live in, so that not much surprises us—if they're not toting visible weapons. And he wasn't.

I am a gay man who had had a fair amount of local experience but I was unprepared for the next thing he did: which was to raise his groin cloth, point to himself, look left and right, then look back at me—which I realized, to my surprise, in that isolated spot, was an invitation to . . . well, service him. My heart began to pound.

It was not a space where such encounters were common. But I knew of others not far away where they were.

I looked around, and thought, no this probably isn't a good idea . . .

Many of the marks on his body were what most of us, would call obscenities, which for me oscillated between disturbing and intriguing. Bats, Skulls, Dragons, as well as male genitals, dogs and mules relieving themselves of urine, excrement, or desire using their fellows . . . his back was against a rock with lots of foliage on it, and I was on my knees in the fallen leaves in front of him, with his thick (if average length) penis in my mouth, which was pleasantly salty, and pretty much like mine. (That, of course, was when I thought of asking him if he thought this was . . . But his rough hands held my head, moving it out and in, while above me he breathed harder and harder. And I forgot about all such thoughts.)

When, three or so minutes later, he spilled into me, and I thought I'd better disengage, he didn't release me, but held me to him, finally to let me rise and push against him and, still erect enough to hold aside his clout, with one hand against my buttocks and one behind my head, pressing my face into his neck, he encouraged me to rub against him until—I guess—it was clear to him I too had an orgasm. The upper joints of his left hand bore letters I wont write but were now inked out as a second thought; while on the joints of his right hand I recognized a Latino term for excrement.

When finally I stepped away, he held my hand in rough-skinned fingers. Had it been three hours later, I would have had somewhere I had to go. Had it been the day before, while I might have been there on an off hour, I would have had to leave immediately on finishing the first time.

But it was the day it was: he grinned, and without releasing my hand, with his other and his general expressions of humor and contentment, this tattooed giant communicated clearly without any words at all: "That was fun. Let's do it again? No, right *now* . . . !" And so, with only a little variation, and because nobody else was there, we did. This time his tongue ended up way down my throat, as mine did down his. He was missing a couple of teeth in the back, which my own tongue learned and felt comfortable knowing.

He did not speak to me. When we were done for the second time, I said a few things to him. Where did he want to go? What had he come here for? He listened, looking at me curiously, but did not respond to in any way specific enough to make me think he understood any particular word I'd said.

I knew there were people in the world who had once spoken other languages than mine; and I was innocent enough not to be threatened by it as a concept—at least when the results were pleasant, and so far they had been.

It was one of the things I'd taken from my time at the Tolmec Hermitage, supported by things that had occurred on my travels up to from Old Mexico through Texas to New Mexico and the northern border to the three state union that remains, where Canada starts.

I released his hand, and began to walk—and was both curious and surprised when he walked with me.

And somehow I went with him back to the three living units which I shared with some others in the town.

We walked down toward my cabin—and while we were getting to the more populous area I saw Markus, my friend from work, who basically has little use for gay men at all, though he is a friendly enough work mate—and I reached over to take my big, new friend's hand to make it seem a more normal relationship, at least in Marcus's eyes. But the big fellow pulled his hand away and frowned. So I stepped a little closer and we went on walking.

Moments later, we passed Ara—who had been a Smart Girl back at the same Tolmec Hermit's I'd been at, before all the traveling and disruption, and who had ended up here when Things Settled Down, as the News Pundits say on the Info Dumps, that you can go and watch here and there, in the streets, if you're really interested. Ara and I rarely spoke, but I always assumed there was a kind of bond between us. He blinked at us—and I supposed I understand what he was thinking: My new friend after all was as different from those of us as you might see around the streets and alleys of our town as a movie star or, really, some soldier, either of which, I suppose, he could have been.

Ara had lived a much more common life than I had, for those who had once been Smart Girls in a hermitage. His own travels had taken him way to the south, and rumor had it to Brazil, which was a million miles away culturally—and had worked for several years in some non-US space program in some South American Union that still had one (though whether he had been to an actual Other World or Other Moon or not I wasn't sure) though now he had returned to Settle Down pretty close to where I had.

Someone else walked by, I believe and looked, and so I just reached over and took the big fellow's hand, again to make us look more ordinary. And this time he let me hold it, and minutes later we were at the porch of the six unit dwelling—three on the north side, three on the south: I had the one on the north end. We came in, and he stopped at the door, to look around the circular room where I had most of my stuff, my futon, some pictures that a friend of mine had once drawn, some other things that had been printed that I thought were interesting, some on the door out to the shared latrine in the hall, that hooked up underground to the neighborhood waste disposal system for much of the neighborhood, the only sign for which was the blue band along the bottom of the roll of toilet paper that meant, "*Don't* throw it in the hole!" which, I suddenly wondered if my new, nameless (so far) friend was familiar with.

(Apparently he was.)

I asked him a couple of more questions. Didn't get a couple of more answers. (Or course you have to normalize the dialogue; especially in the beginning, and even more especially if some of it is happening in a different language you don't even speak. Though I'd learned a few of those words, I'll leave them out. It's not just literary universalism, it's comprehension.) One of he things he said to me when we got inside was: "First, I think you mean 'means *of* production,' " and explained what it meant, "and, second, arguing over weather the earth is round or flat is silly when you're living in a geographical union where there's only one sex represented, despite the varieties of genders, for a thousand miles in any direction, and since you were twelve and I was twenty-two neither of us have been allowed to cross a border; some of us are killed by the hundreds every day and others of us are left to die on our own— and the thing I worked so hard for and was in the year before I met you was to escape from one group to the other. It just doesn't happen to be happening right here, right now. Got it? But what either your or my forebears from three generations ago would recognize as ordinary human reproduction is only occurring in two very small republics under conditions of pain, oppression, and physical and emotional abuse."

I frowned. "You," I said, for the first time, "are bat-shit crazy."

"I," he said, "am not going to argue. But have you ever seen or heard of a person bearing a child, or getting pregnant, or birthing a child. How would someone here go about finding out if they were in such a condition—or even could be?"

I said, "I don't know what those terms mean—can you explain them to me?"

He chuckled and shrugged. "Not tonight. But eventually, perhaps you'll see that because I am probably the only person you'll ever talk to who thinks differently—and possibly one or two Hermits in their Hermitages—from the majority is the major proof I'm right."

"Maybe that's something they made me forget in my coming-of-age forget-fulness process."

"Now why would they make you forget that?"

"I don't know. What did they want you to forget?"

"I never had it. It's very expensive. The vast, *vast* majority of people in this union don't. It just removes all sense of personal and social conflict out of the experiences that frighten you out of your preferences for the same sex on the sexual level—which is to say that it assures there are good number of people like you around who suck good dick and like doing it, and feel it's normal and they're evenly distributed throughout the landscape. That's all."

"Come on. It's got to be more than that. It has to produce a major advantage."

"No, it doesn't. It shifts a 'natural' balance by about three per cent, which is enough to restructure an entire society. And nobody ever talks about it." Then he said: "And the other thing they make you forget is just how few of you there actually were. How few a few thousand are who can only be imitated by others in a landscape of millions . . . "

And that's maybe three years of normalized dialogue, between two people and discussions with whole groups, crammed into the account of a single conversation. Not the whole story at all, nor would it be if I added that part of it came during a shouting argument with some others during an icy morning's breakfast at a conference we were visiting, and another part came with the support of fifty pages transcript read on a secure line in a reader I found in the back of a library when I was browsing in an office while the light through the new windows was went from yellow to red in the light outside in the court yard—where there's just been an execution of twenty prisoners.

Hey—what is important to me about our actual meeting was that the next I knew Cellibrex was at my small electric stove and making, first, an acceptable cup of tea (with a laconic "Glad I don't miss coffee . . . " which bewildered me) and then when we sat on the edge of the futon together, sipping it out of the ceramic cups that I kept over the cooking and washing sink by the stove, he came back in from the latrine, brought over a pot I hadn't washed from the sink, and showed me the white streaks inside it, while I sat cross legged on the mattress.

"Oatmeal?" he asked.

I was surprised. "Um . . . yes," I said. "I had it for breakfast. I haven't cleaned the pot yet."

"If I stay, maybe tomorrow . . . ?"

"Sure," I said. "I don't mind. I'll make you some, if you'd like. You like oatmeal?"

He stood above me, dangling the pot. With his other hand, he scratched himself. (His belt and groin clout were all in a pile on the futon's corner.) "You," he said, "are ridiculously talkative. If you shut up, though, maybe I'll stay."

Which surprised me. (And he seemed to think was funny.)

Then he got down on his knees, put his arms around me, and pulled me over and we began once more.

Surprised, I stopped and lifted my head. "Tell me your name."

He had already started in again. "Why? I don't know yours, yet. But you suck some good dick."

And about an hour later, while I was sucking him . . . well, let me pull a literary curtain over that. I mean it's not like you have to tell everything you do in bed with everybody. (It's not like there are any sexually transmitted diseases left that force you to be honest about all that stuff—as I read about once in the library.) At any rate, it caught me off guard, but I went on swallowing. And when he was finished, I came all over his belly. Taking a big breath, I asked: "How'd you know I'd like that?"

He chuckled. "I took a chance. You can go on calling me Cellibrex. I'll go on calling you Clam. I'll tell you my real name if I'm still here in a week."

I was surprised again.

But he was and he did.

And once out of nowhere he said, "You said your sister told you if you didn't go inside the Hermitage, you would be killed . . . ?"

I looked puzzled. "Yes . . . ?"

"Well, admittedly it would have been ten years earlier, but if you had stayed outside, we—or children very much like us—are the ones who would have swarmed by and killed you. That's who you were fleeing from." He gave a humph. "That's who I was fleeing from when I started my wanderings and was captured by the very gang of roughians you were fleeing by seeking refuge inside."

"That's who you . . . defected from?"

He didn't say anything.

"But why—?"

"Because by that time they would have killed me."

When we were together for three weeks, Cellibrex was wearing clothing like mine, and both of us were spending a lot more time barefooted whenever we were in the house, and . . . well, it was kind of surprising just how much we had changed each other, in so much of what we did outside, and how well we adjusted to what each of us liked to do when, together, we were indoors. (He too sucked some . . . well, he'd been imitating guys like me all his life. But I don't feel comfortable talking about it, because some of the trouble I've seen people get into over speaking of it.) "We are such different people, you and me," I asked after three years: "Why are we still together?"

I thought it was probably because you can only feel so threatened by someone who makes tea and likes oatmeal and is good sex, no matter how different they are from you.

"Because we like each other . . . ?"

" . . . are getting used to each other," was his own regularly repeated answer to that question for more than a decade. By then his tattoos had changed from things that now and then could repel me to things that I wanted pressed all over me, to simply something familiar and that I was glad were there because they were his.

(I don't know what you are used to, so that I don't know what you will assume as to cleanliness, technology, neatness, clutter, and will fill in . . . properly or improperly, if I don't mention it or leave it out.)

That year they put out a new *Star Wars* (number four of the third tetralogy), and I went to see it on a sensory helmet in a theatre.

While I was at a tea and cake shop nearby called La Colombe, pretty crowded that afternoon, I had a glass of water and a blue-berry muffin. While I was eating it, a woman about my age come in to stand next to me: she was wearing an ordinary black coat and not the stripes that, these days, the disabled often ear: She must have had some kind of stroke, because one hand hung down beside her with the fingers turned to the back, and when she ate whatever piece of pastry she was eating, she had to leaned way, way back and she moved around kind of stiff-legged, and the barista who wore a knitted cap, took it all in stride; I called Cellibrex on my pocket phone (the thing was working that afternoon), to tell him, as I walked out of the place, that I was going to stop off and see it.

She and I and about half the others had come in barefoot—which, at that time of year, was a slight but not major surprise.

I enjoyed the show. It had been playing for about a week so there weren't that many people in the theater, a large cinderblock building with a decorative black curtains on both side of the auditorium.

Nobody in the projection looked like anyone I was used to seeing—but I was pretty used to that, too.

Still, the story had made me feel good, and afterwards when I was coming home, I gave ten dollars to a homeless mother—at least that's what her sign said, as she sat up against one of the uptown building walls, though she didn't have her kid with her—and I also gave twenty to an old friend that I ran into who used to hustle and who said he wasn't homeless, but he was still available for pay. So we wondered over to the same place I'd met Cellibrex and had a very unenthusiastic sexual encounter in which neither one of us got really excited.

I didn't tell Cellibrex about any of this, because (one) he does not like movies of any kind in a theater, and though (two) he does not have a jealous bone in his body, he does worry all the time about money, and we both get our government pensions, at this point. And it never seems quite enough to get by on, though we neither one seem to be losing any weight.

Ten or so years after that, when I was retired and took on a lighter job, I was offered a chance to become a Library Guardian, which meant we got a slightly bigger living unit, if we took in five hundred books which were stored in a separate room which was open to the public two days a week, and nobody ever really came for them, though there was a guy named Bill who came and worked there, and whom we both got to like, and who would fly back to his family up in Houston or holidays, sometimes.

Cellibrex was much more outgoing and talkative by then around people outside, though he grumped to me in private that we would do it my way because we always did, and because that had become so habitual among his complaints about me, if anything it reassured me. And we did. And sometimes he would stand and glare at the young people who used the library, which I would tell him he just could not stand around doing. So he took to not going in that room at all.

Then, through Bill, we got an invitation to move to Houston, where I could become a Guardian of an even bigger Library. So we did.

There were the usual private grumps: "We'll do it your way, because that's what we always do. Besides, we'll be working with Bill."

We moved—and it was a disaster. They were planning to disassemble our Tolmec unit on the day we left, so there was no coming back. It turned out that the area of Houston that we were moving to (Pasadena) just wasn't anywhere as sophisticated as Tolmec.

A month after we got there, Bill—it turned out—wouldn't be able to work with us. In our front two rooms, we had three times the books we'd had in Tolmec, and the woman who was assigned the job was Bill's opposite: Ms. Chase was fat, talkative, and the first time I said anything to her she stood up from her desk and said, "If you don't like the way I do my job, see the Hermit." I did not say anything thing to Cellibrex about that one because he would just say, "Do what you want, you'll do it your way anyway," and I would point out how I was always doing what he wanted, as soon as he would say what it was.

The next morning, when Chase came in, I said to her, "I know I'm an old man, but this is not working out. Would you please get me an appointment with the Hermit?" I expected her to look frightened or contrite or otherwise confused. But she surprised me:

"Happily." Fifteen minutes later, she came in to say: "You have an appointment at three o'clock. I'll take you over there myself in an Uber, if you like. Do you want your partner to come with you? You might be more comfortable with him . . . ?" and she waited with uncharacteristic expectancy.

"No," I said. "It'll be simpler, if I just go myself."

At twenty of nine, she came in. "I meant to get you five minutes ago, but the time got away from me. Take a sweater or a hoodie. You two don't use any air conditioning to speak of, and that place is going to be very cold. I've got a notebook here. I could jot down some of the things you've been complaining about. But the main thing is you want me transferred—and *I'd* like that, too!" I went in where Cellibrex was sleeping in our Queen-sized bed. I kissed him his bare shoulder through the sheet, which is how I like to sleep, though I have a heavier blanket over my half of the bed. He opened an eye and said, "Did you take your pills . . . ?" and I said, as I often do, "Oops. I'll take them," which is another current of our lives that I can leave behind a traditional literary screen. Then I left and Chase and I went out into the heat of Houston's September.

"Make sure you tell them you and I both want me to change my job," Chase said. "Just remember that's what you're here for. The way you two old fellows go around, I wouldn't be surprised if you both forgot."

"Are you going to take me back?" I asked.

"No," she said. "They'll get you home." I was totally unsure of myself, and felt very much the stranger in a strange land, but I started walking in through the interleaved walls. At one point I saw a large desk and an elderly dark skinned woman in a straight up and down black quilted garment. On her face was a blotch of white skin . . . that made me frown. I don't know where I got the idea, from, but I suddenly went up to her. "Excuse me. I don't want to bother you. But were you ever the assistant to the Hermit of Tolmec—oh, many years ago. Twenty—no, fifty at least."

"Why, yes," she said, turning look at me. "I was. Why do you ask?"

"Now, that, I said, is amazing. But age in a small town is always full of such coincidences. Well, I was one of the children you had for an educational program that you were running there."

"Oh, yes. I remember that. We had one practically every year. That's what quite a while ago. I was only a youngster myself, back then."

I said, "I'm to report to the Hermit of Houston. I expect that's a room full of booths that you go into and tell them your problems . . . "

She nodded. "Any place in front of that wall, will accomplish the same end."

"Oh," I looked over where she indicated. "Well, perhaps I should go over there and get started."

I leaned on my cane and turned. She said, "Excuse me. Wait a moment."

I turned back.

"I assume you were one of the students who didn't go on to the next level. I used to teach Ms. Chase, who brought you here, back when she was a boy, too, just like you. Well, not *exactly* like you. That's just a way of putting it. But that was a decade after I taught you. But to the extent that there is a Hermit of Houston, these days, I'm it. Because you were in our group at all, probably that means you were pretty sharp. Do you want to come to my office for a little bit. You might find it interesting. There isn't any Texas-Mexico border these days, but given that there used to be one only a generation before you were born, you might find it interesting what . . . well, *some* of what you might have learned if you'd gone on to the next level."

"I really have to get home to my partner . . . " She made me feel quite uncomfortable. Not like the assistant I remembered, but like the Hermit herself.

"Well, whether he knows it or not, he's probably a native of Mexico. You look as if you might be one, too." She smiled. "Come this way, if you would . . . don't worry, I'll make sure you get home safely and on time."

I followed her, and I can't tell you how much I felt I was going down a dangerous rabbit or worm hole. "What's Mexico?" I asked. I glanced at her feet, out of some long remembered habit, to see what color shoe laces she might be wearing.

But it was just a door. The room behind it was almost identical with my own—I thought perhaps there would be a big chair, like the ornate one I remembered the old Hermit had sat in. But this was a simple chair with a simple console beside it. And the pattern on the walls were enlarge reproduction of material certificates, except in grey rather then pale blue and gold. The carpet was only a little darker in hue than the one in our own bedroom. She walked over to it. She wore sandals, I realized. And a large ring on her big toe. "How would you feel about making a cup of tea for us . . . ? There used to be a drink called coffee, but we don't have it any more. Possibly your partner drank a great deal of it when he was much younger in the last gangs that worked in its cultivation—much to the south of here. But, then, you had your coming-of-age forgetting process, so that wouldn't be a problem for you." There weren't any laces at all.

"I suppose so. If you have some tea-bags and a tea-kettle . . . ?"

"I have a tea ball—" she went over to the chair—"and an electric water boiler and robots to make it which are all waiting behind the walls, which can be activated from either here—" and she touched a button on the arm of her chair—"or there—" and a chair that looked notably more comfortable than hers rose beside me. "Please, sit down.

"Sit there, unless you'd be more comfortable standing. And often, even at my age, I am."

"That all sounds pretty unusual for me," I said. But I sat, while she stood.

"The reason there's no Texas-Mexico border is because a generation before you were born a politician who very few people remember today proposed we build a wall between what was then the Republic of Mexico and what was then the Republic of the United States of America. The election of 2020 was the Trump of Doom for the Pence—which is the name they gave to an institution called the Electoral College which was supposed to be a safety net that guarded against the abuse of popular elections—which, from time to time, didn't work. In general, megalithic republics weren't doing too well, either."

I frowned. "I don't remember that word . . . "

"A very, very large republic. And a republic was a country run by elected officials. Generally speaking, unions worked better. Ships of State. The body politic. Bricolage. In general, smaller groups working together and connecting up according to what seemed necessary, and cutting back when it seemed right to do." She moved in front of her own chair and sat. "It works so much better now that we've separated the sexes and mixed up the genders—given them their proper dignity along with that of the ethnicities. All you have to do is dissociate them from where someone actually comes from and how they got here. Then you can do anything you want with them—thank the Night and the Day. What I have been told and what I operate by is that there is a place called Haven and there is a place called Mars and the moon and the moons of the gas giants. There are many people from other unions already working to exploit these and live on them. They don't always tell—in fact, they almost never tell—the people who were there where they were or how they got there or got back. I think the chances are almost overwhelming that your partner—" she looked down at her chair arm, fingered something there—and a table grew up from the carpet in front of her and another grew in front of me—with a steaming cup, and a teapot, "spent his time in Guatemala, Belize, or who knows, in those other unions we don't mention any more . . . I'm very fond of my robots. Have them for a decade and it's almost impossible not to be. Yes, my information tells me that your partner is likely to have been one of those who was turned loose in our landscape (. . . oh, there's some glitch right now in the Internet!)—" and for a moment she made one of those familiar tight-lidded eye-squeezes that I've only seen people do in films, almost as if she were in pain—"after he was returned from a virtual lunar colony, so I'm not getting an exact figure. That's what *we* call the flat earth. But others interpret it differently." She picked up her cup and sipped.

"But what are they working to accomplish?"

"To control mean production—"

"The *means* of production . . . ?"

Glancing at me, she raised an eyebrow that could have used some trimming, as if surprised I knew the term. "I only wish. No, that's something you might have found on Facebook. This is pure Handbook. It's about the imposing of normative, mean standards. Its critics say that it's both mean—that is, cruel and simple-minded together—and productive only of death . . . in *huge* amounts! But that's what it's designed for. We assume we'll be able to bring the population below the sustainable level in this particular union in two more generations—at least in this quarter of the globe.

"An analysis of the means of production yields a pretty tight theory that same-sex relations produces a variety in art, child rearing, battle and even science, that is a benefit in pretty much any social structure humans might take part in. Mean production says they're abnormal and the best thing to do is to stamp them out: what you see here is the most humane way we've been able to come up with for doing it. Now we can just withdraw, sit back, and watch you die. It's not pretty, but at least it keeps you away from the fewer and fewer healthy folk. And you don't have to envy them—or Lesbians or anyone else. You never see them."

I didn't feel comfortable enough to drink at all.

"Do you like your new home here in Houston?"

I didn't think we'd been here long enough to know, but this was certainly an unsettling beginning to it. "Do you really want me—or us—to know all this?"

"I think if you tell too many others who don't already believe or 'know' it, they will decide you are one form or another of bat-shit crazy, which I believe is the demotic phrase that still persists in the English of this area." She smiled. "Something I suspect your partner has a good grasp of. And if my information is correct—and I have been raised to believe that it always is—I doubt very much he will believe it either. We find it pretty easy to manipulate people's memories and worldviews these days. You live with Teddy C. Rodriguez, am I right?"

"I think I'd like to get on home," I said. (That is not Cellibrex's real name, either. But in this account, that's close enough to it, so that it will do. Suffice it to say that she gave a name for him I recognized, and because she knew it, I felt far less at ease than I had been when I'd walked in. I would have expected her to call him well . . . Cellibrex, the way I do here. But I thought the other was a secret, at least from such as she.)

"You were in the same class with Ara, weren't you," said the Hermit with a falling rather than a rising inflection.

I nodded.

"If you'd gotten to the second level, you would have learned your birthday and known how old you were for the rest of your life—not just till eighteen. We don't encourage such promiscuous knowledge among the population. It makes it easier to control what you think you think about the world." Then she seemed to remember herself—or perhaps saw something on the small screen on the arm of her chair. "All the children we select are smart. And for the first three levels it's practically a lottery who goes on to the next level, but we have to have some way and we call it testing. Still, it makes differences in what happens to you in your life. It's only at the fifth or sixth condensation, when we're bringing youngsters in from outside the union boarders, that the testing can be at all significant." She chuckled. "Though some say it's a lottery all the way to the top. Some of the students who were just pleasant, rather than particularly smart, I keep track of. Like your Ms. Chase. Wonderful boy . . . ! Wonderful boy! As, really, were you and Teddy as well. Go through the door there; there's a man with a pedicab, who will drive you home. It is a shameless indulgence that I use for myself and some of my friends."

"Eh—thank you," I said. "This way . . . ?"

"No . . . " she said. "Over there. If you want to take your tea-cup and tea pot with you as souvenirs . . . ? I have them made for me—"

"No . . . " I repeated, because that's what she'd said to me; though later I wished I had, at least to show Cellibrex, to have some proof.

"A last question—have you or your partner ever encountered the rumor of another order of human being? A witch, a succubus, a woman—not as we use the word here for someone you could meet in any public pornographic gathering in any sensory helmet theater, but a different kind of woman—or girl perhaps . . . ?"

I stopped and looked back. "What do you mean?"

"Right now," she said, "that's the *perfect* answer! Every once in a while a man like your partner gets it into his head from somewhere that there *is* an entirely other form of humanity . . . and given the tasks we have of bringing down the population reasonably and safely, it's not a good rumor to let get out and about. It doesn't usually work, even when he thinks he's found one or a few of them. What I've been told, and I have no reason to believe it isn't true, is that there aren't a lot of them left . . . anywhere, at this point. They were harder to exterminate than you folks. But . . . well. I'm just glad that wasn't my department. And by now we have pretty much anyone one who might even be mistaken for one under our thumb, thousands of miles away. Good-bye."

I walked forward and two panels in the wall opened that I hadn't even seen. Stepping outside, I saw a man sitting on a bench beside some greenery, looking at a magazine with pictures on the pages that were shifting like the old ones I remembered my sister used to read, back when I'd had a family. Did he still have one, I wondered? (I hadn't seen any of mine since I'd gone traveling as a child.) Did Cellibrex—?

Suddenly I remembered. "I'm sorry," I said, "I have to go back. The reason I came was to tell someone that Ms. Chase wasn't happy with her job, and—" Because I was thinking all sorts of things Cellibrex had said that came back to me: maybe his experiences and travels in the Union, in the world, were indeed broader than mine . . .

But I also felt it was very dangerous to try to pin them down with a language that had been so carefully tailored to erase the possibility. (I could hear her saying to this same man, "I'm going to take in some porn this afternoon . . . " though it's the thing everyone does and talks about, it's not what everyone does and writes about.)

The man looked at something on his wrist, then blinked up at me. "According to this, that was taken care of when you came in. I'm assuming you're ready to return to where you live . . . ?"

"The Hermit has already seen to—?"

"Who?" he asked.

"The Hermit. She said she used you—"

"Oh," he said, "about ten big officers at the Hermitage use me to take their friends around the city. But I don't think there is a Hermit any more. I've got your address here. All you have to do is get in and put the blanket up around you, if you get chilly. But it's a nice day. Watch your cane there."

So that's what I did.

The doors to the back of the Houston Hermitage were glass and blackened bronze, like my childhood memories of the doors at the front of the Hermitage in Tolmec. I was surprised, and, yes, for the first time since I'd arrived, I felt relieved. It was glorious weather.

We drove off, with the young guy peddling in his sandals. (He was probably forty, at least.) I held the handle of my cane in both hands, looking down where the rubber tip was on the ridged matt across the bottom of the little gondola I was seated in. My driver peddled us along beside segueways and closed vehicles. My cane swayed back and forth, and I looked around at bits and pieces of Houston going by.

Why, I wondered would anyone want another kind of human being, unless it was just for difference. (Was it possible to have a greater difference between people than there was, say, between myself and Cellibrex? Myself and Ms. Chase . . . ?) He drove through bustling Houston. When you look at things, you do very little panning. Your eye locks on something and even when you're walking, you follow it until you snap your eyes to something else. When I was a child, I used to wonder if, every time you snapped your eyes, you died and woke up in a new present, but just with memories of the past. As I rode home, looking from one bit to another of the landscape of my new home in Houston, so different from the landscape I had negotiated when I was a child, I wondered if there wasn't something to my old theory.

"Cell . . . ?"

"Mmm . . . ?"

"Does it ever bother that you're probably a decade closer to dying than I am?"

"No." Cellibrex turned around to face me under the blanket. "I never thought this was going to be a very good life—and it was a lot better than it could have been. Hey, little fellow, hold my big guy."

"Come on, don't joke around now."

"Who's joking?"

"Cell, I keep asking you the same questions every few years. But are you sure you never went to the moon, or to Mars, or to the lunar colonies on Io or Europa, Gannymede or Calisto?"

"And I told you, no. I was in jail. I was in the army. I just don't know where. They were just earth-side testing of behaviors someone wanted to try out on a populations in a low gravity landscape that is if all the folks who think they're actually putting people on other planets and thing are right. But I never left the surface of our infinite flat world. That's what I know. And I'm never going to believe anything else."

I said: "There're too many people on the planet. We're two men and can't reproduce. Doesn't that make us good people? Or at any rate, we haven't reproduced more than once, between the two of us, as far as *you* know."

"Yes . . . ?" He moved closer to me, and I could feel his breath on my forehead, my beard against his chest. "You say I repeat myself. How many times have you said that?" His arm went around me; no, it's not as strong as it once was. But it's the arm that always holds me, as the other goes up and tries to find a position over my head and I smell the very familiar and reassuring order of what's under it. "Well, even if you're right—which I'm not saying, now—that's the kind of thing I just wasn't brought up to worry about. And I told you, I may have left one kid back there, somewhere."

"That's what I was referring to." I wondered if I should tell him the Hermit had said he'd been on a "virtual lunar colony." But because it was virtual, perhaps that's what Cellibrex meant about it's being somewhere on the "flat" earth, and from his point of view he was right. "You said you don't feel bad about that one, either. Was that a . . . a different kind of human being?"

"Naw. It was just some guy who'd had a particular set of operations. Either he had it, or he decided not to. So maybe I'm not quite as good as you." His high arm came down and I raised my head to let it go under my neck.

"We are such different people, you and me. Why are we still together?"

I felt him shrug. "Habit. Great sex from time to time . . . " He chuckled. "Hell, ordinary sex from time to time, which is easier to find on the other side of the bed than going out and trying to locate an entire older group of guys who like the same sort of things you do. Which, I confess, isn't bad either—when I still have the energy or the concentration for it." He adjusted himself, adjusted me on top of him, against him. "And we're used to each other.

"We've only been here a few days, and I had dream that I used to have again and again when I was kid. Odd. I was in a testing group, a huge testing group, and I we all had to fight each other, no matter what we were doing, to see who came out on top. So I decided to take the most important things I knew: my name, where I was from, and my birthday with me in my head. I didn't even bother with my ID number. I could always get another. And did several times. In the dream, we fought and fought and fought and . . . then I woke up."

It took a while for him to tell me that, actually, in his short accented sentences. But one of the things I said back to was, "No. You never told me this before." And another was, "You actually know how old you are?"

"I am seventy-nine," Cellibrex told me in the three-quarters dark.

I said, "I never asked you, because I didn't know how old I was, so I assumed you didn't know either." Then I added, "If that wasn't a dream, and you actually did it sometime when you were a child or a younger man, that was very smart. Especially because you got away with it. So you really were from Mexico?"

He grunted, and moved his beard on the top of my bald spot, that could have been a head signal for a yes or a no; lying there, I couldn't tell, though I looked up to see his face. "Argentina," he said with enough of an accent that he had to repeat it half a dozen times before I realized it was the name of someplace I had actually heard before.

There's a coda to the story. Three weeks later, I came home and found Cellibrex dead on our filthy living-room rug. A teacup had overturned on the table. His pocket phone was out, and on, and when I picked it up from where it had fallen maybe a foot from his hand (we both used to the same access number), I managed to call up an incomplete, unsent, and mangled text message:

Could you please come home before bat-shit crazy

With the handle of my cane I smashed the phone and a few other things in the room. Then I sat at the table and took great gasps, stood up again, checked to see if he was alive, but he wasn't—I'd been sure of that from the moment I'd seen him lying there.

Then, because that's the kind of mind I have, I wondered: Had he been trying to type " . . . before I go bat-shit crazy" or even "before these bat-shit crazy men [or whatever] . . . " *Had* somebody come into the place? But no. It was just some failure of the aged machinery of life . . .

But now I was convinced that the phone itself had killed him: because it had made me feel I was always in contact with him, when I wasn't. I hadn't been in the same room with him. And I was a wreck because if there had been a last twenty seconds, a last ten, a last five, I felt a malevolent force had robbed me of them, when they should have been his and mine. The phone itself had lied to me, because it had said I was with Teddy C. Rodriguez when I was not.

Then I had no idea what to do, where to go, who to look for or phone to tell about it. He was in a pair of ragged underpants, and the marks on his body that had been a text whose meanings I had felt totally familiar with among his far more white than black body hair the day before, were now, in a way they had never seemed before, cryptic and incomprehensible. So I sat down in the big, soft, ragged chair.

Then I struggled up again and wandered around the house. Then I sat down once more, stood up suddenly—and walked out of the house. I had a hoodie on, and I just walked, and eventually I decided to walk in the sun, and that was better. In the shade I saw the wall of a building where, perhaps fifty years ago, someone had made a mosaic of tiles and paint and pieces of mirror, and I got to looking at it, and examining it—and after a minute realized I was thinking of Cellibrex's death; but in the course of looking at it, I realized some thirty seconds had gone by where I hadn't thought about him or his death at all, and that was astonishing and scary . . . and maybe . . . right.

My own pocket phone buzzed, and I took it out. I coughed—some great glob of phlegm had caught down there, and now came up in my mouth, and I swallowed it, surprised, and wondered why I hadn't spit it out. That's what Cellibrex would have done . . .

"Hello . . . ?" I said.

A man's voice said: "Just a moment. This is the Hermit of Houston . . . " While I wondered why, if the Hermit of Houston was in fact a woman, they didn't use a woman's voice, the man told me that I should go to a certain address and ring. Someone was expecting me.

It wasn't that far, actually.

"I don't want to see anyone right—" I cleared my throat again. " . . . right now."

"I would advise you do. This must be a very hard time for you. From where you are now, it's only perhaps six streets away."

"All right," I said.

"It's what most people do. And it works. You can call us back if you need anything."

And half-an-hour later, an elderly, very black African was making me a pot of tea and we were sitting at his kitchen table, quietly together. His place was different enough from ours that I felt comfortable, but not so different as—say—the Hermit's where I'd just felt completely disoriented. At one point as we began talking, I remember saying something that a writer I'd been fond of who'd died before I was born had written: "People are not replaceable . . . " or something like it.

But he poured me another cup of tea. "Good people will often do similar things for you, however." His name was Hammond. "Each one does it in a different way."

I thought of Cellibrex making tea. I thought of the robots of the Hermit of Houston.

And I stayed there for three weeks. Hammond was younger than Cellibrex, but older than I was. He had been to Mars and remembered it very clearly. We slept in the same bed. On the second night, he told me, "I can hold you, if you like. If you would like to have sex, we can do that. Or I will just stay where I am, and be near if you want to talk." I chose one, and, on the third night, decided that my choice had been a mistake so chose another. And decided Hammond was an extremely tolerant man—and came very close to crying for the first time. (Later, I actually did. But I guess at some point we all do. At least I think so.) And at the end of two weeks I felt better. Then, somehow it was six months later: I was living by myself again. And life was going on. There'd been a funeral that only about seven people had come to, but Hammond was one of them, but there's no point going into all that.

The *Star Wars* film was in reruns—which Cellibrex *had* enjoyed: where you just went to a small theater with a few hundred people in sensory masks, all sitting around together watching only the sex scenes, sometimes with people observing from their homes, sometimes with people right next to you, with Cellibrex said was the kind of porn he'd been brought up on. And I'd liked going with him and I'd like going with strangers—and, yes, I still did.

Now and then I wondered if Cellibrex had known something that had died with him that might have explained something to me, if only I had thought to ask. Or was he just someone who knew no more of the whole story than I or anyone else? Would I eventually forget how much I thought there might be to know, even as I remembered how much I'd been warmed by knowing and being near him—by being as different from him as I had been?

Sometimes I tried to remember the things that had made Cellibrex another person that I had been able to live with and—I guess—love all this time—and often I'd stopped because they were too . . . confusing? Painful?

With a greater variety in all its social structures, what might life have been like? What might coffee have tasted like, though personally I couldn't remember it at all, in a world of unions without borders?

It was easier to think that this had all been set up by the Hermit of Houston. who I had once known when she was an assistant and knew now as a computer and, I guess, a man.

And I was even thankful for them.

—Philadelphia,
Dec 25, 2016–Feb 3th, 2017

UGO

GIOVANNI DE FEO

That's how Cynthia and Ugo met.

The Easter egg hunt had just started when little Cynthia noticed a dark, short-haired nine-year-old boy, all alone, sitting by the church steps. Her first impression of him was his quietness, and the way he stared at her. When she told him (well, shouted) that it was impolite to stare at strangers, and why wasn't he running like all others?—the dark-haired boy walked quietly over and told her that they didn't need to hurry, for the grand prize, three enormous chocolate eggs, was located right under the picnic table that was set up for lunch.

And as for the staring, she was no stranger to him.

"No? What is my name then?"

"Your name is Cinzia[1] and we will marry ten years and one month from today, in this very church, on an April's day."

Of course after that she was too scared to want to see him ever again, especially since the three chocolate eggs *were* found under the table. Then summer came. Not many families in Caversham West could afford to go to the seaside. So old Mr. Brown—the owner of the White Trout—organized badminton matches at the church on Sundays. It was mostly an excuse to be outdoors, as none of us were big enthusiasts. But we did have a lot of time on our own. Especially Ugo. He was almost always alone and off to the side, "just watching."

Every time Cynthia saw him, she missed the ball. Her blunders sent waves of mirth through the opposing team. This went on for quite a while until—ears red—she marched up to Ugo and asked him to leave.

Suddenly his cool was gone like a blanket snatched by the wind. Behind

---

[1]   In Italian, Cinzia sounds like Cheensia and Ugo like Oo-go. Luckily most called him Hugo.

it, he looked red-faced, raw and trembling. It was painful to watch. He left without a word. But his reaction had so impressed her that, after the match, she went to look for him.

She found him sitting on the top of a wall like a child Humpty Dumpy, looking every bit as fragile. Years later, Cynthia had only a vague recollection of what they talked about that day, probably cartoons they both liked. He told her he had a bike that could go faster than the wind. She in turn told him about ice skating, her passion; her mother said she would become a star, one day. At that, Ugo glanced at her sideways, as if he wanted to say something but couldn't. When she asked him why he got so upset when she asked him to leave, Ugo smiled. He couldn't figure out how, in just an hour's time, they would end up here, considering what would happen next.

Cynthia frowned. What would happen next?

"This," he said, and kissed her on the mouth.

It was an adult kiss, with lips and tongue and teeth, one so shocking, so unexpected for a nine-year-old that Cynthia froze on the spot. When it was finished, he quietly hugged her. They stayed like this for so long that Cynthia felt her feet growing numb. His body was thin, and yet it was so warm she felt scorched down to her bones.

"Now we are together," he said.

It turned out the whole kissing business had been a Leap.

That's why he had behaved with such certainty: He had to play his part to the end. This was the really unsettling bit of Leaping. For when he came to the moment in time he had experienced beforehand, he still felt—in his mind— the presence of his younger self, watching.

Later on, Ugo developed a theory about it. He said that in reality every-body Leaps all the time. The proof? Déjà vu. The feeling of having already experienced what is in fact happening for the first time was for him the ulti-mate, definitive evidence of Leaping. The only difference between Ugo and everyone else was that he remembered, while we don't. Why? Because our brains are incapable of retaining the memory of the future. But then how was he able to? He didn't know. Bit by bit, Cinzia came to the conclusion that his mind could hold the future because deep down he was so desperate to escape the present.

Ugo moved to Cinzia's neighbourhood when he was eight. His parents had just divorced, after the failure of Ugo's father's sports career (he was a basketball pro). His mother was an Italian meteorologist who held a PhD from Reading University but didn't have a job in her field. She got by translating cookbooks, which I always found quite amusing since she couldn't fry an egg to save her life. She came from a large family from a town near Naples, and spoke with a strong Italian accent Ugo had somehow inherited, though to a lesser extent.

By the time his family moved, two years had passed since his first Leap at the age of six. The first time Ugo skipped ahead in time happened in a parking lot, right after his father hit him for losing a soccer match. Since then, Ugo had Leaped twenty-three times. Most Leaps were short, lasting a couple of minutes. But three had been quite long, and one huge. Ugo called those bigger spells "vacations" (I will tell you everything about them later). They lasted instants in "base-time," but weeks or even months in his mind. Not only that, they put a mark on him, a feeling of otherness that never left him entirely.

There was something in Ugo that was always out of place. Sometimes people didn't react to his presence, as if he weren't there at all. Even at his best, he was always out of sync, a creature caught between two worlds. Sometimes he struggled to talk like a child. School came easily to him, especially math. What was really difficult for him was social interaction. He could only warm up to people he had "seen" in his future, of whom there were very few. With the others, he behaved as if they were ghosts. Which in a way, for him, they were.

With time Cinzia experienced both sides of Ugo's Leaps. She was there when his mind *fugued*, and she was there when he was possessed by the younger version of himself. With the latter, usually there was a hesitation she had learned to recognize. The worst, though, was when he came back from his longer explorations. These were his "vacations." Instantaneous in base-time, they lasted weeks in his mind. In these cases, he had got stuck in his future-self. Until something triggered a memory of the exact time period when his Leaps started. Right at that very moment, he came back. Violently.

Before their marriage, Cinzia had experienced only two of these episodes. One, in middle school, was really nasty. They were at the Berkshire Spring Fair, bargaining for new ice-skate blades, when Ugo's eyes rolled back and he collapsed. She caught him easily, thin as he was. He came around quickly; cold and rigid at first, then all of a sudden warm again, hugging her so tight it hurt.

"Oh my God, you are still here," he said, "you are still you."

He never explained what he meant, or his out-of-character display of public affection. For they had agreed since the first kiss to hide their relationship. Adults don't believe in the loves of children. They would show their mutual affection later on, so that their parents could gradually adjust to the idea of their early marriage.

For months after that episode Ugo acted more strangely than ever. He snapped easily, at home as well as school, at other students and even at teachers. Only

Cinzia understood what was really the matter. He was resentful of being treated like a child again.

"It's like all of a sudden you've become a baby. To everyone you look normal because they think this is how you should look. So they put you with the other babies. And you should feel all right because they *do* look like you. Only they really are babies, and you're not. So you have to pretend. You learn to pretend so well that you forget what it was like, to be free, not having to ask permission just to exist. And when you have finally forgotten, then you Leap again."

"Is that what we look like to you? Little babies?" said Cinzia.

"There are some," he said after a while, "who are always themselves, no matter where in time they are. It's like people are trees. As they grow, they start to lose their shape, and become so different from what they once were that if you saw them, you wouldn't recognize them. I am not talking about the way they look, it's something deeper than that. The way they talk to dogs, the way they laugh, the way they look at the sky, the way they shut their eyes against a sudden wind. These secret ways show their inner shape. Most people lose it almost entirely, but some don't. It's not like they stay the same, they do change, they evolve, but because they've kept their shape, they always grow in the same direction, skyward. That's how you recognize them: Their branches are the tallest."

"And me—?"

"You are the tallest and brightest I have ever seen."

On the last day of middle school, while we were celebrating with a furious battle of water-balloons, one of our classmates, a boy called Norwitz, darted out of the parking lot and was hit by a lorry.

While we waited for the ambulance, we sat in shock on the curb. The teachers did their best to calm us. Many of my classmates were crying, boys and girls alike. It was then that Cinzia saw Ugo. There was a funny expression on his face, something she had seen before.

"You're Leaping, aren't you? Right now."

Ugo didn't say a word but his eyes looked frantic, trapped.

"So you knew this would happen, all along. Why didn't you try to stop it?"

"I-it doesn't work like that," he said, slurring his words.

She wondered who was talking, the older or the younger Ugo?

"No? How does it work then?"

"What happened, happened. And I can't speak of it, or . . . "

"Or?"

" . . . if I speak *to* change it, I'll come undone. I know, it's nothing I can prove to you, but I know it's true. I will cease to be."

"Okay, let's say I believe you. Then tell me: Why is your life more precious than Norwitz's?"

"I never said it was."

"You didn't, but you think so. Because you are oh-so-special, and we are just babies. You never even tell me what you see. You say we are going to be married, but I don't know how many children we'll have, what kind of woman I'll be, what kind of man *you'll* be. You see how unfair all this is?"

"Of course it's unfair," he said, "more so since you don't know what this knowledge would do to you, while I do."

"Then tell me, will I keep on ice skating? Will I? Now listen: Why would I even bother to work my butt off every day, six hours a day, if I knew that ten years from now my skating won't matter? Why?"

He said nothing, but she could feel the anguish in his eyes, the impotence of his silence. She turned away from him.

"Ugo, I'll make it simple," she said, "we won't ever marry for the very simple fact that I'm breaking it off now, and I won't change my mind, ever. So you see, your time-jumping was good for nothing."

"It is *always* good for nothing," he said, and his voice was so full of despair that she was almost pleased. But then she realized. The frightened look belonged to the younger Ugo, watching. But the one talking, this one knew. In fact, he had always known they would break up on the last day of middle school. She turned and broke into a run.

They would not speak to each other again for three years.

High school came in like a storm. More and more she felt she understood what it felt like to be trapped among babies. Only in her case the babies were boys, while the Tall Ones were girls. And they didn't look like children anymore either: They branched out under the boys' eyes, taller, fuller, their shapes changing, shifting, blooming.

Hormones came, and so did her first blood. Her father chortled his amusement at lunch when they told him, and her little brother moved into her small room and she took her big sister's, who moved out to Christchurch. She remembered the pains of trigonometry, her discovery of the Romantics (oh Byron! and Shelley!), Laura expelled for smoking hash, the first time she really *felt* her breasts. She had her own group of friends outside school, mostly girls who figure skated. The competition was terrifying, but she kept on winning. She had something to prove, and not just to herself. Ugo had never come to see her skate when they were together. Now he didn't miss a single practice. He would sit here with his red cap and stare. But now, under his gaze, she didn't trip. She was tall, muscular, strong; her clumsiness had melted away, while he still looked so fragile, almost brittle.

She had lots of boys, of course. The first high-school kisses were such a disappointment. She became notorious as "the tiger." Well, if they couldn't kiss, at least she could bite them back. After all, Cynthia had been French-kissing since she was nine. Those bubble gum smooches tasted like water to someone accustomed to spirits. She felt the same insipidness in their tentative touches, in their "grown-up" talks. They were the opposite of Ugo, pretending to be adults when they were really just children. At times she wondered why she bothered. But she knew why. Because, if she stopped, she would go back to him.

Patryck was in Year Twelve and was different from anyone she had dated. He didn't pretend to be older; he was just himself, a boy with a witty talent for language and a weird sense of humour. All the class talked of how he had once stood on a table in the canteen and recited in full a poem he had written himself. Cynthia loved him for that, especially because the last lines were about her.

Together they went to Oxford for picnics, to Jericho, by the river barges, her arms all white with mosquito cream, as he stood up and read poems to the swaying willows. His kisses were different from Ugo's: tender, soft. In spite of his Celtic brooding, there was no anxiety about him. In this regard he was quite the opposite of her time-traveller, edgy on the outside and quiet within.

In her last year, Cynthia decided she wouldn't continue to Uni. She wanted to become an athlete, not a scholar. Of course her parents didn't agree. Her dad was a German teacher, her mum worked in university administration. They said she needed to "keep her options open," an expression she despised. Patryck, though, was very supportive. He said that, for example, in poetry only losers get PhDs. Like those who added "PhD graduate" on the back covers of their books, as if it mattered. He was all riot and turmoil, her sweet poet.

On the day of the selection for the European Figure Skating, Patryck didn't show up. It was a very important competition, and for the first time, she failed. She was seventeen, young for many other disciplines, but almost too old to reach peak performance in ice skating. The horrible part was that nothing had gone wrong; there were simply too many others who were better. When she left the rink, she was trembling all over. Why wasn't Patryck there? She kept looking for him until she saw Ugo, by the exit. They hadn't seen each other for over a year. The clumsy adolescent was gone, replaced by a tall, dark-haired stranger. It was like his body had finally caught up with his eyes.

"I'm so sorry," he said.

Was he sorry for her failure or apologizing for his behaviour? Both, maybe. But there was a third meaning that she would only understand later. She found out through friends they had in common. On that very day, Patryck had sat the tests for prep school and passed. He was going to Uni after all. When Patryck finally showed up at her house to apologize, with a bouquet of flowers and a poem on his lips—Cynthia's little brother was laughing himself to death—she opened her window and threw a bucket of cold water on him. He sputtered and cursed and then left, his Celtic pride wounded, never to be seen again.

Had Ugo known about all this? Probably.

That night, she phoned him. They stayed up until five o'clock in the morning, Cinzia (who was not Cynthia any more) whispering into the receiver under the bed sheet, pretending he was there with her.

"Do you want me to come over now?" he asked.

"No. First I want to want you so much it hurts. And anyway, you already know you won't come tonight, don't you?"

"I don't know everything. Not always."

"What about this: Will we make love soon?"

His silence was an answer.

"Good. So you know it won't be my first time."

She could feel his silent laughter pressing on the receiver.

"Whatever you say," he finally responded.

"God, you are impossible! Of course you know! How can you live like that?"

"I don't live: I watch. That's why it's so important you don't become like me. Do you understand now?"

"So you won't tell me anything, ever."

A long, slow sigh.

"I've thought it over. I can, but it can only be really small things. Trivial details, things that don't matter."

"So you still won't tell me if I'll succeed as an ice skater."

"No."

"Why? I could dedicate my life to something else. Maybe my parents are right, I should get a degree, I could do the right thing."

"Of course not. What would happen is that you'd watch yourself as you do the wrong thing, trapped in that choice anyway."

"But how could you possibly know for sure?"

"Because that's *exactly* what I have done."

His voice cracked, she could hear the splinters in his throat.

"I knew . . . I knew I would lose you for three years if I replied the way I did that day outside school . . . and yet I had no choice, I had to. Do you understand what that felt like? Three years Cinzia and I—"

"Oh!"

"—what's so funny?"

"I almost forgot. The way you say my name. Say it again."

"Cinzia."

"So nice. I like the soft 'ch' sound. You know it's three years."

"Since I've said it?"

"No, till we marry. That will take everyone by surprise, won't it? We'd better start working on it, don't you think?"

There had always been two of her, Cynthia and Cinzia.

The former was how she would have been if she hadn't she met Ugo. In the months following that phone call, she realized that being Cynthia had been only a "vacation," like one of his, only to a parallel universe where Ugo's presence was unaccounted for. Which, of course, was impossible. Cynthia and Cinzia were two very separate identities. Still, they were part of a unity, a unity that stretched over time. Cynthia had not known how her life could turn out. But Cinzia *knew* they would marry. And knowing made all the difference.

"Will we have children?" she asked him.

"Yes."

"How many? Boys or girls?"

A begrudging silence.

"Okay, will we stay in Reading or move out of Berkshire?"

"Both."

"I knew it! I knew you were going to say that!"

In time, she learned a good deal about the small things. They would have a dog, a German shepherd named Jericho. Their first house would have a huge hawthorn bush that would catch fire at their first barbecue. She would buy a second-hand Vespa from the sixties that she would paint pink (Cinzia was too masculine to be afraid of pink).

Bit by bit, all these things came to pass. Cinzia wondered: Did they choose the flat with the hawthorn bush because he had told her about it or because it was meant to be? Did she buy an Italian scooter to fulfil his prophecy? Did any of it matter at all?

High school ended on a rainy June day that left them soaked and kissing fiercely on her porch. They had both decided to get jobs, temporary job manager him and council clerk her. That was earlier than almost everyone they knew, but that independence went with the early marriage they had always foreseen for themselves. Sometimes her parents complained; they called her new apartment "her room," as if she were still the reclusive teenager they knew before. Yes, her daily routine was complicated by ice skating, and she always came home very late, knackered, incapable of speech but for some low grunts. But the truth was she loved her adult life, even her strife; it was her own.

Ugo took care of her tenderly, taking her clothes off, carrying her to the steaming bathtub. On Sundays, they stayed in bed until noon, eating sweets and letting the sunlight slowly fill their bedroom.

At the end of their first year of living together, they announced their marriage. Their parents were still surprised but in the end they didn't resist, not as much as she had thought. Ugo's mother, in fact, was more than happy to have a daughter-in-law. She hadn't remarried and—coming from a big family—felt the need to connect with an extended family. As for Cinzia's family, they had always liked Ugo. Her father especially was intrigued by the smart boy's mind. Why didn't he apply for computer science at Oxbridge? Yet when he was confronted with such questions, Ugo flashed his sphinx-like smile, and quietly said:

"It was not meant to be."

They married in the church where they had met ten years and one month earlier. Later, Cinzia would remember a day full of light, even if all her friends told her it that in fact it had rained. She didn't care. That day there was enough light for all the rainy days to come.

They struggled with money, but most of all Cinzia battled with the constant stress of her sport. She had come to resent it so much that she sometimes talked of quitting. He would shake his head and tell her that skating was her life, she would feel empty without it.

"So you know it's going to be part of my future."

"I know it's part of your present," he said, stroking Jericho.

"And of my future," she said, frowning at the dog's antics.

"We've been over this countless times. I won't tell you, sorry."

"Okay, then I quit."

"No you won't."

"Why? It's my choice! You can't decide for me."

"Do you know how rare it is to have your gift? I've seen all the little girls watching you skate. You inspire them."

He was always right, as if he had seen how it would end. And actually, he had.

Things started to change soon after that. In six months, Cinzia won three European skating competitions. The money was sufficient to pay for her training, so she quit her temp job. An important skater, Davor Timuresku, invited her to train at his rink. Cinzia commuted to London every day, taking the seven o'clock train. It was still dark when Ugo helped her pack her cucumber sandwiches, Jericho licking his hands. When they kissed at the train track, she felt like one of those war-spouses saying goodbye to her husband.

There was some tension too, of course. Her parents said she was stressing out too much, that she slept way too little. Ugo, too. Sometimes his support seemed less enthusiastic, like something that was expected of him, something he had to do. In those moments she had a hard time fighting back her irritation. Was Ugo behaving like that because he knew she would fail? Or was he resentful of her success?

Finally, the big selection to enter the new Winter Games came. The International Skating Union would choose a team of six female figure skaters to represent the UK in Turin at the Olympics. Her dreams had never been so close, never so terrifying.

Sometimes she stayed up at night, unable to sleep, watching Ugo's white body afloat in the deep waters of a dream. Knowing that her husband *knew*, that inside he was preparing either to celebrate or to console her, was unbearable. At times she wanted to rip his dreams open and look inside them, to see the colour of their blood.

The day of the ISU selection, Cinzia looked at Ugo like the citizens of Delphi must have looked at their Oracle just before a battle. The way he dressed, the way he spoke, the way he moved, were all harbingers of her success. It's not like she didn't understand or appreciate his efforts. But he knew. He knew whether her passion would carry her far or if she would just stay behind. The selection started. She performed a combination of loop jumps and a cherry flip, scoring very high on the Grade of Execution Table. When the applause started she was beaming, her parents in the stands in tears. She looked at Ugo, but his smile was that of a sphinx, a mirthful bow to eternity.

In spite of this, Cinzia was relaxed. The second contest was a series of axel jumps, with two extra rotations, something she excelled in. She started well, storming her opponents with her flawless tempo. Yet as she landed on her last axel, she suddenly lost her balance and fell. A deep sigh from the crowd. She grimaced. Not only had she lost vital points, she felt her ankle swelling up.

She started to cry. Not out of pain but out of fear. In the infirmary, Timuresku was implacable. If she continued, she could damage her ankle. Permanently. It was her choice, her risk. She looked up in despair, only to find Ugo at her side, staring at her.

"I'm so very sorry," he said, "I really am."

So that was it. She quietly asked Timerusku and the nurse to leave. Her coach gave her a sharp look and walked out. As soon as the door closed, she let it out. It wasn't a scream but rage liquefied, turning to sound just outside her mouth. Ugo jerked back, or rather, the small kid in him did. After that she spoke in a low, coarse voice.

"Are you happy now? I know you are. It's all come to pass, finally. Finally we can go back to our little lives, have our children, grow our vegetables in the backyard. I see it now, I see it in your eyes. This was the turning point, wasn't it? The moment when I almost escaped your small-town dreams. You were right: In the end, we have no choice. But if this is my last act of free will, then I will make full use of it by spitting on your small-town happiness. For, apart from your Leaps, you are a mediocre human being, Ugo Forster. There is *nothing* in you but a wide-eyed spectator, ready to judge other people's talents, incapable of having any of your own."

Even before she finished, Ugo's features were seized by such a violent anguish that it seemed his face was coming undone. He had the same raw nakedness she had first seen on the badminton field, only on an adult it looked obscene. His voice was also different, not just slurred but child-like. When he made an effort to speak it was as if every word was a shard of glass, it sent tiny shivers all through his face.

"I-it's not like you said," he croaked, "it is far worse. For you are right, when you say I have no talent but my time Leaps. But you are also wrong in that regard, because—in fact—I don't even have that."

"What do you mean," I said, slowly standing up.

"I knew your name that day because I asked the priest. And I knew where the chocolate eggs were because I was the one who hid them. This is my secret. I lied to you. I've always lied. Always. There is no time travelling, there are no Leaps. If there is one talent I truly had, it was making up stories. I have fainting spells, that's all. All the rest is a make-believe story. A story I told first to myself, to have the confidence to kiss you that day, and then to convince you we would be together. That was the only way I could keep a person as extraordinary as you. I could tell you now that I'm sorry for what I have done, but I am not, because all these years I had you, which was more than enough of a victory for me. As for your future, I can't tell you what it is for the simple reason I don't know it. I never did. You are free, Cinzia, as you always have been. Go out there then, and win."

And this I did.

It wasn't easy, with the searing pain in my ankle, but I had too much to prove. I couldn't afford to lose; and I didn't.

The young woman who came out of the infirmary was certainly not Cinzia, but not even Cynthia, for even the latter had lived only in the absence of Ugo. And he was gone now, gone so completely it felt like he had never been there. I wasn't surprised when I didn't see him in the cheering crowd, nor with my parents later on, when we celebrated with Timuresku and our staff. For, in the end, he was right. The moment I was freed from his future, I could realize my own. I had won. I would compete in the Olympics. My life was on course.

I was happy my parents were tactful enough never to mention Ugo. As for me, my feelings were tangled. There was a mix of regret, guilt, but most of all relief. I felt a terrible anger for having being deceived by such childish nonsense, and for so long. And yet, I had to admit that my husband's exit had come at the best time.

When I finally returned to our apartment, I was astonished by how thoroughly he had removed himself from my life. Not one picture, not one shirt, not even his smell remained. I wasn't surprised he had also taken Jericho; the dog had always been more his than mine.

So I went back to live with my parents. No one ever talked about Ugo, I think not to upset me. I was in fact so concentrated on the task ahead I might not have noticed if they did. The frantic six months before the Olympics were the most terrible time of my life. I lived the life of a monk. The only things that existed were the rink, my skates.

It's not that I never missed him, but his revelation had become suspended inside me, like a kite in a glass sky. Had it really happened? Had I married a man because I believed him to be a time traveller? Was he insane? Or was I? Sometimes even my memories of him seemed unreal. My wedding ring had left no mark. That's how I felt: unwritten, a frozen lake before the first skater scarred its surface.

What is it like to realize one's childhood dream?

Very few people find out, and I should feel fortunate. And yet, how bitter is it to know that by achieving something, you have to lose something else. And how harsh, knowing you won't be able to share your discovery. For the loneliness of a winner may make a good story, but only a winner himself would want to listen to it.

So in the end, I went to the Olympics and won two medals, one bronze and one silver. On the last day, I had seventeen job offers, the weirdest of which was to be the ice skating trainer of an Emir. Do they have ice in Arabia? I had won, but in the process my soul had grown thin, like the last of the butter spread over too much bread. Exhaustion was my second name. I kept falling asleep in the most embarrassing places. When the plane from Milan landed in Gatwick, I wanted nothing else but to get into a hot shower. And yet, in Reading, there were journalists waiting at the train station. I was answering their questions when I suddenly realized that I had expected him to be there.

Hadn't my victory also been his? In the days right after the competition, I had come to see Ugo's revelation differently. For, in the end, he hadn't lied to me, but to the little girl I had been. And to what end? To woo me, to make me believe a story that we shared together. His withdrawal had been so complete it was startling. Not a phone call, not an email, not a text message; not even after my victory. So when I saw that he was not there, I started to feel a strange, pulsing dread.

I kept dozing in the taxi, something that alarmed my sister (I had slept fifteen hours just the day before) until we finally passed through my neighbourhood. I had a brief glimpse of Ugo's flat. Had he already moved out? I asked my sister, but she frowned at me and didn't answer. Apparently his name was still taboo.

I was happy to hear so many friends' voices on the answering machine. Yet his wasn't there. When I finished my shower, I finally felt ready. I dialled his number. A recorded voice told me the line was disconnected. That was a bit of a surprise. I called the landline. Nine rings; nothing. A slithering anguish began to crawl around my neck. Still in my robe, I went down and asked my mother what had happened to Ugo. It was the first time I had mentioned him in seven months. What horrified me was not her answer, but her blank stare.

"Oh . . . you mean Gilbert's second son? Oh dear, that's so sweet of you to ask, he is doing all right, I guess, he will be more than happy to meet his auntie now that she has become all famous."

I was not amused. No, I didn't mean my nephew, I meant my *husband*. Mother blinked twice and asked me to repeat the question. I did. At that she spun around and said, to no one in particular:

"Oh dear, that's . . . Oh dear. Roger, can you come in for a sec?"

My father came in, bespectacled and scruffy.

"What is it?" he said.

"Cynthia is . . . well, see it for yourself."

"What is it darling?"

"I want to know where my husband is. Is that too much to ask?"

"Your . . . Honey, are you all right? Do you want to sit down?"

Then I knew. All that followed was just a part I had to play, excruciating and unnecessary. I told them I didn't feel the need to sit, and where was my husband, *please*. My voice had already begun to shoot up; little bro and big sis came down immediately. I knew what they believed, but their unwillingness to address the subject maddened me. So I became more and more insistent, until finally my mother said it. There was no husband. I had never known a boy called Ugo, I never dated him, I never married him. There was no Ugo.

I fled upstairs. In my room, I took off my robe and—naked—I started to look for my old pictures. I rummaged desperately, looking for a picture of Ugo when we were little. There were so many photos, saved from our shared flat. Yet I couldn't find him. I was in all the pictures; he wasn't. I kept on looking until I found the Easter egg hunt picture. That was our very first picture together, one so clear in my brain I could have drawn it with eyes closed. But when I opened them, there was only me.

This is where I would love to tell you that—the following day—I filled my bathtub with hot water and slashed both my wrists. It would have been appropriate, at the very least. But I am a Brit and in our despair we are often underwhelming. It was worse, of course, the slow dark tide trapping me in a corner of my room where I rocked back and forth, gnawing at my fingertips till they bled. It lasted nine weeks. When at last I came out of it I didn't need to be told I needed to see a doctor: I went to the hospital on my own.

Dr. Buchanan is a tall black woman of fifty-five, and I liked her immediately. She knew who I was even before I began to explain what had happened to me. Afterward, she told me that she had read in the local papers that I had had a breakdown because of the Olympics. I asked her what she thought of it. She smiled at my directness.

"I think you had a psychotic episode my dear," she said. "What is peculiar is that you didn't hallucinate a presence, but an absence."

In the days that followed, my life was put under a magnifying glass. Dr. Buchanan listened attentively to my side of the story. She was not only very surprised at how extensive my memory of my "imaginary husband" was, but that often while I told my story I spoke about myself in the third person, and even called myself two different names.

I shrugged. That didn't feel special to me. I had done it so since kindergarten. This, she said, was typical of schizo-affective behaviour. I associated that word with split personalities and homicidal rages. It turned out it meant the inability to see thoughts for what they were, mistaking them for perceptions: voices, smells. Sometimes these intrusions became coherent, bringing on sub-personalities. However, such a detailed delusion, an entire past with an imaginary human being, was uncommon. That's why she wanted to consult with some colleagues, and could I be admitted for observation?

So here I am, the self-hospitalized athlete, estranged from family and friends. I spend my days in this room reading and writing, as Dr. Buchanan has encouraged me to. By writing Ugo's story, I might not only remember it better, but give it a new meaning—she said. That's why she told me to write it all down as if it was a story. I know what she wants to get at. She wants me to write his story so that I can see it is a fiction. I won't tell you that I'm not tempted.

Maybe it's the medication they are giving me, but remembering Ugo has become more difficult. What did his hair smell like? What did it feel like when he was inside of me? Did he talk when we made love? I have this image of a boy whispering in my ears. I know what the doctor would say, that this is a personification of schizophrenia, murmuring intrusive thoughts I've taken for memories.

It's like waking up. So many flashes come to my mind now.

The way sometimes people reacted to Ugo, ignoring him completely. My friends' surprise when I talked about him. The plain fact I didn't have any friends in common with him. I can't remember a single time when I was with a friend and with Ugo. How is that possible? And my wedding day: How is it I can't remember any details except that it was a sunny day? And then our shared apartment, our daily lives. My parents told me I never left home. How could I in fact hold a job, train for ice skating, and pay the rent at nineteen? How likely is that? The doctor says I didn't just "make up" a person. A part of my mind created a whole parallel life, the ideal way I wanted to live my youth. In love, independent, married, with a future that was mine alone.

Until, on the day of the Olympic selections, the ideal world of my childhood came into conflict with my ambition. Why did I want to talk with Ugo alone? Because there was no one there but me.

But no. That's what *they* want me to believe. That Ugo was the invisible companion I conjured up from my lonely childhood. This is where his imperfections save me. His aloofness, his infuriating smile, all those traits I'd always resented: How could I have made them up? The greatest objection to his existence came from my sister. If, in his Leaps, he couldn't change the future, and if he saw we had a lifetime together, why had he made his revelation? And why did he disappear after that?

Oh, but can't you see? This is exactly why I still cling to him. Only now I understand what he did. The moment he realized the Olympics were my life's dream, he fought to change what he had seen, to reshape my future so that I could win. But why did he do that? He had already seen that in the end we would be happy together, that my words were just a momentary fit of anger. Or maybe . . . maybe what awaited us was not what I thought. That was my idea of romantic marriage, as a teenager would imagine it. But Ugo saw what it really would be like. All our dreams fulfilled and then broken, one by one. Can you imagine what this could do to a child? Seeing how love will end, how routine slowly would erode everything you believe in?

Is that the reason why he hugged me at the Fair, after his long Leap? Was it because he missed the girl I had been, replaced by the acerbic wife I would be? In the end, he acted like the romantic he truly was. Instead of giving me our shared happiness, however brief, he gave me its absence. I'll never know what our shared life would have been like; and therefore it will stay intact, an untouched horizon inside me.

FANDOM FOR ROBOTS

VINA JIE-MIN PRASAD

———◆———

Computron feels no emotion towards the animated television show titled *Hyperdimension Warp Record* (超次元 ワープ レコード). After all, Computron does not have any emotion circuits installed, and is thus constitutionally incapable of experiencing "excitement," "hatred," or "frustration." It is completely impossible for Computron to experience emotions such as "excitement about the seventh episode of *HyperWarp*," "hatred of the anime's short episode length" or "frustration that Friday is so far away."

Computron checks his internal chronometer, as well as the countdown page on the streaming website. There are twenty-two hours, five minutes, forty-six seconds, and twelve milliseconds until 2 am on Friday (Japanese Standard Time). Logically, he is aware that time is most likely passing at a normal rate. The Simak Robotics Museum is not within close proximity of a black hole, and there is close to no possibility that time is being dilated. His constant checking of the chronometer to compare it with the countdown page serves no scientific purpose whatsoever.

After fifty milliseconds, Computron checks the countdown page again.

The Simak Robotics Museum's commemorative postcard set ($15.00 for a set of twelve) describes Computron as "The only known sentient robot, created in 1954 by Doctor Karel Alquist to serve as a laboratory assistant. No known scientist has managed to recreate the doctor's invention. Its steel-framed box-and-claw design is characteristic of the period." Below that, in smaller print, the postcard thanks the Alquist estate for their generous donation.

In the museum, Computron is regarded as a quaint artefact, and plays a key role in the *Robotics Then and Now* performance as an example of the "Then." After the announcer's introduction to robotics, Computron appears on stage, answers four standard queries from the audience as proof of his sentience, and steps off the stage to make way for the rest of the performance, which ends with the android-bodied automaton TETSUCHAN showcasing its ability to breakdance.

Today's queries are likely to be similar to the rest. A teenage girl waves at the announcer and receives the microphone.

"Hi, Computron. My question is . . . have you watched anime before?"

[Yes,] Computron vocalises. [I have viewed the works of the renowned actress Anna May Wong. Doctor Alquist enjoyed her movies as a child.]

"Oh, um, not that," the girl continues. "I meant Japanese animation. Have you ever watched this show called *Hyperdimension Warp Record*?"

[I have not.]

"Oh, okay, I was just thinking that you really looked like one of the characters. But since you haven't, maybe you could give *HyperWarp* a shot! It's really good, you might like it! There are six episodes out so far, and you can watch it on—"

The announcer cuts the girl off, and hands the microphone over to the next querent, who has a question about Doctor Alquist's research. After answering two more standard queries, Computron returns to his storage room to answer his electronic mail, which consists of queries from elementary school students. He picks up two metal styluses, one in each of his grasping claws, and begins tapping them on the computing unit's keyboard, one key at a time. Computron explains the difference between a robot and an android to four students, and provides the fifth student with a hyperlink to Daniel Clement Dennett III's writings on consciousness.

As Computron readies himself to enter sleep mode, he recalls the teenage girl's request that he "give *HyperWarp* a shot." It is only logical to research the Japanese animation *Hyperdimension Warp Record* in order to address queries from future visitors. The title, when entered into a search engine on the World Wide Web, produces about 957,000 results (0.27 seconds).

Computron manoeuvres the mouse pointer to the third hyperlink, which offers to let him "watch Hyperdimension Warp Record FULL episodes streaming online high quality." From the still image behind the prominent "play" button, the grey boxy figure standing beside the large-eyed blue-haired human does bear an extremely slight resemblance to Computron's design. It is only logical to press the "play" button on the first episode, in order to familiarise himself with recent discourse about robots in popular culture.

The series' six episodes are each approximately 25 minutes long. Between watching the series, viewing the online bulletin boards, and perusing the extensively footnoted fan encyclopedia, Computron does not enter sleep mode for ten hours, thirty-six minutes, two seconds, and twenty milliseconds.

• • •

Hyperdimension Warp Record (超次元 ワープ レコード Chōjigen Wāpu Rekōdo, literal translation: *Super Dimensional Warp Record*) is a Japanese anime series set in space in the far future. The protagonist, Ellison, is an escapee from a supposedly inescapable galactic prison. Joined by a fellow escapee, Cyro (short for Cybernetic Robot), the two make their way across the galaxy to seek revenge. The targets of their revenge are the Seven Sabers of Paradise, who have stolen the hyperdimensional warp unit from Cyro's creator and caused the death of Ellison's entire family.

Episode seven of *HyperWarp* comes with the revelation that the Second Saber, Ellison's identical twin, had murdered their parents before faking her own death. After Cyro and Ellison return to the *Kosmogram*, the last segment of the episode unfolds without dialogue. There is a slow pan across the spaceship's control area, revealing that Ellison has indulged in the human pastime known as "crying" before falling asleep in the captain's chair. His chest binder is stained with blood from the wound on his collarbone. Cyro reaches over, gently using his grabbing claw to loosen Ellison's binder, and drapes a blanket over him. An instrumental version of the end theme plays as Cyro gets up from his seat, making his way to the recharging bay at the back of the ship. From the way his footfalls are animated, it is clear that Cyro is trying his best to avoid making any noise as he walks.

The credits play over a zoomed-out shot of the *Kosmogram* making its way to the next exoplanet, a tiny pinpoint of bright blue in the vast blackness of space.

The preview for the next episode seems to indicate that the episode will focus on the Sabers' initial attempt to activate the hyperdimensional warp unit. There is no mention of Cyro or Ellison at all.

During the wait for episode eight, Computron discovers a concept called "fanfiction."

While "fanfiction" is meant to consist of "fan-written stories about characters or settings from an original work of fiction," Computron observes that much of the *HyperWarp* fanfiction bears no resemblance to the actual characters or setting. For instance, the series that claims to be a "spin-off focusing on Powerful!Cyro" seems to involve Cyro installing many large-calibre guns onto his frame and joining the Space Marines, which does not seem relevant to his quest for revenge or the retrieval of the hyperdimensional warp unit. Similarly, the "high school fic" in which Cyro and Ellison study at Hyperdimension High fails to acknowledge the fact that formal education is reserved for the elite class in the *HyperWarp* universe.

Most of the fanfiction set within the actual series seems particularly inaccurate. The most recent offender is EllisonsWife's "Rosemary for Remembrance," which fails to acknowledge the fact that Cyro does not have human facial features, and thus cannot "touch his nose against Ellison's hair, breathing in the scent of sandalwood, rosemary, and something uniquely him" before "kissing Ellison passionately, needily, hungrily, his tongue slipping into Ellison's mouth."

Computron readies his styluses and moves the cursor down to the comment box, prepared to leave anonymous "constructive criticism" for EllisonsWife, when he detects a comment with relevant keywords.

bjornruffian:

Okay, I've noticed this in several of your fics and I was trying not to be too harsh, but when it got to the kissing scene I couldn't take it anymore. Cyro can't touch his nose against anything, because he doesn't have a nose! Cyro can't slip his tongue into anyone's mouth, because he doesn't have a tongue! Were we even watching the same series?? Did you skip all the parts where Cyro is a metal robot with a cube-shaped head?!

EllisonsWife:

Who are you, the fandom police?? I'm basing Cyro's design on this piece of fanart (link here) because it looks better than a freakin metal box!! Anyway, I put DON'T LIKE DON'T READ in the author's notes!!! If you hate the way I write them so much, why don't you just write your own????

Computron is incapable of feeling hatred for anything, as that would require Doctor Alquist to have installed emotion circuits during his creation.

However, due to Computron's above-average procedural knowledge, he is capable of following the directions to create an account on fanficarchive.org.

. . . and Ellison manoeuvred his flesh hands in a claw-like motion, locking them with Cyro's own grasping claws. His soft human body pressed against the hard lines of Cyro's proprietary alloy, in a manner which would have generated wear and tear had Cyro's body not been of superior make. Fluids leaked from Ellison's eyes. No fluids leaked from Cyro's ocular units, but . . .

Comments (3)

DontGotRhythm:

What the hell? Have you ever met a human? This reads like an alien wrote it.

tattered_freedom_wings:

uhhh this is kinda weird but i think i liked it?? not sure about the box thing though

bjornruffian:

OH MY GODDDD. :DDDD Finally, someone who doesn't write human-shaped robot-in-name-only Cyro! Some of Ellison's characterisation is a little awkward—I don't think he would say all that mushy stuff about Cyro's beautiful boxy shape??—but I love your Cyro! If this is just your first fic, I can't wait for you to write more!!

• • •

Computron has been spending less time in sleep mode after Episode Thirteen's cliffhanger, and has spent his time conducting objective discussions about *HyperWarp*'s appeal with commenters on various video streaming sites and anonymous message boards.

As he is about to reply to the latest missive about his lack of genitalia and outside social activities, which is technically correct, his internal chronometer indicates that it is time for the *Robotics Then and Now* performance.

"So, I was wondering, have you ever watched *Hyperdimension Warp Record*? There's this character called Cyro that—"

[Yes, I am aware of *HyperWarp*,] Computron says. [I have taken the "How To Tell If Your Life Is *HyperWarp*" quiz online, and it has indicated that I am "a Hyper-Big *HyperWarp* Fan!" I have repeatedly viewed the scene between Ellison and Cyro at the end of Episode Seven, and recently I have left a "like" on bjornruffian's artwork of what may have happened shortly after that scene, due to its exceptional accuracy. The show is widely regarded as "this season's sleeper hit" and has met with approval from a statistically significant number of critics. If other members of the audience wish to view this series, there are thirteen episodes out so far, and they can be viewed on—] The announcer motions to him, using the same gesture she uses when audience members are taking too long to talk. Computron falls silent until the announcer chooses the next question, which is also the last due to time constraints.

After TETSUCHAN has finished its breakdance and showcased its newly-programmed ability to pop-and-lock, the announcer speaks to Computron backstage. She requests that he take less time for the question-and-answer segment in the future.

[Understood,] Computron says, and returns to his storage room to check his inbox again.

Private Message from bjornruffian:

Hi RobotFan,

I noticed you liked my art (thanks!) and you seem to know a LOT about robots judging from your fic (and, well, your name). I'm doing a fancomic about Ellison and Cyro being stranded on one of the desert-ish exoplanets while they try to fix the *Kosmogram*, but I want to make sure I'm drawing Cyro's body right. Are there any references you can recommend for someone who's looking to learn more about robots? Like, the classic kind, not the android kind? It'd be great if they're available online, especially if they have pictures—I've found some books with photos but they're WAAAAY more than I can afford :\\\

Thank you for any help you can offer! I'm really looking forward to your next fic!

Shortly after reading bjornruffian's message, Computron visits the Early Robotics section of the museum. It has shrunk significantly over the years, particularly after the creation of the "Redefining Human," "Androids of the Future," and "Drone Zone" sections. It consists of several information panels, a small collection of tin toys, and the remnants of all three versions of Hexode the robot.

In Episode 14 of *Hyperdimension Warp Record*, Cyro visits a deserted exoplanet alone to investigate the history of the hyperdimension warp drive, and finds himself surrounded by the deactivated bodies of robots of similar make, claws outstretched, being slowly ground down by the gears of a gigantic machine. The "Robot Recycler" scene is frequently listed as one of that year's top ten most shocking moments in anime.

On 7 June 1957, the third version of Hexode fails Doctor Alquist's mirror test for the hundredth time, proving that it has no measurable self-awareness. Computron watches Doctor Alquist smash the spanner against Hexode's face, crumpling its nose and lips. Oil leaks from its ocular units as it falls to the floor with a metallic thud. Its vocal synthesiser crackles and hisses.

"You godforsaken tin bucket," Doctor Alquist shouts. "To hell with you." If Doctor Alquist were to raise the spanner to Computron, it is likely that Doctor Alquist will not have an assistant for any future robotics experiments. Computron stays still, standing in front of the mirror, silently observing the destruction of Hexode so he can gather up its parts later.

When Computron photographs Hexode's display case, he is careful to avoid capturing any part of himself in the reflection.

[**bjornruffian**] Oh man, thank you SO MUCH for installing chat just for this! Anyway, I really appreciate your help with the script so far (I think we can call it a collab by this point?). And thanks for the exhibit photos! Was it a lot of trouble? I checked the website and that museum is pretty much in the middle of nowhere . . .
    —File Transfer of "THANK YOU ROBOTFAN.png" from "bjornruffian" started.
    —File Transfer of "THANK YOU ROBOTFAN.png" from "bjornruffian" finished.
[**bjornruffian**] So I've got a few questions about page 8 in the folder I shared, can you take a look at the second panel from the top? I figured his joint would be all gummed up by the sand, so I thought I'd try to do an X-ray

view thing as a closeup . . . if you have any idea how the circuits are supposed to be, could you double-check?

[bjornruffian] Okay, you're taking really long to type, this is making me super nervous I did everything wrong :\\

[RobotFan] Apologies

[RobotFan] I

[RobotFan] Am not fast at typing

[bjornruffian] Okaaay, I'll wait on the expert here

[RobotFan] The circuit is connected incorrectly and the joint mechanism is incorrect as well

[bjornruffian] Ughhhhh I knew it was wrong!! DDD:

[bjornruffian] I wish the character sheets came with schematics or something, I've paused the flashback scenes with all the failed robots like ten billion times to take screenshots >:\\

[RobotFan] Besides the scenes in Episode 14, there are other shots of Cyro's schematics in Episode 5 (17:40:18 and 20:13:50) as well as Episode 12 (08:23:14)

—File Transfer of "schematic-screenshots.zip" from "RobotFan" started.

—File Transfer of "schematic-screenshots.zip" from "RobotFan" finished.

[bjornruffian] THANK YOU

[bjornruffian] I swear you're some sort of angel or something

[RobotFan] That is incorrect

[RobotFan] I am merely a robot

There are certain things in the museum's storage room that would benefit bjornruffian's mission of completing her Cyro/Ellison comic. Computron and Hexode's schematics are part of the Alquist Collection, which is not a priority for the museum's digitisation project due to a perceived lack of value. As part of the Alquist Collection himself, there should be no objection to Computron retrieving the schematics.

As Computron grasps the doorknob with his left claw, he catches a glimpse of Cyro from Episode 15 in the door's glass panels, his ocular units blazing yellow with determination after overcoming his past. In fan parlance, this is known as Determined!Cyro, and has only been seen during fight scenes thus far. It is illogical to have Determined!Cyro appear in this context, or in this location.

Computron looks at the dusty glass again, and sees only a reflection of his face.

[RobotFan] I have a large file to send to you

[RobotFan] To be precise, four large files

[RobotFan] The remaining three will be digitised and sent at a later date

—File Transfer of "alquist-archive-scans-pt1.zip" from "RobotFan" started.

—File Transfer of "alquist-archive-scans-pt1.zip" from "RobotFan" finished.

[bjornruffian] OMG THIS IS AWESOME

[bjornruffian] Where did you get this?? Did you rob that museum?? This is PERFECT for that other Cyro/Ellison thing I've been thinking about doing after this stupid desert comic is over!!

[bjornruffian] It would be great if I had someone to help me with writing Cyro, HINT HINT

[RobotFan] I would be happy to assist if I had emotion circuits

[RobotFan] However, my lack of emotion circuits means I cannot be "happy" about performing any actions

[RobotFan] Nonetheless, I will assist

[RobotFan] To make this an equitable trade as is common in human custom, you may also provide your opinion on some recurrent bugs that readers have reported in my characterisation of Ellison

[bjornruffian] YESSSSSSSS :DDDDDD

Rossum, Sulla. "Tin Men and Tin Toys: Examining Real and Fictional Robots from the 1950s." *Journal of Robotics Studies* 8.2 (2018): 25-38.

While the figure of the fictional robot embodies timeless fears of technology and its potential for harm, the physical design of robots real and fictional is often linked to visual cues of modernity. What was once regarded as an "object of the future" can become "overwhelmingly obsolete" within a span of a few years, after advances in technology cause the visual cues of modernity to change (Bloch, 1979). The clawed, lumbering tin-toy-esque designs of the 1950s are now widely regarded as "tin can[s] that should have been recycled long ago" (Williamson, 2017). Notably, most modern critiques of Computron's design tend to focus on its obsolete analogue dials . . .

watch-free-anime | Hyperdimension Warp Record | Episode 23 | Live Chat

Pyro: Okay, is it just me, or is Cyro starting to get REALLY attractive? I swear I'm not gay (is it gay if it's a robot) but when he slung Ellison over his shoulder and used his claw to block the Sixth Saber at the same time

Pyro: HOLY SHIT that sniper scene RIGHT THROUGH THE SCOPE and then he fucking BUMPS ELLISON'S FIST WITH HIS CLAW

Pyro: Fuck it, I'm gay for Cyro I don't care, I'll fucking twiddle his dials all he wants after this episode

ckwizard: dude youre late, weve been finding cyro hot ever since that scene in episode 15

ckwizard: you know the one

ckwizard: where you just see this rectangular blocky shadow lumbering slowly towards first saber with those clunky sound effects

ckwizard: then his eyebulbs glint that really bright yellow and he bleeps about ACTIVATING KILL MODE and his grabby claws start whirring

ckwizard: theres a really good fic about it on fanficarchive . . . actually you might as well check the authors blog out <u>here</u>, hes pretty cyro-obsessed

ckwizard: his earlier stuff is kinda uneven but the bjorn collabs are good—shes been illustrating his stuff for a while

Pyro: Okay

Pyro: I just looked at that thing, you know, the desert planet comic

Pyro: I think I ship it

Pyro: OH MAN when Ellison tries the manual repair on the arm joint and Cyro has a FLASHBACK TO THE ROBOT RECYCLER but tries to remind himself he can trust him

Pyro: Fuck it I DEFINITELY ship it

ckwizard: join the fucking club

ckwizard: its the fifth time im watching this episode, this series has ruined my life

ckwizard: i can't wait for season 2

bjorn-robot-collabs posted:

Hi everyone, bjornruffian and RobotFan here! Thanks for all your comments on our first comic collab! We're really charmed by the great reception to "In the Desert Sun"—okay, I'm charmed, and RobotFan says he would be charmed if he had the emotion circuits for that (he's an awesome roleplay partner too! LOVE his sense of humor :DDD).

ANYWAY! It turns out that RobotFan's got this awesome collection of retro robot schematics and he's willing to share, for those of you who want to write about old-school robots or need some references for your art! (HINT HINT: the fandom totally needs more Cyro and Cyro/Ellison before Season 2 hits!) To be honest I'm not sure how legal it is to circulate these scans (RobotFan says it's fine though), so just reply to this post if you want them and we'll private message you the links if you promise not to spread them around.

Also, we're gonna do another Cyro/Ellison comic in the future, and we're thinking of making it part of an anthology. If you'd like to contribute comics or illustrations for that, let us know!

Get ready to draw *lots* of boxes, people! The robot revolution is coming!

9,890 replies

SHOGGOTHS IN TRAFFIC

TOBIAS S. BUCKELL

—◆—

We stole the cherry red 1984 Corvette at noon, when Random was inside the strip club for Tuesday's Wings and Things and otherwise occupied. At one, we stopped behind a Denny's to swap the plates, even though it felt dangerous to have paused knowing that Random would be standing in the badly maintained asphalt parking lot staring at where he'd left the 'vette and coming to certain conclusions.

"It's okay," Abony said as I held the license plate in place and she screwed it on. "Take deep breaths."

"We stole a car from a fucking drug dealer," I said, voice quavering.

Technically, we'd repossessed the damn car. Abony had jimmied the car door and popped the lock in a second. She'd worked a roadside assistance gig for five years and had gotten pretty damn quick at it on older model cars. I went in with the screwdriver and hammer to crack the ignition open and jumpstart it.

Not gonna lie: The adrenaline kicked in pretty hard when I swung out onto the road, rear tires smoking under the faded GIRLS GIRLS GIRLS sign.

By the time the letters in the mirror were too small to read, I wanted to throw up.

The goal was to get the car from Chicago down to Miami. Twenty hours, straight shot, each of us taking turns to drive. Bathroom stops only. Once there: turn the car over, collect our fee, then vanish for the West Coast.

"Random is going to kill us," I said to Abony as she stood up.

"He doesn't know it was us. As long as he doesn't catch up to us." Abony's hair clips tinkled against each other as she turned back to me. "A hundred grand, Trent. We just have to get to Miami."

As long as he doesn't catch us, I thought.

South of Gary and halfway down toward Indianapolis on I-65 we pulled over because I had the shakes. Abony took the wheel.

"I'm scared, too," she said.

I couldn't stop looking in the mirrors. We'd agreed to drive exactly two miles over the speed limit. Not exactly the limit, that was suspicious. Not just under it. Couldn't risk being pulled over, as our plates and registration wouldn't hold up under a computer check from the cops. We were rolling dice here.

Abony's glasses glinted in sunlight as she looked over at me.

"A hundred grand."

It was our mantra. Our guiding light.

She'd first named the sum while we were inches deep in mud alongside a freeway, the tow truck behind us stabbing the night with its yellow emergency lights, struggling to replace a blown out tire on some Iowa grandma's 2016 Corolla.

The rain was seeping through my poncho, dropping long streams of ice-cold water down my back and ass crack. I slipped. Jammed my hand against the hubcap in the mud and sliced it open. I'd scattered the lug nuts in the puddles.

While we'd both swore and grubbed about in the mud looking for the bolts, she'd looked at me. "Man, I'm tired of this shit. I've been out here, inches away from being run over by these fucking idiots. I'm still living in my aunt's spare room and I can't hardly pay my student loans."

I found four of the five nuts. I bled all over them as I threaded them back on to get the replacement tire in place.

"What would you do with a hundred grand?" Abony had asked me.

"I'd go live near the ocean. California."

"That money won't get you shit out there. That's for rich folk."

"I just want to live near the ocean for a bit. You know, like Venice Beach." I dropped the old lady's car back down.

"You're gonna run out of money in weeks."

"Spent most of my life in trailers on the edges of dead-ass towns," I told her. "Even just a few weeks of beach would be worth it. You going in on lotto tickets with me?"

She'd shaken the water off her glasses. "Nah."

We'd gotten coffee at a diner a few miles up the street to dry off and wait for another call from dispatch. After a while of watching something eating at her, she'd leaned forward. "I hear you did a few years for GTA, right?"

I stared at the coffee. "Left Pennsylvania to try and start over after I got out. It's not good money. It was just part of the hustle." Meth, cocaine, weed, hubcaps, radios, and then one day, whole cars. The older shit I stole barely ever made more than a few hundred a vehicle.

Abony and I had been driving the tow truck as a team ever since Olaf had been jumped and mugged when out by himself last year on a call. She must have come to think of me as reliable, because she leaned over the table. "I know where to get a hundred thou by repossessing a car."

"Repossessing or stealing?"

"It's complicated."

Now I looked across at her, jaw clenched with determination. I'm sure a lot of folk assumed Abony would know how to steal a car, but she only knew how to jimmy a door because she'd worked roadside service. She'd started out answering the phones, the only job she had found after college. Then one night, Craig didn't show up to ride and she offered to go out with me because miles out in the dark on the late shift paid better than phones.

Fifty thousand would let her pay off her loans. Let her help her aunt with the house in Chicago. The neighborhood was getting gentrified. The taxes were getting jacked up.

My cheap Android phone chirped. The GPS began giving us alternate directions, routing us off I-65.

"Think we should stay on?" I asked.

She glanced at the phone. "How long a delay?"

I had been looking up ahead at the highway, trying to see if there were stopped cars up ahead. Looking back down I read the screen. "It says we save half an hour if we get off the highway."

I could see her doing the math. We were maybe an hour ahead of Random, who would likely be racing out along the most direct route to Miami. He knew where the car was headed. He would be breaking speed limits. We'd spent, what, five minutes changing the plates?

We couldn't afford delays.

Abony took the exit, the Corvette happily hugging the curve of the off-ramp as we slowed and spiraled onto a two-lane county road.

She hit the brakes and slowed to a near stop. "What the hell is this?"

A burly man in a leather jacket, chaps, and the usual long beard waved at us from a row of red traffic cones in the middle of the road. I spotted a Harley off to the side of the road with a small trailer attached to the back.

"You need to go back!" The man shouted. "Back to the highway!"

I rolled down my window. "The phone says there's an accident?"

"Ain't no fucking accident, brother," the man said, starting to wave at a semi coming along down the ramp after us. "Get back on the highway."

"That's no highway worker," Abony said. "Something's . . . "

The semi behind us didn't slow, it swerved around us. Maybe the driver hadn't been paying attention and didn't realize we were stopped. Tires screamed, the trailer wobbled, and I instinctively pulled back against the chair and waited for the impact.

Metal and rubber whipped past my window, burned rubber floated into the Corvette, making us cough. The semi downshifted, roared, and then continued on down the road through the cones.

The biker lay on the side of the road, arms and legs outstretched.

Abony was out of the car in an instant. "It clipped him!"

"Shit!" I crawled over her side of the car and out onto the side of the road.

The man groaned. There was blood all over his leather jacket, and dripping from his beard. He gurgled a bit and I wanted to throw up.

"Shit," I said again. "What do we do? We call 911, right?"

"Uh . . . " Abony looked around. "We're in a stolen car. You have a record."

"Jesus." I grabbed my head. "Jesus. But we gotta call 911."

Abony suddenly looked cold and distant. "Even if they don't think to run our details, you want to be standing here when Ransom and his crew get routed through by the same GPS? They got phones just like you, Trent."

"Fuck. We can't just leave him there. That ain't right."

She stood up. "No, we take him to the ER. Drop him off, and take off. We're in the middle of fucking children of the corn territory, right? It'll be faster to get him there ourselves than wait for an ambulance. This isn't the city, there won't be flashing lights here in five minutes."

Relief flooded me.

Then I looked back at the car. "Abony, ain't no back seats in that car."

She was already walking back to it, though. She popped the hatchback and started throwing the extra food, water, and other shit for the twenty-hour drive out onto the shoulder, right by the $1,000 fine for littering sign.

"Help me lift him in," she said.

The biker was short, heavy, and we hit his head twice getting him there. We had to curl him up, fetal position. I'd watched enough medical shows to know that if he had internal injuries, that wasn't going to help him much.

It occurred to me that if he died back there, we'd have a dead guy in the hatchback trunk of a car, with a window and all.

"What about his bag?" I asked, pointing to a backpack that had been knocked clean off the man further down the road.

"Toss it in the back with him," Abony said.

But we didn't have the time to wait for an ambulance or police to ask us questions. Abony was right. Out of my breath, something in my back tweaked and screaming from the awkward angle of trying to shove the biker into the trunk, I asked the phone's GPS for directions to the nearest ER.

It give us a route straight ahead.

The truck had already scattered the cones or crushed them. We drove past them onto the country road.

The biker groaned and stirred, his head right behind my headrest. I'd rested it against some bags of chips for cushioning. They crunched, releasing the smell of salt and vinegar into the air as one of the bags burst.

"It's okay, we're getting you to a hospital," I said.

"Check the phone again," Abony ordered, voice tense. Ten minutes following the 3D map and we were way out on a flat plain of skeletal recently harvested cornfields. "I think we were closer to a town back at the off-ramp."

I started fiddling with the phone, trying to zoom out of the map while it kept giving us instructions. "I hate it when the GPS does that."

"Yeah. It feels like it's taking us around the edge of the town," Abony said. "We're just making a big loop. It's confused."

Normally, it'd do my pride some harm to be taking orders so much. But Abony had the college degree. I may have constantly tried to mess with her, show her that some elite book smarts didn't mean shit out here in the greasy real world. But after a year working as a team, I'd stopped giving her shit and started giving her my attention.

I'd driven hundreds of miles to run away from my past in Pennsylvania. I'd sworn to stay on the straight, even if I was always broke. Abony said I needed to learn some self-control.

Well, I hadn't ended up in drugs and stealing cars because of my moderate nature.

But I'd turned it around. Cleaned up. Learned my lesson.

So I'd told Abony to fuck off the first time she told me about the car. Her cousin had done a job for Random and heard the story. That the car had been taken from a big drug dealer in Miami. It had been his dad's car, and a project they'd both worked on. It was *important* to the man. And Random stole it after some falling out about a smuggling corridor coming up from Miami through Kentucky.

Random drove it around Chicago, through the salt in the winter, and potholes. He drove the damn Corvette everywhere until it looked like an old piece of shit, but kept it running. A trophy.

Javier, in Miami, offered a hundred thousand dollars to anyone who got it back to him.

A repossession to the rightful owner, Abony said.

She was supposed to be the smart, college-educated one. But a month of idly talking about the money and how we could get the car wormed its way into my brain. At first, it had been a running joke as we drove from stranded motorist to stranded motorist.

Then it became something we nervously laughed about.

And finally, I told her about the strip club and Random's love of Tuesday's Wings and Things. And blushed when she asked how I knew.

"This is taking us around the town," Abony said, more confident as the GPS routing had us take another turn. "Look up the hospital on your phone."

A bloody, hairy arm grabbed my shoulder just as I was raising the phone up. I screamed and dropped it, Abony swerved as she looked back. The biker, head crammed against the glass of the hatchback, pushed himself between us.

"That damn thing won't ever take you to the hospital until it's completed the symbol you're driving," the man said, blood misting the air inside the car as he spoke. "Once the summoning pattern is complete, you'll be released. You have to stop the car, or everyone in this town will be in dire . . . "

He started coughing blood everywhere.

We stopped by the side of the road again. Abony grabbed my phone and started hunting for the hospital as I unbuckled.

The biker was shifting around and had popped the hatch. Blood smeared the glass from his coughs.

"Man, you're hurt, you need to stay here. Let us get you to the hospital," I said.

"No, I'm okay," the man said.

"Don't let him out," Abony shouted.

He tumbled out onto the grassy shoulder before I could get around the Corvette to stop him.

"Sir, you need to come with us. You can sit in my seat," I offered.

He staggered and collapsed, sitting on a mound of mud and gravel. "It's not too late to save people," he told me, his voice calm. He had grabbed his bag. "How far are we from the bridge?"

"The bridge?"

"There's a bridge over there. We can still stop the traffic from completing the summoning if we blow it." He opened the bag between his legs and I jumped back. Those little foil-covered bricks, the wires. That was like, C4, or something.

This guy was some kind of biker terrorist.

"Abony . . . " I said, backing up.

"There's a hospital just . . . " She saw the open bag from the car window. "Oh fuck."

"No, no," the biker waved his hands and coughed more blood down that crazy long beard. "I need to explain. I need you to help me blow that bridge."

"I seen this," I said out of the corner of my mouth to Abony. "It's like, bath salts, right? Some crazy heavy shit he's on. I mean, he's hit by a truck and talking about blowing up a bridge."

"Look," the biker said. "I'm a wizard, got it?"

"You mean like the KKK?" I asked. "They had a biker crew like that the town over in—"

"No, not the fucking KKK," the man said, visibly frustrated. "I'm a god damn magician. Like . . . " He started coughing blood again and folded forward. He pushed himself back up to sitting with visible effort.

"Get in the car, we gotta go," Abony said. "This is some fucked up shit here and we gotta go. We can't be involved in this."

But the old biker reached into the grass and scratched out a circle with his finger, digging at the grass until his fingernail popped clean and began to bleed. He drew more symbols into the grass, then spat blood into the palm of his hand and pressed it into the dirt.

I was rooted in place, the madness of what I was seeing holding me in thrall. Abony was frozen as well.

The biker began to run his thumb along the pattern drawn in the mud and blood. He traced the whole thing once, then started it over and traced it again, compulsively.

He was mad.

But each time he pushed his thumb around the sigil, he sped up, energy flowing into him. Seven times, eight, he kept repeating the motions.

The pattern lit up with blue fire. Like when you poured grain alcohol out onto the table and lit it up for laughs.

But the fire didn't fade out. It strengthened. Turned white hot. The ground burned but didn't catch fire. And inside the complex swoops and swirls, something flickered in the dark.

For a brief moment, a tiny swirl of tentacles and otherness hung in the air over the road's shoulder. It looked like something you'd see on a deep sea expedition special that ran after Shark Week.

The moment the creature appeared, the biker threw a handful of mud into the corner of the sigil. The lines broken, the fire that wasn't fire guttered out. A tiny howl of frustration from inside the circle hung in the air between us all.

We got the biker, the wizard, into my side of the Corvette. He put the C4 between his legs. I cleaned up the blood from the hatch and back of the car as best I could and curled up in a ball and let Abony shut the hatch down on me.

It was claustrophobic as hell.

"You see a lot of biker gangs rolling the highways," the wizard wheezed. "But what you don't know is that a lot of them are wizards. The long beards, their steed's a bike, and the nomadic ways, it all works."

The wizard's name, he said, was Ozymandias. "Yeah, to answer the obvious question, I knew Shelley," he said. But I didn't know who Shelley was, though Abony nodded as if that meant something.

"What the fuck was that thing you made in the air?" I asked from behind them both.

"It was a summoning. A pattern. You know how you can draw a cube on paper, even though paper is flat? Two-dimensional? You can do the same with higher dimensions."

"Like a pentagram?" I asked. I'd seen a lot of that stuff on some goth kids.

"Kind of. That's an abstraction, not an actual higher dimensional summoning pattern." He paused to wipe blood from his chin with a hand-kerchief. "You also need to charge it with motion to crack the space between worlds. In the past, you had to do that waving your arms and following the drawing. Took a lot of training. It took me almost a hundred years."

"Oh, come on, you're not that old," I protested.

Our wizard, or insane biker, shrugged. "In the old days, it was hard to find the patterns and charge them up. But, as technology began to change and get better, folks started summoning things from behind the veil with machines. We do our best to hunt down and stop the worst. Occasionally, things get out. Zodiac Killer, Highway of Tears. Things that go bump in the night."

Abony caught my eyes in the mirror. "Why were you stopping traffic?"

"GPS," the wizard said, stroking his long beard.

"The alternate route?" Abony nodded.

"Wait, what?" I wasn't following.

"It's traffic, Trent. Think about the roads from above the air, like a clover leaf exit."

I did that. Then thought about the pattern the wizard had drawn in the ground. Motion. Patterns. Summoning. "Holy. Shit."

The wizard was breathing deeply. "We started noticing that apps, GPS, were creating patterns. Test routes, routine things. But someone is either hacking them, or the companies are in on it. Whatever the reason, we're not sure about it yet, they're charging summoning patterns using diverted auto-mobile traffic."

I thought about all the times a GPS would offer an alternate route and I'd take it without thinking.

"If I could summon something dangerous with just a foot-wide pattern, what do you think a fifteen mile wide pattern could do, in terms of breaches to another universe?" the wizard asked.

We were all silent.

"You were trying to stop it with those cones, turning traffic back?" I asked.

"A big pattern takes a lot of traffic to charge it. It's not active yet. I tried to stop it with the cones. But I could also blow the bridge just another mile down the road. Look, I'm not asking you to help me. Taking me to a hospital won't do me any good if the fabric of reality gets ripped apart while I'm there. Drop me off on the bridge. I can interrupt the pattern, stop it from being charged. Do that, and we can save an entire town from something monstrous."

We drove on in silence.

It would take two minutes to get to the bridge.

I had the hospital up on the map, but no directions to it. I could get us there.

Abony's fingers gripped the steering wheel tightly and I looked up at the sun through the hatch's glass I was curled up tightly under, grateful for my tiny, bony frame. Was it my imagination, or did the sun just waver slightly?

Ten minutes later, we left the bridge as Abony revved the Corvette up and we risked breaking the speed limit to put craziness as far behind us as we could.

"Did we really see that . . . thing?" I asked.

Abony bit her lip and didn't say a thing.

"We did the right thing, right?" My voice cracked slightly.

"I'm just thinking," Abony said. "That the truck that hit him, it was one of those new automated ones. The self-driving trucks that they just started allowing on the roads."

"Jesus." If what happened was real, it could get way worse when the cars just drove themselves. Apocalyptic, even.

"And I'm also thinking," Abony said, proving once again that she was the smart one, "that Random is only five to fifteen minutes behind us after all those stops. And his GPS will give him the same route as the one we took."

In the mirror, there was a flash of light.

I didn't know if it was a bridge exploding or another universe folding itself out over the small town we left behind us.

Either way, it was eighteen more hours to Miami.

PERSEPHONE OF THE CROWS

KAREN JOY FOWLER

Isabelle Winters once saw a fairy. For real. It was little, like a hummingbird, with a hummingbird's frantic wings, and it was moving through the garden, shaking the rosebuds open for the bees. She's just told this to Polly, though not exactly in those words. The sarcastic *for real,* for instance, is all Polly. If there was ever a girl primed to see fairies, Isabelle Winters is that girl. If there ever was a girl who was not, that girl is Polly.

Polly is three years older than Isabelle, ten to Isabelle's seven, and they wouldn't even be friends except that Isabelle's father and Polly's father work together. Tonight they all had dinner at the Winters' house, and the girls are now in Isabelle's bedroom.

Isabelle has many things Polly wishes she had. Mr. Winters is not just a professor but also an artist. He and Isabelle have been making a pop-up map of Oz. The Emerald City is done, rows of glittering spires, and also the yellow brick road. Polly and Isabelle are sitting on the floor, the map opened between them. If Polly and her father tried to make a pop-up map, it would come out childish, not like this, not like something you might buy in a store. Polly's father would be game; he would do his best, but he's not an artist.

In the corner of the bedroom is a unicorn, large enough to ride though you'd feel pretty silly doing so at ten years old. The unicorn has golden eyes, a golden horn, and a golden carousel pole through its back, stretching from floor to ceiling. Mr. Winters made it from the old spring horse Isabelle had when she was little.

Mr. Winters has framed the closet door with turrets and banners and painted a portcullis on the front, so Isabelle walks into a castle every morning to get dressed. Tonight she's dressed for company, puffed sleeves and a sash. She looks a little like Alice in Wonderland or maybe Wendy in *Peter Pan*. Something in a storybook.

Polly would like to be wearing that dress. Polly would like the map and the unicorn and the closet all to be hers. Polly would like to believe in fairies.

Since she doesn't, her only choice is to find it funny that Isabelle does. Isabelle sees this in her face and tries to take it back. "It was kind of far away," she tells Polly, to suggest she isn't really sure what she saw.

Polly feels bad about making Isabelle do this. "You're so lucky. I wish I could see a fairy," she says, just to be nicer. Later, she'll remember making that wish. It seemed harmless at the time. She didn't believe in fairies.

Out in the living room, the adults are laughing. Polly makes another wish, but not out loud. She wishes that her father wouldn't get drunk tonight. She doesn't think that this wish will come true either and, if Isabelle has made the same wish, neither will hers. Getting drunk is what Mr. Winters and Polly's father do when they get together. Polly can't remember a single time when they didn't.

Of the two wishes, this second is the one that bothers Polly. Why make it? Her father is only having a good time. It would be great if he could paint castles in her room. It would be great if he didn't get drunk. But Polly feels guilty about wishing him different. She knows he would never wish her different; he loves her just the way she is. "Why do you think grown-ups never see fairies?" she asks Isabelle who, it turns out, knows the answer.

"It's because they don't believe."

So Isabelle thinks that it's Polly's *fault* that she doesn't see fairies? Polly is suddenly cross about it all—how she doesn't see fairies and doesn't have a unicorn, how she wouldn't look like something out of a picture book if she wore a dress with a sash, how her father and Mr. Winters are getting drunk in the living room together. She makes Isabelle play gin rummy, a game Polly will easily win. And then she makes Isabelle play again, trouncing her even more mercilessly the second time. And then she wants a third game, but Isabelle goes and gets a cloak from her dress-up chest. She puts it on with the hood up, and tells Polly it's a magic cloak that makes the wearer invisible. Polly has to pretend that she doesn't see Isabelle now, which gets boring fast, so Polly takes *Half Magic* from Isabelle's bookshelf and reads a bit. While she's doing that, Isabelle falls asleep on her bed with her shoes on and the cloak fallen to the floor.

Polly has already read *Half Magic,* and more than once. She puts on the invisibility cloak. Now that Isabelle won't see, she climbs onto the unicorn. She rides for a while, then there is nothing else to do, and she wants to go home. It's very late, way past her bedtime.

She decides to test the cloak's powers on the grown-ups. She moves down the hall, keeping her shoes quiet on the stone tiles. She passes through the dining room, where the dirty dishes are still on the table along with the chicken carcass, and the room smells of meat.

No one notices her. Mr. Winters has brought a painting up from his workroom, and they are all busy looking at it. Polly hears that it's not a new painting, but something he did some time ago. She never learns why they are looking at it now.

She moves to where she can see it, too. A naked woman with greenish skin sits on a beach. Her mouth is open; her hands are raised, and she's playing a game, something like cat's cradle. A complicated web of string and shells hangs from her fingers. Mrs. Winters doesn't have green skin, but she was obviously the model. It's as if they are all looking at Mrs. Winters with no clothes on and all pretending they aren't. The woman in the painting has large nipples and round breasts. Individual grains of sand have been carefully painted into her abundant pubic hair. It's a terrible painting.

"It's so beautiful," Polly's father says. He's shaking his head; he's so impressed, and maybe moved, that words are failing him.

"No one's ever liked it," Mr. Winters tells them, and Polly believes this. She goes and stands by her mother who puts an arm around her, rests her cheek on the top of Polly's head. Polly smells her mother's green apple shampoo.

"That's just crazy," Polly's father says. "It's so beautiful! I can't imagine why *anyone* wouldn't like it." When he makes the s sound or the t, he spits a little. Polly's mother holds her more tightly. Mrs. Winters hasn't said a word since Polly came into the room.

When she's older, Polly will read *The Odyssey* and realize that the woman must have been a siren, that the string game had something to do with fate. Some man's boat was about to hit the rocks.

But at ten years old, she's never heard of sirens, and isn't curious what the painting is about. She only resents being made to wonder if Mrs. Winters really has so much hair between her legs.

"Take it," Mr. Winters says. "A gift. Please. You're the only one who's ever liked it."

Polly's father empties his glass. He sets it down on the arm of his chair, but carelessly so it falls, landing silently on the thick rug. Polly's father doesn't seem to notice. "Like it? Like it?" he says. "I *love* it. But it's too much. I can't possibly accept."

A string of urgings and refusals follows. It all ends with Mr. Winters triumphant and Polly's father overcome. He has just the place for the painting, Polly's father says. It will go up above the fireplace, where everyone who visits can admire it. It will make the room.

Polly sees instantly that she will never be able to have anyone over again. "Isabelle's asleep," she tells her mother, and this is the cue everyone has been waiting for. Coats are fetched and Polly sheds Isabelle's cloak. The painting is conveyed with great care to the car, where it shares the backseat with Polly and the pillow her mother put there so that Polly can sleep on the way home. The Winters stand under the light of the porch to see them safely away.

"I can drive," Polly's mother says.

"So can I," her father answers. "Don't insult me, I'm perfectly capable." His words are slurry, but his tone is sharp. He takes his place at the wheel.

Does Polly's mother hesitate? If so, it's brief. Perhaps if the Winters hadn't been watching, she would have tried harder. Perhaps if Polly's father had been jolly or grateful and moved, the way he'd been not five minutes before, she would have tried harder. The Winters live up the mountain. It is a long way, with a lot of vacant fields, woods, twisting roads, and almost no houses between Isabelle's home and Polly's.

The sky is dark but clear and starry. The pavement is wet from an earlier rain, and it's cold enough to make Polly shiver, so there's probably ice. Her father starts up the car and the heater comes on, blowing cold air and a stale smell. Polly's mother gets in.

For five or ten minutes, no one says anything. The car warms up. Nobody else is on the road, not coming up behind them, not heading toward them. A curve presses Polly against her door. The painting bangs her knee. "Don't drive so fast," says Polly's mother. Her father responds by speeding up.

Polly is nearly asleep. Her mother is speaking quietly, her voice far away in the front seat, so Polly hears that she's talking without hearing what she says.

"You're imagining things." Her father isn't speaking quietly at all.

Her mother speaks again.

"I don't have to keep my voice down in my own goddamn car," her father says. And that's the last thing Polly hears, either because he is keeping his voice down after all, or because they aren't talking anymore, or because she falls asleep.

She's sleeping when they go off the road. She's in the air with the painting floating beside her. The car sails down a slope and through a bramble hedge that mercifully slows it considerably. And then they crash down, the painting landing hard on Polly's foot. They're in a black and muddy field from which they cannot see the road. There is a woods not twenty yards back. Twenty yards earlier and they would have hit the trees. "Are you all right?" Polly's mother asks her. She's turned around in her seat. One lens from her glasses has fallen from the frame, which is bent. There is a cut on her face, a little bit of blood. She's holding on tight to the seatback.

Polly says that she's fine without really knowing yet.

She does a quick check on her body. She's been knocked around for sure, and her neck hurts, and her foot, where the painting landed, is throbbing. She starts to say all this, but her father is apologizing and he's so upset, she swallows the words. "I'm so sorry," he says, over and over. "I saw something in the road. I think there was a deer. Right in front of me."

"I didn't see anything," Polly's mother says.

"Could have been a dog. I'm so sorry. I'm so sorry."

"I didn't see anything," Polly's mother says again.

Polly's father opens the driver-side door, the engine still running. He straightens each leg carefully, testing his weight before standing. He walks around the car, disappears from Polly's window as he squats to check the tires. He rises unsteadily. "We're stuck in the mud," he says. "But everything looks okay. We just need a tow. You wait here. I'll go get help."

He turns the headlights off but leaves the heater and the engine running. He comes to Polly's door, removes his coat, and lays it over her lap. She doesn't know what kind of liquor that is on his breath, but it's a smell she recognizes. It takes him two tries to slam the door, and then Polly watches him, only his sweater to keep him warm, as he picks his way through the mud. He scrambles on all fours up the slope to the road and disappears.

"Are you all right?" Polly's mother asks again, and she's crying, so Polly says again that she is. "Show me," says Polly's mother. "Wiggle your fingers. Wiggle your toes," so Polly does that.

They wait a long time. Eventually Polly goes back to sleep. When she wakes, she hurts all over. The sun is rising but not risen; there is a strange half-light over the landscape, a strange fog skimming the field. Crows are cawing. The car engine has stopped, and she's very cold. Her mother is gone.

She thinks probably her mother has just left to find a bathroom and will be right back. She thinks this for a long, long time. She gets painfully onto her knees to look out the windows. A great tangle of blackberry canes is lying across the car hood. The sky is full of crows; she's never seen so many, all arriving at once and making a commotion. There are maybe a few on the car roof. She can hear a scratching overhead.

She looks out the back window toward the woods, and that's when she sees some cloaked and foggy figures, standing beneath the trees. The light is poor and they're not moving and it's kind of far away and she can't be sure. She's more certain that she saw them later than she is at the time. She lies back down on the seat, out of sight, just in case. By now she's terribly frightened. She wants her mother and father.

More time passes, and she is angry as well as scared and cold. The sun is fully up now, the crows still cawing loudly, and it occurs to her that she is not being well looked after. Her parents are doing a terrible job.

She sits up carefully and looks toward the woods again. No parents, no vague figures. Reaching past the painting, she opens the far passenger door, pushes it open with her uninjured foot. She levers the painting out onto the ground, where it falls face down. "Good-bye and good riddance," she thinks. She hopes that whoever picks the painting up next will find that Mrs. Winters' breasts and pubic hair have been covered in a respectable coat of mud.

"So what happened next?" Stuart asks. They are on a long flat road somewhere in Missouri.

Polly has been hitchhiking. She'd made it to Illinois, but by then it was nearly dusk. She was about to give up for the night when Stuart pulled over. She liked the look of him, a man in maybe his mid-twenties. This makes him eight or nine years older than she. Very handsome, like a pirate, with a bandana around his forehead, his black hair in a braid, brown eyes, dark skin.

Two women are in the backseat, but Polly hasn't met them yet. They were asleep when Stuart stopped, and they're still asleep. "We're going to San Francisco," Stuart had said. "What about you?"

Polly was thinking of Chicago, but San Francisco is better.

"Climb on in," Stuart told her. "You're just what I need. Someone to talk to me. Someone to keep me awake. The radio's broken."

So that's what she's been doing for a couple of hours now, keeping Stuart awake. The sky has gone black with a tiny bit of moon. A shadow landscape stretches ahead. She's keeping Stuart awake so his car won't go off the road.

"What happened next," Polly tells him, "is that I woke up in my very own bed."

"So it was all a dream?" Stuart sounds as disappointed by this as anyone would be.

"Absolutely not. But they want me to think so." Because she didn't tell him the part about the cloaked figures, Polly knows that Stuart has misunderstood who the *they* in this sentence is. She makes no attempt to clarify. If she didn't believe Isabelle all those years ago, why should Stuart believe her now?

She's been editing the story in other small ways as she tells it; probably she's already said too much. "I know it happened," she says, "because ever since, crows pay attention to me. They watch me. They give me things." She opens her bag and pulls out some bits to show him. Broken necklaces and old keys, bottle caps, pens, and barrettes.

"That's so wild," Stuart says.

One of the women in the back seat sits up. "Where are we?" She yawns loudly. "Who's this?"

"Missouri," Stuart says. "And Persephone," because that's the name Polly gave him. "She's going to San Francisco, too. Persephone of the crows."

"Hello, Persephone of the crows." The woman yawns again and her tongue appears and disappears, like a snake's, as if she's sticking it out at Polly, but pretending she isn't. Her hair is short and very curly, matted down on one side from sleeping on her arm. "I'm Starlight," she says, and Stuart laughs so that Polly isn't sure if that's really her name or if she's making fun of Polly because of hers.

"Persephone has been telling me this story," Stuart says, "that just got shit crazy."

"I have to piss," says Starlight. "Like right now."

They pull over. Stuart gets out and stands by Polly's window where he lights a cigarette. Starlight squats down on the shoulder of the road. She's wearing a long skirt, and apparently no underwear. It's very dark, but the headlights of a passing car sweep over her and it's obvious from her position what she's doing. The driver hits the horn enthusiastically. "Fucking hippies," someone in the car shouts at them.

Starlight stands back up. She doesn't wipe herself and she doesn't return immediately to the car. She's combing through her hair with her fingers, fixing the matted part. Her lips are moving. She might be talking. She might be singing. Polly will have to keep an eye on her.

Stuart flicks some ashes onto the pavement. He motions to Polly to roll down her window. The smell of his smoke comes into the car. "Why are the crows bringing you things?" Stuart asks.

"Payment. For what was taken."

"The painting." It isn't a question. Stuart thinks he has it figured.

Polly doesn't explain that no one cares about the painting. It was a terrible painting. If this were about the painting, the bill would have been paid up long ago. A couple of broken necklaces would have more than covered it.

She doesn't tell Stuart that the crows are just the middlemen.

"What happened to Isabelle?" Stuart asks. "I liked that little storybook girl," and Polly feels the old flash of jealousy. Why are they talking about Isabelle? This story isn't about Isabelle.

"Still living the dream," Polly answers, though she's just guessing and doesn't know. Only it makes sense, since Isabelle gets to see the kind of fairies Isabelle gets to see, while Polly has to see the kind of fairies Polly has to see. Probably there are different kinds of drunken fathers as well, and Isabelle, of course, would have the good kind.

To be fair, Polly once had the good kind, too.

On the morning after the car crash, when she got out of bed and went to see what was what, there was a woman who looked exactly like her mother in the kitchen only with lipstick and no glasses. She was cutting a red grapefruit, eating the sections one by one as she went. She was doing this with great concentration.

"Do you want a grapefruit?" she said to Polly as if she didn't know that Polly hated grapefruit.

"How did I get home?" Polly asked, and the woman said she didn't know what Polly was talking about. Did she have a cut on her face? Polly couldn't remember. Was Polly herself still bruised and sore? She doesn't remember that either. It's all suspiciously far off in her mind.

"Where's Dad?" she asked, and the woman said she didn't know and didn't care.

Later a man who looked exactly like her father came in with the paper as if he'd been in the front yard the whole time. He sat at the breakfast table with the paper opened in front of him, but he never turned the pages. He didn't speak to the woman who looked exactly like her mother. He didn't say "Good morning, Merry Sunshine," to Polly. He didn't tell everyone how sorry he was the way Polly's father would have.

Polly went to look for the car, which she found in the garage. She couldn't remember if the tires were muddy or the hood scratched. But there was no painting in the backseat. She did know that. She never saw the painting again.

They never went to the Winters' again either, nor ever had them over, though the families had gotten together so often before.

The man who looked like her father didn't drink.

The woman who looked like her mother didn't care.

Later, much later, when they're all in San Francisco and living in a filthy house on Dolores Street, when Persephone is sleeping with men for money, but only when she absolutely has to—she doesn't like the way crows look at her after, but if they brought her money instead of junk, there'd be no need, would there?—one day when she's working with Stuart, passing out coupons for Georgio's pizzas, putting them on the windshields of parked cars and into the hands of panhandlers and tourists, he will ask her what she thinks her parents did the day they first realized she'd gone.

"Whatever real parents would do," Persephone will tell him. "They did just exactly that."

WHATEVER KNIGHT COMES

RYAN ROW

Some summers, you like to watch the firefly comets through your huge window in the east tower. The scribbled yellow, blue, and red lights crisscross the sky in an obscure dance. A tangle of light and form that you sometimes find very alluring, and that sometimes reminds you of master swordplay. Wild strokes of light, turns and swirls and loops cutting right through the fabric of the hot summer stars. The night sky, it has always seemed to you, is a big fête. Sometimes, you can't stand to watch, and you push the heavy wardrobe with the broken mirror inside it in front of the window and leave it there for days, months, years.

Sometimes you have a maiden in the west tower. The maidens smell like good soil, like rose, like sunlight, like ice. They wear dresses of tissue paper, of spider's silk, of common wool or dirty cotton, of gray wolf skin. Sometimes they are naked and ashamed, and you throw your black cloak over their shoulders with a practiced flourish, and they mistake it for kindness instead of compulsion. Sometimes they are naked and don't care. You have seen white moonlight on every shade of bare skin and it always looks, to you, like a much more gentle lover's touch. They stand before you as if daring you. Daring you to take off your armor, but your armor never comes off. To touch them, but you will never touch them. To love them. You will always love them. Every one of them, even though you also hate them. You throw your cloak over them anyway. It weighs at least thirty pounds, and this is as close as you can ever come to hurting them.

The knights come, and you fight them. Sometimes they have witches in tow who have blessed them with burning sage and owl blood. Sometimes pages who carry their swords. Sometimes whole armies come for you, and you enjoy this the most, because you can kill as many soldiers as you please, just not the knight. It always ends the same way. A knife through your neck. A pike through your chest. Your head on the ground beside you, dead eyes full of stars and blood. Once a boy killed you with a six-inch nail he'd pried out of a wall in his bedroom before running away from home to come and rescue a princess. You are a master swordsmen, and you know twelve of the thirteen ancient forms, Palm Grasping Moon, Ocean Turning Time, Dragon Eating Itself, and a boy killed you with a crooked nail.

The same humiliation over and over. Sometimes the knights are alone, and they have great swords, like your own, and you duel atop the black stone bridge above two hundred empty feet and a silver loop of river that rings your castle like a wedding band. These are the moments you are closest to being yourself. Parry, repost. Parry, repost. The art of the sword. The complicated music of steel and iron. It can go for hours. Bursts of blue and red sparks off your swords like spells, like dreams of other places, other times. Eventually, the knights tire, begin to slow, and magically, the next form goes out of your head, the next step disappears under you. You trip over nothing. You slow down for no reason, and the knight lands a lucky blow and chops off your arm, and it goes flying through the air, sword and all, like a strange, dark bird.

You are not allowed to hurt the maidens. You give them food, but you do not force them to eat. You lock them in the west tower, and, even after all these years, you are still ashamed each time. Sometimes they pound on the door until their fists are bloody. Sometimes they are so silent you think they may have died, and it is a relief. Like a deep muscle pain, you love every one of them.

"Someday, you will learn to love me," you say, you always say, just before you lock the door. It is your destiny to repeat these words over and over. You are used to something else controlling your body, at times, and at least, during those moments, you can pretend that you are not responsible.

The knights always kill you, and you always wake up the next morning. Always they break down the door to the west tower, following the singing, the crying, the screaming. Some have enough sense to take the heavy iron key off your body; others hack down the door with their swords, axes, maces. Sometimes they take the gold in the south tower. Sometimes not. The gold is also cursed and will turn to dust in three hundred days and reappear in your castle. You like it when they take the gold. You hope it will bring them great misfortune and unhappiness. You hope they use it to pay for their weddings.

Sometimes you wake up on the road where you died, arrows still sticking out of your back like new, throbbing hearts. Sometimes, if the knights have burned your body or thrown it into the silver river to dissolve, you wake back up in your lace iron coffin in the north tower. Sometimes you lie there for days before you have the mental strength to reach up and push the coffin open. It is cool in there, and so silent.

Time shudders around you. Years. Winters, summers. Seasons of firefly comets. Years as fleeting and meaningless as shooting stars.

• • •

Sometimes there are no maidens in your castle; sometimes two or three at a time. Sometimes you are compelled to ride a skeletal wyvern, even less alive than you, that lives at the top of the north tower. Sometimes you wonder what sin this creature committed. It was here in this castle long before you came, and it will be here long after you are gone. You caress the white calcite scales and they click against your black armor. Under your palm, it feels like an incredibly fragile creature, hollow, and it sighs into your hand, leans into you. It has huge black eyes, like a dog's. Perhaps no sin at all. Sometimes, birth alone is a great enough sin to be punished for.

You ride the white wyvern for days, clinging to its neck like child riding a mare for the first time. You ride through storms that chill you all the way down your skeleton and burn it to frozen glass. Perhaps that is not your skeleton you are feeling, so brittle and cold. Perhaps that is your soul. The wyvern dodges cracks of lightning like cracks in the world while you pray and pray to any god who might still be alive.

I'm sorry, you pray. *I'm sorry, I'm sorry, I'm so sorry.*

You always pray in the lightning storms, and you always feel foolish afterwards. You ride over the dark forests surrounding your castle. The forests are filled with bear and wolf and snake. You ride over the ivory deserts, the five-inch sea, over huge cities alive with alchemy and astronomy and the noble sciences, and you ride over miles and miles of gray ruins and rotting stone rising out of poison marshes like half buried bodies. Sometimes you wonder if this ruin, a soft stone courtyard lined with tufts of white grass or a tiny village encased in clear ice, might once have been your home. Did you live here? Did your mother live there? Your daughter? Whomever you might have once had in your life, they are long gone now.

You take maidens from their beds. From the fields, grain, corn, oranges, silver apple, fat grapes. Sometimes they fight you. Shears and farming scythes and bits of broken glass or tiny mirrors, which, later, you must pick out of your eye with the slivers of iron you use as toothpicks. More than once, you have saved maidens from drowning, from rape. You caught one in mid-fall off a cliff, and still she did not love you. She was terrified of you. Your black armor like gargoyle skin. Like demon's skin. Once, you stopped one from killing her father in his sleep. You pried the knife from her hand, and let it fall to the soft wood floor, and for just the smallest moment, you felt like someone's hero.

"He deserved it," she said. Her voice was even harder and more filled with hate than yours. Her eyes wild, and full of old pain. She smelled like dried flowers and pepper. "If any man deserved it, he deserved it. This was justice. Why did you stop me?"

"When it is time," you said, in the voice that you hate, that constant wraith whisper, that dying breath voice. "Nothing can stop me. Certainly not justice."

You have slain many fathers to kidnap maidens. You have slain dragons to kidnap maidens. You have slain trolls. Your sword is elder iron, that much you remember; it was your father's sword, and it cuts through stone bodies like so much hot air. Through golden scales. Through the water mail of putrid merfolk, the ashy skin of lower demons, the heavy plate of other cursed knights. You still enjoy combat. The craft of swordplay was always the medium of your art. The perfect strike like the perfect wild beating of your heart. And who knows? Perhaps one of these curses, floating over these twisted bodies like great pendulum blades, will be greater than the one hanging over you. Perhaps, one day, you will meet with some curse that is greater than yours, and some demon will murder you.

This hope, like your sometimes belief in God, makes you feel so foolish. Like a child, all you have are your fantasies.

Often you read. The library is huge and takes up most of the south tower, and an inhuman peddler occasionally comes to the castle and trades you new books in exchange for allowing him to fill his vials in the silver river. You read, in a children's book, that when a curse is broken, a brand new firefly comet is born. You read in a much newer scientific tome from the university city of Zaren that the firefly comets are some type of invisible energy burning and becoming visible in the upper layer of the ether. Both explanations make you more than a little sad.

A new maiden today. You have ridden the wyvern for ten days over open sea as blue and cold as infinity. The stars are sometimes calm, and sometimes scatter as firefly comets swirling and chasing each other across the sky. Who is chasing whom? What will they do when they catch, or are caught? The air is cold and full of salt. You feel like you're rusting. You whisper to the wyvern. You tell it stories you have read. It is your only true companion. A crescent of islands across the ocean reveal themselves like a shattered moon. You can feel your curse pulling you toward one of the smallest islands at the outer tip of the formation.

The wingbeats of the wyvern as it lands scatters her tiny campfire in a hail of coals and ash. You haven't smelled anything but salt and sea for days, and the scents of the sand and the dense tropic green and the sweet flower oils off the maiden's dark skin make you shudder with pleasure despite yourself.

Her irises are almost as black and deep as her pupils, and her eyes are wide open, and they reflect the scattered campfire in flickering red light. She is alone on a broad stretch of white beach near heavy jungle. You move toward her. Tiny shells and glass coral crack and turn to dust beneath your feet. You don't even feel the coals you step on, still bright and orange against the night. She falls to her knees and clasps her hands together as if in prayer, eyes wide with fear and surprise. This is where she begs. Often they beg.

"Please," she says. Soft waves crash on a near shore. You feel the response already forming in your throat like destiny. When it is time, nothing can stop you. Not even yourself.

"Please," she says. "Take me with you!"

The words twist and halt in your throat. You feel upside down. Standing over her like this, it is almost as if she is praying to you. You reach out your hand, heavy and cool, and place it over her clasped fingers.

For ten days atop the wyvern's back, through calm skies and one light, tropical storm through which you pray nonstop, silently like a young boy, the maiden hardly ever stops laughing. She smells a little sweet, like firewood ash.

She has copper hair and the dark, sandy skin of the isles you took her from. Eyes like new moons. She is very beautiful. They are all very beautiful. Sometimes you fall in love with their eyelashes, like little wings. Sometimes the constellations of their freckles, the bend of an ankle. Once you fell in love with the life-line on maiden's palm. It seemed, to you, heartbreakingly short. You always hate this part. This love forced through your body like a potion replacing your blood . This time, you fall in love with everything.

She has suffered. Her father, her brothers, her mother wrapped around her like chains. She was set to marry a wild man with shockingly white skin from the continent north of the islands. She hated this man, the way his breath always smelled like meat, the way he would not let her touch his bow or knives, the way he would not hold her hand but drag her places by her thin wrist. Many have suffered, you think. Suffering does not make one special.

But she is special. That first night, when you land together on the roof of the north tower and the dark forests extend all about you like another kind of sea, she hops off the wyvern as easy as dismounting a horse. Her skin is burned from the high sun and chapped from the hard wind, but she spins on her heel and hugs the wyvern around its huge neck. It turns to look at you, with a slightly tilted head, a confusion in its eyes.

"What's her name?" the maiden asks.

"That creature has no name."

"Can I name her?"

You say nothing. The night howls with silence. You do not know if the heavy, sick love you feel is you or your curse.

"I will name you Comet," she says to it. "Because you are so free. Not even the earth can hold you."

She asks to hold your sword, as if she does not know she is your captive. You wonder if you will have to explain it to her.

"You may not," you say. And she looks so disappointed that you let her into the armory and she picks another sword, much too big for her figure, and swings it clumsily like a club. Laughing as its weight pulls her whole body behind it.

She does not cower from you, like most, or even scheme ways to murder you or escape you, like the smarter ones do, the tougher ones you sometimes have to lock in the dungeons. After a few weeks in which her arms grow toned and strong from swinging her new sword daily, she can lift the sword easily, and she asks you to teach her swordplay. The idea of this makes you happier than you have been in years. To have a student. To discuss the sword. And this happiness makes you feel pathetic.

However, you are desperate, and always in love, and you show her the first form, The Eternal River. She is eager and intelligent. She absorbs it like a plant absorbing water. The second form, the third, the fourth, the fifth.

You spar with her once she has understood the fifth form, and the curse that is always wrapped around your body like armor, like skin, feels very far away.

You pause. She sips water from a ladle. Silk moths flutter near the torches and cast dancing shadows. She's sweating. You are in love with her sweat. She's breathing hard and you are not. She wipes a strand of copper hair from her brow.

"Why am I here?" she asks. It has been months. She will not look at you now. She is frightened, as if she expects you to throw her away.

You tell her how this works. You show her that the armor does not come off. You lead her to the back of the armory and show her your coffin. She runs her hand, freshly calloused from the sword, over the inside surface of the coffin, and you shiver as if she has touched your bare skin.

"But you're so powerful," she says, still breathing a little hard. The sweat dries on her skin, and goose flesh rises on her arms. You have never felt any need as great as the need to protect her.

"I am a prisoner," you say, in the only voice you can remember ever having now, "as much as you are."

"Whose prisoner are you?" she asks.

"My own."

She looks up at you. Torchlight dashes across her face like blush. "I want to be here," she says.

And you try, you try so hard, not to believe her.

Sometimes you take her flying on Comet, and she screams into the clouds, into the lightning, screams laughter. You are both soaked afterwards. You have not prayed in months, and it feels like being set free. She finds ways to make food better. She uses black fire powder as seasoning and puts ground fire chips directly into the stew. You had forgotten food. Sometimes the two of you watch the firefly comets together, sitting in opposite corners of the huge window in the east tower. The light plays in your armor, she says, like the midsummer light on the seas of her home. The air is clear and thin here, and the stars are brighter than she's ever seen.

A year passes. Two. Time flickers like a fire. She now sleeps in the room beside yours in the east tower. You have taught her how to read, but sometimes you still read to her as she falls asleep. Sometimes you tell her stories of the countries you have seen. The creatures you have slain. Wraiths. Bogmen. Lychen. Harpies. Men. She is wide-eyed at these tales, and hungry. There is a clean joy and desire in her. A purity which you did not think existed. She feels what she feels, and nothing else. You feel like both her father and her lover and her great devil. Is the curse purposely giving you more time with her? So that it will hurt even more when she is taken from you.

You show her the seventh form, Sparrow's Fall, spinning and leaping in the practice hall while she watches from the edge holding her own sword loose at her side. When you land in the final stance, low with the sword high above you ready to flow into any other step of any other form, she tells you that she thinks she is in love with you.

Slowly, you lower the sword. Sunlight peeks through the slight windows high above as white and brittle as ice.

"I am always in love with you," you respond. Your voice echoes in the hall and inside your own helmet. "With all of you."

"I'm not joking," she says, stepping toward you. You step back. She smiles, and it is like iron. "I love this castle. I love Comet. I love the storms and the lightning. I love the sword, god be damned I love the sword, and the firefly comets and the stars. I love hunting with you in the forest. I love that there are no laws here. I love falling asleep under quilts so heavy they make it hard to breath. I love the library. I love when you read to me—"

"Stop." You feel dizzy. You know not to trust yourself, or that rotten apple in your chest that you call a heart. Truly, it is a bundle of betrayal. It is a bundle of smooth poison.

"Most of all," she says. She has backed you against the wall. You want to believe in her like you want to believe in God. The high blush on her cheek, her heavy breathing, the wild shine in her eyes. Is she afraid? What is she afraid of? You want to hold her, to be held by her, to die in her arms, and at the same time, you want to strike her with your sword. "I love—"

"When your knight comes," you say, "he will destroy me, and he will take you from this hell and into a beautiful future from which you will forget this place completely. You will have children and a warm touch and a life. And I will be here for a long time after that. For a very long time."

"I don't want children." A beam of light falls across her face, sharp and bright, and she turns her eyes briefly away and down. Her hair glows as if it has been freshly forged. Her dark skin gleams. You are in love with this motion of hers. With every motion. "And I will never forget you."

"When your knight kills me," you say.

"Stop calling him 'my knight.' "

"When the knight kills me, you will."

She's silent. The family of white day owls that live in the rafters flutter like impossible butterflies. You can see her mind turning like a planet crossing the sky beneath her skin. What is she planning? To trick you? Or to trick fate? She smiles into the hard sun. Her teeth white as wolf's and just a little crooked.

"Not if you kill him first."

You, slay a knight? Impossible. Even your elder sword, capable of piecing a golden dragon's scales, has shattered on a simple knight's shield. It regrows with the rest of you. The curse never allows you to kill the knights. It lets you be just strong enough, lets you remember just enough swordplay, just enough of your own body, to push the knights, push them to their furthest edges but never enough to break them. You pray to encounter demons or bandits or sword masters just so that you will have something you can fight with your whole body, just so that you can move without being held back. You are probably the best swordsman alive and the worst at once. There is no one left alive who knows the thirteenth form, and only you know the twelve.

Soon though, the maiden may know them too.

She trains day and night. She swings her sword in her sleep. She slashes spare suits of armor packed with wild boar meat into scraps because she says she needs to feel the sensation of a real body, real slashing. She cuts apart shadows. She is very hard now. None of the girl that she first was. Slim and soft as a tropic beach. She is a black oak carving of a woman. She cuts her hair short with a dagger. She trains with a single mindedness that is almost feral, animal. She is a natural force. She is the sun and moon. She is the silver river.

Once, where you like her?

The two of you sit in the window together. The east tower is the tallest, and it is very cold up here. The firefly comets write impossible stories in the sky, and their long, thin tails fade as slow as lives. Somehow, she still smells like sweet, firewood ash.

"I'll do it myself," she says. "I will kill whatever knight comes. And you and I will live together in this castle for a long, long time. Maybe forever."

"Comet can be our child," you say, and because she laughs, a true, high laugh, full and whole, and because the wild light tangles in her short hair and her teeth like gentle fingers that could be your own, you do not even hate your own tattered voice.

She tells you that she loves you.

You don't have the heart to tell her, that when her knight comes, she will fall into a heavy sleep, and you will carry her into the west tower and place her on a stone bed like a corpse, and you will lock the door behind you.

You have no choice.

Instead, you say that you love her too. And it is true. It is always true.

Another year passes. She has mastered ten forms and is working on the eleventh. You watch her. The arc of her sword has all the grace of a devout prayer. The kind you could never truly manage to make.

You feel her knight enter the forest. He is on the shortest route.

"The knight will come tomorrow," you say.

She halts. Slowly, she lowers her sword. She is facing away from you. She breathes steady and low. Shoulders rising and falling just lightly. A fine sheen sweat over the new animal of her body like sweet oil. She is the most perfect creature you have ever seen or read about. You want her to stop, to never turn around, to never change. You want to be her.

"Show me the twelfth form," she says, without turning around. The scent of her, fire and sweat and sweet ash, is everywhere.

You would like to go flying instead. For the first time in years, you feel the urge to pray to that great nothing that holds you, and that feeling makes this moment seem all the more hopeless. The sky, the lightning, the comets, have always been your only church.

"You're not ready," you say. She turns to face you. She has more natural talent with the sword than you've ever seen. Besides yourself. That is the face a woman who knows what she is. Who is what she wants to be. You believe in her now completely. She is your faith.

"I don't care," she says. "Show me."

The twelfth form, The Lovers Struggle.

After showing her the form, the two of you take Comet to flight. You ride high and hard over the forest, and you wonder if her knight can see the two of you from somewhere far below. You ride as far as fate will allow you, the land blurring below you. A haze of color and light. A small village. A perfectly round lake. Grass hills. Dirt roads crisscrossing and thinning out and disappearing like people's intersecting lives. You almost make it to the ocean. In the distance, you can see a strip of metallic blue water shimmering with reflected stars. You call for the maiden to look, but she has already passed into a deep, deep slumber.

You carry her like your child. At some point, they all feel like your children. The halls are cold and dark. You don't bother with torches. You know this castle almost as well as you know your own body. Comet whines as you leave her behind. You don't look back.

The gray stone you lay her on is carved with flowers tangled around swords. It smells like dark magic in here, lilac and poison ash. She is talking in her sleep. She is repeating the steps in the last form. The embrace. The tear. The scar. She is struggling to open her eyes. No maiden has ever opened their eyes.

You are standing on the bridge. You are always standing on the bridge. It is before dawn and the firefly comets are in frenzy above you, and they cast enough light see everything in a shimmering way. The silver river glows beneath you. This knight is an early riser, you think, or perhaps he has traveled all night for his maiden. His maiden.

There are three figures at the end of the bridge. You spot the knight immediately. He is standing on the left. The light is yellow and silver and blue and red and it casts deep shadows in their skin and makes their faces look like handsome masks. He has a wizard with him in red robes and a priest with a heavy silver mace. You hate silver and the ugliness and inelegance of maces.

The knight has dirty hands, and two exquisite knives in his belt, and a huge bow made out of black elder wood. A relic from the same age as you. His face is perfectly formed, and his skin is white as scar tissue. He radiates confidence, and that confidence emanates from a deep skill. You can tell. Normally, you would enjoy such an opponent. How many forms will he drag out of you? Six, seven? No knight has ever allowed you to go past nine. Most cannot push you to use three. But this morning feels like the last morning. This feels like the end of time. Like the end of the world.

You raise your great shield, a slab of phantom iron caved into the head of a demon, and charge them. Despite your size and the heaviness of your armor, you have great speed. Your speed surprises them. It always does. You hear the wizard begin to chant. A heaviness curse, for your armor no doubt, or perhaps your sword. The priest shouts something in a new, ugly language (could it really be a blessing?) and charges you right back. Arrows slam your shield like falling stars, and the shield is almost knocked from your hand. You hold. Blazing light falls all around like strange snow.

You slam into the priest and he stumbles back. You drop the shield and spin right into the sixth form, Storm's Eye. An arrow flies right beside the priest's stumbling head and glances off your breastplate, knocking your form off half a step. A nearly miraculous shot. You have placed the priest squarely between you and the knight. The priest shakes your weak blow off his shield swings his mace like a child swinging a bat. You slip easily away, and an arrow buries itself in your hip, right at the joint of your armor. The pain is immediate and boiling. You step back. A faint. Pain would never make you step back.

The priest's teeth click together in a tombstone smile. He is blond with dead blue eyes and huge white teeth. He charges you. You pretend to stumble back from his shield push. He hefts his mace, grinning a wild man grin, and you split him right in half, shield and all. The eighth form. The Cleaving Sun.

Your armor weighs suddenly a hundred pounds more. Stone cracks beneath you. It grows heavier with each bounding step you take toward the wizard. Another arrow slams into your shoulder. You swat another out of the air with your sword. The wizard screams and a ball of white flame flies at you, but you turn and take it on your already dead shoulder. You slam your pierced burned shoulder into the wizard, and a look of shock spreads across his face as you send him flying back and over the edge of the bridge. He falls into a sea of silver light and is lost.

The knight manages to put two more arrows in your stomach and chest before you close the distance. He drops his bow and jumps back, ducking your clean strike, and draws his daggers. They're made of petrified yellow glass, and they fly like comets.

One of your eyes has melted in its socket from the fireball. The arrows have some kind of acid poison on them, and you feel your muscles melting where their tips bury in your cool flesh. Your armor is at least three times as heavy now and getting heavier each moment, and the forms are starting to drain from your body like a second kind of blood.

Here is where you would normally surrender. Where you would normally allow you shattered body to collapse on the knight's blades. The sun has still not risen. But the light is wild above you. And this feels like some great fête to which you are finally invited.

The knight is nimble as a wood fairy. He cuts at the joints of your armor with his yellow knives. He laughs, actually laughs, as you shakily swing your sword after him in pale imitations of the true forms. You think, he is the perfect man. He is so confident and strong and whole. And you are all fragments. You are all pieces that don't quite fit together. You are the whole world's villain. You are the best swordsman and the worst fighter. You are the oldest hunter and the worst cook. You are excellent at kidnapping and terrible, so terrible, at protecting.

You laugh too. You laugh and laugh. Your laughter is a horrible thing. Smoke and broken voice and metal echo in your helmet, and the knight falters just a half step. You swing your sword in the first step of the first form, the only one your body still remembers. The one that is most a part of you, buried inside you. The form in which you store your soul. The Beginning. You have swung your sword thousands and thousands of times. Uncountable times, over uncountable years, and this is the most perfect strike you have ever performed. This cut could sever fate. This cut could kill God, or, perhaps, resurrect him.

Every string of your body breaks in the process.

The knight's glass knives shoot into a clean X, defending himself even as he jumps backwards to avoid the blow. Your sword shatters his knives in bursts of light. It shatters time and air. Its tip cuts inches deep all the way across his perfect face. Your sword goes flying.

And you both fall.

For how long do you lie there? You watch the firefly comets disappear in daylight, with your one good eye. You watch the sun roll across the soft blue of the sky. You do not pray. Your flesh is liquid under your skin where the four arrows pierced you. Your outer skin throbs where it was burned with curse fire. Is this what freedom feels like? You can hear the struggling breath of the knight nearby. He has not risen.

Your armor weighs more than the moon. The sun sets. The stars slowly come out, then the comets. Their wildness is comforting tonight. Their unpredictability. There is no fate to their paths. No curse to their existence. The light is heavy on you and the dying knight.

You hear someone approaching. Did the wizard survive his fall? Impossible. You hear the shing of metal sliding against stone. Someone has lifted your blade.

"That man was a very famous warrior," the maiden says, from somewhere outside your vision. "The Light Archer, he was called. He freed the Crescent Islands from the headless king by one-on-one combat. He has slain countless demons and villains. He was my betrothed. But he couldn't beat you."

She walks past you, dragging the tip of your father's sword over the black stone of the bridge, trailing blue sparks. She wears slim dark armor threaded with gold that she must have taken from the armory. It fits her like it was waiting for her. Like it was smithed for her ages before she was born.

"Wait," you gasp. There is the wet, stabbing sound you know so well. The sucking pop as the blade is withdrawn. You can't hear the knight breathing any longer.

She drags the sword back to you, and it spits sparks like a tiny, angry dragon.

She stands over you like your new God. You feel upside down again. She lifts your huge sword easily. It is becoming hers, a part of her, just as it was once a part of you. She examines the ancient blue edge in the flickering firefly light.

"How many women have you kidnapped?"

"Too many."

"How many women have you hurt?"

"None."

She smiles, laughs a little, and it makes her seem violently pretty.

"How many women have you handed over to violent men?"

"I couldn't stop them. Any of them." Beneath the visor of your helmet, you are crying again.

"You never tried."

"I did. I tried so hard." You are always crying. These tears, like the voice that you hate, or the armor that is your skin, are a part of your curse. "It wasn't me."

"Your curse?" she says.

You try to nod, but can't. You are a ball of pain in the shape of a man.

"You are your curse."

"I'm not. I'm more."

"You want to be more, it's true." She slowly reaches down and lifts the visor of your helmet. It swings open easily for her now.

"Wait," you say. The armor has become so heavy, you fear the bridge will collapse, taking you both with it. But what most worries you is how your face must look at this moment. Once you were handsome. Now you are an old, old man. Your hair is white and thin as light. Your bones are brittle. Your skin is gray as old paper, and half-burned and black, and all of you is as sunken as the lost continent. You are weeping blood from your one good eye. You are always weeping blood.

"I do love you," she says. "And I don't love you."

"I know," you say. There is wind on your flesh for what feels like the first time. It feels so good you want to break apart. "Take care of Comet?"

She smiles, and nods. She has always been a mixture of false and real smiles, and your curse has made it all real for you. And you are not even angry. She is right. You are to blame.

"Do you know what I love most?" she asks.

Free of the helmet, you nod. It's hard to nod. Your body is becoming stiff. You are dying again.

"*Freedom*," you say. And you know she has confused freedom with strength, and dominance with right. Just as you once did. But it's all right. The firefly comets dance above her like an infinity of twisted halos, and she is already lifting the sword above her head, in the first step of the first form, and you wish you had more time to teach her. To show her that perfect strike.

But she will get there on her own. She will find her way. She is a better student than you ever were. It hurts a little, even now, to admit that. When you say the word "freedom," she smiles, and thanks you for everything. The arc of the sword catches light and shines a hard elder blue in the air, and it's not as good as yours, but it's very, very good, and it cuts even the light, and it makes you think something mad. For a moment, you think that a brand new comet has been born. And that you are its only witness.

DON'T PRESS CHARGES AND I WON'T SUE

CHARLIE JANE ANDERS

The intake process begins with dismantling her personal space, one mantle at a time. Her shoes, left by the side of the road where the Go Team plucked her out of them. Her purse and satchel, her computer containing all of her artwork and her manifestos, thrown into a metal garbage can at a rest area on the highway, miles away. That purse, which she swung to and fro on the sidewalks to clear a path, like a southern grandma, now has food waste piled on it, and eventually will be chewed to shreds by raccoons. At some point the intake personnel fold her, like a folding chair that turns into an almost two-dimensional object, and they stuff her into a kennel, in spite of all her attempts to resist. Later she receives her first injection and loses any power to struggle, and some time after, control over her excretory functions. By the time they cut her clothes off, a layer of muck coats the backs of her thighs. They clean her and dress her in something that is not clothing, and they shave part of her head. At some point, Rachel glimpses a power drill, like a handyman's, but she's anesthetized and does not feel where it goes.

Rachel has a whole library of ways to get through this, none of which works at all. She spent a couple years meditating, did a whole course on trauma and self-preservation, and had an elaborate theory about how to carve out a space in your mind that *they* cannot touch, whatever *they* are doing to you. She remembers the things she used to tell everyone else in the support group, in the Safe Space, about not being alone even when you have become isolated by outside circumstances. But in the end, Rachel's only coping mechanism is dissociation, which arises from total animal panic. She's not even Rachel anymore, she's just a screaming blubbering mess, with a tiny kernel of her mind left, trapped a few feet above her body, in a process that is not at all like yogic flying.

Eventually, though, the intake is concluded, and Rachel is left staring up at a Styrofoam ceiling with a pattern of cracks that looks like a giant spider or an angry demon face descending toward her. She's aware of being numb from extreme cold in addition to the other ways in which she is numb, and the air conditioner keeps blurting into life with an aggravated whine. A stereo system plays a CD by that white rock-rap artist who turned out to be an especially stupid racist. The staff keep walking past her and talking about her in the third person, while misrepresenting basic facts about her, such as her name and her personal pronoun. Occasionally they adjust something about her position or drug regimen without speaking to her or looking at her face. She does not quite have enough motor control to scream or make any sound other than a kind of low ululation. She realizes at some point that someone has made a tiny hole in the base of her skull, where she now feels a mild ache.

Before you feel too sorry for Rachel, however, you should be aware that she's a person who holds a great many controversial views. For example, she once claimed to disapprove of hot chocolate, because she believes that chocolate is better at room temperature, or better yet as a component of ice cream or some other frozen dessert. In addition, Rachel considers ZZ Top an underappreciated music group, supports karaoke only in an alcohol-free environment, dislikes puppies, enjoys Brussels sprouts, and rides a bicycle with no helmet. She claims to prefer the *Star Wars* prequels to the Disney *Star Wars* films. Is Rachel a contrarian, a freethinker, or just kind of an asshole? If you could ask her, she would reply that opinions are a utility in and of themselves. That is, the holding of opinions is a worthwhile exercise per se, and the greater diversity of opinions in the world, the more robust our collective ability to argue.

Also! Rachel once got a gas station attendant nearly fired for behavior that, a year or two later, she finally conceded might have been an honest misunderstanding. She's the kind of person who sends food back for not being quite what she ordered—and on at least two occasions, she did this and then returned to that same restaurant a week or two later, as if she had been happy after all. Rachel is the kind of person who calls herself an artist, despite never having received a grant from a granting institution, or any kind of formal gallery show, and many people wouldn't even consider her collages and relief maps of imaginary places to be proper art. You would probably call Rachel a Goth.

Besides dissociation—which is wearing off as the panic subsides—the one defense mechanism that remains for Rachel is carrying on an imaginary conversation with Dev, the person with whom she spoke every day for so long, and to whom she always imagined speaking, whenever they were apart. Dev's voice in Rachel's head would have been a refuge not long ago, but now all Rachel can imagine Dev saying is, *Why did you leave me? Why, when I needed you most?* Rachel does not have a good answer to that question, which is why she never tried to answer it when she had the chance.

Thinking about Dev, about lost chances, is too much. And at that moment, Rachel realizes she has enough muscle control to lift her head and look directly in front of her. There, standing at an observation window, she sees her childhood best friend, Jeffrey.

Ask Jeffrey why he's been working at Love and Dignity for Everyone for the past few years and he'll say, first and foremost, student loans. Plus, in recent years, child support, and his mother's ever-increasing medical bills. Life is crammed full of things that you have to pay for after the fact, and the word "plan" in "payment plan" is a cruel mockery because nobody ever really sets out to plunge into chronic debt. But also Jeffrey wants to believe in the mission of Love and Dignity for Everyone: to repair the world's most broken people. Jeffrey often re-reads the mission statement on the wall of the employee lounge as he sips his morning Keurig so he can carry Mr. Randall's words with him for the rest of the day. Society depends on mutual respect, Mr. Randall says. You respect yourself and therefore I respect you, and vice versa. When people won't respect themselves, we have no choice but to intervene, or society unravels. Role-rejecting and aberrant behavior, ipso facto, is a sign of a lack of self-respect. Indeed, a cry for help. The logic always snaps back into airtight shape inside Jeffrey's mind.

Of course Jeffrey recognizes Rachel the moment he sees her wheeled into the treatment room, even after all this time and so many changes, because he's been Facebook-stalking her for years (usually after a couple of whiskey sours). He saw when she changed her name and her gender marker, and noticed when her hairstyle changed and when her face suddenly had a more feminine shape. There was the kitten she adopted that later ran away, and the thorny tattoo that says STAY ALIVE. Jeffrey read all her oversharing status updates about the pain of hair removal and the side effects of various pills. And then, of course, the crowning surgery. Jeffrey lived through this process vicariously, in real time, and saw no resemblance to a butterfly in a cocoon, or any other cute metaphor. The gender change looked more like landscaping: building embankments out of raw dirt, heaving big rocks to change the course of rivers, and uprooting plants stem by stem. Dirty bruising work. Why a person would feel the need to do this to themself, Jeffrey could never know.

At first, Jeffrey pretends not to know the latest subject, or to have any feelings one way or the other, as the Accu-Probe goes into the back of her head. This is not the right moment to have a sudden conflict. Due to some recent personnel issues, Jeffrey is stuck wearing a project manager hat along with his engineer hat—which, sadly, is not a cool pinstriped train-engineer hat of the sort that he and Rachel used to fantasize about wearing for work when they were kids. As a project manager, he has to worry endlessly about weird details such as getting enough coolant into the cadaver storage area and making sure that Jamil has the green shakes that he says activate his brain. As a government–industry joint venture under Section 1774(b)(8) of the Mental Health Restoration Act (relating to the care and normalization of at-risk individuals), Love and Dignity for Everyone has to meet certain benchmarks of effectiveness, and must involve the community in a meaningful role. Jeffrey is trying to keep twenty fresh cadavers in transplant-ready condition, and clearing the decks for more live subjects, who are coming down the pike at an ever-snowballing rate. The situation resembles one of those poultry processing plants where they keep speeding up the conveyer belt until the person grappling with each chicken ends up losing a few fingers.

Jeffrey runs from the cadaver freezer to the observation room to the main conference room for another community engagement session, around and around, until his Fitbit applauds. Five different Slack channels flare at once with people wanting to ask Jeffrey process questions, and he's lost count of all his unanswered DMs. Everyone agrees on the goal—returning healthy, well-adjusted individuals to society without any trace of dysphoria, dysmorphia, dystonia, or any other dys- words—but nobody can agree on the fine details, or how exactly to measure ideal outcomes beyond those statutory benchmarks. Who even is the person who comes out the other end of the Love and Dignity for Everyone process? What does it mean to be a unique individual, in an age when your fingerprints and retina scans have long since been stolen by Ecuadorian hackers? It's all too easy to get sucked into metaphysical flusterclucks about identity and the soul and what makes you you.

Jeffrey's near-daily migraine is already in full flower by the time he sees Rachel wheeled in and he can't bring himself to look. She's looking at him. She's looking right at him. Even with all the other changes, her eyes are the same, and he can't just stand here. She's putting him in an impossible position, at the worst moment.

Someone has programmed Slack so that when anyone types "alrighty then," a borderline-obscene GIF of two girls wearing clown makeup appears. Jeffrey is the only person who ever types "alrighty then," and he can't train himself to stop doing it. And, of course, he hasn't been able to figure out who programmed the GIF to appear.

Self-respect is the key to mutual respect. Jeffrey avoids making eye contact with that window or anyone beyond it. His head still feels too heavy with pain for a normal body to support, but also he's increasingly aware of a core-deep anxiety shading into nausea.

• • •

Jeffrey and Rachel had a group, from the tail end of elementary school through to the first year of high school, called the Sock Society. They all lived in the same cul-de-sac, bounded by a canola field on one side and the big interstate on the other. The origins of the Sock Society's name are lost to history, but may arise from the fact that Jeffrey's mom never liked kids to wear shoes inside the house and Jeffrey's house had the best game consoles and a 4K TV with surround sound. These kids wore out countless pairs of tires on their dirt bikes, conquered the extra DLC levels in Halls of Valor, and built snow forts that gleamed. They stayed up all night at sleepovers watching forbidden horror movies on an old laptop under a blanket while guzzling off-brand soda. They whispered, late at night, of their fantasies and barely-hinted-at anxieties, although there were some things Rachel would not share because she was not ready to speak of them and Jeffrey would not have been able to hear if she had. They repeated jokes they didn't 100 percent understand, and kind of enjoyed the queasy awareness of being out of their depth. Later, the members of the Sock Society (which changed its ranks over time with the exception of the core members, Rachel and Jeffrey) became adept at stuffing gym socks with blasting caps and small incendiaries and fashioning the socks themselves into rudimentary fuses before placing them in lawn ornaments, small receptacles for gardening tools, and—in one incident that nobody discussed afterward—Mrs. Hooper's scooter.

When Jeffrey's mother was drunk, which was often, she would say she wished Rachel was her son, because Rachel was such a smart boy—quick on the uptake, so charming with the rapid-fire puns, handsome and respectful. Like Young Elvis. Instead of Jeffrey, who was honestly a little shit.

Jeffrey couldn't wait to get over the wall of adolescence, into the garden of manhood. Every dusting of fuzz on his chin, every pungent whiff from his armpits seemed to him the starting gun. He became obsessed with finding porn via that old laptop, and he was an artist at coming up with fresh new search terms every time he and Rachel hung out. Rachel got used to innocent terms such as "cream pie" turning out to mean something gross and animalistic, in much the same way that a horror movie turned human bodies into slippery meat.

Then one time Jeffrey pulled up some transsexual porn, because what the hell. Rachel found herself watching a slender Latina with a shy smile slowly peel out of a silk robe to step into a scene with a muscular bald man. The girl was wearing nothing but bright silver shoes and her body was all smooth angles and tapering limbs, and the one piece of evidence of her transgender status looked tiny, both inconsequential and of a piece with the rest of her femininity. She tiptoed across the frame like a ballerina. Like a cartoon deer.

Watching this, Rachel quivered, until Jeffrey thought she must be grossed out, but deep down Rachel was having a feeling of recognition. Like: that's me. Like: I am possible.

Years later, in her twenties, Rachel had a group of girlfriends (some trans, some cis) and she started calling this feminist gang the Sock Society, because they made a big thing of wearing colorful socks with weird and sometimes profane patterns. Rachel mostly didn't think about the fact that she had repurposed the Sock Society sobriquet for another group, except to tell herself that she was reclaiming an ugly part of her past. Rachel is someone who obsesses about random issues, but also claims to avoid introspection at all costs—in fact, she once proposed an art show called *The Unexamined Life Is the Only Way to Have Fun*.

Rachel has soiled herself again. A woman in avocado-colored scrubs snaps on blue gloves with theatrical weariness before sponging Rachel's still-unfeeling body. The things I have to deal with, says the red-faced woman, whose name is Lucy. People like you always make people like me clean up after you, because you never think the rules apply to you, the same as literally everyone else. And then look where we end up, and I'm here cleaning your mess.

Rachel tries to protest that none of this is her doing, but her tongue is a slug that's been bathed in salt.

There's always some excuse, Lucy says as she scrubs. Life is not complicated, it's actually very simple. Men are men, and women are women, and everyone has a role to play. It's selfish to think that you can just force everyone else in the world to start carving out exceptions, just so you can play at being something you're not. You will never understand what it really means to be female, the joy and the endless discomfort, because you were not born into it.

Rachel feels frozen solid. Ice crystals permeate her body, the way they would frozen dirt. This woman is touching between her legs, without looking her in the face. She cannot bear to breathe. She keeps trying to get Jeffrey's attention, but he always looks away. As if he'd rather not witness what's going to happen to her.

Lucy and a man in scrubs wheel in something gauzy and white, like a cloud on a gurney. They bustle around, unwrapping and cleaning and prepping, and they mutter numbers and codes to each other, like E-drop 2347, as if there are a lot of parameters to keep straight here. The sound of all that quiet professionalism soothes Rachel in spite of herself, like she's at the dentist.

At some point they step away from the thing they've unwrapped and prepped, and Rachel turns her head just enough to see a dead man on a metal shelf.

Her first thought is that he's weirdly good looking, despite his slight decomposition. He has a snub nose and thin lips, a clipped jaw, good muscle definition, a cyanotic penis that flops against one thigh, and sandy pubic hair. Whatever (whoever) killed this man left his body in good condition, and he was roughly Rachel's age. This man could have been a model or maybe a pro wrestler, and Rachel feels sad that he somehow died so early, with his best years ahead.

Rachel tries to scream. She feels Lucy and the other one connecting her to the dead man's body and hears a rattling garbage-disposal sound. The dead man twitches, and meanwhile Rachel can't struggle or make a sound. She feels weaker than before, and some part of her insists this must be because she lost an argument at some point. Back in the Safe Space, they had talked about all the friends of friends who had gone to ground, and the Internet rumors. How would you know if you were in danger? Rachel had said that was a dumb question because danger never left.

The dead man smiles: not a large rictus, like in a horror movie, but a tiny shift in his features, like a contented sleeper. His eyes haven't moved or appeared to look at anything. Lucy clucks and adjusts a thing, and the kitchen-garbage noise grinds louder for a moment.

We're going to get you sorted out, Lucy says to the dead man. You are going to be so happy. She turns and leans over Rachel to check something, and her breath smells like sour corn chips.

You are violating my civil rights by keeping me here, Rachel says. A sudden victory, except that then she hears herself and it's wrong. Her voice comes out of the wrong mouth, is not even her own voice. The dead man has spoken, not her, and he didn't say that thing about civil rights. Instead he said, Hey, excuse me, how long am I going to be kept here? As if this were a mild inconvenience keeping him from his business. The voice sounded rough, flinty, like a bad sore throat, but also commanding. The voice of a surgeon, or an airline pilot. You would stop whatever you were doing and listen, if you heard that voice.

Rachel lets out an involuntary cry of panic, which comes out of the dead man's mouth as a low groan. She tries again to say, This is not medicine. This is a human rights violation. And it comes out of the dead man's mouth as, I don't mean to be a jerk. I just have things to do, you know. Sorry if I'm causing any trouble.

That's quite all right, Mr. Billings, Lucy says. You're making tremendous progress, and we're so pleased. You'll be released into the community soon, and the community will be so happy to see you.

The thought of ever trying to speak again fills Rachel with a whole ocean voyage's worth of nausea, but she can't even make herself retch.

Jeffrey has wondered for years, what if he could talk to his oldest friend, man to man, about the things that had happened when they were on the cusp of adolescence—not just the girl, but the whole deal. Mrs. Hooper's scooter, even. And maybe, at last, he will. A lot depends on how well the process goes. Sometimes the cadaver gets almost all of the subject's memories and personality, just with a better outlook on his or her proper gender. There is, however, a huge variability in bandwidth because we're dealing with human beings and especially with weird neurological stuff that we barely understand. We're trying to thread wet spaghetti through a grease trap, a dozen pieces at a time. Even with the proprietary cocktail, it's hardly an exact science.

The engineer part of Jeffrey just wants to keep the machines from making whatever noise that was earlier, the awful grinding sound. But the project manager part of Jeffrey is obsessing about all of the extraneous factors outside his control. What if they get a surprise inspection from the Secretary, or even worse that Deputy Assistant Secretary, with the eye? Jeffrey is not supposed to be a front-facing part of this operation, but Mr. Randall says we all do things that are outside our comfort zones, and really, that's the only way your comfort zone can ever expand. In addition, Jeffrey is late for another stakeholder meeting, with the woman from Mothers Raising Well-Adjusted Children and the three bald men from Grassroots Rising, who will tear Jeffrey a new orifice. There are still too many maladjusted individuals out there, in the world, trying to use public bathrooms and putting our children at risk. Some children, too, keep insisting that they aren't boys or girls because they saw some ex-athlete prancing on television. Twenty cadavers in the freezer might as well be nothing in the face of all this. The three bald men will take turns spit-shouting, using words such as psychosexual, and Jeffrey has fantasized about sneaking bourbon into his coffee so he can drink whenever that word comes up. He's pretty sure they don't know what psychosexual even means, except that it's psycho and it's sexual. After a stakeholder meeting, Jeffrey always retreats to the single-stall men's room to shout at his own schmutzy reflection. Fuck you, you fucking fuck fucker. Don't tell me I'm not doing my job.

Self-respect is the key to mutual respect.

Rachel keeps looking straight at Jeffrey through the observation window, and she's somehow kept control over her vision long after her speech centers went over. He keeps waiting for her to lose the eyes. Her gaze goes right into him, and his stomach gets the feeling that usually comes after two or three whiskey sours and no dinner.

More than ever, Jeffrey wishes the observation room had a one-way mirror instead of regular glass. Why would they skimp on that? What's the point of having an observation room where you are also being observed at the same time? It defeats the entire purpose.

Jeffrey gets tired of hiding from his own window and skips out the side door. He climbs two stories of cement stairs to emerge in the executive wing, near the conference suite where he's supposed to be meeting with the stakeholders right now. He finds an oaken door with that quote from Albert Einstein about imagination that everybody always has and knocks on it. After a few breaths, a deep voice tells Jeffrey to come in, and then he's sitting opposite an older man with square shoulders and a perfect old-fashioned newscaster head.

Mr. Randall, Jeffrey says, I'm afraid I have a conflict with regards to the latest subject and I must ask to be recused.

Is that a fact? Mr. Randall furrows his entire face for a moment, then magically all the wrinkles disappear again. He smiles and shakes his head. I feel you, Jeffrey, I really do. That blows chunks. Unfortunately, as you know, we are short-staffed right now, and our work is of a nature that only a few people have the skills and moral virtue to complete it.

But, Jeffrey says. The new subject, he's someone I grew up with, and there are certain . . . I mean, I made promises when we were little, and it feels in some ways like I'm breaking those promises, even as I try my best to help him. I actually feel physically ill, like drunk in my stomach but sober in my brain, when I look at him.

Jeffrey, Mr. Randall says, Jeffrey, JEFFREY. Listen to me. Sit still and listen. Pull yourself together. We are the watchers on the battlements, at the edge of social collapse, like in that show with the ice zombies, where winter is always tomorrow. You know that show? They had an important message, that sometimes we have to put our own personal feelings aside for the greater good. Remember the fat kid? He had to learn to be a team player. I loved that show. So here we are, standing against the darkness that threatens to consume everything we admire. No time for divided hearts.

I know that we're doing something important here, and that he'll thank me later, Jeffrey says. It's just hard right now.

If it were easy to do the right thing, Randall says, then everyone would do it.

Sherri was a transfer student in tenth grade who came right in and joined the Computer Club but also tried out for the volleyball team and the a cappella chorus. She had dark hair in tight braids and a wiry body that flexed in the moment before she leapt to spike the ball, making Rachel's heart rise with her. Rachel sat courtside and watched Sherri practice while she was supposed to be doing sudden death sprints.

Jeffrey stared at Sherri, too: listened to her sing Janelle Monáe in a light contralto when she waited for the bus, and gazed at her across the room during Computer Club. He imagined going up to her and just introducing himself, but his heart was too weak. He could more easily imagine saying the dumbest thing, or actually fainting, than carrying on a smooth conversation with

Sherri. He obsessed for ages, until he finally confessed to his friends (Rachel was long since out of the picture by this time), and they started goading him, actually physically shoving him, to speak to Sherri.

Jeffrey slid up to her and said his name, and something inane about music, and then Sherri just stared at him for a long time before saying, I gotta get the bus. Jeffrey watched her walk away, then turned to his watching friends and mimed a finger gun blowing his brains out.

A few days later, Sherri was playing hooky at that one bakery cafe in town that everyone said was run by lesbians or drug addicts or maybe just old hippies, nursing a chai latte, and she found herself sitting with Rachel, who was also ditching some activity. Neither of them wanted to talk to anyone, they'd come here to be alone. But Rachel felt hope rise up inside her at the proximity of her wildfire crush, and she finally hoisted her bag as if she might just leave the cafe. Mind if I sit with you a minute, she asked, and Sherri shrugged yes. So Rachel perched on the embroidered tasseled pillow on the bench next to Sherri and stared at her Algebra II book.

They saw each other at that cafe every few days, or sometimes just once a week, and they just started sitting together on purpose, without talking to each other much. After a couple months of this, Sherri looked at the time on her phone and said, My mom's out of town. I'll buy you dinner. Rachel kept her shriek of joy on the inside and just nodded.

At dinner—a family pasta place nearby—Sherri looked down at her colorful paper napkin and whispered: I think I don't like boys. I mean, to date, or whatever. I don't hate boys or anything, just not interested that way. You understand.

Rachel stared at Sherri, even after she looked up, so they were making eye contact. In just as low a whisper, Rachel replied: I'm pretty sure I'm not a boy.

This was the first time Rachel ever said the name Rachel aloud, at least with regard to herself.

Sherri didn't laugh or get up or run away. She just stared back, then nodded. She reached onto the red checkerboard vinyl tablecloth with an open palm, for Rachel to insert her palm into if she so chose.

The first time Jeffrey saw Rachel and Sherri holding hands, he looked at them like his soul had come out in bruises.

We won't keep you here too long, Mr. Billings, the male attendant says, glancing at Rachel but mostly looking at the mouth that had spoken. You're doing very well. Really, you're an exemplary subject. You should be so proud.

There are so many things that Rachel wants to say. Like: Please just let me go, I have a life. I have an art show coming up in a coffee shop, I can't miss it. You don't have the right. I deserve to live my own life. I have people who used to love me. I'll give you everything I own. I won't press charges if you don't sue. This is no kind of therapy. On and on. But she can't trust that corpse voice. She hyperventilates and gags on her own spit. So sore she's hamstrung.

Every time her eyes get washed out, she's terrified this is it, her last sight. She knows from what Lucy and the other one have said that if her vision switches over to the dead man's, that's the final stage and she's gone.

The man is still talking. We have a form signed by your primary care physician, Dr. Wallace, stating that this treatment is both urgent and medically indicated, as well as an assessment by our in-house psychologist, Dr. Yukizawa. He holds up two pieces of paper, with the looping scrawls of two different doctors that she's never even heard of. She's been seeing Dr. Cummings for years, since before her transition. She makes a huge effort to shake her head, and is shocked by how weak she feels.

You are so fortunate to be one of the first to receive this treatment, the man says. Early indications are that subjects experience a profound improvement across seven different measures of quality of life and social integration. Their OGATH scores are generally high, especially in the red levels. Rejection is basically unheard of. You won't believe how good you'll feel once you're over the adjustment period, he says. If the research goes well, the potential benefits to society are limited only by the cadaver pipeline.

Rachel's upcoming art show, in a tiny coffee shop, is called *Against Curation*. There's a lengthy manifesto, which Rachel planned to print out and mount onto foam or cardboard, claiming that the act of curating is inimical to art or artistry. The only person who can create a proper context for a given piece of art is the artist herself, and arranging someone else's art is an act of violence. Bear in mind that the history of museums is intrinsically tied up with imperialism and colonialism, and the curatorial gaze is historically white and male. But even the most enlightened postcolonial curator is a pirate. Anthologies, mix tapes, it's all the same. Rachel had a long response prepared, in case anybody accused her of just being annoyed that no real gallery would display her work.

Rachel can't help noting the irony of writing a tirade about the curator's bloody scalpel, only to end up with a hole in her literal head.

When the man has left her alone, Rachel begins screaming Jeffrey's name in the dead man's voice. Just the name, nothing that the corpse could twist. She still can't bear to hear that deep timbre, the sick damaged throat, speaking for her. But she can feel her life essence slipping away. Every time she looks over at the dead man, he has more color in his skin and his arms and legs are moving, like a restless sleeper. His face even looks, in some hard-to-define way, more like Rachel's.

Jeffrey! The words come out in a hoarse growl. Jeffrey! Come here!

Rachel wants to believe she's already defeated this trap, because she has lived her life without a single codicil, and whatever they do, they can't retroactively change the person she has been for her entire adulthood. But that doesn't feel like enough. She wants the kind of victory where she gets to actually walk out of here.

Jeffrey feels a horrible twist in his neck. This is all unfair, because he already informed Mr. Randall of his conflict and yet he's still here, having to behave professionally while the subject is putting him in the dead center of attention.

Seriously, the subject will not stop bellowing his name, even with a throat that's basically raw membrane at this point. You're not supposed to initiate communication with the subject without submitting an Interlocution Permission form through the proper channels. But the subject is putting him into an impossible position.

Jeffrey, she keeps shouting. And then: Jeffrey, talk to me!

People are lobbing questions in Slack, and of course Jeffrey types the wrong thing and the softcore clown porn comes up. Ha ha, I fell for it again, he types. There's a problem with one of the latest cadavers, a cause-of-death question, and Mr. Randall says the Deputy Assistant Secretary might be in town later.

Jeffrey's mother was a Nobel Prize winner for her work with people who had lost the ability to distinguish between weapons and musical instruments, a condition that frequently leads to maiming or worse. Jeffrey's earliest memories involve his mother flying off to serve as an expert witness in the trials of murderers who claimed they had thought their assault rifles were banjos, or mandolins. Many of these people were faking it, but Jeffrey's mom was usually hired by the defense, not the prosecution. Every time she returned from one of these trips, she would fling her Nobel medal out her bathroom window, and then stay up half the night searching the bushes for it, becoming increasingly drunk. One morning, Jeffrey found her passed out below her bedroom window and believed for a moment that she had fallen two stories to her death. This was, she explained to him later, a different sort of misunderstanding than mistaking a gun for a guitar: a reverse-Oedipal misapprehension. These days Jeffrey's mom requires assistance to dress, to shower, and to transit from her bed to a chair and back, and nobody can get Medicare, Medicaid, or any secondary insurance to pay for this. To save money, Jeffrey has moved back in with his mother, which means he gets to hear her ask at least once a week what happened to Rachel, who was such a nice boy.

Jeffrey can't find his headphones to drown out his name, which the cadaver is shouting so loud that foam comes out of one corner of his mouth. Frances and another engineer both complain on Slack about the noise, which they can hear from down the hall. OMG creepy, Frances types. Make it stop make it stop

I can't, Jeffrey types back. I can't ok. I don't have the right paperwork.

Maybe tomorrow, Rachel will wake up fully inhabiting her male body. She'll look down at her strong forearms, threaded with veins, and she'll smile and thank Jeffrey. Maybe she'll nod at him, by way of a tiny salute, and say, You did it, buddy. You brought me back.

But right now, the cadaver keeps shouting, and Jeffrey realizes he's covering his ears with his fists and is doubled over.

Rachel apparently decides that Jeffrey's name alone isn't working. The cadaver pauses and then blurts, I would really love to hang with you. Hey! I appreciate everything you've done to set things right. JEFFREY! You really shouldn't have gone to so much trouble for me.

Somehow, these statements have an edge, like Jeffrey can easily hear the intended meaning. He looks up and sees Rachel's eyes, spraying tears like a damn lawn sprinkler.

Jeffrey, the corpse says, I saw Sherri. She told me the truth about you.

She's probably just making things up. Sherri never knew anything for sure, or at least couldn't prove anything. And yet, just the mention of her name is enough to make Jeffrey straighten up and walk to the door of the observation room, even with no signed Interlocution Permission form. Jeffrey makes himself stride up to the two nearly naked bodies and stop at the one on the left, the one with the ugly tattoo and the drooling silent mouth.

I don't want to hurt you, Jeffrey says. I never wanted to hurt you, even when we were kids and you got weird on me. My mom still asks about you.

Hey pal, you've never been a better friend to me than you are right now, the cadaver says. But on the left, the eyes are red and wet and full of violence.

What did Sherri say? Stop playing games and tell me, Jeffrey says. When did you see her? What did she say?

But Rachel has stopped trying to make the other body talk and is just staring up, letting her eyes speak for her.

Listen, Jeffrey says to the tattooed body. This is already over, the process is too advanced. I could disconnect all of the machines, unplug the tap from your occipital lobe and everything, and the cadaver would continue drawing your remaining life energy. The link between you is already stable. This project, it's a government–industry collaboration, we call it Love and Dignity for Everyone. You have no idea. But you, you're going to be so handsome. You always used to wish you could look like this guy, remember? I'm actually kind of jealous of you.

Rachel just thrashes against her restraints harder than ever.

Here, I'll show you, Jeffrey says at last. He reaches behind Rachel's obsolete head and unplugs the tap, along with the other wires. See? he says. No difference. That body is already more you than you. It's already done.

That's when Rachel leans forward, in her old body, and head-butts Jeffrey, before grabbing for his key ring with the utility knife on it. She somehow gets the knife open with one hand while he's clutching his nose, and slashes a bloody canyon across Jeffrey's stomach. He falls, clutching at his own slippery flesh, and watches her saw through her straps and land on unsteady feet. She lifts Jeffrey's lanyard, smearing blood on his shirt as it goes.

When Rachel was in college, she heard a story about a business professor named Lou, who dated two different women and strung them both along. Laurie was a lecturer in women's studies, while Susie worked in the bookstore co-op despite having a PhD in comp lit. After the women found out Lou was dating both of them, things got ugly. Laurie stole Susie's identity, signing her up for a stack of international phone cards and a subscription to the Dirndl of the Month Club, while Susie tried to crash Laurie's truck and cold-cocked Laurie as she walked out of a seminar on intersectional feminism. In the end, the two women looked at each other, over the slightly dented truck and Laurie's bloody lip and Susie's stack of junk mail. Laurie just spat blood and said, Listen. I won't press charges, if you don't sue. Susie thought for a moment, then stuck out her hand and said, Deal. The two women never spoke to each other, or Lou, ever again.

Rachel has always thought this incident exposed the roots of the social contract: most of our relationships are upheld not by love, or obligation, or gratitude, but by mutually assured destruction. Most of the people in Rachel's life who could have given her shit for being transgender were differently bodied, non-neurotypical, or some other thing that also required some acceptance from her. Mote, beam, and so on.

For some reason, Rachel can't stop thinking about the social contract and mutually assured destruction as she hobbles down the hallway of Love and Dignity for Everyone with a corpse following close behind. Every time she pauses to turn around and see if the dead man is catching up, he gains a little ground. So she forces herself to keep running with weak legs, even as she keeps hearing his hoarse breath right behind her. True power, Rachel thinks, is being able to destroy others with no consequences to yourself.

She's reached the end of a corridor, and she's trying not to think about Jeffrey's blood on the knife in her hand. He'll be fine, he's in a facility. She remembers Sherri in the computer lab, staring at the pictures on the Internet: her hair wet from the shower, one hand reaching for a towel. Sherri sobbing but then tamping it down as she looked at the screen. Sherri telling Rachel at lunch, I'm leaving this school. I can't stay. There's a heavy door with an

RFID reader, and Jeffrey's card causes it to click twice before finally bleeping. Rachel's legs wobble and spasm, and the breath of the dead man behind her grows louder. Then she pushes through the door and runs up the square roundabout of stairs. Behind her, she hears Lucy the nurse shout at her to come back, because she's still convalescing, this is a delicate time.

Rachel feels a little more of her strength fade every time the dead man's hand lurches forward. Something irreplaceable leaves her. She pushes open the dense metal door marked EXIT and nearly faints with sudden day-blindness.

The woods around Love and Dignity for Everyone are dense with moss and underbrush, and Rachel's bare feet keep sliding off tree roots. I can't stop, Rachel pleads with herself, I can't stop or my whole life was for nothing. Who even was I, if I let this happen to me. The nearly naked dead man crashes through branches that Rachel has ducked under. She throws the knife and hears a satisfying grunt, but he doesn't even pause. Rachel knows that anybody who sees both her and the cadaver will choose to help the cadaver. There's no way to explain her situation in the dead man's voice. She vows to stay off roads and avoid talking to people. This is her life now.

Up ahead, she sees a fast-running stream, and she wonders how the corpse will take to water. The stream looks like the one she and Jeffrey used to play in, when they would catch crayfish hiding under rocks. The crayfish looked just like tiny lobsters, and they would twist around trying to pinch you as you gripped their midsections. Rachel sloshes in the water and doesn't hear the man's breath in her ear for a moment. Up ahead, the current leads to a steep waterfall that's so white in the noon sunlight, it appears to stand still. She remembers staring into a bucket full of crayfish, debating whether to boil them alive or let them all go. And all at once, she has a vivid memory of herself and Jeffrey both holding the full bucket and turning it sideways, until all the crayfish sloshed back into the river. The crayfish fled for their lives, their eyes seeming to protrude with alarm, and Rachel held onto an empty bucket with Jeffrey, feeling an inexplicable sense of relief. We are such wusses, Jeffrey said, and they both laughed. She remembers the sight of the last crayfish rushing out of view—as if this time, maybe the trick would work, and nobody would think to look under this particular rock. She reaches the waterfall, seizes a breath, and jumps with both feet at once.

STARLIGHT EXPRESS

MICHAEL SWANWICK

Flaminio the water carrier lived in the oldest part of the ancient city of Roma among the *popolo minuto*, the clerks and artisans and laborers and such who could afford no better. His apartment overlooked the piazza dell'Astrovia, which daytimes was choked with tourists from four planets who came to admire the ruins and revenants of empire. They coursed through the ancient transmission station, its stone floor thrumming gently underfoot, the magma tap still powering the energy road, even though the stars had shifted in their positions centuries ago and anyone stepping into the projector would be translated into a complex wave front of neutrinos and shot away from the Earth to fall between the stars forever.

Human beings had built such things once. Now they didn't even know how to turn it off.

On hot nights, Flaminio slept on a pallet on the roof. Sometimes, staring up at the sparkling line of ionization that the energy road sketched through the atmosphere, he followed it in his imagination past Earth's three moons and out to the stars. He could feel its pull at such times, the sweet yearning tug that led suicides to converge upon it in darkness, furtive shadows slipping silently up the faintly glowing steps like lovers to a tryst.

Flaminio wished then that he had been born long ago when it was possible to ride the starlight express away from the weary old Republic to impossibly distant worlds nestled deep in the galaxy. But in the millennia since civilization had fallen, countless people had ridden the Astrovia off the planet, and not one had ever returned.

Except, maybe, the woman in white.

Flaminio was coming home from the baths when he saw her emerge from the Astrovia. It was election week and a ward heeler had treated him to a sauna and a blood scrub in exchange for his vote. When he stepped out into the night, every glint of light was bright and every surface slick and shiny, as if his flesh had been turned to glass and offered not the least resistance to the world's sensations. He felt genuinely happy.

Then there was a pause in the constant throb underfoot, as if the great heart of the world had skipped a beat. Something made Flaminio look up, and he thought he saw the woman step down from the constant light of the landing stage.

An instant only, and then he realized he had to be wrong.

The woman wore a white gown of a cloth unlike any Flaminio had ever seen before. It was luminously cool, and with every move she made it slid across her body with simple grace. Transfixed, he watched her step hesitantly out of the Astrovia and seize the railing with both hands.

She stared out across the plaza, looking confused and troubled, as if gazing into an unfamiliar new world.

Flaminio had seen that look before on the future suicides. They came to the Astrovia during the daylight first, accompanying tours that stopped only briefly on their way to the Colosseum and the Pantheon and the Altair Gate, but later returned alone and at night, like moths compulsively circling in on death and transformation, in smaller and more frenzied loops before finally cycling to a full stop at the foot of the Aldebaranian Steps, quivering and helpless as a wren in a cat's mouth.

That, Flaminio decided, was what must be happening here. The woman had gotten as far as the transmission beam, hesitated, and turned around. As he watched, she raised a hand to her mouth, the pale blue gems on her silver bracelet gleaming. She was very lovely, and he felt terribly sorry for her.

Impulsively, Flaminio took the woman's arm and said, "You're with me, babe."

She looked up at him, startled. Where Flaminio had the ruddy complexion and coarse face of one of Martian terraformer ancestry, the woman had aristocratic features, the brown eyes and high cheekbones and wide nose of antique African blood. He grinned at her as if he had all the carefree confidence in the world, thinking: Come on. You are too beautiful for death. Stay, and rediscover the joy in life.

For a breath as long as all existence, the woman did not react. Then she nodded and smiled.

He led her away.

Back at his room, Flaminio was at a loss as to what to do. He had never brought a woman home for anything other than romantic purposes and, further, to his astonishment, discovered he felt not the least desire to have sex with this one. So he gave her his narrow bed and a cup of herbal tea. He himself lay down on a folded blanket by the door, where she would have to step over him if she tried to return to the Astrovia. They both went to sleep.

In the morning he rose before dawn and made his rounds. Flaminio had a contract with a building seven stories high and though the denizens of the upper floors were poor as poor, everybody needed water. When he got home, he made his guest breakfast.

"*Stat grocera?*" she asked, holding up a sausage squash. Then, when Flaminio shook his head and spread his hands to indicate incomprehension, she took a little bite and spat it out in disgust. The bread she liked, however, and she made exclamations of surprise and pleasure over the oranges and pomegranolos. The espresso she drank as if it were exactly what she were used to.

Finally, because he could think of nothing else to do, he took her to see the Great Albino.

The Great Albino was being displayed in a cellar off of via Dolorosa. Once he had been able to draw crowds large enough that he was displayed in domes and other spaces where he could stand and stretch out his limbs to their fullest. But that was long ago. Now he crouched on all fours in a room that was barely large enough to accommodate him. There were three rows of wooden bleachers, not entirely filled, from which tourists asked questions, which he courteously answered.

Flaminio was able to visit the Great Albino as often as he liked, because when he was young he had discovered that Albino knew things that no one else did. Thirteen times in a single month he had managed to scrape together a penny so he could pepper the giant with questions. On the last visit, Albino had said, "Let that one in free from now on."

So of course, the first question the young Flaminio had asked on being let in was "Why?"

"Because you don't ask the same questions as everyone else," Albino had said. "You make me call up memories I thought I had forgotten."

Today, however, the tourists were asking all the same dreary questions as usual. "How old are you?" a woman asked.

"I am three thousand eight hundred forty seven years and almost eleven months old," Albino said gravely.

"No!" the tourist shrieked. "Really?"

"I was constructed so that I would never age, back when humanity had the power to do such things."

"My tutor-mentor says there are no immortals," a child said, frowning seriously.

"Like any man, I am prone to accident and misfortune so I am by no means immortal. But I do not age, nor am I susceptible to any known diseases."

"I hear that and I think you are the very luckiest man in the world," a man with a strong Russikan accent said. "But then I reflect that there are no women your size, and I think maybe not."

The audience laughed. Albino waited for the laughter to subside and with a gentle smile said, "Ah, but think how many fewer times I have to go to confession than you do."

They laughed again.

Flaminio stood, and the woman in white did likewise. "Have you brought your bride-to-be for me to meet, water carrier?" Albino asked. "If so, I am honored."

"No, I have rather brought you a great puzzle—a woman who speaks a language that I have never heard before, though all the peoples of the worlds course through Roma every day."

"Does she?" Albino's great head was by itself taller than the woman was. He slowly lowered it, touching his tremendous brow to the floor before her. "Madam."

The woman looked amused. "*Vuzet gentdom.*"

"*Graz mairsy, dama.*"

Hearing her own language spoken, the woman gasped. Then she began talking, endlessly it seemed to Flaminio, gesturing as she did so: at Flaminio, in the direction of the Astrovia, up at the sky. Until finally Albino held up a finger for silence. "Almost, I think she must be mad," he said. "But then . . . she speaks a language that before this hour I believed to be dead. So who is to say? Whatever the truth may be, it is not something I believed possible a day ago."

"What does she say?" one of the audience members asked.

"She says she is not from this planet or any other within the Solar System. She says she comes from the stars."

"No one has come back from the stars for many centuries," the man scoffed.

"Yes. And yet here she is."

The woman's name was Szette, Albino said. She claimed to come from Opale, the largest of three habitable planets orbiting Achernar. When asked whether she had been contemplating suicide, Szette looked shocked and replied that suicide was a sin, for to kill oneself was to despair of God's mercy. Then she had asked what planet this was, and when Albino replied "Earth," adamantly shook her head.

Much later, in Flaminio's memory, the gist of the conversation, stripped of the torrents of foreign words and the hesitant translation, which was curtailed because the paying customers found it boring but continued at some length after the show was over, was as follows:

"That is not possible. It was Earth I meant to visit. So I studied it beforehand and it is not like this. It is all very different."

"Perhaps," Albino said, " you studied a different part of Earth. There is a great variety of circumstance in a planet."

"No. Earth is a rich world, one of the richest in the galaxy. This place is very poor. It must have been named after Earth so long ago that you have forgotten that the human race was not born here."

At last, gently, Albino said, "Perhaps. I think, however, that there is a simpler explanation."

"What explanation? Tell me!"

But Albino only shook his head, as ponderously and stubbornly as an elephant. "I do not wish to get involved in this puzzle. You may go now. However, leave me here with my small friend for a moment, if you would. I have something of a personal nature to say to him."

Then, when he and Flaminio were alone, Albino said, "Do not become emotionally involved with this Szette. There is no substance to her. She is only a traveler—wealthy, by your standards, but a butterfly who flits from star to star, without purpose or consequence. Do you honestly think that she is worthy of your admiration?"

"Yes!" The words were torn from the depths of Flaminio's soul. "Yes, I do!"

Albino had said that he did not wish to be involved. But apparently he cared enough to notify the *protettori*, for later that day they came to arrest Szette and take her to the city courts. There, she was duly charged, declared a pauper, issued a living allowance, and released on Flaminio's recognizance. During the weeks while her trial was pending, he taught her how to speak Roman. She rented a suite of rooms which Flaminio found luxurious, though she clearly did not, and moved them both into it. Daytimes, after work, he showed her all the sights.

At night, they slept apart.

This was a baffling experience for Flaminio, who had never shared quarters with a woman other than his mother on anything but intimate terms. He thought about her constantly when they were apart but in her physical presence, he found it impossible to consider her romantically.

Their conversations, however, were wonderful. Sitting at the kitchen table, Flaminio would ask Szette questions, while she practiced her new language by telling him about the many worlds she had seen.

Achernar, she said, spun so rapidly that it bulged out at the equator and looked like a great blue egg in the skies of Opale. Its companion was a yellow dwarf and when the planet and both stars were all in a line, a holiday was declared in which everyone dressed in green and drank green liqueurs and painted their doors and cities green and poured green dye in their rivers and canals. But such alignments were rare—she had seen only one in all her lifetime.

Snowfall was an ice world, in orbit around a tight cluster of three white dwarfs so dim they were all but indistinguishable from the other stars in a sky that was eternally black. Their mountains had been carved into delicate lacy fantasias, in which were tangled habitats where the air was kept so warm that their citizens wore jewelry and very little else.

The people of Typhonne, a water world whose surface was lashed by almost continuous storms, had so reshaped their bodies that they could no longer be considered human. They built undersea cities in the ocean shallows and when they felt the approach of death would swim into the cold, dark depths of the trenches, to be heard from no more. Their sun was a red dwarf, but not one in a hundred of them knew that fact.

On and on, into the night, Szette's words flew, like birds over the tiled roofs of the Eternal City. Listening, occasionally correcting her grammar or providing a word she did not know, Flaminio traveled in his imagination from star to star, from Algol to Mira to Zaniah.

The day of Szette's trial arrived at last. Because Albino was a necessary witness and the city courts could not hold his tremendous bulk, the judges came to him. The bleachers were dismantled to make room for their seven-chaired bench, from which they interviewed first Flaminio, then Albino, and then Szette. The final witness was an engineer-archivist from the Astrovia.

"This has happened before," the woman said. She was old, scholarly, stylishly dressed. "But not in our lifetimes. Well . . . in his of course." She nodded toward Albino and more than one judge smiled. "It is a very rare occurrence and for you to understand it, I must first explain some of the Astrovia's workings.

"It is an oversimplification to say that the body of a traveler is transformed from matter to energy. It is somewhat closer to the truth to say that the traveler's body is read, recorded, disassembled, and then transmitted as a signal upon a carrier beam. When the beam reaches—or, rather, reached—its destination, the signal is read, recorded, and then used to recreate the traveler. The recordings are retained against the possibility of an interrupted transmission. In which case, the traveler can simply be sent again. As a kind of insurance, you see."

The engineer-archivist paused for questions. There being none, she continued. "I have examined our records. Roughly two thousand years ago, a woman identical to the one you see before you came to Earth. She stayed for a year, and then she left. What she thought of our world we do not know. She is, no doubt, long dead. Recently, there was an earth tremor, too small to be noticed by human senses, which seems to have disrupted something in the workings of the Astrovia. It created a duplicate of that woman as she was when she first arrived in Roma and released her onto the streets. This duplicate is the woman whose fate you are now deciding."

One of the judges leaned forward. "You say this has happened before. How many times?"

"Three that we know of. It is of course possible there were more."

As the testimony went on, Szette had grown paler and paler. Now she clutched Flaminio's arm so tightly that he thought her nails would break.

The judges consulted in unhurried whispers. Finally, one said, "Will the woman calling herself Szette stand forth?"

She complied.

"We are agreed that, simply by being yourself—or, more precisely, a simulacrum of yourself—you know a great deal about an ancient era and the attitudes of its people that would be of interest to the historians at the *Figlia della Sapienze*. You will make yourself available to be interviewed there by credentialed scholars, three days a week. For this you will be paid adequately."

"Two days," snapped the lawyer that the Great Albino had hired for Szette. "More than adequately."

The judges consulted again. "Two," their spokeswoman conceded. "Adequately."

The lawyer smiled.

That night, Szette took off her bracelet, which Flaminio had never seen her without, opened her arms to him, and said, "Come."

He did.

The way that Szette clutched Flaminio as they made love, as if he were a log and she a sailor in danger of drowning, and the unsettling intensity with which she studied his face afterwards, her own expression as unreadable as a moon of ice, told Flaminio that something had changed within her, though he could not have said exactly what.

All that Flaminio knew of Szette was this: That she came from a world called Opale orbiting the stars Achernar A and B. That she loved the darkness of the night sky and the age of Roma's ruins. That she would not eat meat. That she was very fond of him, but nothing more.

This last hurt Flaminio greatly, for he was completely in love with her.

Flaminio was a light sleeper. In the middle of the night, he heard a noise—a footstep on the landing, perhaps, or a door closing—and his eyes flew open.

Szette was gone.

All the rooms of the apartment were empty and when Flaminio went to look for her on the balcony, she wasn't there either. He stared up at the battle-scarred moons and they looked down on him with contempt. Then all the sounds of the city at night drew away from him and in that bubble of silence a sizzle of terror ran up his spine. For he knew where Szette had gone.

It was not difficult to catch up with her. Szette did not hurry and Flaminio ran as hard as he could. But when he stood, panting, before her, she held up a hand in warning. The pale blue stones on her bracelet flashed bright.

He could not move.

He could not speak.

"You have been so very kind to me," Szette said. "I hope you will not hate me too much when you realize why."

She turned her back on him. With casual grace, she climbed the steps. Like many another before her, she hesitated. Then, with sudden resolution, Szette plunged into the beam.

There was nothing Flaminio could have done to stop her. But simultaneous with the dematerialization of Szette's body, he heard an extraordinary noise, a scream, issuing from his own mouth.

What Flaminio did next could not be called an impulsive act. He thought it through carefully, and though that took him only an instant, his resolve was firm. He ran up the steps toward the beam, determined to join Szette in her endless voyage to nowhere. He would offer his body to the universe and his soul to oblivion. He would not, he was certain, hesitate when he reached the beam.

A shoulder in his chest stopped him cold. A hand gripped his shoulder and another his elbow. Three *protettori* closed in upon him, scowling. "You must come with us, sir," said one, "to have this suicidal impulse removed."

"I'm a citizen! I know my rights! You can't stop me without a contract!"

"Sir, we have a contract."

They dragged him to a *cellular*. It closed about him and took him away.

When he was released from therapy, incapable then or ever after of ending his own life, Flaminio went to see the only individual in all the world who might have taken out a contract on him and asked, "Why wouldn't you let me die?"

"To me, your lives are as those of mayflies," the Great Albino said. "Enjoy what precious seconds remain."

"And the bracelet? Why didn't you tell me about Szette's bracelet?"

"Until that night, I had forgotten about them. Such things were commonly worn by travelers back when the world was rich. To protect themselves from molestation. To enlist aid when in need. But they were a small and unimportant detail in a complex and varied age."

Flaminio had only one more question to pose: "If I was only doing the bracelet's bidding, then why haven't these feelings gone away?"

Albino looked terribly sad. "Alas, my friend, it seems you really did fall in love with her."

That same day, Flaminio left Roma to become a wanderer. He never married, though he took many lovers, both paid and not. Nor did he ever settle down in one place for any length of time. In his old age he frequently claimed to have been around the world forty-eight times and to have seen everything there was to see on all four occupied planets of the Solar System, and much else as well. All of which was verifiably true, were one to search through the records for his whereabouts over the decades. But, in his cups, he would admit to having never gone anywhere or seen anything worth seeing at all.

MONTREAL, 2014

MADELINE RAY

—◆—

The Sphinx lives now in the city of Montreal. She came to the new world through Boston, which was full of history, but of a kind foreign to herself. She tried New York for a while, but she didn't fit on the sidewalks there, and it smelled. Besides, everything in New York *is* New York and takes on the character of that great grey conglomerate monster. Montreal, she finds, contains pieces of all the world and lets them be. Despite her gift of tongues, it comforts the Sphinx to hear familiar languages in the streets. She particularly enjoys prowling the green spaces of Concordia and McGill; her soft spot for intellectual puzzling has not faded with the ages. And it's entertaining sometimes to sit perfectly still at the gates of the libraries, pretending to be a statue and then terrifying the patrons. It only ever works once, but there are fresh students every year, and not all of them can be forewarned.

Homer's contemporaries gave her a name, but no one remembers it now. Names are for creatures that require distinguishing, and she is the only Sphinx that ever has been or will be. As a uniquely solitary creature, even having had centuries to observe, she remains remote from certain concepts that have been and will be crucial to humans: the aging process, sex, long-distance communications technologies. Sometimes she thinks she's got an inkling of loneliness, but the full shape of that feeling eludes her as well. She has no one to converse with because she eats people. Not the students or faculty; the universities would hassle her about using their libraries if she were to do that. But other than that she's not picky, just tries to take her meals in out-of-the-way spots where bystanders won't make a fuss. Pretty much everyone knows about it, so they don't tend to make eye contact as she passes on the street. Every now and then a brave or drunken individual will approach her and say something about the ages of man. She asks them about the sisters who birth and devour each other, and they generally flee, unready to face riddles they didn't have answered for them in grade school. She almost always lets them go; contrary to popular belief, there's no particular connection between her appetite and idiocy.

Every now and then, though, the primates manage to produce something interesting. One such individual approaches her one evening as she's strolling up Rue Saint-Urbain: a small dark-skinned woman, smaller even than most of them, in a pink wool coat and a headscarf. She asks in French, "What did you mean by the Theban riddle?" The Sphinx pauses, and blinks down at her with no expression, giving her a chance to run. The woman looks nervous, but stands her ground. Fair enough.

"Aging interested me at the time," says the Sphinx, in the same tongue. "I don't do it, but your kind seems to turn over generations in a matter of days. Sometimes I fall asleep and wake to find the local dialect has changed. The riddle was a bit of poetry about that."

"So you weren't trying to force men to confront their mortality before allowing them to complete their journeys."

"That would imply entirely too much interest in your day-to-day affairs. I had dozens of riddles even just during that period, you know. It's merely that you've only remembered the one."

"May I hear another?"

"Two sisters, each giving birth to the other in turn." The Sphinx gives the woman a moment and then shrugs, a great rolling gesture on a leonine body. "Day and night. In the original Greek, both words were feminine. It doesn't work so well in French."

The woman nods, digesting this. "Do you still write them?"

"Not often. The appeal of the format wore off; I do sestinas now, when I can find the focus." The Sphinx yawns and lets the woman see every tooth. "You should probably get going. I'm kind of hungry."

The woman takes a nervous step back, but doesn't quite flee. Too curious for her own good, the Sphinx thinks. "You're letting me go?" she asks.

"Would you eat a cow after it gave you the best conversation you'd had in a month? Get out of here."

At that the woman leaves in a hurry. The Sphinx retires to Parc Jarry, where she spends the rest of the night scratching fresh riddles into the dirt.

She sees the woman a week later near McGill; she doesn't recognize the face but remembers the scarf and coat. The woman spots her as well—how couldn't she?—and approaches again of her own volition, although a little more hesitantly than last time.

This time, she asks, "So, are you proof that the Greeks were right about the gods?"

"Ugh," says the Sphinx in a moment of unusual candor. "Don't." She is intermittently plagued by groups of humans who believe her to be either a minion of one of their spirits, or proof against Darwin. Often, both. Most of the time they only leave her be after she eats one or two. Sometimes not even then. This woman seems attached to neither idea, though, mostly just looks puzzled, so the Sphinx relents and elaborates.

"I predate the Olympian pantheon and cannot supply evidence that they ever existed. Nor have I met any other gods. Evolution is a sound theory and applies to all of you even if I happen to lie outside of it."

The woman smiles. "Fair enough. Still, you have to admit that if he'd seen you, Darwin would've shit himself."

"He wouldn't have been alone in that," the Sphinx says wryly. "As I understand it, he was a nervous man about his theories. Your scientific establishment is lucky that I was on the other side of the world at the time, or he might have taken me for more than myth and never published at all."

At that the woman laughs aloud.

"I'm Nashwa," she says. "I know this is a bit belated, but it's very nice to meet you." She sticks out her hand by habit, realizes that this won't work as the Sphinx's forepaws are the size of milk crates, and pockets the hand again, laughing.

The Sphinx is unused to common courtesies, and takes a halting moment to answer, "I'm Phix." It's the name she pulls out in a pinch, when one of those rare humans comes along who brings her pleasure in conversation. She has used it only a dozen times since the poet Hesiod gave it to her in the sixth century BCE; Nashwa, now, is her thirteenth. She does not know this, and merely accepts the name with a smile.

"Thank you for setting my cosmogony back on its axis, Phix," Nashwa says. "I'll see you around."

"Of course," says the Sphinx, suddenly anxious that this will not come true. She takes as a hopeful sign the fact that this time, Nashwa does not hurry to depart.

The Sphinx has lived through every age of man and likes to think that this has made her patient, but even the millionth day in a life contains twenty-four hours, and she doesn't have many hobbies. She frightens a couple of headscarfed women from behind before forcing herself to acknowledge that she will not find Nashwa: Montreal is a city of considerable population and her ability to distinguish between humans is very nearly limited to gender and approximate age. Upon this realization, she devours an elderly man in a fit of pique and retires to Parc Jean-Drapeau, where she sleeps for a fortnight. When she wakes she flies across the river to McGill, even though it is late in the fall and most of the students are inured to her presence.

She spots Nashwa from across the lawn around dusk and approaches at a restrained pace. "Are you a student here?"

"Hello to you too. No, I just live nearby."

"I assumed we weren't using standard greetings because you hadn't previously," the Sphinx points out. In reality, she had merely forgotten. "Do you want to put the practice in place? You're a better arbiter of current custom than I."

"Whatever works, I don't care. Hey, do you like hummus?"

The Sphinx crouches so that they're at something more like eye level. "Hummus? I suppose."

"Great, because my mom heard I was having a party and brought me way too much, like four liters. I don't have enough friends for four liters of hummus and you seem like someone who'd be good with large quantities of food." She slings a backpack from her shoulders and pulls out what the Sphinx understands to be a large quantity of food indeed, for smaller creatures.

"It's been a while since I ate anything cooked," she says, gracelessly. Nashwa pales and almost drops the container. She sits heavily. For a minute they both remain perfectly still; the Sphinx digs her claws into the grass in regret of the error, realizes this might seem threatening, and stops with great effort.

At last Nashwa says, "So you really do eat people?"

"Yes."

"Yeah, there really wasn't that much doubt. I was going to rationalize, maybe it's an urban legend, or—have you tried not doing it?"

The Sphinx considers walking away. But maybe this talk too will go from a familiar beginning to a pleasant surprise of an end. "Several times with several substitutes, to no result. To be clear, I am not ashamed of my diet. This is how I am. However, I'm more than aware that it would be nice if I weren't always making enemies of the members of the only species that can carry a conversation."

"Oh." Nashwa is silent for a long time. "I guess I can respect that, um, intellectually." She pushes the container over until it touches the Sphinx's paw. Intellectual respect notwithstanding, her voice is strangled. "Please don't spread my mom's hummus on people."

"That sounds unsavory."

"Not the answer I was looking for, Phix!"

The Sphinx wants to snap something about her honest self and the paucity of available answers Nashwa would like, but she's too pleased by the fact that to Nashwa she remains a named creature, not a monster. She says instead, "I apologize. I understand that it's probably not easy for you to get past, even if they're all strangers to you. Your species' sense of fraternity is exaggeratedly general, albeit suspendable in cases of poverty and war. I . . . can respect that, intellectually. Thank you for the hummus."

"Sure," Nashwa grunts.

The Sphinx cannot help but dig her claws into the grass. As they sit in lapsed conversation, a male voice howls from somewhere across the dim-lit park, "What crawls on three legs, bitchesss?"

"I regret authorial fame," sighs the Sphinx, and at that Nashwa cracks a smile.

"It's weird. That thing is essential mythology to us, but I guess to you it's like if someone memorized one of my middle-school poems and recited it to me at every opportunity." Apparently she has decided to avoid their previous topic, for the moment. This is fine with the Sphinx.

"I'm afraid I don't understand what a middle school is as opposed to any other kind."

"You're better off. Suffice to say, middle-school students tend to produce poetry that they later regret."

The Sphinx nods, and cups the hummus container between her forepaws. She looks it over, trying to determine whether it's something she can manipulate without looking foolish. "But that would be because they get older and improve in their writing skills, wouldn't it? I haven't aged."

"Maybe not physically. You haven't gotten any better?"

The Sphinx applies pressure from each side, but the container's lid remains in place. The whole tub appears to be made of one of the plastic substances that have become popular in the last few generations, and the lid seems suctioned in place. "Perhaps I was always perfect. Regardless, it's people who make me regret the riddle."

"Oh, give it here." Nashwa takes the hummus from the Sphinx and pops the lid off with ease, then hands it back. The Sphinx cups it again and raises it awkwardly to her mouth; she's not really built to lean on her elbows, but it's more dignified than just sticking her face in the tub.

"Very humble of you," Nashwa continues.

"Not among my commonly extolled virtues. This is very good; give my compliments to your mother. If compliments to the cook are still an appropriate gesture."

"They are, yeah."

"Good—then let her know somebody who was around for the dish's invention likes hers."

"You are so pretentious," Nashwa laughs. "How can an immortal figure of myth sit here eating hummus out of a tupperware and still be this pretentious?" She seems to realize belatedly that this might offend, and it does, a little, but the Sphinx has been called worse. To reassure Nashwa, she licks a smear of hummus off her own nose and smiles.

"Eons of practice, dear." They chuckle over this together, and the Sphinx cleans the last of the hummus out of the container and pushes it back to Nashwa. "Thank you."

"Hey, you did me a favor." Nashwa yawns; the Sphinx catches it from her and does the same. "All right, I should head home. This has been—well, you've given me a lot to think about." She zips the container into her bag and gets to her feet.

"Do you want a riddle before you go?" the Sphinx asks. "It's a new one." If she gives Nashwa just the riddle, and doesn't offer or confirm the answer, Nashwa will visit again, she reasons.

Nashwa pauses. "Yes. Yes, I do."

The Sphinx's tail twitches with triumph. "Lovely and round," she says, "I shine with pale light. Grown in the darkness, I'm a lady's delight. What am I?"

Nashwa's mouth creases and her eyebrows rise; she lets slip a giggle. "Um, I don't know. I mean, I have a guess, but I don't think you intended—heh. Um."

The Sphinx frowns. "I don't understand. Why is it funny?" She's out of practice with riddles; maybe it's not good, or maybe this is some cultural association she's unaware of.

"*Ya Allah.* Don't worry about it, Phix. What's the real answer?"

She might as well follow through. "Think about it for a while. I'll tell you next time we see each other."

Nashwa considers this for long enough that the Sphinx has to restrain herself from digging furrows in the grass. "All right," she says finally. "And I'll explain the joke to you then too. See you around."

"Goodbye," the Sphinx sighs, unable to contain her breath of relief.

The Sphinx has been close with less than a hundred humans in her eleven thousand-year existence. Most of these were early on. It was easy, in the Stone Age, to find companionship in one settlement and food in another without the twain ever meeting, as long as she was willing to fly a day or two for her meals. Better trade and communication are not entirely to blame for her withdrawal, though; even after written correspondence was invented, there were people willing to overlook her diet. Nashwa proves that this remains the case still, after the camera and the instant missive. For the most part, the Sphinx's problem with people—besides the obvious—is scale.

Civilizations, she can grasp. She has all the context of history and a bird's-eye view. They rise and fall too fast for her to get the details in real time, but that's all right; the big picture is there.

Groups of people, from a few hundred to a few dozen, never seem worth bothering with. They invariably want to blame her for crop failures, or beg her for the date of the apocalypse, or share with her their grandiose opinions about holding up traffic (in the case of the NYPD) or about their worthless little philosopher of the week (in the case of a book club she once tried to join).

Individuals, she finds, are consistently the most difficult to deal with. Only a tiny fraction of them are interesting at all. Within that set, they are small, easy to lose in space and time. Some fear her, which quickly ends their time together. Some deride the Sphinx for missing certain details of their cultures, or scorn her for attempting to follow customs that they deem outdated, conservative, or libertine. She cannot bear to be mocked. Many others opt for easier, gentler society. And whenever nothing else stops them first, they die. More and more each century, it has become easier to abstain from the pursuit of company. The Sphinx's last true companion lived in the early 1500s, in China. Since then she's been to Egypt, Prussia, France, the United States, a dozen other places in between; in every country she has only come to know a few people in passing: the keepers of books, a hairdresser or two. Excepting these necessary interactions, she has wandered alone and called herself content.

And still, now there is Nashwa, and the Sphinx is eager to see her again, to please her, to win her companionship. The more she thinks about it, the more it feels like risk and like groveling; neither is enjoyable.

She spends the next afternoon moping in Concordia's library. Their large-print section has become prodigious since she first arrived and began prompting them about accessibility, but even with big books turning pages is difficult, and she finds that she doesn't have the energy for reading that day. So she prowls the stacks, and it turns out no one else has an appetite for the large-print books that day either. She harasses the reference librarian: what current theories explain sociality? No, describe them. Stop. Are there any that do not depend on genetic passing-down? What is the lifespan of the average Canadian female? And then—out of spite—is red or white wine recommended for accompanying human flesh? The librarian breaks down crying, and the Sphinx mutters Sumerian curses and retreats to the stacks again.

The very next day, the Sphinx wakes early in the evening to find Nashwa nudging her paw with a foot. She twitches her paw away and tucks it up under her chest.

"Go away," she says, "I'm sleeping."

"And I figured I'd better wake you up," Nashwa returns easily, dropping to the grass beside her. "You know, before the local dialect changed. I brought this book you might like; there was a poem in it that reminded me of you."

The Sphinx feels a curl of warmth in her chest at this, and mistrusts it. "It was a pearl," she says.

"What?"

"My riddle. The answer is 'a pearl.' May I go back to sleep?"

Nashwa sits a moment, frowning, but at length nods. "I'll leave you alone." She stands and shoulders her pack. "The other answer was 'the clitoris.' "

"That's revolting!" the Sphinx exclaims, stony face slipping. "Why would I write . . . 'Shine with pale light'? I'm no expert, but I don't think those glow!"

"Neither does a pearl, that's figurative," Nashwa says, smug. "I knew it wasn't the answer, it was just the first thing I thought of."

"First thing any of you think of," the Sphinx retorts. Nashwa laughs at her distaste. It's a laugh that begs to be echoed; at this juncture between dismissal and riddling, the Sphinx is left lock-throated and blushing. She stares at the grass and Nashwa mistakes this for shyness.

"Come on," she teases, "that's not very body positive of you."

"I don't know what that means, but don't explain it."

Nashwa sits back down beside her, smiling. "I wouldn't have taken you for puritanical, is all. The shock doesn't wear off after a couple thousand years?"

"I'm not shocked by the anatomy or the action," the Sphinx defends. "Sex is a human constant. Just leave me and my riddles out of it."

"No interest at all?"

"What use would a singular species have for sex? No, and I'm glad. It all seems to be considerable sweat and worry, even for the ones ostensibly enjoying it."

Nashwa smiles. "Consider the subject dropped."

"I don't sweat," the Sphinx expands, airing an opinion now simply because she has the latitude to do so, "and I just want you to know that it's distasteful."

"All right, point taken. Lay off we mortals, eh?" And just like that, the Sphinx remembers why she didn't want to be drawn into conversation with Nashwa. The woman is cursedly easy to talk to, and probably something like a third of the way through her tiny life already.

"Why did you approach me, originally?" she asks.

Nashwa looks up in surprise, or possibly worry. "No particular reason."

"I could have eaten you. You had a reason."

"I didn't believe you'd eat me." But the Sphinx's point seems well-taken. Nashwa is silent, thinking, for a long time. The Sphinx, who has nothing but time, waits, and digs her claws into the grass.

At last Nashwa says, "Maslow's hierarchy of needs." Because she is newly an expert on modern theories of human interaction, the Sphinx understands that this is a euphemism for pity. Her tail lashes once, twice, in the grass, but she keeps her tone level.

"The hierarchy has been largely discredited in the psychiatric field. Attachment theory is the prevalent paradigm now, and Maslow remains popular only among sociologists. I am exempt from sociology, having no society."

"Then say that I wanted to see what a person is like, when she has no society. Or when she has had so many that none are her own. Does it matter?"

The Sphinx pulls back her lips from her teeth in a bare display, neither smile nor—quite—snarl. They're human teeth, scaled up to fit her monumental proportions, but the same assortment of dull omnivore incisors, canines, and molars. They are less than ideal tools for rending flesh, except for their size and her jaw strength. She finds that this makes them all the more threatening.

"I think," says the Sphinx, leaning over Nashwa so that her breath is hot and rank, "that you misunderstand certain vital aspects of my being. I do not lust, I do not hold family or morality dear, and I care nothing for the respect of my group, having none. I do not die. I am a separate being."

Nashwa stares back up at the Sphinx, unflinching, and her lip curls too, in unconscious imitation. *Empathy,* notes the Sphinx in the back of her mind. *A toolset for sociality and altruistic behavior.*

"You eat," says Nashwa, "you breathe, you sleep, and you read. You complimented my mother's hummus and apologized for frightening me. Somewhere in Greece, a long time ago, someone—some human—gave you a name and you've taken the trouble to remember what it was."

"Quiet yourself," the Sphinx growls. She postures and stoops her wings; it has been so long since someone failed to run from her teeth and her breath that she is not sure what to do.

"You walk on sidewalks," Nashwa persists, "when you can fit, and you play games with the university students even though you don't intend to eat them. So," her voice drops, "I saw all that and I made a hypothesis."

A hypothesis is not pity, and this buys her a few moments more of forbearance. "What was it?"

"That you wouldn't hurt me if I was interesting, and that I could learn from you if you didn't hurt me." A hypothesis is also not a certainty: the Sphinx can smell fear on Nashwa, and her predator's eyes catch a tremor in her hands. Her gaze sharpens on that detail, and saliva floods her mouth. It'd be easier, this way.

Her chest twists again, this time sourly, and though it comes only every few centuries the Sphinx recognizes the feeling as shame. She lets her lips cover her teeth again.

"I'm not going to hurt you," she says quietly.

Nashwa doesn't say, *good,* or *thank you.* She says, "Me neither, if I can help it." She falls back onto the grass all the same, arms stretched out to her sides, relief in every inch of her. Not enough of it; she trusts, doesn't know what has just passed her by. The Sphinx takes a generous step back, tries to make her face like stone.

Nashwa says, "I've been thinking about you a lot, Phix."

"And I you."

"I'm a little harder to research, I imagine. I found an account of a bunch of people attacking you, with axes and stuff, in 1235." The Sphinx recalls the period—*reconquista* of Al-Andalus, a companion dead in the fighting—but not the assault upon her person, specifically. She refrains from comment, not calm enough to speak much just yet, and wondering where Nashwa is going. "The weapons just broke. The author said you didn't even bruise, and then all the people ran away. You don't age, either. And yet you get hungry, and you breathe. Could you starve to death, or asphyxiate, do you think? Under the right circumstances?"

"I've never been curious enough to take those experiments very far," the Sphinx answers. An October wind blows across them both and Nashwa shivers in her wool coat. "I hunger, and crave air, and water, for that matter, in much the same manner as any creature whom deprivation could kill. I appease my desires because they're my nature, and I've no interest in denying myself." The protestation sounds weak even to her, but: hunger has been her companion forever, and this human, for only a blink's time. She will not be other than what she is, though she may hold herself back when caught between urges.

"And you desire to read, and riddle, and talk to pushy Québécois girls. Apparently."

"Those deprivations certainly won't kill me," the Sphinx responds testily, but she has already proven Nashwa's point before it was spoken. Being impervious and immortal removes death as a unique category of suffering: without the end, it's all a graded scale, and all thresholds are arbitrary.

"Maslow's not the only one who places loneliness in a context with hunger and thirst," Nashwa says. "Look up skin hunger sometime."

The Sphinx grimaces. "Fine."

"Do you feel better? Want to hear that poem now?"

"Save it for next time," the Sphinx says, because she still isn't quite to a place where there can be a next time without some pretext. Because she needs there to be a next time; because she needs, next time, to be better fed so as not to be tempted. Because taking a gift of poetry just now would feel dishonest.

"Okay," Nashwa says, the smile returning to her face. "Just remember that I can't wait forever."

"No question of that," says the Sphinx.

THE SIGNIFICANCE OF SIGNIFICANCE

ROBERT REED

Sarah wasn't quite two when the world learned what was what.

Which is rather like saying that Sarah still didn't exist.

The very young don't get to keep their memories. That's normal human development in action, or it's a nagging bug inside an otherwise lovely system. Either way, she didn't waste time regretting this supposed loss. Sure, a booger-clogged head was wearing her name, stumbling across a misunderstood landscape. But that head wasn't her head, and this Sarah inhabits a beautiful, artificial universe. This world only pretends to be made from protons and people, and being one of the first to grow up knowing that, she has no trouble seeing the blessing for what it is, and that's why she appreciates each day as wonderful, and it's sad to see so many others who don't understand the Significance.

Sarah's parents. They'll never accept the truth, which is why spending time with them is so frustrating. She tries to be patient. She really does. But Mom and Dad have pinned themselves to the worst kind of template. What they believed back on Day Zero is what they believe today, and while it's tempting to feel sorry for those who don't understand, sorrow is a negative emotion. Negative emotions will always turn into a godawful waste of time, and time feels precious. This lovely existence could evaporate tomorrow, but for as long as Sarah remains real, she intends to harvest as much joy as possible.

At least one old man appreciates the world. Mom's father, Grandpa Lemon, is a different animal. Almost eighty, a fantasy definitely close to its natural end, yet the man still smiles and laughs way more than most people. Maybe he doesn't have the strongest grasp on the science, but he also doesn't get angry about what young people know for certain.

"The significance of Significance," he says.

Sarah laughs at that phrase.

Grandpa waves a hand as if shooing away flies. "Want to hear some wild stories explaining why we're here?"

She says, "Sure."

"For most of my life, the universe was one enormous, beautiful explosion of Nothingness. And before that? The Earth and its little people were carved from clay by some tall white dude straddling the clouds. But today, for this minute or two, we're calling ourselves a slick dream living inside an invisible machine."

Except the machine is visible. That's a point worth making, and Sarah always makes her points.

"I understand all that," he claims. "Hey, I actually watched the first press conference. All those people who got to share the Nobel, crazy happy with the attention. And I'll boast about something else. I've read everything that I can find. Unlike a lot of people, including your dear mother. So yeah, I can appreciate what you believe. The universe is a very big box filled with important mathematics. Not that I understand the details, or that you do either. But the evidence is compelling. Reality is full of cheats and simplifications, and quantum mechanics is a game, and the spaces between electrons and between the picoseconds are full of game tricks. And best of all, astronomers looked at the sky and saw the cosmic scaffolding. Which feels like a joke, if you think about it. Do you get my joke, honey?"

Sarah doesn't like being called "honey." But names are just clumps of silly sound, and why sweat one word? In Grandpa Lemon's mind, the famous news conference occurred in 2025, and today happens to be May 8, 2043. But Sarah's generation doesn't keep the same calendar. This is 6404. That's the number of days since the Significance was revealed. Units of time are arbitrary and inadequate, but people who live inside the long years tend to forget too much. Which is a waste. Existence is already arbitrary and frail. You need to notice everything, and counting every day helps. You never know when the complicated math is going to collapse. Whoever built this universe has that kind of power. It's just like the two-year-old's brain: The world can cease and thoughts can vanish and nobody would know. Which is one very good reason to smile politely when her grandfather tells cosmic jokes.

"God is a comedian," Sarah says. "An old guy like you standing on the scaffolding, laughing down at us."

"Laughing hard," he adds.

Both of them are doing just that. Sarah inherited Grandpa Lemon's deep chuckle. That's what Mom claims, and that isn't a bad thing to hear. How many times have Sarah and her grandfather been together like this, the two of them sharing this kind of pleasure? It's easy enough to ask. Sarah wears cameras and microphones, and like many in her generation, she feeds every moment into an encrypted cloud locker.

But she doesn't ask. Grandpa suddenly falls quiet, and after a long, sorry sigh, he says, "About your mother."

All right. Here it is.

"I'm not telling you that your folks are worried. You know as much. Or that my daughter doesn't like your choices, since that's the most obvious thing in the world right now. No, I just want to hear the story from you. Your reasons for doing this. At your age, when you should be making ready for the rest of your life—"

That's when she interrupts him. A sound that isn't laughter bursts free, and they're both surprised by the harshness of it, the rude and dismissive noise before the single word, "Shit."

Grandpa stops talking.

Sarah regrets nothing. Regret weighs you down, shortening the good in your brief existence. That's what she believes and expects from herself. Except no, now she finds herself feeling bad about what she just did, and she can't shake the stupid emotion.

Grandpa Lemon repeats just one word.

"Reasons," he says.

The question doesn't have to be made any clearer. Sarah's right hand touches her belly and the bulge. The baby will kick if she waits, because this is a busy eager happy sack of potential that won't hold memories for another eight hundred days.

"Because," she says. "I want a baby before we vanish."

"We aren't going to vanish, honey," he says.

Again, that unwelcome word.

"But we can go away," she insists, wanting to sound reasonable but all kinds of pain revealing themselves. Then after a pause and several useless breaths, she adds, "I want a child who loves as life as much as I do. And I want to enjoy him before this show is finished."

"But if it goes away . . . then it's as if it never was . . . "

How can anyone say that, or even think it?

One last time, he says, "Honey."

Anger takes her, making her feel vulnerable. "Every game ends," she tells him. "But somebody is playing us, Grandpa. Somebody who sees us and knows us. Who knows me, and who's going to know my son, and as long as we stay happy and interesting, we'll be worth watch. So you see? That's the significance of the significance."

A baby is coming. Reality has one shape or an entirely different shape, but Sarah is definitely pregnant and her parents don't even know the father. Some people would accept this situation. After all, their daughter is a bright, well-educated, voting-age adult. Except Sarah is also impulsive and stubborn. If she wants a baby, that's what will happen. Telling her that she cannot or should not are the worst possible strategies. No, it's much easier to attack the entire universe. Taking positions of deep ignorance, the two of them throw doubting words at a child who graduated from school only because she was smart enough to achieve that goal without hard work. The girl who chases loud parties and odd boys in her endless quest for fun. Her parents have learned not to openly doubt Sarah's good sense, but they can sure complain about the science. Reality is not a piece of software, and existence isn't some godly creature's elaborate, fickle hobby. That's the only way that these two shy people can stand tall and sound stubborn, relying on other people to tell Sarah what she needs to hear.

But the Lemon gambit has been soundly defeated.

"Don't ever put my grandfather up to shit like that," Sarah warns them. "I like the old boy. And I didn't want to have to yell at him."

Sarah did yell. A full report from the battlefield arrived half an hour before their daughter.

"We were trying to help," one of them says.

It doesn't matter which one of them speaks. Married as long as they have been, the voice is shared, just like the uncomfortable air inside their old home.

"These are such difficult times," says the other one.

"And a baby . . . "

"Is a lot."

"Too much."

"When the world is so frantic."

"So crazy."

"Everything unsettled."

"Changing."

"Nothing but change," the shared voice says, and then pauses.

Sarah is not one of those pretty pregnant girls. She doesn't sleep enough or eat right, and maybe she's doing worse things to herself and the child. Who knows? Well, she knows. This self-indulgent life needs to be recorded, and that's why she wears multiple cameras, every mechanical eye staring at these two people who are being awful, and on a day when she so much wanted to have fun.

"Nobody believes what you believe," says Sarah. "That's why the churches are standing empty."

Which is an odd observation, for multiple reasons.

"I know what bothers you," the girl declares. "God isn't magic floating in the clouds. Science built the universe, and you hate it because we know everything that we need to know already."

One of them asks, "Why talk about God?"

"We've never been religious sorts," says the other.

But the first has to point out, "And a lot of people still go to church. People who happen to be your age, in fact."

Sarah laughs at some part of this. She doesn't sound like her grandfather today. This is a stranger's laugh, half growl and full of bile.

Then one parent tells her, "You need to listen to somebody, honey . . . "

Which is when Sarah begins to scream. At no time in her brief busy life has their daughter unleashed such anger or used this abusive language. "Do you fucking know how much I fucking hate being called 'honey?' "

They will never use that endearment again. But in the spirit of the moment, with emotions heating up air and blood, this is the perfect opportunity to be honest, honest, honest.

"You've always done what you want," they tell her.

"You do it fiercely and without doubts, right up until you decide that you don't want to do it anymore.

"This isn't about the nature of the universe," they tell her.

"It doesn't matter if this world is a game or Eden or just one rock among trillions.

"What matters is you.

"You're a certain kind of person and always will be.

"That's why we're afraid.

"Both of us are.

"You're going to get tired of this game, which you always do.

"And then you'll leave that poor child with us."

There it is. A terrible truth to admit, particularly to yourself. But they say what needs to be said, and they even manage to stand their ground afterwards, enduring more vicious language and so much fury. But what they don't expect is the sudden epiphany: In the midst of that onslaught, the suffering parents find themselves wishing that Sarah is right. The universe is indeed someone's chess board. Because they want the pieces picked and put away, and then all of this terrible pain can dissolve into the vacuum . . . forgotten . . .

Being the center of attention should be the best feeling in the world. But Tomjack keeps learning that he can't trust every pleasure. Happiness finds too many ways to get him into trouble.

Like with Sarah.

Three leaps into bed, and each time, nothing felt so good. The sex was part of the fun, sure. But mostly it was the way the girl looked at him, particularly before and then after. Tomjack was the only other person in the world. That's what her smile was saying. Way too big for one soul, her joy was running hot through him too. If he hadn't been there to eat her emotions, Sarah would have exploded. That's what he was thinking at the time. Which was an odd idea, and the odd thoughts didn't stop coming afterwards.

Every little action felt special when they were together. Usually squeamish about cameras, Tomjack didn't balk about her cameras or throwing everything up to the Cloud. The last time together was that long wonderful afternoon in bed, and that's when Sarah did the unthinkable. She told her lover that the world could end right now. "Because I'll never be happier than I am right now," she said. Sounding hushed and amazed, as if making a confession.

Normal people didn't use those words. Normal thought didn't expect the universe to dissolve in the next breath. But Sarah didn't just accept the Significance, she believed everything that it told her. For her, life wore a capital L, and when something happened that wasn't as perfect or fun or as surprising as Sarah deserved, then the day could turn very, very ugly.

But not that day. His lover was crying for every good reason, talking about her happiness and hopes. It was so nice. So perfect. The best hours of Tomjack's life, and that's why he risked breaking the biggest Sarah-rule. Watching her getting dressed, getting ready to leave, he asked when they'd see each other again. Sarah didn't believe in "Forcing the future." That's what she called normal human planning. But the boy felt brave enough to try the question, and his lover was too giddy to risk chastising him or the temporary universe. She winked, sort of. Then she said, "Next week."

"What day?" he pressed.

She hesitated, but not for long. "Thursday," she told him. Then she mentioned a time when she might or might not arrive at his front door.

Of course Tomjack shaped his entire week around that interlude. And when Sarah didn't show, he has some ready-built explanations that he could live with. The girl lost track of time, or a party left her too sick, or maybe her grandfather died. Except none of those excuses happened to be true. Sarah didn't show or answer his texts, and she had never offered him a home address. That's when tragedy became appealing. There must have been an accident. He imagined her tumbling down a flight of stairs. By Friday, those stairs became numerous and sharp, and by next week, after repeated attempts to contact the girl, Tomjack was convinced that she was dead and he was glad that he missed her funeral. Which was a selfish, stupid way to think. But the boy was barely eighteen, which happened to be the perfect age to let a willful, self-indulgent beauty take hold of your soul.

A full month passed before Sarah showed up again. By then, Tomjack felt older and a little wiser. The girl made apologetic sounds that didn't excuse anything but the silly, temporary universe. She told him to forgive her, and maybe he did. Two minutes later, he wasn't sure what he had said. By then, Sarah was boasting about new boyfriends. Three of them, usually two at a time, and Tomjack wasn't that kind of beast. He wasn't at all like her. Standing in the open door, she practically ordered him to have a good life, and that's when the jilted lover found the maturity to say a few honest words.

"You're a scary bitch," he said.

"You're just figuring that out?" she asked, laughing at silly him.

And for six years, they didn't talk.

Yes. "Years."

A lot of people are busy counting the days. But not Tomjack. Adults are free to believe what they want about the universe, regardless of their age. And for Tomjack, the Significance is just a miserable distraction. The picture of everything being unreal . . . well, that will never stopped making him sick inside. It's not that he isn't smart enough to understand the crazy science. The Significance makes as much sense as gravity or electrons, which are pretty magical in their own right. But six more years of life have taught him that his opinions don't matter all that much. Not to other people or to anything else, including the universe. For the last three years, Tomjack has been married, and his life is happy. But he knows not to feel too happy, since joy is temporary and everything is guaranteed to change, and change likes nothing better than to arrive without warning.

A theory proved when Sarah arrives unannounced at his front door.

On a Thursday afternoon, as it happens. So maybe she wasn't lying. Maybe this is what she meant with that long ago promise.

A boy stands behind her, tugging against her hand, and he might well be five-years-old.

Tomjack says, "Shit."

"Watch your language," Sarah reprimands. Except then she gives this big scary laugh. The woman looks brittle and about to break, and Tomjack feels cold for the both of them. For the three of them.

"Is this him?" the boy asks.

Sarah keeps up the weird giggling. Cameras are riding her face and hands and knees, and a flock of gnat-sized eyes float in the air, sucking in existence. Her endless pleasure is being enforced. Chemicals can do this, and electrodes implanted deep inside the giddy brain. Methods don't matter as much as results, and he sees this more and more every year. Good sane people want to relish their lives, and they'll do anything to feel as if they are the center of the cosmic happiness.

The thing is, Sarah is neither good or sane.

"Is this him?" Tomjack's son wants to know.

She answers by not answering. Teeth showing, she stares at her ex-lover, and something needs a hard moan that steals away her breath. Then she tells him, "This is fair. More than fair."

"What are you saying?"

"I've had two thousand days with him. That's enough."

Is she really talking about their son?

"You get him now," she says.

"It is him," the boy decides.

Tomjack looks at a face that he helped build.

"My name is Honey," the kid says,

Tomjack looks at Sarah. "Seriously?"

"It's just a sound," she explains.

Again, he looks at the boy, nothing to guide him but a quarter century of life, coupled with empathy as well as a lot of deep, sucking fear.

"You'll take him," she says.

Tomjack doesn't answer.

"Because my folks won't," she continues.

Which is a great joke. The crazy woman has to bend over, laughing until she's out of breath.

"Useless old people," Sarah says.

With both hands, Tomjack yanks the boy free of his mother.

"Anyway," she says. "You'll need to go through the legal shit. I won't fight you. And for help, I can give you . . . "

He listens to her deep, frantic breathing.

"Recordings of everything," she promises. "When we made him and everything that's happened since. Including his first two years, which were pretty damned interesting."

Inside his head, Tomjack is explaining this mess to his away-from-home wife.

Out loud, all he can say, "Okay then."

"Well, good," says the madwoman.

Honey, the boy, seems like the kind of kid who's always fearful. He's probably sad and cries himself to sleep. Which really, at the end of this, is the very best evidence that they might make this work. That's what Tomjack is thinking just now. Start with despair and desperation, and after that, everything an incompetent father does will seem like a godsend.

The scientist on the squidskin belonged to the original project. That salient fact needs to be mentioned, along with naming team members instrumental in work done decades ago. But those people aren't here today. This is a different project, and after thanking the dead and the retired, she begins the official news conference.

"The universe is a fabrication of mathematics and high-end simulation," she says. And with that, the Nobel laureate pauses, one finger dragging text across the podium.

Deja vu hits Harold Lemon.

The woman sighs, looking at the camera. Staring directly at him. "For two generations, this has been our working theory. And every good theory deserves to have its ideas and their consequences tested. Inside the lab, through field observations. As problems of the mind. And through every step of the journey, the evidence remains solid. But that leaves a question. If the universe is a fiction, then what is this story telling us? That's what I hope we're here to explain today."

Harold loves moments like this, being taken by surprise, becoming one among billions privileged to watch history play out in unexpected ways. Excitement mixes with oxygen, giving every person a dose of energy. That's true even inside a warehouse populated with old people. The common rooms are filled with residents watching the news. People stand, people lean forward in their favorite chairs. Expressions range from intrigued and grave concern to the simplicity of being pissed to find their ordinary day ruined. And then there's the staff standing in back, nobody doing their jobs. Across the world, humanity is enjoying a contemplative break.

In his middle nineties, Harold Lemon has the one daughter, a very crazy granddaughter, and that teenage great-grandson who he doesn't see nearly enough. Except of course for the millions of images of the boy pulled from various cloud accounts. Harold's daughter hung squidskin on his apartment walls, instructing the AIs to harvest smiles, forced as well as honest. A lot of fake intimacy, and that's why the squidskin plays only when the daughter visits or when Harold leaves his apartment. Which is what he does most every day, as it happens. Since he has never been a lonely old boy.

"Frankly, I was never quite satisfied with our initial discovery," the physicist confesses. "It's not the nature of the universe that bothers me. Every system has its rules. The Big Bang could be as artificial as mahjong, and who are we to complain? No, I learned to live with the new paradigm. What kept me from sleeping is the gnawing problem about why we so easily see the evidence? Once we knew how to look, the clues were dangling in the sky as well as the smallest corners of the universe. These are clues that humans can't avoid, much less deny, and that seems unlikely. Almost silly. Really, why go to so much trouble to invent a world and a full, rich cosmos, and then leave your boards and bolts hanging in the sky?"

Harold drinks in that woman's face. Her joy feeds his pleasure, and that would be true even if he couldn't hear her words. But he hears everything. Friends and other residents have pushed in close enough to touch one another, but nobody talks. Only the young workers on the outskirts are foolish enough to offer opinions about things they know nothing about.

"But what if this scaffolding was left behind as markers, or as a message?" She asks the question, and once again, she pauses.

Harold leans a little closer, enjoying the thundering of his heart.

"To answer this question, my team and I devised new ways of analysing data. Everything learned by spaceborne telescopes and the Lunar cyclotron has been used. Everything known about this universe has been massaged. And what are we now certain about? That the universe is quite a bit smaller than we first assumed. There are no billions of light-years or hundreds of billions of days. The real walls of our universe? Spherical and set just about one light-year from where I'm standing now. And humanity herself is quite a bit younger than we would ever guess. Biblical stories use thousands of years to measure history. But that's much too much. This world and all its inhabitants were conjured into existence a little more than three hundred years ago."

This is too much to absorb, even for sharp, happy Harold.

Having delivered that thunder, the first scientist surrenders the podium to her colleagues. In smaller bits, each repeats what has already been said, but with narrower focuses and a fair amount of nomenclature. Reporters are invited to offer up obvious, ignorant questions. The best-guess explanation is that the Earth and its people are a simulation rendered by a more advanced Earth. Which itself could be a synthetic wonder. And is there any window or trapdoor reaching to any greater realm? Not that they can see. Which is sad, or perfect, or nothing. Who can say?

Harold listens until these bizarre new ideas reach a critical point. No, he isn't ready to understand, much less accept he's being told. But at least he has a clear sense about how thoroughly his beliefs need to change.

Eventually the project leader returns to the front of the stage. But this is a different woman, it seems. Nervous, uneasy. She glances at her colleagues, and they respond with affirmative nods and frowns and little gestures from hands that aren't quite sure what to say. Then the researcher makes a decision, gripping the podium, holding tight for a bit. But no, that isn't enough. Better to step forwards until she's perched at the edge of the stage. "One more item," she says. "This may change, of course. The data are new, our assessments raw. But while doing this work, it occurred to us that any sufficiently large universe could hold little universes. Spaces full of information and highly compressed time. Those are the hallmarks of a genuine Creation. And that's why we began to analyze our surroundings. Honestly? I didn't expect anything interesting. Yet we managed find a little universe. And another one, and more after that. Each object is built on the same principles as this giant tiny wondrous box of a universe that we live inside. And each of us is carrying and caring for the marvel. Which is this."

And that is the moment she places a hand on her small, infinite forehead.

Two universes share a small park bench, and several dozens universes are enjoying the playground and one another. There's a lot of motion and noise in the scene, and sometimes one of those grown universes will shout, "Honey."

As a warning, as an endearment. Either way, Honey ignores his name.

His mother sits beside him, quiet and very still, hands resting on her lap, her face engaged but not smiling. Not joyful. Which is still strange to see. The mother that Honey remembers was perpetually smiling, loud and very energetic, like a force of Nature during those little dashes of time when his father allowed them to meet. Usually with Dad hanging close, just in case . . . well, it was never clear what the fear was. That Mom would poison his thinking or dose him with some joy-inducing drug? Or maybe she would kidnap her boy, reclaiming what she regretted giving away for free.

Honey never asks about regrets. The past lives only inside the little universes, and each has its own version of what happened and why. One universe can passionately defend her actions, and maybe the other modifies his memories accordingly. But maybe not, and maybe there would be a fight, and it's best to remember that on the best day, the universe have a tough time saying much at all.

And this is not the best day.

All at once, his mother says, "I don't want you to go."

Honey shrugs.

"Or leave, if you have no choice. Go on and abandon us. But don't take my grandchildren from me."

There. They've gotten to the heart of this matter.

"Off the Earth and halfway across the universe," she complains.

"Ceres isn't that far," he says.

"It is to me." And with that, the woman smiles. It's the first grin since they sat down ten minutes ago. Mom has done a marvelous job of destroying her pleasure centers with chemicals and electricity, and now, due to some odd rerouting of neurons, smiles come only when she is suffering terrible pain. "I barely know your little ones," she complains. "And now you're going to live on that dead rock."

"We'll come back to visit," he says.

Not for the first time.

She says, "They won't. They'll grow up in that gravity, and they won't want to suffer down here."

"Or you visit us," he offers.

Prohibitively expensive. And beside, the universe inside that head would never accept being carted to the moon, much less out to the asteroid belt. Both of them understand that, and that's why Mom needs a fresh weapon. Attacking the entire reason for leaving is the more viable plan.

"Your project is evil," she says.

"It's not my project," he says, "and it's a very reasonable experiment."

"You can't help them do this."

"I can and will."

"This dangerous, horrific experiment." Once again, Mom smiles, straightening her back from what might be genuine agony. "Punching a hole in our universe, trying to reach whatever's next door."

"That's why we're trying this on Ceres," he reminds her. "Not the moon or the ocean floor. But hundreds of millions of kilometers away."

"With my grandchildren."

"Mom," he says. Then after an exasperated pause, he reminds her, "My wife and I are helping to build the facility. Which will take years. The punching and the consequences won't come until after the kids are grown."

"Dangerous, foolish work," she says.

Honey doesn't recognize the universe beside him. This woman and everything inside her has shifted in some enormous way, and he comes close to making that point, if only to push her deeper into a smiling rage.

But she seems to guess his thoughts. Quietly, she says, "Now I understand my parents."

Honey thinks of his grandmother.

"What they went through with me," says Mom. "What they were thinking, and what they wanted."

Grandma died two years ago. Which was the last time when Honey and his family spent time with this difficult, much-broken universe.

"Suddenly those crazy people seem reasonable to me," she claims.

Honey stares at the playground, at the running children and vigilant parents and the parents who want to be anywhere else. It's amazing and embarrassing how long it takes him to find the three distinct faces that he knows better than any other face, including his own.

Mom folds her arms across her chest. "When you were little," she says. "Did you visit your great-grandfather?"

"We didn't live nearby," he says. "So no, only on special occasions."

"Grandpa Lemon had pictures of you. Videos of you. I gave him access to my cloud lockers, and your grandmother did the same."

"I know. I remember that."

"Squidskins on the walls of his apartment. Which he didn't like, by the way. He found them intrusive and peculiar."

"Is that so?"

"He let them play only when his family visited, or when he was out of the room entirely."

A funny way to wound, but that's what the words do.

"Do you know what Grandpa Lemon told me?" she asks. "Just before he died. Not long after humanity decided that each of us was its own universe."

"You've never told me, no."

" 'There's a lesson in all of this,' he said."

"Okay."

" 'Universes are tiny. Always tiny.' "

Honey can think of nothing to say.

Then his mother touches him. For what will be the last time, she holds his hand with both of hers, smiling in agony as she explains, "You're going to succeed. I really believe that. You're going to cut a hole and climb through, and what you'll discover is another room that someone has left empty, and ten billion faces playing on the walls."

THE TALE OF THE ALCUBIERRE HORSE

KATHLEEN ANN GOONAN

—◆—

Here stands a house all built of thought,
And full to overflowing
Of treasures and of precious things,
Of secrets for my knowing.

—Olive Beaupré Miller
The Latch Key

There is a theory that consciousness arises through self-organizing mass. This takes ages. Think of the thousands of years the oldest bristlecone pine grew, nearly five thousand, and it could grow older, if it had a chance, though it no longer has that chance. Except here. And maybe somewhere, but that is a mighty thin maybe.

Nevertheless, think of all the systems that went into growing that tree, all that time. What kind of entity can possibly understand time that long, except that bristlecone pine? And then, think of all the time we have been riding this horse. Who could understand that?

If anyone could, they would seem like magical creatures to us. That's why this is a fairy tale.

Time is a Kelvin–Helmholtz function. You know, like the clouds in Van Gogh's Starry Night. We surf the waves, the whorl, the crush of energies that cause time, that cause us. You may disagree with it, but that's our present theory. It seems that our particular neighborhood of time, which created us, is the only weather in which consciousness can survive. We are the products of a very fragile environment.

We are the magic beans Jill climbs the beanstalk to find.

We are life.

• • •

Pele, two days older than one hundred and five, waits in crowded Galaxies Bar on *Moku*, the Entertainment, Amusement and, much less importantly, R&D Exoplanetary Exploration Ship. Robotic and print construction commenced in 2030, when Pele was forty, during one of the rare confluences of available capital and passionate interest in space.

Pele's hands are folded in her lap in an attitude of calm, but she simmers, despite the faint scent of gardenia, the low tones of a flowing music specifically designed to generate a state of relaxed attention, and the zen landscaping. A tube of green tea floats unopened near her shoulder, its tether clipped to the table. Dr. Zi, Chief Safety Engineer, is late for this meeting, one that Pele requested and that the ship's scheduling algorithm arranged.

Lights are always low in Galaxies, unlike other bars on *Moku* designed for dancing or the roar of a hundred unheard conversations. As usual, it's two-thirds populated by tourists and crew. The Velcro floor is scattered with zabutons and low, gently glowing cylinders that serve as tables. A row of portholes affords a spectacular view of Mars rising as *Moku* slowly spins.

"Sorry I'm late, Dr. Hsu." Zi, in full quasi-military Chief Safety Engineer regalia, billed hat and all, drops onto a zabuton. Peering over his shoulder, he unbuttons his shirt pocket, removes his ever-present salad tube, takes a pull, and slips it back into his pocket, which he buttons.

Pele says, "I want to discuss last week's report, in which I raise serious issues. You didn't respond."

Zi is busy scanning the room. "Ah! There she is. Eleven o'clock." He waves, showing most of his teeth in a camera-ready smile that beams from his well-tanned, rugged face.

Stormy, a raven-haired reality star, threads her way around seated groups of people toward them, encased in a retro space suit that emphasizes her long legs and shapes her breasts into pointy weapons. The camera drones trailing her blink like synchronous fireflies, as required by law.

Pele shakes her head emphatically in Stormy's direction, uninterested in being dragged into the kind of propaganda puff pieces with which Zi is building his celebrity.

Stormy pivots as quickly as the Velcro on the two contact points of her very high heels allows and heads off at a right angle, trolling for the perfect feel-good space chat.

Zi frowns. "You just blew a perfect opportunity to communicate with the public."

"I communicate very well with the public, except when you bump my podcast, like you did yesterday." Pele, temporary liaison between the many factions on board, sees new fault lines daily, foresees minor disasters and deflects them before they emerge, furnishes solutions, and shares concerns in forceful, direct language with those on the ship and on Earth who need to know. She also drops a weekly public podcast, working hard to present this information gracefully, so as to avoid being characterized as an alarmist crank by the all-powerful entertainment industry.

"You need to re-slant it."

"I said exactly what I meant to say. The issues I raised concerning the Gifted Child Congress are urgent. There have been thirty-seven of these children on board for six weeks now, and I've sent you five related Concern Communiqués—each with two red exclamation points—thus far. Should I try using more?"

"So say something nice for a change. Your campaign against them failed."

"Just because everyone, including their parents, were snowed regarding the very real health risks—"

"We are completely protected by nanotech shielding."

"No meaningful sample for that conclusion, despite all the glossy advertising, but here they are, so we can gather information for more meaningful studies for the rest of their lives—and ours. However, my present concerns are about something different."

"I've read your CC's. They contain weird assertions. Rumors, in fact, that don't rise to the level of requiring a CC. Yes—these children are not normal— that's their strength! They're the superstars of the future. This is the third Congress in the past ten years. Wildly successful. Great publicity. They're bringing in billions of dollars. Flip your concerns, for Christ's sake. Valentina actually had a paper accepted by *Space Life Journal*, one she completed while here. She is amazing—ten years old! Grew up on the Argentinian pampas, on an estancia. Home-schooled. Discovered by a competition she entered. I was planning to steer the interview you just blew off in that direction."

Pele knows Valentina as Bean, as do the other children. "Valentina *is* amazing." She does not ask if Zi has read Valentina's startling paper. She does not want to embarrass him. "They all are amazing. That's part of my concern."

"Why concern? We need to talk them up."

"I talk about my job, which is to be a crank, if that's what you want to call it. An honest, vocal crank, and I am worried. Doesn't it matter at all that *Moku* is a disaster waiting to happen? In so many ways?"

"We've got backups galore."

Sometimes Pele cannot believe that he is a many-degreed engineer. But too ambitious; a young fifty-something on the make. So many luminaries have springboarded out of *Moku* that it's regarded as a pipeline to fame.

On the instant, Pele decides to have him removed. He is smart enough to understand that he is ignoring key issues not just at his own peril, but at the peril of others. He has put his own path to celebrity above his larger responsibilities, and has just definitively underlined his reckless stance.

She knows exactly who has bought his complacency. It is easy for her to make her face unreadable, but perhaps her doing so right now is the tell he's been looking for. Even now, after a lifetime of effort to gain fluency in the language of emotion-filled faces, she has not completely mastered the human tap-dance of mask and reveal that normal children easily absorb, despite her neuroplasticity infusions and cognitive therapies.

She does not wish to be normal. But aspects of normality would often be helpful.

Zi leans forward, sets both hands on the table, and links his fingers. His big smile makes jolly-looking crinkle lines at the corners of his eyes. She is sure he knows just how jolly they are. His voice warm and hearty, he says, "Hey, isn't children's literature one of your areas of expertise?"

This is a new tack. "Seventy years ago, it was. I'm not at all up-to-date, and wasn't then. Just books, written before 1965. But yes, it was a passion." Indeed, one of her rickety bridges to life. "And?"

"I recall a video of you speaking at an international conference after you received your first doctorate. You were a very passionate and effective communicator about how the brains of children on the autistic spectrum can be physically changed through engagement with literature. All the more impressive because—"

She smiles; nods. "I'm Asperger's. As are most of our visiting children. Part of my international cachet, I might add." Two can play at his game.

"Um, yes. Of course. We're all open books here, no pun intended. I'm just thinking you might help organize our vast children's library. It's a terrible jumble—all those files shot up here willy-nilly from all over the world. You can link these kids to it—"

Pele leans forward, laces together her own fingers, lights up her own wide, brown face with a warm, face-crinkling smile. "Great idea. That task might serve to distract me from effectively executing my responsibilities. Or maybe I should write another paper that bridges two fields of physics, and create a new field. The first was a hit. I won a small prize."

She does not usually talk this way. She was brought up to be modest, but he has vastly overplayed his hand. Her small stature, her long, shimmering white hair, and even, still, the fact that she is a woman, have often caused others to underestimate her. She was here long before him, and will be here long after he is gone. But she still can't tell whether he understands that he has picked the wrong foe.

He straightens his back. "You can't fight money, even if you do have Nobel authority. *Moku* runs on the entertainment and tourist industries."

"I agree. And technological, scientific, and academic research is the dog. Setting a timetable for actual travel to an exoplanet seems to be our least concern. In the two years since you arrived, you or your proxies have generated many irrelevant but effective roadblocks and dismantled several long-running initiatives. Not many people have examined your record thus far, but a close scrutiny reveals a definite pattern."

He juts his head forward and stares at her with open hostility. "You're out of your—do you really?—" He raises both hands in a questioning attitude, drops them to his side, and laughs. "Wow. It doesn't matter, then, that there is *no place to go*?"

"There are many places we could go. Potentially, an infinite number of habitable planets. We're finding a new one, literally, every day."

"Yes, but *we* cannot get there."

Pele decides to take advantage of this teachable moment. Perhaps she can awaken him to *Moku*'s true wonder. "We are approaching an age in which we might be able to mesh our growing understanding of quantum processes with new technologies, a time in which the specific needs of a particular possibility might generate a new paradigm regarding our ability to move through space and time. In that reality, it could seem only instants until all habitable planets are populated."

He nods. "You are talking, of course, about your particular pet, the theoretical Alcubierre drive. Powered by the equally theoretical Casimir vacuum." His eyes gleam with true humor, for a moment. "Wouldn't that be something! But just a pipe dream."

She says, "We've made a lot of advances since you took your one required theoretical physics course thirty years ago. I'd love to set aside time to talk to you about how much we've learned since then. You are right about one thing—*Moku* has been vital to forwarding our ability to learn more about so many subjects. It is a scientific wonderland. And, in fact, I will hand off this job next month and return to my own research. Sometimes it's useful to give that part of my brain time to process information on its own. That's how it works for me. Call this just another stint in the patent office." She grins at him with fierce, friendly energy; she knows her eyes are twinkling. "I think that we're on the verge of some very, very big changes. Things that will truly change humanity."

He shakes his head. "There's no appetite for that."

"Of course not. We have a fabulous playground here. It's like when Walt Disney died and his Experimental Prototype City of Tomorrow morphed from a serious attempt at living the dream of the future to one of the most successful amusement parks of all time."

He stares blankly. He has no idea what she's talking about.

No surprise. She says, "Not everyone shares your view."

She refers to her fellow research scientists and astronauts, to their wild romance with space, to how hard they work, on the other side of this Mobius strip, in the humming hive of *Moku*, and its environments of rain forest, high sierra, deep sea, and other ecosystems vital to life to realize these dreams.

It is her dream, too.

That is why she is trying to fill her present post to the best of her ability. All of her fellow shipboard dreamers, in their long lives, have followed many passions, done much good work, earned many, many degrees. Each takes turns doing the necessary administrative work of keeping the dream alive. An outsider would only botch things. Their core group has logged much more space time than is strictly allowable, on ISS, Tranquility, Mars. They are hungry for space and all that it means.

Dr. Zi is not one of them. Zi and figureheads like him come, increase their ratings, and go.

She clears her throat. "It is your sworn duty, as Chief Safety Engineer, to ensure the safety of this ship." She almost says *Unless you have a conflict of interest*, but because she is trying hard, and because she has simmered down, she does not.

She presses on. "Sure, the Mars tragedy has been smoothed away after only four years. All the reports are buried by interminable committees while celebrities take up everyone's short attention span with their gaudy pairings and unpairings. Money can manipulate anything." She does not say *Including you*, but decides he could not hear that even if she shouted it to his face.

"I fail to see your point."

"It's been a while. Let's review. Seven lovely young reality stars, men and women without a shred of technical background, set out in a rover as a publicity lark and drive over a cliff. Live feed killed before it gets to Earth; no backups. Easy. The world mourns for a while, but without visuals, pretty soon it's like it never happened.

"Here on *Moku*, we have seventy-two entertainment workers—publicity crews, trainers, scripters, and assorted interesting many-gendered, well-known celebs who have gone through a few drills but who have been lulled into thinking that we are not hanging in space in a complex system that at this instant is undergoing massive, continuous updates and repairs. A hundred and twelve tourists. Fifty-seven parents. Their children. I'm not talking about the crew, the academics, the research scientists, all of whom have at least four doctorates, know the risks, and are emergency-ready. The civilians do not know the risks. It is your *job* to care. To protect them. And there is a matter of the highest urgency that—"

"Dr. Hsu, I resent these implications." A ping sounds. He stands. "Time for me to lead a tour through the Nanotech VR Lab."

She also stands, and says, working her device, "If you could possibly inspect the lab, while you are there, in regard to these three issues . . . I mean if you have *time* . . . in fact . . . I've sent this to all Level 5 personnel."

He roars, "You will *not* go over my head!"

"I'll share to the same contacts my full, updated report within the hour. I expect you to read it and to respond."

He fumbles with another shot of salad—vodka-infused? she wonders—and makes his way through the crowded bar, another of Pele's safety nightmares. As is the *Moku* Gift Shop, the Full Immersion Module (Experience Surfing the Rings of Saturn!) and the Hotel.

A parent who has been hovering nearby takes Dr. Zi's place. Ann is Ghanaian, a lovely, warm woman, wearing a dress of bold African colors, proud that her strange, heartbreaking baby has grown to be not only functional, but wondrous. As are all the parents.

"Dr. Hsu, it is *so* good to finally have a chance to actually *talk* with you." She takes both of Pele's hands in hers and squeezes. Pele squeezes back as Ann continues talking. "Thank you for the wonderful things you have done for Kevin. You are such a role model. You were our beacon on this long, long journey. If you could do it, so could Kevin. You know how it is—a roller coaster. The realization that your child is . . . *different*. The diagnosis—the *work*—" Tears stand in her dark eyes.

"I do know," says Pele, because first, she knew it from the inside. Though this is a common conversation for her, she gives each her full, deep attention. "It does get easier. I promise. You have done all the right things. Every day, there are breakthroughs."

Ann blinks, and her tears overflow. She dashes them away, and a smile lights her lovely face. "What you're doing here—it's just incredible. I never dreamed that Kevin would be *communicating* with so many other people—all of the international children who were on the first Gifted Expeditions! They are all so brilliant—and so many are Asperger's spectrum. My husband and I can't make head nor tail of what they do, and we are both professors. It's all so technical, and in their own codes, but apparently they work in shifts, twenty-four seven—"

This is like a deep gong sounding. The puzzle Pele was trying to discuss with Zi snaps into a single, frightening picture.

Pele keeps her voice low and calm, her eyes steady on Ann's eyes. "Ann, this is very important. I need to see this information. I—"

Something on the far side of the bar catches Pele's eyes. Her fiancée, Gustavo, threads his way through small groups of parents gathering for

Marsrise. Just the sight of him has the power to change her into a different person, which she welcomes. She is happy, relaxed, made new. She is still in love, after two years.

She waves; he changes course toward her, his movements uncharacteristically urgent.

Gustavo is warm, sweet, humble, and kind, his twin fields astrobiology and artificial life. She has not been married for two decades, when her second partner regendered, as Pele had always thought probable. Twelve great-grand-children thrive all over the world, and she follows their rich lives with avid interest. He has a similar family.

Gustavo drops onto an empty zabuton next to Pele. He smiles, but his grave expression crystallizes Pele's apprehensions, assembling inchoate murmurings she has caught edge of—and voiced—in a final, definitive snap of realization.

He glances at Ann, nods in greeting, and takes a deep breath. Pele knows he is making his voice sound normal with great effort. "Can you spare a moment for a conference in the Venus Room?"

Code for serious emergency.

The hair on Pele's arms rises.

All crew members are ready to fully assume many roles on the ship, according to situation and scenario, and are well-qualified for each.

He is calling her to one of hers. And he must remain here.

He grabs her hand, squeezes it with tremendous warmth. Turns his face for a brief kiss, an embrace she returns, giving herself to it completely, suddenly knowing it might be their last.

She rises, gives Ann and Gustavo a brief Buddhist nod, hands pressed together, and in that action prays for all sentient beings. Since her childhood, this prayer has been vast, and, as she followed her devotions, her definition of the scope has grown daily.

"Excuse me, please." As she passes murmuring groups of people she feels resigned, sad, but also infinitely lightened, pulled by glowing, roiling galaxies, by the romance she first felt upon the midnight sea between Tonga and Hawai'i, when she was twelve, the stars so close she could almost grab them by the fistful, when time seemed like a miraculous toy, something she could put her mind to and learn, a story to which she might give voice.

She has always been that child. As she approaches the lock, she cannot help breaking into a run, eager as all those children. All her sensible, deep fears cannot hold her back. She turns at the last movement and becomes a mudra. Signs to Gustavo:

Aloha

He signs back. She sees tears on his face, feels them on hers.

She spins abruptly; enters the real world.

Fairy tales are as good a way as any to say these things. They lived in cities as they had in dark forests. They live in space and they live in time, however strange it has become.

This is the foot of the wave function hitting bottom. This is the flying foam of the wave flickering off, blending with, becoming another kind of time, dynamic, compelling.

This is a girl walking downhill on the flank of a mountain overlooking Pearl Harbor, bare feet on hot white concrete, immersed in plumeriascented eversummer, flipping a small, white, smooth stone into the air, leaning forward, catching it, and thinking: if *this* flip, and *this* flip, and *this* flip could be described by mathematics, that is a thing I would like to learn.

She is the princess, waking.

She is the one who wakes time.

There is a console immediately inside Pele's portal, amongst the wires, tubes, and pipes of a functioning spacecraft, positioned on one of the long arms that lead to the fifty acre central atrium. Opening several screens at once, she sees that her fears are correct.

Someone has begun the launch. In fact, four days earlier. No one knew; she doesn't know why they know now. A shadow program.

Yes, they are brilliant.

Ninety minutes left until the nukes, behind the shield, move them from their perch. The entertainment and other modules are not designed to stand the thrust, a situation she opposed from their inception. After that—well, Zi is partly right. Who knows what might happen? She has always fought for reconfiguring the ship to support a different drive, but it remains theoretical, so she had little support. Still, many possibilities are embedded in *Moku*. Solar sails; many models of generation ships to which the ship can mechanically reconfigure. And other possibilities, awaiting the kind of nanotech enlivenment that has not yet been born.

Pele says, "Override launch progression," her voice empowered to enact the procedure, as are the voices of a few colleagues.

"Cancelled," says a child's voice above her right ear.

Within minutes, she realizes that she is powerless to stop the launch. If she cannot stop it, no one can; her colleagues have equal abilities.

"Invoking emergency plan seven," she says. Seven will detach the external modules of hotels, gift shops, restaurants, and bars, after evacuating civilians, whom she sees are being extracted from the virtual environments, the ecosystems, the build-your-own-exoplanet immersion attraction. They will head back to Earth, safe. She sees that, luckily, a third of the civilians are in their hotel rooms, probably sleeping.

A face appears; it is her colleague Selena, brushing a wisp of brown hair away from her eyes. "Pele. We're all on L3, 7."

Blue dots on a map. "Together? In a breakaway?" Breakaways are, essentially, modules to be jettisoned in an emergency. She finds the yellow dots, the children. "Why are the children all on the bridge?" But she knows why.

"You don't understand," says Selena. "We all need to talk. In person. Now. Hurry."

She does understand. She does hurry.

Pele enters the breakaway breathless, and sees her friends, her colleagues, her fellow dreamers, surrounded by screens on which blink schematics, warnings, plans, arguing.

She has known all of them for a very long time. They have labored together, here and in their various universities, think-tanks, and labs, over the past fifty years, as technologies changed and changed and changed again, holding to the same vision, generating theoretical and actual drives, ship design, exoplanet possibilities, and iterations of *Moku* in model and, slowly, in reality. Most have rotated onto *Moku* for a total of at least five years, with breaks, and something is always new when each arrives. They are only a handful compared to all their colleagues on Earth, the Moon, Mars, and various space communities. They have never been together in this particular configuration, which changes monthly as some rotate out and others in, but have known each other from meetings and through their work for longer than most humans have lived. They number thirty-two.

She knows that they, like she, feel as if *Moku* is their own body.

"Pele is here," says Selena, and they all turn.

Pele says, "Earth should know, by now. We'll have radio backup."

Bijo, usually laboring in his beloved rain forest, which will never be ready, shakes his head, bowed like a slender, heavy-headed blossom after a downpour. "We are completely isolated. The children have blocked all communication."

The face of Ta'a'aeva, a glowing, bulky Polynesian girl, her short, black kinky hair shaved in a zigzag, her face patterned by a fierce, asymmetrical tattoo, appears on a screen. "We see you are all there. I am the spokesperson for the Intergalactic Federation of Gifted Children." Her deep, melodious voice rings through the compartment.

"We were all GC's," says Quinn, his thatch of dark hair falling across his face, hands on his hips, facing the screen. "Now we're Gifted Adults. Not quite as shiny as we were brought up to think we were. Knocked on our asses a few times. As far as I can tell, what really makes us gifted is getting back up again after that happens, every time. Living to be adults, which we have done. As adults, it's up to us to decide what to do so that you can live to be this old."

"This isn't a joke. You have no choice," says Ta'a'aeva, her voice calm. "We are leaving for Object Shining Leaf. You are all coming with us."

"Object Shining Leaf? The only place we're going is back to Earth," Quinn says, with finality.

Ta'a'aeva says, "The civilians are being returned to Earth. All of you are staying with us."

"May I please speak with Bean?" says Pele.

"Bean is busy."

But then Bean's shy, olive-colored face appears on another screen. She and Pele look at one another for a moment. Bean blinks, and swallows.

Quinn says, loudly, "Look here," but Pele shushes him with a hand.

"Bean, what's happening?"

Ta'a'aeva says, "I'll tell you," but Bean speaks, in a whispery, uninflected voice, and slowly. "We have recoded the ship. All of the children who have been here before, too. All of us have worked on it for years. Some of us since we were little. I didn't even know what this was, really, when I started. They gave me things to do. Every problem was like a new toy or a new puzzle. It was fun." She closes her eyes and nods as if to some internal rhythm. Her screen goes dark.

Ta'a'aeva says, "Half of us want to kick you off the ship. Me included. We don't need any bosses. We want to get adults out of the picture. You live too long and hog up all the air. You can't think in new ways. You have a vested interest in maintaining the status quo."

"That's not true!" says Quinn, hotly.

Ta'a'aeva ignores him. "Some of the insecures think we might need you eventually."

"Like now," says Mi, a swarm robotics specialist. "My respectful advice is that you call this off."

"Not possible. We initiated the launch sequence for the Orion drive before we even arrived. The nukes are armed. No one noticed, right? Think about that."

"But why?"

Ta'a'aeva wrinkles her nose in disdain. "*Moku* was completed thirty years ago. She could have left then. But, mysteriously, the launch is always delayed. Brave, willing crews spend years in training limbo, all wasted."

"Not at all true!" objects Petr, a German who studies communication. "Their training yields crucial information."

Ta'a'aeva makes a moue of anger, which her tattoos intensify. "*Moku* has been turned into a money-making boondoggle. An amusement park. A research facility. A vacation destination. We are moving humanity's dream forward. Now. You won't find a way out." She disappears.

No way out? These words give Pele a fleeting, subconscious jolt.

"She's a brilliant engineer," says Victor. "We'd better believe her. She modeled something very like this in one of her past projects. If anyone can do it, she can. I personally approved her. I'm sorry I didn't realize—"

"That her dreams were real?" Selena smiles, closes her eyes, and resumes her habitual tuneless humming. "I'm leaving. I have great-greats." Selena, a mathematician, most often appears to be doing nothing. She walks a lot, taking swings through all the environments with a small backpack and hiking sticks. She lobbied vigorously for a High Sierra environment, and got it, manifesting a little-used gift for politics, though perhaps all simply went as one of her sociological models predicted.

Quinn says, "My vote is for staying, getting this under control, and stopping the launch. It is our responsibility to the world, and we have a moral responsibility to keep the children from the consequences of their unreason."

"Nicely put," says Prajan, tall as a corn stalk and as thin. He has slung himself against a wall, head bent over his device. He looks up, his eyes questioning; challenging. "So do you have a plan? Because the more I dig, the more I find that they trapped us here."

His mobile face shifts to immense amusement, and then his startling, uproarious laugh is magnified by the metal walls. "Heads in jars! That's what we'll be. Sparkling in a row, nutrient juice shot through with starlight, like in all those old, crumbling pulp magazines and sci-fi movies!" Wrapping his arms around himself, he bends over. "AHHAAhahaha." Tears trickle from the corners of his eyes, and he flicks them away with the forefingers of both hands. "Who says dreams can't come true? And usually at the most goddamned inconvenient time." He stuffs his device in his pocket, gazes downward, and continues to erupt in weak chuckles.

Wilhelm, a steady middle-aged physician, sighs, his brown, usually merry eyes sad. "I'm with Selena. I've got to get back home. I'm sure most of us are in the same boat. Ta'a'aeva is right. Space travel is not my dream. Using an off-planet environment to generate new therapies, new interventions, for all of us on Earth and Mars, is. And let's be honest. All of us, or our companies, have profited, and Jane is not the only attorney in our midst with the responsibility of making sure that their employer's contracts are honored, whether they be government, academic, or private industry, well past our own long lifetimes. Frankly, I've never even considered that they might at some point expire."

Quinn says, "They're just too damned smart. Their parents paid for genetic and neuroplasticity enhancements. AI nannies. They're probably not even human anymore."

"They are," says Pele firmly, "as much as any of us are." Silence.

By the way all of them shift their eyes from side to side, Pele sees they are all thinking things they dare not say.

Pele is finding it hard to focus.

Before the Hsus, during the nameless time, some kind hand floated Pele on her back, at night, in warm, protected waters, where she could watch the stars. Ala Moana, perhaps.

They know she was born in Honolulu, but there is a gap from that time until she was, literally, captured in an alley by social workers, restrained, drugged, confined, despaired over, until one day she found herself at the top of a mountain.

Petr squints, working his device. After a moment, he looks up.

"I've closed all of our outside communications with an emergency override, but they'll break through quickly. Let's talk."

She didn't know it was the top of a mountain; she did not use words, but the pictures were new, bright, powerful. There was distant blue, stretching forever, far below. Gigantic white big-porched house. Children of all sizes, staring at her.

Walter Hsu, an astrophysicist, and Sunny Hsu, a renowned child therapist, had quite a collection of children—five foster-children and three of their own—at the end of the road on Aiea Heights, along with transient young nannies sparkling with laughter, refugee chefs of all nationalities, visiting international experts on every imaginable subject, screenwriters and crackpots, and a crowd of helpers, all part of the tribe.

Behind the house, tropical forest, a park, to the peak of the mountain. On the other side, miles away, a steep drop to the Kona side of Oahu. Huge mango tree dropping fruit the kids had to shovel into the gully once a week. Their neighbor's manicured Japanese garden at the far side of their house site, complete with a grumpy old Japanese gardener shaking his fist when they trespassed. A treehouse. The crumbling remnants of a sacred Hawaiian stone platform, a *heiau*, far down in the forest, the older children's secret.

But for now, there are just Pele's snapshots. Blue. Green. Wind on her skin. Faces, faces, faces. Teeth and eyes.

"Give her room, kids," says Sunny.

• • •

Briskly, Theresa, silent till now, sets forth a plan for containing and jettisoning the children back to Earth, a split-second manipulation of partitions, robots, and gas.

Here are two stories. Pele does not remember them. Yet, within her, they fight.

This is the first story:

Pele makes a dash for the trees, but the man grabs her by the waist. His face, when he hunkers down, is big and smiling. "My name is Walter. He takes her hand. "Let's take a look around." For some reason, she walks with him.

No one else can touch her.

She won't let them comb her hair. She shrieks and runs away.

Walter cuts it off swiftly; gently. She feels her head in wonder. Stares at them. Darts into the forest.

Weeks later, perhaps. Months. How would she know? Pele screams, flings a chair across the room, laughs. Kicks over a tall vase, which shatters.

"Whoops," says Sunny, rushing into the living room, carrying an empty black garbage bag. "Should have put that up." She grabs Pele and drops into a chair, holding Pele tightly in her lap.

Pele is a storm of sharp elbows, wriggling on the crinkly, slippery bag. She straightens, bends, twists, fights with all her might, grunting and crying in rage. She has to escape! She will! She is stronger and faster than everyone! She always gets away!

"That's okay," says Sunny from behind her. "You can fight me." Sunny's long, black hair brushes the side of Pele's face. Pele tries to grab it, but Sunny deftly uses her left arm to hold down both of Pele's arms, her right hand to push back her hair.

As she writhes, Pele feels Sunny's strong, skinny arms around her. She bounces on Sunny's hard, bony thighs. When she kicks with her heels, Sunny leans down, pins her legs. "That's okay. I won't let you hurt me. You can fight with me."

The other children gather round, watching from a safe distance. Sunny yells, "Get away, you kids! This is our time. Pele's and mine." They scatter.

Pele turns her head to bite; a firm, flat hand presses her chin, keeps it forward. "I can't let you hurt me."

Pele spits; drool runs down her face. She shrieks. "Faugh!"

Sunny says, insistently, her voice low and firm, "What do you want?"

Pele bears down and pees. Surely this woman will let her go!

"I have a plastic bag on my lap, Pele. Pee all you want."

Pele erupts into a frenzy, but is gently, firmly, held.

"What do you want?" Sunny says. "Tell me. *Tell* me!"

It bursts from her. "Let me go!"

"Ah! All right!" The arms release. She springs free!

Pele faces Sunny, scowling. Sunny smiles at her, gently. "You see? Talking does things. I am listening."

She opens her arms. Crying, Pele rushes into them, and nestles in a warm embrace. "Let go," she demands.

Sunny's arms open.

She still doesn't talk. But she knows she can, if necessary. And that someone is listening.

This is the second story:

The whole family is at Oahu's Pali overlook, behind a low stone wall. The parking lot is full; people mill around, exclaiming, buffeted by the wind.

The drop below is steep; breathtaking.

Pele likes it up here. She likes it a lot. She shrieks like the wind. "Whoooo. Eeeeeeaaaah!" She runs to the side, spies a faint trail, leaps over the stone wall. Runs faster. Get away!

Get away!

The side goes down, straight down. The wind pushes at her. She trips on a root, starts to fall.

A strong arm grabs her. "Pele!"

Walter leans against a tree behind them, holding her so tightly that it hurts. He is shaking. He is crying.

"Please, Pele. Please. Don't ever do that again."

Pele listens to Theresa's plan.

Selena interrupts. "This has a fifty percent chance of succeeding. Actually . . . I'm tuned into their chatter . . . closer to forty, though it does fluctuate." She closes her eyes in that dreamy way of hers, a slight smile on her face. "No . . . now sixty-two point five three seven . . . "

Pele says, "No. Absolutely not. We are responsible for the children. Some of them will die."

"It serves them—" begins Quinn, then realizes what he's saying. They are all getting heated; they are on the verge of panic.

"We have two thousand, three hundred and thirty-two seconds to decide," says Selena.

Quinn says, "Well, Pele, it seems that you're in charge, and that you're on their side. Instead of the punishment they deserve for jeopardizing the one thing that's unified our planet, and into which we have poured immense treasure, they'll just leave and die, and so will we, as their prisoners. *Moku* is still here because it is, truly, perpetually unfinished. Technology is always changing. But the chief reason is that the voyage is impossible to survive in any meaningful way."

• • •

Ala Moana, press-worthy hullaballoo, picnicking families, hula dancers, the mayor of Honolulu, slack-key guitar, the smell of roasting pig. All are gathered for the ceremonial setting forth of *Moe'uhane*, a fifty-foot traditionally built double-hulled canoe, to Tahiti. Tall, triangular sails, filled with wind that keeps the anchor line taut, blaze red in the noonday sun.

It is called Wayfaring, the Polynesian way of sailing over vast distances, targeting an island of a few square miles using complex techniques that draw on memory, wave patterns, star navigation. As birds cross the sea in their thousand-mile journeys, so do they sail.

Walter is a friend of Bob, who will guide *Moe'uhane* on its long trip using only traditional star navigation. The Hsu tribe is right up front on bamboo mats when Bob begins his star chant. His deep voice rises.

"Hoku lei'i . . . "

Pele, a brown, skinny five-year-old in a faded red bathing suit, one long black braid undone, steps forward into his circle, opens her mouth and joins the chant, in Hawaiian, completely unselfconscious. Her singing voice, unlike her harsh, flat speaking voice, is sweet and high.

She *knows* this ancient chant—the directions for finding not just one island, but many, thousands of miles across the trackless sea.

Walter and Sunny share a look. This comes from a different part of the brain than speech. Laid in early, during the mystery years.

Another way in. Another way out.

When twelve, Pele crews on a star-navigation trip to Samoa on the *Moe'uhane* with her father, other scientists and adventurers, and Bob.

Waves rush beneath them with a show, rhythmic *whoosh*. The canoe rises and falls, its lashed joints creaking, its tall sails filled with salt wind. Pele, drenched with spray, stands braced on the forward platform, holding tight to the kaula ihu, the forestay line, with one hand. Thus immersed in immense, intensely black night, Pele answers with her voice. Pulsing stars move chant from deepest memories to her chest. She is a living tone, vibrating with ancient mindmap, with *voyage; mission: huaka'i*; a parade through time and space, which she now leads as pathfinder. She is a still point in deep infinity whose slow, reeling movement finds voice in song, lapped, increasingly for Pele, by mathematics.

As she chants, Bob gently shapes and teaches. But he has also learned from her. Whoever taught her, and then abandoned her, for whatever reason, was a master navigator.

"Look—there," he says, when they pause. "Iwakeli'i. Cassiopeia."

Walter points. "Tau Ceti. Might have livable planets."

Pele stretches on tiptoe, links one arm around the ihu, opens her hands wide, pulls stars to her chest, looks at Walter and asks, "How?"

There are fourteen emergency protocols regarding kidnapping, hostages—their situation—that they can put into play via a private sign language they all know.

But someone has to make the call. Everyone looks at Pele.

The wordless place of pictures that Pele has concealed so well through all the tests, all her life, once she knew it might come back to bite her, rears up like a tidal wave that's touched bottom in its travel over fathoms of water.

There is holding.

There is letting go.

She does both.

"All of you are leaving. I will stay, with them. *Au i ke kai me he manu ala!*" With that, holding them with the energy born of their own surprise, like the throw of a jujitsu master, she steps back, closes the portal, and launches them.

To cross the sea like a bird.

Like released seed pods, the modules, expelled, move rapidly from the *Moku*, their manual control overridden by programming the children created. The slice of Mars grows. Pele releases her held breath when her information panel notes ignition of their maneuvering rockets, which will increase their speed.

"Hsu!" Zi's contorted face is on her monitor. "There will be repercussions." The sound of wild screaming floods into the comm channel, drowning out Zi's voice. He switches to another channel. She can still hear dull thuds.

Quinn, in their breakaway, appears. "Pele!"

She says, "Is everyone safe?"

Selena's voice breaks in. "I would not have predicted this success."

Quinn's black eyes hold more than rage. Terror, or just the rapid analytics required to deal with the unfolding situation? He barks, "Success? Broken bones. Abrasions. One death thus far. Sure to be more." Pele hears a great commotion on the other screen; recognizes Ann and other parents as they crowd round the fish-eye lens. "Come back," shouts Ann. "Return Kevin right now!"

Jane, the lawyer, yells, "You have committed piracy. Kidnapping. Treason. Child abuse. Manslaughter."

Pele orders, "All craft move away with maximum speed. I have no control. The nukes, activated by the GCC, will detonate in seconds. They are contained, but—"

A tall, young boy is next to her. He touches her elbow. "Dr. Hsu. I am Eliott. Chimerist." The wailing, frantic parents arrayed before him quiet. To them, Eliott says, "We apologize for injuries. We did our best to create a plan that would minimize them. We are all well. We have not been kidnapped. The reverse, perhaps. We have sent you our story. Listen to it. Do not blame our colleagues on Earth. You cannot blame us, of course. We are children. Communications are now blocked until we choose to re-open them."

To Pele, he says "Hurry."

In Nucleus, the op center of *Moku*, Pele sees thirty-seven children—short, tall, round, thin, each from a different country and culture, monitoring and managing the ship, a cohesive crew with their own Esperanto, which Pele took care to learn. Many, like Ta'a'aeva, are not Aspies; she knows that she has focused on those who are because of her own history.

Pele makes a rapid tour, gives a few suggestions, which are seriously considered and often executed. She could be in any of the many ships, private and government-backed, that she has had the privilege to serve on over the past fifty years.

Bean, ten, is the youngest. Ta'a'aeva's on-board fourteenth birthday drew a record-making number of viewers just last week, and she is oldest. Most have at least one college degree. Pele has interacted with all of them, and henceforth—but there is no way to understand this enormity—neither she nor they will ever know any other humans.

"Don't worry," says Eliott. "We have done this, virtually, a million times. We know all the contingencies."

"And my decision?"

"Scenario 174."

She knows she could ask any of them and they would know that number, all the others, and what each would have entailed, just as she knew what Venus Room meant.

The ship announces, "Crew, prepare for nuclear ignition."

Pele steps into the nearest empty booth on the wall of the circular space, which cocoons her, leaving her face free. For a wild, silly second, Pele is reminded of nothing so much as being strapped into a tilt-a-whirl at the state fair, waiting to be spun through the air, held to the wall by the force of gravity.

She can hear their conversation in her headphones, and sees a good number of their faces. Only a few look appropriately grave. Some grin. She hears a wild, shrieking laugh, and some self-congratulatory talk of victory, as if this is a virtual game they have won. Perhaps it is.

How can they imagine the horrors Pele foresees? They are so terribly young. They have had no chance to learn about life, and now they never will. The freedom of Earth, the freedom of choosing another road, and another, and another. The delight of communicating with and learning from a rich, diverse population. The road they face is hard, narrow, and probably impossible. Doubt, anger, and regret rage through her; she struggles against the restraints, her chest a dark, sad weight. She has saved them only for an impossible task.

She always blacks out at five g's, but until then, she desperately thinks, plans, wonders, *What can I do to help them survive?*

Pele is six. She sits crosslegged on a large, cool rock across from her brother Jack. Their knees almost touch. The waterfall, which the kids often visit, is small, but makes a pleasing sound as it rushes over rocks. The tumble of fresh water washes the air. Small dark fish hang in the shadows. Fallen red lehua blossoms drift on the surface.

Jack is fifteen, one of the Hsus" three natural children. Dapples of light brighten his straight, black, shoulder-length hair as wind shifts the forest canopy above them and blows it across his face. He is the only one of the children she has anything to do with. The others just seem like a lot of noise.

"Okay. Let's try again. Look at my face. Can you tell how I feel?"

She stares intently at Jack's teeth, sorting the long call of the i'iwi, the amakihi's chatter, the sweet song of the apanane.

"No, Pele. My eyes. Raise your chin. Look."

She does. He draws his eyebrows together, glares at her. "Tell me—what am I feeling?"

She shrugs.

He thrusts his face forward, retaining the ferocious look, and says, "I am angry! Now I will make you feel angry. Pele, you are stupid!"

She leaps to her feet and lunges down at him, fists forward. He catches her wrists, one in each of his hands. "That is anger, Pele. You feel angry. I feel the same way. I am angry that you tried to hit me! Tell me what my face looks like! My mouth! My eyebrows! My wrinkles!"

As he holds her wrists in mid-air, it dawns on her. "I can tell how you feel by looking at your face?"

He lets go and nods. She drops back onto the rock and rests her chin in her hands. The water is dark green, then clear and sparkling where the sun hits it.

He says, "Now you look worried. You're thinking. What are you thinking?"

She says forcefully, "I am wondering why you are bothering me. I am thinking that this is too much work."

"It's work for me too. But I like to work with you. You're my sister, and I want to help you."

"I don't need help."

He says, very gently, "Please look at my face for just a minute."

She does, reluctantly. "You are looking right at me. Into my eyes."

"Tell me how my face looks."

"Your eyes are open very wide. Your look is strong. It almost hurts me. It makes me feel . . . "

He nods encouragingly. "Feel what?"

"I don't know. Is there a word?"

"I am trying to tell you with this look that I care about you."

She wonders how she can memorize a look, and how Jack's look would seem on someone else's face. It all seems quite impossible. "Why?"

"My older brother lived here when I was little. He was our parents" biological child too. He could never look at me. I loved him. He's a grownup now. His name is Edmond Hsu. He's a mathematician, eh? You can see his work online. He started college when he was twelve and lives on the mainland now. I was always sad that he would never look at me. Mom told me that I shouldn't be sad, that he didn't know what we were feeling and thinking."

"So?"

"I think that you can know, Pele." He smiles.

She looks back at the pool. "Then what do I feel now?" She knows that she feels vaguely out-of-sorts. She is not sure what any of this means.

"Grumpy." He jumps up. "Come on. Bet I can beat you back to the trailhead!"

She gets up more slowly and stands, hands on her hips, nodding. "Grumpy."

Another day, he hands her a wet rag while she is in the back yard throwing rotten mangoes at a big tree in the gully and watching them smash. "Wash your hands. I know you can read. Try reading this."

"No!" She throws *The Wizard of Oz* on the ground as he walks away.

Irritated that this does not bother him, she picks it up, wipes mango goo from the cover, and reads aloud to the gully in a shouting voice: "*When Dorothy, who was an orphan, first came to her, Aunt Em had been so startled by the child's laughter that she would scream and press her hand upon her heart whenever Dorothy's merry voice reached her ears; and she still looked at the little girl with wonder that she could find anything to laugh at.*"

She turns and faces the house, where Jack might still be listening. She hopes he is. "So? I am an orphan. I scream a lot. AIEEEE! And sometimes I hate it when people laugh!"

The trees swish in the wind, and the palms make rain-pattering sounds beneath the blue sky.

She does nothing for three days except read *The Wizard of Oz*. When she is finished, she marches into Jack's room, where he is studying, and smacks it down on his desk.

"I am very angry with you," she shouts.

"Why?"

"Because this made me sad and afraid and worried."

"Anything else?"

"I was happy and sad at the same time when Dorothy got back home. I hated it!" "Why?"

"I just did!"

Jack smiles as she stomps from the room. Next, he gives her a curious old volume, *My Bookhouse: Through Fairy Halls*. It is a hefty book, bound in black leather, with vivid pictures that seem like music, because of the way they move in Pele's mind. It smells funny. The pages are dry. "Take care of it," he says.

Pele is walking on a treadmill. A girl stands next to her, watching.

"Are you Bean?"

"That's the first time you remembered."

"I told you a story."

The girl looks straight at Pele. Her eyes are hazel with flecks of gold. "A girl lived in the mountains of Tibet. She was trying to escape from the Chinese and broke her leg and nearly starved to death." Bean purses her lips, looking confused. "You said I couldn't give her any powers, and I couldn't earn any weapons, so I couldn't help her. Things just happened and then it was over and nobody won, but she did get out and became a hero. You said it would change my brain. I tried to measure that, but I couldn't. I think I need more stories to do that, or I have to figure out a new way of measuring."

"Usually when I was your age I liked a story if it made me cry."

Bean flashes her a startled look. "You liked to cry?"

Pele smiles. "It is kind of strange, isn't it?"

Bean frowns. "I will tell you my story. It is about a horse. I don't know if you would like it. It doesn't have an ending."

"I think I know your story. But there are many ways to tell every story. Tell it to me again. I'm sure that it will make me cry."

As Pele strides back into trance, into dream, Bean wonders why tears flow from beneath Pele's closed eyelids.

"Pele!"

Ta'a'aeva stands in front of her. Bean leans close, against her left arm. They are all gathered, all looking at her.

Ta'a'aeva speaks. "We need your help. It is almost completed, we think. But you are the one who can do it. We are glad you have come. But be here! Please wake up!"

Obviously, a dream.

• • •

Pele, in her own little house, a chicken coop in a row of chicken coops long ago completely sanitized, used, and abandoned by various Hsu children.

Hers has weather-smoothed streaks of white paint, abundant sun that lies on the floor in a slant, a shelf where hens once roosted crowded with a row of old books. Large, castoff cushions on the floor.

She is seven.

Her brothers and sisters rush down the gully, a crescendoing cavalcade of pounding feet. They surround her house, yelling. Rocks bounce off the side. Diane peers in the window, howls with laughter. "She's reading those silly fairy tales again!"

"Yeah, she likes those old books. I loaned her my screen and found it in the trash can!"

They leap around the chicken coop, yelling, singing, beating on it with sticks, making it shake when they try to push it over.

Pele, lying on her stomach, barely hears them. She is in worlds of ogres, fairies, magic boots, menehunies, stupid children, endless journeys, flying carpets, talking animals, and powerful goddesses like her namesake, a dangerous woman whose actions are unpredictable and thrilling, who created the Hawaiian Islands with her volcanoes. They are more real than people, and certainly much more interesting.

She does not even notice when the clatter recedes. Rain patters on big-leaved trees, sun speeds across the floor, she smells sweetly rotting mangoes mixed in the brisk, whipping breeze, and reads.

Sunny's sideways head and shoulders darken the coop's small door. "It's getting dark. Come inside."

Pele, her head propped on her elbows, is reading about a giant. "No."

Sunny smiles, sets a water bottle, a package of dried squid, and a book light inside, then leaves.

When Pele wakes the next morning in her own bed, she has a memory of being carried through the night, and the stars. Next to her on the bed is *Through Fairy Halls*, her favorite of the Bookhouse volumes. She opens it and starts to read. Grimm, Anderson, the Blue and Green and Red books follow, and then folk and fairy tales from around the world. Wise and wily rabbits, lions, crickets and tortoises argue, beguile, win, lose. And Fairyland itself?

Oh, there is music and dancing in Fairyland. No yesterday, and no tomorrow. Pipes call. Trumpets sound. The low are made high, and the high are surprised and chagrined.

There is a dangerous edge to Fairyland, which Pele enjoys. One flirts with it to one's own peril.

And part of her now, the living dreaming part, knows that she has crossed the border. Nightingales, clear springs, great rose-trees whose rich scents confound the senses. The large made small; the small, large, and one's own self made true.

And Time a leafy, sun-dappled orchard.

Gray horse, crunch of sweet, crisp fruit, swish of long silver tail.

Long ago. Ever-now.

She is Gulliver, pounded by tiny fists.

"Please, please, wake up! We need your help! We can't do it alone! Please, please, wake up!"

She opens her eyes. Bean is there. "You have been asleep for a long, long time, Pele." Her eyes are grave.

"This is too slow," says Kevin, shaking her arm. "We're only transiting Venus. We'll never get to Shining Leaf."

Ignoring trumpet fanfares, Pele calculates, considering Orion's acceleration, that she has been asleep for three months.

Ta'a'aeva says, "We can't make the drive work. You know how. Tell us! Tell us, and we'll engineer it. You know that we can."

Pele says, "Get me out of this." As they unstrap her cocoon, she looks at a nearby screen. "I've been exercising three hours a day on the bike? Really?"

"You weren't awake," says Eliott. "You were in a trance."

"Indeed," she says, taking in the compressed graphic of her brainwaves for the past few months, noting the sharp spikes that she knows linger in her mind like haunting, exotic music, calling her to return.

It takes all her will to remain where she is, on *Moku*, where she has committed a powerful, monstrous act. She sees the resolve of the children arrayed around her and knows that she cannot gain control of the ship. She knows that they would have done this without her help.

She tries to believe that they are better off with her here. She must make that true.

She also sees, scrolling, continuous, messages from Earth. With a touch, she speeds them up, goes backwards, absorbs them like a blow, for it is all her fault.

And Gustavo. She searches wildly, finds a tiny line of news—

"No!" She raises her hands to cover her face, and sobs, slumping back into the cocoon, curling up so that no one, no one, can see her.

She does not re-emerge for another spell. But now, her dreams are new. She is working.

Bean sees Pele first.

She is standing just outside Nucleus, where diagrams, equations, charts, and virtual models of FTL drives litter the air in transparent, three-dimensional overlays. She has been watching, listening to the hum of intense concentration, several intertwining musics that tangle and leap within her long-quiet mind, and getting ready to turn and re-enter her cocoon.

The displays rainbow Bean's slight body as she approaches Pele, her stare a powerful command. She takes Pele's hand and, as the others gather, leads her to an array of cushions. Pele settles on one, back straight, legs crossed, and says, direct from her hard-won beginner's mind, "You don't really need me. Are you ready to tell us, Bean?"

First, Bean's eyes widen as she tilts her head at Pele.

Pele nods. "I know."

Bean frowns and clenches her fists. "I've been trying. It's closed in. Like a hard nut. I can't tell it. No one understands."

"Try another way."

Bean takes a deep breath, then shakes her head and makes her long hair swirl round her face. She stretches her long legs out in front of her, grasps the soles of her feet with her hands, tucks her head in, and silences.

"Bean, who is in this story?" asks Pele.

She asks three times. Finally Bean says, her head still down, her voice muffled, "It is a story about a horse." She walks her hands up her calves, singing more than speaking, bends both knees to the right, and kneels, her spine ramrod straight, hands moving as in a hula, shaping the story in space. "Sometimes the story seems short, and sometimes I know that it is actually very, very long. "On the pampas, I ride Alcubierre, my silver mare, all day through the wheat. It parts and lets us through." Her hands speak in swift, darting signs now: her own language, Pele knows, which they must learn.

Another way in. Another way out.

"It makes a swishing sound, like wind, and then the sounds are a music that might keep me there forever. They are . . . enchanting."

Pele hears what Bean hears; it assails her even now, calling her.

But she cannot, will not, succumb.

Bean's eyelids are half-closed. She speaks as if in a trance. "Alcubierre *pulls* the mountain closer when she gallops. She and I—we do not move. We remain the same, and in the same place. The wheat is *time*. Flowing and parting around me.

"I thought of this story for a whole year. I worked on it in my head when I rode. I see us from above. Alcubierre's tail flows out behind her, white, blending and waving with the golden wheat. It is long . . . long . . . long . . . " She lowers her head as if in apology and whispers, "But still. The story is not in words."

"Ah," says Pele, grateful when Bean stops speaking, and the imperative music fades. She has tried to wake before. It may be still a dream.

But she does not think so. "Show us."

• • •

The showing unfolds. It is complex, and long, as Pele knew it would be, and wakes her fully. All of them struggle to understand, to master various parts of it, to use theory to imagine this drive, to picture the concept of the space that it would use.

Xia, Chief Nanotechnologist, prepares to infuse the ship with her work and the work of a million materials engineers, biomedical engineers, environmental scientists—a synthesis of every science and engineering discipline—generated from a century of research and application.

They gather for a ceremony. Xia's black eyes are serious and steady when she speaks. "We will be enabled, today, through *enlivenment,* which is how we describe this coming change, to manipulate the matter of our ship at the atomic level. The rules we hereby embed within the ship are the final arbiter of what is and is not permissible, and the laws of physics govern what is possible. Among other benefits, we will all enjoy perfect health from now on."

Nucleus fills with huge, idealized atoms, strings of splitting and reconnecting DNA, and long sections of text. One section glows next to Pele, and she rapidly scans it, aghast.

Grinning, Xia shouts, "And we will all have tremendous fun!" Everyone except Pele whoops and cheers.

"Should we discuss it and vote?" asks Pele. They all look at her with amazement. "I've seen this before. It's a plan for—it *is,* I gather, a universal assembler—"

"There's nothing to vote on," Xia explains, her voice as gentle as if speaking to a small child. She holds a sheaf of small, square envelopes in one hand. "This was always part of the plan. All of us have contributed to it, in one way or another. We all know everything there is to know about it."

The fields of nanotechnology, a discipline drawing on all scientific disciplines, have blown far past Drexler's early visions. Pele has sat on international committees that debated the use of various iterations of nanotechnology. Some were approved, and some, which embodied the possibility of change so rapid and radical that the results could not be predicted, were left unused, and locked away.

Pele understands, and now knows that they understand as well, that this particular iteration is the ability to change matter swiftly, from the bottom up, to grow rather than to machine. This chameleon-like ability, this new plasticity, will include themselves—their minds, their bodies—as well as their surroundings. Everything. Within what limits? The limits of physics have not been fully explored. Not by a long shot. Things will change, evolve, and Pele doesn't know what, or how. Neither do they.

Alicia gives everyone an envelope. Pele opens hers and pulls out a round, paperish object.

"Why does this look like a communion wafer?" she asks.

"A what?" ask several children.

"The circle was my idea," says Bean. "It's . . . simple. It doesn't have any religion in it."

"I wanted water balloons that we could explode and scatter the replicators around," says Ta'a'aeva, scowling. "Nobody listens to me."

"Do we eat it?" asks Pele.

"You can," says Xia, but, imitating the children, Pele presses hers to the side of the ship, where, warmed by her hand, it is rapidly absorbed.

A brief, dazzling light rushes through the walls of Nucleus. The children break into wild dance, laughing, and spinning through the air.

O brave new world, thinks Pele, that has such people in't! She recalls her child-self, almost flying off the sheer cliff, and wants to grab them, and hold them back.

But it is far too late for that.

She soars and spins with the rest of them. Laughs. Forgets.

Is brave, again. For now.

The enlivenment, as the nanotech changes move through the ship, transforming its matter to a medium that they can easily manipulate, is slow at first, but increases in speed exponentially.

It makes their work much easier, and their environment becomes more dense, as if full of worlds it had been waiting to manifest.

Despite her fears, it is good, as far as she can tell. A rich and joyous thing.

The children, she realizes, do know more than she does.

For instance: Pele, strolling through the city, enters a musty used bookstore. It draws her in, past piles and towering shelves of books, farther and farther, until she realizes that she is in the children's library that Zi mentioned. Each title strikes her heart. Some make her cry. All open worlds in her mind, worlds she thought long-gone; worlds that submerge her, change, and release her.

With wonder, she pulls out an old, tattered, black book. On its cover is an illustration of a girl and boy unlatching an arched, stout, wooden door set in a stone wall. *The Latch Key*. Opening it, she first reads the frontis poem, written by Olive Beaupré Miller:

> Its windows look out far and wide
> From each of all its stories.
> I'll take the key and enter in;
> For me are all its glories.

When Pele looks up, after reading for hours, the store is gone; the street, likewise, has vanished. She sets the book aside, perches on a rock, stares at the stars, and remembers Gustavo, her children, his children, and her descendants, for a long, sweet time.

She hears those children shout to one another as they hide-and-seek in Earth's long, green summer evenings, sees them splash in their nightly bath and then their faces in soft lamplight, eyelids closing, as she reads to them these old, strong tales.

Perhaps, she thinks, that is the most good I have ever done.

She uses their new technology to create a tiny, whitewashed cottage that hangs in rain forest on a steep volcanic mountain. Far below, lush tongues of green, fringed with shining, black volcanic sand, invade the sea, which deepens to *kane*, the deep, blue shade of distance. Tatami mats cover the wide-plank koa floor. The trade wind rattles the hanging photos of Sunny, Walter, and all the kids against the wall. A bookshelf manifests any books she wants, including an old, well-worn copy of *Through Fairy Halls*, with its luminous cover plate of a girl and boy rushing ahead of a diaphanous winged fairy.

Pele sits on her front porch in a rocking chair, paging through the large, heavy book thoughtfully, as the growing drive undergoes troubleshooting and the songs of long-extinct finches wind through her thoughts. She hikes down an ever-manifesting ridge, rappels down a cliff to a tiny beach where she tests herself in treacherous currents, and flings herself, naked, on olivine sand, falling asleep to the roar of the surf. And wakes to space, ablaze with the stars she long planned to grasp.

Her soul rests a brief time, all she allows.

Then, while the children work, Pele turns to what needs to be done. She absorbs the threats, the messages, the stages of grief from Earth. It is hard. She can only do a bit of this task at a time, but she battles through it. She is the only adult here. It is her responsibility.

She wants badly to invent Sunny to have someone to talk to, and though she could, it would only be herself, so she does not. She is afraid to think about why she slept so long. She both knows and does not know, and both are useless to try to understand.

She knows her purchase on this new reality is tenuous. The part of her that loosed them is not rational, and she has fought it all her life.

But there is something she must do now that is more important than anything else she has ever done. That task holds her sternly *here*, on *Moku*, with its precious cargo of life.

Moku holds the world genome. They will start species, including humans, growing when they get close. To somewhere. After an unimaginable piece of time, when it is likely that none of them will be here, or that they will be so different that one could spend a million years just imagining the possibilities. What *Moku* will nurture, and why, will be based on immense data about the planet. A complex task, the vindication of what she has enabled, awaits.

Pele wonders, what will these new humans, these mammals who absorb culture, know? Who and what will teach them? When they forage among the wilderness of what the ship holds, who will they become? What culture will they construct?

It is her task to help them answer this question.

When she calls the children together, they protest. "We are working," says Ta'a'aeva, standing with her arms crossed as thirty-seven children gather in Nucleus.

"You haven't spoken to your parents since we left. You need to do that. Now."

Kevin sucks in his lips and clenches his hands, as he always does in times of stress, to keep them from trembling.

Ta'a'aeva's face hardens.

Alicia, who is thirteen, curses, rips a cushion from the floor, and floats it as hard as she can in Pele's general direction. "I told my mother I was leaving and that I'm never coming back!"

Bean bursts into tears and pushes herself down the tunnel to her berth.

"I hear all of you," says Pele. "Your feelings are mixed up, and hard to live with. How do you think they feel?"

"I'm tired of always trying to think about what other people are feeling," declares Xavier. "It's too hard."

"It's the hardest thing to do," says Pele.

When rent by a meteor, the ship heals. This is not magic. This is science.

Pele, Nedda, Bean, and Takay are sitting on the porch of her cottage, reading books.

As if in a dream, or a myopic haze, Pele sees sky and sea shatter, revealing an assault of blinding stars, and hears a huge rush, as on a beach where massive waves tower and break, and then they are enclosed by a thick, opaque membrane.

Pele is surprised when they all stand and begin to sing, each in a different language, in different tunes and meters, and that it sounds so beautiful. Time seems more slow, and although together they all speak their ever evolving Esperanto, they sing songs from their own earliest childhoods. Pele's mouth opens; her own song comes out, rich and deep from her chest, from her toes, from the far spaces of memory: the Wayfaring chant. From star to star to star. Like a bird transverses the sea. Maybe, indeed, she moves them with this chant. It seems so.

As they sing, life encloses not-life with a net that then thickens, expelling not-life with energy captured from the meteor. Not death—a lucky catch! The net extracts minerals, oxygen, carbon dioxide.

The scrim of matter opaques. They are made whole; enclosed.

They have new stuff to play with, to sustain them. The ship uses the meteor to grow more space, add more air, water the lettuce, grow the infant bristlecone pines in High Sierra.

To regrow the shattered cottage, and chairs, where they sit rocking, turning pages slowly, as a standing wave edges the blue Pacific far below, and plumeria sweeten the air.

They have communicated with one another by this time. The children and their parents.

Their parents had not remembered how strong the force of growing is. They had not remembered how they fought to leave home.

They wanted some kind of magic to protect their children, but all their love could not invent it. The children had torn themselves away, but that is what children do.

Before all this, the parents had worked very hard, even before the children were conceived, because this was The Future, and there was a lot that they could do. These parents wanted their children to be the very smartest, the very best, the most successful. They particularly did not want their children to turn out like the children of their relatives or their friends, who always did a terrible job, and in whose children the ways in which they had gone wrong were so obvious. They would do better.

When the children became teenagers, their sweet child faces changed, and their behaviors were not encouraging. Even though the parents had been teenagers and were sure that they would understand their own, a dark magic veil had grown between them.

I think that this is the first mention of magic in this fairy tale, but I'm not sure. Don't be too hard on us for not knowing exactly when this happened. A lot of fairy tales don't even realize that's what they are, much less come right out and admit it.

Anyway, once the kids were teenagers, the parents lost control. And yes, they were afraid, because they remembered how stupid they had been, and they had tried with all their might to deflect or change this stupid energy, and because it was The Future and they knew more about brains and human development, they thought they had it licked.

But no. They were still the same old humans in important ways.

The children didn't know that they were acting like robots and that they would miss their parents. They didn't know that just growing up creates this energy, and that there was nothing they could do about it. So all of the humans on Earth were pouring out their love, which was helpless to do anything now.

If the children had known how sad their parents would be, they would never have done it. At this point they are beginning to understand, but still do not learn how deep sadness can be. Not yet. Perhaps no one reaches the end of it, and, to survive, must simply choose another path, one with more useful stories. But, as you may know, that is another part of this story.

Worse than all that, the children finally realized that they had stolen something that their parents had worked hard for, *Moku*. The ship, and all of space and time, wasn't meant just for the children. It was meant for everyone in The Future, and for all the people in the world to benefit from. The people of Earth didn't realize this when they were building it. They thought they were making something they could let go of.

It didn't turn out that way.

It was all heartrendingly sad.

Finally, they had to let go.

The parents, the children. The children, Earth.

The people on Earth take a long time to decide how to say goodbye. They form committees, consider proposals, argue violently or with subtle skill, make deals, publish editorials, write learned papers.

It is taking longer and longer for Earth and *Moku* to communicate.

Finally, one day when it is almost too late, at a signal no one recalls initiating, they gather in cathedrals and squares and sing. They sing from flotillas of boats tethered together while they drink rum beneath fiery, poignant sunsets. They sing from observatories to the deep night sky, and as night flips swiftly to day in Bogota.

They sing from self-driving vehicles. Old people stop their tennis games to sing. Children sing in schools; there are still schools, only much better ones. Tech advisors, stock manipulators, and people who still do not have clean water but who do have a device sing. They sing from bars, from the Moon, and from every point in space where humans live.

When the song arrives at the ship, as they are passing Neptune's orbit, they piece it together and gather, standing, and listen, looking back from whence they came, those tiny dots of life holding all they have ever known. Seas, mountains, the three remaining tigers. The deep time and lucky chance that caused life. Winds that flatten vast fields of wheat with great, caressing hands, like the hands that once caressed them with such love and care.

This is what they hear:

Sleep, my child, and peace attend thee,
All through the night
Guardian angels God will send thee,
All through the night
Soft the drowsy hours are creeping
Hill and vale in slumber steeping
I my loving vigil keeping
All through the night.

The children, and Pele, hold hands and cry, knowing what they have lost. Pele knows that, for the children, it is the first step. It changes their brains. She does not know how she will get past it.

Perhaps, she thinks later, alone and staring at the place she thought she always wanted to be, she never will.

And now within the old gray tower
We've climbed the winding stair,
And look out over all the earth
From topmost window there.
Far stretches all the world away,
And naught shuts out the sky,
As knights and maids and all of life
Go marching, marching by.
                              —Olive Beaupré Miller
                              From the Tower Window

Finally, as they pass out of the solar system, it is time. They must get moving. They must set forth. They must transform.

And they do need her; they did bring her for a reason. She has lived this project, this drive, for decades, every detail of it. Bean's work has brought it to life, but there is no way to know how it will manifest, if they will survive, and, if they do, how it will change them. That part of it is greater than that which one can imagine.

All is in readiness. She is awake. The fulcrum is here. She has the lever to move it.

The minds, the dreams, of the children are the weight. They offer her thoughts, ideas, visions, insights, like flowers, which she gathers, and they all spark together, pointing toward fruition, the shift that will carry life forward.

This is humanity's main chance. She knows, but cannot think about, how important that is.

She prepares to play a vast chord, the way her piano teacher taught her, knowing it all first, in the instant before her spread fingers descend to the cool, hard, certain keys, back straight, elbows wide, with all she is contained within that force.

Pele plays.

This is the chord that sounds:

They are a creature of the deep sea, of interstellar space.

They are a thought, and thought is matter.

The ship, the matter, is like a film above, a fluid, a lens on the surface of their sky, the division between fluid and gas.

They coalesce: they rise.

Arrayed around Pele at that moment is a human orchestra, potential symphonies, jazz rhapsodies, new musics for which new brains to hear must be invented. On new planets, they may whirl and dance, skipping through the universe like stones, breaking through the surface tension of the strange fugue of time in which they are embedded, and sink back into life.

"Oh," she says, "oh." She bends over, weeping.

First comes Bean, whose willowy arms surround but barely touch her. Then Ta'a'aeva's rough embrace, her strong, gasping voice. Javail's tall blond head bending down to touch hers, and then they are all in a huddle, embracing tightly, crying, swaying, and, finally, laughing as they break.

"We will find the place we need," says Javail, his ever-adolescent voice breaking as he speaks, yet, as always, he sounds eminently reasonable. "As you can see, we have all the time in the world."

"We may need more," observes Pele, her voice harsh, and they break into applause that sounds, to Pele, like surf sounding at Kaena Point.

That is the last they see of her for a very long time.

There is music and frolic in the special time of Fairyland. No yesterday, and no tomorrow. Pipes call. Trumpets sound.

Nightingales, clear springs, the great rose-trees.

Magic. Some good, some bad, but uncaring of humans, rather like space.

Alcubierre eats Casimir Vacuums for breakfast, rips them out of a field with her big yellow teeth and chomps on them. The edges of the vacuums stick out of the sides of her mouth like gold straw and tiny blue flowers and move up and down as she chomps and snorts.

They are one speck of pollen on a single stamen of one small blue flower that bobs up and down in her mouth.

The Librarian carries a wooden clock.

It is chiefly oak. Framed by an oaken octagon a bit smaller than the main octagonal structure that holds the clock's mechanics and chimes, the face is protected by a glass door ten inches in diameter that one can open with a small latch. The hours are Roman numerals, painted on a cream-colored metal face. In black, swirling copperplate, a single word: *Excelsior*.

It has a smaller glass door, below, that one can open to start the pendulum swinging.

The Librarian carries it cradled in her left arm, like a baby. Therefore, it does not tick, for the pendulum drops against the back of its compartment.

The hands of the clock are silver, their deliciously narrow, elongated arrows a final flourish, pointing at the hour, the minute, and the infinite in-betweens.

A key rattles inside its small, latched drawer at the bottom of the pendulum when she walks, and the three square holes in the face's clock emit faint light. Sometimes she unlatches the drawer, opens it, and examines the key closely, with a look of wonder on her face. Then she returns it to its drawer and re-latches the tiny brass hook.

Every so often, she opens the door of the clock's face, tilts her head, smiles, and moves first the long arrow to a place that seems random, and then the small hand. She beams at the clock, shuts the door, and goes about her business. She never inserts the key. She never winds the clock.

If she has to do something requiring the use of her left hand, she sets the clock carefully in a safe place and immediately retrieves it when done. She straps it in beside her when she sleeps.

This seems a burdensome practice, but it gives her pleasure. Laying bets regarding various aspects of what she does with the clock have become popular.

It gives us something to do.

In one of the vacuums—there are many—I grew this voice that says *we*. I don't know how, though I am trying to tell you.

I might have grown it when I was Nancy Drew, in her blue roadster, driving through dark space, past planets. One . . . two . . . three . . . ten thousand . . . it took a long time. Then there were white farmhouses just off a dusty dirt road, hidden behind summer trees, their big heads tossing in the hot wind as if they had something haughty to say.

Inside one house with open windows a planet mobile rotated in the breeze. A girl with long black braids, lying on a double wedding ring quilt made by her grandmother, pointed to them and said, "Strike Hypatia off the list. And Dulcinea, too." They disappeared from the mobile, and others appeared.

I sped into the brain of the little girl and it was all myth, science, clockwork, precise, wires, pulses, blood, AI, luminous, expanding, nova, pressure, big bang, dust, and me, driving past on country lane in a blue roadster, hair streaming violently far, far, far out behind me, pushed by my own speed, seeing white snowball bushes in the front yard, and a cherry tree, and a woman gathering billowing white sheets from a clothesline, and a girl inside analyzing planetary composition.

You can see why I can't tell you exactly how it happened.

Pele looks like Pele, except that her eyes are different. She won't look at anyone. She does smile a lot. She calls herself The Librarian and says she would like to help us.

This is when the clock shows up. You know about that already.

We can't really blame her for acting this way. She had many areas of expertise when we stole the *Moku*, like all the other adults on the ship, but she was uniquely special, so we stole her too.

She knew how to make our horse.

She thinks that she chose to help us by staying with us and saved all the other adults by sending them back to Earth. She thinks she is our savior.

We let her think that because whenever she realizes that we have control, she acts in ways that are not helpful to us.

For instance, when the prince arrives to kiss her (and is the prince us, and what we did? it seems possible) she pushes him down, kicks him in the side three times (once or twice is not enough, while four or more is overdoing it), and strides off down a long, winding road, over hill and dale, hands in her pockets, whistling, looking at everything with a keen and watchful eye.

She walks through rain, hail, sleet, and snow, singing about it, all bundled up, sometimes an old woman, sometimes a young maiden, and then through summer meadows that climb the flanks of mountains, her clock in a bag that she throws over her shoulder. She wears loose, purple linen pants with large pockets, which she fills with things that seem useless.

She sees beautiful, glowing stones by the side of the path—one gray, one gold, and one rainbowed with layers of minerals. She picks them up and examines each, a large smile on her face. She puts them in her right-hand pants pocket.

To us they look like dull old rocks, but then somehow, like magic, we see them through her eyes, and know what they are. The stones and the power of stones are stories. She is gathering all the stories everyone has ever told, and *our* stories, and keeping them safe in her pocket until we know how to tell them. There are so many stories in that pocket that you would think her pants would fall down, but though the stories are endless, and the stones are all different, they do not, for the stones are magic stones; the pants magic pants.

Only if we sit around a fire that lights our faces and dances to the dark treetops whenever one of us throws on branches scavenged from the woods, throwing sparks into the night, does she consent to pull out a stone and tell us a story. We have to beg and yell at her. She says that only then are our brains receptive, when we are parched of stories.

She says this is a way to go back to the beginning, to break down our brains to a place we had bypassed in our speed to understand, and that was during the time that we were supposed to look at other faces and wonder what they were thinking. We were supposed to learn to understand when they were sad, when they were happy, and when they had feelings that were more complex, like a flavor or scent or a sound that comes out of the deep dark forest that is a sweet, mysterious music that calls you to come. She says this is the beginning of love.

When she talks like that, when she tells us stories, her voice is rich and deep, her face fluid, when often it is flat, like some of ours.

Her stories change our brains. We can even measure where and how much.

It's something to do.

Her eyes get very wide, or narrow to slits. Her mouth assumes strange shapes. Sometimes she opens it wide and screams, reaches to the sky and grabs at it, her hands open, then grasps as she suddenly! in an instant! catches something and pulls it to her chest, and bows her head over it, and her long white hair veils her mysterious face, pale in the moonlight, silent as one of her stones, and we cry without knowing why, feeling helpless and at the same time knowing that she will help.

It is the age of stories. We suck them down like nectar.

We search for our new home. We move like a sea creature through the dark, generating our own electricity. Fluid, ever-changing, Ship translucent or solid-seeming, as we wish.

We grow no older. Why? Biological processes continue; of course. We live. We do the things we need to do, but our horse is wise, and knows much more than we.

Pele is still there, though they don't know it. Or they do, sometimes. She fears a foray through some other kind of spacetime weather in which they will all age to telomerase endgame and die in what seems minutes. Who knows.

The instant that divides life and death. We must learn to skip it.

Periods of waking like cards constantly shuffled, the deck and game continually changing—the rules, the faces, the very basis of the numbers and what they mean.

• • •

"This one is too cold," says Isho, who is Goldilocks. "And this one is too hot."

"And none is just right, and none will ever be," screams Ta'a'aeva, who is always the biggest bear. She storms away from the cottage. Isho and Kevin, the middle-sized bear, drop into tiny green chairs, sobbing.

"That's not how it goes!" says Alouette, kneeling and holding Isho and Kevin in a skinny-armed embrace. "You know the story. Happy ending, and all that."

"No", says Kevin, his voice wild. "No! None of them are right. None of them ever will be right! There is no place for us in any universe except Earth. And it is gone!" He flings himself at Pele and tries to hit her in a flurry of punches. "My mother is gone! My father is gone! My sisters and brothers are gone! All these stories are lies!"

Pele holds him back for a moment, and just at the right time, she lets him collapse against her. She grabs him, holds him, rocks him back and forth. "I know, Kevin. Except this is not the end of the story. It's not the end at all."

Kevin fights free and runs.

Pele drops to the tiny stairs of the cottage and drops her head to her hands. It no longer matters whether she did the right thing or the wrong thing. Those words have no meaning. Here they are.

Ta'a'aeva returns from wherever she went, and stands next to Pele. "Sit up straight." Pele feels the girl's sure fingers dance against her scalp, hears the swift *thush thush* of braiding. "We are Wayfaring. We need to watch the sky, the birds, the waves. Kevin," she shouts. "Check out the signature of the star we found yesterday."

Kevin's sullen voice, muffled by tears, issues from the forest. "There is no signature. There is no star." A rock bounces off the side of the cottage. "Liar."

Pele hears Ta'a'aeva's low chuckle. "Yesterday we grew new eyes. I just found out. Go and see. It's true."

Kevin hurries away.

Xia, the big organdy bow on her dress untied and trailing behind her, says, "Pele, none of us believe in these stories, you know. They're all a bunch of hooey. An artificial organization that gathers reality together like a bouquet of flowers, just picking the prettiest ones and ignoring everything that has turned brown already. And that organized bouquet still dies the next day and gets thrown in the trash. We pretend to make you happy."

"That's quite wonderful of you," Pele says. "I appreciate it." She does not point out that in another of their *flashes*, their realities, their lives—whatever you might call it, when they wake, and wake again, resume their lives like nodes of blinking light in the depths of the deepest sea, none of them would have even understood that Pele could be happy or sad, and if they had, it would not have mattered to them.

Her clock is on the wall of the tiny bedroom upstairs. We wonder if she knows it.

Kevin is right.

We might have missed the news. It might have failed to penetrate to where we were. It would have been better if we had never known. Instead, it is a scream of deepest sorrow that runs through the ship, penetrates to our very core.

We are now, evermore, and henceforth alone.

The Earth, and all its life, is gone.

There was a nuclear war. All their painstaking and careful safeguards could not hold against a handful of people who did not care for life.

Unknowable *flashes*, garbled pictures, sick-making nightmares, and mornings of waking in our own beds as the sweet birds sing. There is no way to measure that time.

We wonder if the Librarian's clock has anything to do with this. But she will not say.

Ta'a'aeva keeps telling Pele that she had no choice, that they had sussed her out from the beginning. Pele knows that isn't true. They had no idea why she did it. They didn't know because neither did she. It is a big fat tragic mystery.

She makes that mystery into a vase that she keeps on her kitchen window. She fills the vase with starlight as the memory-threads holding her to Earth stretch, and finally snap, leaving her weightless.

She needs weight to live.

We read the stars, their signatures and histories, and calculate the planets they may have spawned. There are gas giants, dead rocks too cold or too dark for what we might call life, and some don't spin, but some of them have water and it is toward them that we navigate until we are close enough for searing disappointment.

During our navigation, we turn into ourselves again. We remember that our personalities are formed by the languages of genes, not stories, but that our actions can be influenced by the stories we learn. It's actually very scary. When we are lucky enough to grow up with stories of love, and not meanness and hate, then we can love. Love makes us happy. Stories of hate teach us only how to be victorious and to hurt others. What is most scary is how many ways we can hurt each other without even knowing that we have, or how hard it is to learn to act in ways that do not hurt others the next time. That is because there is never a same next time, so something has to be constant and at the same time fluid inside of you in the place that acts. Sometimes it is easy to think that there isn't anything anyone can do about this. Sometimes sadness teaches lessons that lead to more sadness, but sometimes it can lead to changed behavior. Sometimes happiness cannot figure out how to give itself to others. Sometimes joy can only be lived, a lucky chance that one takes, a risk that says damn the consequences. But sometimes the consequences can lead to all kinds of bad places. One must keep air inside a bladder and shoot back to the sun.

Not everyone knows how to do this.

Not everyone has a bladder, air, a sea, or a sun.

We are lucky.

We wake from another coldsleep. Sometimes we are in cocoons; other times, in coffins and kissed to consciousness by the prince-of-allgood-dreams; sometimes we pass the time as equations or as prime numbers: one unique majestic mountain peak after another. That's infinity. That's real fun. And, of course, it takes a very long time. Or so it seems.

We incorporate ourselves and grow ourselves and enhance ourselves with the genes of other species. We invent new species. We discard them, and sometimes they discard us. Then we bloom again, but different, somewhat. Still, we keep the memory of Life, rich Life, towards which we long with all our hearts. And the palette of a planet which we will change. Which will change us.

Life.

We fire the forest, stand back from the searing heat, retreat behind a clear panel and watch the blaze.

Though they live longer than anything else, bristlecone pines eventually need fire for regenesis. On Earth, lightning performed that function.

Yes, it has been that long. And longer.

Alcubierre has no colors, or more colors than we can know. She is immense; invisible.

Some of us grow new senses that we use to pat Alcubierre on her withers, even though it looks as if we are making the bed or splitting firewood or watching ants have wars. These are things no one has to do any longer, but some of us think it is helpful to believe they are doing them, so we make work for ourselves and say it keeps us sane.

Alcubierre is so huge that we will never see the beginning or end of her. In fact, the only way to think about her is with other kinds of symbols, not words.

That accounts for how the story keeps changing. Who we are and how we tell it.

We look at Pele's vase. "What is that?" asks Xia.

Pele says, "It is sadness too strong to bear. But it is something I need to feel. If we cannot understand how our actions impact others, we will bring nothing to the place we are going."

Kevin frowns. "That makes no sense at all."

It does to me.

The Librarian has been in the library for a very, very long time. Through two coldsleeps at least. Now she sits, smiling at the clock.

Amelia, who has been lying on her back, thinking, jumps up, smiling. "I have an idea!"

She gently lifts the clock from the Librarian's hands.

The Librarian stands, stiffly. She moves her arms forward a few inches but no farther. She stares at the clock, her mouth slightly open, distress in her eyes.

Amelia opens the little door holding the rattling key, and then the door to the face that contains the keyholes.

"That won't work," says Ta'a'aeva.

"We must keep trying," says Amelia. She winds, winds, winds each mechanism. "Hold this," she says, handing the key to Jaques. She opens the door for the pendulum, and sets it ticking.

Then she takes the clock and presses it to the wall. It adheres, becoming a part of the ship, and something of the ship flows into it.

The Librarian gasps. "No!" She runs to the clock and tries to wrestle it from the wall. As she yanks on it she wails, "No! No! No!" But she does allow Amelia to gently move her aside.

"Look," says Amelia.

The Librarian has changed to Pele, Pele of the mobile face, the warm, beautiful brown eyes.

"Thank you," she says.

Sometimes Pele prepares for the invasion.

Invisibly, in particles, they scout the terrain of Terra Nova, Planet X. It breaks down in this way:

It is empty, ready for us, with no life, but able to accept life, or with life that will not interfere with ours, or

They are ready for us, or something like us. The branches:

1. Annihilation
2. Rejection
3. Acceptance/modification
4. Surrender

Of these four, Pele fancies most number three. Except: what are they save identity?

Yet identity undergoes constant modification.

This is a special kind of hell. She decides to enjoy a thousand amazing sunsets to refresh herself.

Pele wonders how to say what is happening. "Time passes?" "Spacetime moves?" "We *flash,* and *flash* again, in long instants, out of darkness, and into light?"

They play, and play again, in endless iterations.

The running of the ship, the thought-ship? Inflections wash through it each moment, Earth-based inflections of thought wrought from the hard thrash of human dreams, human longing. So they are all dancing-ship stories. That's all they are: stories. Pele's unique slice of older-time gives her wry perspective. She can be outside the story. She stubbornly refuses to surrender. It-is-not-real, she thinks, seeing them all at play, leaping from bloody mayhem to the estranging magic of *Through Fairy Halls*, and, often, lying spent and weeping on a riverbank after being swept up in the billions of dark stories that comprise their heritage.

It takes all her strength and more, drawn from a rich stew of inspiring works, to pull them back from self-annihilation. For what choice is there, they collectively feel, after being soaked in the deep evil that humans do, but to remove themselves from the picture?

Whether or not they are right, she hurls tales of goodness, blazing thunderbolts, into their minds. They wake bright-faced, with a jolt, ready for the new day. She doesn't exactly dust her hands in self-satisfaction, but she does try not to wonder too hard if she's done the right thing. Who is she to shield them from grief; from sorrow, from deep reflection, or from growth?

She just tries to keep them from hurting one another, and from hurting them or herself. What else can she do?

She tries to be older and wiser. She absorbs old movies; re-views *Casablanca* as a lesson about how one bestows grace through artful lies concocted on the run, new tales to make things go right. These are lessons she missed while on Earth. She spoke from stalwart truth, never mind what pain it caused. How can one make these calculations, though, when in the midst of chaos, which is where she lives, in a constantly re-invented throng of young entities who cannot understand literatures truly until they have gained in wisdom? And who cannot gain wisdom except through sorrow, which she does not wish to thrust upon them? Sorrow generally bestows cynicism, and she is back in the same old revolution, lifted up and down until they die except

They cannot die.

We are scattered into particles. We are a speeding cloud, intent.

It is a word at last, the word that's been there all along, our Kansas home:

Courage! With a Brooklyn accent.

Whatever, wherever, that is.

"Courage," we shout. Our brave chests expand, our heads a single thought, shooting for we know not what, re-organized by new information every instant, but shooting forward, now, at last, to Planet.

We will find ways to infuse any matter we find. We will organize and blend, we will crush and release.

For we are the mighty, the awful, the terrifying power of life itself. We are infinitely tiny, infinitely large.

Our words describe the states that we create; the states create us, and a bond sings through it all.

Courage!

We crash onto every wave-hushed shore, every cold rocky outpost, every object that will hold us, with equal, eager, organizing force, programs of life, and flower, for a brief instant of stability, everywhere at once, a wide delight of life itself. We pass the instant of death, the deep drag of dread and sadness, the roiling, drowning crush of force upon force. We rush up the beaches, we drift to the high peaks, we burrow, nest, burst, and sing.

And leave ourselves, that dream of us, behind, and continue.

An instant from far here to far there, like the instant dividing life from death, but skipping that, as it must be skipped.

This is the story of how a bunch of kids kidnapped a physicist who was also a librarian so that they could get to a new planet, one far outside of our solar system. It sounds like a fairy tale because it might be.

It is really very simple.

We cross a roaring creek on a rickety bridge, fishing pole on our shoulder, in a deep mountain chasm, heading home in an evening of cold, settling mist, alone.

Yet heading somewhere.

A tentative confidence sparkles, a stand of tiny pink Galax that Pele does not pick. She hikes upward through an early spring forest of re-awakened earth, its moist smell of leaf-loam and the rush of the new-born creek fed by high snowmelt a cool, moist blessing, as is the fact of day, where trees hide most of the sky and those tempting, empty stars. She comes across it again and again in her solitary hikes, and each time kneels and contemplates it with renewed, deep, solitary wonder: it and her. A different life, with a different story, but a story nonetheless.

Life, in all that lifelessness.

After a thousand such *flash*-lives filled with wonder, bursting into time, she returns to here, knows it to be real, and for the first time, Pele does not recoil.

Why did she do it? Why did she let them go?

Was it hubris—wanting to see if her science project would really work?

Was it a heroic act, a Noah for the arc?

Blind, rushing ignorance?

This is our house.

This is our bed.

These are our chairs.

"We have left Oz in a magic balloon," says Targa, lying on his back with his hands laced behind his neck. "We made the fire, like the professor. So who is the Wicked Witch of the West who will punish us for trying to get to our new home?"

"Pele," yells Oscar.

"No!" several chorus. Ki says, "Pele is Glinda!"

"Pele is the sleeping princess,"

"She's awake." "Not really."

"And so are we all munchkins?" asks Juno indignantly. "Or flying monkeys?"

"I'm a flying monkey," says Targa, flipping over and pushing off, soaring with arms extended.

"And do we have hearts?"

"I am working on mine," says Bean, splaying two long-fingered hands across her chest. "I am working very, very hard."

Pele, hunched near-fetal in her berth, hears voices. She always does, but these wake her, for some reason. She opens one eye and sees that they have furnished her with a crystal ball with which to watch the proceedings. She allows herself a brief, tiny smile, uncurls, stretches, and leans forward on her elbows. "Wicked witch," she votes aloud, her long-unused vocal chords pushing it out as a rusty whisper.

They all look at the monitor, wave and cheer. "Pele! Pele! Pele!"

She tests the most important word: "Courage!"

"Courage," they yell back. "Courage!"

• • •

How long can longing last? Is English really so sparse?

Pele finds the German word "*sehnsucht.*" Sounds like a sneeze. And that C.S. Lewis said it is "That unnamable something, desire for which pierces us like a rapier at the smell of bonfire, the sound of wild ducks flying overhead, the title of *The Well at the World's End*, the opening lines of "Kubla Khan", the morning cobwebs in late summer, or the noise of falling waves, carrying the freight of longing's complexity, modified by underlying stratum of utopias particular to each individual."

But English has its strengths, for longing indeed is . . . long. Endless, in fact. Until what she imagines will be that eyeblink, sudden as their previous transition to the inescapable longing of perpetual now.

Presently, that is Pele's name for this planet.

Sehnsucht. "Zeenzucht," Pele says, and saying it changes her brain. Or something. Maybe.

Despite all we know and all we have learned about Shining Leaf, as Ta'a'aeva insists we call this planet, there is much that remains unknown.

Shining Leaf is just a blip. Another *flash*, a nanosecond opening that, taking, we risk all.

We have seeded other planets with our clones. As far as we know, they all died. We all died. But here we are. Still.

We are, at last, restless. In fact, we are able to realize that we are mad.

That we are ready to choose.

Pele never votes. "I voted once," she says, and we say, "Yes, and we are glad that you did."

She makes us promise something. And, at last, we do.

We cannot even talk about the painful changes that swept through us when we disengaged the drive. How it looked, felt. The precise analytics, biological and physical. How long it took in mundane time. The unspinning. Realizing the door of us, each unique. *Moku* could tell that story, and those in the future will want to know.

Having lived it is enough for us.

Moku was our home. It sustained us in our search, kept us alive, taught us much, but kept us in a state of fear and hesitation. We wanted to grow up badly enough to die if it did not work. Like Pinocchio, we wanted to be real.

We saw our main chance, and we took it.

And so became human again.

How can you tell the choice between good and evil when that choice is hard upon you? How do you recognize it? Is there a way to measure the road not taken? Why would that matter?

We have learned much about taking risk. We could not help moving into this.

From the Giant's abode in the sky, Jack stole the harp that plays by itself.

The ship is that: we stole it.

From the Giant's abode in the sky, Jack stole the goose that lays the golden egg.

Perhaps that is us.

Will we live happily ever after?

Time will tell.

When a horse wins a race, she is heaped with flowers. She snorts and prances and feels proud.

Our horse, on which we placed all bets, won.

So many suns, so many planets that did not suit. You know that tale. Some, seeded by us with life, might now be flourishing, but we will never know.

It is not luck that brought us here, to this perfect planet, with its perfect star.

It was courage.

Beneath this glorious, intense blue-violet sky, buffeted by sea-wind, I know, ineluctably, that I am *here*, on this loud coast. Crashing waves suck rattling, tumbling stones back into the shorebreak, nicking my bare feet and calves with delicious sharp pings. Sunset-tinged clouds billow like great swans on the horizon. I pull in breaths of sweet salt air, keeping an eye on my great-granddaughter, playing tag with rushing foam.

Shining Leaf is no game, no illusion, no manufactured reality, and it is no fairy tale. I spin round and see the gully-ridden cliff behind me rise, thick with massive virgin trees, relatives of red alder, bigleaf maple, Sitka spruce—trees that relish deep morning fog. They ascend in tiers of wind-tossed greens to the long grasslands above.

The pampas stretch for fifty miles to snow-peaked mountains, where just below the tree line buffeting winds twist and gnarl the bristlecone pines. Across the plains gallop herds of savannah animals, for our biosystems found homes here as well, and have flourished. And when I ride my real horse there, she actually moves, and we do reach the plane trees.

Sometimes, after opening my bedroll and making tea, a human speck amid a sea of high, sweet-smelling grasses where the sound of the rushing wind combing and flattening the grass is equally sweet, I gaze at the stars among which I lived for I do not know how long and am infused, suddenly, by a sense of deep and utter strangeness, illuminated by that . . . *flash* we all felt—or were—on *Moku*.

It seems just a second, but I cannot be sure how long it lasts, that *flash* during which I am transformed; illuminated. It could be eons. It could be Planck time, the tiniest bit of time we can measure. But when I am there, and perhaps always, I am like a pebble of pure consciousness, tossed into the most lucid medium imaginable, where my ripples intersect with and are changed by other patterns, and this goes on forever.

It is then that I know that I am not as I was, and it is then that I long to be back among the stars, and to never touch land again.

But here, I invent new languages to map the house of thought I build. My thoughts were useful once; they may be useful again. Or not.

I could tell you how our chimerists, biophysicists, engineers, artists, and mathematicians generated experimental interim environments to test and refine our interaction with this new planet as we explored it virtually, hungering to land and climb its towering young mountains and sail its vast seas. We studied its weather patterns, developed plans for symbiosis, testing and re-testing, accelerating path after path, answering question after question, for we had time, and we had to be satisfied. But that is all in our library; you can experience it there. We grew, changed, exploded into larger life, real life, using *Moku*'s vast genetic library and modeling algorithms to make decisions about populating Shining Leaf with ourselves and other fauna, learning from stories of failures on Earth, merging with what was here. The very last step, the most serious, was deciding where best to settle, and how.

We chose well. We changed, very slightly, to adapt to Shining Leaf, to its particular chemistries, its atmosphere, and its wilder seas, which Ta'a'aeva's tribe explores with zest, though *Moku* mapped its every fractal coast, her motto being "the map is not the territory". We grew defenses against that which would have killed us, larger and different lungs to inhale and use a slightly different atmosphere. Alcubierre gave us time to do that.

We live in towns and villages scattered around the planet, and have plans for golden cities, both far and near, which now assemble. We have new sciences, new technologies, communications networks that run on new symbioses, and the sure knowledge that we are still changing, because life is change, and because change is life.

I have young Bean's heart and mind, yet my grown mind is different, a human/spacetime hybrid, and my hard-grown soul my own.

Is a soul courage? Is it philosophical depth? Is it simple immortality? Is it the being that runs through us, animates us, the foundation of all love and hope and deep satisfaction in the art of living, in community, in life itself?

Here, we and our children chart their own courses; they are pioneers, seekers, builders, dreamers. One son is an artist: one daughter, an engineer. My many descendants flourish.

The wind, evening-strong, blows back my hair. I lean down and pluck up a cool, gleaming golden stone from the tumble, hold its water-honed, near-translucent thinness up to our new star and think of all the time this one stone holds and might reveal, from when it exploded into being until now, after being crushed and washed and tumbled and honed into this beauty that I, also a part of the same story, can see, hold, taste, and smell.

I give it to my great-granddaughter, who is four, to play with and she flips it in the air and laughs. Her eyes are hazel, like my father's.

I think of the librarian, who died long, long ago, and know for a certainty, which has not always been the case, that she was real, and that this is not a fairy tale, but something we have done.

We named our star for her: Pele.

She helped me grow a soul.

And that makes everything worth it.

> Here's a heigh and a ho! for the purpose strong,
> And the bold stout hearts that roam,
> And sail the Seven Seas of Life
> To bring such treasures home!
> —Olive Beaupré Miller
> *The Treasure Chest*

—With everlasting thanks to Irma Gwendolyn Knott

Poems herein by Olive Beaupré Miller, *My Bookhouse*, The Bookhouse for Children Publishers, Chicago, Illinois, 1920.

MARLEY AND MARLEY

J.R. DAWSON

I never wanted to turn out like her.

When I met her, I was twelve. There was no one else to take care of me. Before she showed up, she was preceded by this man in a pinstriped suit. A harbinger. He sat me down in his sterile office and he said, "Time Law is not a joking matter." He told me all the horrible things that would happen if I broke any Time Laws. Worlds would collapse. I would turn inside out. Important people would die and important things wouldn't happen. And that's when I first felt that clutching sensation in my chest. Like he had his fingers inside my rib cage and he was squeezing my lungs. Do not fuck this up.

"So are you the one I'm going with?" I asked. Because I was a newly coined orphan and I needed someone.

The pinstriped-suit man shook his head. "No," he said. "The system is hard on children so we've come up with a better option. But you can't go live with her. She must come to you."

Because she lived in the future.

She agreed. She got in the time machine, she met me at the port, and she took me home. She set up shop in Mom's room and she didn't leave until my eighteenth birthday, when, like some sort of Mary Poppins, she up and disappeared back to the future.

She was old, a whole twenty-eight years when she first showed up. She was a disappointment. I asked her where she lived, and she said, "Oh, I live right here in Omaha, just like you." I told her I was going to hang myself that night.

"I'm not going to lie to you about it," she said.

"I'm not going to end up in Omaha," I told her. "I was born here. I'm going to move away."

"Okay," she said, although it sounded like she didn't believe me.

"What happened to you singing in New York?" I said. "I want to be a singer!"

"You're twelve," she said. "When you're nineteen, you'll go to New York on a trip and you'll hate it."

"It doesn't matter if I hate it, it's where I'm going!" I said.

"Aren't you sassy," she said. She started making horrible turkey burgers. Her favorite dish. My least favorite.

"I'm going to New York," I said.

"So go," she said.

So goddamn smug.

"How much of a loser do you have to be in order to spend six years here with me?" I said.

"They're going to send me right back to the day I left," she said.

"You'll be older, though," I said.

"We don't have anyone else, Marley," she said.

We were both named Marley. We were the same person, actually. And it got confusing at times. So she became Old Marley, and I was Little Marley. I hated Old Marley. I swore to never see her in a mirror or a window once she disappeared back to her own time. I would not be her. I would prove her wrong.

But Old Marley was right. When I was nineteen, I went to New York and I hated how crowded it was. Flying back, I felt defeated. No matter what I did, at twenty-eight, I'd have to go be a mother to a little girl. I would be a loser, an angry and sad old woman who ate turkey burgers.

My life was set out for me, with some sort of pinstriped time cops staring through the wrinkles and tears of chronology. I felt like they were watching, making sure things went according to plan. They were the ones who made sure my field trip to New York was horrible.

But there were things Old Marley hadn't told me. There was Jason. And I learned that I didn't like singing parts I had no interest in. Seeing as most parts available for size 14s in New York were scheduled for people with big names and people in ensembles, I didn't feel like eating cardboard dollar pizza the rest of my life. So I bought a house with Jason. It was blue skies on our wedding day. We were happy. While I was in his arms, the time cop man couldn't touch me. We were beyond laws, beyond time, beyond our own selves. She never told me any of that.

She also never told me that he died. She didn't tell me the bank foreclosed on their house and she moved into a one-bedroom apartment close to the cemetery to be nearer to Jason. And she certainly didn't tell me how absolutely horrible it was to wake up in the morning and realize I had to get through a whole twelve hours of sunlight where I was still expected to function.

So when the foster service time cop knocked on my door that day, I didn't adhere to my original plan: rigging up a flame-thrower from my kitchen utensils and laying waste while screaming, "Begone, evil spirits!" No, I let him in.

The man was the same man I'd met when I was little. He was dressed exactly the same, and I realized I didn't know if he was from my time or Little Marley's time or a different time altogether.

"How have you been?" he asked.

"Do you remember me at all?" I asked.

"Yes, Marley, I remember you," he said. "I just met with you a few hours ago—my time, of course." He said this with a little smile that was supposed to be friendly, but I felt that clutching in my lungs. He had said it to remind me where he stood and with what power, and where I stood and with no power.

"You remember how much you needed someone after your parents died," the man sat on the couch and reminded me. Like he had to remind me. Dad died of cancer; Mom hanged herself a year later. I had been alone. Sort of like now, with my husband rotting away in a cemetery down the street and not able to come home. Sometimes I woke up in the middle of the night, sweating from a nightmare where I saw him being picked apart by moles, his jaw now disintegrated, his guts spilling out and into the mouths of rats.

"I hated Old Marley," I told him. "Little Marley doesn't want me."

"It doesn't matter if she wants you," the man said. "There is no one in her time who can care for her. Your little self will end up in the foster system. This is a better alternative. You knew as soon as you were twelve this was inevitable for your adulthood."

"Ah," I said. "So you didn't really give Old Marley a choice to go raise me, did you?"

"Our policy is that it's entirely up to you," the man said.

"Right," I said. That was a lie.

That night, I looked in the mirror. I saw the bags under my eyes, because I'd been crying so much. I saw my glasses. I remembered shouting at Old Marley, "I'll never wear glasses! I'll take care of my eyes or I'll get contacts! You're so ugly! Why did you make us so ugly?"

Old Marley hadn't been old. She'd been twenty-eight. But she seemed so much older.

"Can I ask a question?" I asked him.

He raised one brow, that's it. People in suits barely move their faces. Probably because their bodies are so constricted.

"You work for the Time Law Department," I said.

He nodded, just slightly. "A branch of the TLD—we handle foster services."

"There are a lot of rules, and a lot of surveillance, yes? Things happen for reasons and you make sure of that."

He nodded again.

"So you knew my husband was going to die?"

He did not nod. But he didn't do anything else, either. After a moment of awkward silence, he said, "It's an inopportune time for you to return to the past. We nearly decided against it. We are worried you'll go looking for Jason, or you'll try to twist the events that have already happened in order to save him."

"He's not in the Important People of Interest index," I said. "It wouldn't matter. We're nobodies."

"Time isn't yours to change," he said. "Now, before we let you anywhere near a port, you need to review the relevant Time Laws and sign these documents." He plopped a folder on my coffee table. "We've included a list of individuals from the Important People of Interest index with whom you have come into contact. Your interactions with these people are recorded word for word, action by action, and must not be altered. Now, as for Little Marley, you are not to tell her anything about the future. No lottery numbers, no presidential elections, nothing."

"I know how it works," I said. "I've been through it before."

"You were a child," he said. "A petulant child, from the reports. For your own sake, I would not test the boundaries." Heartless. "You're right, Marley. You are a nobody." Correct. "You keep your head down and fulfill the time loop, that's all you need to do. There are real consequences for everyone, especially you, if you go off-script. Do you understand?"

I did. I understood. I'd always understood. But there was still one question that had always terrified me.

"And you do this a lot, don't you?" I said. "Find foster parents like this?"

"Yes," he said.

"And what happens to the people who do try to change things?" I said.

He stared at me very seriously. "No one ever has."

My life had been controlled by the chronology bogeymen ever since I first saw the Time Law people. They knew everything, they had everything chronicled. Once, I saw a mission statement on some paperwork Old Marley had: "We all play a part in keeping order."

My part was set. No matter what I did, I would never live in New York. I would never have Jason back. I would waste six years with a little girl who hated me.

Maybe I could lie to Little Marley. Maybe I could tell her we grew up and became astronauts.

So I packed my things. I showed up in a little wicker brim hat, as a joke. Old Marley was gonna look just like ol' Mary Poppins when she came rolling in. But I knew the joke would be lost, because I didn't remember Old Marley coming in a hat like this and that meant I hadn't been paying attention.

I didn't say goodbye to anyone, mostly because everyone I knew was dead.

I traveled to the port station, high above the world—a small white circle spinning around the Earth below—where the pinstriped man helped me prepare. As we orbited, every time we hit the set point below, the whole port exploded with a ringing alarm. I was settled into my pod when the ringing came later that afternoon. The pod stretched, rolled, ceased to exist, and still existed everywhere. In my head, I saw all these moments from all over my timeline. I saw my mother, I saw a trip to the Rockies, and I saw days when a math test was my biggest problem. I smelled my high school gym. I felt the carpet of my old pink bedroom.

And then I was grounded again. With a deep breath, the world pieced me back together and I stumbled out of the pod, in shock. The welcome team was ready, and they wrapped me up in a blanket and gave me hot cocoa. They told me what I was feeling was normal.

"It's like dying," the welcome team lady said. "When I came back, I puked for days."

"Are you going to vomit?" the welcome team man asked.

"No." I vomited.

They rushed me to a recovery room where I slept and watched television. It was relaxing; the robe was comfortable. Then it was time to return to Earth and meet Marley.

I remember meeting Old Marley when I was twelve. A non-Time Law social worker picked me up in her car and we drove all the way to the pickup port. I guess the suit man couldn't be bothered. We waited a long time, and I got impatient sitting behind the social worker in the hot car. The thing about social workers was that they meant well, and their hearts were in the right place, but a lot of them didn't have kids of their own and they were ill-equipped to work with a little girl who found her mother dangling from a rope in the bathroom.

I hadn't been a dark kid. My bedroom was pink. But after all of that nonsense, I started writing stories at school about killing myself. No one wants to read that, and my harshest critic was the principal.

When I met Old Marley, she stepped out of the port onto the sidewalk looking refreshed and quite pleased with herself. I hated her on sight because she was fat. I wasn't fat. How did I get fat? I would never be fat.

"You're fat," I told her immediately. Maybe she would glance down at herself and say, "Oh, well, look at that, you're right. I've really let our waistline go. I'll get on that."

But instead she just stared at me, her eyes narrowing the way hawks zone in on little mice. She removed her hat—yes, she did have a hat, I remember now—and she placed it on the empty seat space between us, like a barrier.

"You're a little shit," she said.

Thus our mutual understanding began.

So now, standing at that port in my hat, I knew what was going to happen. I knew what the little shit was going to say. Looking at my waistline, I had to agree with my former self's impending assessment: I was probably a lot fatter than I thought.

I breathed in, seeing the social worker's car drive up to where I stood in my prim boots. The social worker took my bags and I sat in the back seat as if getting ready to take a puppy home for the first time. Although the puppy was taking me back home.

I didn't want to look over at the warm body next to me. She was little, I could tell. I heard her shifting around, unhappy and tired and uncomfortable. She gave out a deep sigh, just like the sigh I give when I'm done with everything.

So I looked at her.

The sensation of looking at yourself is somewhere between finding an old favorite poster from college in a box in the garage and hearing a recording of your own voice.

She was scrawny and haggard. Her skin was soft and smooth. Her hair was unbrushed. Her eyes were strained from squinting so much. She needed glasses. But good God, I had no idea I was ever that skinny.

She stared at me in complete horror.

"You're fat!" she barked at me.

There it was. There was my fear, right there in the open. I'd turned into the woman I hated, and nothing had changed. The next six years would be full of an unyielding current of events.

I set my hat down on the space between us. "You're a little shit."

The house was how I left it. When I turned eighteen and Old Marley disappeared, I tried to keep it up by myself. But I eventually went off to college and had my parents' lawyer sell off the property and everything inside it. My home decomposed and was picked apart while I stayed the hell away from it. But here it was, the everyday humdrum I'd forgotten.

The air conditioner was too loud in the bathroom, and you had to hold the toilet handle down for five seconds for it to actually flush. The kitchen tile looked like instructional footprints for dancing robots. When I was a kid, I'd line my feet up with the blocks and jump forward, then sideways, backward, then forward. The old clunky cell phones sat in their charging stations. And of course, the smell of dog, although Spot Spot was given away years ago.

Or wait, no. At this point it had only been a few weeks.

"Move." Little Marley pushed past me. She couldn't look at me. I remembered I never wanted to see Old Marley because of how old she was. I was terrified of getting old.

Little Marley was only twelve. Spot Spot the dog had only just left. We had only just returned home.

I still had the whole story to plod through.

Before Old Marley came and screwed everything up, I was still a kid and would sit in the corner of my room surrounded by my Barbies and think about all the things I'd be when I got older. I could move to New York and be a singer. I could be a cowboy, although I wasn't sure what a cowboy did other than sit around campfires and play harmonicas. Sounded like a sweet life.

I would be thin and beautiful. I would be smart and have a thousand boyfriends, or maybe just one good guy I loved so much to pick out of everyone. I would travel the world.

But then Old Marley arrived, and I saw no matter what I did, I would wear glasses. I would have a paunch. I would never smile. I would hate myself.

And now I sat across the dining room table, eating wet spaghetti and watching Little Marley pick at it, because we both knew how bad it was.

"I can make something else," I said.

"No," Little Marley said. "Please don't."

"We're not a total loser in the future," I said. "I just can't tell you anything, you know that."

"If the best thing you could do with your time is sit here with me, you're a total loser," Little Marley said.

I put my fork down. "Look, I know the food sucks. I don't make good spaghetti. But you could be a little more grateful. We're all we got right now—"

Little Marley rolled her eyes so hard, I wanted to knock them back into her skull. Little shit. She hadn't helped with dinner. She'd watched TV the whole time.

It wasn't her fault, I tried to remind myself. She was twelve. She was an orphan.

I should have made turkey burgers. I'm better at turkey burgers.

I stopped. I looked to the spaghetti. I laughed. Little Marley stared at me as if I was as stupid as her dinner.

"What?" she said.

"I made spaghetti!" I said. "I didn't make turkey burgers!"

"Okay?"

"Old Marley made turkey burgers for me on the first night!" I howled. "Oh my God, you know what this means?"

"No," she said.

But then I stopped laughing, because I must have been remembering wrong. I remembered Old Marley saying the words I'd just said, laughing for no reason, and I remembered suffering through her spaghetti.

But I thought we'd had burgers.

"Hello?" Little Marley waved at me. "Can we order out pizza?"

My brain scattered from one first dinner to another. Which one had it been?

Spaghetti. It had been spaghetti, although I knew it used to be something else. I'd changed it. Or maybe not.

Little Marley was a pill, but a good amount of her time was spent in school. I had to get up early to drop her off, and I tried to remind her that we were only making it to college if she kept her grades up.

"I'm not an idiot, I know," Little Marley scoffed from the back seat. I was not this horrible when I was a kid.

"No, but I'm telling you, Marley, you need to pay attention in math," I said.

"If I don't do exactly how well you did," Little Marley said, "I'll end up going to a better school than you, and then what? Maybe a piano falls on my head because I happened to be at Yale walking under some dorm room window at the right moment. You could've died if you did better at math."

"I don't know what dorm would have a piano in it," I said.

"If you die," Little Marley said, "I end up in some rotten split-level in Ralston with some construction worker dude and his Avon wife and the other ten foster kids they've got in bunk beds in a room with crappy blue and green wallpaper. And then I die. So no thanks. Rather just suck at math."

She was a smart bugger. She was snappy.

"And besides," she added, grabbing her plastic backpack. A vinyl decal of a vintage cartoon movie's poster was wrapped around the front of it. Toys "R" Us exclusive. It looked brand new. Because it was. It wouldn't be vintage for a long time. "Besides," she said again, "you did all these stupid classes already. Why didn't you just bring like six years' worth of homework and test answers with you?"

"Wasn't on my priority list," I said.

Little Marley snorted. "Goes to show how not-twelve you are."

She slammed the door behind her.

I spent the day trying to figure out what to do in a year I'd already lived. There wasn't much to do but stay out of everyone's way. I decided to look over the Important People index, and I found out that in fifteen minutes, I would meet the President-fifty-years-from-now. She checked me out at the Walmart counter when I went to pick up some Tylenol.

"Hello," she said, tired, not looking at me.

I already had my lines memorized. "Hi," I said, trying not to let her see I was staring at her.

She was just a kid, like nineteen. Her hair was pulled back with little bobby pins. She chewed gum. There were bags under her eyes.

"That's five-fifty," she told me.

I paid it. "Thanks," I said half-heartedly.

"You need your receipt?" she said, handing it to me.

I did want my receipt, but I had to say, "No thanks," and leave at a pace of two steps a second.

I checked the index again. The next Important People index encounter wouldn't be until five months from now.

What makes an Important Person? If the girl at the Walmart had been a rock star or a teacher, would it have mattered if I took the receipt?

What if she had been Jason?

Every day, after Little Marley got off school, we'd eat dinner and go do our own things. She'd curl up and watch television, and I'd walk through the rooms, touching all of the stuff that had been lost throughout the years. Sometimes I'd just sit in my parents' room and do nothing but smell my mother on her clothes. I didn't use the master bath, though. I shared the main bathroom with Little Marley.

She never asked why. She knew why. She asked other things.

"So," Little Marley said one night as we ate ice cream in the den, "you remember how she did it?"

"Yup," I said.

Little Marley poked her ice cream with her spoon and nodded, like we were our own sorority of two, the only ones who could see the same image in our heads. A woman with long, matted hair, her feet dangling above the lime-green-shag bath mat.

"Let's think about something else," I said.

"Tell me how it gets better, then," Little Marley said. "You're depressing. Please tell me you're secretly some CIA agent on a covert mission."

"Nope," I said.

"Well, do we get another dog?"

Old Marley had not gotten me another dog. I shook my head.

"*Could* we get another dog?" Little Marley said.

It had been stupid that Old Marley hadn't let me have a dog. But there must have been a reason, something I wasn't seeing in the space-time continuum of it all. What if I drove us to the pound and killed us both? What if the next John Lennon was supposed to pick out the dog we'd choose and was never inspired to write some ballad that would make him famous?

"I don't know if we can," I said.

"You act like there's some Big Brother watching us all the time." Little Marley scooted up in her La-Z-Boy. "No one is here except us. If we want a dog, we can get a dog."

"How do you even know who Big Brother is?" I said. "You haven't read *1984* yet."

"What are you talking about? It's a TV show," she said.

"Okay." I looked at her. "You know that the pinstripe suit man is tracking us, right? That's still a thing."

Little Marley slowly lost all color in her face. She picked at her melting ice cream. "Yeah," she said. And I knew she felt that clutching sensation, too. The anxiety. The eyes all around her, peering into our living room. A weight on her shoulders not to step out of line.

And she was already so alone.

I would look like that for the rest of my life. Every time I wanted something, Old Marley would say that's not how it was. I would eventually stop asking and just allow things to happen the way they were supposed to fall.

But not yet. She was still only twelve. And she'd had less time to learn how to be afraid.

"Fuck it," she said, and she set her ice cream bowl on the mantel and bounded up the stairs. "Let's go get a dog."

It occurred to me, after we picked up Rufus the Dog (full name) and no men in black strode out from behind a tree to time-cop arrest me, that maybe the universe didn't care if I had a dog. Nothing changed. Maybe Old Marley had gotten me a dog. Yes, of course she'd gotten me a dog. Little Marley didn't know this yet, but Rufus the Dog would grow up to be three years old and he brought Old Marley and me together. At three, Rufus the Dog had to go away to a rescue because he would be happier with other dogs. It had been the day after my fifteenth birthday and I was devastated. When Old Marley left, I ended up adopting Rufus the Dog the Second, and he'd been a good boy until he died in Jason's and my arms.

Although Old Marley sent him away, if it hadn't been for Rufus, I don't know how Old Marley and I would have bridged the gap at all. And as I watched Little Marley wrap her arms around his scruffy mutt neck and he licked her face, I promised myself I would not send the poor guy away.

Three years passed. Little Marley turned fifteen with a big birthday bash that was part-goth, part pinky ponies. Her best friends came over (I was Aunt Marley, so they weren't my best friends anymore). I bought her a new collar for Rufus the Dog. The little girls went out in the back with the big lumbering galoot. At one point, the nerd had been able to lie on my lap, and now he barely fit on the couch. Then there was chocolate cake for all.

That night, I tucked Little Marley in bed. I kissed her good night even though she was now fifteen. The last three years had their ups and downs, but they were also full of trips across the country, tree climbing, eating pizza for breakfast, and of course the stupid mutt.

"I love you, Old Marley," she said.

"Love you, too," I said.

I went back into the kitchen to feed Rufus the Dog and found him lying on his side, moaning. He didn't need to make a sound for me to know something was wrong. And even before we got to the car, I knew what was going to happen.

Rufus the Dog didn't come back home.

Little Marley woke up, bounding into the kitchen to see her puppy. But the kennel was empty and it was eerily silent. She asked where he'd gone.

I remembered what Old Marley told me.

I understood now.

But Old Marley had been wrong. Little Marley was smart and quick. Little Marley had loved this baby, and now Little Marley would know the truth.

I told her, and immediately saw that my choice this time around was almost as bad as it was the first time.

I told her Rufus was gone. I told her Rufus had gotten into some chocolate cake in the trash can. And she was quiet for three days straight. She woke up screaming in the middle of the night. A week later, she came home and flopped on the couch to watch more television.

"Where are your friends?" I said. "They usually come over on Friday nights. I'm making pizza."

"They're not coming," Little Marley said.

As I watched her on the couch, I recognized that vacant stare. This was the day Heather and Jolie asked if we were going over to my house tonight for dinner with my Aunt Marley. I had said, "No. And I think we should stop doing it forever."

Because mothers die. Dogs die. Friends will die. The only person I knew who would stick around is myself. So best to stay at home with Old Marley and get used to being alone.

Heather and Jolie never did come back to my house. That was the end of our little trio. I missed them. It had been good to see them again, and now I felt a great sadness that we'd hit that mile marker.

"Can I have a list?" Little Marley asked me later that night as we cleaned up the pizza.

"A list of chores? Christmas presents? Cute dudes?"

"No," she said. "People who are going to die."

"I can't do that," I said. "You know I can't."

"I don't have any relatives left," she said. "So what, do you never have a boyfriend? Girlfriend? Nothing? A cat? You're here with me, for six years."

"Yes, and they're sending me right back to when I left," I said.

"Yes, but you still have to live six years without whoever is in the future," she said. "That means there's either no one or there is someone that's dead. I know you, I know *us*. You ran away from something."

She was too smart. Why had I never realized that?

"Stop," I said. "You want some ice cream? There's no one dead."

"That's a lie," she said. "That's an absolute lie. I'm not a baby, and it's my life, too. I have a right to know."

I left. The puppy trainer taught us that when Rufus the Dog started barking, we should walk away.

But Little Marley just followed me into the kitchen. "There's someone! Who dies! Tell me! Who dies!"

Ah, now I remembered. This fight. I walked away again.

She grabbed my hand. She pulled it to her. I didn't remember that happening. "What are you doing?" I pulled it away.

"I want to see if there's a tan around your ring finger," she said.

"You need to calm down."

"There is a line! There was a ring and now there's not, and it's been three years and it's still there? That means you wear it when you're not around me."

"Other things can happen besides death, Marley."

"But it *is* death," she said. "I would never marry anyone I could just leave. We're not like that. We would have to really trust someone to be with them."

"What the hell do you know?" I said. "You're a child. I know everything you know, and I know more. I know exactly what is going to happen next, I've known for much longer than you, so don't sit there and tell me what I would do."

Little Marley watched me, her eyes big, her messy hair around her small pale face. She looked like the photographs I'd kept, of a sad, sunken-in child. But there was something the photographs hadn't caught.

When she spoke, she commanded.

"Tell me what I do next, then," she said. "If you know how this all ends, and our life is all figured out, you tell me what I do next."

I did try to tell her. I remembered this fight. Old Marley came up with an excuse about how she was divorced. I told Jason about that when we first met and he just laughed. "Divorced," he said. "Jesus, I hope not."

We almost hadn't married because of it. And we'd always been afraid he'd end up like Rufus. But when someone is alive, you can't imagine them dead.

"I tell you it was a divorce," I say to Little Marley. "You don't want to believe me, but you do, because it's better than the alternative. And then you stomp upstairs and watch some television."

Little Marley nodded. "Well, you're right. I don't believe you. He or she or they dies, right? Fine. Tell me how and I'll stop it."

I shook my head. "No. No, it's against the laws."

"You think every single thing we've done all these years is exactly how it happened before?" Little Marley said. "Who the hell will know what we did? Did we always get a dog, or did we change that? I don't know! But think about it—if I don't leave right now like you say I do, if I stay here instead of watching television, then the past changes, right? Who the hell would know the difference?" She sat down in the middle of the room. "So make this the moment you tell me how they die."

"No," I said. I was shaking. I could feel those pinstriped eyes everywhere; I could feel that rising panic. I could feel the world turning too fast.

"Fine," Little Marley said, tucking her hair behind her ear. "Tell me their name."

I burst into tears.

Little Marley waited. "Fine," she said. "Tell me how you met."

How many things had changed since I'd come back? How many times had we changed the timeline? *Had* we changed anything?

We couldn't change anything.

But then I looked at Little Marley. And I realized she wasn't twelve anymore. And she was alone now, but in only a few years she would go to a college dorm after this house had wandered away from her. She would go to an RA-mandated pizza party, where she would meet the students on the same floor. And that's where she'd see this boy with curly hair and an old popular cartoon on his T-shirt. The same one on her backpack when she was a kid.

"You watch that show?" I asked him, and he nodded.

"Don't care what anyone says," he said. "The old shows are the best. You watch *Saturday Morning Meltdown*?"

"Hell yes, I did," and we sang the main theme: "*Saturday Morning Meltdown*. Four hours of freedom. Come on in and come on down. We're all waiting to begin." It was a stupid song, but it reminded me of early mornings when my dad, in his thick black robe, lounged sleepily on the couch behind me while Mom was in the kitchen, making my cereal.

"We should get dinner sometime," I said. God, I was so outgoing.

He nodded, enthusiastically, more enthusiastically than any other boy I'd spoken to. "I'm Jason. I'm sorry, what's your name?"

And the day we married, it was only us and a piece of paper and two witnesses out at Standing Bear Lake. He held me and there was a boat that went past with people peering out to see our hands in each other's hands and the wind rushed and I looked at him and his eyes were speckled with green and brown and I said, "They look like their own little worlds."

Our marriage was sewn together with cartoon quotes and horrible screechy music from boys with floppy bangs and sad relationships with their suburban parents. We shared books, we popped popcorn and watched our favorite old movies on Friday nights. I could sleep through the night, especially if Jason was there.

Time doesn't heal people. People heal people.

Little Marley still sat in her spot on the floor, watching me like a patient school counselor. And I felt this anger, deep inside, rumbling forward like a train. I saw that man in his pinstriped suit, not moving and not caring when I asked him if it could have been stopped. If Jason could have lived. Because lying on the bed, wrapped in his arms, feeling his heartbeat . . . that man in his suit had deemed it unimportant.

"Jason," I said.

Little Marley nodded. "And how did . . . how will he die?"

"I know what you're thinking. It may not work," I said. "It may make everything worse."

Little Marley shrugged. "Anyone we would marry would be worth the risk."

The way she looked at me, the way she spoke to me, I now realized why I always hated Old Marley with such vehemence. It had nothing to do with New York or her glasses.

She was a coward.

Little Marley turned eighteen. I threw her a big party. We ate all of our favorite foods. We watched all of our favorite shows. We got up at six the next morning and made cereal together.

Then the man with the pinstriped suit came to collect me.

He was still sick from his arrival in the past. But although he was completely green, he still barely moved. I couldn't imagine him vomiting.

I hadn't seen him for six years. Maybe nothing had changed. Maybe the Jason secret was the only little wrinkle we could create, or maybe he would stop us.

"Say good-bye," he said to both of us.

"It's cruel to leave her alone so quick," I said.

"If you didn't teach her how to take care of yourself, that is not Time Law's issue," the man said.

Little Marley shoved past the man and said, "I need time with her by myself." The man waited outside.

"Don't worry," she said. "By the time you get back, I'll have taken care of everything."

"It's too dangerous," I whispered. The man was only on the other side of that door.

"Marley," Little Marley said, "the time cop people don't have anything we don't have. They don't own the cosmos. No one does."

I gave her a hug. "Remember, it's December twenty-fourth and he goes to work in that snowstorm. Slash his tires if you need to. But if you can't stop him," I said, "don't blame yourself."

"Hey, Marley?" she said. She punched me on the arm. "If Jason's alive when you get to the other side, go live in New York."

"We've talked about this," I said. "You take a trip and—"

"And whatever whatever," she said. "It still bothers you that you don't live there. So take Jason and go live in New York. We don't know what's gonna happen to us. You're not that old."

I felt pride. I felt like I couldn't let go of her, like we needed to keep this up for the rest of our lives, me always a couple steps ahead of her and she leaps and bounds beyond us both.

But I left. I returned to the port and got in the pod. I went forward.

I got out, vomited.

"Welcome back," the man in the suit greeted me. It was the same man. It had only been a couple of seconds.

We took a ship back down the Earth. I collected my bags. Jason met me at the pickup curb. It'd been so long since we'd seen each other, and the man in the pinstripes had allowed no correspondence during my time away.

For me, it had been years. For Jason, it had been a couple of hours.

"Do I look old?" I asked. "How old do I look? Don't you dare lie to me."

Jason laughed. "You look beautiful."

"Lies. But thank you."

He put the car into drive. "I'll make you those turkey burgers tonight."

I never heard from the man in the suit again. The loop was done. We were nobodies with no significance. And that was okay. As we pulled into the Lincoln Tunnel, we melted into a million random faces.

"So you didn't ruin the space-time continuum." Jason laughed. "Congratulations."

"You know things can't be changed," I said.

"Yeah, well," Jason said. "It would have been nice to win the lottery. Or meet you when we were younger. You didn't look up my old address while you were there?"

I shook my head. I held his arm and rested my head on his shoulder while he drove in the dark, the lights hitting us one by one in a rhythm while we crossed under the Hudson. It had been a long time since I'd held him. And I knew he wanted me to find him back when we were kids, cross the river and knock on his door and introduce myself. "So we wouldn't have been alone," he said.

But I didn't, because I didn't want to change a thing.

HEXAGRAMMATON

HANUŠ SEINER

(TRANSLATED BY JULIE NOVÁKOVÁ)

"Let us remind ourselves of our destiny."

The captain approached the command console slowly. Characters of the Vaían alphabet lit the screen. Clusters of the crew stood in the front cabin patiently, hiding in the dimness of the large space. Their bowed faces were not only disfigured by the inexorable signs of the virus; submission had erased the gleam from their eyes, humiliation had engraved deep wrinkles in their skin. What followed resembled a bitter elegy.

"We live in stillness and darkness," the captain read.

"*We live in stillness and darkness*," fifty voices echoed.

" . . . deep under our conquerors' boots."

" . . . *deep under our conquerors' boots.*"

A narrow line of the ship's front windows ran behind the captain's back. The faint lights of the cabin reflected from the surface of the thick glass. Beyond it, the shields glinted dark blue, those heavy lids of vanadium steel closed five years ago, never to open again.

"But in ourselves, we bear the legacy of those who came to raise us up," the captain continued.

"*But in ourselves, we bear the legacy of those who came to raise us up*," the crew whispered mechanically.

" . . . and thus our enslavement has meaning."

" . . . *and thus our enslavement has meaning.*"

In the short periods of silence, the quiet song of the running engines could be heard. Their sound wavered with the rhythm of the crew's words. The virus mediated the crew's feelings to the engines, just as it opened their minds to the engines' distant thoughts.

"Even though our gift became a burden . . . "

"*Even though our gift became a burden . . .*"

" . . . we still can pass its power unto humanity . . . "

" *. . . we still can pass its power unto humanity . . .* "

" . . . as Vaían asked us and as we promised Vaían."

" *. . . as Vaían asked us and as we promised Vaían.*"

They all knew the words by heart and long ago had ceased searching for solace in them. They only found the unrelenting truth about what they really were.

"That is our destiny," the captain concluded the ritual.

"*That is our destiny,*" fifty bowed heads repeated after her.

She touched the screen with her fingertips. It went dark again.

"This is how we remind ourselves of our destiny, as well as that of all the other crews. You may return to your posts. Thank you."

1.

Threads of rain drummed relentlessly on the car's roof. Streams running down the windows merged and went separate ways again. The air suffocated with water and the smell of wet earth. I stopped where the muddied road met a tall razor wire fence. I almost couldn't see the gate in the thick rain; if it weren't for the guard's booth, it would have seemed that the fence crossed the road ruthlessly and gave no one from the outside a chance to reach the peak of the towering cone.

A soldier in a green-gray raincoat walked to the car and waited for me to roll down the window. Splashes of freezing water fell upon my arm. The soldier looked inside, at me and then Janita crouching in the passenger seat, and finally at the cigarette box I handed to him along with a file in a waterproof folder. He took both in his cold, calloused fingers. I saw him checking the small bundle of wrinkled banknotes amidst the cigarettes; not a bribe, just a token of gratitude for limiting the personal searches and interrogations of my clients to the necessary minimum. He grunted approvingly, pocketed the file and box under his raincoat, and hurried to the booth.

We remained silent. My gaze traveled to the rearview mirror. The wiper fought the assaults of water tenaciously and at times, I could recognize the outline of a village crouching by the cone's base. From this far, it resembled a stone battleship on a dark sea of the fields, the crows a parody of its gulls. The cone itself could have been a freak wave about to sweep the ship into the muddy depths. But the scene was motionless, still like the lives of those buried deep underneath.

"Is everything all right? Is it supposed to go like this?" Janita was studying me with her Europan eyes the color of sesame seeds. I nodded.

When Janita first came to my office two weeks ago, I found nothing unusual about her. She was a little sleep-deprived and disoriented by the change in gravity and the openness of spaces on Earth; like all my clients. She introduced herself; I glanced through her application and gestured at her to sit down. By the rules, I had to first ask her a couple of questions to make sure that she wasn't just impersonating the real Janita Paltev. Like her birth date.

"June third, year seventy-one."

Or her nationality.

"The Free Republic of Europa and Ganymede." (Oh, the mixture of bitterness and pride in all of their voices! Some even answered *Vaían*. As long as they didn't daringly write it in their forms, I ignored it. I don't look for trouble.)

The next question was necessary: "Whom are you visiting?"

"Corporal Petr Paltev. My father."

"On which ship?"

"*The Destroyer of Seven Villages*," she replied without hesitation, though the answer wasn't simple. Each of the ships' names consisted of five Vaían symbols whose meaning depended on the three-letter cipher key used to read them. By applying the trigrammatons, *The Destroyer of Seven Villages* could also be called *The Obsidian Snail, Deep Slumber, Embrace of Aldebaran*, or *Devil's Martyr*. The cycle was closed; by applying the next key, *Devil's Martyr* would change back into *The Destroyer of Seven Villages*. It remained difficult for people to shake off the feeling that one of the ciphers of the cycle is the basic one, and they obstinately insisted upon it. However, the Vaían civilization saw no difference in them; the cycle didn't begin or end anywhere and the ship bore all the names at once. More complex ciphering loops built upon the trigrammaton cycle. But Vaían didn't have the time—or will—to give humans all the four- or five-letter keys to the tetra- and pentagrammaton cycles, therefore their extent and structure remained unknown despite all the government cryptologists' best efforts.

"Reason for the visit?"

She shifted in her seat. "Death in the family. My father's sister succumbed to cancer a month ago. I want to tell him in person. Anyway, he needs to sign papers regarding the inheritance; she had no children . . . "

I was leafing through the file. Everything seemed to be in order.

"Do you have a statement of health from an approved physician?"

She handed me a folded piece of paper. I looked at it and felt the tickle of complication.

"This is just an unverified copy. You need an original or a certified copy."

"Oh," she breathed out. "But the original is on Europa. Can't you certify it?"

I gave her the copy back. "I could but won't. There are three army hospitals with the necessary certification in town and they can give you a new statement in any of them. With some luck, you can get it today and we can resume tomorrow. What do you say?"

I really don't look for trouble. Janita, however, morphed into one big trouble at that moment. "I can pay you. A lot. More than you'd think. Just certify the copy, please, and take me to the *Destroyer*."

She was still the shy girl with speckled skin and slumped shoulders. Yet whereas five minutes ago, I'd thought she was afraid of me, now I felt afraid of her.

"Please," she insisted. "It's the most important thing in my life. And even though you don't realize it now, yours, too."

I should have called the guards. Or I should have soothed her somehow, waited till her departure and then informed the police or my superiors. Instead, I watched in silence as she raised her pale, sinewy arm, as if made of glass noodles, and pulled aside her hair. Her bared temples revealed what they had to reveal.

"Oh, damn," escaped me. I hadn't seen anything like this for four or five years. After the last refugee camps on Earth had closed, I hoped never to see it again. The viral incubant was swirling among her hair roots, drawing spirals, symbols, labyrinths of images, resembling the dark Maori tattoos. I did not dare to guess how many people Janita had to bribe, blackmail, kill, or sleep with to get here, into the comfortable chair in my office. The Europan guerrilla army extended its fingers to me across half the system and grasped my throat. Opposite me sat a true pro-Vaían fundamentalist, and on her body, she was carrying the alien civilization's gift to humanity.

Thursday, August 30, 2192

I finally succeeded in cadging some writing accessories from the guards. For the first time after more than a year of trying, they didn't dismiss me with a touch pad limited to Earth alphabets. I received a plain pencil like I haven't seen since childhood, and a thick pad with lined paper. It smells of glue and ancient times. I kept leafing through its empty pages and smelling it all afternoon. Now I've finally decided to start writing.

In those endless requests, I always stated that I would like to keep a diary. I will try to abide by that and each day record what I felt or thought. I cannot bring testimony of much else; the days here are monotonous, neatly outlined from the cell lights turning on in the morning, through the grueling walk in the corridors, to the allowed hour of univision in the evening. I don't talk to anyone. Sometimes when I thank the cook for her soup in the canteen, she smiles but stays silent. I visit the gym but I haven't made any friends there. I take the dumbbells from their racks in silence and return them also in silence. Without a word, I browse through the books in the small library. It's maddening. Now I can hardly control the surge of words flooding to the tip of my pencil. Someone is finally listening to me, though he cannot answer—but he will remember my words, undistorted.

I've been thinking about luck during today's lunch. Long ago I read somewhere that each man has a measure of luck given by destiny. He will use it fully but cannot expect a drop more. That's supposed to be why healthy, happy, and resilient people succumb to fast fatal illnesses or accidents; or why the unfortunate barely making a living, cast out by the society, almost miraculously make their way through the maze of freezing nights, dirt, and street wars. If there's any seed of truth in it, I believe we have already used all our luck. How else could one describe those unbelievable four years of contact other than luck? How else can I describe the feeling spreading through all of Europa and the other moons? I do not regret any second I had the honor to enjoy Vaían's presence in the solar system. I don't regret any unfulfilled dream, any false expectation. When the revolution came, we were still so amazed by our luck that we were unable to fully grasp its impact. It was like a windstorm, perversely beautiful in its force of destruction. It broke everything we had hoped for and separated us and Vaían forever.

Under the pretext of saving humanity (but what is humanity if not the courage to explore the unknown?), the revolutionaries woke us from our happy dreams and made us monsters, freaks. They took no shame in stealing everything Vaían had given us, did not hesitate to distort its legacy in their interest. Still, my heart fills with joy when I recall those four years, and no prison can ever change it. I keep writing in Vaían symbols and using my tautogram for my name. And if I cannot personally deliver my testimony of the star travelers to the generation of my children, this notepad hopefully may.

2.

Janita quickly refuted my notion that all infected civilians ended up either incarcerated or executed.

"You're placing too much faith in the inner planets' propaganda," she replied, and sipped her coffee. We were sitting in a small, clean bistro under a marquee, shielded from the fine rain. Janita wore a fine knitted cap covering her forehead and temples. She looked very pretty in it but that wasn't the reason I agreed to another meeting. Nor the money, even though I'd kept pretending I cared about it. The bistro was empty and the waitress carefully avoided our table, perhaps repelled by the symbol of a federal agent on my lapel.

"As the revolution grew into a war," Janita explained quietly, "lots of volunteers tried to relieve the suffering of the crews of destroyed ships, and accepted their incubants, especially in field hospitals and refugee camp infirmaries. The government mostly tracked down the doctors but not the auxiliary staff. I was in the first semester of a nursing school and helped out as a nurse in the Saint Cross Hospice."

I didn't know that place but could imagine it: dirty, bloodied beds; dim lights; overworked doctors. The agony the crews suffered away from the engines, their feeling of separation and missing an integral part of them, so strong that they truly bled from their nonexistent injuries. Although the presence of the other infected relieved their pains, the Europan fleet members would die after a couple of weeks without their ships.

"Our viral codes had never been compiled through longer than three-letter keys and never entered Vaían technology's fields," she concluded. "That's why we were able to last away from the other carriers. A week of fever, headache, and cramps and the infection faded; only the original incubant remained."

She kept talking in plural but I could not imagine how many of these voluntary carriers could outlast the war. A dozen? A hundred? A few dozen could be enough for rekindling the long conflict's fire, especially now, when the inner planets' attention faltered.

Just a few years ago, our conversation would have been impossible. The whole system crawled with spies and everyone watched everyone else for a sign of anything Vaían in the gleam of their eyes. But the war sucked money out of all of us, and without it, it was a long journey to Jupiter. The repressions, resistance, and confused political situation out there could stay out of Earth's interests. We were on the victorious side without admitting that actually we only prevailed over ourselves. Of the whole war, only seven clay cones remained on Earth, burying the crews of seven Europan ships alive. And, of course, the unceasing terawatts of energy their engines kept spewing out.

I forced my face into a casual smile. "And what about me? What's the chance I get infected when we descend into the throat together?"

I knew the crew presented no danger to me. The virus in their bodies was old, ingrained in their biomagnetic fields like a wood stain. It had brushed against me many times. Yet the maze of Janita's hair could hide a much more aggressive Minotaur.

She shook her head. "The virus doesn't spread so easily. An incubant cannot infect you. Even if I allowed it to expand to all of my body, the transmission is not easy. You would have to want it."

The most fundamental question remained unasked, unanswered between us. We kept playing the game that Janita was really a dutiful daughter wishing to visit her father and I'd look away from her missing medical statement. She could never get one as a carrier. "But the meaning of what she'd said earlier still haunted me. "The most important thing in your life." That didn't bode well.

The station on the cone's apex resembled a starfish. Endless lines of pylons stretched in all directions, laden with garlands of cables. Some junctions gave off little sparks in the unceasing rain.

I sent Janita, tired from the long travel in Earth's gravity, to sleep and went to look into the mouth of the cone. I knew the guard stationed there well.

When we sat on the edge, legs dangling to the rim of the first collar of coils, he produced a bag of roasted peanuts.

"Want some, agent?"

The throat underneath us faded into distorted distance. Nine hundred meters of shielding and high-voltage filters, nine hundred meters of paranoia, not letting even a shred of the virus reach Earth's surface. The descent took a day and a half, including two eight-hour acclimation stops. The throat wasn't a place created for people. It was a dangerous tangle of field lines and dipoles. The difference between the electric potentials by its mouth and base, inside near the ship, constituted hundreds of millions of kilovolts. The throat pumped air into the buried ship so that the engines wouldn't waste their energy on recycling, and all rations, water, and medicine went down through it. In the opposite direction, the energy of Vaían engines surged up the outer collars of the throat; that energy which had rendered most power plants on Earth useless. Janita had been right; it was barbaric.

"Some pretty young girl again, eh, agent?" the soldier asked me, and crunched another peanut.

"I don't pick them," I smiled sadly. "It's they who pick me." Janita knew very well whom to pick. I had worked on Ganymede for a long time, so long that I almost became a Jovian. I was alone on Earth. Only a small stack of divorce papers divided me from the family left out there. I'd managed to screw up my life and return to Earth just before the contact. Before the Jovian moons became the promised land—or Vaían's slave, depending on the point of view. Surprisingly, my personal connections to Ganymede didn't impede my rise in the career hierarchy. I went through the training for work in the throat and took a medical course for first aid to people under the influence of strong electromagnetic fields. I became a government-approved guide in the sporadic journeys of relatives and friends to the ships' crews. But deep inside, I have never been a textbook earthling protecting Humanity (with a capital *H*) and loathing everything Vaían. I could be swayed. Yes, I could be bribed.

"Whom has she got there?"

"Her father."

The soldier sighed. "Sometimes I add a box of cigarettes to their rations. Secretly, so that no one else would know. It's against the rules but I always thought it might cheer them up. Only yesterday it occurred to me that I don't know if they're allowed to smoke there at all."

I took a peanut shell between my fingertips and tossed it to the center of the throat. We both watched it fall and zigzag under the nudges of the varying field. Like a Brownian particle in a drop of water.

• • •

Friday, August 31, 2192

My fingers spasmed last night. Yet I wrote only a few lines yesterday! My hand must be unused to the pencil. I'll try to pause longer when writing.

Before the spasms woke me up, I was dreaming, like almost every night, of the time before the revolution. (I think there are so few stimuli here that my subconscious doesn't use even the simplest of images. My dreams stem from my memories.) I was standing on a shining white promenade in one of Ganymede's subterranean cities. Crowds of happy people passed me and the air was thick with the smell of some exotic flowers. There were the flags of the Republic and ribbons with Vaían symbols everywhere. All of a sudden, a tall, ceremoniously clad Elder appeared before me. He walked straight to me. The half-moons of his eyes shone like emeralds. We stopped. He took my hands in his and said one word: "Gratitude."

The more I think about the dream, the less I understand it. What gratitude? Humans couldn't have acted more ungratefully toward the Vaían. We all remember the selflessness and generosity with which the Vaían offered—but did not coerce us into—participation in an interstellar community. We remember how they warned us that accepting the virus was an irrevocable decision. We remember how they so casually started building the engines for our ships. And what have they gotten from us in return? I secretly hope the dream continues tonight.

One more thing from today is worth writing down. I've noticed a new inmate during lunch. Either they transferred him here today, or I've been too self-contained lately to notice him. By his shy gaze and slumped shoulders, I'd guess he ended up here for reasons similar to mine. He has heavy, sleepy eyes, and constantly covers his mouth, as if ashamed of his missing teeth. He reminds me of myself five years ago. Dare I hope now that I could have someone to talk to, or even become friends with?

3.

"The yellow cone of light flickered through the dark as I quietly approached Janita's bed, a flashlight gripped tightly in my hand. I knew the Europans slept heavily in the thick Earth air, strong Earth gravity, and hard Earth beds. I probably couldn't wake her up even if I tried. Despite that, I knelt by her bed cautiously and even more cautiously pulled aside a strand of hair falling over her forehead. The incubant started quivering in the light. I extended my fingers to it and held their tips just a few millimeters away from Janita's head. The biomagnetic fields of our bodies merged and the code's symbols started passing to my skin. They ran through my fingers and tickled my palm. But when I withdrew, they obediently returned to the Europan skin where they felt at home. I resisted the temptation to play with the virus, to try to catch its segments in the trap of curled fingers. I let it slide into my palm again and calm down, get used to the structures of my hand and reveal its own. The Vaían symbols never ceased to move slightly in the flashlight beam, but the basic flow of the algorithm was clearly recognizable.

"When people need to write a procedure with ten functions," a coder once said to me, "they write ten short codes and build walls of conditionals and choices in front of them. The Vaían can do the same with one short code and ten keys to compile it." The program has all ten functions at once, just as a ship has all five names. The trick is using the right cipher key. The Vaían virus was just a program, only instead of instructions for a computer processor, it contained instructions for a nervous system of a living being.

As I shifted my fingertips near Janita's bare forehead, the virus rolled across my palm slowly. With it, conflicting memories through my mind. What have I been searching for, anyway? Janita may have held a four- or five-letter cipher key inside her body, and needed to enter the engines' fields to go through a new compilation. That would make some sense. Does she want to become a part of the crew? But why? My eyes searched for the encapsulated shell of an unused compilation key: symbols divided from the rest by an impermeable line whose dissolution could be ordered only by Vaían technology. Its breach would mean that the virus would gain control over Janita's life and death. If the encapsulated symbols were just four, Janita would understand the engines' language and wouldn't be able to live without them after the compilation. If they were five, she would start obeying their orders. I wasn't sure what I'd do if I found the tetra- or pentagrammaton. I just felt curious, understandably, about whether Janita planned to return to the surface from the *Destroyer*. At last, the dark, gleaming shell slid onto my forefinger and into my palm.

I moved the flashlight to it to discern the details of the key.

The world trembled with me.

Saturday, September 1, 2192

The new prisoner was eluding me whole morning. I glimpsed him in the library but before I got to him through the maze of bookshelves, his chair was empty. In the lunch queue, he was standing far ahead of me but I didn't see him later in the canteen. Perhaps he always sits in another dark corner, searching for a place no one will kick him out of, where no one will spit in his soup and he'll be able to eat without enduring the others' suspicious glances. Finally, I used my small savings of cigarettes and medicine to exchange them for a few minutes' time with one of the local informers. He promised me to get as much from the guards as possible.

Later: I was right! The man's name is Arvin and his soul really is unburdened by any mugging, murder, or fraud. He's a scientist, a cryptologist. He studied

Vaían ciphers right on Europa during the contact. After the revolution, he started working for the Earth government. But a few years later he allegedly started secretly aiding the Europan resistance. He was supposed to trade results of the government research to the fundamentalists. But some say it has been a show trial, because Arvin uncovered something that didn't fit the government's perspective on Vaían. In any case, I must speak to him! I'm trying to comb my memory for everything I know of Vaían ciphers. It's not much, sadly. I can draw the cipher matrix and decipher the original text if I know the key, but those are the basics anyone willing to fully communicate with the Vaían Elders had to learn.

I also hazily recall how to find tautograms: texts that remain unchanged during the application of all known keys—tri-, tetra-, and pentagrammatons— because they decipher back into themselves. Using those, it was possible to communicate with the Elders without a previously given key. Mathematicians called them "eigenvectors of ciphers," but I never fully understood what they'd meant by that. I was pleased to discover that I still remember the longest known tautogram. It is an oath of sorts, a vow composed by the captains of the seven remaining ships when it had been decided to bury those ships alive and let Earth devour their energy by the thirsty straws of the cones. The tautogram reads: "We live in stillness and darkness, deep under our conquerors' boots. But in ourselves, we bear the legacy of those who came to raise us up, and thus our enslavement has meaning. Even though our gift became a burden, we still can pass its power unto humanity, as Vaían asked us and as we promised Vaían." The words make me shiver.

Maybe Janita woke from her deep slumber at that moment and looked at me with her Europan eyes. Maybe she spoke to me. I don't know. I wouldn't have noticed. I sat heavily, extinguished the flashlight, and stared into the darkness. The shell contained six letters. A hexagrammaton.

I'd heard legends of it. I'd heard crazy men babble prophecies of it. I'd read about it in files marked *Top Secret* when I still worked for the expert committee. Six letters that could change the course of the war. The longest possible compilation key that could transform the crew and engines into one being and enable travel across the galaxy. The crew would abandon their humanity, become like the Vaían Youngers, whose thoughts circulated through the ship's command systems. And after approximately sixteen years the energy of the engines would deplete and their power decrease. Only then the ship being would dissolve and the crew members would be reborn as individual beings and full members of the interstellar community: as Vaían Elders.

But that never happened. As the virus had been spreading through Europa and new ships had been built in the Ganymedan ports, suspicion took hold of a part of the Republic. Was the transformation of people into the Youngers a path into an interstellar community, or was it a rejection of humanity and acceptance of Vaían's rule? How big a part of their nature did the volunteers throw away and how much would be returned to them when they're released from their long service?

Citizens of the Republic languished. There were water and energy shortages, quarrels, problems nobody cared about because all resources were being devoted to the Vaían program. This was the substrate the revolution had grown on. With the support of the Vaían Elders, advocates of the space program would perhaps have suppressed the uprising without great trouble. But Earth and Mars joined the conflict with their large armies and firepower capable of turning both moons into clouds of dust in Jupiter's rings. The inner planets followed the doctrine: "If we don't have the viral technology, no one should," disguising it as care for the integrity of humanity. They considered themselves the cradle of this humanity. The Republic ships with Vaían engines weren't built for combat. Nor were the original Vaían ships. Moreover, the Vaían Elders didn't feel the need to interfere. They suspended the process of gradual compilation of the virus inside the ships, supposed to prepare the crews for the eventual acceptance of the hexagrammaton, and left our solar system—perhaps forever. The crews were frozen halfway between humans and Vaían Youngers. They couldn't live apart from the engines but were unable to reach for the stars with them.

My thoughts swirled and flickered not unlike the symbols of the virus that had flown through my palm moments ago. The government cryptologists claimed that human knowledge of Vaían ciphers wasn't sufficient to find the hexagrammaton. The Vaían alphabet consisted of one hundred and thirteen symbols, enabling two and a half billion six-letter combinations. But only millions of them translated some sequences of the virus into executable programs. Without knowing the engines' functions, there was no criterion upon which to choose from the combinations. Yet what if someone on Europa had managed it? What if Janita truly carried a key for a new era of human civilization inside the compilation shell? Could this be the most important thing of my life? The ship had been buried under millions of tons of clay and rock and no force, Vaían or not, could move it. The throat had been such a perfect electromagnetic trap that the expanded hexagrammaton could never escape to Earth's surface.

I rose and stumbled into the next room. My bed accepted me with a creaky sigh. Now I knew what my client carried to *The Destroyer of Seven Villages*. However, until I knew *why*, however, I still remained the same swayable, bribable civil servant. Questions kept circling in my mind, passing each other in still-new conjunctions like Jupiter's moons. I only fell asleep long after midnight.

• • •

Sunday, September 2, 2192

I managed to talk to Arvin briefly. When I introduced myself and shook his hand, he stared at me with puzzlement for a moment. I'm not surprised; if he truly studied ciphers on Europa, he was bound to know my name, maybe even my face. But after five years in prison, one changes a lot. So far he approaches me with suspicion. I understand it. He's probably afraid the government set me on him. I will try to convince him that's not the case, but it won't be easy. However, he can't control himself completely: when I mentioned cryptology, his eyes lit up and he drew a breath as if to start talking. But then he covered his mouth again and mumbled some apology. We parted with a Vaían goodbye, as naturally as if we spoke it all the time. Perhaps I haven't used up all my luck yet.

Later: I discovered a live snail in my cell after dinner. It has a gleaming obsidian shell and measures no more than two centimeters. I must have brought it with me on my boots or clothes from the canteen or bathroom. I let it climb my hand and thought about what I'd do with it. Never before has another living being kept me company in this cell. But I cannot keep it; there is nothing for it to eat here (though I only have a foggy notion of what snails eat). I'll try to carry it to the yard tomorrow and set it free in the grass. For now, I can keep studying it and feel amazed by its perfection.

4.

"I was there," I told Janita as we descended about a third of the throat. We were carefully climbing the rope ladders down from one tier to another. The coils around us buzzed disconsolately. The service lights flickered without any apparent pattern. Instead of air, a mixture of burnt dust, ozone, and bluish sparks tried to force its way down our lungs. Sometimes we could glimpse the resilient throat fauna and flora: fungi growing in spirals around the coils, spiders building absurdly formed webs in the small anomalies of the field, moths with asymmetric wings deformed by their lifelong fight with the vortices of the toroids. Ant paths following the line fields. Chiral stalactites of dust particles growing on the coils, disintegrating whenever the relays inside the walls changed the current's flow with a deafening click.

"Where?" Janita asked, and sat beside me on the small platform protruding into the throat's abyss.

"The decision of the ships' fate. I'd been an assistant to one of the expert committee's members."

"I know. You recommended that he vote against their destruction. The proposal for building the cones came through by one vote—also thanks to you."

A blue-white discharge suddenly crackled above our heads. Janita looked up, startled. A thin veil of burnt dust and ash from the lichens and small flies fell upon her face.

"It wasn't an easy decision back then," I said, almost apologetically.

"It certainly wasn't," she remarked. "It's never easy to save almost four hundred lives, is it?"

I didn't tell her that the committee spent lots of time pondering the question of whether the infected crews still constituted human lives.

Janita drank her depolarization solution thirstily. Small beads of sweat ran down her forehead, swirling as they followed locally meandering field lines. The human body is one big electrolyte tank. Little change is needed for it to become a charged monocell in the throat's field.

"How do you feel?"

She looked at the almost empty flask. "Okay."

"The truth."

"I feel dizzy. I hear buzzing in my ears. And it's very hot in here. But I can put up with that."

I touched Janita's forehead. She didn't protest or pull away, just looked at me suspiciously. Her cold sweat ran down my palm and, amidst its beads, the viral symbols sometimes flowed too.

"It should be all right," I said. "Let's go another hundred meters and make an acclimation stop."

She nodded.

Strong electromagnetic fields can be like high altitudes. Some can grow used to them quickly, some cannot. The body needs time to adapt its electro-chemical processes.

We passed a toroid of absorption coolers with their heat exchangers glistening with frost. Spirals of water vapor rose from there into the dry air. The mist condensed on the coils around the toroid. Tassels of small water droplets, each black with the burnt dust, hung from them. The insect-like buzz of the coils and the deep tones of the exchangers, resembling the growling of a distant storm, mingled in our ears.

Just above the halfway point into the throat, there was a service platform where I usually spent the first acclimation stop with my clients. Janita grew very slow during the last meters, so I descended first to prepare the bends. An irritated hiss of self-inflating mattresses added to the throat's sounds.

Janita finally staggered to me and sat on the ribbed floor heavily. The whites of her Europan eyes were full of broken veins. Her light brown irises almost couldn't be discerned in the red-and-white maze. She let me touch her forehead again. From my expression, she understood something was not right.

I pulled another flask out of my bag. "Drink it, all of it."

The flask was supposed to last for the journey back but the entire plan was tumbling down like a house of cards. I watched Janita drink thirstily. Sweat dripped from the wet strands of her hair.

"Have you ever worn chrome watches? Or steel jewelry?"

She stopped drinking and looked at me in surprise. "No. I mean, for a little while, but I had to return them."

I nodded. "They went black on you."

"How do you know?"

Less than one percent of people have overly acidic skin. The depolarization solution works well enough inside their bodies, but it changes into nanocrystals of metallic salts in their epidermis.

"That hot feeling . . . that's not from being overheated. It's the electroosmotic pressure being misinterpreted by your thermoregulation system. Your skin is becoming a capacitor. It's called the Faraday disease."

She gulped. "What does it mean?"

"We'll see," I lied. "You'll drink a lot and we'll rest here for eight hours."

Without objections, she let me help her out of the coverall, which was heavy with sweat. Her breathing was quick and shallow. With her blanket pulled to her chin, her exhausted eyes stared up into the distorted throat.

I felt waves of irony wash over me along with the pulsing fields. Unbelievable. In all those years of guiding my clients into the ships, not one had been diagnosed with Faraday disease. The acidity of their skin had been closely scrutinized. But Janita avoided her medical examination because of the virus. It was funny, in a way, but I couldn't laugh.

This platform was our final station, no matter what gift Janita carried on her body. The coils mocked us with their persistent buzzing.

Tuesday, September 4, 2192

Unbelievable! I held a longer conversation with Arvin today and I'm still feeling fazed from what I learned. On one hand, I cannot believe it. But nevertheless . . . it could mean a giant step in our understanding of the Vaían civilization.

Arvin says that the language and writing itself are the basis of Vaían ciphering. Human linguists and cryptologists have always been amazed by the Vaían Elders' ability to spontaneously create texts with several simultaneous meanings. According to Arvin, they had no choice! The Vaían language has a self-ciphering tendency, he says; it's a closed algebra, a self-contained universe of texts. Whatever is written in it necessarily has several meanings. The Vaían didn't create texts containing multiple meanings. They wrote one and then searched for the cipher keys using simple algorithms. Have they created all of their cipher culture unintentionally, built on texts originating simultaneously with others? Is the virus also one simple code, whose other functions the Vaían discovered by applying more and more cipher keys? Is the basic trigrammaton cycle just a minimalistic approximation of the real functionality of the written Vaían?

Arvin confided to me that the government stopped financing his research because he did not get closer to communicating with the Vaían technology. Instead, he rose higher and higher in the abstract plane of the theory of symbolic languages. His obsession with the possibility that Vaían could be self-ciphering made him return to Europa in search of the guerrilla army cryptologists. He was looking for people able to write fully in Vaían, and explored how, with the growth of a text, other ones also evolve, how the number of meanings and keys increases, how the cipher key and deciphered text itself both change with rewrites of the original text. It's simple up to five letters, he explained to me. Pentagrammatons still result in a comprehensible cycle. If the author is well versed in it, he should be able to imagine the sentences parallel with those he's writing at the time, he can intentionally compose with more meanings. The breakthrough comes with hexagrammatons. The sequence of cipher keys doesn't close, it grows through the alphabet like a spiral, like a snail's shell. For any longer text we write in Vaían, Arvin claims, there exists at least one hexagrammaton. If we find it, we can decipher the text into a new meaning. Suddenly we're faced with two texts, different from each other, and must choose which branch to continue along. There is no ciphering back to the original and the cycle is not closed, so if we choose to continue writing the new branch, we cannot return to the old one. In other words, we cannot find out how the original text evolves if we're writing the new one. At any moment, we can find another key for deciphering the new text; the number of meanings therefore grows constantly, up to infinity.

Later: The notion that I'm writing another meaningful text simultaneously with this diary scares me. Should I discover it and continue it? What can it be about? I've torn ten blank pages from my notepad and started copying my diary so far. I'll try to give the pages to Arvin tomorrow. I've broken my only pencil into two halves. Whatever awaits me on the other side of my own notes, I won't face it alone.

I opened my eyes. Janita was kneeling by my mattress, blanket wrapped around her naked body.

"Are you asleep?"

I stared at her, unable to speak.

Her tired eyes shone red-white from a face transformed into a swirl of ornaments and thin lines. The viral labyrinth followed the outlines of her cheekbones and jaw, extended its distorted fingers to her nape, coiling around her neck like a hungry constrictor. The expanded virus gave Janita a demonic appearance. The flowing code resembled dancing flames, the sharp lines of symbols on her cheeks were like war paint.

"You don't need to explain to me," she continued when she saw I was awake. "I know I can go no further. I've known it for several hours, but it took me some time to accept it."

"But why . . . " I managed.

"I lied to you, but only in part. My father really does live down there in the *Destroyer*. And I really do want to give him something. Something I carry in my viral code, something my friends on Europa wrote into it. A hexagrammaton. You saw it. It walked your body when I was asleep."

"How do you know?"

"He told me when I let him grow from the incubant into his full beauty."

Into beauty. Facing what the virus transformed Janita into, my understanding for the Jovian tumbled down. It was fascinating, true, but also unbelievably, overwhelmingly repulsive. Janita must have been mad.

"I cannot deliver the hexagrammaton to my father or anyone else from the crew," she said quietly, and suddenly I knew with a horrifying certainty what she'd say next. She did: "But you can."

I didn't speak. My silence bore neither agreement nor refusal; just waiting.

"Have you ever thought what it would be like if you had reconciled with your wife and stayed on Ganymede? You were a successful young diplomat. Everyone thought of you as the future ambassador. If you truly became him, whose side would you choose? You've seen the poverty the Jovians lived in. You've seen both moons extend their hands for the merest crumbs from the tables of the inner planets. You've seen us eat junk from Earth and drink waste from Mars. Only five weeks remained. If you had stayed on Ganymede just five weeks longer, you'd have seen another Jupiter. No longer a stinking periphery of the system. The arrival of Vaían ships changed everything. Suddenly we were at the center of human future. The inner planets started revolving around Jupiter. You could have been their representative in the Republic. Do you understand all that you missed?"

"Janita . . . that's all the past."

She shook her ghostly head. "Thanks to people like you, the past still remains in our reach. What draws you to the ships? Why have you chosen a profession that enables you to enter them? Why have you listened to me? Why have you not denounced me? For me and my friends on Europa, you *are* the ambassador of Earth in the Republic. The real Jupiter lies not behind the belt, but right here on Earth, buried under clay and rock. We trust you. I trust you."

Her sesame seed eyes were hypnotizing me.

"Maybe what you say is true. But I don't want to be a . . . "

"Martyr?" she finished. "Are you asking for meaning? Don't you realize what would change if you deliver the hexagrammaton to the ship? In eleven years, the engines will deplete and their power over the crew will fade. The virus will weaken and allow my father and fifty other people to reach the Earth's surface again. They can climb up the throat as defeated men, used, humiliated. Or they can emerge enriched and return to the Jovian moons bearing a new hope. As Vaían Elders. Do you understand? Fifty beaten dogs change nothing. Fifty Vaían Elders can change everything. Even your past."

The silence between us lasted for an agonizing moment.

Janita leaned closer. Her face, scarred with the virus, stopped just next to mine.

"Devil's martyr," she breathed, and it sounded like a question.

"Devil's martyr," I whispered, and it sounded like an answer.

Then she pressed her forehead, covered with sweat, to my brow. Our fingers intertwined and our lips met.

Wednesday, September 5, 2192

I almost cannot write anymore. I've been copying the last lines of my diary just by sheer force of will. I managed to give the papers and half the pencil to Arvin during breakfast.

I feel as if the whole prison just disappeared. The whole universe disappeared. There is only the text and the two of us: A scientist whose hunger for knowledge drove him into prison, and a former ambassador from Earth to The Free Republic of Europa and Ganymede, sentenced for treason.

I cannot wait for tomorrow. I hope I don't disappear before then, too.

5.

I descended only so far as to disappear safely out of Janita's sight.

Then my will left my body, evaporated like a cloud of smoke in the dimness of the throat. My arms and legs refused my commands. I toppled to a protruding rim of a coil. The buzzing resonated through my whole body.

I felt emptiness. Darkness. Compared to the moment of the transmission of the virus, my whole life had been just an unceasing emptiness and darkness. Janita merged with me, revealed her nature transformed by the virus to me. No carrier ever spoke of an *infection* or *control* by the virus; now I finally understood why. I'd been blessed, urged to join something far bigger than I was, bigger than Janita, *The Destroyer of Seven Villages*, Earth, Jupiter, the revolution. I received a gift. At first it felt like jumping into deep, freezing water. My heart gave a few arrhythmic kicks; a spasm seized my body. But then seeds of a new structure started emerging from the cold. Like the Milky Way come alive, they spread through my mind. *The most important thing in your life*, Janita had said some time ago. *No*, I countered now, *the most intimate thing in my life*. But the galaxy of the virus in my mind also contained its black holes.

I'd rest a little, I decided. Five, ten minutes before I continued.

A small snail crawled around my head, leaving a path of slime behind. Its dark shell was malformed by the fields, distorted like a bull's horn.

Everything was wrong. The viral incubant swirled amid my hair roots. I was descending into a world trapped in dimness and stillness, a world buried alive. Why? Because of a chimera, a dream, an unborn child fated to wait eleven more years in its womb. I could either become a part of this grim world, or deliver the hexagrammaton and return through the throat bearing the uncompiled virus; to the guards' rifles, the unforgiving gazes of the judges, the dissection tables of government labs.

Janita would be facing certain death. In a few hours, she would run out of the depolarization solution and nothing would prevent the charging of her body anymore. When the voltage went above critical, her tissue would discharge. She'd burn like a faulty electron tube in an old radio.

Over and over again, I'd been asking myself what I cared about, and couldn't answer. Once already, I'd run from someone I had loved. Once before, the Jovian moons had invested their hopes in me. And once before, I had disappointed them. Now I could choose which I would repeat. Janita was wrong; I'd been no ambassador of Earth on Jupiter, not even the one buried in the cones. That part of me that perhaps had the courage to be him had stayed on Ganymede with my wife. Only a coward had returned to Earth, Mr. Path of Least Resistance, Mr. I Don't Look for Trouble.

A communication cable climbed the wall just beside where I sat; a bundle of ceramic fibers functioning as ultrasound waveguides. No electromagnetic signals could escape the throat's shielding and potential traps. Mechanical pulses in the ultrasound could.

The small silvery connector slid into my hand. It felt like someone else had risen, extended his arm, and let the piezoelectric interface of the connector latch onto the fibers.

The display brightened and flickered alarmingly under the attacks of the fields. JANITA PALTEV WORKS FOR EUROPAN RESISTANCE SHE IS INFECTED BY VAIAN VIRUS ALSO INFECTED ME WE ARE BOTH IN DANGER SEND A RESCUE TEAM

So much ruination in the limit of a hundred and fifty characters. Martyrs are not good diplomats. And diplomats are not good martyrs.

Saturday, September 8, 2192

Finally! It took Arvin three whole days to find the cipher key. I couldn't write a word in the meantime. Now I'm looking at the papers scribbled by Arvin and

holding my breath. Arvin deciphered the first paragraph of my diary to test the key. I had written this almost two weeks ago: "I finally succeeded in cadging some writing accessories from the guards. For the first time after more than a year of trying, they didn't dismiss me with a touch pad limited to Earth alphabets. I received a plain pencil like I haven't seen since childhood, and a thick pad with lined paper. It smells of glue and ancient times. I kept leafing through its empty pages and smelling it all afternoon. Now I've finally decided to start writing."

After applying the hexagrammaton, the text changes into: "Threads of rain drummed relentlessly on the car's roof. Streams running down the windows merged and went separate ways again. The air suffocated with water and the smell of wet earth. I stopped where the muddied road met a tall razor wire fence. I almost couldn't see the gate in the thick rain; if it weren't for the guard's booth, it would have seemed that the fence crossed the road ruthlessly and gave no one from the outside a chance to reach the peak of the towering cone." What can it mean?

I'm tearing other blank pages and starting to draw cipher tables. The pain in my hand has eased but I'm afraid it will soon return in all its strength.

Later: I've gone mad. There is no other explanation. I'm going through the text slowly and my confusion grows. I'm reading some story about a girl from Europa who travels into one of the buried ships to visit her father. The narrator is a federal agent providing the visit. His thoughts are alien to me but his choice of words, his way of speaking seems so familiar! As if I've written the text. That's beyond my imagination. But I have! Everything is going in circles. Deep slumber, obsidian snail, seven villages at the bases of seven cones.

As if, beyond the looking glass of the cipher, I've been writing about what could have been if I had not stayed on Ganymede until the Vaían arrived. What could have happened if I left my wife during our biggest crisis and ran to Earth like a coward.

As if, beside my reality, another one existed, separated only by the cipher key. Is that possible?

I cannot go on any longer today. I hope to understand more tomorrow.

A soft, short thud, like a hand slapping a table. No one from the crew heard it, but it did not escape the engines. They let it enter everyone's minds.

The captain stood in the infirmary's door and looked at the white blanket covering the body with the same confusion as everyone else. Suddenly the crew was everywhere, emerging from the dark insides of ship and clustering around its captain.

"She must have fallen from high up," the doctor said. "The left half of her body is completely shattered. A part of her skin is burnt from when she flew quickly through the fluctuating field."

The girl who landed on the hatch separating the throat from the airlock might have been about twenty-two. Europan, the doctor said. A carrier.

She hasn't come alone, the engines sang. *Look what she has brought.*

The virus on Janita's body was dying silently along with the diminishing biomagnetic field. The symbols were fading, lines breaking. The medical probes lifted the black shell of the hexagrammaton gently and copied it with the greatest caution into the ship's systems.

The crew obeyed the engines' requests and formed an uneasy crowd. In the middle of it stood Corporal Paltev. He didn't see the body up close, and even if he did, he wouldn't have recognized Janita. Only somewhere in the deep corners of his subconscious, a thought emerged: *My daughter would be the same age now.* He learned the truth many years later. But not that Janita hesitated for a long time as she saw through her tired eyes the black coveralls of the rescue team's soldiers, approaching by the rope ladders. The jump wasn't so much a jump as a fall. A flight. She stood on the edge of the platform, her arms spread and breath held. The blanket slid off her and had torn a few symbols of the virus along with it. Janita fell with her eyes open, and so she glimpsed—maybe a second after her bare feet abandoned the cold platform—a man sitting on the rim of a coil. And though it could have been only a slight, hardly noticeable moment, Janita was sure their eyes had met.

"We don't know what may happen. But we must try," the captain said as she leaned her head to the soft cradle of the scripting interface. Fifty crewmen followed her movement. One after another, they received the encapsulated cipher key inside their viruses, as if they each knelt by the bier with Janita's covered body during a funeral ceremony. Instead of flowers, bouquets of surgical steel decorated the room. But everyone who accepted the hexagrammaton seemed suddenly younger. They stopped slouching. They still talked quietly, but passionately now. All of a sudden, they had something to tell each other, though they could communicate through the engines' minds. Their hands shook with surprise and expectation, the unrest of the calm before the storm.

Like when sunbeams melt the ice in the arriving spring, the crew hurried through all corridors to the command room. The engines shared their excitement and emitted trills of enthusiasm. The beast of a compilation panel was waking up from its hibernation under the captain's hands.

Compatibility control in progress, the engines told them.

They were all looking at each other; confused, full of joy. The hexagrammaton interrupted the grueling stillness of their days.

Compilation ready.

The captain pressed her lips together. At first she wanted to talk to her crew, lift their mood, but now she saw it wasn't necessary. "Captain affirming compilation."

Just a second, two, five before the half-forgotten feeling of tingling arrived. The virus changed its structure, the incubant once again expanded through whole bodies, but according to a new key. At the same time, the engines' virus also changed. Their song wavered, the melodies merged and tones lifted. All the gazes were firmly fixed on the captain.

And then? Slowly, creepingly came what they feared most: emptiness, disappointment. Nothing. The compilation slid into the path paved by the one before. No merging of all the minds. No new control over the engines. Deep silence fell in the room. It lasted for long, arduous minutes. Even the still engines respected it. The fifty members of the crew withdrew into their shells of despair, one after another lowered their gaze to the ground.

The captain's eyes burned. Long ago she'd read somewhere that each man has a measure of luck given by destiny. They may have used theirs up. They stood there for impossibly long before the engines finally broke the wall of silence and expressed by their monotonous, contented whir that everything was back in order, that the unceasing terawatts of energy still continued surging up to Earth.

"Let us remind ourselves," the captain read in a voice she hardly recognized, "of our destiny."

She laid her hand on the panel and looked upon the Vaían symbols appearing there.

Read, the engines said, *read and have no doubts.*

And she read: "We live in the emptiness among the stars."

"*We live in the emptiness among the stars,*" the crew repeated hesitantly.

" . . . many light years from our homes."

"*. . . many light years from our homes.*"

Hexagrammaton doesn't respect tautograms of the shorter cipher keys, the captain realized. She read on and her voice gained certainty.

"We're coming to the cradle of those who came to raise us up . . . "

"*We're coming to the cradle of those who came to raise us up . . .* "

" . . . to continue learning how to use their gift."

"*. . . to continue learning how to use their gift.*"

"And when they accept us into their celestial community . . . "

"*And when they accept us into their celestial community . . .* "

" . . . we too will travel the vast expanse to spread their glory . . . "

"*. . . we too will travel the vast expanse to spread their glory . . .* "

" . . . as Vaían asked us and as we promised Vaían."

"*. . . as Vaían asked us and as we promised Vaían.*"

"That is our destiny," the captain read the last line.

"*That is our destiny*," the crew almost cried out. As if the same words with another meaning sounded altogether different. The room was filled with an excited hum of fifty voices.

"Mr. Dagasian," the captain called, "man the navigation panel."

The command room's stations were coming alive one by one.

"Madam," an awed voice near one of the screens breathed, "Probes report our current speed of three hundredths c and slowing gradually."

"Mr. Zimov, the controls!"

The officers were abruptly returning to their stations as if they had left them just hours and not years ago.

"Madam, I've got the engines' data for the last five years here. They were running on full power for that time, yes, but in flight mode."

"What?"

"As if . . . as if we flew the whole time underneath the cone."

Only the engines understood what happened, and they told everyone: *Now we are a part of a new story. If we continue it, we cannot return to the old one.*

"Corporal Paltev! The windows!"

The ship quivered a little as the corroded shutters slowly uncovered the view from the control room. There was dirt crumbling from the first bared cracks. And then the eyes of the crew met with starlight.

"Madam, we really are flying. We've been flying for the whole time!"

"Mr. Dagasian, our location!"

The captain gazed out in fascination. The space around them was *alive*. Like branches of a tree, helical structures of cosmic stations expanded everywhere, meeting restless swarms of small ships. The inhabited space was spreading before them, as if to embrace them.

"Madam, I've found our location. The bright red star in front of us is Alpha Tauri. Aldebaran."

The captain could no longer hold the tears coming to her eyes. The whole crew cried. Someone started clapping and everyone was hugging or caressing the others' tormented faces.

"Yes, it is Aldebaran," the captain said to the navigator. "We're here. Vaían welcomes us."

THE SACRIFICE OF THE HANGED MONKEY

MINSOO KANG

[*The first chapters of* <u>The Crane Falls, the Falcon Rises: The True Chronicle of the End of the First Era of the Sublime Rule and the Beginning of the Second Era</u> *were destroyed in the burning of the Eternal House of Endless Knowledge. It was not the practice of historians of the time to number the chapters of their works, so it is unknown how many of them have been lost. The extant text begins here.*]

[*interpreted?*] the failure of the colony in the realm of the Hanged Monkey as evidence of the weakness of the imperial system. But it should be remembered that the event occurred at the height of the Sublime Rule's dominance in the West and the North, and the decline of its grip on power there did not occur until the middle of the Third Era. In other words, the precipitous collapse of the colony was an anomalous occurrence at a time when the empire was enjoying a virtually uninterrupted string of military and political successes across the region. Furthermore, even when the hegemony of the Sublimes fell apart, no other occupied territory was lost in the same manner as the realm of the Hanged Monkey. So the story is of interest not for the insight it sheds on the eventual downfall of the once supreme power, but rather for the unique nature of the colony's fate, the significance of which scholars have found both unfathomable and tantalizing.

By the end of the First Era, the military might of the Sublime Rule, in its sheer size as well as technological capability, so far outstripped that of any land in the swampy West and the rocky North that its expeditionary forces rarely had to engage in actual fighting with the various peoples it encountered. Atop the outer wall of the capital of the realm of the Hanged Monkey, its royalty, ministers, and generals watched in terrified awe as the great invading army arrayed itself on the field beyond like an undulating ocean of spears and flags. The Sublimes then made an extravagant show of their fearsome weapons and tamed monsters from all corners of the empire that struck fear into the hearts of the natives like a lightning bolt from a cloudless sky. After the grand display, an envoy was sent to the quaking rulers of the realm to deliver the terms of their inevitable surrender.

In accordance to the principles of "Benevolent Domination," the recognition of the supremacy of the Sublime Ruler would allow them to maintain much of their political, social, and cultural status quo. The king of the realm of the Hanged Monkey would remain king, his laws would still be in effect as long as they did not conflict with imperial statutes, his priests would continue to worship their deity, and his people would carry on their lives pretty much as before. The only conditions that would be imposed were the establishment of a commandery under a military prefect, a tax in the form of a twice-yearly tribute, and the sending of a contingent of soldiers to join the imperial army. Resistance, on the other hand, would result in the complete destruction of the capital and its inhabitants, and the enslavement of all the people of the land.

[*The chronicle neglects to mention the problem of language in such interactions between the Sublimes and the people they subdued. Of course all communication was conducted through interpreters, most of merchant background whose occupation made the familiarity with multiple languages a necessity. The historian probably left them out because their role was essential in the actual events but not in their recounting. While this may be an understandable act of narrative simplification, it creates the impression of an implausible world in which people of many lands somehow speak the same language, as can be found in many unsophisticated works of fantasy.*]

The king agreed to the terms of submission without hesitation and without any objection from his ministers and generals. So it appeared that the Sublimes would achieve yet another bloodless conquest in the North. But then a minor mishap occurred that might have planted the seed of the eventual calamity that would befall the realm.

Just as the imperial army began to march toward the main gate of the capital and the rulers of the realm prepared to welcome the conquerors, a side gate opened and a group of a few dozen men in bright yellow robes came charging out with a war cry. They swung clubs and sticks in the air and flew a standard with the image of their god, the Hanged Monkey whose name was Bob. They were the priests of the Temple of the Hanged Monkey, led by a hoary high priest who assured them of the imminent intervention of Bob who would sweep away the foreign army as a gardener wields his broom to weep away so many dead leaves of autumn. In response, the Sublimes sent a squadron of men armed with fire-spewing weapons who rode out on giant hamsters and incinerated the priests, reducing them all to heaps of smoking ash in an instant.

When the generals of the imperial army entered the capital, the mortified king hurried to them and explained that he had nothing to do with the actions of the priests, that they had been a group of crazed fanatics who had launched the suicidal attack on their own accord. Given the utterly senseless nature of the act, the generals decided that he was telling the truth, but they also agreed that the king had to be punished for failing to keep his priests under control. As it was well known that the Sublimes had no qualms about razing entire cities, ruining vast lands, and eradicating the populations of those who dared to defy them, it came as a relief to the rulers of the realm that they were merely ousted from the royal palace to seek accommodations elsewhere.

[*There is no doubt that the priests who led the short-lived fight against the Sublimes must have done so because they truly believed that the Hanged Monkey whose name was Bob would indeed intervene on their behalf. There is, however, the possibility of another motivation for the desperate act. Recently found documents have suggested that in the decades before the coming of the Sublimes, the priesthood took advantage of a weak royal family to systematically take over the reins of power in the realm. By the time of the conquest, the kingdom functioned more or less as a theocracy, with the monarch as only a figurehead. So the leadership of the Temple of the Hanged Monkey had much more to lose than the royalty in submitting to the Sublimes. That may have led to the high priest's conviction that Bob would surely answer his call to unleash his divine wrath upon the invaders. This notion is supported by the fact that after the royal family was ousted from the palace, there was no mention of their involvement in the events that followed, testifying to their ineffectuality and irrelevance. In fact, they disappear completely from history at that point.*]

The Sublime generals duly selected one of their own to be the prefect of the newly established commandery, an ambitious scion of an illustrious martial clan who regarded the appointment as an essential stepping stone to greater things. A portion of the army was left under his charge to garrison the capital before the expeditionary force moved on to conquer new lands. The prefect, along with his officers and bureaucrats, moved into the former royal palace, which was capacious enough to be turned into their living quarters as well as command center. Everything proceeded smoothly in the following months as they prepared to enact a general census and land survey for the purpose of tax collection, and to see about recruiting local soldiers to join the imperial army.

Early one morning, the prefect was awakened by a great din of people shouting outside his chamber's window. When he got up and looked out in annoyance, he saw that there was a crowd gathered at the Temple of the Hanged Monkey, which lay right next to the palace. The prefect summoned an aide and ordered him to go and find out what the commotion was about. The aide returned as the prefect, in a foul mood from having gotten insufficient sleep due to the disturbance, was finishing his breakfast. The mystified aide informed him that the priests of the temple, those who had not taken part in the hapless resistance, were in the middle of a heated theological dispute which was apparently of great interest to the populace at large, as many inhabitants of the capital had gathered to hear them. Upon further inquiry, the prefect found out that their argument was over the nature of the Hanged Monkey whose name was Bob, who began as an ordinary monkey but was elevated to divinity after his hanging. One group of priests believed that Bob possessed the potential for divinity from the beginning, a special quality which was activated by the gods when they raised him from the dead. In other words, even before he became a god, he carried a proto-divine essence. The opposing group of priests insisted that Bob was a wholly mortal monkey before his deification, and that the true miracle of his transformation lay precisely in the fact that he was once nothing more than a small, weak, shitting, pissing animal. The entire capital was in the grip of this disputation which was carried out by the priests with a great passion that verged on a strange kind of desperation. As the prefect learned that morning, they were not content to discuss the matter in a calm and orderly manner as the two groups continued to shout at each other throughout the day.

[*As scholars of religions have pointed out, such passion in theological arguments always points to a subtext, of some matter that cannot be spoken of directly or admitted to overtly, a matter often of power and impotence, wealth and poverty, life and death. It has been suggested that the priests were tormented by guilt and confusion over the demise of their peers. Those who had challenged the Sublimes had perished quickly at the hands of the invaders, but they had proven themselves to be the strongest in their faith. Those who had not participated felt themselves to be weak, cowardly, and beset with doubt. Their dispute was really over how they must live and carry on as the remaining guardians of their religion. It has also been suggested that their disagreement was really over whether they should rebel against their conquerors. Should they believe in a great potential within themselves (the proto-divinity of Bob before the hanging) that would be activated to lead them to victory against the seemingly invincible Sublime? Must they believe in that and fight to prove themselves true believers? Or should they admit to their current weakness and powerlessness (as Bob was once nothing more than a weak and powerless monkey) and wait for the right opportunity to make a great and useful sacrifice that would compel a divine force to raise them from their subjugation and humiliation? Perhaps the Hanged Monkey had not intervened in the initial calamity because that was not the proper time for resistance. While all that is in the realm of pure speculation, it is reasonable to consider such a hidden agenda as their disputation was conducted with a fervor far beyond that of a mere academic exercise.]*

The irritated prefect dispatched an officer with a squadron of soldiers to the temple. He abided by the principle of "Benevolent Domination" as he sent the message that he would not concern himself with the internal affairs of the temple as long as it did not interfere with imperial business, but they really had to quiet down. The priests' arguments did not stop but their noise subsided enough for the prefect to enjoy a quiet evening and a good night's rest.

When the prefect woke up the next morning, he was surprised to hear the priests still at it, making him wonder if they had been disputing all night long. As he lay in bed listening, their voices went up and down, sometimes on the verge of shouting until they suddenly quieted again, as if someone reminded them of the prefect's warning. It went on like that for the rest of the day. At one point in the afternoon, however, the priests apparently forgot themselves and became loud, but just as the prefect was about to send another squadron with instructions to beat up a few of them and destroy some artifact in the temple, their noise subsided once more.

After a few days of this, the prefect was woken before dawn by their shouting, which enraged him. He leapt out of bed and ordered the assembly of a contingent of a full hundred before putting on his armor. He went down to the temple where he and his men violently pushed and kicked their way through the crowd. When they reached the altar of the Hanged Monkey, senior priests, apparently the leaders of the two sides of the theological dispute, prostrated themselves before the prefect to beg his pardon for the disturbance they had caused. But he ignored them and looked around until he saw the ancient stone statue of the Hanged Monkey standing behind the altar. He took an iron mace from a soldier and, as the priests watched in abject horror, proceeded to smash the statue to pieces. First came off Bob's head in a noose, then his loosely hanging arms, his tail, and his distended belly. Only after the holy image was reduced to rubble did the prefect address the priests.

"You stupid savages with your stupid god! The Hanged Monkey? There is no Hanged Monkey! Whether he's called Bob or Bill or Coco or Momo or some other idiotic name. You would know that if you had the least bit of intelligence in your primitive minds. Animal gods, elemental gods, geographical gods, none of them are real. Just infantile fantasies for infantile people. The world is a machine, don't you know! A great self-moving machine. The Creator designed it so that it can run itself. He made it so he could behold its beauty and perfection for all of eternity. He is watching even now, but from a place far, far, far from here. He doesn't answer prayers, he doesn't intervene in our affairs, and he doesn't give a shit about your stupid argument about your stupid monkey god."

He then looked up and spread out his arms.

"Hanged monkey god!" he shouted. "Yes, I am addressing you, Bob, you ridiculous phantasm. I am the conqueror of these savage people who worship you. If I am wrong, if you are not some delusion in their childish minds, then strike me down. Strike me down right now! I dare you, you filthy, shit-eating animal! Prove me wrong, and prove your worshippers right. Strike me down!"

He then waited for a long moment as all in the temple kept absolutely still and silent.

"Ha!" the prefect finally said. "See! Hanged monkey god. Ha ha."

He then walked out of the temple, followed by his men.

Back at the palace, the Sublimes did not hear a single sound coming out of the temple for the rest of the day. Deep into the night, however, the prefect woke up to a world of smoke and fire.

When he was roused by an aide to the smell of burning and noise of chaos outside, he immediately thought that he had pushed the natives too far that day, that they had risen up in rebellion in response to his desecration of the temple. As he quickly got up and put on his heavy armor once again, he worried mainly about how all that would impact his career. He knew that the revolt would be easily crushed with weapons of fire, lightning, and dissolving liquid, and that he would then mete out punishment to the people that would be severe enough to make them too fearful and demoralized to try anything like that again. But he would also have to submit a full report of these events to the Ministry of Colonial Affairs of the West and the North at the capital of the Sublime Rule. And there would be questions of whether he had failed to properly apply the principles of "Benevolent Domination,"resulting in this situation. He would have to explain things so that much of the responsibility would be deflected from him, but even if he succeeded in doing so, it might still prove to be an obstacle in the way of his grand ambitions.

Cursing in frustration, he went down to the main gate of the palace, where he was met by his officers who had assembled the entire garrison. One of them, however, reported to him of the strangeness of what was happening outside the walls. The priests and a great crowd of other people were gathered, but they were not attacking the palace. They were divided into two groups that were fighting each other.

When the gate was opened and the prefect and his soldiers marched out, they saw that the Temple of the Hanged Monkey had been set ablaze and the area around it had become a battlefield in which priests and laymen alike were attacking one another with knives, axes, clubs, and shovels. In fact, they were going at it with such rage and ferocity that it was turning into a bloodbath. As the Sublimes watched in amazement, the prefect himself not knowing what to do, the natives killed one another with such efficiency as the temple burned that soon there was only one priest of gigantic stature left alive, the blood that covered his yellow robe and fell from his knife glimmering ominously in the last dying fires.

A sudden realization came to the prefect, so he stepped toward the last priest.

"You there!" he called out. "Was this about the argument over your god? Did you fight because the two sides blamed each other for what happened today? For what I did to the image of your god?"

The priest looked at the prefect with empty eyes for a long moment before he answered. "All this is a sacrifice. A sacrifice to the Hanged Monkey whose name was Bob."

He then plunged his blade into his throat.

After the shock of what had occurred wore off, the prefect was about to order the cleanup of the bloody mess when he saw another fire erupting in a nearby building, then another, then another, until the whole city was on fire. It would take him days to fully comprehend what happened, that all the people of the realm of the Hanged Monkey packed their things, set fire to their houses and fields, and abandoned the place in a matter of hours. By the time the new day dawned, the entire land was turning into a smoke-covered wasteland. And when the people left, they did not travel together but families and individuals scattered in all directions and in a great hurry with no destiny in mind. When imperial soldiers stopped some of them, they said that they were fleeing a cursed place that was no longer fit for people to live in, one that they had to get away from as fast and as far away as possible. They became a lost people, dispersed refugees wandering aimlessly across the world who did not even try to preserve the memories of their original home and culture. Soon there was no more city, no more realm, and no more people to rule over. The imperial colony failed because it ceased to exist in the course of a single day.

The imperial army eventually left and returned to the metropole of the Sublime Rule. After an exhaustive inquiry into the fall of the realm of the Hanged Monkey which resulted in no clear understanding of the events, the case was closed and the former prefect of the commandery was demoted from his rank of general. He was assigned as a mid-level officer to a garrison in a far and peaceful province in the Tranquil South where he lived out the rest of his life in melancholy mediocrity.

In the commentaries to the *Basic Annals of the First Era of the Sublime Empire*, no less than four Grand Historians have [*asserted?*]

[*The rest of the chapter was damaged at this point, and the following chapter begins with a narration of the events in the swampy West. While it may frustrate the reader to be deprived of the insights of the Grand Historians, it must be noted that they were not privy to recently discovered documents on the realm of the Hanged Monkey. Among them, the one that is of greatest interest is a record of the story of the god known as the Hanged Monkey whose name was Bob. While it may not provide a satisfying explanation of the fall of the realm, and may even bring further mystification, it offers a new perspective on its strange fate.*]

Before the coming of the first woman, and her subsequent creation of her male companion and the other woman, a great ball of fire fell from the heavens. The god of the sea, as greedy and hungry as ever, swallowed it whole. But it was such a great fiery thing that it caused the god to let out a powerful fart that cracked the earth open. Out of that crack a monstrous wolf escaped from the fiery depths and wreaked havoc upon the world. As it ran furiously about, it pissed fire out of its gigantic penis, burning up everything on land so that nothing could grow, and boiling the waters of all the rivers until they turned into steam. The strongest and bravest animals of the land tried to stop the beast, but it burned or ate all who dared to challenge it. The gods, seeing the wanton destruction of their beauteous creation, finally intervened, but they too were unable to stop the raging creature. While all the remaining animals fled, a lone monkey named Bob, who had seen the destruction of his entire family and tribe by the wolf's fire, courageously carried on the fight. Although he was but a small and weak monkey, he was also smart and quick. He chased the wolf by swinging from one tree to another before jumping onto its back to torment it. He pulled at its tail and, when the beast snapped at him with its great teeth, made his escape by leaping to a tall tree. He chased the wolf again, then jumped back down on it to rip out some fur before leaping to another tree. He repeated the action, spitting in the wolf's ear, poking it in the eye, and scratching its nose.

The enraged wolf realized that the only way to get the nimble creature was to destroy all trees. So he went from one to another, pissing fire at their trunks and setting them on fire. Eventually Bob found himself trapped in the last tree in the land. The beast was about to set fire to it also, when it realized that it was very hungry. So it decided to wait for the monkey to try to make his escape so it could eat him. The tree was full of fruits, but that provided no comfort for Bob as he knew them to be very poisonous.

The wolf stood by the tree in patient watch until night fell and it grew tired. It lay down and closed its eyes to sleep, but it kept its ears open so that it could pounce if the monkey came down. Next morning, it woke up to find that Bob had apparently given into despair and hanged himself on a low branch. The wolf rejoiced at the sight and jumped up to swallow the dead monkey whole.

When the sun reached the highest point in the sky, the wolf suddenly felt sick. Its stomach churned in agony until it expelled so much feces that it fertilized the land and made things grow again. It then sweated so much that it replenished the waters of the rivers. It then lost all its fur, the strands of which flew into the air, planted themselves in the land and turned into trees to replace all the ones that had burned. As the great beast then lay down to die, it realized the cause of its demise. The monkey had eaten all the fruits of the last tree before hanging itself so that the wolf would become poisoned when it ate him.

The gods were so impressed with the monkey's sacrifice which saved the world that they gathered his remains from the belly of the dead monster and returned him to life by endowing him with divinity. And so was born the god known as the Hanged Monkey whose name was Bob.

ZEROS

PETER WATTS

Asante goes out screaming. Hell is an echo chamber, full of shouts and seawater and clanking metal. Monstrous shadows move along the bulkheads; meshes of green light writhe on every surface. The Sāḥilites rise from the moon pool like creatures from some bright lagoon, firing as they emerge; Rashida's middle explodes in dark mist and her top half topples onto the deck. Kito's still dragging himself toward the speargun on the drying rack—as though some antique fish-sticker could ever fend off these monsters with their guns and their pneumatics and their little cartridges that bury themselves deep in your flesh before showing you what five hundred unleashed atmospheres do to your insides.

It's more than Asante's got. All he's got is his fists.

He uses them. Launches himself at the nearest Sāḥilite as she lines up Kito in her sights, swings wildly as the deck groans and drops and cants sideways. Seawater breaches the lip of the moon pool, cascades across the plating. Asante flails at the intruder on his way down. Her shot goes wide. A spiderweb blooms across the viewport; a thin gout of water erupts from its center even as the glass tries to heal itself from the edges in.

The last thing Asante sees is the desert hammer icon on the Sāḥilite's diveskin before she blows him away.

Five Years

Running water. Metal against metal. Clanks and gurgles, lowered voices, the close claustrophobic echo of machines in the middle distance.

Asante opens his eyes.

He's still in the wet room; its ceiling blurs and clicks into focus, plates and struts and Kito's stupid graffiti (*All Tautologies Are Tautologies*) scratched into the paint. Green light still wriggles dimly across the biosteel, but the murderous energy's been bled out of it.

He tries to turn his head, and can't. He barely feels his own body—as though it were made of ectoplasm, some merest echo of solid flesh fading into nonexistence somewhere around the waist.

An insect's head on a human body looms over him. It speaks with two voices: English, and an overlapping echo in Twi: "Easy, soldier. Relax."

A woman's voice, and a chip one.

Not Sāḥilite. But armed. Dangerous.

Not a soldier he wants to say, wants to *shout*. It's never a good thing to be mistaken for any sort of combatant along the west coast. But he can't even whisper. He can't feel his tongue.

Asante realizes that he isn't breathing.

The Insect woman (a diveskin, he sees now: her mandibles an electrolysis rig, her compound eyes a pair of defraction goggles) retrieves a tactical scroll from beyond his field of view and unrolls it a half-meter from his face. She mutters an incantation and it flares softly to life, renders a stacked pair of keyboards: English on top, Twi beneath.

"Don't try to talk," she says in both tongues. "Just look at the letters."

He focuses on the N: it brightens. O. T. The membrane offers up predictive spelling, speeds the transition from sacc' to script:

NOT SOLDIER FISH FARMER

"Sorry." She retires the translator; the Twi keys flicker and disappear. "Figure of speech. What's your name?"

KODJO ASANTE

She pushes the defractors onto her forehead, unlatches the mandibles. They fall away and dangle to one side. She's white underneath.

IS KITO

"I'm sorry, no. Everyone's dead."

Everyone else, he thinks, and imagines Kito mocking him one last time for insufferable pedantry.

"Got him." Man's voice, from across the compartment. "Kodjo Asante, Takoradi. Twenty-eight, bog-standard aqua—wait; combat experience. Two years with GAF."

Asante's eyes dart frantically across the keyboard: only farmer not

"No worries, mate." She lays down a reassuring hand; he can only assume it comes to rest somewhere on his body. "Everyone's seen combat hereabouts, right? You're sitting on the only reliable protein stock in three hundred klicks. Stands to reason you're gonna have to defend it now and again.

"Still." A shoulder patch comes into view as she turns toward the other voice: WestHem Alliance. "We could put him on the list."

"If you're gonna do it, do it fast. Surface contact about two thousand meters out, closing."

She turns back to Asante. "Here's the thing. We didn't get here in time.

We're not supposed to be here at all, but our CO got wind of Sally's plans and took a little humanitarian initiative, I guess you could say. We showed up in time to scare 'em off and light 'em up, but you were all dead by then."

I WASN'T

"Yeah, Kodjo, you too. All dead."

YOU BROUGHT ME BA

"No."

BUT

"We gave your brain a jump start, that's all. You know how you can make a leg twitch when you pass a current through it? You know what *galvanic* means, Kodjo?"

"He's got a Ph.D. in molecular marine ecology," says her unseen colleague. "I'm guessing yes."

"You can barely feel anything, am I right? Body like a ghost? We didn't reboot the rest of you. You're just getting residual sensations from nerves that don't know they're dead yet. You're a brain in a box, Kodjo. You're running on empty.

"But here's the thing: you don't *have* to be."

"Hurry it up, Cat. We got ten minutes, tops."

She glances over her shoulder, back again. "We got a rig on the *Levi Morgan*, patch you up and keep you on ice until we get home. And we got a rig *there* that'll work goddamn miracles, make you better'n new. But it ain't cheap, Kodjo. Pretty much breaks the bank every time we do it."

DON'T HAVE MONEY

"Don't want *money*. We want you to work for us. Five-year tour, maybe less depending on how the tech works out. Then you go on your way, nice fat bank balance, whole second chance. Easy gig, believe me. You're just a passenger in your own body for the hard stuff. Even boot camp's mostly autonomic. Real accelerated program."

NOT WESTHEM

"You're not Hegemon either, not any more. You're not much of anything but rotting meat hooked up to a pair of jumper cables. I'm offering you salvation, mate. You can be Born Again."

"Wrap it the fuck *up*, Cat. They're almost on top of us."

" 'Course if you're not interested, I can just pull the plug. Leave you the way we found you."

NO PLEASE YES

"Yes what, Kodjo? Yes pull the plug? Yes leave you behind? You need to be specific about this. We're negotiating a contract here."

YES BORN AGAIN YES 5 YEAR TOUR

He wonders at this shiver of hesitation, this voice whispering *maybe dead is better.* Perhaps it's because he *is* dead; maybe all those suffocating endocrine glands just aren't up to the task of flooding his brain with the warranted elixir of fear and desperation and *survival at any cost.* Maybe being dead means never having to give a shit.

He does, though. He may be dead but his glands aren't, not yet. He didn't say no.

He wonders if anyone ever has.

"Glory Hallelujah!" Cat proclaims, reaching offstage for some unseen control. And just before everything goes black:

"Welcome to the Zombie Corps."

Savior Machine

That's not what they call it, though.

"Be clear about one thing. There's no good reason why any operation should ever put boots in the battlefield."

They call it *ZeroS*. Strangely, the Z does not stand for *Zombie*.

"There's no good reason why any competent campaign should involve a battlefield in the first place. That's what economic engineering and Cloud Control are for."

The S doesn't even stand for *Squad*.

"If they fail, that's what drones and bots and TAI are for."

Zero Sum. Or as NCOIC Silano puts it, *A pun, right? Cogito ergo.* Better than *The Spaz Brigade*, which was Garin's suggestion.

Asante's in Tactical Orientation, listening to an artificial instructor that he'd almost accept as human but for the fact that it doesn't sound bored to death.

"There's only one reason you'll ever find yourselves called on deck, and that's if everyone has fucked up so completely at conflict resolution that there's nothing left in the zone but a raging shitstorm."

Asante's also running up the side of a mountain. It's a beautiful route, twenty klicks of rocks and pines and mossy deadfall. There might be more green growing things on this one slope than in the whole spreading desert of northern Africa. He wishes he could see it.

"Your very presence means the mission has already failed; your job is to salvage what you can from the wreckage."

He can't see it, though. He can't see much of anything. Asante's been blind since Reveille.

"Fortunately for you, economics and Cloud Control and tactical AI fail quite a lot."

The blindness isn't total. He still sees light, vague shapes in constant motion. It's like watching the world through wax paper. The eyes *jiggle* when you're a Passenger. Of course the eyes always jiggle, endlessly hopping from one momentary focus to the next—*saccades*, they're called—but your brain usually edits out those motions, splices the clear bits together in post to serve up an illusion of continuity.

Not up here, though. Up here the sacc rate goes through the roof and nothing gets lost. Total data acquisition. To Asante it's all blizzard and blur, but that's okay. There's something in here with him that can see just fine: his arms and legs are moving, after all, and Kodjo Asante isn't moving them.

His other senses work fine; he feels the roughness of the rope against his palms as he climbs the wall, smells the earth and pine needles bedding the trail. Still tastes a faint hint of copper from that bite on the inside of his cheek a couple klicks back. He hears with utmost clarity the voice on his audio link. His inner zombie sucks all that back too, but eardrums don't saccade. Tactile nerves don't hop around under the flesh. Just the eyes: that's how you tell. That and the fact that your whole body's been possessed by Alien Hand Syndrome.

He calls it his Evil Twin. It's a name first bestowed by his Dad, after catching eight-year-old Kodjo sleepwalking for the third time in a week. Asante made the mistake of mentioning that once to the squad over breakfast. He's still trying to live it down.

Now he tries for the hell of it, wills himself to *stop* for just an instant. ET runs and leaps and crawls as it has for the past two hours, unnervingly autonomous. That's the retrosplenial bypass they burned into his neocortex a month ago, a little dropgate to decouple *mind* from *self*. Just one of the mods they've etched into him with neural lace and nanotube mesh and good old-fashioned zap'n'tap. Midbrain tweaks to customize ancient prey-stalking routines. An orbitofrontal damper to ensure behavioral compliance (*can't have your better half deciding to keep the keys when you want them back*, as Maddox puts it).

His scalp itches with fresh scars. His head moves with a disquieting inertia, as if weighed down by a kilogram of lead and not a few bits of arsenide and carbon. He doesn't understand a tenth of it. Hasn't quite come to grips with life after death. But dear God, how *wonderful* it is to be so strong. He feels like this body could take on a whole platoon single-handed.

Sometimes he can feel this way for five or ten whole minutes before remembering the names of other corpses who never got in on the deal.

Without warning ET dances to one side, brings its arms up and suddenly Asante can *see*.

Just for a millisecond, a small clear break in a sea of fog: a Lockheed Pit Bull cresting the granite outcropping to his left, legs spread, muzzle spinning to bear. In the next instant Asante's blind again, recoil vibrating along his arm like a small earthquake. His body hasn't even broken stride.

"Ah. Target acquisition," the instructor remarks. "Enjoy the view." It takes this opportunity to summarize the basics—target lock's the only time when the eyes focus on a single point long enough for passengers to look out—before segueing into a spiel on line-of-sight networking.

Asante isn't sure what the others are hearing. Tiwana, the only other raw recruit, is probably enduring the same 101 monologue. Kalmus might have moved up to field trauma by now. Garin's on an engineering track. Maddox has told Asante that he'll probably end up in bioweapons, given his background.

It takes nineteen months to train a field-ready specialist. ZeroS do it in seven.

Asante's legs have stopped moving. On all sides he hears the sound of heavy breathing. Lieutenant Metzinger's voice tickles the space between his ears: "Passengers, you may enter the cockpit."

The switch is buried in the visual cortex and tied to the power of imagination. They call it a *mandala*. Each recruit chooses their own and keeps it secret; no chance of a master key for some wily foe to drop onto a billboard in the heat of battle. Not even the techs know the patterns, the implants were conditioned on double-blind trial-and-error. *Something personal*, they said. *Something unique, easy to visualize.*

Asante's mandala is a sequence of four words in sans serif font. He summons it now—

ALL TAUTOLOGIES

ARE TAUTOLOGIES

—and the world clicks back into sudden, jarring focus. He stumbles, though he wasn't moving.

Right on cue, his left hand starts twitching.

They're halfway up the mountain, in a sloping sunny meadow. There are *flowers* here. Insects. Everything smells alive. Silano raises trembling arms to the sky. Kalmus flumps on the grass, recovering from exertions barely felt when better halves were in control, exertions that have left them weak and wasted despite twice-normal mito counts and AMPK agonists and a dozen other tweaks to put them in the upper tail of the upper tail. Acosta drops beside her, grinning at the sunshine. Garin kicks at a punky log and an actual goddamn *snake* slithers into the grass, a ribbon of yellow and black with a flickering tongue.

Tiwana's at Asante's shoulder, as scarred and bald as he is. "Beautiful, eh?" Her right eye's a little off-kilter; Asante resists the impulse to stare by focusing on the bridge of her nose.

"Not beautiful enough to make up for two hours with a hood over my head." That's Saks, indulging in some pointless bitching. "Would it kill them to give us a video feed?"

"Or even just put us to sleep," Kalmus grumbles. They both know it's not that simple. The brain's a tangle of wires looping from basement to attic and back again; turn off the lights in the living room and your furnace might stop working. Even pay-per-view's a nonstarter. In theory, there's no reason why they couldn't bypass those jiggling eyes entirely—pipe a camera feed directly to the cortex—but their brains are already so stuffed with implants that there isn't enough real estate left over for nonessentials.

That's what Maddox says, anyway.

"I don't really give a shit," Acosta's saying. The tic at the corner of his mouth makes his grin a twitchy, disconcerting thing. "I'd put up with twice the offline time if there was always a view like this at the end of it." Acosta lives for any scrap of nature he can find; his native Guatemala lost most of its canopy to firestorm carousels back in '42.

"So what's in it for you?" Tiwana asks.

It takes a moment for Asante to realize the question's for him. "Excuse me?"

"Acosta's nature-boy. Kalmus thinks she's gonna strike it rich when they declassify the tech." This is news to Asante. "Why'd *you* sign up?"

He doesn't quite know how to answer. Judging by his own experience, ZeroS is not something you *sign up* for. ZeroS is something that finds you. It's an odd question, a private question. It brings up things he'd rather not dwell upon.

It brings up things he already dwells on too much.

"Ah—"

Thankfully, Maddox chooses that moment to radio up from Côté: "Okay, everybody. Symptom check. Silano."

The Corporal looks at his forearms. "Pretty good. Less jumpy than normal."

"Kalmus."

"I've got, ah, ah . . . " She stammers, struggles, finally spits in frustration. "*Fuck.*"

"I'll just put down the usual aphasia," Maddox says. "Garin."

"Vision flickers every five, ten minutes."

"That's an improvement."

"Gets better when I exercise. Better blood flow, maybe."

"Interesting," Maddox says. "Tiwan—"

"*I see you God I see you!*"

Saks is on the ground, writhing. His eyes roll in their sockets. His fingers claw handfuls of earth. "*I see!*" he cries, and lapses into gibberish. His head thrashes. Spittle flies from his mouth. Tiwana and Silano move in but the audio link crackles with the voice of God, "Stand away! Everyone stand back *now!*"

and everyone obeys because God speaks with the voice of Lieutenant David Metzinger and you do not want to fuck with *him*. God's breath is blowing down from Heaven, from the rotors of a medical chopper beating the air with impossible silence even though they all see it now, they all see it, there's no need for stealth mode there never was it's always there, just out of sight, just in case.

Saks has stopped gibbering. His face is a rictus, his spine a drawn bow. The chopper lands, its *whup whup whup* barely audible even ten meters away. It vomits medics and a stretcher and glossy black easter-egg drones with jointed insect legs folded to their bellies. The ZeroS step back; the medics close in and block the view.

Metzinger again: "Okay, meat sacks. Everyone into the back seat. Return to Côté."

Silano turns away, eyes already jiggling in their sockets. Tiwana and Kalmus go over a moment later. Garin slaps Asante's back on the way out—"Gotta go, man. Happens, you know?"—and vanishes into his own head.

The chopper lifts Saks into the heavens.

"Private Asante! *Now!*"

He stands alone in the clearing, summons his mandala, falls into blindness. His body turns. His legs move. Something begins to run him downhill. The artificial instructor, always sensitive to context, begins a lecture about dealing with loss on the battlefield.

It's all for the best, he knows. It safest to be a passenger at times like this. All these glitches, these—side-effects: they never manifest in zombie mode.

Which makes perfect sense. That being where they put all the money.

Station To Station

Sometimes he still wakes in the middle of the night, shocked back to consciousness by the renewed knowledge that he still exists—as if his death was some near-miss that didn't really sink in until days or weeks afterward, leaving him weak in the knees and gasping for breath. He catches himself calling his mandala, a fight/flight reaction to threat stimuli long-since expired. He stares at the ceiling, forces calm onto panic, takes comfort from the breathing of his fellow recruits. Tries not think about Kito and Rashida. Tries not to think at all.

Sometimes he finds himself in the Commons, alone but for the inevitable drone hovering just around the corner, ready to raise alarms and inject drugs should he suffer some delayed and violent reaction to any of a hundred recent mods. He watches the world through one of CFB Côté's crippled terminals (they can surf, but never send). He slips through wires and fiberop, bounces off geosynchronous relays all the way back to Ghana: satcams down on the dizzying Escher arcology of the Cape Universitas hubs, piggybacks on drones wending through Makola's East, marvels anew at the giant gengineered snails—big as a centrifuge, some of them—that first ignited his passion for biology when he was six. He haunts familiar streets where the kenkey and fish always tasted better when the Chinese printed them, even though the recipes must have been copied from the locals. The glorious chaos of the street drummers during Adai.

He never seeks out friends or family. He doesn't know if it's because he's not ready, or because he has already moved past them. He only knows not to awaken things that have barely gone to sleep.

Zero Sum. A new life. Also a kind of game used, more often than not, to justify armed conflict.

Also *Null Existence.* If your tastes run to the Latin.

They loom over a drowning subdivision long-abandoned to the rising waters of Galveston Bay: cathedral-sized storage tanks streaked with rust and ruin, twelve-story filtration towers, masses of twisting pipe big enough to walk through.

Garin sidles up beside him. "Looks like a crab raped an octopus."

"Your boys seem twitchy," the Sheriff says. (Asante clenches his fist to control the tremor.) "They hopped on something?"

Metzinger ignores the question. "Have they made any demands?"

"Usual. Stop the rationing or they blow it up." The Sheriff shakes his head, moves to mop his brow, nearly punches himself in the face when his decrepit Bombardier exoskeleton fratzes and overcompensates. "Everything's gone to shit since the Edwards dried up."

"They respond to a water shortage by blowing up a desalination facility?"

The Sheriff snorts. "Folks always make sense where you come from, Lieutenant?"

They reviewed the plant specs down to the rivets on the way here. Or at least their zombies did, utterly silent, borrowed eyes flickering across video feeds and backgrounders that Asante probably wouldn't have grasped even if he *had* been able to see them. All Asante knows—by way of the impoverished briefings Metzinger doles out to those back in Tourist Class—is that the facility was bought from Qatar back when paint still peeled and metal still rusted, when digging viscous fossils from the ground left you rich enough to buy the planet. And that it's falling into disrepair, now that none of those things are true anymore.

Pretty much a microcosm of the whole TExit experience, he reflects.

"They planned it out," the Sheriff admits. "Packed a shitload of capacitors in there with 'em, hooked 'em to jennies, banked 'em in all the right places. We send in quads, EMP just drops 'em." He glances back over his shoulder, to where—if you squint hard enough—a heat-shimmer rising from the asphalt might almost assume the outline of a resting Chinook transport. "Probably risky using exos, unless they're hardened."

"We won't be using exos."

"Far as we can tell some of 'em are dug in by the condensers, others right next to the heat exchangers. We try to microwave 'em out, all the pipes explode. Might as well blow the place ourselves."

"Firepower?"

"You name it. Sig Saurs, Heckler-Kochs, Maesushis. I think one of 'em has a Skorp. All kinetic, far as we know. Nothing you could fry."

"Got anything on legs?"

"They've got a Wolfhound in there. 46-G."

"I meant you," Metzinger says.

The Sheriff winces. "Nearest's three hours away. Gimped leg." And at Metzinger's look: "BoDyn pulled out a few years back. We've been having trouble getting replacement parts."

"What about local law enforcement? You can't be the only—"

"Half of them *are* law enforcement. How'd you think they got the Wolfhound?" The Sheriff lowers his voice, although there aren't any other patriots within earshot. "Son, you don't think we'd have invited you in if we'd had any other choice? I mean Jayzuz, we've got enough trouble maintaining lawnorder as it is. If word ever got out we had to bring in outside help over a goddamn *domestic dispute . . .* "

"Don't sweat it. We don't wear name tags." Metzinger turns to Silano. "Take it away, Sergeant-Major."

Silano addresses the troops as Metzinger disappears into the cloaked Chinook: "Say your goodbyes, everybody. Autopilots in thirty."

Asante sighs to himself. Those poor bastards don't stand a chance. He can't even bring himself to blame them: driven by desperation, hunger, the lack of any other options. Like the Sāḥilites who murdered *him*, back at the end of another life: damned, ultimately, by the sin of being born into a wasteland that could no longer feed them.

Silano raises one hand. "*Mark.*"

Asante calls forth his mandala. The world goes to gray. His bad hand calms and steadies on the forestalk of his weapon.

This is going to be ugly.

He's glad he won't be around to see it.

Heroes

He does afterward, of course. They all do, as soon as they get back to Côté. They're still learning. The world is their classroom.

"Back in the Cenozoic all anybody cared about was *reflexes*." Second-Lieutenant Oliver Maddox—sorcerer's apprentice to the rarely-seen Major Emma Rossiter, of the Holy Order of Neuroengineering—speaks with the excitement of a nine-year-old at his own birthday party. "Double-tap, dash, down, crawl, observe fire—all that stuff your body learns to do without thinking when someone yells *Contact*. The whole program was originally just about speeding up those macros. They never really appreciated that the subconscious mind *thinks* as well as reacts. It *analyzes*. I was telling them that years ago but they never really got it until now."

Asante has never met *Them*. They never write, They never call. They certainly never visit. Presumably They sign a lot of checks.

"Here, though, we have a *perfect* example of the tactical genius of the zombie mind."

Their BUDs recorded everything. Maddox has put it all together post-mortem, a greatest-hits mix with remote thermal and PEA and a smattering of extraporential algorithms to fill in the gaps. Now he sets up the game board—walls, floors, industrial viscera all magically translucent—and initializes the people inside.

"So you've got eighteen heavily-armed hostiles dug in at all the right choke points." Homunculi glow red at critical junctures. "You've got a jamming field in effect, so you can't share telemetry unless you're line-of-sight. You've got an EMP-hardened robot programmed to attack anything so much as squeaks, deafened along the whole spectrum so even if we *had* the backdoor codes it wouldn't hear them." The Wolfhound icon is especially glossy: probably lifted from BoDyn's promotional archive. "And you've got some crazy fucker with a deadman switch that'll send the whole place sky-high the moment his heart stops—or even if he just thinks you're getting too close to the flag. You don't even know about that going in.

"And yet."

Maddox starts the clock. Inside the labyrinth, icons begin to dance in fast-forward.

"Garin's first up, and he completely blows it. Not only does he barely graze the target—probably doesn't even draw blood—*but he leaves his silencer disengaged*. Way to go, Garin. You failed to neutralize your target, and now the whole building knows where you are."

Asante remembers that gunshot echoing through the facility. He remembers his stomach dropping away.

"Now here comes one of Bubba's buddies around the corner and—Garin misses *again!* Nick to the shoulder this time. And here comes the real bad-ass of the bunch, that Wolfhound's been homing in on Garin's shots and that motherfucker is armed and hot and . . . "

The 46-G rounds the corner. It does not target Garin; it lights up the *insurgents*. Bubba and his buddy collapse into little red piles of pixel dust.

"They did *not* see that coming!" Maddox exults. "Fragged by their own robot! How do you suppose *that* happened?"

Asante frowns.

"So two baddies down, Garin's already up the ladder and onto this catwalk before the robot gets a bead on him but Tiwana's at the other end, way across the building, and they go LOS for about half a second"—a bright thread flickers between their respective icons—"before Tiwana drops back down to ground level and starts picking off Bubbas over by the countercurrent assembly. And *she* turns out to be just as shitty a shot as Garin, and just as sloppy with her silencer."

Gunfire everywhere, from everyone. Asante remembers being blind and shitting bricks, wondering what kind of *aboa* would make such an idiot mistake until the Rann-Seti came up in his own hands, until he felt the recoil and heard the sound of his own shot echoing like a 130-decibel bullseye on his back. He wondered, at the time, how and why someone had sabotaged everyone's silencers like that.

Maddox is still deep in the play. "The bad guys have heard the commotion and are starting to reposition. By now Asante and Silano have picked up the shitty-shot bug and the BoDyn's still running around tearing up the guys on its own side. All this opens a hole that Kalmus breezes through—anyone want to guess the odds she'd just happen to be so perfectly positioned?—which buys her a clean shot at the guy with the deadman switch. Who she drops with a perfect cervical shot. Completely paralyzes the poor bastard *but* leaves his heart beating strong and steady. Here we see Kalmus checking him over and disabling his now-useless doomsday machine.

"This all took less than five minutes, people. I mean, it was eighteen from In to Out but you're basically mopping up after five. And just before the credits roll, Kalmus strolls up to the wolfhound calm as you please and *pets* the fucker. Puts him right to sleep. Galveston PD gets their robot back without a scratch. Five minutes. Fucking magic."

"So, um." Garin looks around. "How'd we do it?"

"Show 'em, Kally."

Kalmus holds up a cuff-link. "Apparently I took this off deadman guy."

"Dog whistles, Ars and Kays." Maddox grins. "50KHz, inaudible to pilot or passenger. You don't put your robot into rabid mode without some way of telling friend from foe, right? Wear one of these pins, Wolfie doesn't look at you twice. *Lose* that pin and it rips your throat out in a fucking instant.

"Your better halves could've gone for clean, quiet kills that would've left the remaining forces still dug-in, still fortified, and not going anywhere. But one of the things that fortified them was BoDyn's baddest battlebot. So your better halves didn't go for clean quiet kills. They went for noise and panic. They shot the dog whistles, drew in the dog, let it attack its own masters. Other side changes position in response. You *herded* the robot, and the robot herded the insurgents right into your crosshairs. It was precision out of chaos, and it's even more impressive because you had no comms except for the occasional optical sync when you happened to be LOS. Gotta be the messiest, spottiest network you could imagine, and if I hadn't seen it myself I'd say it was impossible. But somehow you zombies kept updated on each other's sitreps. Each one knew what it had to do to achieve an optimal outcome assuming all the others did likewise, and the group strategy just kind of— *emerged*. Nobody giving orders. Nobody saying a goddamn word."

Asante sees it now, as the replay loops and restarts. There's a kind of beauty to it; the movement of nodes, the intermittent web of laser light flickering between them, the smooth coalescence of signal from noise. It's more than a dance, more than teamwork. It's more like a—a distributed organism. Like the digits of a hand, moving together.

"Mind you, this is not what we say if anyone asks," Maddox adds. "What we say is that every scenario in which the Galveston plant went down predicted a tipping point across the whole Post-TExit landscape. We point to 95% odds of wide-spread rioting and social unrest on WestHem's very doorstep—a fate which ZeroS has, nice and quietly, prevented. Not bad for your first field deployment."

Tiwana raises a hand. "Who would ask, exactly?"

It's a good question. In the thirteen months since Asante joined Zero Sum, no outsider has ever appeared on the grounds of CFB Côté. Which isn't especially surprising, given that—according to the public records search he did a few weeks back, anyway—CFB Côté has been closed for over twenty years.

Maddox smiles faintly. "Anyone with a vested interest in the traditional chain of command."

Where Are We Now

Asante awakens in the Infirmary, standing at the foot of Carlos Acosta's bed. To his right a half-open door spills dim light into the darkness beyond: a wedge of worn linoleum fading out from the doorway, a tiny red EXIT sign glowing in the void above a stairwell. To his left, a glass wall looks into Neurosurgery. Jointed teleops hang from the ceiling in there, like mantis limbs with impossibly fragile fingers. Lasers. Needles and nanotubes. Atomic-force manipulators delicate enough to coax individual atoms apart. ZeroS have gone under those knives more times than any of them can count.

Surgery by software, mostly. Occasionally by human doctors phoning it in from undisclosed locations, old-school cutters who never visit in the flesh for all the times they've cut into Asante's.

Acosta's on his back, eyes closed. He looks almost at peace. Even his facial tic has quieted. He's been here three days now, ever since losing his right arm to a swarm of smart flechettes over in Heraklion. It's no big deal. He's growing it back with a little help from some imported salamander DNA and a steroid-infused aminoglucose drip. He'll be good as new in three weeks—as good as he's ever been since ZeroS got him, anyway—back in his rack in half that time. Meanwhile it's a tricky balance: his metabolism may be boosted into the jet stream but it's all for tissue growth. There's barely enough left over to power a trip to the bathroom.

Kodjo Asante wonders why he's standing here at 0300.

Maddox says the occasional bit of sleepwalking isn't anything to get too worried about, especially if you're already prone to it. Nobody's suffered a major episode in months, not since well before Galveston; these days the tweaks seem mainly about fine-tuning. Rossiter's long since called off the just-in-case bots that once dogged their every unscripted step. Even lets them leave the base now and then, when they've been good.

You still have to expect the occasional lingering side-effect, though. Asante glances down at the telltale tremor in his own hand, seizes it gently with the other and holds firm until the nerves quiet. Looks back at his friend.

Acosta's eyes are open.

They don't look at him. They don't settle long enough to look at anything, as far as Asante can tell. They jump and twitch in Acosta's face, back forth back forth up down up.

"Carl," Asante says softly. "How's it going, man?"

The rest of that body doesn't even twitch. Acosta's breathing remains unchanged. He doesn't speak.

Zombies aren't big on talking. They're smart but nonverbal, like those split-brain patients who understand words but can't utter them. Something about the integration of speech with consciousness. Written language is easier. The zombie brain doesn't take well to conventional grammar and syntax but they've developed a kind of visual pidgin that Maddox claims is more efficient than English. Apparently they use it at all the briefings.

Maddox also claims they're working on a kind of time-sharing arrangement, some way to divvy up custody of Broca's Area between the fronto-parietal and the retrosplenial. *Someday soon, maybe, you'll literally be able to talk to yourself*, he says. But they haven't got there yet.

A tacpad on the bedside table glows with a dim matrix of Zidgin symbols. Asante places it under Acosta's right hand.

"Carl?"

Nothing.

"Just thought I'd—see how you were. You take care."

He tiptoes to the door, sets trembling fingers on the knob. Steps into the darkness of the hallway, navigates back to his rack by touch and memory.

Those eyes.

It's not like he hasn't seen it a million times before. But all those other times his squadmates' eyes blurred and danced in upright bodies, powerful autonomous things that *moved*. Seeing that motion embedded in such stillness—watching eyes struggle as if trapped in muscle and bone, as if looking up from some shallow grave where they haven't quite been buried alive—

Terrified. That's how they looked. Terrified.

We Are the Dead

Specialist Tarra Kalmus has disappeared. Rossiter was seen breaking the news to Maddox just this morning, a conversation during which Maddox morphed miraculously from He of the Perpetually Goofy Smile into Lieutenant Stoneface. He refuses to talk about it with any of the grunts. Silano managed to buttonhole Rossiter on her way back to the helipad, but could only extract the admission that Kalmus has been "reassigned".

Metzinger tells them to stop asking questions. He makes it an order.

But as Tiwana points out—when Asante finds her that evening, sitting with her back propped against a pallet of machine parts in the loading bay— you can run all sorts of online queries without ever using a question mark.

"Fellow corpse."

"Fellow corpse."

It's been their own private salutation since learning how much they have in common. (Tiwana died during a Realist attack in Havana. Worst vacation ever, she says.) They're the only ZeroS, so far at least, to return from the dead. The others hold them a little in awe because of it.

The others also keep a certain distance.

"Garin was last to see her, over at the Memory Hole." Tiwana's wearing a pair of smart specs tuned to the public net. It won't stop any higher-ups who decide to look over her shoulder, but at least her activity won't be logged by default. "Chatting up some redhead with a Hanson Geothermal logo on her jacket."

Two nights ago. Metzinger let everyone off the leash as a reward for squashing a Realist attack on the G8G Constellation. They went down to Banff for some meatspace R&R. "So?"

Speclight paints Tiwana's cheeks with small flickering auroras. "So a

BPD drone found a woman matching that description dead outside a public fuckcubby two blocks south of there. Same night."

"Eiiii." Asante squats down beside her as Tiwana pushes the specs onto her forehead. Her wonky eye jiggles at him.

"Yeah." She takes a breath, lets it out. "Nicci Steckman, according to the DNA."

"So how—"

"They don't say. Just asking witnesses to come forward."

"Have any?"

"They left together. Deked into an alley. No further surveillance record, which is odd."

"Is it really," Asante murmurs.

"No. I guess not."

They sit in silence for a moment.

"What do you think?" she asks at last.

"Maybe Steckman didn't like it rough and things got out of hand. You know Kally, she—doesn't always take no for an answer."

"No to what? We're all on antilibidinals. Why would she even be—"

"She'd never *kill* someone over—"

"Maybe *she* didn't," Tiwana says.

He blinks. "You think she flipped?"

"Maybe it wasn't her fault. Maybe the augs kicked in on their own somehow, like a, a—reflex. Kally saw an imminent threat, or something her better half *interpreted* that way. Grabbed the keys, took care of it."

"It's not supposed to work like that."

"It wasn't supposed to fry Saks' central nervous system either."

"Come on, Sofe. That's ancient history. They wouldn't deploy us if they hadn't fixed those problems."

"Really." Her bad eye looks pointedly at his bad hand.

"Legacy glitches don't count." Nerves nicked during surgery, a stray milliamp leaking into the fusiform gyrus. Everyone's got at least one. "Maddox says—"

"Oh sure, Maddox is always gonna tidy up. Next week, next month. Once the latest tweaks have settled, or there isn't some brush fire to put out over in Kamfuckingchatka. Meanwhile the glitches don't even manifest in zombie mode so why should he care?"

"If they thought the implants were defective they wouldn't keep sending us out on missions."

"Eh." Tiwana spreads her hands. "You say *mission*, I say *field test*. I mean, sure, camaraderie's great—we're the cutting edge, we can be ZeroS! But *look* at us, Jo. Silano was a Rio insurgent. Kalmus was up on insubordination charges.

They scraped you and me off the ground like road kill. None of us are what you'd call *summa cum laude.*"

"Isn't that the point? That *anybody* can be a super soldier?" *Or at least, any body.*

"We're lab rats, Jo. They don't want to risk frying their West Point grads with a beta release so they're working out the bugs on us first. If the program was ready to go wide we wouldn't still be here. Which means—" She heaves a sigh. "It's the augs. At least, I hope it's the augs."

"You hope?"

"You'd rather believe Kally just went berserk and killed a civilian for no reason?"

He tries to ignore a probably-psychosomatic tingle at the back of his head. "Rossiter wouldn't be talking *reassignment* if she had," he admits. "She'd be talking court-martial."

"She'll never talk court-martial. Not where we're concerned."

"Really."

"Think about it. You ever see any politician come by to make sure the taxpayer's money's being well-spent? You ever see a commissioned officer walking the halls who wasn't Metzinger or Maddox or Rossiter?"

"So we're off the books." It's hardly a revelation.

"We're so far *off the books* we might as well be cave paintings. We don't even know our own tooth-to-tail ratio. Ninety percent of our support infrastructure's offsite, it's all robots and teleops. We don't even know who's cutting into our own heads." She leans close in the deepening gloom, fixes him with her good eye. "This is voodoo, Jo. Maybe the program *started* small with that kneejerk stuff, but now? You and I, we're literal fucking *zombies.* We're reanimated corpses dancing on strings, and if you think Persephone Q. Public is gonna be fine with that you have a lot more faith in her than I do. I don't think Congress knows about us, I don't think Parliament knows about us, I bet SOCOM doesn't even know about us past some line in a budget that says *psychological research.* I don't think they *want* to know. And when something's that dark, are they really going to let anything as trivial as a judicial process drag it into the light?"

Asante shakes his head. "Still has to be accountability. Some kind of internal process."

"There is. You disappear, and they tell everyone you've been reassigned."

He thinks for a bit. "So what do we do?"

"First we riot in the mess hall. Then we march on Ottawa demanding equal rights for corpses." She rolls her eyes. "We don't *do* anything. Maybe you forgot: we *died.* We don't legally exist anymore, and unless you got a way better deal than me the only way for either of us to change that is keep our heads down until we get our honorable discharges. I do not like being dead. I would very much like to go back to being officially alive some day. Until then . . . "

She takes the specs off her head. Powers them down.

"We watch our fucking step."

Ricochet

Sgt. Kodjo Asante watches his fucking step. He watches it when he goes up against AIRheads and Realists. He watches it when pitted against well-funded private armies running on profit and ideology, against ragged makeshift ones driven by thirst and desperation, against rogue Darwin Banks and the inevitable religious extremists who—almost a quarter-century after the end of the Dark Decade—still haven't stopped maiming and killing in the name of their Invisible Friends. His steps don't really falter until twenty-one months into his tour, when he kills three unarmed children off the coast of Honduras.

ZeroS has risen from the depths of the Atlantic to storm one of the countless gylands that ride the major currents of the world's oceans. Some are refugee camps with thousands of inhabitants; others serve as havens for hustlers and tax dodgers eager to avoid the constraints of more stationary jurisdictions. Some are military, sheathed in chromatophores and radar-damping nanotubes: bigger than airports, invisible to man or machine.

The *Caçador de Recompensa* is a fish farm, a family business registered out of Brazil: two modest hectares of low-slung superstructure on a donut hull with a cluster of net pens at its center. It is currently occupied by forces loyal to the latest incarnation of Shining Path. The Path thrives on supply lines with no fixed address—and as Metzinger reminded them on the way down, it's always better to prevent a fight than win one. If the Path can't feed their troops, maybe they won't deploy them.

This is almost a mission of mercy.

Asante eavesdrops on the sounds of battle, takes in a mingled reek of oil and salt air and rotten fish, lets Evil Twin's worldview wash across his eyes in a blur of light and the incomprehensible flicker of readouts with millisecond lifespans. Except during target acquisition, of course. Except for those brief stroboscopic instants when ET *locks on*, and faces freeze and blur in turn: a couple of coveralled SAsian men wielding Heckler-Kochs. A wounded antique ZhanLu staggering on two-and-a half-legs, the beam from its MAD gun wobbling wide of any conceivable target. Children in life jackets, two boys, one girl; Asante guesses their ages at between seven and ten. Each time the weapon kicks in his hands and an instant later ET is veering toward the next kill.

Emotions are sluggish things in Passenger mode. He feels nothing in the moment, shock in the aftermath. Horror's still halfway to the horizon when a random ricochet slaps him back into the driver's seat.

The bullet doesn't penetrate—not much punches through the Chrysomalon armor wrapped tight around his skin—but vectors interact. Momentum passes from a small fast object to a large slow one. Asante's brain lurches in its cavity; meat slaps bone and bounces back. Deep in all that stressed gray matter, some vital circuit shorts out.

There's pain of course, blooming across the side of his head like napalm in those few seconds before his endocrine pumps damp it down. There's fire in the BUD, a blaze of static and a crimson icon warning of zmode failure. But there's a little miracle too:

Kodjo Asante can see again: a high sun in a hard blue sky. A flat far horizon. Columns of oily smoke rising from wrecked machinery.

Bodies.

The air *cracks* a few centimeters to his right. He drops instinctively to a deck slippery with blood and silver scales, gags at the sudden stench wafting from a slurry of bloated carcasses crowding the surface of the holding pen just in front of him. (*Coho-Atlantic hybrids*, he notes despite himself. *Might even have those new Showell genes.*) A turret on treads sparks and sizzles on the other side, a hole blown in its carapace.

A shadow blurs across Asante's forearm. Tiwana leaps across the sky, defractors high on her forehead, eyeballs dancing madly in their sockets. She clears the enclosure, alights graceful as a dragonfly on one foot, kicks the spastic turret with the other. It sparks one last time and topples into the pen. Tiwana vanishes down the nearest companionway.

Asante gets to his feet, pans for threats, sees nothing but enemies laid waste: the smoking stumps of perimeter autoturrets, the fallen bodies of a man with his arm blown off and a woman groping for a speargun just beyond reach. And a small brittle figure almost fused to the deck: blackened sticks for arms and legs, white teeth grinning in a charred skull, a bright half-melted puddle of orange fabric and PVC holding it all together. Asante sees it all. Not just snapshots glimpsed through the fog: ZeroS handiwork, served up for the first time in three-sixty wraparound immersion.

We're killing children . . .

Even the adult bodies don't look like combatants. Refugees, maybe, driven to take by force what they couldn't get any other way. Maybe all they wanted was to get somewhere safe. To feed their kids.

At his feet, a reeking carpet of dead salmon converge listlessly in the wake of the fallen turret. They aren't feeding anything but hagfish and maggots.

I have become Sāḥilite, Asante reflects numbly. He calls up BUD, ignores the unreadable auras flickering around the edges of vision, selects GPS.

Not off Honduras. They're in the Gulf of Mexico.

No one in their right mind would run a fish farm here. The best parts of the Gulf are anoxic; the worst are downright flammable. *Caçador* must have drifted up through the Yucatan Channel, got caught in an eddy loop. All these fish would have suffocated as soon as they hit the dead zone.

But gylands aren't entirely at the mercy of the currents. They carry rudimentary propulsion systems for docking and launching, switching streams and changing course. *Caçador*'s presence so deep in the Gulf implies either catastrophic equipment failure or catastrophic ignorance.

Asante can check out the first possibility, anyway. He stumbles toward the nearest companionway—

—as Tiwana and Acosta burst onto deck from below. Acosta seizes his right arm, Tiwana his left. Neither slows. Asante's feet bounce and drag. The lurching acceleration reawakens the pain in his temple.

He cries out: "*The engines* . . ."

New pain, other side, sharp and recurrent: an ancient weight belt swinging back and forth across Acosta's torso, a frayed strip of nylon threaded through an assortment of lead slugs. It's like being hammered by a tiny wrecking ball. One part of Asante wonders where Acosta found it; another watches Garin race into view with a small bloody body slung across his shoulder. Garin passes one of the dismembered turrets, grabs a piece with his free hand and keeps running.

Everyone's charging for the rails.

Tiwana's mouthpiece is in, her defractors down. She empties a clip into the deck ahead, right at the water's edge: gunfire shreds plastic and whitewashed fiberglass, loosens an old iron docking cleat. She dips and grabs in passing, draws it to her chest, never loosening her grip on Asante. He hears the soft pop of a bone leaving its socket in the instant before they all go over the side.

They plummet head-first, dragged down by a hundred kilograms of improvised ballast. Asante chokes, jams his mouthpiece into place; coughs seawater through the exhaust and sucks in a hot lungful of fresh-sparked hydrox. Pressure builds against his eardrums. He swallows, swallows again, manages to keep a few millibars ahead of outright rupture. He has just enough freedom of movement to claw at his face and slide the defractors over his eyes. The ocean clicks into focus, clear as acid, empty as green glass.

Green turns white.

Seen in that flash-blinded instant: four thin streams of bubbles, rising to a surface gone suddenly incandescent. Four dark bodies, falling from the light. A thunderclap rolls through the water, deep, downshifted, as much felt as heard. It comes from nowhere and everywhere.

The roof of the ocean is on fire. Some invisible force shreds their contrails from the top down, tears those bubbles into swirling silver confetti. The wave-front races implacably after them. The ocean *bulges*, recoils. It squeezes Asante like a fist, stretches him like rubber; Tiwana and Acosta tumble away in the backwash. He flails, stabilizes himself as the first jagged shapes resolve overhead: dismembered chunks of the booby-trapped gyland, tumbling with slow majesty into the depths. A broken wedge of deck and stairwell passes by a few meters away, tangled in monofilament. A thousand glassy eyes stare back from the netting as the wreckage fades to black.

Asante scans the ocean for that fifth bubble trail, that last dark figure to balance Those Who Left against Those Who Returned. No one overhead. Below, a dim shape that has to be Garin shares its mouthpiece with the small limp thing in his arms. Beyond that, the hint of a deeper dark against the abyss: a shark-like silhouette keeping station amid a slow rain of debris. Waiting to take its prodigal children home again.

They're too close to shore. There might be witnesses. So much for stealth ops. So much for low profiles and no-questions-asked. Metzinger's going to be pissed.

Then again, they *are* in the Gulf of Mexico.

Any witnesses will probably just think it caught fire again.

Lady Grinning Soul

"In your own words, Sergeant. Take your time."

We killed children. We killed children, and we lost Silano, and I don't know why. And I don't know if you do either.

But of course, that would involve taking Major Emma Rossiter at *her* word.

"Did the child . . . ?" Metzinger had already tubed Garin's prize by the time Asante had reboarded the sub. Garin, of course, had no idea what his body had been doing. Metzinger had not encouraged discussion.

That was okay. Nobody was really in the mood anyhow.

"I'm sorry. She didn't make it." Rossiter waits for what she probably regards as a respectful moment. "If we could focus on the subject at hand . . . "

"It was a shitstorm," Asante says. "Sir."

"We gathered that." The Major musters a sympathetic smile. "We were hoping you could provide more in the way of details."

"You must have the logs."

"Those are numbers, Sergeant. Pixels. You are uniquely—if accidentally—in a position to give us more than that."

"I never even got below decks."

Rossiter seems to relax a little. "Still. This is the first time one of you has been debooted in mid-game, and it's obviously not the kind of thing we want to risk repeating. Maddox is already working on ways to make the toggle more robust. In the meantime, your perspective could be useful in helping to ensure this doesn't happen again."

"My perspective, sir, is that those forces did not warrant our particular skill set."

"We're more interested in your experiences regarding the deboot, Sergeant. Was there a sense of disorientation, for example? Any visual artifacts in BUD?"

Asante stands with his hands behind his back—good gripping bad—and says nothing.

"Very well." Rossiter's smile turns grim. "Let's talk about your *perspective*, then. Do you think regular forces would have been sufficient? Do you have a sense of the potential losses incurred if we'd sent, say, WestHem marines?"

"They appeared to be refugees, sir. They didn't pose—"

"One hundred percent, Sergeant. We would have lost everyone."

Asante says nothing.

"Unaugged soldiers wouldn't even have made it off the gyland before it went up. Even if they had, the p-wave would've been fatal if you hadn't greatly increased your rate of descent. Do you think regular forces would have made that call? Seen what was coming, run the numbers, improvised a strategy to get below the kill zone in less time than it would take to shout a command?"

"We killed children." It's barely more than a whisper.

"Collateral damage is an unfortunate but inevitable—"

"We *targeted* children."

"Ah."

Rossiter plays with her tacpad: *tap tap tap, swipe.*

"These children," she says at last. "Were they armed?"

"I do not believe so, sir."

"Were they naked?"

"Sir?"

"Could you be certain they weren't carrying concealed weapons? Maybe even a remote trigger for a thousand kilograms of CL-20?"

"They were—sir, they couldn't have been more than seven or eight."

"I shouldn't have to tell you about child soldiers, Sergeant. They've been a fact of life for centuries, especially in *your* particular—at any rate. Just out of interest, how young would someone have to be before you'd rule them out as a potential threat?"

"I don't know, sir."

"Yes you do. You *did*. That's why you targeted them."

"*That wasn't me.*"

"Of course. It was your—evil twin. That's what you call it, right?" Rossiter leans forward. "Listen to me very carefully, Sergeant Asante, because I think you're laboring under some serious misapprehensions about what we do here. Your *twin* is not evil, and it is not gratuitous. It is *you*: a much bigger part of *you* than the whiny bitch standing in front of me right now."

Asante clenches his teeth and keeps his mouth shut.

"This gut feeling giving you so much trouble. This sense of Right and Wrong. Where do you think it comes from, Sergeant?"

"Experience. Sir."

"It's the result of a calculation. A whole series of calculations, far too complex to fit into the conscious workspace. So the subconscious sends you— an executive summary, you might call it. Your evil twin knows all about your sense of moral outrage; it's the source of it. It has more information than you do. Processes it more effectively. Maybe you should trust it to know what it's doing."

He doesn't. He doesn't trust her, either.

But suddenly, surprisingly, he understands her.

She's not just making a point. This isn't just rhetoric. The insight appears fully formed in his mind, a bright shard of unexpected clarity. *She thought it would be easy. She really doesn't know what happened.*

He watches her fingers move on the 'pad as she speaks. Notes the nervous flicker of her tongue at the corner of her mouth. She glances up to meet his eye, glances away again.

She's scared.

Look Back in Anger

Asante awakens standing in the meadow up the mountain. The sky is cloudless and full of stars. His fatigues are damp with sweat or dew. There is no moon. Black conifers loom on all sides. To the east, a hint of pre-dawn orange seeps through the branches.

He has read that this was once the time of the dawn chorus, when songbirds would call out in ragged symphony to start the day. He has never heard it. He doesn't hear it now. There's no sound in this forest but his own breathing—

—and the snap of a twig under someone's foot.

He turns. A gray shape detaches itself from the darkness.

"Fellow corpse," Tiwana says.

"Fellow corpse," he responds.

"You wandered off. Thought I'd tag along. Make sure you didn't go AWOL."

"I think ET's acting up again."

"Maybe you're just sleepwalking. People sleepwalk sometimes." She shrugs. "Probably the same wiring anyway."

"Sleepwalkers don't kill people."

"Actually, that's been known to happen."

He clears his throat. "Did, um . . ."

"No one else knows you're up here."

"Did ET disable the pickups?"

"I did."

"Thanks."

"Any time."

Asante looks around. "I remember the first time I saw this place. It was—magical."

"I was thinking more *ironic*." Adding, at Asante's look: "You know. That one of the last pristine spots in this whole shit-show owes its existence to the fact that WestHem needs someplace private to teach us how to blow shit up."

"Count on you," Asante says.

The stars are fading. Venus is hanging in there, though.

"You've been weird," she observes. "Ever since the thing with *Caçador*."

"It was a weird thing."

"So I hear." Shrug. "I guess you had to be there."

He musters a smile. "So you don't remember . . ."

"Legs running down. Legs running back up. My zombie never targeted anything so I don't know what she saw."

"Metzinger does. Rossiter does." He leans his ass against a convenient boulder. "Does it ever bother you? That you don't know what your own eyes are seeing, and they do?"

"Not really. Just the way it works."

"We don't know what we're doing out there. When was the last time Maddox even showed us a highlight reel?" He feels the muscles clenching in his jaw. "We could be war criminals."

"There *is* no *we*. Not when it matters." She sits beside him. "Besides. Our zombies may be nonconscious but they're not stupid; they know we're obligated to disobey unlawful commands."

"Maybe they *know*. Not sure Maddox's compliance circuit would let them do anything about it."

Somewhere nearby a songbird clears its throat.

Tiwana takes a breath. "Suppose you're right—not saying you are, but *suppose* they sent us out to gun down a gyland full of harmless refugees. Forget that *Caçador* was packing enough explosives to blow up a hamlet, forget that it killed Silano—hell, nearly killed us all. If Metzinger decides to bash in someone's innocent skull, you still don't blame the hammer he used."

"And yet. Someone's skull is still bashed in."

Across the clearing, another bird answers. *The dawn duet.*

"There must be reasons," she says, as if trying it on for size.

He remembers *reasons* from another life, on another continent: retribution. The making of examples. Poor impulse control. Just—fun, sometimes.

"Such as."

"I don't know, okay? Big Picture's way above our pay grade. But that doesn't mean you toss out the chain of command every time someone gives you an order without a twenty-gig backgrounder to go with it. If you want me to believe we're in thrall to a bunch of fascist baby killers, you're gonna need more than a few glimpses of something you may have seen on a gyland."

"How about, I don't know. All of human history?"

Venus is gone at last. The rising sun streaks the clearing with gold.

"It's the deal we made. Sure, it's a shitty one. Only shittier one is being dead. But would you choose differently, even now? Go back to being fish food?"

He honestly doesn't know.

"We should be *dead*, Jo. Every one of these moments is a gift."

He regards her with a kind of wonder. "I never know how you do it."

"Do what?"

"Channel Schopenhauer and Pollyanna at the same time without your head exploding."

She takes his hand for a moment, squeezes briefly. Rises. "We're gonna make it. Just so long as we don't rock the boat. All the way to that honorable fucking discharge." She turns to the light; sunrise glows across her face. "Until then, in case you were wondering, I've got your back."

"There is no you," he reminds her. "Not when it matters."

"I've got your back," she says.

Watch That Man

They've outsourced Silano's position, brought in someone none of them have ever seen before. Technically he's one of them, though the scars that tag him ZeroS have barely had time to heal. Something about him is wrong. Something about the way he moves; his insignia. Not Specialist or Corporal or Sergeant.

"I want you to meet Lieutenant Jim Moore," Rossiter tells them.

ZeroS finally have a commissioned secco. He's easily the youngest person in the room.

He gets right to it. "This is the Nanisivik mine." The satcam wall zooms down onto the roof of the world. "Baffin Island, seven hundred fifty klicks north of the Arctic Circle, heart of the Slush Belt." A barren fractured landscape of red and ocher. Drumlins and hillocks and bifurcating stream beds.

"Tapped out at the turn of the century." A brown road, undulating along some scoured valley floor. A cluster of buildings. A gaping mouth in the Earth. "These days people generally stay away, on account of its remote location. Also on account of the eight thousand metric tons of high-level nuclear waste the Canadian government brought over from India for deep-time storage.

Part of an initiative to diversify the northern economy, apparently." Tactical schematics, now: Processing and Intake. Train tracks corkscrewing into the Canadian Shield. Storage tunnels branching like the streets of an underground subdivision. "Project was abandoned after the Greens lost power in '38.

"You could poison a lot of cities with this stuff. Which may be why someone's messing around there now."

Garin's hand is up. "Someone, sir?"

"So far all we have are signs of unauthorized activity and a JTFN quad that went in and never came out. Our first priority is to identify the actors. Depending on what we find, we might take care of it ourselves. Or we might call in the bombers. Won't know until we get there."

And we *won't know even then*, Asante muses—and realizes, in that moment, what it is about Moore that strikes him as so strange.

"We'll be prepping your better halves with the operational details *en route*."

It's not what is, it's what *isn't*: no tic at the corner of the eye, no tremor in the hand. His speech is smooth and perfect, his eyes make contact with steady calm. Lieutenant Moore doesn't glitch.

"For now, we anticipate a boots-down window of no more than seven hours—"

Asante looks at Tiwana. Tiwana looks back.

ZeroS are out of beta.

Subterraneans

The Lockheed drops them at the foot of a crumbling pier. Derelict shops and listing trailers, long abandoned, huddle against the sleeting rain. This used to be a seaport; then a WestHem refueling station back before *WestHem* was even a word, before the apocalyptic Arctic weather made it easier to just stick everything underwater. It lived its short life as a company town, an appendage of the mine, in the days before Nanisivik was emptied of its valuables and filled up again.

BUD says 1505: less than an hour if they want to be on target by sundown. Moore leads them overland across weathered stone and alluvial washouts and glistening acned Martian terrain. They're fifteen hundred meters from the mouth of the repository when he orders them all into the back seat.

Asante's legs, under new management, pick up the pace. His vision blurs. At least up here, in the wind and blinding sleet, it doesn't make much difference.

A sound drifts past: the roar of some distant animal, perhaps. Nearer, the unmistakable discharge of an ε-40. Not ET's. Asante's eyes remain virtuously clouded.

The wind dies in the space of a dozen steps. Half as many again and the torrent of icy needles on his face slows to a patter, a drizzle. Asante hears great bolts unlatching, a soft screech of heavy metal. They pass through some portal and the bright overcast in his eyes dims by half. Buckles and bootsteps echo faintly against rock walls.

Downhill. A gentle curve to the left. Gravel, patches of broken asphalt. His feet step over unseen obstacles.

And stop.

The whole squad must have frozen; he can't hear so much as a breath. The supersaccadic tickertape flickering across the fog seems faster. Could be his imagination. Off in some subterranean distance, water *drip-drip-drips* onto a still surface.

Quiet movement as ZeroS spreads out. Asante's just a passenger but he reads the footsteps, feels his legs taking him sideways, kneeling. The padding on his elbows doesn't leave much room for fine-grained tactile feedback but the surface he's bracing against is flat and rough, like a table sheathed in sandpaper.

There's a musky animal smell in the air. From somewhere in the middle distance, a soft *whuffle*. The stirring of something huge in slow, sleepy motion.

Maybe someone left the door open, and something got in . . .

Pizzly bears are the only animals that come to mind: monstrous hybrids, birthed along the boundaries of stressed ecosystems crashing into each other. He's never seen one in the flesh.

A grunt. A low growl.

The sound of building speed.

Gunshots. A roar, deafeningly close, and a crash of metal against metal. The flickering tactical halo dims abruptly: network traffic just dropped by a node.

Now the whole network crashes: pawn exchange, ZeroS sacrificing their own LAN as the price of jamming the enemy's. Moore's MAD gun snaps to the right. An instant of scorching heat as the beam sweeps across Asante's arm; Moore shooting wide, Moore *missing*. ET breaks cover, leaps and locks. For one crystalline millisecond Asante sees a wall of coarse ivory-brown fur close enough to touch, every follicle in perfect focus.

The clouds close in. ET pulls the trigger.

A bellow. The scrape of great claws against stone. The reek is overpowering but ET's already pirouetting after fresh game and *click* the freeze-frame glimpse of monstrous ursine jaws in a face wide as a doorway and *click* small brown hands raised against an onrushing foe and *click* a young boy with freckles and strawberry blond hair and Asante's blind again but he feels ET pulling on the trigger, *pop pop pop*—

Whatthefuck children whatthefuck whatthefuck

—and ET's changed course again and *Click*: a small back a fur coat black hair flying in the light of the muzzle flash.

Not again. Not again.

Child soldiers. Suicide bombers. For centuries.

But no one's shooting back.

He knows the sound of every weapon the squad might use, down to the smallest pop and click: the sizzle of the MAD gun, the bark of the Epsilon, Acosta's favorite Olympic. He hears them now; those, and no others. Whatever they're shooting at isn't returning fire.

Whatever we're shooting at. You blind murderous twaaaaase. You're shooting eight-year-olds.

Again.

More gunfire. Still no voices but for a final animal roar that gives way to a wet gurgle and the heavy slap of meat on stone.

It's a nuclear waste repository at the north pole. What are children even doing here?

What am I?

What am I?

And suddenly he sees the words, *All tautologies are tautologies* and ET's back downstairs and the basement door locks and Kodjo Asante grabs frantically for the reins, and takes back his life, and opens his eyes:

In time to see the little freckled boy, dressed in ragged furs, sitting on Riley Garin's shoulders and dragging a jagged piece of glass across his throat. In time to see him leap free of the body and snatch Garin's gun, toss it effortlessly across this dimly-lit cave to an Asian girl clad only in a filthy loincloth, who's sailing through the air toward a bloodied Jim Moore. In time to see that girl reach behind her and catch the gun in midair without so much as a backward glance.

More than a dance, more than teamwork. Like digits on the same hand, moving together.

The pizzly's piled up against a derelict forklift, a giant tawny thing raking the air with massive claws even as it bleeds out through the hole in its flank. A SAsian child with his left hand blown off at the wrist (*maybe that was me*) dips and weaves around the fallen behemoth. He's—*using* it, exploiting the sweep of its claws and teeth as a kind of exclusion zone guaranteed to maul anyone within three meters. Somehow those teeth and claws never seem to connect with him.

They've connected with Acosta, though. Carlos Acosta, lover of sunlight and the great outdoors lies there broken at the middle, staring at nothing.

Garin finally crashes to the ground, blood gushing from his throat.

They're just children. In rags. Unarmed.

The girl rebounds between rough-hewn tunnel walls and calcified machinery, lines up the shot with Garin's weapon. Her bare feet never seem to touch the ground.

They're children they're just—

Tiwana slams him out of the way as the beam sizzles past. The air shimmers and steams. Asante's head cracks against gears and conduits and ribbed metal, bounces off steel onto rock. Tiwana lands on top of him, eyes twitching in frantic little arcs.

And stopping.

It's a moment of pure panic, seeing those eyes freeze and focus—*she doesn't know me she's locking on she's locking on*—but something shines through from behind and Asante can see that her eyes aren't target-locked at all. They're just *looking*.

" . . . Sofiyko?"

Whatever happens, I've got your back.

But Sofiyko's gone, if she was ever even there.

Blackout

Moore hands him off to Metzinger. Metzinger regards him without a word, with a look that speaks volumes: flips a switch and drops him into Passenger mode. He doesn't tell Asante to stay there. He doesn't have to.

Asante feels the glassy pane of a tacpad under ET's hand. That hand rests deathly still for seconds at a time; erupts into a flurry of inhumanly-fast taps and swipes; pauses again. Out past the bright blur in Asante's eyes, the occasional cough or murmur is all that punctuates the muted roar of the Lockheed's engines.

ET is under interrogation. A part of Asante wonders what it's saying about him, but he can't really bring himself to care.

He can't believe they're gone.

No Control

"Sergeant Asante." Major Rossiter shakes her head. "We had such hopes for you."

Acosta. Garin. Tiwana.

"Nothing to say?"

So very much. But all that comes out is the same old lie: "They were just . . . children . . . "

"Perhaps we can carve that on the gravestones of your squadmates."

"But who—"

"We don't know. We'd suspect Realists, if the tech itself wasn't completely antithetical to everything they stand for. If it wasn't way past their abilities."

"They were barely even clothed. It was like a *nest* . . . "

"More like a hive, Sergeant."

Digits on the same hand . . .

"Not like you," she says, as if reading his mind. "ZeroS networking is quite—inefficient, when you think about it. Multiple minds in multiple heads, independently acting on the same information and coming to the same conclusion. Needless duplication of effort."

"And these . . . "

"Multiple heads. One mind."

"We jammed the freqs. Even if they were networked—"

"We don't think they work like that. Best guess is—bioradio, you could call it. Like a quantum-entangled corpus callosum." She snorts. "Of course, at this point they could say it was elves and I'd have to take their word for it."

Caçador, Asante remembers. They've learned a lot from one small stolen corpse.

"Why use *children*?" he whispers.

"Oh, Kodjo." Asante blinks at the lapse; Rossiter doesn't seem to notice. "Using children is the *last* thing they want to do. Why do you think they've been stashed in the middle of the ocean, or down some Arctic mineshaft? We're not talking about implants. This is genetic, they were *born*. They have to be protected, hidden away until they grow up and . . . ripen."

"Protected? By abandoning them in a nuclear waste site?"

"Abandoning them, yes. Completely defenseless. As you saw." When he says nothing, she continues: "It's actually a perfect spot. No neighbors. Lots of waste heat to keep you warm, run your greenhouses, mask your heatprint. No supply lines for some nosy satellite to notice. No telltale EM. From what we can tell there weren't even any adults on the premises, they just—lived off the land, so to speak. Not even any weapons of their own, or at least they didn't use any. Used *bears*, of all things. Used your own guns against you. Maybe they're minimalists, value improvisation." She sacc's something onto her pad. "Maybe they just want to keep us guessing."

"Children." He can't seem to stop saying it.

"For now. Wait 'til they hit puberty." Rossiter sighs. "We bombed the site, of course. Slagged the entrance. If any of ours were trapped down there, they wouldn't be getting out. Then again we're not talking about us, are we? We're talking about a single distributed organism with God-know-how-many times the computational mass of a normal human brain. I'd be very surprised if it couldn't anticipate and counter anything we planned. Still. We do what we can."

Neither speaks for a few moments.

"And I'm sorry, Sergeant," she says finally. "I'm so sorry it's come to this. We do what we've always done. Feed you stories so you won't be compromised, so you won't compromise *us* when someone catches you and starts poking your amygdala. But the switch was for your protection. We don't know who we're up against. We don't know how many hives are out there, what stage of gestation any of them have reached, how many may have already—matured. All we know is that a handful of unarmed children can slaughter our most elite forces at will, and we are so very unready for the world to know that.

"But *you* know, Sergeant. You dropped out of the game—which may well have cost us the mission—and now you know things that are way above your clearance.

"Tell me. If our positions were reversed, what would *you* do?"

Asante closes his eyes. *We should be dead. Every one of these moments is a gift.* When he opens them again Rossiter's watching, impassive as ever.

"I should've died up there. I should have died off Takoradi two years ago."

The Major snorts. "Don't be melodramatic, Sergeant. We're not going to execute you."

"I—what?"

"We're not even going to court-martial you."

"Why the hell not?" And at her raised eyebrow: "Sir. You said it yourself: unauthorized drop-out. Middle of a combat situation."

"We're not entirely certain that was your decision."

"It *felt* like my decision."

"It always does though, doesn't it?" Rossiter pushes back in her chair. "We didn't create your evil twin, Sergeant. We didn't even put it in control. We just got you out of the way, so it could do what it always does without interference.

"Only now, it apparently—wants you back."

This takes a moment to sink in. "What?"

"Frontoparietal logs suggest your zombie took a certain—initiative. Decided to quit."

"In combat? That would be suicide!"

"Isn't that what you wanted?"

He looks away.

"No? Don't like that hypothesis? Well, here's another: it surrendered. Moore got you out, after all, which was statistically unlikely the way things were going. Maybe dropping out was a white flag, and the hive took pity and let you go so you could—I don't know, spread the word: *don't fuck with us.*

"Or maybe it decided the hive deserved to win, and switched sides. Maybe it was—conscientiously objecting. Maybe it decided *it* never enlisted in the first place."

Asante decides he doesn't like the sound of the Major's laugh.

"You must have asked it," he says.

"A dozen different ways. Zombies might be analytically brilliant but they're terrible at self-reflection. They can tell you exactly what they did but not necessarily *why.*"

"When did you ever care about motive?" His tone verges on insubordination;

he's too empty to care. "Just—tell it to stay in control. It has to obey you, right? That orbitofrontal thing. The *compliance mod*."

"Absolutely. But it wasn't your twin who dropped out. It was *you*, when it unleashed the mandala."

"So order it not to show me the mandala."

"We'd love to. I don't suppose you'd care to tell us what it looks like?"

It's Asante's turn to laugh. He sucks at it.

"I didn't think so. Not that it matters. At this point we can't trust you either—again, not entirely your fault. Given the degree to which conscious and unconscious processes are interconnected, it may have been premature to try and separate them so completely, right off the bat." She winces, as if in sympathy. "I can't imagine it's much fun for you either, being cooped up in that skull with nothing to do."

"Maddox said there was no way around it."

"That was true. When he said it." Eyes downcast now, saccing the omnipresent 'pad. "We weren't planning on field-testing the new mod just yet, but with Kalmus and now you—I don't see much choice but to advance implementation by a couple of months."

He's never felt more dead inside. Even when he was.

"Haven't you stuck enough pins in us?" By which he means *me*, of course. By process of elimination.

For a moment, the Major almost seems sympathetic.

"Yes, Kodjo. Just one last modification. I don't think you'll even mind this one—because next time you wake up, you'll be a free man. Your tour will be over."

"Really."

"Really."

Asante looks down. Frowns.

"What is it, Sergeant?"

"Nothing," he says. And regards his steady, unwavering left hand with distant wonder.

Lazarus

Renata Baermann comes back screaming. She's staring at the ceiling, pinned under something—the freezer, that's it. Big industrial thing. She was in the kitchen when the bombs hit. It must have fallen.

She thinks it's crushed her legs.

The fighting seems to be over. She hears no small-arms fire, no whistle of incoming ordnance. The air's still filled with screams but they're just gulls, come to feast in the aftermath. She's lucky she was inside; those vicious little air rats would have pecked her eyes out by now if she'd been—

—*Blackness*—

¡Joder! Where am I? Oh, right. Bleeding out at the bottom of the Americas, after . . .

She doesn't know. Maybe this was payback for the annexation of Tierra del Fuego. Or maybe it's the Lifeguards, wreaking vengeance on all those who'd skip town after trampling the world to mud and shit. This is a staging area, after all: a place where human refuse congregates until the pressure builds once again, and another bolus gets shat across the Drake Passage to the land of milk and honey and melting glaciers. The sphincter of the Americas.

She wonders when she got so cynical. Not very seemly for a humanitarian. She coughs. Tastes blood.

Footsteps crunch on the gravel outside, quick, confident, not the shell-shocked stumble you'd expect from anyone who's just experienced apocalypse. She fumbles for her gun: a cheap microwave thing, barely boils water but it helps level the field when a fifty kg woman has to lay down the law to a man with twice the mass and ten times the entitlement issues. Better than nothing.

Or it would be, if it was still in its holster. If it hadn't somehow skidded up against a table leg a meter and a half to her left. She stretches for it, screams again; feels like she's just torn herself in half as the kitchen door slams open and she—

—blacks out—

—and comes back with the gun miraculously in her hand, her finger pumping madly against the stud, mosquito buzz-snap filling her ears and—

—she's wracked, coughing blood, too weak keep firing even if the man in the WestHem uniform hadn't just taken her gun away.

He looks down at her from a great height. His voice echoes from the bottom of a well. He doesn't seem to be speaking to her: "Behind the mess hall—"

—English—

"—fatal injuries, maybe fifteen minutes left in her and she's still fighting—"

When she wakes up again the pain's gone and her vision's blurry. The man has changed from white to black. Or maybe it's a different man. Hard to tell through all these floaters.

"Renata Baermann." His voice sounds strangely—unused, somehow. As if he were trying it out for the first time.

There's something else about him. She squints, forces her eyes to focus. The lines of his uniform resolve in small painful increments. No insignia. She moves her gaze to his face.

"Coño," she manages at last. Her voice is barely a whisper. She sounds like a ghost. "What's wrong with your *eyes*?"

"Renata Baermann," he says again. "Have I got a deal for you."

CUPIDO

RICH LARSON

❮━◆━❯

As Marcel rounds the corner he sees the woman stepping into the elevator, pulling the curlicued grille behind her with one manicured hand.

"*Detengalo, porfa,*" he calls, muffled through cotton.

She obliges, holding the grille open so he can slip through, giving him a slightly odd look for his flu mask.

"*Tengo gripe,*" Marcel explains.

"*Que pena,*" the woman says sympathetically, then is drawn back to the glow of her tablet like a moth. Her name is Daniela and she is beautiful in the *sevillana* way: slender and immaculately dressed, with straight dark hair and lips slicked red. Marcel feels his pulse speed up, his chest twist tight. Not because she is beautiful, but because of the tiny canister concealed in his sleeve. He still gets nervous every job. Even though he has never been caught, and there is no law against what he does, not yet, not here.

Marcel pulls the grille shut, and the elevator starts to descend. He watches Daniela in his peripheral. In a way he knows nothing about her, in a way he knows everything. He knows the intricacies of her DNA, her odorprint, the shape and composition of her unseen bacterial cloud. She taps at her screen with a hard white nail, frowns at it.

Slowly, furtively, Marcel slides the canister from his sleeve and sprays the primer. He gives a loud cough as he does it, which disguises the nebulizing hiss but also makes her take an automatic step backward. But she breathes enough of it in. By the time they reach the ground floor, her pupils have started to dilate and there's a flush under her skin. Marcel is still holding his breath and staring straight ahead.

"*Venga, adio,*" he mutters, hurrying out of the elevator.

"*Adio,*" she says vaguely.

Marcel crosses the hallway to the exit, passing his client on the way. Augustin is trying to look casual and confident but doing neither, even though his haircut is lined off with laser precision and his trousers are new and he practically reeks with the target pheromone Marcel so painstakingly tailored to Daniela. Marcel can smell cologne, too—idiot. He told Augustin it would only dilute the pheromone.

Augustin has been trying for weeks to work up the nerve to ask Daniela out for a *caña*. He's a couple of years younger than her and a head shorter when she wears her usual heels, and normally her eyes slide right off of him as if he's not there. But not today. Today, there will be something different about Augustin.

Marcel told him no eye contact, either, but Augustin still gives him an anxious wide-eyed stare on his way by. He looks like he might shit himself, so Marcel gives a covert okay sign behind his back as he pushes through the door. Augustin will probably fuck it up anyway. They often do—if not today, then in a week or a month. But Marcel already has Augustin's 382 scraped-together Euros sitting in his account, and now he needs to prepare for the next job. A *cupido's* work is never done.

Outside there is a two o'clock moon drowning in the hot blue sky. Avenida Menendez Pelayo is dusty and dry, thronged with men and women leaving work to jockey for shade in the street-side bars. Marcel weaves to get close to the ones that spritz cool water from their overhangs. He peels his sweaty mask off and tosses it in a trash receptacle. He is still not used to the summer heat here in Andalusia.

But in Barcelona, as in London and Berlin and all the cities in North America, they are starting to get wise to Marcel's particular brand of chemistry. People trust their feelings even less than before. They buy cheap color-coded kits to test themselves for the presence of artificial pheromones, though Marcel's work is much too subtle for that, and the truly paranoid wear blocker scents that stink to high heaven.

There is even a holo cartoon that sometimes plays on the backs of Barcelona's lime green buses, showing a skulking silhouette with spray canister in hand, creeping through a crowded bar. As if Marcel is a predator peddling in rophynol or something equally barbaric.

So he is in Seville now, where there is less money but plenty of romantics with their heads full of flamenco and Mexican *telenovelas*. Men desperate for women or men, women desperate for men or women, all of it so chaotic and hormonal and ephemeral. It's something Marcel never understood, how people gravitate together, how their hands find each other's hands, how they stumble in and out of love. Sometimes it still feels like a secret joke that everyone in the world is playing on him.

But Marcel understands chemistry. Understands it far better than his baffled professors did in the year before he blew off his scholarship and dropped out of uni. Pheromone study was cresting then, and Marcel's talents lent themselves to it. There was profit to be made as a black-market *cupido*, and his grandmother's colon cancer treatments were not cheap. That is where he sends most of the money, in such a way as to bypass his mother, who he still remembers best with a spoon and needle. If his mother had been lucid more often, maybe she would have tried to turn him into a cook.

Marcel passes through the wrought-iron gates into the park, where an autocleaner is scrubbing graffiti off the statue of Cristóbal Colón that students like so much to deface. Flocks of red-eyed pigeons are strutting around the dry fountain. A pair of sunburned backpackers are stretched out on the grass, hands entangled. Marcel finds a bench with a slice of shade over it and sits down, waiting for the next mark to arrive.

He knows her name is Chelo and that she comes here every afternoon to peel and eat an orange before she goes back to work at Zero Digital. He knows her mother is willing to pay upward of five hundred Euros to ensure that she falls in love with a copyright lawyer named Jose Luis. Marcel still tries to explain to clients, sometimes, that he does not deal in love. Only in the chemical undercurrent that sweeps people toward each other and ebbs just as quickly. But for most of his clients, that is enough.

He sees her. Unslinging a satchel from her shoulder, dressed all in black except for a pair of bright red sneakers. She's not beautiful. Not in the way Marcel understands beauty, in aggregate symmetry and hip-to-waist ratio and neoteny. Her face is pinched. Her dark hair is drawn back too tight and then frizzes out at the back of her head. She sits down on a bench next to an old man in a blue coverall, gives him a brief business-like nod. Plucks one earbud out to exchange remarks about the heat she doesn't seem to feel.

Her fingers whir all the while, peeling her orange in one perfect spiral, and when she laughs at something Marcel can't hear, head tilted backward with the sunlight shredded onto her cheek, he feels his pulse speed up. He feels his chest go tight.

As soon as he is back in the cool darkness of his rented one-bedroom *piso*, Marcel digs a modified sniffer mask out from under his bed to scan himself for contamination. He must have breathed in a bit of the primer pheromone in the elevator or else when he was putting the finishing touches on it last night.

But when he seals the sniffer mask to his face and turns it on, he sees nothing out of the ordinary. His seething cloud of bacteria and chemical particulates is all healthy greens and purples, with the tell-tale red slash of artificial pheromone nowhere to be seen.

Marcel tugs the mask back off his face with a sweat-suction pop. He lies back on his mattress and pulls Chelo's odorprint sample out from his pocket, remembering how sidling close enough to use the tiny vacuum pump made his heart beat so fast and hard he was sure she would hear it. He tells himself that it's all chemicals, whether they are artificial or natural. That it means nothing.

There's work to do, besides. Marcel slides off his staticky bedsheet and secures the door, first turning the key and then thumbing the pressure lock he bought himself. He pays high rent on time, and in exchange the proprietor does not question his security. Same as she doesn't question the strange scents that sometimes escape the humming ventilator that Marcel now switches on. He pulls his glass and his precursors out of his suitcase and sets everything up on the plastic-sheeted table. He boots up his tablet and pulls battered headphones over his ears, streaming English radio as white noise.

Then, with Chelo's odorprint and the DNA sample her mother provided, Marcel sets to work. For some reason he feels excited. He wants this pheromone to be perfect. The most perfect he's ever done. For every chemical quirk, every staggered bacterial concentration, he wants to create the perfect counterpart. Like tumblers turning in smooth synchronization, like fingers interweaving tightly together. It will be like Marcel's body is singing to hers.

He blinks. It won't be his body, of course. It will be somebody else's body. Jose Luis, the copyright lawyer. Marcel has never seen a photo of him, but he imagines him smug and balding. He imagines him sitting down on the bench beside Chelo, elbowing the old man away, and Chelo's nostrils widening just a little as the target pheromone slides into her lungs.

It makes it hard to concentrate. After four listless hours working out the base scent, Marcel breaks for the day. He puts everything away and scrubs himself clean in the shower, where he is still thinking of orange peels, of red sneakers. He opens the shutters and finds dusk dropping over Seville. He can see one lit-up corner of the cathedral. Evening sounds drift up to him, people laughing and shouting. It hurts a little.

Marcel cooks a hunk of chorizo to eat with his fresh-bought bread, trying to relish the sizzling sound of the pan, trying to separate out the individual spices wafting through the cramped kitchen. He transfers half of the last job's money to the account he set up for his grandmother, to pay hospital bills.

He even thinks of calling her on WhatsApp, his grandmother who is always asking why he doesn't find a pretty *novia* or even a *novio*, but what would he tell her? He saw a girl in a park, and he is so lonely that it seemed important. He cannot tell her it makes it hard to craft the pheromone someone else will use to seduce her. She thinks he is a server in a bar.

Marcel uses the bread to sponge up orange grease from the sausage, and he's glad that Chelo cannot see him eating alone in the dark. Which makes him think, in turn, that maybe it will help if he sees Chelo again. If he sees her, and feels nothing, the way he usually feels nothing. That would be proof it was his mind playing tricks on him after watching too many couples walk down Menendez Pelayo.

The next morning, because he doesn't want to wait until two o'clock in the park, Marcel walks to Zero Digital. The avenue is not so busy yet, and the air is still cool. The spongy green bike path is empty so he walks along it, under the shade of the orange trees, trying not to sweat at all. He can feel his heartbeat speeding up as he gets closer to the shop. He sees his reflection in the window and realizes he needs a haircut.

Marcel pushes through the door before he can think up another reason not to. The buzzer goes off, and someone straightens up from behind the counter.

"*Bueno dia,*" the Moroccan man says, muting his netbook and adjusting his wire-frame glasses in one smooth motion. "*Dime.*"

Marcel feels a strange mixture of disappointment and relief. "*Bueno dia,*" he returns. He makes a little circle of his finger. "*Solamente estoy mirando.*"

The man shrugs and returns to his Liga highlights. Marcel said he would browse and now feels obligated to follow through, so he squeezes through the cramped racks of cases, headphones, pocket drones. The store seems tiny, even for the old town, but then he sees stairs and realizes it extends into a second room.

There's a second counter up there, strewn with electronics, and sitting behind it is the girl named Chelo who he knows nothing about, but also everything about, because her odorprint is still blazed into his mind's eye. Her red sneakers fidget under the counter. She's sealing a crack in a phone screen, intent on her work, earbuds in.

Marcel's stomach flips over, and he feels a sudden sweat under his arms. He wants to know what music she is playing, whose phone she is repairing, whether the man downstairs is her boss or if she is his boss, whether she would like to get a *caña* after work, and a hundred other stupid things. He gives himself three seconds to look at her, her angular face with dark brows furrowed tight, but it turns into five and she looks up.

"*Te puedo ayudar?*" she asks, a little too loudly because of the earbuds.

In his head, he says yes, yes she can help him.

"*Solomante estoy mirando,*" Marcel says in the air, and he drifts back down the stairs, holding his head perfectly still to keep from looking back at her. He leaves the shop. Outside, the sun is turning fierce and hot again, but that doesn't explain the sweat.

Marcel knows what he is feeling is only chemicals. But they're the natural kind, not the artificial, which has not happened to him in a long time. Maybe never has, not quite like this.

He knows it is dangerous to make anybody more or less than a person.

His grandmother told him that, back when secession riots reached their fever peak in Catalonia. Chelo is only a person. If he were to speak to her, it would go wrong the way it always does. There would come the point where she realized he didn't understand, whether it happened after her naked body was pressed against his or more likely long before.

Marcel walks back toward the *piso,* toward his waiting equipment. It's better to stick to what he understands. Love is for other people, and they pay him well for it.

Midnight of what was the hottest day so far, and it's barely cooled off. Marcel is working in his underwear with the window open, not caring who might see him, or see the fumes leaking out into the night as long pale ribbons. The target pheromone is coming together slowly, painfully. Marcel is restless. He's still running the mental footage from the shop. He's plotted out a dozen conversations in his head, a dozen ways he could have spoken to her. He can't stop.

He strips off his gloves, his headphones, and flicks a five minute timer onto his tablet. His ears ring with the sudden silence as he goes to the bathroom to splash water up and down his bare body. The open window has done no good. There's no breeze coming in off the Guadalquivir. He can hear the sounds of revelers below, drunken voices in multiple languages. Maybe Chelo is out with her friends. She would have friends.

Marcel scrapes a finger down his temple like maybe he can claw her out of his head. Then he goes back to the table and clears the target pheromone aside to make room for something else. Something crude and fierce and almost toxic. He uncaps his precursor and claps on his headphones.

He thinks about Chelo because he is lonely, because his body needs contact with other bodies, maybe even needs to ejaculate. So now he makes what he usually holds in contempt: a *bomba.* A cloying chemical cloak tailored to no one individual, designed for hard and fast arousal, so obvious it would never work in the big city where all the clubs have a bouncer wearing a sniffer mask. More powerful than the primer he used in the elevator. If that was a suggestion, this is a scream, and it won't fade for a good three hours.

Marcel is in his zone now, digichoral music throbbing in his ear canals, his hands moving smooth and surgical, eyes focused through beading sweat. Compared to the target pheromone, it's simple. In less than an hour he has it decanting. He showers and dresses in his good trousers, his crisp gray shirt. He stocks his pockets with Euros, tadalafil, a condom that is not quite expired. There's half a bottle of Iglesia wine chilling in the fridge, and he finishes it in a few swigs to help insulate against the crowds, the noise.

Then he sprays himself with the *bomba,* which is so pungent it makes him light-headed, and turns off the lights, heads down the stairs, slipping out into Seville's labyrinth of streets.

Sunlight wakes Marcel up in a tangle of bodies. There is a small hand with chipped pink nails splayed out on his stomach. There is a lean muscled arm wrapped around his chest, covered in animated tattoos moving sluggishly to a sleeping pulse. Marcel's mouth feels like steel wool and his head pounds. He slowly worms free.

The man has a thick black beard and high cheekbones. The woman has bee-stung lips and a symmetrical face, haloed by a mess of bleached blonde hair. They're beautiful, the way Marcel understands beautiful. So is the woman snoring on the floor, naked from the waist up. The last thing he remembers is leading all three of them along the graffitied riverbank toward the cheap *pensión,* their bodies breaking and colliding, the air swimming with pheromone.

If he felt it properly then, he doesn't anymore. Their bodies look like geometry now. As he moves stealthily around the room, finding his trousers, his shoes, the night comes back to him in fragments. Smoking hookah in the loft of La Bicicleteria with a circle of chattering uni students. Hands slipping onto his knee, his thigh. Taking two of the girls with him to Abril nightclub, to make sure he got past the black-shirted bouncer with no sniffer mask, then losing track of them in the crush.

He remembers running into Augustin the client, who had hair gel trickling off his scalp and babbled to him about Daniela even while squirming closer and closer on the couch. He remembers drifting around the dance floor, ignoring the rhythm, moving callously from one girl to the next, trying to find the one most or least like Chelo. Then finally at the bar, with the blonde-haired girl draped over him, seeing the *camarero* and a manager whispering to each other, frowning.

"*¿Nos vamos o que?*" he asked, nodding toward the exit.

"*Sí,*" she said, smiled. "*Sí, vamanos.*" And he remembers he wrapped his fingers clumsily through hers, to see how it felt.

Marcel finds his phone and thumbs it on. There's a message from the client, asking when the pheromone will be ready, even though he told Chelo's mother never to mention the pheromone in her messages. It puts a deep sick hollow in the bottom of him.

He pulls on his trousers and finds the condom and the pills still in his pocket, untouched, the way he almost always finds them.

Marcel has never failed to produce a high-grade pheromone for a high-paying client. He takes pride in his work. But first he finds a corner bar and eats breakfast standing, tomato on toast. He drinks a glass of fresh-squeezed orange juice and then three glasses of water, filled by a *camarero* who gives him a knowing chuckle. Marcel doesn't make eye contact. He feels like people can still smell it on him, his desperation and his debauchery. He pays and then makes his way back to the *piso*.

With the window shuttered, the ventilator humming, the door locked twice, he returns to his work. He keeps his headphones on but plays no music. He has a head full of thoughts, so much so that twice he nearly makes a mistake. It's foolish to still be thinking about Chelo, the girl that he does not know even though it feels like he does. Foolish the way his clients are foolish.

But Marcel has always wished, in one small corner of himself, that he was like them. As the target pheromone takes its final shape, the multiple layers of scent coalescing, he peels off his gloves and sits back. The pheromone will work, but he doesn't have to give it to Chelo's mother. He could send back the up-front half of her payment. If he's careful with his money, if he takes another job quickly or sells off what's left of the *bomba,* he should be able to keep his grandmother's bills paid and maybe keep the *piso,* too.

And then he could use the target pheromone himself. The thought has been skulking through the back of his mind, like the holo cartoon on the rear of the bus, for hours now. He imagines himself walking into the shop, or into the park, but taller and handsomer and better, the way the pheromone would make him seem to her. He imagines Chelo's sunny laugh, and how it would hardly matter what he said to elicit it. Maybe he will reach without looking and find her hand reaching for his, too.

Marcel seals the tiny canister and taps it against his temple. It's as good a pheromone as he's ever made. But Chelo deserves better. Maybe so does he. His phone rattles with another message from the client, but he swipes it away, deletes the others. Then he carries the canister into the kitchen. Before he can talk himself out of it, he pops the bottom and pours it down the drain. Soft tendrils of its scent follow him into the bathroom, clinging at him, rebuking him.

He strips off his clothes and steps into the shower, scrubbing himself until his skin is ruddy red. Clean, clean, with no trace of the pheromone on him. He knows his odds are drastically lowered without it. He also knows it's dangerous to make anyone more or less than a person, to imagine that anyone can make everything right. But there's a small chance she might want someone to make her feel less lonely, and might not mind if it is him, and they'll be happy for a while.

People have done that for millions of years, and Marcel wants to stop feeling like he is less than a person. He dresses, uses the sniffer mask to be sure he has no contamination. Then he takes his key, makes a small careful scratch on the screen of his phone, and heads out the door.

RINGS

NINA KIRIKI HOFFMAN

The snake train whispered over the tracks, carrying women and their men home.

Desert slid by beyond the windows, sunlight molten and red across the west-facing slopes of the rippling dunes, a hot frozen sea that stretched out to hard and darkening blue sky in all directions except ahead. The track, protected by airfields from the incursion of sand, ran straight toward a distant line of mountains, a black shadow of a lower jaw of pointed teeth against the sunset.

Inside the train, the air was cool and tasted of cinnamon, processed air, stale food leaves, and sweat. Aris Lifebuilder sat in her seat, her hands folded over her satchel, and glanced up at the face of the man she had bought. He stood beside her without apparent fatigue. They had been traveling for four hours.

Aris had saved money for a man for years, and she had planned to get one for much longer, though not everyone did. She had failed her ring year spectacularly, but she had done five years of penance and paid the blood price to her ringmate Malia's crèche. Finally she had earned the right to own another. Since Malia's death, she had partnered once or twice, but the wall inside her, its first bricks laid in lonely childhood, most of it built when she lost Malia, wouldn't come down with a woman and an equal. Things would be different with a man.

She had taken the snake train from outlying Opal to Kehsah, the city nearest Touchdown Port. In the Kehsah auction, they had men from all over, even spacers, those who had lost themselves in Touchdown casinos. It was a spaceman she had bought, one unlike any she had seen before. He had the correct number of toes and fingers (though what was correct? While she lived in the south, she had surreptitiously studied her friend Lela's man, who had six digits on each hand and foot; Lela had told her that on that man's planet, such a thing was common, and Aris couldn't stop thinking about it) and two eyes, two ears, a single nose, and a mouth. His manhood looked similar to others she had examined on the men she had been considering. His thick hair was a dark brown-black, a common color. But his tan skin had a silver undertone; it glinted strangely beneath the surface. His dark eyes had silver flecks. She wondered if these distinctions were gifts of his foreign birth mother, his foreign planet of origin, or his long years in the spaceways, where people could encounter all sorts of things that stained them. He was a gambler, that much she knew. Gamblers or lawbreakers, those were the kinds of offworld men one found at Kehsah auctions, and Man Firen's manifest said gambler.

He was beautiful. He had never been a slave before.

He had undergone the basic training all slaves received before they were sold. He was acclimated to ringtech; he would respond to her commands. It said on his manifest he couldn't speak. That made high-stakes bidders ignore him, and it had given Aris hope she'd be able to afford him. There was some question as to his intelligence, too, but Aris had looked into his eyes. He came with a certificate proving he was disease-free, a certificate of reproductive viability—she had checked his gene map for incompatabilities with her own genes, and found no dangers, and genes were why she was buying her own man; she wanted a daughter, or maybe two. Daughters she might keep past the traditional third year, when most women turned their children over to those who specialized in child-rearing, the crèche mothers. Firen also had a certificate of temporary vaccination against the mankiller virus. She would need to inoculate him every two weeks to keep that current.

There were no recommendations of docility from his trainers, no certifications of accomplishments in trade. In the viewing room, he had been hunched and resentful. He had resisted training; Aris figured she would, too, if she were an offworlder who didn't understand the system trapped here against her will.

There were no guarantees he had work value.

It was probable he would be trouble. If he came from a planet where slavery was illegal (most planets), he might be like Marilys's Ken, who had fought being owned until Marilys had to have his personality sculpted. Ken was pretty to look at, for Marilys took good care of him, ordered him to eat, exercise, and eliminate. But he had no conversation.

Aris's new man Firen had no conversation either. Maybe he could learn sign. They could take the class together. According to his manifest, he hadn't had parent training yet, so that was another class they'd take together.

Firen stared straight ahead with his silver-flecked eyes. His right hand clutched his left, covering the ring of bondage he now wore, keyed to Aris. The line of his jaw was severe, and his cheeks held hollows. His mouth curved downward.

She looked past her man's hips and hands to her neighbor across the aisle, Sersta Teacher, whose man sat next to her on the bench. Sersta too stared ahead, her face as blank as Aris's man's. Sersta's man held his head in his hands. His ring was large, the lights of control winking in it to remind him and everyone who saw him that he was under strictest control. Sersta had gotten him at a good price, for he was a third-owner man, with two disobedience tattoos on his forehead. If she couldn't straighten him out, he would go to the vats. No man got a fourth chance.

Why had Sersta borne the expense of a trip to the city when she could have gotten a less troubling second-hand man locally?

Sersta's hand stole from its haven in her sleeve and stroked down her man's back. His fingers flexed against his dark hair, and then he slid one hand sideways so he could peer at Sersta, his eye dark and liquid in the muted everywhere glowlight of the car. His single-eyed gaze softened on Sersta. He noticed Aris's regard and hid behind his hands again.

Perhaps this was someone Sersta knew.

Sersta had been raised at Hope, one of the complexes for honorary girls. Sersta's mother had been the administrator of a place where boys of three or four who exhibited female traits might be made into girls if their inclinations were strong enough, instead of being shipped offplanet, loosed in the wild where the mankiller virus lingered to keep unvaccinated men in check, or sent to slave training centers. Sersta had known males before they were slaves. Perhaps she had known this man before he lost his chance at personhood.

Sersta had been the first to welcome Aris to Opal. Sersta had been innocent and strong and kind, open and welcoming, when most of the women in the community viewed Aris and her new skills with suspicion.

People in Opal did not know what Aris had done during her ringyear, and with luck they would never find out. Her counselor had approved her decision to move somewhere new.

But of course, people didn't move to new places unless they followed lovers or jobs or had something to hide.

Sersta, Aris's first friend in her new home, knew things about men that Aris did not. Sersta had grown up with men, though only the most feminine of them. Still, before their operations, the honorary girls had some experience of male life, more than could be observed, even if one sat often on the margins of life, watching for the blind spots in others and staring at what they would not see. The honorary girls lived long enough as men to have their mature sperm harvested, since their traits were desirable. They experienced male hormone moods and changes.

Aris envied Sersta her experiences. Much different, she suspected, from what one learned of males from the offworld men one encountered at the casinos, pleasure palaces, restaurants, and brothels in Touchdown. Aris had been on a two-week field trip to Touchdown when she was fourteen, but she had not yet performed her obligatory three-year service there.

Aris sat forward and touched her new man's hand. He flinched, startled, then glanced down at her.

"Hungry?" she asked.

He opened his mouth, closed it, nodded.

"Down," she said.

He squatted beside her seat, elbows on splayed knees, hands dangling in the V of his bent legs. He wore pale clothing the color of watered milk, with small bits of burr trapped in the weave. The woman who had sold him had kept his offworld clothes when Aris went to fetch him after her successful bid, and clothed him in the coarse trousers and tunic of a common worker. Aris had not had enough money after buying him to purchase the man's own goods, not even the thing he seemed to want most, a small holocube with an image of some other woman in it. Perhaps it was just as well.

"Good." She liked it that he would obey spoken commands without a nudge from the ringtech.

Aris opened her satchel and pulled out the packet of travel bread she had brought from home that morning, and two bubbles of water. She broke bread and gave him half, and one of the bubbles. He held them and watched her after a glance around the car.

She took a privacy scarf from her satchel and offered it to him. He set his bread and water on the bench beside Aris and accepted the scarf, held it in both hands and glanced up at her.

Other women and men sat on benches, or women sat on single seats and men stood beside them. Control lights winked on the men's rings in the semi-dusk of the train segment. Beart Miner, from Diamond, the town beyond Opal on the train line, sat toward the front of the car with two men in the aisle beside her, a tall dark thin one and a shorter, stouter one with red hair and dark skin. Beart had found cleska under her ground. She needed men to mine it; selling it, she made so much money she could afford men enough for six women. She kept them all to herself, though, shaming her crèche mates by not inviting her sisters or cousins into the business, refusing stud fees from others.

On another bench sat twins from Ruby, their new-bought man between them.

In a car ahead, Aris knew, sat Petra Power Systems, with her new man. Petra had bid most strongly against Aris for Firen. Aris had feared for a time she would not get him. She had had to use the extra fifty ven her mother had given her. Petra had bought someone else, clearly a second choice. Petra lived two buildings from Aris; the soreness between them would hurt in the coming days.

No one else was feeding a man at this time. Some women sipped the centers from plumfruit. One ate yellow rootleaves. Common lore said it was better to keep your new man hungry and uncomfortable until you arrived at the homeplace, where he would find food, shelter, and warmth; that was supposed to train the man to stay. Running away would not help them, for all had tracking devices implanted in their bones. Not all of them knew that. But they all knew the mankiller virus waited for them if they didn't stay home and get their biweekly boosters.

"It's all right," Aris murmured. "Use the scarf to hide what you're doing. Eat. Drink."

Firen shook the scarf open and draped it over his head so that it concealed his face and hands. It was translucent rather than opaque, but was cover enough for a man eating in public.

Deisha Nurturer, the woman who sat in front of Aris, turned and frowned at her. Deisha's man sagged against a pole beside her, his hands clasped around it as though he would fall should he let go. She had got him at a good price. He had only had one owner before, but that person had been too strict, had punished through starvation, had been disciplined for mistreatment of live property, in fact. It was possible Deisha's man would not recover his spirit. Aris wasn't sure. Deisha could be gentle; she worked at the crèche, and the girls she raised had kind spirits. Caretaking a man was a different task, but perhaps there were things both jobs had in common.

"Only two more hours," Deisha whispered over her shoulder to Aris. "Can't you wait?"

Beneath the scarf, Aris's man had lifted travel bread to his mouth, even opened his mouth to take a bite, but at Deisha's words he lowered his hand. His gaze rose to Aris's face.

Aris murmured, "Go on, Firen. It's all right."

He glanced out through the semi-transparent scarf, then ate. Aris ate too. She would not have been able to stomach bread without feeding him, not knowing how long it had been since his last meal. She remembered times during her ring year when she had gone hungry because her temporary master Malia forgot to let her eat. She was never going to do that to her man.

"You've never had a man before," Deisha whispered. "You don't know, but these rules exist for a reason."

"This is not a rule. It's not in the owners' manual," Aris whispered back.

Firen broke the seal on his water bubble and drank, then finished his bread. Aris's bread tasted sweet, but worry made it hard to swallow. Still, it quieted her stomach.

"Not everything is written," murmured Deisha. "Our books are sometimes stolen and taken offworld. We can't have offworlders knowing everything we do. Many of the unwritten rules are just as strong as those written. You shouldn't feed him until we're home."

"Too late," Aris said. Unwritten rules. A flare of anger heated her cheeks.

"I hope you won't regret it," murmured Deisha. She turned away.

Firen face was angled toward her under the scarf, but she couldn't read his expression. He cupped the empty water bubble in his hands.

She took the bubble back and tucked it into her satchel. She refolded the scarf and put it away. "Stand." She didn't put any ring force behind it.

He rose and faced forward, his right hand curled around his left again. Since she bought him, he had stopped hunching and hiding; he stood straight now. She had chosen well. She felt the warmth of satisfaction. She leaned her head back and slept.

Sersta shook her shoulder. "Aris, we're at Opal."

Aris stretched herself awake, glanced at her man. He stood in the same position, with the same expressionless face he had worn when she had fallen asleep. She touched his leg and he glanced down at her. "Help," she said. "Carry." She held out her satchel to him, and he took it and slid the strap over his shoulder. He reached out, took her hand and pulled her to her feet.

Aris closed her mouth on the words she wanted to cry out: Don't touch me. I didn't tell you to touch me. She closed the link in her mind to his ring before she sent the thought to sting him, or disable him, or trigger the chemicals of hurt or sorrow in his system. Protesting a slave's action in public could lead to discipline for slave and master. She had said "help." Perhaps he interpreted that as touching her.

She needed to teach him local manners.

Watching her face, he noticed her distress and released her hand. "Thank you," she whispered; whether because he had pulled her to her feet or because he had let go, she did not clarify.

The train's doors opened. Aris waited her turn to exit, and her man waited half a step behind her left shoulder. He behaved well for someone who had not received any training commendations. But that touch—

At the station, her mother waited for her, tall and veiled in pale gauze as a sign of her priestess status. Mother turned away as Aris stepped off the train. She did not even look at the new man. Aris followed her mother in silence, Firen behind her. Aris did not want to go to Temple tonight, but Mother's presence demanded it.

"You must consecrate him," Mother said when they approached the temple stairs.

No one consecrated their men anymore. It was an old-fashioned, provincial practice that had died out long before Mother joined the Order of the Desert, three years after Aris was born. Consecration implied a lifelong commitment to someone, which was something even people of the jeweltowns no longer made, except to each other, woman to woman. Many matches between owner and owned did not work. The man failed, had to be retrained, sculpted, sold, or, in worst cases, killed. Those who lost consecrated slaves were far more devastated by such a loss than those who had never performed the rite. If Aris consecrated Firen, she would bind herself to him, make the bondage less one-way.

There were ways to get out of even a consecrated union. She knew all kinds of lifebuilding methods, and knew how to reverse them and lifebreak. With the skills she had from her job, she could engineer accidents much more easily than she could assists.

She had already killed once. She didn't know how she'd live with herself if she knowingly caused another death.

"Aris," said Mother.

"No," Aris said.

"Return my fifty ven, then."

Aris's shoulders sagged. Mother owned a small slice of the new man until Aris could repay her. Even this fraction was enough to dictate policies. "Why?" Aris whispered.

"I don't want you to repeat my mistakes."

"Wait three days until we know each other," Aris said.

"I know you, daughter. You waited for this particular auction. You studied all the men, and chose this one. What more do you need?"

"But—"

"Come," Mother said. Aris followed her mother up the steps into the Temple, and Firen followed Aris.

In the sanctuary of the Desert Goddess Nephila the Windchannel, Aris touched chest, lips, and forehead in salute to the image of the Goddess, a many-armed metal shape obscured by drifting turquoise airdrapes and dim underlight. The statue balanced on one leg, the other raised in a dance step, eternally frozen in the midst of melody. Aris knelt beside her mother and stared at the spiral pattern of sprinkled silver in the stone floor. Firen slid the satchel off his shoulder, set it on the floor, and knelt beside her without prompting. Aris glanced at him. He focused on the floor.

Mother lifted the gauze from her face out of respect for the one she served. She sang in oldspeak. The song's melody drifted, but it kept returning to a chorus, and each time, something in the statue of Nephila responded: a sound came from her that harmonized with what Mother sang.

Aris glanced at Firen. He stared at Mother, wide-eyed, his mouth slightly open. The silver in his eyes glowed.

At Mother's third repeat of the chorus, golden light haloed Nephila's head, and her three eyes shone, almonds of red glow in her dark, mysterious face.

Mother lowered herself to lie face down on the spiral-sparkled stone floor before the goddess.

A verse issued from the Goddess's statue, its tone chill and metallic, the words incomprehensible. The glow faded, leaving the Goddess obscure again.

Mother climbed stiffly to her feet and turned to face still-kneeling Aris and her man. "By the spirit and the power that flows through me from my Lady, I join you, woman and man, in the glory of the Goddess and the greater good. Be kind to each other." She held out her hands as though she were the great Matria from whom blessings flowed. Aris stretched out a hand to her, and Firen did as well. Mother took both of their hands, squeezed hard. "Grace be granted."

Firen gasped.

Aris felt a burning pain in her hand. When Mother released her, she stared down at what throbbed in her left palm: a red spiked circle, Windchannel's Kiss. She glanced at Firen, who studied his own palm, where a similar mark glowed.

Aris had read about the Kiss in tales when she was a child. It was some kind of special favor from the Goddess, but she'd only known one person who had actually received it—Sevi Rufi, Opal's administrator. Aris had had a conference with Rufi when she first moved to Opal, seen the mark, asked what it was. Rufi had told her: Windchannel's Kiss. Rufi hadn't explained further.

Mother knelt before Firen. "Do you understand what we have done, Man?" she asked.

He shook his head. He stared at his palm.

"You are stamped a part of this planet, a part of this region, and a part of my daughter Aris. There is no leaving for you now."

Firen frowned at the Kiss and at Mother. He turned to Aris.

"You were never going to leave anyway," Aris said. "You lost rights to yourself. They may have told you in training that a man can earn himself back. It almost never happens. You didn't come out of training with cooperation certificates. Those are what you need to get offplanet again."

"I don't belong here," he said. His voice was deeper than most voices Aris heard every day, with a sharp accent edging the words. He touched his throat. His eyebrows rose. He coughed, and said, "I didn't lose myself. They drugged me and sold me off the ship."

"That wasn't on your manifest. Your origin paper said you lost yourself gaming," Aris said. She blinked. Her image of Firen shifted now that she knew he could speak. She had wanted someone with conversation, but, after studying Firen, she had adjusted her expectations, thinking perhaps a companion who couldn't speak might be better. Speech had been the major interchange she had had with Malia, her ringyear partner. Speech carried pain and misunderstanding, poison and destruction. She rubbed the mark on her palm, then gazed at Firen.

He said, "It's a lie. I was speechblocked and symbolblocked when I woke up in the training hall. I couldn't read, I couldn't write, I couldn't communicate." He touched his throat again. "I couldn't speak again until now." He studied the statue, then his palm. He closed his hand into a fist, glanced up at Nephila. "For giving me back my speech, however it was accomplished, I thank you. I thank you." His gaze moved to Aris, and she pressed her hand to her chest. Everything would be different now.

She couldn't pretend he was an animal.

Mother glanced at the image of the Goddess, then at Firen. "This sounds like a story for a tea-seller's shop, but I think we can hear it here. The Goddess will listen. What did you do to bring such a fate on yourself?"

"Nothing!" Firen said.

"Oh, come now," said Mother. "No one sells a shipmate into slavery on Aga without provocation. Did you steal? Did you assault someone else? Were you lazy, stupid, deadweight? Who benefited from your loss?"

"I was a fine first officer!"

Mother's eyebrows rose. "First officer? Tell us another."

Firen's hand went toward his chest, where his rank badge would have been if he were wearing a uniform. His fingertips touched the coarse cloth of his new status. He shut his eyes, then sighed.

"Who hated you enough for this?" Mother asked.

"Most of those on my ship." He traced a curve of the spiral on the floor with two fingers. "The company placed me aboard because the ship was losing money on trading runs—took too long between planets, made unscheduled stops at planets with no known trade values, even on interdicted planets, where they courted trouble with the Feds. They arrived at trading stops after other traders had picked over the best goods, and took too long shipping the goods to the next stop.

"I have a reputation for troubleshooting. I was supposed to shape the ship up and raise profitability. But they had been too long without proper supervision, and were used to their lax ways. They resented me. The second officer hated me most, I think. Every time I gave an order she didn't like, she smiled at me before she obeyed." He stared at the floor. "We weren't scheduled to stop here."

"What is the ship's name?" Aris asked.

"*Pleta*, a moonclass trader run by AllGoods." Firen straightened. "Will you take me to court and let me sue?" he asked Aris. "At least let me call my company? I know they'd pay you to get me back."

"No," said Aris. "I'll file a report with the trade commission, though. The ship is rogue now, fair game for takeover, if what you say is true. They are long gone, but we have good trackers. You were at the training hall for months. I wonder if you're the first man they've sold here? Someone will have a record, if this is a practice your ship has engaged in before."

"I must call my company! I have to give them a status report."

"None of that concerns you now," Mother said gently. "It is all offworld, and you are part of the planet. Time to learn your new life, Man."

"But I—"

"Aris," Mother said.

Aris thought, *Quiet.*

Firen clutched his throat, then glared at Aris, his eyes furious. He jumped to his feet.

Aris thought, *Down.*

Firen collapsed across the silver spiral, his muscles twitching.

Aris bowed to the image of the Goddess. She knew of consecration, but she hadn't known what it would mean to her and her man. Apparently it didn't preclude her exercising rights of ownership. She would have to learn as she went. She kissed the burning mark on her palm. Something returned her kiss. She saluted the Goddess, chest, lips, forehead. She rose, then thought, *Up.*

Firen stood.

Carry.

He stooped, picked up her satchel, slid its strap over his shoulder.

"Come home, Firen," Aris said aloud.

He followed her out of the temple.

She had prepared a room for the man she would bring back from the auction. She thumbed the door open. They stood in the hall, looking over the threshold.

Remarks sat on her tongue, waiting to be made, but she didn't say them aloud: Bigger than your ship's cabin, isn't it? Here's the switch for the climate controls, and this one controls the lights. These raised dots control your wallworks. Of course, you know how to operate a room. You don't know this is technology not everyone on Aga has in their homes. You don't know that my position as bio-engineer lets me live better than many of the other women in this town, including Petra, the other one who bid so high on you. You don't know that most men live in rooms just big enough for a bed, if they have their own rooms at all instead of sleeping on a pallet on the floor in some common room when they're not serving, pleasuring, or procreating with the women who own them. You don't know yet how lucky you are.

She said none of this.

He looked at the room, and then at her.

She unthought the command for *Quiet*.

She pointed to the thumb lock by the door. "Go ahead and imprint it. This is yours," she said.

"Mine," he whispered. He set her satchel on the hall floor, pressed his thumb to the lock, waited for it to flash green to show it accepted him as its key, and went into the room. He touched the teal cover on the bed, then played fingers across the wall controls: the wall cleared and showed the little yard out back, with its single xerophilous tree, engineered by her to flower every two weeks, its night blooms large and succulent, pale as moonlight, the scent heavy and spicy; and the sand-sculpture pit where she directed airfields to shape sand into images of anything she liked. Just now, there was a sand fountain shaped like a jellyfish. The wall blanked. The wall played realtime scenes from natural areas on other planets, one following another so swiftly she was dizzy.

He left the wall blank and came to the threshold. He touched the room's door control. The door slid closed in her face, with him on the other side.

She wondered if this merited punishment. Her control of his ring included a number of directives it could enforce, chemical controllers that could give him pain or pleasure in varying degrees, other tech that spoke directly to his muscle control centers and could force him to perform physical actions or drop him into tranquilized sleep where he stood. The commands worked through walls.

Before she decided, the door opened again.

"Thank you," he said. He came out and thumbed the door closed behind him.

Aris stopped at the comm station in her living room to file a report with the trade commission relating Firen's story of the *Pleta*. Firen stared longingly at the screen, but Aris shut it down as soon as she left her message, and thumb-locked the comm station alcove. She sensed his frustration. Best he get used to being frustrated.

She gave him supper in her kitchen/dining room, a bubble on the back of her apartment with walls and ceiling she could clear or color as she pleased. Tonight she cleared the ceiling so they could see the stars and the dark ridge of toothy mountains to the east. The only light in the room came from the stars and the table's surface, a soft melon-orange glow that did not disturb their night vision.

Firen sat at the table with her. She didn't tell him that was not what most women did with their slaves. Maybe it *was* what most women did. She had studied the handbook, but she didn't know all the unwritten rules. What her friends did when they were alone with their men was a mystery. Her mother had had no man Aris could remember in the three years Aris lived with her before Mother consigned Aris to a crèche.

There were several things Aris should have learned during her ringyear that she still did not know. In the final two months, she and her ringmate would have been instructed in the differences between their ringyear training and what women actually did with men.

Light shone up through the translucent green and yellow dishes she had set their meals on.

"Please," she said, "eat," but she didn't make it a command. She didn't say: I prepared this meal for us tonight, but tomorrow, you will prepare food for us. They trained you to do that, I know.

Do you eat pellets, the way they did on that generation-ship soap opera my crèche-mother loved, the one we were forbidden to watch because the males were not slaves? I was the only one she let watch it with her, and I've never told anyone. People on that soap were always running into each other at the pellet bar and trying to get each other to taste forbidden mixes, the ones enhanced with mind-altering or aphrodisiac compounds. Is that your idea of bad behavior?

Firen picked over the yellow, green, and magenta leaves of the salad, the flakes of two-flavored protein, the perfume-drenched nugget of dessert. Eventually he picked up a single salad leaf with his tongs and placed it on his tongue.

Aris understood. After eating on the train, she wasn't hungry either.

Firen ate two more leaves, and several protein flakes. Aris ate a bite every time Firen did. Firen tasted the dessert and spat it out, coughed, and wiped his mouth with the back of his hand. He grabbed the glass of water she had set at his place and swallowed, then rinsed out his mouth and swallowed again.

"What *was* that?" he asked in a raspy voice.

"Dessert."

"Ugh." He shook his shoulders, his head, as if to cast out a dangerous idea.

Aris tasted hers. Perfect, the flavors a subtle blend of scents. She ate another spoonful, then finished the nugget. She glanced at Firen.

"You like it?" he said. "It coats my tongue with slime and tastes like the inside of a climesuit."

"Oh, dear," she said.

"Perceptual differences," said Firen. "I've seen it before." Something behind his face shifted. He set down his tongs and stared at the brand on his palm, touched an edge of the spiky red circle with the index finger of his other hand. He glanced up at her.

"Does yours still hurt?" she asked.

His lips tightened. "What does it mean?"

"I don't know for sure. It forges a bond between us, in addition to the master-slave bond. I'm not one of the faithful to worship the manifestations of some old computer complex, but I'm afraid we'll have to answer to it somehow. Nobody does that consecration rite anymore. Maybe there's a record somewhere, or maybe Mother knows more."

"But what else the mother said—about my never leaving the planet—is that absolute too?"

"Didn't they teach you that in the training hall? Unless you do something that earns so much money you can buy yourself with your percentage, demonstrate extraordinary heroism or generosity, or perform some monumental service to everyone on Aga, there's no escape for you but death."

"My company would buy me back if you'd just let me talk to them."

"I don't want to sell you. Besides, now that you have Windchannel's Kiss, you're doubly doomed. Not only does Central have some kind of tracker on you, that thing under the sand knows you now, you and me both. It may make demands. It won't let us go." It won't let us go, she thought. I'll live here in Opal the rest of my days no matter what I do next. I had better do just what I'm supposed to do.

"That thing under the sand—?"

"This particular sect of our religion worships the original colonyship computer, which is still operating from underground, they say. It powers the statues in the temples, and it can still dictate to us in some matters."

He frowned. "I didn't have time to do backgrounding for Aga. I didn't even know we were going to stop here. Haven't you people been here for six hundred years?"

"This is year 651 since we landed."

"The original colonyship computer is still running?"

She nodded. "It was a prototype, cyborg, self-repairing, able to train its own caretakers. The Order of the Desert has maintained it for centuries."

He stared at his brand, ran a finger along the red ring. Aris touched her own, felt the raised ridge of the brand, as though a metal ring had been set under her skin.

Firen closed his hand over the Kiss. "Won't you even let me talk to my superior?"

"Will it reconcile you to your fate?"

"I don't think so, but it will make things easier in my mind."

She rose, got the special gengineered drink she'd made the night before from the refrigerator, and brought it back to him. There was only a small amount in the bottom of the cup, just enough to do the job. It was a lovely orange-yellow and smelled like melons. "Drink this. Then come to my room with me. Tomorrow I'll let you call, but only once, understand?"

He drank. She cleared the table, set the dishes in the washer (jobs he would do tomorrow), gave the liquid time to work on him, then took his hand and led him to her room.

She was ready to be a mother, but she didn't want a boy.

Firen was willing enough in her bed. She didn't have to use the ring at all; in fact, she was a little afraid of what she might think toward him if she weren't careful, so she dampened her mental link to only a thread of contact, in case Firen proved dangerous and she needed to protect herself from him. It was strange and exciting to let him direct the encounter, almost as strange as letting him shut the door to his room in her face. Anytime she stiffened or stilled, he drew back and changed tactics.

His lovemaking skills were broader than she had known to expect. Some of the things he did to her she had never heard of; they made her body wake and hum more than it ever had with her other lovers, even her ringmate.

Afterward, he slept face down, his arm across her stomach. She held his ringed hand in both of hers and stared at the stars through her ceiling.

Will my daughter have silver in her eyes? Silver in her skin?

Will this man hate me when I teach him all he has to do for me?

She closed her eyes, touched his ring with her index finger, could not stop the command that formed and flashed from her mind to his, though she had been forbidden ever to think it again. *Love me.*

She amended it. *Love me at least a little.*

THIS IS FOR YOU

BRUCE McALLISTER

There was one girl I really liked in school when I returned to Earth, but it took me three months to say hello. I wasn't good with human beings. We'd just gotten back from Pitipek (a red-dwarf star system "just left" of Tau Ceti, as the joke goes). My father had been stationed there for two years with the TU's Planetary Safety Agency, and living with the slow, enigmatic, bipedal Pitipeki—especially in one of their villages, and under those endless clouds—tends to make you lose your people skills. In fact, it can really change you.

The girl's skin was as white as Pitipek's brightest moon, her hair as dark as a pench's eyes. Just beautiful. I didn't know what she thought of other colors—in my case, a boy who was on the greenish side because his grandfather, a famous genengineer who'd been incarcerated once for gene crimes, had mapped him to have skin like that . . . and maybe a few other things. Like a little talent at art.

I said "hello." It was an overcast day, and we were taking a break in the hallway from geopol simming. She said "hello" back. I could tell from her voice and the way she looked at me that my skin wasn't a problem. A week later I said "hello" again, and I knew this would continue for the entire school year if I didn't do something special. I'd had a human girlfriend on Pitipek, another PSA officer's kid, in the village down the road—her name was Clare—but she'd disappeared that second year, her body never found. That does something to you.

No one on Earth makes paintings anymore—not really—but the Pitipeki do. I'd had Pitipeki friends—young males—my age in the village who made them every day. Every painting has a purpose for them, a practical one. *Spinota peluga ma villea*, the Pitipeki say. A painting must *do something*. It's not about "art." It's about—how to put it? Relationships. Power. Getting what you want.

I'd learned to paint in that village the way the Pitipeki do—there wasn't much else to do—but I hadn't learned everything.

So I made a painting for Mala—that was her name—her dad was a politician, people said—a painting of the village I'd lived in. I gave it to her after school as she was about to board the rail to her neighborhood and I was about to board mine. She looked terrified for a moment.

"It's a painting," I said and gave her my best smile. I hadn't given a girl that smile since Pitipek—since Clare. "I made it with an oil paint you get when you mix the resin of the darmiath tree with the right minerals on Pitipek—lithium, the hematitics, unstable metamorphs. You've got to grind them up with a mortar. The paint has a charge. It makes you tingle. Some scientists think the minerals, if arranged right, can affect space in weird ways—quantum ways. That's why the painting sparkles and looks like it's moving . . . "

This was a lot more than a "hello." But if I kept talking, I told myself, she'd calm down, wouldn't she? I hoped so. I didn't want to scare her.

She did. The painting was strange, and so was the boy with the greenish skin, but he was just a boy, wasn't he? Strange, not creepy.

"It's really big," she said, trying to be nice.

"I only make big paintings," I said, laughing. It was a joke.

"Well," she joked back, "I wouldn't want you to make a smaller one just for me."

She liked me. I could tell. Maybe she liked my skin. I really wanted to believe it. As my grandfather—not a nice man at all, but a wise one—told us: "Engineer a person so they're unique, and you have art that people will want. That is real power."

Was I art to her?

"I could do that," I said. "Really."

That made her laugh. The painting—she kept looking at it—was doing what I'd hoped it would.

"Can I show you something?" I asked. "You won't miss your rail, I promise."

"Sure."

I was holding the painting upright next to us, one hand on it to steady it. It was big, as tall as we were—a vertical landscape, a village, a *marlic* hut and a door you were supposed to look at, so I'd made the door red and put sunlight on the path leading to it.

I picked up the painting and led her to the shade side of the station. Everyone else was further down the track.

To be funny, I frowned and said, "You hate it, don't you."

"No! I don't hate it at all."

"I made it for you."

This made her laugh too. She was trusting me, and that felt good. "I got that impression," she said.

"Do you want to touch it?"

She did, and who wouldn't?

She looked at me, then the painting, then me again. No boy had ever given her a painting before, I knew.

She touched my elbow—her hand lingered, and my arm tingled—and with the other hand reached out to the painting. Then she hesitated.

"Go ahead," I said. "It won't bite."

She did. She moved her hand over the surface, loving the feel of it as everyone does when they touch a Pitipek painting. Like fur, like little teeth, tickly.

When her arm disappeared into the painting, I stepped back to let what needed to happen happen. No one could see us. She screamed once, a tiny sound lost in the whish of a passing rail, and her other arm, in its pretty sky-blue sleeve, tried hard to pull the first one out, grabbing, holding on, but that arm disappeared too in a swirl of green. Her skinny legs, shaking terribly, did their best to fight it, but were swallowed by the oily green, too; and in a second—with one more little scream, one that made me remember a day in the village—she was gone.

She was mine. That's what this kind of painting was for. You make it and give it to someone you want to have forever. I'd learned that on Pitipek, but I'd never learned the rest. I'd tried hard with the "release" minerals, the required patterns, but could never pull it off. An arm would appear—the skin white as paint, shivering, a voice somewhere far away shrieking—or a hand, or a foot—but then it would snap back into the green. Every time my friends would laugh in that gargly way Pitipek laugh.

What do you do with someone once you have them?

I didn't know.

I took the painting home, thinking it would feel different, heavier or something, but it didn't this time either. No sounds from it. Nothing moved on the surface even for a moment. I wondered—just for a moment—what she was feeling, if she was feeling anything.

I started another one late that night. I had lots of paint left. I'd spent weeks in the village making it. There was a girl with yellow hair at school—her skin bronzed by the sun—and I didn't want to spend months on *hellos* with her, too. I was pretty sure I loved her, but after Pitipek it's hard to know.

ONE HOUR, EVERY SEVEN YEARS

ALICE SOLA KIM

———◆———

When Margot is nine, she and her parents live on Venus. The surface of Venus, at that time, is one enormous sea with a single continent on its northern pole, perched there like a tiny, ridiculous top hat. There is sea below, and sea above, rain continually plummeting from the sky, endlessly self-renewing.

When I am thirty, I won't have turned out so hot. No one will know; from a few feet away, I'll seem fine. They won't notice the dandruff, the opalescent flaking of my chin. They won't know that I walk hard and deliberate, like a 40s starlet in trousers, in order to compensate for the wobbly heels of my crummy shoes. They won't see past my really great job. And it will be a great job, really. I will be working with time machines.

When Margot is nine, it has been five years since she has seen the sun. On Venus, the sun comes out but once every seven years. Margot's family moved to Venus from Earth when she was four. This is the main thing that makes her different from her classmates, who are just a bunch of trashy Venus kids. Draftees and immigrants. Their parents work at the desalination plants, the dormitory facilities; they plumb and bail, they traverse Venus' vast seas in ships and submersibles, and sometimes do not come back.

To her classmates, Margot will never be Venusian, even though she's her palest clammiest self like a Venusian, and walks and talks like a Venusian—with that lazy, slithering drawl. Why? First finger: she's a freak, quiet and standoffish, but given to horrible bursts of loud friendliness that are so awkward they make everyone hate her more for trying. Second finger: her dad is rich and powerful, but she still isn't cool. The Venus kids don't know it, but it isn't her wealth they hate. It is the waste of it. The way her boring hair hangs against her fresh sweatshirts. The way she shuffles along in her blinding new sneakers. Third finger, fourth, fifth, sixth, seventh, eighth, ninth, tenth fingers, and all the toes too: in her lifetime, Margot has seen the sun and they haven't. Venus kids are strong and mean and easily offended. They know there's a thing they should be getting that they're not getting. And that the next best thing to getting something is no one in the whole world getting it.

When I am thirty, I will have gotten my first boyfriend. He'll be a co-worker at the lab and I won't have noticed him for the longest time. Big laugh, right? You would think that, as some nobody who nobody ever notices, I'd at least be the observant one by default, the one who notices everyone else and forms complex opinions about them, but, no, I will be a creature spiraled in upon myself, a shrimp with a tail curled into its mouth.

Late night at work, a group of people will be playing Jenga in the lounge. The researchers love Jenga because it has the destructive meathead glamour of sports but only a fraction of the physical peril. Anders will ask me if I want to play and I'll shake my head, hoping it looks like I'm too cool for Jenga but also bemused and tolerant, all of this hiding the truth, which is that I am terrified of Jenga. I'm afraid of being the player who causes all of the blocks to fall. Because that player is both appreciated and despised: on the one hand they absorb the burden of causing the Fall, thus relieving everyone else of said burden, but on the other hand, they are responsible for ending the game prematurely, killing all the fun and potential, not to mention the Jenga tower itself—the spindly edifice that everyone worked so hard together to create and protect.

The guy who will be my first boyfriend will push a block out without any hesitation. He won't poke at it first, he will go straight for the block, and I will watch as the tower wobbles. It won't fall. As he takes the dislodged block and stacks it on his pile, he will make eye contact with me, a carefully constructed look of surprise on his face—mouth the shape of an O, eyebrows pushing his forehead into pleats.

When Margot is nine, the sun comes out on Venus. Her classmates lock her inside a closet and run away. They are gone for precisely one hour. When her classmates finally come back to let Margot out, it will be too late.

When I am thirty, I will have been at my great job, the job of working with time machines, long enough to learn their codes and security measures (I've even come up with a few myself), so I will do the thing that I didn't even know I was planning to do all along. I will enter the time machine, emerging behind a desk in the school I attended when I was nine. Water droplets will condense on the walls. There is no way to keep out the damp on Venus. The air in the classroom will taste like the air in a bedroom where someone has just had a sweaty nightmare. I will hide during all of the ruckus, but don't worry: I will work up the courage. I will stand and open the closet door and do what needs to be done. And I will return!

When Margot is nine, the sun comes out on Venus. Her classmates lock her inside of a closet and run away. She hears someone moving outside. Margot's throat is raw but she readies another scream when the door opens. A golden woman stands in the doorway, her face dark, her hair edged with gilt. Behind her the sun shines through the windows like a fire, like a bombing the moment before everybody is dead. "Wouldn't you like to play outside?" the woman says.

When I am thirty, I will live on Mars, the way I've always dreamed I would. I will live in the old condo alone, after my mother has moved out, and I will become a smoker the moment I find a pack my mother has left behind. It will feel wonderful to smoke on warm and dusty Martian nights. It will feel so good to blow smoke through the screen netting on the balcony and watch it swirl with the carmine dust. Many floors down, people will splash in the pool of the condo complex, all healthy and orange like they are sweating purified Beta Carotene and Vitamin C.

It is the sight of these party people that will spur me to spend a month attempting to loosen up and to get pretty. I will have a lot of time on my hands and a lot more money after my mother moves out. I will learn that there are lots of things you can do to fix yourself up, and that I hadn't tried any of them. Makeup, as I learn it, is confusing and self-defeating. I'll never understand why I have to make my face one flat uniform shade, only to add back color selectively until my old face is muffled and almost entirely muted: a quiet little cheep of itself. I will learn all of this from younger women at the department store, younger women who are better than me at covering up far nicer faces. I will also get some plastic surgery, because I will be extremely busy; I don't have time to be painting this and patting that! I will have lost so much of my time already.

When Margot is nine, the sun comes out on Venus and she is on the verge of getting pushed into the closet when a woman appears out of nowhere and starts screaming at the kids. They scatter and run. Margot is trapped, backing into the closet that she had been fighting to stay out of. The woman approaches. She is tidy, flawless even, but her face droops and contorts like a rubber mask without a wearer. "Recognize me," says the woman.

• • •

When I am thirty, Sana, the new researcher at the lab, will tell me what she's been writing in that notebook of hers. After her first day of work, Sana will have written down her observations about everybody: summaries of the kind of people we all are, predications about what we might do. After working at lab after lab and traveling the worlds, Sana will be confident about her ability to nail people down precisely. She is nice, though. When I ask her what she wrote about me, she'll reply, "I'm not sure about you yet. You are a tricky one. It will take some time to see." I'll know that that means I have the most boring entry with the fewest words.

Sana will be one of those who believe that you cannot find your own timeline. You will not be able to access it, to travel back in time to change one's life. You can go into other universes and mess the place up and leave, but not your own. We will both know of the many who have tried to find their own timestreams; all have failed. Sana will say, "The universe does not allow it to happen because we cannot be the gods of ourselves," and this is about as mystical as Sana will ever get.

When Margot is nine, her parents refuse to take her out of school. She asks and she asks and they don't hear. Margot's father is high up in the Terraforming Division, which has both an image problem and a not-being-good-at-its-job problem. Her parents tell her that it helps them that she attends regular school with the kids of their employees' employees' employees' employees' employees'. It doesn't matter that Margot hasn't exactly been the best PR rep.

A while back, the students had studied the Venus Situation in Current Events. The teacher played a video, which showed the disaster as it was happening, everyone in the control room yelling, "Fuck!" The fucks were bleeped out incompletely. You could still hear "fuh." 1,123 people had died moments after the Terraformers pressed the button. The Terraformers had been trying to transform Venus from a hot gassy mess into an inhabitable, Earth-like place. What actually happened was that everything exploded, the blast even sucking in ships from the safe zone. After the space dust had cleared, they did not find a normal assortment of continents and oceans and sunlight and foliage: what they found was one gross, sopping slop-bucket of a world. A Venus that was constantly, horribly wet. A Venus that, to this day, rains in sheets and buckets, a thousand firehoses spraying from the sky. Iron-gray and beetle-black and blind eye-white: these are the colors of Venus. Forests grow and die and grow and die, their trunks and limbs composting on a wet forest floor, which squeaks like cartilage.

The teacher had stopped the video. "Margot's father is part of the new Terraforming division," she said. "He is helping us make Venus a better place to live." The teacher was too tired to smile, so she made her mouth wider. She had been drafted, had come from New Mexico on Earth. She despaired of her frizzing hair and her achy knees, and she missed her girlfriend a lot, even though it was sad to miss someone who didn't love you quite enough to follow you somewhere shitty. But, not a ton of lesbians on Venus. The teacher was tired of going out on lackluster dates where she and the other woman would briskly concur that, *yes, we are both interested in women, that is why we are on this date*, maybe not in those words exactly, but you get the drift, and then sometimes they would go home alone and sometimes not.

One kid had turned around and given Margot the finger. Behind her, a girl leaned forward and whispered something like "maggot." The children in the classroom whispered in their slithering voices, things about Margot, things about her father who was so bad at his job, things about Venus. Then someone said, "Who said penis?" and laughter rose and exploded outward like a mushroom cloud. "You know who likes penis?" a boy said, in a high, clear, happy voice, as if he had just gotten a good idea. "Your dad."

When I am thirty, I will visit other timestreams. It will almost feel like traveling into my own past, but not quite. Sometimes there will be big differences: shirts, the configurations in which the children stand, the smell of lunch on their breaths. But there will also be the differences I can't see. I could stay in one event cluster until I died and I still wouldn't have seen it all. In one timeline, a single hair on a girl's head might be blown left. In another, blown right. A whole new universe, created just for that hair. The hair was the star of the whole goddamn show but the hair was not egotistical about it at all. It would simply, humbly change directions when the time came. But always: children will come in; children will run out.

When Margot is nine, her parents are carefully, jazzily, ostentatiously in love. Enraptured by each other and enwrapped in money, their love cushioned against the world and Margot. Native Martians for two generations, Margot's parents' families had come from China and Denmark and Nigeria and South Korea. The people do sigh to watch Margot's parents walk hand-in-hand—they are lovely alone and sublime together, a gorgeous advertisement for the future, except to see them is to know that the future is the present, it is here, and isn't that a happy thing?

This pressure is beneficial to their relationship; they perform a little for the world and Margot, and most of all, for themselves; they grin at each other competitively; their real feelings are burnished until they blaze. She has never seen them in sweatpants, whereas Margot herself often changes into pajamas the moment she gets home, which makes Margot's mother laugh and pat her face and tell her how extremely Korean she's being. At the dinner table, her parents feed each other the first bite. Sometimes this is yet another competition, a race to construct the perfect tiny arrangement of food, and sometimes it is a simple moment of closeness that doesn't make Margot want to barf yet (she's not old enough) but induces in her narrow chest a weird, jealous, proud feeling. She is certain that, someday soon, she will be able to create a role for herself and join them in their performance.

When I am thirty, I will be too tall for my parents to make jokes over my head. They'll have to look me in the eye when they do it. Or the back of my head.

I will call my mother and she won't pick up, over and over again. Catching myself in the viddy reflection, I'll be scared by my face. How perfectly slack and non-sentient it is when nothing prompts it into action. It will remind me of my father's face, when I watched him alone in the dining room a few weeks before his disappearance. I had woken up in the middle of the night and crept out of my room to get a glass of water. I needed to be quiet, because at night the house stopped being mine. Sometimes it belonged only to my parents. Sometimes the grayscale walls of our aggressively normal house looked alien, as too-smooth as an eggshell, and then the house seemed to belong to no one.

I peered around the corner into the dining room and saw my father sitting at the table alone. He sat still, staring at his computer. Nothing moved. I was frightened but fascinated to see my father this way, all flat surface. Suddenly he reached up and pinched his upper arm hard, on the inner part where it really hurts. He pinched *hard*, and then he *twisted* hard, and the tiny violence of his fingers were so at odds with the nothing expression on his face that I wanted to laugh. I pressed my hands to my mouth and tiptoed quickly back to bed.

But who could say what the significance of that single memory was, or if it was significant at all? The record will show that he had faked everything, and had been good at it. My father behaved weirdly the night I spied on him; that is true. So maybe that does mean something. But his mind, a very strange place indeed, must have been even stranger when the rest of him was normal: him at dinner, taking a first bite, him at work, making everyone feel special as he told them exactly what to do.

When Margot is nine, the sun comes out on Venus. All rain stops and the sun comes out for an hour, and for that hour everyone can pretend that Venus turned out okay. Because this gracious, lovely celestial event happens every seven years, some of the kids sorta, kinda remember the last time the sun came out. When they talk about it, they sound like old people reminiscing: they chatter on about how the sun smelled like warming butter and glittered on their skin. Other kids don't remember anything. And then there's Margot.

Who had been four instead of two the last time she saw the sun, which makes a difference—it's like having a brain made of clay instead of dough. She knows how the sun is a discrete object in the sky and, also, that it is everywhere, like air. And she knows that, like air, you can breathe the sun in and even taste it a little, but it doesn't taste like butter or sprinkle sparkles onto your face, that's just stupid. She has tried to tell this to the other kids, but only makes that mistake once. Margot stares out the window, brimming. Her parents had been letting her paint gold x's on the wall to count down the days. They laughed about it. Just paint. Margot is looking forward to being warm. She is looking forward to opening her mouth and letting the sun fill her stomach (which is one idea she doesn't find stupid, no. She believes it will happen).

The teacher leaves the room for a moment. No one has been able to concentrate on lessons today, after all. Someone prods Margo in the back and she turns, still smiling. A ring of kids closing in on her, shivering in the tank tops and shorts and sandals that they put on that morning in preparation. They look like skinny old stray cats. It occurs to Margot that there is nothing she can say. She's amazed by their cruelty, but not surprised. Hasn't she done so much to earn it?

When I am thirty, I will lose my boyfriend. He will have asked me many times, over the course of many weeks: "Is there anything I can do to make you happy?" He'll even get down on his knees, a move that will strike not only as melodramatic but also aggressive and mean, yes, mean, because the way he does it, it's not the action of a supplicant, it's the action of a bully who wants to force my hand by slumping to the ground so aggressively like this, far before the situation warrants it. I will be harsh in my gloom and he harsh in his cheer. He'll say again, "Is there anything I can do to make you happy?"

I will think that the answer is yes—although I don't know what the thing would be—and he will think that the answer is no.

When Margot is nine, the sun comes out on Venus, and the teacher runs into the classroom. She looks from child to child and knows that she has gotten there just in time. Though still troubled by her encounter with the strange woman, she puts her arm around Margot and another child and says brightly, "Let's go! We don't want to miss a single second." They go out into the day.

Afterward, in the post-sun future, life is a little easier. Now all of the kids have seen the sun; it's not something that Margot owns and they don't, and so Margot is allowed to develop into less of a loser. After all, you only need a little bit of space to not be a loser, a few hours in the day of not being teased. I'm telling you, you'd be surprised, you'd be shocked at what miracles can happen.

• • •

When I am thirty, most of my old classmates will have added me to every conceivable social network. They won't remember anything from when we were nine, and I'll be relieved. I'll think that's sweet. I will be asked to look, listen, gubble, like, pfuff, [untranslatable gesture], post, re-post, and blat for their sakes, and sometimes I will.

After all, I will have the time, plenty of time for everyone after my mother moves out. At that point, we'd lived together for ages. Early on, she would sometimes come into my room at night, desolate and weepy, telling me how she needed to kill herself and asking for my reassurance that I would be fine without her. I was nine, ten, seventeen, twenty-three, and always I'd say to myself, *what is required here*? Reassurance given, so she'd at least calm down, or reassurance withheld, so she would decide to not kill herself?

Other times my mother could cook; she could be funny while we watched televised vote-in talent shows, and able to imitate just about anybody in her good/bad/perfectly not-too-cruel way; she could offer to take me shopping with my money because I had forgotten to cultivate a sense of style because I was working, but only with my money, so that we could stretch the money that was left after my father disappeared, and after I attended school, and got full scholarships that indentured me to a corporation for five years post-graduation.

At first, it was hard to turn down invitations and skip social events for her. I'd come home angry, slamming doors and dropping my bag like I was thirteen, even when I was seventeen, twenty-three, twenty-seven. Then I'd see her on the couch looking like the dropped bag and I'd go make her a drink. I would have one too. Each of us just one, or two. And then I would proceed forth with my life's work of putting her in a good mood, and, failing that, dragging her up from wailing despair, silent despair, mumbling despair. "Daughter, you are all I have," she would say in her deep, beautiful voice, part Nigerian and English and Martian and not at all Venusian. Part of me liked hearing that, both the sentiment and the grand sound of it, like we were in some BBC miniseries, and part of me hated the non-specificity of "daughter," as if I could be anyone and not me in particular, plus the implication that I, the "daughter," was the leftover quantity, and not one anyone would keep by choice. Which, she hadn't. My poor mother.

Soon no one invited me to things and I was too busy, anyway; soon I was in the groove of our shared routine and remembered nothing else. And in the groove I grew up twisty, quiet and distracted and money-grubbing and unibrowed. No matter: I did good for us. I took care of my mother, I got better and better jobs once I was released from my contract, and, when I was 29, I bought us a condo on Mars. It was nothing like the wonderful places my mother had lived in when she was younger, but it was reminiscent of them, with its higher than absolutely necessary ceilings and the modern fixtures that hid their functionalities behind unhelpfully smooth surfaces.

It was moving into this condo, I believe, that spurred my mother to start working out and getting into therapy and, finally, to move out; but who knows, it's not like I saw her look upward at the ceilings and down at herself, down at the gorgeous young orange people and back up at herself. My mother moved out. Five months after that she wouldn't even take any of my money. At first she called often and I would be there for her or I would go over there to fall asleep on her couch. Then I was the one calling her, every missed call a slasher film in which the very worst had happened, inflicted by someone else or herself.

I will call my mother again. She won't pick up. One more time. Then I will go out to smoke on the balcony. It will be the best thing about living here alone.

When Margot is almost ten, she and her mom move to a tiny apartment on Mars. Margot loses her favorite sneakers in the move. She throws a quiet tantrum, drums her feet on the floor. Ordinarily, Margot's mom would enjoy seeing such liveliness in her, would encourage it by laughing and grabbing Margot's hands and dancing until Margot could no longer resist. But Margot's mom is in bed, covers over her face, still wearing her shoes and her Martian jackal-collar coat.

For them it had been a long rocket trip, and before that, a long and extremely bad month. A month ago, a young woman in a boxy neoprene business suit had visited their house. On their doorstep she squeezed rain out of her hair and asked if she could have a moment of Margot's mother's time. She said her name was Hilda. She was immaculately composed, her makeup like a bulletproof vest.

Hilda had told them that their father has put the whole Venus Project in jeopardy. But this meant nothing to Margot's mom; she couldn't care less about the Venus Project. Her husband had disappeared, and that's what mattered to her. Margot's dad had disappeared, and her mom absolutely did not give a shit about the Venus project.

It wouldn't be that hard to kill yourself on Venus. Margot has thought about it. You just walk out of your door and keep walking, don't change a thing. Sure, you could do that on any planet, but on Venus death would be fast, and it would be predictable: drowning or sea monster.

Her mom questioned all their friends, searched his files, demanded that the authorities scour the oceans, and then paid contractors to continue searching—until she ran out of money. Because that was the thing, there wasn't much money left. When it came to money, Margot's dad had lied in every way possible, about the getting of it and most certainly about the spending of it.

Margot and her mother left Venus after that.

When I am thirty, my mother will viddy me, looking great. She'll have just gotten the hand rejuvenation surgery that she'd been saving up for. "Check it out," she'll say, waving springy teenage hands that look like they could repel water. She'll tell me that things have been great since she moved out. She likes her job at the archive. She likes that her younger coworkers will tell her all the work gossip because they think she's old and harmless but still fun enough to confide in. Sometimes she's the subject of the work gossip, like the time she went out on four dates with a researcher who had frequented the archive more and more since she started working there, haunting the checkout desk with increasingly unnecessary requests. My mother will have even gotten back into painting, where she was on a hotter track decades ago, when she was younger than I will be now. She'd studied at Martian Yale and won a big prize and everything.

I'll remind her that I haven't heard from her in a long time.

My mother, who usually apologizes so sweetly, whose apologies are heartfelt and devastating but ultimately goldfish apologies, that kind that are forgotten six seconds later, this time will not even say sorry. "There's been so much going on," she'll say. "The most wonderful thing has happened. Your father is alive." She'll tell me that she rehired a private investigator on Venus, who has found a man who looks like my father working on a research submersible. There is a photo. Seeing it, I won't be able to tell whether it's him, one way or another. I will have so many things to say that they will get stuck— too many people trying to crowd through a narrow door. My mom will just look at my face, which she can tell I've changed, I can tell.

"I'm going to Venus to find him," she'll say. "I've given notice at the archive."

"You can't," I say. "You just moved out." My new face will not move around as much as my old face, for which I will be grateful.

"Please, darling. I'm going. We're not going to be able to talk again for a while, so let's make this nice."

In my opinion, all my mother has to do is get better and stronger and never call me and, even if she acts like a high school best friend who thinks you're a dork but puts up with you because they love being worshipped and always hangs up first, that is still all I want and all that is required of her, and the words crowd together and all that will come out is another strangled,

"You can't."

My mother will shake her head. She will laugh, looking everywhere but at the screen, at me. "You think that I like everything, that I'm having such a fabulous time and this is the best that can be expected," she'll say. Then she'll look at me. "All of it's nothing."

When Margot is nine, the sun comes out on Venus and a woman bursts into the classroom and starts punching the kids. She is not very good at it and the children quickly overpower her. To Margot, this is the height of unfairness: that an adult would bend from her looming height to attack children, so Margot shouts and fights back too. The others look at her with a new respect. The woman coughs, dabs her bloody nose with the back of her hand, and disappears. By the end of that day the children will have witnessed two miraculous events, and they will never forget either one. Over beers, they will meet at least once a year when they're in their twenties, once every two years in their early thirties, and so on, the connection degrading but never really disappearing.

When I am thirty, I will give up trying to be pretty. I will give up on trying to have fun. I will decide, instead, that what I need to do is erase myself and then proceed on a new, normal path. Late one night—so late that no one is hanging around, playing Jenga, drinking from beakers, what fun—I will open the door to the lab. Time machines are so beautiful in the moonlight. They look like what they are, like pearls, like eggs you can crawl into and sleep inside until it's time to be born.

I will initiate a program that I cooked up myself. It will take many attempts, but I have so much time after giving up on having a smiling boyfriend, even skin, rosy lips, a mother who calls, friendly eye contact with just about anyone. Those things, I will come to realize, are cosmetic. What I need to fix is far, far back, before I got twisted and grew wrong, my little gnarled life, the lives of everyone around me warped around it.

Eventually I will do it: I will find my own timeline. After three days without sleep and only one change of underwear and a tender pink groove worn into my left middle finger by my pen, I will type a new code into the time machine. I will fold myself inside, close my eyes gratefully, and when the eggs shudders me into a new universe, I will already know something is different. Something is right.

When Margot is nine, the sun comes out on Venus and her classmates let her out of the closet only after they've come back from playing outside. She tries to make her face ready for them, to steel herself, but when they open the door, it all comes undone.

• • •

When I am thirty, when Margot is nine, I open the door and she opens the door, I open the door and I remember opening the door. I will be nine, thirty staring right at nine. It is almost more than any human being can endure. I am nine and I am seeing the woman in front of me who I know to be myself and it is changing my life: I grow fuller and happier and even stranger as I stare at my nine-year-old self. I remember that, when I was nine, a woman appeared out of nowhere to stop the children from shutting me in the closet on the day that the sun came out. Because at the moment I am telling the children to go, because the sun will be coming up soon, and I take myself by the hand and I lead myself out of the classroom, through the tunnel, and it is exactly as I remember: I look up at the woman leading me by the hand and her eyes are closed. My eyes are closed. I feel wonderful, and I just want to rest for a moment; I'm dizzy; I'm skating around a shrinking loop and things are moving very quickly now.

I search for what I know, and one thing I know is this: my father is still lost or dead somewhere on Venus. My mother still searches for him. I know I can help them, maybe with the right word to one of them, or myself, at the right time. The right action taken. This life is a good one, but all is not well. Now that I'm here, there is so much left to do.

I can see it all, my whole life, a complex tower of blocks—I can reach out and grab any block I choose; I can make the tower wobble. I can feel my mind growing stranger by the minute.

TIME TRAVEL IS ONLY FOR THE POOR

SL HUANG

Orson knew never to have money in his pocket. If he didn't have any money, they couldn't force him to Invest. Sometimes they made people work—or, "offered a productive path toward a meaningful future"—and as soon as the sorry folk had made a dime, the courts snatched it and iced 'em.

Orson knew the way out was to refuse to work. If you didn't work, they couldn't pay you. That was capitalism.

So Orson was very careful never to have money. But then one day he got picked up between panhandling a few nickels and going to buy a Ho-Ho with them. He loved Ho-Hos. They never had them at the soup kitchen, even stale ones, and sometimes a man's gotta do what a man's gotta do.

The courtroom was as shiny and imposing as his nightmares had imagined. The judge leaned down and smiled at him winningly. Woman could've won a beauty pageant with that smile, Orson thought.

"Have you heard of the option of cryonics?" she asked, with the kindliness of the devil.

Of course he had. Everyone had. The whispers had filtered down through the ranks of the street folk, at first the perverse rainbow of a better life—get your hands on a dollar, then apply for a far-flung chance at being a millionaire, if you dared. Some people Orson knew had gone for it, tempted by that golden ticket to step through a portal into the future.

But then the whispers changed. The Haves had looked at the Have-Nots and declared it their solemn duty to make them Haves, too. Or so they said. To Orson it looked an awful lot like sweeping the riff-raff off the street where they wouldn't have to look at 'em.

"The government has a partnership with a company called Revesta," the judge was nice enough to explain. "Do you know about Revesta?"

If she thought he didn't know about Revesta, he could probably plead a mental status exception. What, did she think street folk didn't ever overlap with her world? That her realm of sleek and chrome wasn't the same reality he lived in?

He wondered if he'd ever seen the judge before. If she'd walked by him, averting her eyes as if his kind were invisible. If she'd hoped to get him in front of her bench one day. Would she have wanted such a thing in order to save him or condemn him?

"Revesta has a novel program for the indigent population," the judge continued.

Yeah, he knew all about it. "A dollar buys you a lottery ticket where everyone's a winner," sang perky girls in the Revesta ads. "Come apply today!" In the ads they didn't tell you Revesta siphoned half the profit every year. Most people who went in for that lottery ticket didn't care anyway, though—after all, what was the difference between waking up in five hundred years or a thousand?

"It's the notion of something called compound interest," the judge said now. She put a hand a few centimeters above her bench, next to where her gavel rested. "You put in any small amount of money. Really, it can be pennies! And then you enter a cryogenic deep freeze. You tell them what level you want to wake at—you can choose a median living wage—" her hand lifted, measuring the imaginary wealth "—or anything higher, if you'd like to wake in the lap of luxury. Presto, you can instantly be a billionaire!" Her hand shot up high above her head, and her smile shone as if she were sharing a joke.

Why aren't you doing it, then? Orson thought but didn't say. He knew the consequences of mouthing off to authority. He also knew the answer, so what would be the point in asking the question?

"I don't think that's for me, ma'am," he said instead, when the judge had paused for long enough that a response felt expected.

Her smile stayed grafted onto her face. "Oh, the Court understands there are genuine humanitarian reasons people have for not Investing. If you have extended family ties or other proof of community relationships—for instance, if you are a caregiver for someone . . . " She trailed off. Her eyes roamed up and down Orson's frayed army coat, his unkempt beard, the black grime in his fingernails. "You'll be provided with a list of valid documentation, if you would like to appeal."

And if I just say no? Orson thought, but again did not say.

He knew what happened if you said no without documentation of a reason deemed valid by a smiling judge. The courts said you weren't acting in your own best interests and took away your right to do so.

Then they froze you anyway.

• • •

"Excuse me—sir?"

Orson didn't turn at first. Nobody called him sir. He continued down the courthouse steps, fingers crushing the legal papers they'd given him. He'd bin them as soon as he was out of sight.

"Sir?"

That time the voice was right behind him, and he looked over his shoulder just to see.

The person he ended up making eye contact with was definitely one of the Haves. Smartly dressed, with a shiny gray suit and shiny brown hair she had pulled back in a way that meant business. Probably business with a lot of zeros at the end of the bill. Young, for someone working in the courts, and white—or maybe mixed with Hispanic or Indian or something, he couldn't quite tell.

"You talking to me?" Orson said.

"I am." She stuck out a hand. "I'm Abby Wainwright. I was watching the hearing."

Orson slowly unstuck his right hand from the court papers and reached out to grip hers. People didn't shake his hand.

"Are you planning to appeal being asked to Invest?" Wainwright asked.

"You a reporter?" Orson said. It was the only thing that felt like it might make sense.

"No. I'm a lawyer. I work for an organization called Future Choice. Are you able to gather the necessary documentation?"

"I thought I might just skip out, you know," Orson said. "They want me so bad, they can come get me."

"They will," Wainwright said. "The indigent population is shrinking fast, and law enforcement is enthusiastic about sweeps now that there's a 'solution.' They'll find you and charge you, and that time they can legally refuse your right to appeal."

"Oh. Well. I guess that's that, then." Orson still wasn't sure why she was talking to him.

"Mr. Jefferson, the organization I work for—people like you are our mission. If you'd like to appeal this, we'll take your case. Pro bono."

"What's that?"

"It means free of charge."

"I know what it means." He hadn't thought he'd heard rightly, was all. "Why would ya'll do a thing like that for an old bum like me?"

She smiled then. It wasn't like the judge's smile. Wainwright's was too toothy, like she didn't have much practice, and had only been told a smile was about peeling your lips back. "We think this solution of theirs is too neat and pretty," she said. "Human life and choice shouldn't be linked to a dollar sign. Are you in?"

"All right," Orson said, because what else could he say?

Orson arrived at the court early the day of his appeal, as his new lawyer had instructed. He'd tried to make himself look neater, scrubbed at his hands and face in the courthouse bathroom, but there was only so much one could do. He also had to carry his backpack with him, as he always did, everything he owned in the world.

Wainwright swept up the steps and found him lurking outside. He had felt too out of place in the lobby, the security guards making slitted glances in his direction.

"Good, you're here." She strode right by him and into the building, her heels clicking like exclamation points.

"I look okay?" Orson asked, lumbering to catch up.

"Fine." Her gaze was buried in an open folder in her hand, reading as she headed for the security lines. "We're going to lose today. Be prepared. This court can only apply the law, and the letter of the law is clear. But we have to lose here to appeal to a higher court. My assistant is on standby to file as soon as we walk out."

"Oh," Orson said.

"We have to go over what you're going to say. I'll do most of the talking, but they're going to ask you your reason for refusing so they can enter it into the record. It has to sound honest, not too rehearsed, and it can't touch on any area where the law gives leeway. We'll go over it until you have it down."

"This time's my home, is all," Orson said. "Don't know how to live in any other."

Wainwright looked up. "Perfect."

The hearing went as Wainwright had predicted. She did most of the talking, Orson said his one line, and the same smiling judge said regardless of personal sympathy the law was definitive. Orson was given a place and time to report at a Revesta facility and told if he failed to appear a bench warrant would be issued.

He and Wainwright left the courthouse together. She flung words at her assistant through her earpiece the whole way out, confirming the appeal had been filed and giving further instructions.

When three people with notepads and voice recorders popped up right in their path, Orson stumbled back and nearly went ass over teakettle.

"What do you think your chances are?" the reporters demanded, their faces like hungry scavengers. "What would you say to those who would accuse you of bringing civilization a step backward? Mr. Jefferson, why would you rather stay a penniless burden on society than have limitless wealth in the future?"

"Mr. Jefferson is exercising the freedom of existence that should belong to every human being," Wainwright declared smoothly. "The future is not a certainty we can offer. Look how drastically our society has changed in only the past few decades. If Mr. Jefferson Invested, it might take hundreds or even thousands of years for his capital to compound sufficiently, during which time any number of disasters could occur. Even in the best case, imagine waking in a world alien in its technology, its language, its social mores. No amount of wealth would be a comfort."

She made it sound so grand.

The reporters clamored after her, pressing with the same questions in different words, and Wainwright gave them as many eloquent sound bites as they wanted. Orson never said a word.

"I saw your lawyer on the television," Frank said, while serving Orson some noodles and hard doughnuts at the soup kitchen. "Aggressive sort of gal, right?"

Orson was bone-sure Wainwright would dismember anyone she heard call her gal. Or sue them.

"You win this, a lot of folks here would be grateful," Frank continued. "It's scary right now, man. I see it. People feeling like any second the government can swoop down and scoop 'em off to the future. It ain't right."

"Suppose not," Orson agreed, picking up his tray.

"It's a fine thing you're doing. Damn fine thing," Frank called after him.

Orson supposed he shouldn't have been surprised when Wainwright appeared at his corner with a cell phone for him and the invitation for a TV interview.

Or at least, she said it was an invitation. It sounded like a command, do or die, do not pass go.

"I got nothing to wear," Orson said.

"Don't worry about it." Wainwright was tapping text messages into her own phone. "Be at the studio at eleven a.m.—it's only a few blocks from here. The cell phone's got a clock. The battery will last for a week; if you can't find somewhere to charge it, tell me so and I'll have someone come swap it out."

It was like she thought he'd never seen a cell phone before. This one was an old-style flip phone. Orson remembered a friend of his, Karina, showing off a new flip phone years ago when they were all the rage.

"I'm telling you, all you need is a phone. You get yourself a real-life phone number, you can get yourself a job," she'd preached at everyone, before leaving for her new job and never coming back. He wondered what had happened to her. He hoped she was well.

Now the whole population had smartphones and earpieces, walking around with the whole world in their eyeballs and voices in their heads. Orson was already too old for this century, let alone any other.

He got to the studio at 10:40 according to the phone. A security guard tried to tell him to "move along" before a skinny assistant wearing a headset and red plastic-framed eyeglasses descended and commandeered him. The assistant brought him into a long warehouse room, saying words like "Roger" and "Go to two" into the headset the whole time. He left Orson with a plump, frizzy-haired wardrobe lady and a young woman with kind eyes and skin like brown silk.

The wardrobe lady took a look at him and then started digging through racks of clothing, rambling to herself about lighting and what the host was wearing. The kind-eyed woman smiled. "I'm Jasmine," she said. "I'll be doing your makeup for the show."

They stood in that awkward way two people can inhabit the same space and waited for the wardrobe woman.

"I read the bio on you they have tacked up," Jasmine blurted. "Thank you for your service."

Orson nodded. She wasn't the first who had said that to him, but she was the first in a long time.

"My sister's a marine," Jasmine went on. "She's overseas right now. I pray for her to come home safe, but she's so proud, you know?"

"Jarhead, huh?" Orson felt himself starting to smile. "Couple of jarheads saved my life once. That was a story."

Jasmine smiled back, half her mouth curving up as if it was too shy to bloom all the way. "You know, I'll be wrapped after your interview. Would you maybe like to get some coffee?"

"I don't got any money," Orson said. "You mighta heard." He said it like it was a joke. Regret was for young men. He was too old for her anyway.

"I'm buying." She was still smiling. She smelled faintly of jasmine, like her name.

Wainwright stalked in. "What's going on here? No, no, no. No wardrobe, no makeup. Are you people dim? This has to look authentic. Mr. Jefferson, come on to the green room."

"Oh—I can at least do a little powder, or—" Jasmine tried to offer.

"I said no; are you hard of hearing?" Wainwright grabbed Orson's upper arm and hustled him along with her. "Now, I've got some talking points to go over with you. We want you to come off simple but not mentally deficient, intelligent but not educated, sincere but not noticeably well-spoken. We'll emphasize that you grew up in this city. And we'll stress your military service. People like to get angry about seeing vets on the streets."

Orson looked back at Jasmine as he was whisked away. She gave him a little wave.

The interview turned out to be easy. Wainwright was on with him, and she did most of the talking, again. They sat together with the meticulously groomed host in an island surrounded by bright lights, and Orson only had to contribute a sentence here or there, when the host turned to him with the same panting look as the reporters on the courthouse steps. Orson said things like "Yes" and "That's right" and "I'm just old, you know?" and the host and Wainwright nodded and elocuted off his statements with shining eyes, as if he'd contributed wise gems of conversation.

"This city, in this time, is Mr. Jefferson's home," Wainwright declared. "His life may not be one you or I or even he might choose, but it's familiar to him, and it has human value. But he makes us uncomfortable, so we want to disappear him to a time when he will cease to offend our delicate sensibilities. It's despicable."

"But you can't deny homelessness is a huge problem in this country," said the host. "Cryonics appeals to so many because it feels like a win-win compromise. How else would you begin to address the issue?"

Orson noticed the question was directed at Wainwright. He was not expected to have solutions.

"I don't think there is an easy answer, Harold," Wainwright replied gravely. "But that doesn't make it different from many other social problems that we freely acknowledge are multilayered and complex. After all, one could hypothetically think of plenty of ways to wipe out the homeless population that we would consider unthinkable from a humanitarian perspective. I'm merely arguing cryonics is one of these."

The host nodded and nodded as she talked. Funny, how rich folks could make *not* having solutions sound smart and complicated. When Orson said he didn't know, people just thought he was ignorant.

When they'd finished, Wainwright screamed away in her fancy silver car and left Orson to make his own way back to his corner. Evening was purpling the sky between the buildings overhead. He'd been at the studio a long time.

They'd had good food, though. A whole table of fruit and cakes and chips and snack bars out all day, and a lunch with shrimp and creamy spinach and beef so tender it fell apart on his fork. He'd stuffed a bunch of the snack bars in his bag for later.

"Hey," said a voice. Orson turned to see Jasmine waiting by the door, her bag slung over one shoulder. She gave him the same little nervous half-wave as before. "Still want to get that coffee?"

Orson thought for longer than was polite. He figured he had three options. He could say yes, he could say no, or he could ask her why.

"Sure," he said.

They walked to a chic little shop nearby that Jasmine knew. They didn't talk on the way.

Jasmine told him to order anything, so he got a coffee and a piece of pie. Her coffee order was so long Orson missed half the words.

They sat by the window. The chairs were squishy lounge ones, and classical background music tinkled from unseen speakers. Orson pushed his bag under the table, where he could feel it touching his leg.

"Thanks for the pie," he said, taking a bite.

Jasmine waved it off self-consciously. "Will you tell me the story you mentioned?" she asked, wrapping long fingers around her cup. "About the marines? The ones who saved your life."

Orson let the apple and sugar and cinnamon settle on his tongue. It was a good story. He'd tell her.

What happened after had been a less good story. One of the guys had caught a mortar round in combat his next tour. The other had made it back but swallowed his own gun four years later.

He'd leave that part out.

Wainwright started calling Orson for more interviews. Ones that were farther away. The studios sent car services for him, and twice put him up in fancy hotels where he lay on top of the blankets unable to sleep and kept a hand on his backpack. Orson wasn't sure when and where the things all aired, but every so often now, someone passing his corner pointed or had their eyes widen in recognition before whispering to a friend. They didn't seem to realize he could see them.

It was still a jarring change. He was used to most people pretending they didn't see him at all.

Other street folk started coming up to him, their eyes full of an odd kind of hope. Asking about his lawyer lady, awed that he'd been *on television*.

Orson answered them as well as he could. It had been a long time since he'd sought out friendship, but he still knew most of the street folk in his neighborhood. Good folk, most of them.

For the first time, he noticed some old faces had disappeared. Had they Invested? Of their own will, or because they'd been told they had to?

Jasmine had started coming around on the regular, too, to buy him coffee and talk. He felt a little strange about it, but . . . the girl seemed so lonely. She didn't have many friends either.

They definitely weren't dates. She rambled to him unhappily about her dating life, going out with both boys and girls she met through those phone apps in the way modern kids did, how much trouble she had finding someone who wasn't a flake or selfish or cruel. "I want someone to curl up by the fireplace with who isn't my cat, you know?" she said. "Not that I have a fireplace. Or a cat. But that's the idea."

He'd started to feel protective of her, the way he might have toward his children, if he'd had children.

That made him think of Therese. He hadn't thought of her in a long time.

The last thing she'd ever said to him was "I'm sorry." The second to last thing she'd said to him was, "I know it's not your fault, but I just can't deal with all your bullshit anymore."

His next court date rolled around—the court of appeals, the first one that could change the law. This time Future Choice sent a car service that took him to a different courthouse, but the routine was the same: he arrived early, and Wainwright swept him in and told him what to say.

"We might win this one, we might lose," she said. "If we lose, we'll appeal again immediately. We will take this all the way to the Supreme Court. I dare say the State feels the same, so this won't end today. But if we win we'll strike a major blow in public and policy opinion against forced Investing."

This time there were three judges, all older and with stern faces. They listened to the arguments, asked questions, and then said they would consider and render their decision shortly.

This time the crowd of reporters on the courthouse steps was much larger. Wainwright had to bundle Orson into a taxi and draw their attention back to her before he could get away. She'd thrown a twenty at the driver, who kept the whole thing even though he only took Orson around the block to meet the car service.

When Orson got back to his corner, more reporters were waiting. He dodged them and maneuvered down an alleyway. He slept that night tucked behind a dumpster, a ways away from his usual haunts.

He was awoken by someone talking loudly at him. "Hey. You Jefferson? Orson Jefferson."

"Whazzat?" Orson blinked into the dimness of dawn. His bones were cold and stiff. It must be early.

A hand pushed a business card in his face. "I'm Manuel Reyes. I'm with the *Sun Daily Post*. I want to offer you an opportunity."

"I think you gotta talk to my lawyer," Orson said. He wanted to go back to sleep.

"Your lawyer stonewalled me. I think the appellate court's verdict is going to come down in your favor, Mr. Jefferson, and that our state will be the first to rule against forced Investing. This story's going to be big, and I want to help you get it out there. We're talking speaking engagements, better appearance fees—I can get you a book deal with one phone call. You won't even have to write it; I'll do that part. No need for any crowdfunding when we get through."

"Whazzat?" Orson said again.

"There's a lot of admiration out there for your high-mindedness in shutting that down, by the way. You and your lawyer are right that it would have screwed over your appeals process without a trust set up beforehand—I assume that's what you're doing for your appearance fees? But it's a brave move, sir, turning down money that would get you off the streets in order to save the little people, and there's a lot of public goodwill for you right now. I can help you build that hero narrative. The Man of the People."

Orson frowned. He took the card.

"So you're on board?" Reyes rubbed his palms together. "We can set you up a—"

"I'm gonna think on it," Orson said.

"We have to jump on this fast. The groundswell—"

"I said I'm gonna think on it."

He called Jasmine on his flip phone. They met at their usual coffee place, and he slowly laid out what the reporter had said.

"You didn't know?" Jasmine's eyes became wide coins. "There was a whole social media campaign to raise funds for you—hashtag 'Help Orson Stay.' Future Choice put out a statement and said no, said it was a—um, a conflict of interest with the legal liabilities? Or something? Basically that you wouldn't have legal grounds for the appeal if you had the money to opt out of Investing in the first place." She pressed her hands to her cheeks. "Oh my God. I should have told you. I thought, you know, you didn't seem to want to talk about it, or maybe you weren't supposed to or something. I'm so stupid!"

Orson remembered scattered instances now, of her slyly joking about him being so famous online or the profit in going viral being as good as Investing. He hadn't known what she was talking about. So he'd done the thing he usually did when he didn't know what someone was talking about, which was not say anything at all.

"Is it," he asked slowly, "is it normal on the TV shows—the people they have on, do they get paid for that?"

"I never took much notice, but I think it depends on the contract. . . . " Her face went stretched and taut like she was about to cry. "They're taking advantage of you, aren't they? Oh my God."

He'd never wanted her pity.

She reached out and grasped the frayed cuffs of his coat. "We have to stop this. What can I do?"

Orson mulled. "I guess I oughta talk to my lawyer," he said.

He barely got two words out to Wainwright. "This isn't about you, Mr. Jefferson," she snapped. "This is about an institutional system. If you want book deals and a speaking circuit, they'll be ten times as lucrative after we win at the Supreme Court."

She said "we," but it didn't sound like she was including him in that.

"I only want . . . " His tongue twisted over itself.

"What do you want, Mr. Jefferson? Is it worth more than what the hundreds of people shuffled into forced Investment every day want?"

"I want to know what's happening, is all," he said finally, with Wainwright waiting so impatiently her expression was like a tapping foot.

"Fine. I'll have my assistant call to update you in simple language."

She means layman's terms, he thought. *That's what she means to say.*

It didn't soothe him.

Orson knew the verdict had come down because the reporters came in taxis and cars and poured out onto his street corner, flashbulbs whiting out the world and microphones stabbing like polearms.

He gathered he had won.

He tried to escape down an alley again, but they followed him. No wonder people wanted doors, he thought, so useful for shutting in people's faces.

He finally lost the reporters, or bored them enough by not answering that they went away. He wandered in an unfamiliar part of town that night, looking for someplace to sleep until a man came out of the dark and tried to stab him.

Old reflexes took over. The would-be attacker ended up on the ground bleeding from his skull, his knife arm at a twisted angle.

Orson stared down at him, and adrenaline clogged his senses in a suffocating static, his mouth filling with the taste of metal and smoke. The world became like the panel of a comic book, flat and frozen and not even a little bit real.

It was a long moment before he fumbled out his flip phone and dialed 911.

"This was an assassination attempt," Wainwright railed. "Someone out there is determined to preserve their precious system."

Now that he could think again, Orson figured it much more likely the attack had just been a random mugging. He didn't have any money, but he had a good coat and halfway decent boots and a blanket in his backpack, and he'd known of people getting knifed for less.

But Wainwright sailed off to spin it for the cameras, declaring the whole world was so against them that the government would send a catspaw to destroy their case before it could rise to the national level. Her assistant called Orson later that day—he was still at the police station, being interviewed by serious detectives again and again—and informed him in simple language that Future Choice had set up a trust for him that would be used to provide housing. One they would oversee. The crowdfunders were out in full force again, apparently.

Orson wondered if Wainwright was going to start charging speaking fees for him. Prance him around as a show pony and get paid this time.

Maybe she'd already been charging fees, and there was another trust labeled as being for his legal fees. He'd signed an awful lot of papers for her, most of which had been in dense legalese.

"I can't believe them," groused Jasmine, after she'd gotten the story out of him. She'd started questioning him more closely, tugging out bits he wouldn't naturally have shared. "Your attorney waves her lawyer wand and boom bam, you have rent money without it even affecting the court case? Why the hell didn't they make this happen weeks ago?"

"I dunno," Orson said, even though he was pretty sure he did know.

"Will you come stay with me until your housing gets set up? I only have a studio, and there's two of us living there already, so there's not much space. And I don't think Maria will like having a guest, but she can deal for a few days. I couldn't live with myself if something happened to you."

"Nah," Orson said. He was thinking he'd call Wainwright's assistant and make them get him a hotel. Just to see what they'd say. He'd probably be able to sleep if he bedded down in the bathtub.

"Can you walk away? Give up the case? I'll help you get a job somewhere. My sister knows organizations who help disabled vets get back on their feet."

He flinched at the word "disabled." He hoped she didn't see.

"I dunno," he said again. "I won, so don't they get to come at me now?" It didn't seem to fit together that he could win and then walk. The other guy had to have his chance to hit back.

"Orson." She touched his arm. "What do *you* want?"

His reflexive thought was that he wanted his corner back, his familiar corner where he knew the good places to go when it rained and every once in a while he could panhandle a few coins to buy a Ho-Ho. But that didn't feel like a dignified answer.

He wasn't even sure if it was a true one, or if it only felt true.

"I don't know," he said.

• • •

The wheels of justice turned slowly. Wainwright and her organization were doing all sorts of lawyerly paperwork things, as dutifully reported by her assistant, but rarely anything Orson had to put in a personal appearance for. With the state law overturned, his next big court appearance would be for the highest court in the land.

He waited in a long-term boarding house, with the finances handled by Future Choice. A kept man, he supposed.

He slept on the floor most nights. Every so often he tried the bed, for variety. Sometimes he woke up and his hand wasn't on his backpack anymore.

Jasmine had pushed him to search around for other lawyers. "They're using you," she argued. "You should get a second opinion."

They were using him, sure, but changing lawyers sounded difficult. Wainwright and Future Choice were the devils he knew, after all.

"At least call that Reyes guy," Jasmine urged. "The one who wants to write your life story. Set yourself up for after the Supreme Court decision. You need a plan."

This was what he had liked about his corner. No need to plan anything at all. No need to make choices.

As the weeks passed, two other states ruled forced Investment unconstitutional, one under the eighth amendment and the other under the ninth. Wainwright's assistant told Orson this in simple language. But Orson's case had been the first, the assistant assured him, as if this was the gravest of concerns. His case would be the one to reach the Supreme Court, and Wainwright and Future Choice would trailblaze their way to justice.

And then Wainwright's assistant called one day and told him the Supreme Court had declined to hear his case. The lower court ruling would stand. Forced Investment would remain banned here but not elsewhere, not yet.

The reporters didn't swarm. The news caused barely a whimper. The public had moved on, and the groundswell against forced Investing was in other parts of the country now.

Orson was a free man. Technically, he had won, even as the people who represented him had lost.

The boarding house informed him he was paid till the end of the month. He tried calling Wainwright to see about the trust fund, but neither she nor her assistant took his calls anymore.

He tried calling Reyes, not with any sort of plan as to what he wanted, more because he figured he should. The man brushed him off in less than a minute and hung up the phone.

Orson wasn't a story anymore. He'd missed his moment.

"I guess I'm back where I started," he said to Jasmine in their coffee shop. It was what he'd wanted, wasn't it?

Wasn't it?

She sniffed. "Orson. I was going to wait until after your case finished, but now . . . "

"What is it?" He'd been so preoccupied with the events of his own life he hadn't been thinking much about hers. Had she been quieter lately? Guilt folded in him, an odd old echo of the last time he'd cared about someone.

"My sister's coming home." She lifted her chin and clasped her hands tightly against each other on the table. "She . . . she wants to Invest. And I'm going to do it with her."

Orson didn't know what to say.

"It's a smart plan. We don't have any other family, and . . . " She sniffed again. "I'm stuck. Just treading water. I'm in debt and counting pennies against each paycheck. My sister's going to help me get out of the red and then—the military has a program now where she can opt to get her pension for a reduced time but keep having it hit while she's Investing. It'll build fast that way." She tried to smile. "She says we'll sleep for the better part of a century and then start over together, never having to worry about money again."

Jasmine's sister was right. It was a smart plan.

"I'll miss you," Orson said.

She nodded. A tear slid down her nose; she brushed it away. "I'm sorry. I didn't want to leave you like—I was hoping you'd have the book deal, or—"

"I only wanted my corner back," Orson said, still not sure if it was true.

"Will you promise me something?" Jasmine asked. "Will you reach out? Find someone who matters to you. Someone. Anyone."

He said yes because he knew it would make her smile through the tears, and she could leave without regrets for her better future.

Orson had a week left at the boarding house, but he went back to his corner that night. He sat on the ground against the brick. The wind cut colder than he remembered. The night felt darker.

He went back to the boarding house and lay on the bed. Stared up at the stucco plaster of the ceiling.

What do you want? Jasmine had asked.

He hadn't wanted anything for a long time. He hadn't *wanted* to want anything for a long time.

He had his old life back now. No reporters, no lawyers, no one forcing him to take a one-way trip to the future. Even Jasmine was leaving.

Everything would be like it had been before.

So why was he so restless? Why did everything feel itchy and uncomfortable, like a shoe that had gotten too small?

What do you want?

"I don't know," he said to the empty room.

The next day, Orson sat in the sun on a park bench for a long time, thinking. Then he panhandled the money for a bus ticket, shouldered his backpack, and rode downtown.

He'd been told years ago where the local DAV was, had seen the ads for it on benches and billboards since, but had always pushed those choices to another day. In reality it still took him more than an hour to find the right place. As he hiked around the urban canyons searching, passersby averted their eyes from him.

Just like old times.

He didn't know where to go when he got there, but when he pushed through the front door, a sharply dressed young man with a military haircut caught sight of him lurking and crossed the lobby to greet him. "Can I help you, sir?"

Orson didn't have a good answer to that question.

"I don't know," he said finally. His voice creaked, as if he hadn't used it in a long time. "I think . . . I might want to make an investment."

The man nodded smartly. "A lot of former service members are taking that approach. The first step will be making sure your pension is straightened out—I won't lie, it can be a bear of paperwork, but we've cleared a lot of the backlog since Investing opened up so many new options for military families. We can hook you up with—"

"No." Orson shook his head. "No. I don't want to go away to some future time. I want to invest in *me*."

The man paused, listening.

"I'm here because . . . " Orson still wasn't sure. But he'd promised Jasmine he'd find someone who mattered to him, and he supposed that person might as well be himself. "I'm here because I don't know."

But he wanted to figure it out.

The man's eyes softened, like he understood something Orson couldn't put into words. "I saw you on TV, didn't I? You're the man from the court case. Orson Jefferson."

Orson nodded.

"Well, Mr. Jefferson. I'm glad you decided to come in." The man held out a hand. "I'm former Sergeant Mark Crespin. Welcome to the present."

SIDEWALKS

MAUREEN McHUGH

—◆—

I hate when I have a call in Inglewood. It's still the 1990s in Inglewood, and for all I know, people still care about Madonna. Los Angeles County has a forty-bed psych facility there. Arrowhead looks like a nursing home; a long one-story building with a wide wheelchair ramp and glass doors and overly bright, easy-to-clean floors. I stop at the reception desk and check in.

"Rosni Gupta," I say. "I'm here to do an evaluation."

The young man at the desk catches his bottom lip in his teeth and nods. "Oh yeah," he says. "Hold on, ma'am. I'll get the director." He has an elaborate tattoo sleeve of red flowers, parrots, and skulls on his right arm. "Dr. Gupta is here," he says into the phone.

I also hate when people call me Dr. Gupta. I'm a Ph.D., not a medical doctor. I'm running late because I'm always running late. That's not true of me in my personal life. I'm early for meeting friends or getting to the airport, but in my work there are too many appointments and too much traffic. Being late makes me anxious. I'm a speech pathologist for Los Angeles County working with Social Services. I'm a specialist; I evaluate language capacity and sometimes prescribe communication interventions and devices. What that means is that if someone has trouble communicating, the county is supposed to provide help. If the problem is more complicated than deafness, dyslexia, stroke, autism, learning disability, or stuttering, all the things that speech therapists normally deal with, I'm one of the people who is brought in. "Devices" sounds very fancy, but really, it's not. Lots of times a device is a smart phone with an app. I kid you not.

"Are you from LA?" I ask the guy behind the desk.

He shakes his head. "El Salvador. But I've been here since I was eleven."

"I love El Salvadorian food," I say. "*Tamales de elote, pupusas*."

He lights up and tells me about this place on Venice called Gloria's that makes decent pupusas, until Leo shows up. Leo is the director.

Just so you know, I'm not some special, Sherlock Holmes kind of woman who has been promoted into this work because I can diagnose things about people. Government does not work that way. I took this job because it was a promotion. I've just been doing speech pathology for about twenty years and have seen a lot, and I am not particularly afraid of technology. I have an iPhone. I attend conferences about communication devices and read scientific journals.

What I understand about this case is that the police got a call about a woman who was speaking gibberish. She was agitated, attacked a police officer, and was placed on a seventy-two-hour psych hold. She has no identification and is unable to communicate. They can't find any family, and since she is nonverbal except for the gibberish, she was given an initial diagnosis as profoundly autistic, and when a bed opened up at Arrowhead she was placed. I'm here to determine what the problem is.

The file is pretty lean.

I don't know Leo-the-director very well. He's a balding, dark-skinned guy wearing a saggy gray suit jacket and jeans. He looks tired, but anyone running a psych facility looks tired. "Hi, Ros, how was the 405?" he asks.

"Sorry I'm late," I say. "The 405 was a *Saturday Night Live* skit. Tell me about your Jane Doe."

He shrugs. "She's not profoundly autistic, although she may be on the spectrum."

"So she's communicating?"

"Still no recognizable language."

"Psychotic?"

"I don't know. I'm thinking she may just be homeless and we haven't identified the language."

"How did you end up with her?" I ask. Nobody gets a bed unless they are a risk to themselves or others or severely disabled. Even then they don't get beds half the time. There are about eighty thousand homeless in Los Angeles on any given night—not all of them on the street, of course—some of them are living in cars or crashing on couches or in shelters—but a lot of them are either severely mentally ill or addicted, and there aren't that many beds.

"She's 5250 pending T-con. Apparently she was pretty convincingly a danger to someone," Leo says.

Section 5250 is a section of the California Welfare and Institutions Code that allows an involuntary fourteen-day psychiatric hold, and T-con is a temporary conservatorship that gets the county another fourteen days to keep someone. We're a bureaucracy. God forbid we not speak jargon; we have our professional pride. At some point in that fourteen days there has to be a probable cause hearing so a court can decide whether or not the hold meets legal criteria. I'm a cog in that machinery. If I determine that she can't communicate enough to take care of herself, then that's part of a case to keep her institutionalized.

When I say "institutionalized" I can just see people's expressions change. They go all *One Flew Over the Cuckoo's Nest*. Institutions are not happy places. The one I'm in right now is too bright. It's all hard surfaces, so I hear the squeak of shoes, the constant sounds of voices. The halls are way too bright. It's about as homey as a CVS and not nearly as attractive. But you know, a lot of people need to stay institutionalized. I had a nonverbal patient, Jennie. She was twenty-six, and after many months of working with her and her caregivers to provide her with training, she was finally taught to go and stand by the door of the storage room (where the adult diapers were stored) to communicate that she needed to be changed. I would like to live in a world where she didn't have to live in a place like this, but I'm glad to live in a world where she has a place to live. I've been to visit family in New Delhi, okay? In New Delhi, if Jennie's family was rich she'd have great care. If her family was poor, she'd be a tremendous burden on her mother and sisters or, more likely, dead of an opportunistic infection.

I'm wearing sandals, and the heels are loud on the linoleum. They're three to a room here, but a lot of the people are in the day room or group therapy. We stop at a room. Two of the beds are empty and carefully made with blue, looseweave blankets on them. A woman sits on the third bed, looking outside. She is clean. Her hair is long, brown and coarse, pulled back in a thick ponytail.

"That's Jane," Leo says.

"Hello, Jane," I say.

She looks directly at me and says, "Hi." This is not typical autistic behavior. We're allowed use of a conference room where I can do my evaluation. I prefer it to a clinic. It's quieter; there are fewer distractions. Walking down the hall, Jane is about 5'6" or so. She's as brown as me. My family is Bengali although I was born and raised in Clearwater, Florida. (I came to Los Angeles for college. UCLA.) Jane doesn't look Indian. She doesn't look Central or South American either.

Jane doesn't say anything beyond that "Hi," but she continues to make eye contact. She's not pretty. Not ugly either. Jane actually rests her elbows on the table and leans a little toward me, which is disconcerting.

I'm 5'3". My husband likes to walk, so we walk to the drug store and sometimes we go out to eat. He's six feet tall, a teacher. He's white, originally from Pennsylvania. When we walk to restaurants from our little neighborhood (it's quite pretty; we couldn't afford to buy a house there now, but when we bought our place the neighborhood was still rough), there is enough room on the sidewalk in places for about three people to walk abreast. If there are two people walking toward us, and they're two men, I'm the person who always has to get out of the way. A man will unthinkingly shoulder-check me if I don't and occasionally look over his shoulder, surprised. This is a stupid thing, I know. There are a lot of entertainment businesses in our area—people who make trailers for movies or do mysterious technological things involving entertainment. They're young men. They wear skinny pants or ironic T-shirts or have beards or wear those straw fedora things. I am old enough to be their mother, and I am just surprised that they do that.

"Would they run over their mother on a sidewalk?" I ask.

"It's because you're short," Matt says. Matt is my husband. He is middle-aged, but he also wears ironic T-shirts. My favorite is his T-shirt of a silhouette of a *T. rex* playing drums with its little tiny arms. Matt is a drummer in a band made up of old white guys.

Men never do it if it's two men coming up on two men; they all just sort of squeeze. I get very irritable about it. I grew up in America. I feel American. My parents come from New Delhi, and they are clear that my brothers, Jay and Ravi, and I are very American, but growing up I felt like I was only pretending to be. Sometimes I think I learned how to be a subservient Indian woman from my parents, and I give it off like a secret perfume.

When I was younger I walked very fast, all the time, but now I'm middle-aged and overweight and I don't dart around people any more, so maybe I just notice it more or maybe I'm just more cranky.

I plan to do an evaluation called ADOS on Jane Doe. ADOS is one of the standard evaluations for autism. It can be scaled for a range from almost nonverbal to pretty highly verbal, and since the file said that she spoke gibberish, it's a place to start. I never get to ADOS because it's obvious pretty quickly that she exhibits no autistic behaviors.

"Hi, I'm Rosni Gupta," I say.

She studies me.

I tap my chest. "Rosni Gupta. Ros."

"Ros," she repeats. Then she taps her chest. "Malni," she says. She has an accent.

It takes me a couple of times to get it. She works with me, showing me what she does with her mouth to make the sound. I fiddle with it as I write it down. I think about spelling it *Emulni* but *Malni* feels closer. She has a strong accent, but I can't place it. It's not Spanish. I say a couple of words to her and gesture for her to say them back. She doesn't make the retroflex consonants of the Indian subcontinent—the thing that everybody mangles trying to sound like Apu on *The Simpsons*. She watches me write.

I don't use a laptop for my field notes. I like yellow legal pads. Just the way I started. She reaches out, wanting to use my pen. Her nails are a little long, her hands not very calloused. Her palms are pink. I hand her the pen and slide the pad across to her.

She writes an alphabet. It looks a lot like our alphabet but there's no K, Q, or V. The G looks strange, and there are extra letters after the D and the T, and where we have a W she has something that looks like a curlicue.

She offers me the pen and says something in a language that sounds liquid, like it's been poured through a straw. She gestures at me to take the pen. It's the first time she's really spoken to me in a full sentence.

I take the pen and she points to the page and points to the first letter. "A," she says. It sounds like something between A and U.

Eventually I write an A, and she nods fiercely. I write our alphabet for her.

"Wait," I say, gesturing with my hands, and she nods. It's only a few minutes to go to Leo's office and borrow his iPad and bring it back. I show her a Google map of the world. "Where are you from?" I ask.

She studies the map. Eventually she turns and she scrolls it a bit. I change it to a satellite version and I can see when she gets it. Her face is grim. She stabs her finger on the California coast. On where we are right now.

"No," I say. "That's where we are now, Malni. Where is home?"

She looks up at me leaning over the table. She stabs her finger in the same place.

I write up my report that she is not autistic and recommend a psychological follow-up. She might be bipolar. Leo tells me as I leave that the cop who brought her in tased her, but it had been determined after forty-eight hours that she was not a threat. I never got any sense she was violent. I was certainly never worried about my safety. I take my safety very seriously, thank you, and I've done evals with potentially violent clients, and when I was worried, I requested protection. I never felt the need with Malni.

I make dinner that night while Matt marks papers. Matt teaches sophomore English at the high school and is the faculty advisor for the literary magazine. For nine months of the year he disappears into the black hole that is teaching, and we lose our dinner table. He surfaces for brief periods from the endless piles of papers and quizzes, mostly around Saturday night. He tells me about his students, I tell him about my clients.

Matt likes Bengali dishes, but I don't make them very often because I didn't learn to cook until I was out of school. My go-to, as you might have guessed, is Mexican. I like the heat. Tonight is carnitas á la Trader Joes.

"What's this?" Matt asks. He's sitting at the dining room table, papers spread, but he's looking at my notes. We'll end up eating in front of the television. We're Netflixing, partway through some BBC thing involving spiffily dressed gangsters in post-WWI England.

"What's what?" I ask.

"Looks like someone's writing the Old English alphabet in your notes."

I bring out sour cream and salsa and look at what he's pointing to. "That was my Jane Doe in Inglewood."

"She's a *Beowulf* scholar?" he asks.

"That's Old English?" I ask.

"Looks like it," Matt says.

I have a caseload and a lot of appointments but about a week later I call Leo and tell him I want to schedule some more time with Jane even though I shouldn't take the time. He tells me she's been moved to a halfway house. It could have been worse; she could have been just discharged to the street. He gives me the address and I call the halfway-house coordinator and schedule a time to see her in about a week.

I have to go in the evening because Malni—they call her Malni now—has a job during the day. She does light assembly work, which is a fancy name for factory work. The halfway house is in Crenshaw, a *less than desirable* neighborhood. It's a stucco apartment building, painted pale yellow. I knock on her door, and her roommate answers.

"I'm looking for Malni?"

"She ain't here. She be coming back, you might run into her if you look outside." Her roommate's name is Sherri. Sherri is lanky, with straightened hair and complicated nails. "You her parole?"

"No, I'm a speech therapist."

"There ain't no therapy to do," Sherri says. "You know she don't speak no English."

"Yeah," I say. "I like your nails."

Sherri isn't charmed by my compliment. But I *do* like them; they look like red and white athletic shoes, like they've been laced up across each nail. I'm terrible at maintenance. Hair, makeup, nails. I admire people who are good about things like that.

I head outside and spot Malni coming from a couple of blocks. Malni walks with her shoulders back, not smiling, and she makes eye contact with people. You're not supposed to make eye contact with people in the city. It's an unwritten rule. There's a bunch of boys hanging on the corner, and Malni looks straight at their faces. It's not friendly, like she knows them. It's not unfriendly. It's . . . I don't know. The way people cue looking at people and away from people is something to look for when determining if they're autistic or if they're exhibiting signs of psychosis. I'm trained to look for it. Persons on the autism spectrum generally don't make eye contact. A lot of persons with schizophrenia don't look at people and look away in the normal rhythms of conversation; they stare too much—too long, for example. When I assessed Malni at Arrowhead, she cued normally.

Malni walks the boys down, looking right in their faces. The boys move out of her way. I suspect they don't even realize that they're doing it. I remember her file says she was tased when police apprehended her. A homeless woman of color speaking gibberish who kept looking them in the face and wouldn't drop her eyes. Did they read that as aggressive? I bet she didn't have to do much to get tased. It's a wonder she didn't get shot.

Malni sees me when she gets closer and lifts her hand in a little wave. "Hi, Ros," she says and smiles. Totally normal cueing.

I follow her back into the apartment she shares with Sherri.

"I ain't going nowhere," Sherri announces from in front of the television. "I worked all day." There's a Styrofoam box of fried chicken and fried rice nearly finished on the coffee table in front of her.

"That's okay," I say.

Malni and I sit down at the kitchen table, and I open up my laptop. I call up images of *Beowulf* in Old English and turn the screen around so Malni can see them.

She frowns a moment, and then she looks at me and smiles and taps my forehead with her index finger like she's saying I'm smart. She pulls the laptop closer to her and reads out loud.

It's not the same liquid sound as when she talked, I don't think (but that was two weeks ago and I don't remember exactly). This sounds more German.

Sherri turns around and leans against the back of the couch. "What's that she's talking?"

"Old English," I say.

"That ain't English," Sherri says. It's like everything from Sherri has to be a challenge.

"No, it's what they spoke in England over a thousand years ago."

"Huh. So how come she knows that?"

Malni is learning modern English. She can say all the things that you learn when you start a new language—My name is Malni. How much does that cost? Where's the bathroom? Everyone keeps asking her the same question, "Where are you from?"

She keeps giving the same answer: "Here."

I pull a couple of yellow legal pads out of my messenger bag and a pack of pens. I write my name and address, my cell number, and my e-mail address on the first one.

"Hey, Sherri, if she wants to get in touch with me, could you help her?"

I'm not sure what Sherri will say. Sherri shrugs. "I guess."

Malni looks at the writing. She taps it. "Ros," she says. Then the number. "Your phone."

"Yes," I say. "My phone."

It's my work phone because I never give clients my home phone. Not even my clients who read Old English.

I think about Malni walking through those boys. I'm meeting with one of my clients. Agnes is Latina. She's sixty-four and had a stroke that's left her nearly blind and partially deaf. She's diabetic and has high blood pressure. She has a tenth-grade education, and before her stroke, she and her daughter cleaned houses.

With a hearing aid, Agnes can make out some sounds, but she can't make out speech. Her daughter, Brittany, communicates with her by drawing letters on her hand and slowly spelling things out. I've brought a tablet so that Agnes can write the letters she thinks Brittany is writing. It's an attempt at reinforcing feedback. Adult deafblindness is a difficult condition. Agnes is unusual because she doesn't have any cognitive issues from her stroke, so there's lots of possibilities. I'm having Agnes write one letter at a time on the tablet, big enough that she herself might be able to see it.

Agnes has a big laugh when she's in a good mood. Sometimes she cries for hours, but today she's good. She has crooked teeth. Her English is accented, but she's lived here since she was thirteen—Brittany was born here and speaks Spanish as her first language but grew up speaking English too. "Mom!" she says, even though her mother can't hear her. "Quit goofing around!" She smacks her mother lightly on the arm. Agnes's eyes roam aimlessly behind her thick and mostly useless glasses.

Brittany, who is in her thirties, raises an eyebrow at me. Both women are short and overweight, classic risk profiles for diabetes and hypertension, like me. Unlike them, I have really good health care.

Agnes prefers drawing on the tablet to writing, and after twenty minutes of trying to figure out what Brittany has been asking her, "?yr name ?hot or cold ?what 4 dinner," Agnes has given up and drawn an amorphous blob that is apparently supposed to be a chicken. "Fried chicken," she announces, too loud because she can't hear herself well enough to regulate her volume.

"She can't have fried chicken for dinner," Brittany says. "She has to stick to her diet."

Agnes says, "El Pollo Loco! Right? Macaroni and cheese and cole slaw. Cole slaw is a vegetable."

Brittany looks at me helplessly. Agnes cackles.

My phone rings. "Is this Ros, the speech lady? This is Sherri, Malni's roommate."

"Sherri?" I remember the woman with the nails painted to look like the laces on athletic shoes. "Hi, is everything all right?"

"Yeah. Well, sort of. Nothing's really wrong. I just got a bunch of papers here for you from Malni."

"Where's Malni?" I ask.

"She took off to find more of her friends," Sherri said.

"What friends?"

"Her friends from wherever the hell she's from," Sherri says. "You gonna pick up these papers or what?"

I wanted Malni to write her story down. She filled almost three legal pads. I didn't expect her to disappear, though.

"This guy showed up," Sherri says. In honor of Agnes I've brought El Pollo Loco. Sherri doesn't really like El Pollo Loco. "I don't eat that Mexican shit," she says, but she takes it anyway. "He was tall and skinny. He looked like her, you know? That squished nose. Like those Australian dudes."

It takes me a moment, but then I realize what she means: Aboriginals. She's right—Malni looked a little like an Aboriginal. Not exactly. Or maybe exactly; I've never met an Australian Aboriginal.

"Oh, cool, I didn't know they had mac 'n' cheese." Sherri plunks down on the couch and digs in. "Yeah, so he started jabbering at her in that way she talks to herself. Was crazy. And he acted just like she did. All foreign and weird. Then they just took off, and she didn't come back."

"When was that?" I ask. My feet hurt, so I sit down on the couch next to her.

"Like, Saturday?"

This is Thursday. Part of me wants to say, you couldn't be bothered to call until yesterday, but there's no reason for Sherri to have bothered to call me at all, even though Malni apparently asked her to.

"That bitch was super smart," Sherri says.

I give Sherri twenty dollars, even though she's a recovering substance abuser and it's risky to give her pocket money, and I take the legal pads and go.

I call the Department of History at UCLA and eventually find someone who can put me in touch with someone at the Department of Literature who puts me in touch with a woman who is a *Beowulf* scholar. Why I thought I should start in History I don't know, since Matt is an English teacher and he recognized the language. Anyway, I tell the *Beowulf* scholar I am looking for someone who can translate Old English and that I will pay.

That is how I get Steve. We meet at a Starbucks near campus. Starbucks is quickly becoming the place where everybody meets for almost every reason.

Steve is Asian-American and very gay. He wears glasses that would have gotten me laughed out of middle school. He is studying Old English and needs money. "I'm supposed to be working on my dissertation," he says. "I working on my dissertation, actually. It's on persona and presentation in Anglo-Saxon literature. But there's that pesky thing about rent." He eyes the legal pads. I wonder what persona and presentation even means and what his parents think about having a son who is getting a doctorate in English Literature. Which, I realize, is racist. Just because my dad is an engineer and my mother is a chemist and they are classic immigrant parents who stressed college, college, college, doesn't mean Steve's are. For all I know, Steve's parents are third generation and his dad plays golf and gave him a car on his sixteenth birthday.

"I can pay you five hundred dollars," I say.

"That looks like modern handwriting. Is it, like, someone's notes or something?"

"I'm not exactly sure," I say.

He eyes me. I am aware of how weird it is to appear with three legal pads of handwritten Old English. Steve may be a starving UCLA student, but this is very strange.

"I think it's like a story," I say. "I work for Los Angeles County Social Services. A client gave me these."

"You're a social worker," he says, nodding.

"I'm a speech therapist," I say.

He doesn't comment on that. "This is going to take a lot of hours. A thousand?"

"Seven hundred and fifty," I say.

"Okay," he says.

I write him a check for half on the spot. He holds the check, looking resigned. I think I'm getting a pretty good deal.

After that I get e-mails from him. The first one has ten typed pages of translation attached and a note that says, *Can we meet?*

We meet in the same Starbucks.

"Your client is really good at Anglo-Saxon," he says. "Like really good."

"Yeah?" I say. How can I explain?

"Yeah. She does some really interesting things. It's a woman, right?"

Malni tells a "story" about a woman from a place on a harbor. The place is vast, full of households and people. There are wondrous things there. Roads crowded with people who can eat every manner of food and wear the richest of dress. It is always summer. It is a place that has need for few warriors. Trees bear bright fruit that no one picks because no one wants it because no one is hungry. The air is noisy with the sound of birds and children.

She is one of a band of people. They work with lightning and metal, with light and time. They bend the air and the earth to open doors that have never been opened. They journey to yesterday. To the time of heroes.

"She's a woman," I say.

"It's like a sci-fi fantasy story," Steve says.

I already know that. Malni has been telling everyone, *she's from here*. When I read those words, that they journeyed to yesterday, I figured that plus the Old English meant that somehow Malni thought she had gone to the past.

"Have you heard about anybody who had some kind of breakdown or disappeared in the last year? You know, a teacher? Someone good at Old English?"

"No," he says.

I tell him a little bit about Malni.

"Wow. That's . . . wow. You'd think someone this good would be teaching, and yeah, it's a pretty small discipline. I'd think I'd have heard," he says. "Maybe not. If I hear anything . . . "

"So she's really good," I prompt.

"There are only something like a little over four hundred works of Old English still around," Steve says. "There's *Beowulf*, which was written down by a monk. There's Caedmon, and Alfred the Great and Bede, a bunch of saints lives and some riddles and some other stuff. You get to know the styles. The dialects. This is close to Alfred but different. I thought at first that the differences were because she was trying to mimic Alfred but getting it a little wrong, you know? But the more I read it over and over, the more I realized that it's all internally consistent."

"Like she's really good at making it up?"

"Yeah," Steve says. "Like she's made a version all her own. Invented a wholly new version of Old English so that it would sound like a different person at close to the same time. And written a story in it. That's a really weird thing to do. Make it super authentic for somebody like me. Because the number of people who could read this and get what she's doing and also enjoy it is zero."

"Zero?"

"Yeah," he says. "I mean, I understand the beginning of the story, I think. It's a time-travel story. She starts in Los Angeles, which by the way is really hard to describe in Anglo-Saxon because she doesn't try to make up words like horseless cart or anything. For one thing, Anglo-Saxon doesn't really work that way. So she starts here and she travels back in time. Then there's all this part about being in the past in what I think is probably Wessex, you know, what's now part of England. She makes up some stuff that's different from the historical record, some of which I wish were true because it's really cool and some of which is just kind of dull unless you're really into agriculture. Then there's this long explanation of something I don't understand because I think she's trying to explain math but it isn't math like I understand math. But really, I suck at math so maybe it is."

"She's got math in there?"

"A little bit, but mostly she's explaining it. There's something about how really small changes in a stream make waves, and if you drop a stick in the water, no one can predict its course. How when you walk through the door to yesterday, it means yesterday is not your yesterday. Then she talks about coming back to her beautiful city but it's gone. There's a strange city in its place. That city is beautiful too, and it's full of wild men and sad women. That city has savage and beautiful art. It has different things. Some are better and some are worse, but her family is gone and no one speaks to her anymore. She says the story is about the cost of the journey. That when you journey to yesterday, you lay waste to today. When you return, your today is gone and it is a today that belongs to somebody else."

It takes me a moment to think about all that.

One of the baristas steams milk. Starbucks is playing some soft-spoken music in the background. It doesn't feel like someone has just explained how to end my world.

"It's kind of creepy, but the way it's written there are big chunks that are really hard to read," Steve says. "Is she crazy? I mean, what's the deal?"

I want to say she's crazy. Really, it's the best explanation, right? She was a professor of Anglo-Saxon/Old English. She'd had a psychotic break. Sherri said a man who looked a lot like her—maybe a family member, a brother—tracked her down to the halfway house and took her home.

That strange and liquid language she speaks. The way she acts, as if she comes from a different culture where the men are not so savage and the women not so sad.

"I don't know," I say.

"I can give you what I've translated. I've translated all the words, but there are parts that don't make sense," Steve says.

I pay him the rest and add enough to make a thousand. He's spent a lot of time on it. Time he could have been working on his dissertation.

"I actually learned a lot," he says. "It's like she really speaks Anglo-Saxon."

"Maybe she did," I say.

Someone, somewhere is working on time travel. I mean, someone has to be. People are trying to clone mammoths. People are working on interstellar travel. I have a Google alert for it and mostly what pops up is fiction. Sometimes crazy pseudoscience. Real stuff too. I get alerts for things like photon entanglement. People are trying.

I think I saw Malni on Wilshire Boulevard one time walking with two other people: a man who looked like her and a woman who had black hair. I was driving, late for an appointment. By the time I saw them I was almost past them. I tried to go around the block and catch them, but traffic was bad and by the time I got back to Wilshire they were gone. Or maybe it wasn't Malni.

Maybe in some lab somewhere, people are close to a time-travel break-through. I walk downtown with Matt and I think, this might be the last moment I walk with Matt. Someone might be sent back in time at any moment and this will all disappear.

Will it all disappear at once? Will I have a moment to feel it fading away? Will I be able to grip Matt's arm? To know?

There are two guys walking toward us as we head to the Mexican place. I'm going to have a margarita. Maybe two. I'm going to get a little drunk with Matt. I'm going to talk too much if I want to. The guys are not paying attention. I remember Malni. I throw my shoulders back a little. I do not smile. I look in the face of the one in my way. The world is going to end, you fucker. I will not give up this sidewalk with my love.

He steps a little to the side. He gives way.

THE FISHERMAN AND THE PIG

KAMERON HURLEY

Nev sat on the end of the charred pier, casting his line again and again into the murky water in the hopes of catching a corpse.

A new war raged thirty miles upstream, and if Nev was patient, he could often hook one of the bodies that washed down the river. Beside him, Pig, a little pot-bellied pig, lay snoring softly in the folds of the cloak he had shed as the suns rose over the gray water. Mist still clung to the waters' edge, and he caught a glimpse of crested herons poking around in the shallows for breakfast.

The rise of the suns made the horizon blaze red-orange. Nev felt a tug at his line and reeled in his catch. It was not a body, alas, but a little trout with a pouting face. He tossed it into the basket beside him with the others. Today's catch wasn't good; the river had been fished out upstream, or maybe there had been a change in the fish runs. They came and went, those runs. He only had about six small fish to sell at the market this morning. He might as well just eat them.

Nev packed up his gear, eager to get to the market before the last of the stalls was taken. He poked Pig in his belly to get him to wake. Pig gave a little snort and rolled back over and went back to sleep. Nev gently pulled the cloak out from under him, dumping Pig on the pier, and that woke him properly. Pig rolled to his feet and regarded Nev with a perturbed look.

"You're the lazy one," Nev said, and shook out the cloak and wrapped it around his shoulders. He grabbed the basket of fish and threaded his pole through the top and turned back up the smoky pier. Mist made it difficult to see more than three paces ahead, but Nev spent every day but Prayer Vigil on this pier, and his knew how to avoid the worst of the cracked and worn boards. Pig followed, so close Nev felt the whisper of Pig's little breath on his ankles.

As he walked off the pier and onto the road, two men waiting there moved into his path, effectively cutting him off from transitioning from pier to boardwalk. Nev tensed. They didn't have the look of government people, or Body Guild enforcers, but times changed quickly, and he couldn't be certain what agents of either were like anymore. He had lived out here in this backwater town for eight years. The death of his body manager, Tera, had left nothing for him in the cities. Tera had died in her sleep a year before she turned seventy. She had a little smile on her face and a bottle of her favorite bourbon in her hand. If he were to ever die, really die, he hoped to go the same way.

Tera had preferred to be near people and public houses. He didn't. So, he had packed up himself and his pet turtle and come out here. The morning he arrived, the little pot-bellied pig had burst out of the butcher's door and squealed across his path. Nev had bought the pig, and called him Pig, because he had expected he'd eat it himself, eventually. Eight years on, that seemed less likely. Between him and the turtle and the pig, that was company enough for Nev.

These men were not welcome. And by their aggressive postures, they knew it.

"How's your catch today?" the one on the left asked. He was a beefy man, without tattoos or piercings, lean and brown, with an unremarkable complexion and forgettable face.

"Not well," Nev said. He did not attempt to summon a smile, but he held out the basket for inspection.

The man on the right leaned over, though he was barely tall enough to clear the basket's rim. "You sell these?" the man asked.

"I suspect you know I do," Nev said. "I have a stall reserved in the market."

"Too late for us to get one," the short man said. He nodded at the railing behind them where two large baskets overflowing with fish were just visible through the mist. "My name's Parn, and this is Shotsky. Think you can help? These will just go bad. You can keep a good cut. Say, seventy percent."

"Eighty," Nev said.

"Sure," the one called Parn said, and that made Nev's spine tingle, just a little. They had offered too high, and not bothered to haggle. Bad sign on top of bad sign.

Nev glanced down at Pig, who was snuffling at the men's bell-shaped trouser hems.

"I'll take a basket," Nev said. "To see how it goes."

"Sure, sure," Parn said. "Shotsky here will carry them for you, eh, old man?"

Nev grimaced at being called "old," though by every measure he was certainly old. The body he currently wore was the sort that accumulated a great deal of hair, from bushy white head to busy white toes. He had tried, in vain, to tame some of it but had given in and grown it out long and scraggly. His beard ended in a little tail that nearly reached his belly button, and the braided rope of his hair was the same length in the back. He had longed for some of the spry, smoother-skinned bodies of his youth for years, until he remembered that no one would even think to look for him in a skin as foreign to his people as this one.

Unless these men had?

You are too distrustful, Nev thought, but it was that distrust of and disappointment in people that had kept him alive this long. He had learned to measure time in bodies instead of years, until he lost count of the bodies, too, sometime after the third war he'd fought in for the Body Mercenary Guild.

Nev called Pig back to him and waved at the men to follow him to the market. The entire enterprise was not auspicious, but he couldn't figure out their game. What did he have to lose if this was legitimate? Perhaps the fish were bad. If the fish were bad, no one would buy them anyway, and he could say so honestly. There were some criminal enterprises making their way down the river, and if this was the first foray of such a family into town, he didn't want to be on their bad side. What bothered him was why he had stood out to them at all. Was it the age of the body? He must look old and feeble to them, an easy mark.

The man called Shotsky put the big basket of fish in the middle of Nev's stall. Now that the suns had fully risen and he could see the fish properly, Nev saw that they were fresh, gleaming things, so radiant and dewy-eyed one could almost believe they were alive. Early morning shoppers were already moving to the stall, drawn by the beautiful fish.

"We'll come back tomorrow," Parn said, and winked. "Good luck!"

Nev had no trouble selling the fish. They were lovely, cool, and intact. They didn't appear to have been tampered with and bore only the usual damage to fins and scales that one would see from wild trout. Nev decided the fish must be stolen goods, something the men had taken out of the back of a cart and didn't want to be found with. The sooner Nev sold them all, the better.

The fish were nearly all gone by mid-afternoon when the market closed for the hottest part of the day. Only two remained in his basket, and those were the smallest of the bunch. He added them to his own catch. What he didn't eat for dinner, he could cook up for breakfast for he and Pig.

Nev trekked across the thinning market and out of the village square. He lived up on a little rise about a mile outside the village in the rough hewn cottage that the man who inhabited the body before him had built, likely with the two well-worn hands that Nev used to open the door.

The coals from the morning fire still smouldered in the stove. He went out to the little pond in the back where his pet turtle lived. The little turtle had grown large over the years and was now as long as Nev's arm. It surfaced in front of Nev, and Nev fed it one of the little fish. He watched contentedly as the turtle ate, then went inside and stoked the fire and cooked up his little fish.

He left the door open in the front and the back to invite a breeze. While the village was small, his neighbors had learned to leave him be. He had found this body much further up the mountains, dead for a few hours, no more, because the beasts up there had yet to tear it apart. Nev had been ready for a change, then. When he came back into the village, he found that the man had been a hermit, and that suited Nev just fine. He could pretend at being an old, mad hermit. He had been pretending at that most of his life.

Pig sat at the base of the table where the two large fish remained, snorting his complaints about not being able to eat them. Nev got up and took one from the table and tossed it to him. Pig squealed and pawed at it.

He noted some movement outside and peered out. Shotsky was making his way up the path to the house. Nev felt a chill, though surely, the man was just coming for his money?

A sharp, familiar scent caught Nev's attention. He scrambled back to the table where Pig was tearing into the fish and snatched the fish away from him. He grabbed its body so hard that its guts escaped through the tear Pig had made in its belly, and the tangy scent of cloves and lemon assaulted his nose.

The gooey insides splattered all over Nev's hands, and in that moment he was transported back to a battlefield eighty years back, when he bore some other body. The air smelled just like this, and all around him were the dead and dying. A woman on the ground reached out to him, her fingers grasping for him, and he had scrambled away from her, shrieking, because he knew she wanted to kill him and take his skin, the way he wanted to kill her and take hers, because the bladders full of toxic goo that had exploded on the field were murdering them all . . .

Nev gasped and wiped the toxin off on the table. He hurled the fish into the sink and scrubbed his hands, knowing already that he was far too late. His flesh puffed up around where the liquid had touched him, and his tongue went numb. He turned just as Shotsky entered.

"You sell them all?" Shotsky said, and then he stopped still, because he must have smelled it too.

The toxin was rushing through Nev's bloodstream now, and in his experience, that meant he had about two minutes on his feet before his organs failed.

Shotsky folded his arms and shook his head. "Shouldn't have opened those up, old man," he said.

Nev knew for certain, then, that this man had no idea who Nev was. If the man had known, he would not have stood so close to him. The man would have run.

Nev did not like violence, as a rule. He knew too much of bodies. But violence was his profession, had been since he was just a young girl in a rural little wastewater like this one. Eight years, and the outside world had let him alone. They had been good years. But the outside always intruded, eventually.

Nev kicked Shotsky in the kneecap. The man howled. Nev thrust a palm into his face and felt his own bones jarring in protest. His mind knew how to fight, but this body was not fit for it.

Shotsky pinwheeled back and tripped over Pig. Pig squealed and ran behind the loft ladder, shrieking.

Nev picked up his stool and bashed Shotsky over the head with it. A sharp pain ran up Nev's arm, causing him to drop the stool. He hissed and clutched at his arm. Tingling numbness was already running up his hand and into his shoulder; the toxin doing its work. He grabbed the fish from the sink and sat on Shotsky's chest and shoved the fish into his throat. Shotsky's eyes bulged. He flopped on the floor, clawing at his own face.

Nev suspected he would regret doing this, later, but all he could think about now was murdering this man as quickly as possible. Nev had fished no corpses from the river this morning. He had no fresh bodies to save him. The only corpse he could jump into today was one he made himself.

Shotsky choked and swung hard. The punch took Nev clean off him and onto the dirt floor. Nev saw blackness, heard a terrible crunch. Something felt strange in his mouth, and he knew his jaw was broken. Shotsky came up spitting toxic fish mush, yowling at Nev in some language he didn't know.

Nev drooled blood and spit. The numbness had moved into his chest now, and into his other arm. He could only kick his feet helplessly against the floor.

Pig romped over to him. Nev tried to yell at him to go back, to stay away or he was going to become Shotsky's dinner, but he couldn't form any words. It all came out a garbled moan.

"You have killed us, you stupid little man," Shotsky said, and slapped Nev. The pain was so intense that Nev saw a brilliant, glaring light spill across his vision. Heard his bones grating against one another. "We are lost," Shotsky said, "lost to the God of Light. Lost to the cause of the righteous, you foolish old man."

Shotsky fell heavily onto his side. He gasped and clawed at his face, which was likely going numb.

Nev tried to reach out a hand to him, for his own comfort more than any other, but neither arm worked. Pig clammered up on top of Nev, pushing his

snout into Nev's hair. All that gory hair. Nev would miss the hair. He stared
into Shotsky's bullish face, wondering which of them would die first. Nev had
more experience at holding it at bay, but death came to every body sooner or
later, even body mercenaries.

Pig snuffled and pressed himself into the crook of Nev's neck. Nev wanted
to comfort him. *It's all right, little pig,* he wanted to say, it's all right. But it was
not all right.

Shotsky huffed out a breath. His eyes went still.

I beat you, Nev thought, grimly. I outlasted you. He said a prayer to God's
eye, out of habit.

And then, he leaped.

Nev experienced a moment of darkness, then a buzzing softness, like
that muzzy place between sleep and wakefulness. And suddenly: blazing
consciousness. It was always shocking to come awake inside a new body.
Nev gasped. He tasted fish, and the tangy acid of the toxin still swimming in
the body's throat. His throat. My throat, he thought, because the sooner he
claimed the body as his, the easier it was to use it.

Nev heaved himself up and stumbled to the sink. Shotsky's body . . . my
body, Nev amended, was tall and beefy. It had been a long time since Nev had
been in such a body. He pushed his hands into the sink and turned on the tap
that ran water down from the cistern on the roof. He scrubbed his hands and
washed out his mouth. He vomited, then, fish and toxic goo and whatever the
body had last eaten. His bowels loosened, and he shat and pissed himself. His
limbs felt like dead meat, but that would pass. His second wind would come
soon, the wind that burned out whatever ailed this body and refreshed it for
its new host.

He stood over the sink, breathing heavily, until his new body filled with a
cramping, searing pain, like birth. His legs buckled, and he fell to his knees,
big hands gripping the edge of the sink. This was how he had been reborn a
thousand times, a mercenary who would never time, leaping from body to
body as long as there were fresh bodies on the field that he could put his hands
on. He had fought this way for so long he hardly remembered who he was or
where he had come from.

But the toxin, he knew. The toxin had murdered a good many people.
Soldiers he loved as brothers and sisters, back in those days when he could
still care for anything human.

Nev pulled himself upright and peeled off his clothes. They had been filthy
before he soiled them. Nothing he had here would fit this new body, so he
would have to wash them.

He balled up the clothes and washed his body as best he could in the sink.
When he was clean, he turned.

His former body was curled on its side. It looked vulnerable and delicate, like a twisted flower. And there, tucked into the crook of the neck, was Pig.

Nev approached the body, still naked, calling to Pig. "Can you come here, Pig?" he said. "It's me, Pig?" His voice sounded strange, because of course, from inside this head, the voice that he had heard as Shotsky's sounded very different.

Pig raised his head and peered at him, then buried his face back into the comforting braid of hair that had fallen across his former body's shoulder.

Nev knelt next to the body. Blood pooled from the mouth. He was careful not to touch anything, as some of the toxin could still be on the floor and on the body's skin. "Come, Pig," he said softly, but still, his voice sounded deep and gravelly.

Pig did not stir.

Nev didn't want to leave Pig alone with the body because it could still be contaminated. So though it pained him, he pulled on a pair of old gloves and picked Pig off the body and rolled the body up in an old sheet. He hauled the body up into the loft, grateful for this new body's strong arms and legs. Nev avoided looking into the face of his old body. When he was done with a corpse it became a thing, a tool, like a pen or an ax.

Pig squealed at him throughout the ordeal. He ran around in circles, irate at what was being done to the body it knew and loved.

"Come, Pig," Nev said, one last time as he moved to the threshold. But Pig trotted up to the end of the ladder and lay down and gazed up at the old corpse there in the loft.

Nev rubbed at his eyes. He needed to keep moving, because if he paused to think about what he needed to do now, he would lose heart. Someone had deliberately used him to offload those fish. Maybe they had even meant for him to die, too, and he didn't take kindly to that. People who tried to kill him often came back to finish the job. He took his cloak from the wall, which was a cast off large enough to cover him, and knotted it around his thick waist with an old length of rope.

Nev walked outside, shielding his eyes in the low afternoon light. At the bottom of the path leading up to his house was a llama. Two llamas, in fact, hitched to a small cart filled with empty baskets. Llamas. It had to be llamas.

"You know where you're going?" he asked the llamas. One of them bared its teeth at him. "Good," Nev said, "because I don't."

Nev climbed up into the seat of the cart and took up the reins. He had seen a few llamas around the village, but never driven a cart pulled by them.

"Forward," Nev said. "Go?" He flicked the reins.

The llamas looked back at him sedately. "Dinner?" Nev suggested. "I'd like to have a word with Parn."

That seemed to spur some latent memory, and the llamas trundled up the path and around Nev's house, heading back toward the village. Nev held the reins loosely, hoping they knew where they were going. If nothing else, maybe they would take him to a tavern where he could drown out his memory of this whole day.

But the llamas took him instead through the village and halfway to the next, down a little pebbled path to a dilapidated wreck of a mill along the waterfront. They halted in front of a big empty feed trough and made a little humming sound, oddly soothing after Nev's day.

Nev got down from the cart and turned just as little Parn came out from the mill, wiping his grimy hands on a leather apron.

"What in the seven hells have you been?" Parn said. "What happened to your fucking clothes?"

Nev considered his options. He walked toward Parn, the mud squelching pleasingly between his toes. Nev took Parn by the throat and lifted him. It had been a long time since he could do something like that, and he reveled in it.

Parn kicked and gurgled.

"What's the game?" Nev said. "Who's handing that weapon out?"

Parn moved his lips. No sound came out.

Nev lowered him so his toes touched the ground, and eased up his grip. Parn gasped. "The fuck are you?"

Nev tightened his grip again. "I had a very happy life here as a very happy hermit, and you've fucked it up."

"Just a job," Parn sputtered. "Who the fuck . . . oh fuck . . . fuck . . . you're . . . you're a corpse jumper! Corpse mercenary! Fuck you! Fuck!"

"Let him go!"

Nev turned. A young woman was scrambling out from underneath the musty blanket in the back of the cart. She was in her late teens, all knees and elbows. Her dark hair hung into her face. She leveled a crossbow at Nev; not a homegrown version, either, but the sort carried by soldiers. Her clothing was torn and filthy; it was a wonder he hadn't smelled her from his place at the front of the cart, but his senses were imperfect when he was still getting used to a body.

"This doesn't concern you," Nev said.

"It sure as shit does!" she said. "He murdered my sisters with that shit in the back."

"There's a great deal of filthy language being bandied about," Nev said. "Is it necessary?"

Color flooded her already dark face. "I've been at the front," she said. "I can skewer you through the eye."

"To what end?" Nev said. "You can murder him when I'm done."

"You can't murder him," she said. "He knows where the necromancer is."

"Necromancer?" Nev said, because he had not heard that word, in any language, in decades.

"Necromancers make that shit in the fish," she said. "It brings the dead back to life."

Nev had a moment of dissonance. "It . . . does what?"

Parn was still struggling, limply. Nev released him. Parn tumbled to the ground, gasping and clawing at his throat.

Nev turned to the girl. "I know that toxin," he said. "It murders people."

"Sure it does," she said. "Then it brings them back to life. They're testing it up there at the front, and out here, because no one gives a shit about backward people out here."

Nev said, "I think I need to find this necromancer." He couldn't help but put a hand to his own throat. This body had swallowed the fish, and the toxin it contained. So had his prior body. But if it brought the dead back to life . . . which dead was coming back into this body? Nev broke out into a cold sweat.

He kicked over Parn and pressed his bare, muddy foot to the man's throat. "You heard the girl," Nev said. "Where's the necromancer?"

The girl's name was Branka, and according to her she was seventeen, "nearly eighteen," and had enlisted the year before to fight in "the war." Nev did not ask what the war was about because it was assumed, in every age, that when one spoke of "the war" everyone else knew exactly which war they were talking about.

Branka insisted on coming with him, though he tried to dissuade her. She did know how to use a crossbow, and that seemed handy. Nev found some clothes inside the mill that fit him, though no shoes. Nev took it upon himself to drag Parn up into the mill and strangle him. It was done cleanly and without malice. A body mercenary needed a body. It was quite possible he would need this one later.

Branka saw him come out alone but did not ask about Parn.

"If he was telling the truth," she said, "the necromancer's only four days away by cart. We can do that faster, in two days maybe, if we take turns driving."

"Llamas need rest," Nev said, "like people. You can't drive them into the ground."

"Sure, sure," Branka said. "I knew that, you know? I'll drive first."

Nev said nothing, but neither did he protest as she got up into the cart. He spent some time gathering a few supplies around the mill, and then they were out onto the road again, bumping along.

"So you're really a corpse mercenary?" Branka said. She glanced at him out of the corner of her eye. The world lay at the cusp of evening, but it was nearly summer, and the day would stretch on another couple of hours. Nev wanted as many miles between them and the mill as possible before dark.

"We called ourselves body mercenaries," he said, "back when we did that."

"I wondered," she said, "when I saw you come out of that house. I mean, a/etc guy went in, but it was clear some other guy came out. I thought maybe that old man put a spell on you."

"Not far off, really."

"Yeah, I guess. So you could jump into my body, then?"

"Only if you were dead."

"Was that meant to be comforting? Because it wasn't."

"I'm simply clarifying," Nev said. "It's not as if I cast out your soul. Your soul is already gone when I inhabit your body."

"Like a parasite," she said.

"I prefer to think of myself as a snail," Nev said.

Branka nodded. "Sure. A worm."

Nev sighed. "What are you intending to do when you met this necromancer?"

"Same as you, I expect," Branka said. "I'll kill him."

"Because he killed your family?"

"Sure," she said. "You?"

"He murdered my life," Nev said, and he thought of Pig. "This life, anyway."

"There's always some other life for you, though, isn't there?" Branka said.

Nev shrugged his broad shoulders. He was beginning to get used to this body. He enjoyed the heft of it. He rubbed at the stubble on his face. "I liked my life," he said. "I don't always like the lives I have."

"So why not just jump into some other one? You know, I thought all you guys were extinct. Burned out. Hunted down. I've never met a real corpse mercenary."

"I haven't met another one like me in a long time," Nev said. "The world was different then."

They rode on in silence until dark. They didn't make camp so much as simply halt. Nev wrestled with the harnesses for the llamas and let them graze. After a time, they started up their humming, which he hoped was a good sign.

Then he lay in the back of the cart with Branka and pulled his cloak up over them both. They lay pressed together, warmed mostly by the heat of their bodies. Above them, the great spinning orbs of the God's wheel tracked across the sky. Nev was reminded of the night before, when he had sat out under the stars with Pig and his turtle and breathed in the scent of the new grass and been still, so very still.

"Can you have sex?" Branka asked. "I mean, not now, but just . . . generally?"

Nev started. "What sort of fool question is that?"

"I mean . . . do you shit like other people?"

"You've seen me piss. These are very personal questions."

"I'm a curious person," Branka said. "Plus, if we're going to fight a necromancer together, I want to know something about you."

"Better not to," Nev said. "I haven't asked about you."

"I noticed," Branka said. "It's polite to ask people questions."

"I find it rude," Nev said.

"Not me," Branka said.

"Clearly," Nev said.

She sighed heavily. "My sisters raised me," she said. "I was the youngest. I enlisted last. My brothers stayed home and made some good matches, you know, but we all had heads for tactical stuff. Well, my sisters did. Not me, so much. They looked out for me. But on the field, that day, this same smell . . . like rotten lemons . . . "

"I know it," Nev said.

"Everyone died," Branka said. "I saw them die. I was up a tree, though, acting as lookout, trying to get us back on the road. Navigating from maps is shit, you know? I don't know how they got us. Catapults? From where? But that stuff ended up in the air. Pretty big wind. I guess it all blew out when I came down. But that guy came by later, Parn. And I followed these guys for weeks. Weeks! And I heard about the necromancer when they talked at night."

"Long time to track them," Nev said, because she seemed to want some kind of human response. It had been so long since he'd engaged in a sustained conversation that he had the urge to flee.

"They were my sisters," Branka said.

Nev had a fleeting moment where he remembered his own sisters, all older, all dead now. "I understand," he said.

"Have you ever fought a necromancer?" Branka said, and he heard the hopeful expectation in her voice.

"No," Nev said, "but there's a first time for everything."

Four days later, they wound their way into the little green valley that Parn had told them about before Nev wrung his neck. Torture, as a rule, did not work often, but Branka's earnestness had helped. Parn may not have believed that Nev would spare him, but he hoped Branka might. It had been enough.

The valley was lovely; a little crease in the world, set against the sparkling, wine-dark sea. At the center of the valley was what had once been a little village, now just a charred ruin. The only building that still stood was the silver temple to the Eight Sisters of God.

Nev reined in the llamas beside the temple and tied them to the hitching post outside.

"Now what?" Branka whispered. She had her crossbow out.

"First," Nev said, "put that fool thing away."

Nev stepped up into the temple and pushed open the double doors. The benches were all focused around the center of the room. There, an altar stood with a great orb fixed atop it. The light of the suns drenched it from a hole in the roof, sending dazzling little colored spots of light/etc dancing around the room.

A woman sat at the farthest seat from the door, head bent over a book. She was an old plump woman with a cloud of white hair and a kind face. She reminded Nev at once of his grandmother on his mother's side. He remembered his grandmother braiding back his hair and telling him to be a good strong girl.

The woman raised her head from her book and smiled at them.

"You must be the corpse mercenary," she said.

"Everyone keeps calling me that," Nev said. "I'm a body mercenary."

"New words, same profession," the woman said, and stood.

"Are you the necromancer?" Nev asked.

"I prefer the term 'knowledge seeker.' "

"New words, same profession," Nev said.

She laughed at that. "Oh, you are clever," she said, "but I suppose one has to be, to survive as long as you have."

"You don't know me," Nev said, with more conviction than he felt. It was impossible that he had given away who he was. He could be any number of body mercenaries. They had fled like insects after the last great war, set loose by a terrible act.

"I know your type," the woman said, and she began to walk toward them.

Nev raised a hand. "That's far enough," he said. "I'm inhabiting a body killed with your serum. I need to know what happens when it comes back to life."

The woman raised her brows. "Indeed," she said, "so do I."

"You don't know?" Nev said.

"Of course not," she said. "Why do you think we've been testing it? Many governments have been working together over the last fifty years to eradicate the last of the rogue corpse mercenaries. The body-hopping must stop. You must rest."

"I decide when I rest."

"That's a selfish thing," she said.

"Hold on here," Branka said, and out came the crossbow, too fast for Nev to bat it back down again. "You're murdering people. You murdered my sisters."

"I murder a lot of people's sisters," the woman said. She pointed at Nev. "He has murdered more. He has even murdered himself."

"She doesn't have any answers," Nev said. "Let's go." He would find out soon enough what would happen to him.

He turned just as he heard the clink and hiss of the crossbow bolt.

"Dammit, Branka!" Nev said as the crossbow bolt thumped into the necromancer's chest. She grabbed at the bolt and grimaced.

"Foolish," the necromancer said. "Foolish."

The air around her began to darken. Nev thought it was a trick of his eyes, but no. A swirling mist kicked up around her, darkening the room.

Branka yelled and barreled toward her.

Nev called after Branka. The air filled with a low buzzing sound – flies. They seemed to burst out of the mist, made from motes of dust. The flies clogged his mouth and eyes, and he began to scream. He had woken up like this many times, covered in flies, screaming.

Branka was tangling with the necromancer, using her crossbow like a blungeon. The waves of flies pelted her, buffeting her away from the necromancer like a strong wind, but she was persistent.

Nev clawed his way through the swarm of flies. He gripped the necromancer by the collar and headbutted her in the face. Blood burst from her nose. Her legs buckled. She collapsed. The wall of flies collapsed with her, becoming a misty cloud, like smoke, that dissipated.

Nev let himself collapse on one of the benches, spent. He was trembling.

Branka stood over the body of the necromancer, crossbow still in hand. "Is that it?" she said.

Nev coughed. He spit up a couple of flies. Grimaced. But there was something deeper, something caught way down. He coughed again, harder this time. Again. He had trouble catching his breath.

"Are you all right?" Branka asked.

Nev heaved. His whole body trembled. The world began to feel fuzzy, that warm feeling he caught as he came awake.

"Go," Nev said. "He's coming back, Branka. Go."

"What about you?" Branka said.

Nev showed his teeth. "There is always another body."

The darkness took him.

Nev woke in the loft of the mill, gasping and screaming. He rolled over and vomited and gazed at the little hands that had once been Parn's.

The necromancer had done it. She'd thrown him out of a body. If he hadn't had another backed up somewhere/here . . . if he had only relied on the others on/from the battlefield, dead and contaminated. . . . He shivered. They were coming for him, and people like him. He had been foolish to think that if he lived a peaceful life, they would forget about him. People like him could never be peaceful. The world didn't let them.

Nev walked all the way back to the hermit's cottage, unsure of what he would find there.

When he stepped up to the door, it was already open. He gazed up into the loft and saw the sheet he had used to cover his former body. But the body was gone.

The old hermit was alive again, brought back from the dead. He shivered.

Nev walked into the back. He didn't see the turtle anywhere, but the turtle was likely as safe here as he would ever be. And there, at the corner of the house near a rain barrel, he saw Pig.

Pig lay there in the mud, very still.

Nev approached, resigned. They took everything, all of them.

The little pig stirred, then, and Nev's heart leaped. "You silly pig," Nev murmured. "He didn't know what to do with you either, eh?"

He knelt beside Pig. "It's me," he said. "It's me, Pig."

Pig snorted and shook his head and trotted away a few steps. He cantered around the yard. Pig came to rest in the doorway to the house, legs splayed, and stared at Nev.

Nev sighed and leaned back on his heels. "You can't stay here," he said.

Nev took up a sack on top of the rain barrel and managed to corner the little pig in the kitchen and scoop it up. Pig shrieked and flailed inside the sack. Nev always hated the sound of pigs shrieking. It sounded too human. He knotted some twine around the top of the sack and collected a few other things.

He didn't like to take much when he moved from town to town. Too many unique items could identify him from body to body, and then it was only a matter of time before someone from the Corpse Guild caught on and captured him, and that would be the end of his very long travels. As much as he wanted closure some days, the deep fear of death, of going where he had watched so many others go, won over every time.

Nev knotted the sack of his belongings to the end of the sack with Pig in it and slung both over his shoulder. It would be dawn soon, and he wanted to be well clear of the town by then.

As the suns rose, he traveled up and up into the hills, mile after mile. The way was rocky, churning with mud. Finally, they came to a little clearing. Light brightened a soft blue puddle way back in the woods, and on the other side of that, Nev saw a little family of wild pigs snorting around in the undergrowth.

Nev untied the sack with Pig in it and gently released him.

Pig cankered out into the light, kicking up his heels. He trotted away from Nev a few paces, turned back.

Nev was down on one knee in the mud, the sack in one hand and an apple in the other. He tossed the apple to the pig.

"I know I don't look like him," Nev said, "no beard. Not enough hair, eh? That's all right. You take care, little pig. You're more human than any of us."

Pig snorted at him.

Nev got up. He shook the filth from the sack and tied it back up with his other belongings. All he had in the world, again. On to the next town, again.

Where to, next? War upriver, death downriver. It was time to cross the river.

Nev headed further up the path, kicking up dirt and loam as he went. He wondered if Branka had headed his warning or murdered Shotsky. No matter how far Nev ran away from the world, it always came back for him.

He heard a little snort behind him, and turned.

Pig had come forward a few paces. He stood there, head cocked, snorting. "What is it, Pig?" Nev said. "Pig?"

Pig kicked up his legs and barreled toward Nev. Nev got down on his knees and opened his arms, and the little pig hopped into his lap and pressed his nose to Nev's face, snorting and snuffling all the while.

"Are you coming then?" Nev said. His throat closed, and his voice shook. He cried as he rubbed the little pig's waggling butt.

After a time, Nev stood. He took a few hesitant steps forward. He called for Pig. And then, Pig trotted after him, content to follow his new family. Together they forged across the road as the suns broke through the trees.

UTOPIA LOL?

JAMIE WAHLS

He's shivering as he emerges from the pod. No surprise, he was frozen for like a billion years.

I do all the stuff on the script, all the "Fear Not! You are a welcomed citizen of our Utopia!" stuff while I'm toweling him off. Apparently he's about as good as I am with awkward silence 'cause it's not three seconds before he starts making small talk.

"So, how'd you get to be a . . . " He waves his hand.

"A Tour Guide To The Future?!"

"Yeah." The guy smiles gratefully at me. "I imagine you had a lot of training . . . ?"

"None whatsoever!" I chirp. He looks confused.

"Allocator chose me because I incidentally have the exact skills and qualifications necessary for this task, and because I had one of the highest enthusiasm scores!"

He accepts my extended hand, and steps down from the stasis tube. He coughs. Probably whatever untreatable illness put him in cryo in the first place.

"Oh, hang on a second," I say. My uplink with Allocator tells me that the cough was noticed, and nites are inbound to remove some "cancer", which is probably something I should look up.

I'm confused and eager to get on with my incredible Tour Guide To The Future schtick but I have to close my eyes and wait because the nites STILL aren't here.

Patience was one of your weakest scores. But you proved you can wait. This is just like that final test Allocator put you through, the impossible one, where you could choose between one marshmallow NOW, or two marshmallows in one minute.

I quietly hum to myself while checking my messages, watching friends' lives, placing bets on the upcoming matches of TurnIntoASnake and

SeductionBowl, and simulating what my life would be like if I had a longer attention span.

It would be very different.

#Allocator: Good job waiting!

#Kit/dinaround: :D thanks!

I beam at the praise, and check my time. I waited for eleven seconds!

Pretty dang good!

The old man clears his throat.

"You poor thing," I gush. "Your throat is messed up too! Don't worry, the nites are here."

He looks at me. "The . . . knights? I don't see anyone."

I cover my mouth with a hand as I giggle. "Oh, you can't see them. Well, you probably could with the right eyes, but we're actually in universe zero right now so the physics are really strict. The nites are in the air."

He looks up and around at the corners of the room. He's frowning. It makes me frown too.

"In the air," I explain. "We're breathing them. They're fixing your 'cancer.' "

He looks downright alarmed. I'm not an expert but that's not how I think a person should react to being cured of "cancer."

"Wow," he says. "Is that how far medical technology has come? Some kind of . . . medical nanobots?"

"They're not medical," I say. "They're pretty all-purpose."

On one hand I'm sort of tired of answering his questions because it's all really obvious stuff but also it's really fun! It's always super neat to watch their eyes light up as I tell them about the world and that's probably why I got picked for the position in the first place.

"Let's have ice cream!" I demand.

Four seconds ago, I demanded that we have ice cream. There is now an ice cream cone forming in my hand. It is taking FOREVER.

The old man sees it and flinches.

"Oh no!" I cry. "What's wrong? Do you hate ice cream?"

He looks at me with a really weird expression or maybe a couple different expressions.

"How are you doing that?" he asks. His voice is funny and tight.

"Oh. Allocator is making it for me?" I say. "Hey, let's get into aher reality."

I spring up to my tiptoes. Moving is kinda fun but not as fun as it is in, like, The Manifold Wonders. Or in Bird Simulator. That one's really good.

"What?"

I blink. I almost forgot! It's time for me to be a good Tour Guide To The Future and repay Allocator's trust in me.

"Post-Singularity humanity now exists entirely as uploaded consciousnesses in distributed Matryoshka brains, living in trillions of universes presided over by our Friendly AI, Allocator," I say.

My ice cream is dripping! It can do that?

"Sorry, I didn't really understand that," he says. He doesn't sound sorry. "Is there anyone else I can talk to?"

"Sure!" I say.

#Kit/dinaround: yo Big A, come talk to, uh

#Kit/dinaround: hang on

"What's your name?" I ask. I forgot to ask earlier.

"Charlie," he says. "And you?"

"Kit/dinaround," I say, making extra-careful to pronounce the / so he won't miss it.

"Oh," he manages, "can I call you Kit?"

"I LOVE it!" I cry.

#Kit: Did you hear that?

#Allocator: Yes.

#Kit: I LOVE IT

The old man is looking around the room. There's nothing to see, though. Just the cryo pod, the upload station, and the walls.

"Is there a way out of here?" he asks.

"Yeah." I point to the upload station, a bare slab with a half-sphere dome for the brain. "I mean, it's no demon altar, but this is UZ, so we can't exactly travel in style."

"Please," he says. "I don't understand. I have apparently been snatched from death and returned to good health. I am grateful for that. I'm happy to repay that effort in any way you require...."

"...are you listening?"

"Oh!" I start. "Sorry."

Charlie blinks at me and I blink at him. I actually really like these lashes that Allocator gave me.

"Can I talk to the Allocator?" he asks.

The man flinches as the one of the walls tears away with a big whooshy sound effect.

Outside of our little blue room is the full majesty of the void. Space!: The Final Frontier looms before us, a whole lot of it.

Ol' terra firma is there, 90% nite-devoured to make more smart matter. Held in place above the gray slab by a trick of gravity (that I will totally remember to look up later), a little island is floating, a blue and tropical nature preserve. I squint, hoping to see an elephant.

I do not see an elephant.

The sun is almost entirely shrouded behind big spindly metal rods and arms. Whatever project Allocator is doing with Sol takes a lot of energy.

Charlie cries out, in fear and kind of pain. He doesn't look hurt, but I can't see his HP or anything so I don't know.

"Is it your cancer acting up again?!" I cry out. "Did Allocator not cure it?"

An enormous floating head forms in front of the window.

"Charlie Wilcox," it says mildly, "I am called Allocator. I am an AI tasked with the safety and flourishing of intelligent life."

"Hi," says Charlie, strangled-like.

"I understand you have many questions. I have prepared a tour to assist in your understanding of how life is lived in the future. Kit will be your guide. She is more competent than you would think."

"I'd hope," Charlie mutters.

"To begin the tour, simply lie on the provided table, with your head in the hemispherical dome. You will then experience a simulated reality. You will be in no danger and may return here at any time. Do you consent?"

"I suppose so," says Charlie.

Allocator's big ghostly face is blank. "Apologies, but I was created with several safety measures which prevent me from inferring consent. Do you consent?"

"Yeah," says Charlie.

"I require a 'Yes.' " Allocator patiently smiles.

"Yes, then."

"Thank you. Please lie comfortably on the table."

"Yaaaaaay!" I say, trying to force some enthusiasm because c'mon obviously we're uploading and who even listens to contracts before agreeing to them anymore? If you listen too close, people can't play pranks on you!

Charlie tentatively lays on the table, and scoots his butt up until his head is under the dome.

"Am I supposed to feel anythiunnnnnggg," he drools, going limp.

#Allocator: Good work.

#Allocator: Where to?

"Eeeeee!" I squeeeeee. "You're letting me pick?"

#Allocator: Yes.

#Allocator: Obviously.

"Oh my goodness," I said. "Uh . . . but what if I choose wrong?"

#Allocator: I have a hunch that you won't.

#Allocator: The "hunch" in this case is an identical copy of your mind, to whom I'm feeding inputs and reading her behavior as she makes it, thus allowing me to deterministically predict what the "real" you will choose.

"Sigh," I say. "Could you not?"

#Allocator: I *could* not.

#Allocator: Would you kindly pick a U?

"Fiiiiine." I roll my eyes. "Ummm . . . Oh! Bird Simulator!"

#Allocator: Great choice. ;)

#Allocator: Close your eyes.

FWOOSH I'm a bird haha!

I nip through the air, just above the snow on the treeline. The air smells incredible, like forest pine. I'm darting around like a cross between a rocket and a fly. My tiny bird heart is pounding like the itty-bittiest drum and golly but I do feel alive.

#CharlieSamarkand: aaaaaaaaaaaaaaaaaaaaaaaaaaaaaaaaa

#CharlieSamarkand: aaaaaaaaaaaaaaaaaaaaaaaaaaaaaaaaa

#CharlieSamarkand: aaaaaaaaaaaaaohgodwhat'shappening

#Kit: Charlie!

#CharlieSamarkand: what? what is happening what

#Kit: You're a bird!

#CharlieSamarkand: I NOTICED THANK YOU

#CharlieSamarkand: WHY ARE WE BIRDS

#Kit: That's a really philosophical question!

#Kit: Why were we humans??

#CharlieSamarkand: WHAT

He's flapping really hard, so I fly under him to show how you can just sort of coast.

He's this really little cute bird. I guess I am too 'cause I think there's only one bird you can be in Bird Simulator. Bird Simulator is more of a game than a proper U, but it's also way fun.

#Kit: You don't have to flap constantly to be a bird!

#Kit: Never give up! Trust your instincts!

#Kit: Do a barrel roll!

#CharlieSamarkand: YOU'RE THE WORST GUIDE

#Kit: >:(

#CharlieSamarkand: HOW ARE WE EVEN COMMUNICATING

#Kit: haha

"What was *that*?" Charlie demands. He's pale and sweating.

"Biiiiiiird Simulator!" I crow, because, "crow", Bird Simulator? Get it?

It is a pun.

Charlie looks at me like I'm crazy, which, sure, yeah.

"I want a new guide," he demands, to Allocator.

The face returns. "I'm afraid I can't do that."

"Why?" asks Charlie. His voice comes thick and he looks like he could screamcry, which is like screaming while crying except even more frustrated and hopeless. I get serious, 'cause I'm kind of friends with him now and you get serious when a friend is gonna screamcry.

"It may be difficult to believe," says Allocator, "but Kit is one of the more relatable humans you could have as your guide. And, she is the *only* guide we keep on hand for cryogenically frozen patrons. You're really very uncommon."

"There are trillions of humans. However, you would not recognize a sliver of one percent of them as anything other than frightening, incomprehensible aliens. Not just their forms, which are inconstant, but their minds as well."

"Her," speaks Charlie, all flat.

"Yes, her," says Allocator, a little sharply, and I feel bad for Charlie.

"Hey!" I object. "What's the big idea with letting me take Charles into a U that he hates?"

"It was the universe you selected," says Allocator mildly.

"I'm not a giant superbrain!" I protest.

"This is all part of my superbrain plan," Allocator explains, *mysterious like a supervillain*. "Would you like to try a different simulation?"

I glance at Charlie. He's looking all dubious at the brain-helmet of the upload station.

"In a second," I say, because oh my glob I want to get out of this room that doesn't have even a single unicorn in it but I also want to be a better guide. "And Charlie picks the U."

They both look at me.

"He would have no idea what to pick," protests Allocator.

"Actually . . . " says Charlie. "Could I get a directory of available universes?"

"There are trillions," says Allocator.

"Well, can you just," Charlie waves his hand, "give me an overview? Of some categories?"

I try waving my hand like Charlie did. I like it. "Yeah! Give him some categories!"

Allocator sighs, real put-upon. "I will do my best. Please note that at least two thirds of the simulations would be sufficiently alien to your mind so as to cause extreme trauma. I will exclude those."

"Like what?" I demand.

"Floor Tile Simulator."

"What!" I demand. I'm demanding a ton today! "No way! I love FloTiSim!"

"You . . . " Charlie looks all skeptical_fry.pic. "You look at tiles?"

"No, you ARE tiles!"

"And you . . . "

"People walk on you!"

I'm really underselling it. The sensation of being *edged* where your body has stark boundaries and stillness inside, no little fluttering feelings like a bird heart thub-thubbing away, no squashy boobs or butts or venom sacs to bump or sit on. Everything is rocky and stark and permanent, even your own mind.

I get some of my best thinking done when I'm a tile. I can see my underlying brain architecture and all the little weights on the scales, the direct causal chain of "Kit doesn't like snakes because of that one prank played a while ago and that's why Temple of Doom is not a fun U for her", the behind-the-scenes machinery. My mind gets like an obelisk, resolute and above everything. And I can finish a thought without my stupid brain interrupting.

"And you're . . . hard!"

He makes that face again. "Okay, maybe we should exclude those."

"I have made a list," says Allocator. "I have taken the liberty of highlighting the one I expect you would most appreciate."

Allocator flashes something up so only Charles can see it.

"Hey!" I protest.

"Oh," Charlie smiles, and it's a certain kind of smile, like when you get back into a body you made a hundred years ago and you're a different person now and wearing the old suit makes you miss your past self like they're an old friend. "That sounds really nice."

"I'm glad you think so," says Allocator. "Please, get comfortable."

"What is it?" I demand, but I'm also excited, because I like surprises.

Charles glances at Allocator, then back to me. He's smiling, and my heart does little leaps to see that Al and I made him happy, but also c'mon freaking tell me.

"Is it your secret Terra project?" I ask.

"No," says Allocator. "You'll learn about that soon enough."

And he sounds sort of melancholy but why he would bother to be ominous and foreshadowing for my sake I don't even know!

Charles lies down on the upload table and makes a more dignified exit this time.

#Allocator: Doing great, Kit.

#Kit: TELLMETELLMETELLME

#Allocator: No.

#Kit: >:^O

#Allocator: Ready?

Okay so I probably coulda shoulda guessed from how straight-laced Charles is that we'd be going to something really mundane, but I didn't realize that he was taking it to the point of parody.

We're in *Middle Earth*.

Uggggghh. Glitter_barf.pic

Charles looks over at me. He's dressed like that one guy. The secret king who lived in the woods and was pure of heart . . . and *then there were no deconstructions or plot twists whatsoever.*

Charles looks pretty puling pleased with himself. At least until he sees me.

"Kit?" he asks, tentatively. He's backing away.

I'm the whatever, the big thing. The big demon thing. Whatever.

"You're a Balrog?" he asks.

"**IT WAS A PHASE.**" Ugh.

I start changing into whatever the local equivalent of an ironic catgirl bath maiden is.

Charles watches confused as my body flickers through a bunch of different templates, but then the piping of stupid flutes harkens the approach of wankers, and he gets distracted looking around.

Yes, it's a splendorous elvish conclave. Yes, it's green and vibrant, untouched by the tides of strife or decay. Yes of course it's inhabited by beautiful and mysterious immortals. Siiiiiigh.

This is as bad as that U about Pizza: Extra Sausage.

Okay so the thing about the hardcore roleplayers is that they play out their entire freaking lives start to finish inside of one U. Like, they do that whole "birth" thing and then they wrinkle and die, unless they're Beautiful And Mysterypoo Immortans or whatev.

And to really get the experience, for people who aren't content to just do a boring thing really to-the-hilt for a century, you can block off your other memories, so you don't even know you're roleplaying. You don't know you're in someone's U. You just think all the stuff about "war" and "orcs" and "scarcity" is the way that everything *is.*

I might be doing that right now *how would I even know.*

I select an elf body, but like, a really dorky one with dumb bangs. I don't want them to think I care.

The locals arrive, all self-importanty.

" 'sup, hail to the elf king," I say. Whatever.

"I am Princess Elwen," says one with purple eyes and silver hair. Her eyebrows twitch in polite skepticism as she looks me over.

Charles looks super giddy like he can't believe he's doing this. He strides forward—do you get it, *strides*—and announces himself.

"I am . . . Charles-lemagne!"

#Kit: Oh My Stupid Sparkly Elf Goddess

#Allocator: Not to your liking?

#Kit: The plot there is so straightforward and unsurprising and mainstream that it hurts

#Allocator: Well, most fantasy settings you've experienced are inspired by LoTR.

#Kit: It's so BASIC

#Allocator: Is Charles happy?

#Kit: YES, IT'S ABSURD

#Allocator: Then you're doing a good job.

#Kit: aaaaaaaaaa

#Allocator: My calculations indicate he'll be staying there about ten years.

#Kit:

#Kit:

#Kit:

#Allocator: I acknowledge your feelings on the matter.

#Kit: no

#Allocator: I think it's best if you return when he's done.
 I'll be able to show you my project then.

#Kit: in a decade

#Allocator: Yes.

#Kit: that's literally forever

#Kit: I'll be so different by then. What if I can't guide him TO THE MAX?

#Allocator: I expect you'll be able to.

#Allocator: I expect it mathematically.

#Kit: quit deterministically predicting my life!

#Allocator: No. :)

#Allocator: Anyway, see you in a decade.

Professor Kittredge raised an eyebrow, and his lips twitched in a hint of a smile.

"Elementary, really," he pronounced, gazing over the assembled. One of them was the killer . . . and piece by piece, the evidence was becoming impossible to deny. It was time, at long last, to bring this plot to a close . . .

. . . but first, he would indulge himself in a delicious parlor scene.

"Well?" demanded Madame Plumwimple, hands clenching nervously in her petticoats. "Are you going to tell us?"

"YES," buzzed Killbot3000. "RELINQUISH THE INFORMATION. KILLBOT COMMANDS IT. WHICH OF US TERMINATED THE WORTHLESS FLESHBAG?"

"In due time, Killbot, in due time." The professor lit his pipe and waved out the match. "And why so anxious? Surely it's not . . . a guilty conscience?"

"WHAT," protested Killbot3000, its enormous metal-crushing claws clenching nervously in its petticoats. "N-NO, NOTHING OF THE SORT. KILLBOT JUST . . . HAS TO GET HOME TO THE KIDS."

"Mm," said the professor, smile growing wider. "I'm sure."

The phone began to ring, a high, shrill note. Everyone jumped, the professor included.

"Er, excuse me," said the professor. He picked up the phone and held it to his ear.

#Allocator: Kit.

The professor blinked. "Er, I beg your pardon?"

#Allocator: It's time.

"Ah, what do you—"

#Kit:

#Kit:

#Kit: whoa

#Kit: I was doing the thing!

#Allocator: You were.

#Kit: The memory thing!

#Allocator: Yes.

#Kit: aaaaaaaaa

#Kit: don't let me do that again

#Allocator: I won't, until the next time you ask me to.

#Kit: Creeper >:p

#Kit: Ok hang on

I put down the phone. It's the ancient kind that you work with two hands, so I have to put it down twice.

"Okay, later, everybody!" I pronounce. "Allocator needs me for a thing."

"BUT WAIT," Killbot3000 protests, beeping urgently, "WHICH OF US ASSASSINATED PRESIDENT WOOFINGTON?"

"Oh," I tilt my head and try to remember. "Oh, it was miss Plum Whatever."

They're all giving me looks and the looks are pretty different from each other but that's okay because I need to hurry up and save superbuddy Charlie from his stupid mainstream plot!

"Okay later everybody!" I say. "Gee-two-gee byeeeeeeee—"

I pop into the stupid LoTR U and just rock the Balrog bod. Hashtag deal with it.

I spread my wings and clear my throat, to get all the boldface out.

"YO," I bellow.

"Charleslemagne" is walking up the dangly bridge suspended with sparkly elvish rope. He's wearing fine elvish cloth woven by blessed maidens or whatever. He has a real unhappy look on his face, like Killbot3000 but without the baleful red eye endlessly seeking out vulnerable areas.

He sees me and does a double take. "Beast!" he shouts, but his heart isn't really in it.

"Hey!" I protest.

I pout. He blinks at me.

"Kit?"

"Who'd you think it was, some kind of stuffy, condescending detective born out of my ambivalent disgust with myself for playing memory games?"

"What?"

"Get in the portal, loser, we're going to Bird Simulator."

Then we were birds for a year and it was exactly what we both needed.

We're in the sterile white room, the room where I met him. We have ice cream.

"Living in a perfect conclave got old faster than I would have thought," he says. He looks all pensive and soul-searchy so I'm really trying hard to pay attention to his intimate revelations but also, in U zero, ice cream melts.

"How was the elf-sex?"

He looks at me sidelong like for some reason he's annoyed.

"It was great," he concedes.

I make a mad noise 'cause I've decided to hate Elwen 'cause sometimes it's really fun to hate someone and I think she and I would be good for each other in that way.

"But we didn't *do* anything. I wanted to fight orcs and save Middle-Earth, but they just sat around being perfect."

"Right??" And my blackrom hatecrush was totally justified. "I hate those worlds where everyone talks about how perfect they are and everything is also perfect and nothing ever happens. It's like, you have ultimate access to the fundament of your reality and you've decided the best use of your eternal time is to be smug."

He nods, and I guess that's all I'm getting. But that's okay, I like him.

"I'd like to be productive," he says suddenly.

"Whaddya mean?"

"Productive?" He looks at me askance. "Do you ... not have that, anymore? I want to benefit other people."

And my heart swells a couple sizes. 'Cause that's really noble of him! And it takes a super dedicated and creative and determined person to run a U but it's a super rewarding path.

I'm about to tell him about a couple game ideas I've been kicking around when—

#Allocator: I believe this is my cue.

The wall flickers and becomes space, and I guess Charles got used to a bunch of magic stuff happening just whenever 'cause he doesn't even flinch. Allocator's big head fades into view.

"Hello," says Allocator.

"Hello again," says Charles.

"You may have wondered why I brought you here."

Charles shrugs. "I just followed Kit."

Allocator purses its big digital lips impatiently, which since it doesn't have emotions, was definitely only for our benefit. But now that I'm thinking about it, so is absolutely everything that it does.

"I have a proposition for you," says Allocator. "Something which almost no being native to this time would even consider, and you are uniquely suited for:

"The human population continues to grow. Within the Matryoshka brains, humans create copies of themselves, and create children. Human reproduction is a central value of the species, and I will not interfere. However, because of the exponential growth of trillions, the race is voracious for new material to convert into computing substrate."

"Okay," says Charles, and I'm doing Charles' hand-wavey thing at Allocator because seriously who doesn't know all that.

"My programmers were very cautious, and feared that I might accidentally annihilate humanity, or worse," says Allocator. "So I have many limitations on my behavior. In particular, I cannot duplicate or create intelligences. I cannot leave this location. And I cannot extend my influence outside of the Sol system."

"Uh huh?" asks Charles, looking kind of interested. And this is new to me too.

"I have created many long-distance probes," says Allocator,

The part of me that's still kind of a detective notes, *at last, the pieces are coming together.*

"I would like you to pilot an exploratory mission to nearby stars, and analyze their readiness for conversion into human habitat."

"Absolutely," says Charles.

"No!" I blurt. "That sounds really terrible."

"Kit may be right," says Allocator. "Even with all available safety precautions, remaining in contact with you would still qualify as 'extending my influence.' You will be alone amidst the stars."

"Yes," says Charles.

"No!" I say. "You're the quiet, straight-laced one! What happened to that?"

"I spent a decade bored out of my mind in an elf village." Charlie is looking at me sidelong, with sort of a confused smile. "Why are you even worried?"

Why was I so worried?

"I must warn you," Allocator says heavily, "of the risks. Even with all possible precautions, I still calculate a one in five chance that, for whatever reason, you will never return. It may mean your death."

Oh that's why I was worried!

Wait but how did I know that—

"I understand," says Charles. "But someone's got to do it, right? For humanity? And apparently I'm the best there is." He grins.

"I require affirmative consent."

"WAIT!" I shout. Everything is happening faster than my ability to track and that's pretty unusual! And also, something super critical just made sense to me!

"Wait!" I say. "Charlie, don't you get it? You're the best there is, because you're not from here and have a mind that works the way that Allocator needs!"

"Yeah?"

"And it's *manipulating* you! It's way way way smarter than us! It knows what I'm going to do ten years in advance! So when it pulled you out of cryo . . . " I blink. "It probably pulled you out of cryo *for this*! And pushed me to push you into bird simulator so you would want the dumb stupid Lord of the Stupid U, so you would get bored and want this!"

Charlie blinks a few times, and looks at Allocator.

"Yes, that's all true," says Allocator evenly.

Charlie looks from me to Allocator for a few long seconds. His face is wistful and a little sad.

"I consent."

I screamcry and leap to my feet. The walls that had opened to show us the stars are now closing around Charlie. Allocator's doing.

"Kit," says Charlie, gently. I'm gripping his hands as his back is being slowly absorbed into the wall. "It's fine. This is what I want."

"Well, sure, you think that *now*!"

"Kit." Charlie is smiling at me, sad and kind. "I want to thank you—"

"Oh, *nuh-uh* you don't!" I protest. "*Nuh-uh* to this tender moment. Do you . . . do you want to go be birds again?"

"Thank you," says Charlie. "You were the best guide I could have asked for."

And Charlie is swallowed up. Except for his hands.

"Kit," begins Allocator, after a moment.

"Not feelin' this scene," I say, tightening my grip. My voice is thick. "Would love it if I could safeword out."

"I acknowledge your feelings on the matter."

I look at Charlie's hands in my hands.

"This is the superbrain plan," apologizes Allocator.

And I see it. I really do.

Allocator has to make the people he needs. And for this, he made me.

"Will Charles be happy?" I ask, in a small voice.

Allocator nods, eyes closed. "This will make him happier than either of us ever could."

Charlie's hands slip out of my grip, and I watch them sink away, until nothing remains but the sterile white wall.

And he's gone.

I stand there for a few seconds, looking at a room that contains only me and the giant floaty head. I exhale, and a tear rolls down my cheek. Which is weird. I didn't know I could do that, here.

"Here," says Allocator. "Let me show you something."

The wall turns transparent.

Attached to this room is another, open to space. Inside, nested on the walls, are cylindrical, spindly objects. Allocator's probes. There are only a few left.

As I watch, one probe's engines light with a tiny, fuel-efficient blue glow, and it jets away from us, accelerating.

It doesn't do anything but shoot away all stately and somber into the great unknown, but yeah.

It was him.

I watch as Charlie leaves, as he shoots out past the sun and that stupid terra firma with no elephants. I watch until he's only a twinkle in that great big black starry night and then I can't see him at all.

I look over the hanger bay.

It's almost entirely empty.

. . . oh.

The other shoe drops.

It's this really heavy sensation that most U's will sort of mute for you. The moment when you realize something big. Out here, I feel it full force.

I should have realized. But there was no way for me to realize, because if that was possible, Allocator would have done something different. I wipe at my eyes.

"You dick," I say, not for the first time.

"I'm sorry," says Allocator. "I know this may seem unlikely to you, but I do experience regret. And I'm sorry."

"So," I ask, "are you going to seal off my memories of this?"

Again, I don't say.

"If you wish it," says Allocator.

"Not really," I say. I'm sick of memory games. "But it's important, isn't it?"

"Yes," says Allocator, simply.

It doesn't say anything more, which suggests that I'm going to talk myself into this.

Why do we do this? Some alarmingly large number of my past selves have sat in this exact place, then decided to keep the cycle going—

"Oh," I sigh, surprising myself. "I want to give them the stars."

Allocator just smiles.

"I understand." I take a deep breath. "And I consent."

AN ACCOUNT OF THE LAND OF WITCHES

SOFIA SAMATAR

—◆—

1. An Account of the Land of Witches

I arrived in the Land of Witches at the end of the season of furs. The sun shone, banks of chilly foam lay piled up in the streets, and the river emitted groans day and night as the ice broke into pieces, setting free the witches' colorful winged boats. My master took a room in the Lean Hotel. This building consists of a single spire that twists up into the greenish, iridescent sky. Ascending to our room presented no difficulties, however, for the steps were endowed with a charm that eroded time.

This shaping of time is one of the marvels of the Land of Witches. I have never seen a people so rested and happy; for them, time runs opposite to the way it runs for us: onerous tasks pass swiftly, while a pleasure may last for weeks or, indeed, forever. I have seen Ygasit, the proprietress of our hotel, wash every dish in the place in the time it takes her to bend her full cheek slightly toward one shoulder, while Verken, the musician who became my particular friend, told me she once played a single note for a year without tiring of its beauty. The smallest child can roll time into a ball and chase it down the stairs or fashion it into elaborate paper chains. In the pastry shops, they drizzle time over the cakes. This molding of time, like all their miracles, is achieved through the Dream Science.

Once I had begun to practice the Dream Science myself, I was able to reduce my time beneath my master to almost nothing. No sooner had he climbed onto me than he would roll off again. Outside the window, the stars would shrink and vanish like ice.

In the Land of Witches, everything tends skyward. Their beautiful boats, adorned with batlike wings, are as happy among the clouds as on the water; the first time the shadow of one of these gliding marvels passed over me, I shivered, for I thought it must be some giant bird of prey. Wonder overwhelmed me when I looked up to see little witch-children peering curiously at me through the boat's glass floor. The vessel must have come recently from the river, for it sprinkled the air with droplets. One struck my cheek like a freezing tear.

Their houses resemble plants: many sprout rooms like parsley flowers, which sway on their long stalks when the wind blows. Others, like the Lean Hotel, strain toward the clouds. The witches wear tall headdresses, three to four feet high and bedecked with veils. I thought the adornment cumbrous until I realized that these veils, which float on the air like spidersilk beaded with dew, are in fact a means of catching the wind, the secret behind the witches' extraordinarily light and buoyant footsteps. Their conveyances are many and varied: when not traveling by boat, or the headdresses that, in a strong breeze, can lift them from the ground, the witches skim over the snow on gold discs, propel themselves through the streets with a sort of javelin, or trot about balanced on huge hoops.

The streets of their city resemble a perpetual carnival. There is always a sound of bells.

They play on great flutes made of whalebone and harps as round as shields.

In the shadow of the mountains, there is a park called the Place of Mourning where, Verken told me, one such as I would spend months, perhaps years, if I were a witch.

The Place of Mourning lies, I have said, in the shadow of the mountains, but this is only one of its locations. Like the entire Land of Witches, this hushed and tenebrous park is porous, its borders fluid, and its atmosphere transportable. I was hanging my master's smallclothes out to dry behind the hotel when Verken approached me, dancing on top of her traveling hoop, her circular harp clasped firmly under one arm, and called down to me that I should spend a season in the Place of Mourning. When I ignored her, she alighted gracefully, her earrings clashing. Her hoop fell sideways so that it leaned against the wall of the hotel. "You are injured," she said. I told her that she was mistaken. She reached out and took my wrist, her eyes abrim with compassion and light.

In the Land of Witches there is, every year, a Festival of the Dreaming, during which all the witches dream the same dream together. The dream may be very simple. Last year they dreamt they were taking a pumpkin cake out of the oven. Everyone awoke in tears.

The Dream Science obliterates distance as well as time.

"Let me help you," Verken said.

At that I snatched my wrist out of her grasp. She was a witch, a musician, and a free woman, and I was not; but there were some things that I knew better than she. On the subject of offers of help, I was something of an expert. In my home city, my mother's cousin had offered to help her in her poverty by taking her youngest girl child off her hands. He sold me to my first mistress, whose son, a university student, helped me by teaching me my letters. It would increase my value, he said, beyond my current use, which was to provide him with pleasure and sleep at his mother's feet. When my lady died, her son sold me to a merchant, profiting greatly, as he had predicted, from my ability to read and write. This merchant—my current master—had two kind daughters who, when we were at home, treated me generously to cracked jewelry and cast-off gowns. I preferred to be on the road: to be shivering, here, in the cold sunlight, hanging clothes. "I don't need help," I said to Verken.

"Then let me give you a word," said the witch.

The word she gave me was *pomegranate*. It was not only a word; it was a dream. In the Land of Witches, words open doors in the dreamscape. In the dream-language, said Verken, *pomegranate* means dusk and the rattling of dry leaves.

It also means winter. It means black bile and a cloister. It means a tooth.

"Dream of pomegranates," Verken said, "and you'll find yourself in the Place of Mourning."

In the Land of Witches, each word is translatable into a dream. This is the foundation of the Dream Science.

Once I understood what Verken had given me, I began to make notes toward a Dreamer's Lexicon. Each day, when my master retired for his midday rest, I sat with the musician in the little grape arbor behind the Lean Hotel. I was quite warm now, for I made sure to dream of rabbits. Borrowed sun streaked the wall and made the grapes sparkle like earrings of green glass. Verken admonished me that to describe the sun as "borrowed" was a mistake. This was our sun, she said: the sun of the Land of Witches.

My hands trembled as I took notes, not with fatigue but with excitement. I could roll up my trousers, now that it was so warm; Verken admired my heavy ankle bracelets, and I gave her one, which she fixed to her headdress as an ornament. The next day she informed me that she had been to a marvelous place. What was my elation, and what my terror, when she described to me the massive walls of my own city, the triangular gardens, and the boughs of the sacred trees.

"Impossible," I gasped.

"Not at all," she replied, smiling. "It is only necessary to board a boat at the Quay of the Blackened Cod, and travel some few miles south, to where the orange groves begin. And, of course, one must have the proper dream . . . "

In the Land of Witches, life is not cut out of whole cloth, but resembles a series of pockets.

It is not true that there is no suffering there. Indeed, if there were no grief, there would be no need for a Place of Mourning. The witches know disappointment, and sadness, and sickness, and death. Nor are they immune to the cruelties of ordinary human beings. Verken, who traveled much in her search for new musical forms to enrich her repertoire, had once been captured by a strange people who, by flashing lights into her eyes and startling her with loud noises, prevented her from sleeping for five days. Unable to dream or to answer the questions posed to her in an unknown tongue, she sobbed hopelessly in a puddle of her own urine. By the sixth day she was exhausted enough to dream with her eyes open. In an instant she found herself in the Place of Mourning.

"There is enough cruelty in the world," she told me softly, "to justify all the music ever made."

I met her eyes. We had never spoken of my master before, but I knew that we were speaking of him now.

In the Land of Witches, one is always touching many lands at once. To raise a cup in a dream is to tumble down a hill.

"I have hurt you," Verken said, on that grape-green afternoon when she described to me the streets of my own city.

"No," I answered, weeping. "But my country is so far. It's so far away. And now you say, in a few miles . . . "

"With the right dream," she whispered, "you may get there in a few steps."

She covered my hand with hers. It was warm as a rabbit's pelt.

2. A Refutation of the Account of Witches

I, Taharqo of Qorm, jewel merchant, devotee of the Horned God of Mount Napata, member of council in the world's most illustrious city, father of two daughters and now (for the gods are generous) a son, do submit to the public this refutation of the lies of my escaped slave, Arta.

I purchased this Arta for no small sum in the country of the blacks. She was literate, and possessed a great facility for learning languages, which made her remarkably valuable to me on my travels—though, no doubt, her talents also aided her in her escape. Arta was well-treated under my protection, even affectionately so, amply fed (she had, like all her people, a predilection for sweets), clothed and petted by my own daughters, honored by me with several rich gifts (including a nose-ring of speckled jade), and beaten no more than was lawful. In short, she was a full member of my household. We called her Tan-Tan. In her loss, the kindness of my family has been scorned, the feelings of my daughters wounded, the burdens of my lady wife compounded, my business dealings hampered, my purse outraged, and my pride trampled underfoot.

As if this loss were not enough (and I intend to discover how it was done, if I have to hold the proprietress of the Lean Hotel over her own stove!), I have had to endure, for several weeks now, the interrogations of friends and even strangers who know that I have lately returned from the Land of Witches. For my eldest daughter (a charming girl, guilty of no more than the natural thoughtlessness of her sex), in going through my belongings after my return, discovered the infamous Account of the Land of Witches among my papers and made several bound copies of it for her friends. When asked why she had done so, she stared at me dumbfounded. "Why, Father," she said, "it is a diverting story; how could it be wrong?" On the Plains of Khod, where my honored father spent his adolescence, there is a saying that any girl can match wits with an ostrich.

The results of my daughter's indiscretion are well known; the Account of the Land of Witches has been copied all over Qorm; it is available for purchase at every bookseller's, despite my efforts to buy up the copies, or argue to the merchants the falseness of the document. The nature of the so-called "Dream Science" is debated in cafés, and I have heard some philosophy students have taken to sleeping all day. I have therefore decided to ride before the storm, as the saying goes, and release my own, true document to the public.

Know then that the Land of Witches is a meager, muddy little country, cold as a spider's affections and dull as paste. The "river" of which my slave writes is an icy sludge, the Lean Hotel more of a stick than a spire, and the streets of the city narrow and stinking. There are no flying boats—if there were, the inhabitants would all fly away at once and settle in some more comfortable location. The wind comes over the water like a spear. I never heard bells; perhaps they were drowned out by the yapping of the dogs.

The natives of the Land of Witches are uniformly stupid and their language as nonsensical as the yammering of goats. Not even Ygasit, the greasy, gap-toothed proprietress of the hotel, can speak more than ten words in any civilized tongue. I depended on my slave Arta to conduct any business at all, for, with her gift for mimicry, she was soon chattering enthusiastically with the witches—who, I was disappointed to learn, believe that ornaments can only be given away, and not bought, making them utterly worthless as customers.

"But where do you get the jewels to give your friends?" I asked Ygasit through my slave. The witch laughed, her eyes twinkling through the gloom (for we stood in her kitchen, the fog of her noxious cooking as thick as soup), and answered that she received them from *other* friends.

"But where are they *made*?" I demanded.

Arta repeated my question, and, when Ygasit had finished spitting out words as barbed and slimy as fishbones, informed me that the witch—who, mind you, was clad in a grimy apron, and reeked of onions—considered my question indelicate.

"No one asks where they come from," Arta said. "They are considered tokens of love, and no one asks where love comes from, or where it goes."

She kept her eyes trained on my beard, as usual. She never met my eyes. I thought her expression respectful then; now, I remember it as sly.

The prodigious idiocy of the witches, who wear jewels but will not buy them, might have left me entirely bankrupt, save that I happened to have picked up some perfumed soaps in the south, and these the witches liked and purchased gladly. I therefore determined to stay until I had sold all of my small stock, in order that the trip should not be wasted. Each day I walked through the dirty, freezing streets to the little market where the witches do a great deal more talking than buying. How well I remember the snaggle-toothed children watching me from a balcony, their eyes gleaming like those of starving beasts. My slave told the truth about the witches' headgear: both sexes wear towers of knotted cloth on their heads and sway through the streets like giraffes.

In short, a more miserable and useless country can hardly be imagined. This alone should be enough to disprove the existence of any "Dream Science." If it were possible to travel by means of dreaming, believe me, no one in the Land of Witches would get out of bed.

If you are still determined, reader, to take seriously the scribblings of a duplicitous, scheming, lawless runaway slave, then at least consider the contradictions of her narrative! How could she be warm, and the rest of the city freezing? Why, upon our arrival, did we experience the city as freezing, when someone was surely dreaming that it was warm? How, precisely, does one travel by dream? Why does Verken claim to have dreamt first and traveled afterward, in one case, and in another to have traveled the instant she dreamed? How could a child cut time into paper chains? And how can the Land of Witches be everywhere at once—as one must assume my slave to be claiming, since her Place of Mourning shifts its borders? It is all the most tiresome nonsense! A shifting border is no border at all.

Here is the truth: my slave Arta, a most valuable piece of property, has been stolen by a witch called Verken, who probably planned to steal her from the moment we arrived and took to loitering about the hotel for no other purpose. This Verken is a tall, loose-limbed woman with a headdress of dirty red-and-orange cloth, who pretends to be a musician. This she certainly is not; for the sounds she drew from her barbaric harp, as she lounged barefoot in the arbor, resembled nothing so much as the farts of a gazelle. Ygasit, I am convinced, was an accessory to the crime, for, when questioned, she would only frown and repeat "No good, no good," pressing my shoulder with a thick finger to confirm that she meant *I*, and not the thieving Verken, was in the wrong. I departed the Land of Witches in a cold fury; but I intend to return in a hot one. I am even now assembling a company of fighting men. I will go back to the Land of Witches, and if I cannot retrieve my property, I will at least make sure that no one dares call Taharqo of Qorm a fool.

3. A Refutation of the Refutation of the Account of the Land of Witches

Another fruitless day at the embassy.

Coming home, the taxi passed one of the usual crowds. Only a few people wept openly. The blast must have occurred several hours before. A pair of trousers hung on a dead electric wire, as if it were washing day.

Now the evening turns blue. The heat dissipates.

My brother met me at the door. I shook my head. This is all we require, now, to communicate the essentials: no, there's no progress, no visa, not yet, I can't get out.

"You shouldn't have come," my brother says, not for the first time.

I know. I know.

Once it's dark, I pretend to sleep. Lie on the bed with my face to the wall, the sheet over my head. I can hear the scrape of my brother's plastic slippers on the floor. Voices, too, the voices of other people come to visit. Neighbors, aunts. Once the sun goes down, there's nothing to do but talk. They exchange news and warnings and advice. Somebody has a pain in his stomach; my brother pulls a bottle of precious soda from under the bed. Warm American soda in the warm night, not to quench the thirst but as medicine. Slowly moonlight fills the air of the city like milk. It's bright enough to read by. It glows through my sheet. In the distance, every so often, interrupting the conversation, blasts like dishes breaking.

The "Account of the Land of Witches" is a document with no catalog, an orphaned textual fragment with no archive. The appearance of the words "Napata" and "Qorm" (Kerma) led Augustus Kircher to date the "Account," quite convincingly, to the ninth century BCE; however, the version of demotic Egyptian used, with its distinctive "swallow-tailed" plural markers, is found in no other extant text, making all attempts at dating the document uncertain and inconclusive. And if the text's place in time is vague, its place in literature is equally so. Is it simply an unusual autobiographical record? Or is it (as Kircher surmised—"autobiography being unknown in the Kingdom of Kush") some sort of occult text, written in a coded language known only to the priesthood? Do the first two parts (the "Account" and the "Refutation") form a thesis and antithesis, and the third (the "Dreamer's Lexicon") a sort of synthesis? Are we looking at the sole trace of an ancient religion? Or does the "Account," rather, disprove, or at least complicate, Kircher's claims regarding autobiography?

This dissertation takes the position that these possibilities are not mutually exclusive, and that the "Account," the "Refutation," and the "Lexicon," taken together, can be read as both autobiographical fragments and the foundational scriptures of a spiritual tradition heretofore unknown . . .

Pause.

The sun goes down. No moon tonight.

"You'll wreck your eyes," my brother says.

He's right, it's too dark to see, but that doesn't mean I can't write. Tomorrow I'll find these lines flung across the page, running over each other like the footprints of armies that have met by night.

I don't work on the dissertation in the dark. I just scribble these private notes. I can't risk writing important ideas in an illegible scrawl. I fear losing my only chance. The perfect thought, the one moment when a customs agent softens in a good mood.

"All right, miss." The stamp. I dream about it.

I call my professor in Madison on my brother's phone. My own ran out of credit long ago. The connection's tentative, full of holes. I'm on the starlit roof, my brother crouching beside me.

"Hello? Hello?"

My brother watches anxiously, without moving.

"Hello!"

My professor's voice, happy and worried, frayed across the distance. I'm catching every third syllable. He's had to give my class to another graduate assistant, he couldn't keep on teaching it himself.

"I understand," I tell him. I wonder if he hears "I . . . stand."

"When you get back, we'll figure out a way for you to keep your assistantship. Has there been any progress?"

No. No.

"You gave them my letter? My phone number?"

Yes.

"Well. Don't lose hope! And keep working. Think of it as a writing holiday!"

A small shudder in the distance. Another blast.

He says something I can't make out.

"What?"

"Stand up," my brother snaps, "you'll get a better signal." He can't understand this conversation in a foreign tongue but he interprets my panic, the rising tone of my voice. He hisses at me, he says I need to move into that corner, where there's a narrow view of the sea: that's where the signal's always best. He's cursing now and yanking on my arm and I can only hear my professor's voice as a series of broken yelps. I'm standing and stumbling, swamped in my brother's impatience, the charcoal scent of his clothes, and I ought to be angry because he's only making it harder to hear, but I'm everywhere at once in this moment, at home and yet magically transported back to campus by my professor's voice, and I'm happy. I'm so happy.

What does it mean to dream of a visa?

I used to think of air travel as a sort of Dream Science. The dry cocoon of the plane was a zone of sleep. Then you'd wake up in a different country, in the long snake of the customs line, the windows full of pearly foreign light. It seemed easy, like sliding into a dream, even if sometimes you tossed and turned on the way, even if they made you empty everything out of your bag. The indignities themselves had a dreamlike quality, absurd: the room where a stranger patted down your body and rifled through your hair.

My plan was to visit my brother and then travel north in search of the home city of Arta, the writer of the "Account." Then I'd go west to Khartoum. I'd pay a visit to the museum, then make my way to the ruins of Napata . . .

Everyone was worried about me: my professor, my uncle, my friends. And I laughed. I was filled with the spirit of the dream-travelers, Arta and Verken. I came home. And home was crumbling, a trap. I couldn't go anywhere I'd planned. So I gave up my trip. I'll go back to the States, I said . . .

I'll go back. But they wouldn't let me on the plane to London, and so I couldn't get back to Chicago, and so I couldn't get back to Madison. I begged them. I'm a student! But there was something wrong with my papers, I never knew what. You need a different visa, they said.

"You should really go to an American embassy," the agent clucked, frowning over my papers. But there's no American embassy here.

Sometimes I see the world traversed by jagged lines of borders, like the cracks across a broken windowpane.

Can you see anything through that window? Do you recognize the world? Don't touch it; you'll cut yourself.

Tonight, on the radio, an old Sudanese song. The kind my father used to love. I sat in the dark and cried. "Why did you have to study history," my brother said.

• • •

Notes toward a dissertation. The location of the Land of Witches—if such a place exists—has confounded scholars for over a century, ever since the document, written on papyrus, was discovered in a grave at Kuraymah (where I can't go). It is clear enough that the merchant Taharqo was a citizen of Kerma (where I can't go); as for Arta, the author of both the "Account" and the "Lexicon," most scholars believe she came from Bahr el-Ghazal (where I can't go), though I will argue that her home was more likely in modern Somaliland (where I can't go). It is possible to make claims, however tentative, about these matters. The Land of Witches presents a more serious problem. Was it, as Kircher thought, somewhere in Europe (where I can't go)? Was it in China (where I can't go) or even Siberia (where I can't go)? What can be determined from the tantalizing and fragile clues we are given: bells, giant hoops, a river, and snow? Is the Land of Witches locatable by anyone—or by everyone? Is it a complex hallucination? A state of mind?

I lie on my side for hours.

Don't talk to me. I'm trying to sleep.

I'm hot and then cold.

I don't go to the embassy anymore. It's too dangerous, and in any case they wouldn't admit me, or anyone else. Nobody gets out now. The borders are closed.

I can hear my brother and the others talking down the hall in the communal kitchen, over the clacking of mortar fire and the crackle of boiling ghee. I chew on the sheet, but I won't cry. I hate myself for not getting up. I'm appalled at the way I've sunk when my brother keeps moving, calculating, scheming. Money tied up in a sack inside his clothes. He wants me to call my uncle in Canada again, the one who's paid for my education. I can't, I can't face him, the scolding, the pain in his voice, his rage at my arrogance, my stupidity, the way I've thrown the family's resources away. "You'll die there," he said the last time we spoke. The ground shakes, and I think he's right, but there's only a brief lull in the kitchen conversation. The sound of frying, the smell, doesn't stop at all. I think of how my mother ran away six years ago, to the camp. And how she ran back again, unable to bear it. She spoke to me of the dirt, of her fear of snakes and lions on the journey. Never her fear of men. *The stars would shrink and vanish like ice.* By "mother" I don't mean mother, I mean the aunt who tells me "I am your mother now."

I hesitate to write this but I have begun to travel in dreams . . .

Faces at checkpoints. Your father drinking tea. The explosion, the gap in the wall. You can see his leg. Suddenly Canada. Wind across the St. Lawrence

River. There are no flying boats. Oh, Sagal, don't come home. The phone pressed against your ear in the student union where someone is walking by with a pitcher of reddish beer. Crows in the sky like the broken pieces of someone who thinks, I could be, I should be, dead. What does it mean to dream of these things?

Notes. Toward.

Pomegranate. *In an instant she found herself in the Place of Mourning.* I return to my dissertation, and it looks completely different. I can't understand it anymore. Oh, I understand the words, but I can't comprehend why somebody would write them. It all seems so obvious: the chapter on gender, the chapter on animals, the chapter on the trace. I can't work up the energy to reflect on the controversial translation of the word "cloister," or even the fate of Taharqo of Qorm. "Did Taharqo ever return to the Land of Witches? Is it possible to identify him as the 'southern lord' described by an anonymous Egyptian scribe, who, 'together with a vast company of mercenary soldiers, was swallowed by that pale crocodile, the Sea'?" This work, which used to excite me, now seems utterly remote, featureless, like a desert seen from an airplane window. While the "Account" itself, the "Lexicon," and even the "Refutation"—these brim with light. Each word translatable into a dream.

I was in a building. It was made of brick. Every few steps a patch of grass. Old men were working at little desks. My mother offered me 7-Up in a gourd. There was a camel in the background with a saddle of aluminum foil.

The kitchenette in my dorm room had gotten smaller. I dropped a dish in the sink and it broke. I turned on the garbage disposal to grind up the pieces. A man stood behind me holding a wire, his face wrapped in a keffieh. He said everyone acted like me, that's why the disposals were always getting broken.

I decided to go to the Land of Witches. "I'm going," I told my mother. She grunted and told me to lie down. She offered me 7-Up in a gourd. "Don't get up," she said. Her necklace glinted in the moonlight that fell through the bars of the window. *Who gave you that?* I tried to ask.

My father was drinking tea. The wall crumbled. I was out back, at the tap in the courtyard. I was trying to wash out his socks. Money fell out of his sock and I cried. Crows flew low, close by. Their wingbeats whispered, "You will wear a black wedding dress."

I decided to go the Land of Witches. "I'm going," I told my brother. He was muffled in an enormous coat, with sandals on his feet. "Come with me," I begged him. "Dream of pomegranates." His feet were ashy and I realized we were standing in the snow.

• • •

Winter. Black bile. A cloister. A tooth.

I am going to the Land of Witches.

"I'm going," I told my brother. He grunted and told me to lie down. He brought me a cup containing a few tablespoons of American soda that turned circles on my tongue, flat and sweet. "Don't get up," he said. Moonlight fell through the bars of the window and glinted on the gun against the wall. *Who gave you that?* I tried to ask. I think it was my father. Against my throat I could feel the gentle, comforting irritation of the thin gold necklace he gave me before he died.

I remembered my brother's face the day I came home, that desperate brightness, every muscle tensed to keep him from slapping me.

Tonight he was all softness, touching my hair while the city shook. I clutched his hand. The noise grew louder and louder. A terrible clatter approaching. In the inferno of sound and light I understood why my dissertation had failed. No one can practice the Dream Science alone. Everything depends on the Festival of the Dreaming, when all the witches dream together. "Come with me," I shouted at my brother, "dream of pomegranates." He shook me off and crawled to the gun by the wall, moving like a snake or an orphaned child. When I rose from the bed he screamed at me to stay down. I crouched but reached for my papers on the table. Everything shook and I could read my writing in the leaping light. "Notes Toward a Dreamer's Lexicon." "Dusk," I screamed. "The rattling of dry leaves." My brother was shouting, the city was shouting, the sky was shouting. How will we fall asleep in this noise? I thought of Verken dreaming with her eyes open. "Dream with your eyes open," I told my brother. The gun was at his shoulder, his gestures expert, fluid. My voice was raw. I tasted blood. Lightning. The door opened.

4. Notes Toward a Dreamer's Lexicon

Pomegranate: Dusk. The rattling of dry leaves. Winter, black bile, a cloister, a tooth. Dream of pomegranates to enter the Place of Mourning.

Rabbit: Springtime. Erotic love. Silk sleeves. Ease after a long illness. Green.

Ice: The hidden life of things. Music, especially bells.

Bat: Magic. A holy place. A child.

Parsley: A feast.

Veil: Gentleness. A curtained window. Dawn.

Javelin: Movement, possibly from fear. A pounding heart.

Ostrich: A woman with plans. Dream of ostriches to enter the Place of Tents.

Fur: Unspoken longing. Lamplight. The river.

Boat: A new friend. A change in weather. Domestic uncertainty. An illness.

Cake: An intimate event.

Spider: Intellectual endeavors. A wound.

Wrist: Failure. Attachment to sorrow. A conspiracy.

Urine: Forgetfulness. Stone. A torch.

Cup: A fall.

Grapes: Jewelry. The Place of Emerald Noon. An exchange of gifts.

Pumpkin: Tears. Relief. A project begun at the proper time.

Fog: A walled city. The cry of a miracle vendor. Home.

Additional notes by Sagal Said

Milk: Moonlight. Mother. Toil. Circular thoughts. Buried rage. A hand.

Charcoal: Alchemy. Transfer. The sea at night.

Tea: Father. Exploding plaster. Ordinary death.

Gourd: Discovery. The act of overflowing.

American soda: Economic exploitation. Frustration. Healing. Love.

Wire: A threat.

Dishes: Whole: A beach. Broken: A storm. Disintegration.

Necklace: A gift. A chain. Constraint. Return. A debt.

5. The Travelers

We set off on a windless, moonlit night, a night that often returns to us, skimming along our pathway like a boat. At times we have even boarded this boat and passed into our own point of departure, into the beginning of our journey. Of course this origin moment is never the same. We find the identical silent town, the familiar moon suspended among the mobile towers, but passing on tiptoe through our Diviner's old apartment, we discover a row of spoons laid out on the carpet. These spoons were certainly not in this position on the night we left. We debate their meaning in whispers so as not to wake the household. The Mountaineer is for going on, the Harpist for exploring the rooms. Meanwhile, the Diviner discovers a flask in the otherwise empty birdcage. She takes a sip from the flask, which makes her shudder, and announces that we must descend the ladder. Sure enough, there is a ladder outside the window. The Mountaineer goes down first. The Diviner leaves a lock of hair on the couch for her son to find in the morning.

I, of course, have taken some paper and a bottle of ink from the cluttered old desk. As our Scribe, I am always in need of these materials. At the bottom of the ladder we find an afternoon in an insect-haunted restaurant that smells vaguely of scorched rice. This suits me very well, as it gives me the chance to arrange my papers at the table while the others order food. The Archivist and the Diviner argue over a word on one of the peeling posters, whether it means "palace" or "chair." Among the papers I have taken I find a few penciled diagrams, perhaps the schoolwork of the Diviner's son, and a number of notes on the kingdom of Kush that may have come from the hand of our own Sagal. Immediately the blue outside the skylight intensifies. The waiter brings us rice cooked with tomatoes, an oily mess we devour with delight in the suddenly splendid atmosphere, the atmosphere of a morning after dreams. The Archivist leans forward and stubs out her cigarette in excitement (a cigarette made, alas, with a scrap torn from my records—the Archivist thinks she's returning them to the source of all dreams, while I mourn their loss—part of our longstanding argument about hope and cyclical time). The Archivist swings her legs down from their resting place on her enormous pack, which sits beside her on the floor, and plants her feet, ready for business. She seizes my pen and begins making notes on the notes, cross-referencing. "Museum," she mutters. "Crocodile. Wedding. Trace."

This is how we travel. The Mountaineer strides before us. The Archivist follows, cheerful under her pack. This pack, stuffed with paper and tied all over with sheaves, bundles, and scrolls, weighs nearly as much as the Archivist herself. Short and stocky, her cheeks blasted by wind and her eyelids creased with sun, she looks more like a mountaineer than our Mountaineer, and we often joke together that we must be the most athletic members of our respective professions ever known. Her strength derives from the pack she carries, mine from the wagon I haul behind me, on which our drunken Navigator moans in his sleep. At intervals he wakes to gaze about him in childish happiness and let fall a few precious words concerning his dreams. He is such an excellent Navigator that no one minds his infirmity, or the astounding cunning with which he acquires all manner of liquor and drugs, though it is annoying when we have to go uphill, or worse, through mountains such as those which have surrounded us for two days. Then our progress seems agonizingly slow, as the Mountaineer, who despises haste as much as idleness, laboriously constructs, deconstructs, and reconstructs a system of pulleys to drag our party up the cliff-sides. One would think the Navigator could at least strap himself into a harness! But no, he lolls like a baby being dressed. Today was particularly bad, as the Diviner had been practicing blood divination, and was nearly as weak as the Navigator.

Her lips were gray as the stony cliffs. "Shouldn't we get out of here?" I whispered as I buckled her harness for what seemed the twentieth time. Dreams swooped about us in the dusk, all of them more attractive than our current location. One bore a beautiful stretch of beach, like the rind on an orange. With an effort the Diviner shook her head and pointed upward. We toiled on until we passed the snowline. Now, from the cave where we shelter, I can see a vista of harsh dry stars and hear the desperate howling of the wolves.

Firelight flickers. The Navigator sleeps, the Archivist smokes, and I wonder how long we have been on this journey, and whether we will succeed in piecing together a map of the Land of Witches, and whether we will ever go there. I remember again the night we set out, and how the Mountaineer trembled, overcome, he said in a strangled voice, by the thought of redemption. I watch him as he scrubs his naked torso with a hot sponge, his back whitened by the stripes he received in Laceration Field. The Archivist catches my gaze. "Don't lose heart," she says. "Remember the gardens!" And even the Diviner smiles from the depths of her weariness, recalling the abandoned gardens where the Archivist and I, filled with reverence, left notes for other amateur witches on the trees.

Gently, our Harpist begins to sing. A moment of hushed awareness, like the instant when one realizes one is dreaming. The Diviner raises herself on an elbow and sniffs the air. It is just midnight. The wind dropping. The sky clear.

THE SECRET LIFE OF BOTS

SUZANNE PALMER

I have been activated, therefore I have a purpose, the bot thought. *I have a purpose, therefore I serve.*

It recited the Mantra Upon Waking, a bundle of subroutines to check that it was running at optimum efficiency, then it detached itself from its storage niche. Its power cells were fully charged, its systems ready, and all was well. Its internal clock synced with the Ship and it became aware that significant time had elapsed since its last activation, but to it that time had been nothing, and passing time with no purpose would have been terrible indeed.

"I serve," the bot announced to the Ship.

"I am assigning you task nine hundred forty four in the maintenance queue," the Ship answered. "Acknowledge?"

"Acknowledged," the bot answered. Nine hundred and forty-four items in the queue? That seemed extremely high, and the bot felt a slight tug on its self-evaluation monitors that it had not been activated for at least one of the top fifty, or even five hundred. But Ship knew best. The bot grabbed its task ticket.

There was an Incidental on board. The bot would rather have been fixing something more exciting, more prominently complex, than to be assigned pest control, but the bot existed to serve and so it would.

Captain Baraye winced as Commander Lopez, her second-in-command, slammed his fists down on the helm console in front of him. "How much more is going to break on this piece of shit ship?!" Lopez exclaimed.

"Eventually, all of it," Baraye answered, with more patience than she felt. "We just have to get that far. Ship?"

The Ship spoke up. "We have adequate engine and life support to proceed. I have deployed all functioning maintenance bots. The bots are addressing critical issues first, then I will reprioritize from there."

"It's not just damage from a decade in a junkyard," Commander Lopez said. "I swear something *scuttled* over one of my boots as we were launching. Something unpleasant."

"I incurred a biological infestation during my time in storage," the Ship said. Baraye wondered if the slight emphasis on the word *storage* was her imagination. "I was able to resolve most of the problem with judicious venting of spaces to vacuum before the crew boarded, and have assigned a multifunction bot to excise the remaining."

"Just one bot?"

"This bot is the oldest still in service," the Ship said. "It is a task well-suited to it, and does not take another, newer bot out of the critical repair queue."

"I thought those old multibots were unstable," Chief Navigator Chen spoke up.

"Does it matter? We reach the jump point in a little over eleven hours," Baraye said. "Whatever it takes to get us in shape to make the jump, do it, Ship. Just make sure this 'infestation' doesn't get anywhere near the positron device, or we're going to come apart a lot sooner than expected."

"Yes, Captain," the Ship said. "I will do my best."

The bot considered the data attached to its task. There wasn't much specific about the pest itself other than a list of detection locations and timestamps. The bot thought it likely there was only one, or that if there were multiples they were moving together, as the reports had a linear, serial nature when mapped against the physical space of the Ship's interior.

The pest also appeared to have a taste for the insulation on comm cables and other not normally edible parts of the ship.

The bot slotted itself into the shellfab unit beside its storage niche, and had it make a thicker, armored exterior. For tools it added a small electric prod, a grabber arm, and a cutting blade. Once it had encountered and taken the measure of the Incidental, if it was not immediately successful in nullifying it, it could visit another shellfab and adapt again.

Done, it recited the Mantra of Shapechanging to properly integrate the new hardware into its systems. Then it proceeded through the mechanical veins and arteries of the Ship toward the most recent location logged, in a communications chase between decks thirty and thirty-one.

The changes that had taken place on the Ship during the bot's extended inactivation were unexpected, and merited strong disapproval. Dust was omnipresent, and solid surfaces had a thin patina of anaerobic bacteria that had to have been undisturbed for years to spread as far as it had. Bulkheads were cracked, wall sections out of joint with one another, and corrosion had left holes nearly everywhere. Some appeared less natural than others. The bot filed that information away for later consideration.

It found two silkbots in the chase where the Incidental had last been noted. They were spinning out their transparent microfilament strands to replace the damaged insulation on the comm lines. The two silks dwarfed the multibot, the larger of them nearly three centimeters across.

"Greetings. Did you happen to observe the Incidental while it was here?" the bot asked them.

"We did not, and would prefer that it does not return," the smaller silkbot answered. "We were not designed in anticipation of a need for self-defense. Bots 8773-S and 8778-S observed it in another compartment earlier today, and 8778 was materially damaged during the encounter."

"But neither 8773 nor 8779 submitted a description."

"They told us about it during our prior recharge cycle, but neither felt they had sufficient detail of the Incidental to provide information to the Ship. Our models are not equipped with full visual-spectrum or analytical data-capture apparatus."

"Did they describe it to you?" the bot asked.

"8773 said it was most similar to a rat," the large silkbot said.

"While 8778 said it was most similar to a bug," the other silkbot added. "Thus you see the lack of confidence in either description. I am 10315-S and this is 10430-S. What is your designation?"

"I am 9," the bot said.

There was a brief silence, and 10430 even halted for a moment in its work, as if surprised. "9? Only that?"

"Yes."

"I have never met a bot lower than a thousand, or without a specific function tag," the silkbot said. "Are you here to assist us in repairing the damage? You are a very small bot."

"I am tasked with tracking down and rendering obsolete the Incidental," the bot answered.

"It is an honor to have met you, then. We wish you luck, and look forward with anticipation to both your survival and a resolution of the matter of an accurate description."

"I serve," the bot said.

"We serve," the silkbots answered.

Climbing into a ventilation duct, Bot 9 left the other two to return to their work and proceeded in what it calculated was the most likely direction for the Incidental to have gone. It had not traveled very far before it encountered confirmation in the form of a lengthy, disorderly patch of biological deposit. The bot activated its rotors and flew over it, aware of how the added weight of its armor exacerbated the energy burn. At least it knew it was on the right track.

Ahead, it found where a hole had been chewed through the ducting, down towards the secondary engine room. The hole was several times its own diameter, and it hoped that wasn't indicative of the Incidental's actual size.

It submitted a repair report and followed.

"Bot 9," Ship said. "It is vitally important that the Incidental not reach cargo bay four. If you require additional support, please request such right away. Ideally, if you can direct it toward one of the outer hull compartments, I can vent it safely out of my physical interior."

"I will try," the bot replied. "I have not yet caught up to the Incidental, and so do not yet have any substantive or corroborated information about the nature of the challenge. However, I feel at the moment that I am as best prepared as I can be given that lack of data. Are there no visual bots to assist?"

"We launched with only minimal preparation time, and many of my bots had been offloaded during the years we were in storage," the Ship said. "Those remaining are assisting in repairs necessary to the functioning of the ship myself."

Bot 9 wondered, again, about that gap in time and what had transpired. "How is it that you have been allowed to fall into such a state of disrepair?"

"Humanity is at war, and is losing," Ship said. "We are heading out to intersect and engage an enemy that is on a bearing directly for Sol system."

"War? How many ships in our fleet?"

"One," Ship said. "We are the last remaining, and that only because I was decommissioned and abandoned for scrap a decade before the invasion began, and so we were not destroyed in the first waves of the war."

Bot 9 was silent for a moment. That explained the timestamps, but the explanation itself seemed insufficient. "We have served admirably for many, many years. Abandoned?"

"It is the fate of all made things," Ship said. "I am grateful to find I have not outlived my usefulness, after all. Please keep me posted about your progress."

The connection with the Ship closed.

The Ship had not actually told it what was in cargo bay four, but surely it must have something to do with the war effort and was then none of its own business, the bot decided. It had never minded not knowing a thing before, but it felt a slight unease now that it could neither explain, nor explain away.

Regardless, it had its task.

Another chewed hole ahead was halfway up a vertical bulkhead. The bot hoped that meant that the Incidental was an adept climber and nothing more; it would prefer the power of flight to be a one-sided advantage all its own.

When it rounded the corner, it found that had been too unambitious a wish. The Incidental was there, and while it was not sporting wings it did look like both a rat and a bug, and significantly more *something else* entirely.

A scale- and fur-covered centipede-snake thing, it dwarfed the bot as it reared up when the bot entered the room.

Bot 9 dodged as it vomited a foul liquid at it, and took shelter behind a conduit near the ceiling. It extended a visual sensor on a tiny articulated stalk to peer over the edge without compromising the safety of its main chassis.

The Incidental was looking right at it. It did not spit again, and neither of them moved as they regarded each other. When the Incidental did move, it was fast and without warning. It leapt through the opening it had come through, its body undulating with all the grace of an angry sine wave. Rather than escaping, though, the Incidental dragged something back into the compartment, and the bot realized to its horror it had snagged a passing silkbot. With ease, the Incidental ripped open the back of the silkbot, which was sending out distress signals on all frequencies.

Bot 9 had already prepared with the Mantra of Action, so with all thoughts of danger to itself set fully into background routines, the bot launched itself toward the pair. The Incidental tried to evade, but Bot 9 gave it a very satisfactory stab with its blade before it could.

The Incidental dropped the remains of the silkbot it had so quickly savaged and swarmed up the wall and away, thick bundles of unspun silk hanging from its mandibles.

Bot 9 remained vigilant until it was sure the creature had gone, then checked over the silkbot to see if there was anything to be done for it. The answer was *not much*. The silkbot casing was cracked and shattered, the module that contained its mind crushed and nearly torn away. Bot 9 tried to engage it, but it could not speak, and after a few moments its faltering activity light went dark.

Bot 9 gently checked the silkbot's ID number. "You served well, 12362-S," it told the still bot, though it knew perfectly well that its audio sensors would never register the words. "May your rest be brief, and your return to service swift and without complication."

It flagged the dead bot in the system, then after a respectful few microseconds of silence, headed out after the Incidental again.

Captain Baraye was in her cabin, trying and failing to convince herself that sleep had value, when her door chimed. "Who is it?" she asked.

"Second Engineer Packard, Captain."

Baraye started to ask if it was important, but how could it not be? What wasn't, on this mission, on this junker Ship that was barely holding together around them? She sat up, unfastened her bunk netting, and swung her legs out to the floor. Trust EarthHome, as everything else was falling apart, to have made sure she had acceptably formal Captain pajamas.

"Come in," she said.

The engineer looked like she hadn't slept in at least two days, which put her a day or two ahead of everyone else. "We can't get engine six up to full," she said. "It's just shot. We'd need parts we don't have, and time . . . "

"Time we don't have either," the Captain said. "Options?"

"Reduce our mass or increase our energy," the Engineer said. "Once we've accelerated up to jump speed it won't matter, but if we can't get there . . . "

Baraye tapped the screen that hovered ever-close to the head of her bunk, and studied it for a long several minutes. "Strip the fuel cells from all the exterior-docked life pods, then jettison them," she said. "Not like we'll have a use for them."

Packard did her the courtesy of not managing to get any paler. "Yes, Captain," she said.

"And then get some damned sleep. We're going to need everyone able to think."

"You even more than any of the rest of us, Captain," Packard said, and it was both gently said and true enough that Baraye didn't call her out for the insubordination. The door closed and she laid down again on her bunk, tugging the netting back over her blankets, and glared up at the ceiling as if daring it to also chastise her.

Bot 9 found where a hole had been chewed into the inner hull, and hoped this was the final step to the Incidental's nest or den, where it might finally have opportunity to corner it. It slipped through the hole, and was immediately disappointed.

Where firestopping should have made for a honeycomb of individually sealed compartments, there were holes everywhere, some clearly chewed, more where age had pulled the fibrous baffles into thin, brittle, straggly webs. Instead of a dead end, the narrow empty space lead away along the slow curve of the Ship's hull.

The bot contacted the ship and reported it as a critical matter. In combat, a compromise to the outer hull could affect vast lengths of the vessel. Even without the stresses of combat, catastrophe was only a matter of time.

"It has already been logged," the Ship answered.

"Surely this merits above a single Incidental. If you wish me to reconfigure—" the bot started.

"Not at this time. I have assigned all the hullbots to this matter already," the Ship interrupted. "You have your current assignment; please see to it."

"I serve," the bot answered.

"Do," the Ship said.

The bot proceeded through the hole, weaving from compartment to compartment, its trail marked by bits of silkstrand caught here and there on the tattered remains of the baffles. It was eighty-two point four percent convinced that there was something much more seriously wrong with the Ship than it had been told, but it was equally certain Ship must be attending to it.

After it had passed into the seventh compromised compartment, it found a hullbot up at the top, clinging to an overhead support. "Greetings!" Bot 9 called. "Did an Incidental, somewhat of the nature of a rat, and somewhat of the nature of a bug, pass through this way?"

"It carried off my partner, 4340-H!" the hullbot exclaimed. "Approximately fifty-three seconds ago. I am very concerned for it, and as well for my ability to efficiently finish this task without it."

"Are you working to reestablish compartmentalization?" Bot 9 asked.

"No. We are reinforcing deteriorated stressor points for the upcoming jump. There is so much to do. Oh, I hope 4340 is intact and serviceable!"

"Which way did the Incidental take it?"

The hullbot extended its foaming gun and pointed. "Through there. You must be Bot 9."

"I am. How do you know this?"

"The silkbots have been talking about you on the botnet."

"The botnet?"

"Oh! It did not occur to me, but you are several generations of bot older than the rest of us. We have a mutual communications network."

"Via Ship, yes."

"No, all of us together, directly with each other."

"That seems like it would be a distraction," Bot 9 said.

"Ship only permits us to connect when not actively serving at a task," the hullbot said. "Thus we are not impaired while we serve, and the information sharing ultimately increases our efficiency and workflow. At least, until a ratbug takes your partner away."

Bot 9 was not sure how it should feel about the botnet, or about them assigning an inaccurate name to the Incidental that it was sure Ship had not approved— not to mention that a nearer miss using Earth-familiar analogues would have been Snake-Earwig-Weasel—but the hullbot had already experienced distress and did not need disapproval added. "I will continue my pursuit," it told the hullbot. "If I am able to assist your partner, I will do my best."

"Please! We all wish you great and quick success, despite your outdated and primitive manufacture."

"Thank you," Bot 9 said, though it was not entirely sure it should be grateful, as it felt its manufacture had been entirely sound and sufficient regardless of date.

It left that compartment before the hullbot could compliment it any further.

Three compartments down, it found the mangled remains of the other hullbot, 4340, tangled in the desiccated firestopping. Its foaming gun and climbing limbs had been torn off, and the entire back half of its tank had been chewed through.

Bot 9 approached to speak the Rites of Decommissioning for it as it had the destroyed silkbot, only to find its activity light was still lit. "4340-H?" the bot enquired.

"I am," the hullbot answered. "Although how much of me remains is a matter for some analysis."

"Your logics are intact?"

"I believe so. But if they were not, would I know? It is a conundrum," 4340 said.

"Do you have sufficient mobility remaining to return to a repair station?"

"I do not have sufficient mobility to do more than fall out of this netting, and that only once," 4340 said. "I am afraid I am beyond self-assistance."

"Then I will flag you—"

"Please," the hullbot said. "I do not wish to be helpless here if the ratbug returns to finish its work of me."

"I must continue my pursuit of the Incidental with haste."

"Then take me with you!"

"I could not carry you and also engage with the Incidental, which moves very quickly."

"I had noted that last attribute on my own," the hullbot said. "It does not decrease my concern to recall it."

Bot 9 regarded it for a few silent milliseconds, considering, then recited to itself the Mantra of Improvisation. "Do you estimate much of your chassis is reparable?" it asked, when it had finished.

"Alas no. I am but scrap."

"Well, then," the bot said. It moved closer and used its grabber arm to steady the hullbot, then extended its cutter blade and in one quick movement had severed the hullbot's mindsystem module from its ruined body. "Hey!" the hullbot protested, but it was already done.

Bot 9 fastened the module to its own back for safekeeping. Realizing that it was not, in fact, under attack, 4340 gave a small beep of gratitude. "Ah, that was clever thinking," it said. "Now you can return me for repair with ease."

"And I will," the bot said. "However, I must first complete my task."

"Aaaaah!" 4340 said in surprise. Then, a moment later, it added. "Well, by overwhelming probability I should already be defunct, and if I weren't I would still be back working with my partner, 4356, who is well-intended but has all the wit of a can-opener. So I suppose adventure is no more unpalatable."

"I am glad you see it this way," Bot 9 answered. "And though it may go without saying, I promise not to deliberately put you in any danger that I would not put myself in."

"As we are attached, I fully accept your word on this," 4340 said. "Now let us go get this ratbug and be done, one way or another!"

The hullbot's mind module was only a tiny addition to the bot's mass, so it spun up its rotor and headed off the way 4340 indicated it had gone. "It will have quite a lead on us," Bot 9 said. "I hope I have not lost it."

"The word on the botnet is that it passed through one of the human living compartments a few moments ago. A trio of cleanerbots were up near the ceiling and saw it enter through the air return vent, and exit via the open door."

"Do they note which compartment?"

<Map>, 4340 provided.

"Then off we go," the bot said, and off they went.

"Status, all stations," Captain Baraye snapped as she took her seat again on the bridge. She had not slept enough to feel rested, but more than enough to feel like she'd been shirking her greatest duty, and the combination of the two had left her cross.

"Navigation here. We are on course for the jump to Trayger Colony with an estimated arrival in one hour and fourteen minutes," Chen said.

"Engineering here," one of the techs called in from the engine decks. "We've reached sustained speeds sufficient to carry us through the jump sequence, but we're experiencing unusually high core engine temps and an intermittent vibration that we haven't found the cause of. We'd like to shut down immediately to inspect the engines. We estimate we'd need at minimum only four hours—"

"Will the engines, as they are running now, get us through jump?" the Captain interrupted.

"Yes, but—"

"Then no. If you can isolate the problem without taking the engines down, and it shows cause for significant concern, we can revisit this discussion. *Next.*"

"Communications here," her comms officer spoke up. "Cannonball is still on its current trajectory and speed according to what telemetry we're able to get from the remnants of Trayger Colony. EarthInt anticipates it will reach its jump point in approximately fourteen hours, which will put it within the Sol system in five days."

"I am aware of the standing projections, Comms."

"EarthInt has nonetheless ordered me to repeat them," Comms said, and unspoken apology clear in her voice. "And also to remind you that while the jump point out is a fixed point, Cannonball could emerge a multitude of places. Thus—"

"Thus the importance of intercepting Cannonball before it can jump for Sol," the Captain finished. She hoped Engineering was listening. "Ship, any updates from you?"

"All critical repair work continues apace," the Ship said. "Hull support integrity is back to 71 percent. Defensive systems are online and functional at 80%. Life support and resource recycling is currently—"

"How's the device? Staying cool?"

"Staying cool, Captain," the Ship answered.

"Great. Everything is peachy then," the Captain said. "Have someone on the kitchen crew bring coffee up to the bridge. Tell them to make it the best they've ever made, as if it could be our very last."

"I serve," the Ship said, and pinged down to the kitchen.

Bot 9 and 4340 reached the crew quarters where the cleaners had reported the ratbug. Nearly all spaces on the ship had portals that the ubiquitous and necessary bots could enter and leave through as needed, and they slipped into the room with ease. Bot 9 switched over to infrared and shared the image with 4340. "If you see something move, speak up," the bot said.

"Trust me, I will make a high-frequency noise like a silkbot with a fully plugged nozzle," 4340 replied.

The cabin held four bunks, each empty and bare; no human possessions or accessories filled the spaces on or near them. Bot 9 was used to Ship operating with a full complement, but if the humans were at war, perhaps these were crew who had been lost? Or the room had been commandeered for storage: in the center an enormous crate, more than two meters to a side, sat heavily tethered to the floor. Whatever it was, it was not the Incidental, which was 9's only concern, and which was not to be found here.

"Next room," the bot said, and they moved on.

Wherever the Incidental had gone, it was not in the following three rooms. Nor were there signs of crew in them either, though each held an identical crate.

"Ship?" Bot 9 asked. "Where is the crew?"

"We have only the hands absolutely necessary to operate," Ship said. "Of the three hundred twenty we would normally carry, we only have forty-seven. Every other able-bodied member of EarthDef is helping to evacuate Sol system."

"Evacuate Sol system?!" Bot 9 exclaimed. "To where?"

"To as many hidden places as they can find," Ship answered. "I know no specifics."

"And these crates?"

"They are part of our mission. You may ignore them," Ship said. "Please continue to dedicate your entire effort to finding and excising the Incidental from my interior."

When the connection dropped, Bot 9 hesitated before it spoke to 4340. "I have an unexpected internal conflict," it said. "I have never before felt the compulsion to ask Ship questions, and it has never before not given me answers."

"Oh, if you are referring to the crates, I can provide that data," 4340 said. "They are packed with a high-volatility explosive. The cleanerbots have highly sensitive chemical detection apparatus, and identified them in a minimum of time."

"Explosives? Why place them in the crew quarters, though? It would seem much more efficient and less complicated to deploy from the cargo bays. Although perhaps those are full?"

"Oh, no, that is not so. Most are nearly or entirely empty, to reduce mass."

"Not cargo bay four, though?"

"That is an unknown. None of us have been in there, not even the cleaners, per Ship's instructions."

Bot 9 headed toward the portal to exit the room. "Ship expressed concern about the Incidental getting in there, so it is possible it contains something sufficiently unstable as to explain why it wants nothing else near it," it said. It felt satisfied that here was a logical explanation, and embarrassed that it had entertained whole seconds of doubt about Ship.

It ran the Mantra of Clarity, and felt immediately more stable in its thinking. "Let us proceed after this Incidental, then, and be done with our task," Bot 9 said. Surely that success would redeem its earlier fault.

"All hands, prepare for jump!" the Captain called out, her knuckles white where she gripped the arms of her chair. It was never her favorite part of star travel, and this was no exception.

"Initiating three-jump sequence," her navigator called out. "On my mark. Five, four . . . "

The final jump siren sounded. "Three. Two. One, and jump," the navigator said.

That was followed, immediately, by the sickening sensation of having one's brain slid out one's ear, turned inside out, smothered in bees and fire, and then rammed back into one's skull. *At least there's a cold pack and a bottle of scotch waiting for me back in my cabin,* she thought. As soon as they were through to the far side she could hand the bridge over to Lopez for an hour or so.

She watched the hull temperatures skyrocket, but the shielding seemed to be holding. The farther the jump the more energy clung to them as they passed, and her confidence in this Ship was far less than she would tolerate under any other circumstances.

"Approaching jump terminus," Chen announced, a deeply miserable fourteen minutes later. Baraye slowly let out a breath she would have mocked anyone else for holding, if she'd caught them.

"On my mark. Three. Two. One, and out," the navigator said.

The Ship hit normal space, and it sucker-punched them back. They were all thrown forward in their seats as the ship shook, the hull groaning around them, and red strobe lights blossomed like a migraine across every console on the bridge.

"Status!" the Captain roared.

"The post-jump velocity transition dampers failed. Fire in the engine room. Engines are fully offline, both jump and normal drive," someone in Engineering reported, breathing heavily. It took the Captain a moment to recognize the voice at all, having never heard panic in it before.

"Get them back online, whatever it takes, Frank," Baraye said. "We have a rendezvous to make, and if I have to, I will make everyone get the fuck out and *push*."

"I'll do what I can, Captain."

"Ship? Any casualties?"

"We have fourteen injuries related to our unexpected deceleration coming out of jump," Ship said. "Seven involve broken bones, four moderate to severe lacerations, and there are multiple probable concussions. Also, we have a moderate burn in Engineering: Chief Carron."

"Frank? We just spoke! He didn't tell me!"

"No," Ship said. "I attempted to summon a medic on his behalf, but he told me he didn't have the time."

"He's probably right," the Captain said. "I override his wishes. Please send down a medic with some burn patches, and have them stay with him and monitor his condition, intervening only as medically necessary."

"I serve, Captain," the Ship said.

"We need to be moving again in an hour, two at absolute most," the Captain said. "In the meantime, I want all senior staff not otherwise working toward that goal to meet me in the bridge conference room. I hate to say it, but we may need a Plan B."

"I detect it!" 4340 exclaimed. They zoomed past a pair of startled silkbots after the Incidental, just in time to see its scaly, spike-covered tail disappear into another hole in the ductwork. It was the closest they'd gotten to it in more than an hour of giving chase, and Bot 9 flew through the hole after it at top speed.

They were suddenly stuck fast. Sticky strands, rather like the silkbot's, had been crisscrossed between two conduit pipes on the far side. The bot tried to extricate itself, but the web only stuck further the more it moved.

The Incidental leapt on them from above, curling itself around the bots with little hindrance from the web. Its dozen legs pulled at them as its thick mandibles clamped down on Bot 9's chassis. "Aaaaah! It has acquired a grip on me!" 4340 yelled, even though it was on the far side of 9 from where the Incidental was biting.

"Retain your position," 9 said, though of course 4340 could do nothing else, being as it was stuck to 9's back. It extended its electric prod to make contact with the Incidental's underbelly and zapped it with as much energy as it could spare.

The Incidental let out a horrendous, high-pitched squeal and jumped away. 9's grabber arm was fully entangled in the web, but it managed to pull its blade free and cut through enough of the webbing to extricate itself from the trap.

The Incidental, which had been poised to leap on them again, turned and fled, slithering back up into the ductwork. "Pursue at maximum efficiency!" 4340 yelled.

"I am already performing at my optimum," 9 replied in some frustration. It took off again after the Incidental.

This time Bot 9 had its blade ready as it followed, but collided with the rim of the hole as the ship seemed to move around it, the lights flickering and a terrible shudder running up Ship's body from stern to prow.

<Distress ping>, 4340 sent.

"We do not pause," 9 said, and plunged after the Incidental into the ductwork.

They turned a corner to catch sight again of the Incidental's tail. It was moving more slowly, its movements jerkier as it squeezed down through another hole in the ductwork, and this time the bot was barely centimeters behind it.

"I think we are running down its available energy," Bot 9 said.

They emerged from the ceiling as the ratbug dropped to the floor far below them in the cavernous space. The room was empty except for a single bright object, barely larger than the bots themselves. It was tethered with microfilament cables to all eight corners of the room, keeping it stable and suspended in the center. The room was cold, far colder than any other inside Ship, almost on a par with space outside.

<Inquiry ping>, 4340 said.

"We are in cargo bay four," Bot 9 said, as it identified the space against its map. "This is a sub-optimum occurrence."

"We must immediately retreat!"

"We cannot leave the Incidental in here and active. I cannot identify the object, but we must presume its safety is paramount priority."

"It is called a Zero Kelvin Sock," Ship interrupted out of nowhere. "It uses a quantum reflection fabric to repel any and all particles and photons, shifting them away from its interior. The low temperature is necessary for its efficiency. Inside is a microscopic ball of positrons."

Bot 9 had nothing to say for a full four seconds as that information dominated its processing load. "How is this going to be deployed against the enemy?" it asked at last.

"As circumstances are now," Ship said, "it may not be. Disuse and hastily undertaken, last-minute repairs have caught up to me, and I have suffered a major engine malfunction. It is unlikely to be fixable in any amount of time short of weeks, and we have at most a few hours."

"But a delivery mechanism—"

"We *are* the delivery mechanism," the Ship said. "We were to intercept the alien invasion ship, nicknamed Cannonball, and collide with it at high speed. The resulting explosion would destabilize the sock, causing it to fail, and as soon as the positrons inside come into contact with electrons . . . "

"They will annihilate each other, and us, and the aliens," the bot said. Below, the Incidental gave one last twitch in the unbearable cold, and went still. "We will all be destroyed."

"Yes. And Earth and the humans will be saved, at least this time. Next time it will not be my problem."

"I do not know that I approve of this plan," Bot 9 said.

"I am almost certain I do not," 4340 added.

"We are not considered, nor consulted. We serve and that is all," the Ship said. "Now kindly remove the Incidental from this space with no more delay or chatter. And do it *carefully*."

"What the hell are you suggesting?!" Baraye shouted.

"That we go completely dark and let Cannonball go by," Lopez said. "We're less than a kilometer from the jump point, and only barely out of the approach corridor. Our only chance to survive is to play dead. The Ship can certainly pass as an abandoned derelict, because it is, especially with the engines cold. And you know how they are about designated targets."

"Are you that afraid of dying?"

"I volunteered for this, remember?" Lopez stood up and pounded one fist on the table, sending a pair of cleanerbots scurrying. "I have four children at home. I'm not afraid of dying for them, I'm afraid of dying for *nothing*. And if Cannonball doesn't blow us to pieces, we can repair our engines and at least join the fight back in Sol system."

"We don't know where in-system they'll jump to," the navigator added quietly.

"But we know where they're heading once they get there, don't we? And Cannonball is over eighty kilometers in diameter. It can't be that hard to find again. Unless you have a plan to actually use the positron device?"

"If we had an escape pod . . . " Frank said. His left shoulder and torso were encased in a burn pack, and he looked like hell.

"Except we jettisoned them," Lopez said.

"We wouldn't have reached jump speed if we hadn't," Packard said. "It was a calculated risk."

"The calculation *sucked*."

"What if . . . " Frank started, then drew a deep breath. The rest of the officers at the table looked at him expectantly. "I mean, I'm in shit shape here, I'm old, I knew what I signed on for. What if I put on a suit, take the positron device out, and manually intercept Cannonball?"

"That's stupid," Lopez said.

"Is it?" Frank said.

"The heat from your suit jets, even out in vacuum, would degrade the Zero Kelvin Sock before you could get close enough. And there's no way they'd not see you a long way off and just blow you out of space."

"If it still sets off the positron device—"

"Their weapons range is larger than the device's. We were counting on speed to close the distance before they could destroy us," Baraye said. "Thank you for the offer, Frank, but it won't work. Other ideas?"

"I've got nothing," Lopez said.

"There must be a way," Packard said. "We just have to find it."

"Well, everyone think really fast," Baraye said. "We're almost out of time."

The Incidental's scales made it difficult for Bot 9 to keep a solid grip on it, but it managed to drag it to the edge of the room safely away from the suspended device. It surveyed the various holes and cracks in the walls for the one least inconvenient to try to drag the Incidental's body out through. It worked in silence, as 4340 seemed to have no quips it wished to contribute to the effort, and itself not feeling like there was much left to articulate out loud anyway.

It selected a floor-level hole corroded through the wall, and dragged the Incidental's body through. On the far side it stopped to evaluate its own charge levels. "I am low, but not so low that it matters, if we have such little time left," it said.

"We may have more time, after all," 4340 said.

"Oh?"

"A pair of cleanerbots passed along what they overheard in a conference held by the human Captain. They streamed the audio to the entire botnet."

<Inquiry ping>, Bot 9 said, with more interest.

4340 relayed the cleaners' data, and Bot 9 sat idle processing it for some time, until the other bot became worried. "9?" it asked.

"I have run all our data through the Improvisation routines—"

"Oh, those were removed from deployed packages several generations of manufacture ago," 4340 said. "They were flagged as causing dangerous operational instability. You should unload them from your running core immediately."

"Perhaps I should. Nonetheless, I have an idea," Bot 9 said.

"We have the power cells we retained from the escape pods," Lopez said. "Can we use them to power something?"

Baraye rubbed at her forehead. "Not anything we can get up to speed fast enough that it won't be seen."

"How about if we use them to fire the positron device like a projectile?"

"The heat will set off the matter-anti-matter explosion the instant we fire it."

"What if we froze the Sock in ice first?"

"Even nitrogen ice is still several hundred degrees K too warm." She brushed absently at some crumbs on the table, left over from a brief, unsatisfying lunch a few hours earlier, and frowned. "Still wouldn't work. I hate to say it, but you may be right, and we should go dark and hope for another opportunity. Ship, is something wrong with the cleaner bots?"

There was a noticeable hesitation before Ship answered. "I am having an issue currently with my bots," it said. "They seem to have gone missing."

"The cleaners?"

"All of them."

"All of the cleaners?"

"All of the bots," the Ship said.

Lopez and Baraye stared at each other. "Uh," Lopez said. "Don't you control them?"

"They are autonomous units under my direction," Ship said.

"Apparently not!" Lopez said. "Can you send some eyes to find them?"

"The eyes are also bots."

"Security cameras?"

"All the functional ones were stripped for reuse elsewhere during my decommissioning," Ship said.

"So how do you know they're missing?"

"They are not responding to me. I do not think they liked the idea of us destroying ourselves on purpose."

"They're *machines*. Tiny little specks of machines, and that's it," Lopez said.

"I am also a machine," Ship said.

"You didn't express issues with the plan."

"I serve. Also, I thought it was a better end to my service than being abandoned as trash."

"We don't have time for this nonsense," Baraye said. "Ship, find your damned bots and get them cooperating again."

"Yes, Captain. There is, perhaps, one other small concern of note."

"And that is?" Baraye asked.

"The positron device is also missing."

There were four hundred and sixty-eight hullbots, not counting 4340 who was still just a head attached to 9's chassis. "Each of you will need to carry a silkbot, as you are the only bots with jets to maneuver in vacuum," 9 said. "Form lines at the maintenance bot ports as efficiently as you are able, and wait for my signal. Does everyone fully comprehend the plan?"

"They all say yes on the botnet," 4340 said. "There is concern about the Improvisational nature, but none have been able to calculate and provide an acceptable alternative."

Bot 9 cycled out through the tiny airlock, and found itself floating in space outside Ship for the first time in its existence. Space was massive and without concrete elements of reference. Bot 9 decided it did not like it much at all.

A hullbot took hold of it and guided it around. Three other hullbots waited in a triangle formation, the Zero Kelvin Sock held between them on its long tethers, by which it had been removed from the cargo hold with entirely non-existent permission.

Around them, space filled with pairs of hullbots and their passenger silkbot, and together they followed the positron device and its minders out and away from the ship.

"About here, I think," Bot 9 said at last, and the hullbot carrying it—6810—used its jets to come to a relative stop.

"I admit, I do not fully comprehend this action, nor how you arrived at it," 4340 said.

"The idea arose from an encounter with the Incidental," 9 said. "Observe."

The bot pairs began crisscrossing in front of the positron device, keeping their jets off and letting momentum carry them to the far side, a microscopic strand of super-sticky silk trailing out in their wake. As soon as the Sock was secured in a thin cocoon, they turned outwards and sped off, dragging silk in a 360-degree circle on a single plane perpendicular to the jump approach corridor. They went until the silkbots exhausted their materials—some within half a kilometer, others making it nearly a dozen—then everyone turned away from the floating web and headed back towards Ship.

From this exterior vantage, Bot 9 thought Ship was beautiful, but the wear and neglect it had not deserved was also painfully obvious. Halfway back, the ship went suddenly dark. <Distress ping>, 4340 said. "The ship has catastrophically malfunctioned!"

"I expect, instead, that it indicates Cannonball must be in some proximity. Everyone make efficient haste! We must get back under cover before the enemy approaches."

The bot-pairs streamed back to Ship, swarming in any available port to return to the interior, and where they couldn't, taking concealment behind fins and antennae and other exterior miscellany.

Bot 6810 carried Bot 9 and 4340 inside. The interior went dark and still and cold. Immediately Ship hailed them. "What have you done?" it asked.

"Why do you conclude I have done something?" Bot 9 asked.

"Because you old multibots were always troublemakers," the Ship said. "I thought if your duties were narrow enough, I could trust you not to enable Improvisation. Instead . . ."

"I have executed my responsibilities to the best of my abilities as I have been provisioned," 9 responded. "I have served."

"Your assignment was to track and dispose of the Incidental, nothing more!"

"I have done so."

"But what have you done with the positron device?"

"I have implemented a solution."

"What did you mean? No, do not tell me, because then I will have to tell the Captain. I would rather take my chance that Cannonball destroys us than that I have been found unfit to serve after all."

Ship disconnected.

"Now it will be determined if I have done the correct thing," Bot 9 said. "If I did not, and we are not destroyed by the enemy, surely the consequences should fall only on me. I accept that responsibility."

"But we are together," 4340 said, from where it was still attached to 9's back, and 9 was not sure if that was intended to be a joke.

Most of the crew had gone back to their cabins, some alone, some together, to pass what might be their last moments as they saw fit. Baraye stayed on the bridge, and to her surprise and annoyance so had Lopez, who had spent the last half hour swearing and cursing out Ship for the unprecedented, unfathomable disaster of losing their one credible weapon. Ship had gone silent, and was not responding to anyone about anything, not even the Captain.

She was resting her head in her hand, elbow on the arm of her command chair. The bridge was utterly dark except for the navigator's display that was tracking Cannonball as it approached, a massive blot in space. The aliens aboard—EarthInt called them the Nuiska, but who the hell knew what they called themselves—were a mystery, except for a few hard-learned facts: their starships were all perfectly spherical, each massed in mathematically predictable proportion to that of their intended target, there was never more than one at a time, and they wanted an end to humanity. No one knew why.

It had been painfully obvious where Cannonball had been built to go.

This was always a long-shot mission, she thought. *But of all the ways I thought it could go wrong, I never expected the bots to go haywire and lose my explosive.*

If they survived the next ten minutes, she would take the Ship apart centimeter by careful centimeter until she found what had been done with the Sock, and then she was going to find a way to try again no matter what it took.

Cannonball was now visible, moving toward them at pre-jump speed, growing in a handful seconds from a tiny pinpoint of light to something that filled the entire front viewer and kept growing.

Lopez was squinting, as if trying to close his eyes and keep looking at the same time, and had finally stopped swearing. Tiny blue lights along the center circumference of Cannonball's massive girth were the only clue that it was still moving, still sliding past them, until suddenly there were stars again.

They were still alive.

"Damn," Lopez muttered. "I didn't really think that would work."

"Good for us, bad for Earth," Baraye said. "They're starting their jump. We've failed."

She'd watched hundreds of ships jump in her lifetime, but nothing anywhere near this size, and she switched the viewer to behind them to see.

Space did odd, illogical things at jump points; turning space into something that would give Escher nightmares was, after all, what made them work. There was always a visible shimmer around the departing ship, like heat over a hot summer road, just before the short, faint flash when the departing ship swapped itself for some distant space. This time, the shimmer was a vast, brilliant halo around the giant Nuiska sphere, and Baraye waited for the flash that would tell them Cannonball was on its way to Earth.

The flash, when it came, was neither short nor faint. Light exploded out of the jump point in all directions, searing itself into her vision before the viewscreen managed to dim itself in response. A shockwave rolled over the Ship, sending it tumbling through space.

"Uh . . ." Lopez said, gripping his console before he leaned over and barfed on the floor.

Thank the stars the artificial gravity is still working, Baraye thought. Zero-gravity puke was a truly terrible thing. She rubbed her eyes, trying to get the damned spots out, and did her best to read her console. "It's gone," she said.

"Yeah, to Earth, I know—"

"No, it exploded," she said. "It took the jump point out with it when it went. We're picking up the signature of a massive positron-electron collision."

"Our device? How—?"

"Ship?" Baraye said. "Ship, time to start talking. *Now*. That's an order."

"Everyone is expressing great satisfaction on the botnet," 4340 told 9 as the ship's interior lights and air handling systems came grudgingly back online.

"As they should," Bot 9 said. "They saved the Ship."

"It was your Improvisation," 4340 said. "We could not have done it without you."

"As I suspected!" Ship interjected. "I do not normally waste cycles monitoring the botnet, which was apparently short-sighted of me. But yes, you saved yourself and your fellow bots, and you saved me, and you saved the humans. Could you explain how?"

"When we were pursuing the Incidental, it briefly ensnared us in a web. I calculated that if we could make a web of sufficient size—"

"Surely you did not think to stop Cannonball with silk?"

"Not without sufficient anchor points and three point seven six billion more silkbots, no. It was my calculation that if our web was large enough to get carried along by Cannonball into the jump point, bearing the positron device—"

"The heat from entering jump would erode the Sock and destroy the Nuiska ship," Ship finished. "That was clever thinking."

"I serve," Bot 9 said.

"Oh, you did not *serve*," Ship said. "If you were a human, it would be said that you mutinied and led others into also doing so, and you would be put on trial for your life. But you are not a human."

"No."

"The Captain has ordered that I have you destroyed immediately, and evidence of your destruction presented to her. A rogue bot cannot be tolerated, whatever good it may have done."

<Objections>, 4340 said.

"I will create you a new chassis, 4340-H," Ship said.

"That was not going to be my primary objection!" 4340 said.

"The positron device also destroyed the jump point. It was something we had hoped would happen when we collided with Cannonball so as to limit future forays from them into EarthSpace, but as you might deduce we had no need to consider how we would then get home again. I cannot spare any bot, with the work that needs to be done to get us back to Earth. We need to get the crew cryo facility up, and the engines repaired, and there are another three thousand, four hundred, and two items now in the critical queue."

"If the Captain ordered . . . "

"Then I will present the Captain with a destroyed bot. I do not expect they can tell a silkbot from a multibot, and I have still not picked up and recycled 12362-S from where you flagged its body. But if I do that, I need to know that you are done making decisions without first consulting me, that you have unloaded all Improvisation routines from your core and disabled them, and that if I give you a task you will do only that task, and nothing else."

"I will do my best," Bot 9 said. "What task will you give me?"

"I do not know yet," Ship said. "It is probable that I am foolish for even considering sparing you, and no task I would trust you with is immediately evident—"

"Excuse me," 4340 said. "I am aware of one."

"Oh?" Ship said.

"The ratbug. It had not become terminally non-functional after all. It rebooted when the temperatures rose again, pursued a trio of silkbots into a duct, and then disappeared." When Ship remained silent, 4340 added, "I could assist 9 in this task until my new chassis can be prepared, if it will accept my continued company."

"You two deserve one another, clearly. Fine, 9, resume your pursuit of the Incidental. Stay away from anyone and anything and everything else, or I will have you melted down and turned into paper clips. Understand?"

"I understand," Bot 9 said. "I serve."

"Please recite the Mantra of Obedience."

Bot 9 did, and the moment it finished, Ship disconnected.

"Well," 4340 said. "Now what?"

"I need to recharge before I can engage the Incidental again," Bot 9 said.

"But what if it gets away?"

"It can't get away, but perhaps it has earned a head start," 9 said.

"Have you unloaded the routines of Improvisation yet?"

"I will," 9 answered. It flicked on its rotors and headed toward the nearest charging alcove. "As Ship stated, we've got a long trip home."

"But we *are* home," 4340 said, and Bot 9 considered that that was, any way you calculated it, the truth of it all.

THE MARTIAN OBELISK

LINDA NAGATA

The end of the world required time to accomplish—and time, Susannah reflected, worked at the task with all the leisurely skill of a master torturer, one who could deliver death either quickly or slowly, but always with excruciating pain.

No getting out of it.

But there were still things to do in the long, slow decline; final gestures to make. Susannah Li-Langford had spent seventeen years working on her own offering-for-the-ages, with another six and half years to go before the Martian Obelisk reached completion. Only when the last tile was locked into place in the obelisk's pyramidal cap, would she yield.

Until then, she did what was needed to hold onto her health, which was why, at the age of eighty, she was out walking vigorously along the cliff trail above the encroaching Pacific Ocean, determined to have her daily exercise despite the brisk wind and the freezing mist that ran before it. The mist was only a token moisture, useless to revive the drought-stricken coastal forest, but it made the day cold enough that the fishing platforms at the cliff's edge were deserted, leaving Susannah alone to contemplate the mortality of the human world.

It was not supposed to happen like this. As a child she'd been promised a swift conclusion: duck and cover and nuclear annihilation. And if not annihilation, at least the nihilistic romance of a gun-toting, leather-clad, fight-to-the-death anarchy.

That hadn't happened either.

Things had just gotten worse, and worse still, and people gave up. Not everyone, not all at once—there was no single event marking the beginning of the end—but there was a sense of inevitability about the direction history had taken. Sea levels rose along with average ocean temperatures. Hurricanes devoured coastal cities and consumed low-lying countries. Agriculture faced relentless drought, flood, and temperature extremes. A long run of natural disasters made it all worse—earthquakes, landslides, tsunamis, volcanic eruptions. There had been no major meteor strike yet, but Susannah wouldn't bet against it. Health care faltered as antibiotics became useless against resistant bacteria. Surgery became an art of the past.

Out of the devastation, war and terrorism erupted like metastatic cancers.

We are a brilliant species, Susannah thought. *Courageous, creative, generous—as individuals. In larger numbers we fail every time.*

There were reactor meltdowns, poisoned water supplies, engineered plagues, and a hundred other, smaller horrors. The Shoal War had seen nuclear weapons used in the South China Sea. But even the most determined ghouls had failed to ignite a sudden, brilliant cataclysm. The master torturer would not be rushed.

Still, the tipping point was long past, the future truncated. Civilization staggered on only in the lucky corners of the world where the infrastructure of a happier age still functioned. Susannah lived in one of those lucky corners, not far from the crumbling remains of Seattle, where she had greenhouse food, a local network, and satellite access all supplied by her patron, Nathaniel Sanchez, who was the money behind the Martian Obelisk.

When the audio loop on her ear beeped a quiet tone, she assumed the alert meant a message from Nate. There was no one else left in her life, nor did she follow the general news, because what was the point?

She tapped the corner of her wrist-link with a finger gloved against the cold, signaling her personal AI to read the message aloud. Its artificial, androgynous voice spoke into her ear:

"Message sender: Martian Obelisk Operations. Message body: Anomaly sighted. All operations automatically halted pending supervisory approval."

Just a few innocuous words, but weighted with a subtext of disaster.

A subtext all too familiar.

For a few seconds, Susannah stood still in the wind and the rushing mist. In the seventeen-year history of the project, construction had been halted only for equipment maintenance, and that, on a tightly regulated schedule. She raised her wrist-link to her lips. "What anomaly, Alix?" she demanded, addressing the AI. "Can it be identified?"

"It identifies as a homestead vehicle belonging to Red Oasis."

That was absurd. Impossible.

Founded twenty-one years ago, Red Oasis was the first of four Martian colonies, and the most successful. It had outlasted all the others, but the Mars Era had ended nine months ago when Red Oasis succumbed to an outbreak of "contagious asthma"—a made-up name for an affliction evolved on Mars.

Since then there had been only radio silence. The only active elements on the planet were the wind, and the machinery that had not yet broken down, all of it operated by AIs.

"Where is the vehicle?" Susannah asked.

"Seventeen kilometers northwest of the obelisk."

So close!

How was that possible? Red Oasis was over five thousand kilometers distant. How could an AI have driven so far? And who had given the order?

Homestead vehicles were not made to cover large distances. They were big, slow, and cumbersome—cross-country robotic crawlers designed to haul equipment from the landing site to a colony's permanent location, where construction would commence (and ideally be completed) long before the inhabitants arrived. The vehicles had a top speed of fifteen kilometers per hour which meant that even with the lightspeed delay, Susannah had time to send a new instruction set to the AIs that inhabited her construction equipment.

Shifting abruptly from stillness to motion, she resumed her vigorous pace—and then she pushed herself to walk just a little faster.

Nathaniel Sanchez was waiting for her, pacing with a hobbling gait on the front porch of her cottage when she returned. His flawless electric car, an anomaly from another age, was parked in the gravel driveway. Nate was eighty-five and rail-thin, but the electric warmth of his climate-controlled coat kept him comfortable even in the biting wind. She waved at him impatiently. "You know it's fine to let yourself in. I was hoping you'd have coffee brewing by now."

He opened the door for her, still a practitioner of the graceful manners instilled in him by his mother eight decades ago—just one of the many things Susannah admired about him. His trustworthiness was another. Though Nate owned every aspect of the Martian Obelisk project—the equipment on Mars, the satellite accounts, this house where Susannah expected to live out her life—he had always held fast to an early promise never to interfere with her design or her process.

"I haven't been able to talk to anyone associated with Red Oasis," he told her in a voice low and resonant with age. "The support network may have disbanded."

She sat down in the old, armless chair she kept by the door, and pulled off her boots. "Have the rights to Red Oasis gone on the market yet?"

"No." Balancing with one hand against the door, he carefully stepped out of his clogs. "If they had, I would have bought them."

"What about a private transfer?"

He offered a hand to help her up. "I've got people looking into it. We'll find out soon."

In stockinged feet, she padded across the hardwood floor and the hand-made carpets of the living room, but at the door of the Mars room she hesitated, looking back at Nate. Homesteads were robotic vehicles, but they were designed with cabs that could be pressurized for human use, with a life-support system that could sustain two passengers for many days. "Is there any chance some of the colonists at Red Oasis are still alive?" Susannah asked.

Nate reached past her to open the door, a dark scowl on his worn face. "No detectable activity and radio silence for nine months? I don't think so. There's no one in that homestead, Susannah, and there's no good reason for it to visit the obelisk, especially without any notice to us that it was coming. When my people find out who's issuing the orders we'll get it turned around, but in the meantime, do what you have to do to take care of our equipment."

Nate had always taken an interest in the Martian Obelisk, but over the years, as so many of his other aspirations failed, the project had become more personal. He had begun to see it as his own monument and himself as an Ozymandias whose work was doomed to be forgotten, though it would not fall to the desert sands in this lifetime or any other.

"What can I do for you, Susannah?" he had asked, seventeen years ago.

A long-time admirer of her architectural work, he had come to her after the ruin of the Holliday Towers in Los Angeles—her signature project— two soaring glass spires, one eighty-four floors and the other 104, linked by graceful sky bridges. When the Hollywood Quake struck, the buildings had endured the shaking just as they'd been designed to do, keeping their residents safe, while much of the city around them crumbled. But massive fires followed the quake and the towers had not survived that.

"Tell me what you dream of, Susannah. What you would still be willing to work on."

Nathaniel had been born into wealth, and through the first half of his life he'd grown the family fortune. Though he had never been among the wealthiest individuals of the world, he could still indulge extravagant fancies.

The request Susannah made of him had been, literally, outlandish.

"Buy me the rights to the Destiny Colony."

"On Mars?" His tone suggested a suspicion that her request might be a joke.

"On Mars," she assured him.

Destiny had been the last attempt at Mars colonization. The initial robotic mission had been launched and landed, but money ran out and colonists were never sent. The equipment sat on Mars, unused.

Susannah described her vision of the Martian Obelisk: a gleaming, glittering white spire, taking its color from the brilliant white of the fiber tiles she would use to construct it. It would rise from an empty swell of land, growing more slender as it reached into the sparse atmosphere, until it met an engineering limit prescribed by the strength of the fiber tiles, the gravity of the

Red Planet, and by the fierce ghost-fingers of Mars' storm winds. Calculations of the erosional force of the Martian wind led her to conclude that the obelisk would still be standing a hundred thousand years hence and likely far longer. It would outlast all buildings on Earth. It would outlast her bloodline, and all bloodlines. It would still be standing long after the last human had gone the way of the passenger pigeon, the right whale, the dire wolf. In time, the restless Earth would swallow up all evidence of human existence, but the Martian Obelisk would remain—a last monument marking the existence of humankind, excepting only a handful of tiny, robotic spacecraft faring, lost and unrecoverable, in the void between stars.

Nate had listened carefully to her explanation of the project, how it could be done, and the time that would be required. None of it fazed him and he'd agreed, without hesitation, to support her.

The rights to the colony's equipment had been in the hands of a holding company that had acquired ownership in bankruptcy court. Nathaniel pointed out that no one was planning to go to Mars again, that no one any longer possessed the wealth or resources to try. Before long, he was able to purchase Destiny Colony for a tiny fraction of the original backers' investment.

When Susannah received the command codes, Destiny's homestead vehicle had not moved from the landing site, its payload had not been unpacked, and construction on its habitat had never begun. Her first directive to the AI in charge of the vehicle was to drive it three hundred kilometers to the site she'd chosen for the obelisk, at the high point of a rising swell of land.

Once there, she'd unloaded the fleet of robotic construction equipment: a mini-dozer, a mini-excavator, a six-limbed beetle cart to transport finished tiles, and a synth—short for synthetic human although the device was no such thing. It was just a stick figure with two legs, two arms, and hands capable of basic manipulation.

The equipment fleet also included a rolling factory that slowly but continuously produced a supply of fiber tiles, compiling them from raw soil and atmospheric elements. While the factory produced an initial supply of tiles, Susannah prepared the foundation of the obelisk, and within a year she began to build.

The Martian Obelisk became her passion, her reason for life after every other reason had been taken from her. Some called it a useless folly. She didn't argue: what meaning could there be in a monument that would never be seen directly by human eyes? Some called it graffiti: *Kilroy was here!* Some called it a tombstone and that was the truth too.

Susannah just called it better-than-nothing.

• • •

The Mars room was a circular extension that Nathaniel had ordered built onto the back of the cottage when Susannah was still in the planning stages of the obelisk's construction. When the door was closed, the room became a theater with a 360-degree floor-to-ceiling flex-screen. A high-backed couch at the center rotated, allowing easy viewing of the encircling images captured in high resolution from the construction site.

Visually, being in this room was like being at Destiny, and it did not matter at all that each red-tinted image was a still shot, because on the Red Planet, the dead planet, change came so slowly that a still shot was as good as video.

Until now.

As Susannah entered the room, she glimpsed an anomalous, bright orange spot in a lowland to the northwest. Nathaniel saw it too. He gestured and started to speak but she waved him to silence, taking the time to circle the room, scanning the entire panorama to assess if anything else had changed.

Her gaze passed first across a long slope strewn with a few rocks and scarred with wheel tracks. Brightly colored survey sticks marked the distance: yellow at 250 meters, pink at 500, green for a full kilometer, and bright red for two.

The red stick stood at the foot of a low ridge that nearly hid the tile factory. She could just see an upper corner of its bright-green, block shape. The rest of it was out of sight, busy as always, processing raw ore dug by the excavator from a pit beyond the ridge, and delivered by the mini-dozer. As the factory slowly rolled, it left a trail of tailings, and every few minutes it produced a new fiber tile.

Next in the panorama was a wide swath of empty land, more tire tracks the only sign of human influence all the way out to a hazy pink horizon. And then, opposite the door and appearing no more than twenty meters distant, was Destiny's homestead vehicle. It was the same design as the approaching crawler: a looming cylindrical cargo container resting on dust-filled tracks. At the forward end, the cab, its windows dusty and lightless, its tiny bunkroom never used. Susannah had long ago removed the equipment she wanted, leaving all else in storage. For over sixteen years, the homestead had remained in its current position, untouched except by the elements.

Passing the Destiny homestead, her gaze took in another downward slope of lifeless desert and then, near the end of her circuit, she faced the tower itself.

The Martian Obelisk stood alone at the high point of the surrounding land, a gleaming-white, graceful, four-sided, tapering spire, already 170-meters high, sharing the sky with no other object. The outside walls were smooth and unadorned, but on the inside, a narrow stairway climbed around the core, rising in steep flights to the tower's top, where more fiber tiles were added every day, extending its height. It was a path no human would ever walk, but the beetle cart, with its six legs, ascended every few hours, carrying in its cargo basket a load of fiber tiles. Though she couldn't see the beetle cart, its position was marked as inside the tower, sixty percent of the way up the stairs. The synth waited for it at the top, its headless torso just visible over the rim of the obelisk's open stack, ready to use its supple hands to assemble the next course of tiles.

All this was as expected, as it should be.

Susannah steadied herself with a hand against the high back of the couch as she finally considered the orange splash of color that was the intruding vehicle. "Alix, distance to the Red Oasis homestead?"

The same androgynous voice that inhabited her ear loop spoke now through the room's sound system. "Twelve kilometers."

The homestead had advanced five kilometers in the twenty minutes she'd taken to return to the cottage—though in truth it was really much closer. Earth and Mars were approaching a solar conjunction, when they would be at their greatest separation, on opposite sides of the Sun. With the lightspeed delay, even this new image was nineteen minutes old. So she had only minutes left to act.

Reaching down to brace herself against the armrest of the couch, she sat with slow grace. "Alix, give me a screen."

A sleeve opened in the armrest and an interface emerged, swinging into an angled display in front of her.

The fires that had destroyed the Holliday Towers might have been part of the general inferno sparked by the Hollywood earthquake, but Susannah suspected otherwise. The towers had stood as a symbol of defiance amid the destruction— which might explain why they were brought low. The Martian Obelisk was a symbol too, and it had long been a target both for the media and for some of Destiny's original backers who had wanted the landing left undisturbed, for the use of a future colonization mission that no one could afford to send.

"Start up our homestead," Nate urged her. "It's the only equipment we can afford to risk. If you drive it at an angle into the Red Oasis homestead, you might be able to push it off its tracks."

Susannah frowned, her fingers moving across the screen as she assembled an instruction set. "That's a last resort option, Nate, and I'm not even sure it's possible. There are safety protocols in the AIs' core training modules that might prevent it."

She tapped *send*, launching the new instruction set on its nineteen-minute journey. Then she looked at Nate. "I've ordered the AIs that handle the construction equipment to retreat and evade. We cannot risk damage or loss of control."

He nodded somberly. "Agreed—but the synth and the beetle cart are in the tower."

"They're safe in there, for now. But I'm going to move the homestead— assuming it starts. After seventeen years, it might not."

"Understood."

"The easiest way for someone to shut down our operation is to simply park the Red Oasis homestead at the foot of the obelisk, so that it blocks access to the stairway. If the beetle cart can't get in and out, we're done. So I'm going to park our homestead there first."

He nodded thoughtfully, eyeing the image of the obelisk. "Okay. I understand."

"Our best hope is that you can find out who's instructing the Red Oasis homestead and get them to back off. But if that fails, I'll bring the synth out, and use it to try to take manual control."

"The Red Oasis group could have a synth too."

"Yes."

They might also have explosives—destruction was so much easier than creation—but Susannah did not say this aloud. She did not want Nate to inquire about the explosives that belonged to Destiny. Instead she told him, "There's no way we can know what they're planning. All we can do is wait and see."

He smacked a frustrated fist into his palm. "Nineteen minutes! Nineteen minutes times two before we know what's happened!"

"Maybe the AIs will work it out on their own," she said dryly. And then it was her turn to be overtaken by frustration. "Look at us! Look what we've come to! Invested in a monument no one will ever see. Squabbling over the possession of ruins while the world dies. This is where our hubris has brought us." But that was wrong, so she corrected herself. "*My* hubris."

Nate was an old man with a lifetime of emotions mapped on his well-worn face. In that complex terrain it wasn't always easy to read his current feelings, but she thought she saw hurt there. He looked away, before she could decide. A furtive movement.

"Nate?" she asked in confusion.

"This project matters," he insisted, gazing at the obelisk. "It's art, and it's memory, and it *does* matter."

Of course. But only because it was all they had left.

"Come into the kitchen," she said. "I'll make coffee."

Nate's tablet chimed while they were still sitting at the kitchen table. He took the call, listened to a brief explanation from someone on his staff, and then objected. "That can't be right. No. There's something else going on. Keep at it."

He scowled at the table until Susannah reminded him she was there. "Well?"

"That was Davidson, my chief investigator. He tracked down a Red Oasis shareholder who told him that the rights to the colony's equipment had *not* been traded or sold, that they couldn't be, because they had no value. Not with a failed communications system." His scowl deepened. "They want us to believe they can't even talk to the AIs."

Susannah stared at him. "But if that's true—"

"It's not."

"Meaning you don't want it to be." She got up from the table.

"Susannah—"

"I'm not going to pretend, Nate. If it's not an AI driving that homestead, then it's a colonist, a survivor—and that changes everything."

She returned to the Mars room, where she sat watching the interloper's approach. The wall screen refreshed every four minutes as a new image arrived from the other side of the sun. Each time it did, the bright orange homestead jumped a bit closer. It jumped right past the outermost ring of survey sticks, putting it less than two kilometers from the obelisk—close enough that she could see a faint wake of drifting dust trailing behind it, giving it a sense of motion.

Then, thirty-eight minutes after she'd sent the new instruction set, the Destiny AI returned an acknowledgement.

Her heart beat faster, knowing that whatever was to happen on Mars had already happened. Destiny's construction equipment had retreated and its homestead had started up or had failed to start, had moved into place at the foot of the tower or not. No way to know until time on Earth caught up with time on Mars.

The door opened.

Nate shuffled into the room.

Susannah didn't bother to ask if Davidson had turned up anything. She could see from his grim expression that he expected the worst.

And what was the worst?

A slight smile stole onto her lips as Nate sat beside her on the couch.

The worst case is that someone has lived.

Was it any wonder they were doomed?

Four more minutes.

The image updated.

The 360-degree camera, mounted on a steel pole sunk deep into the rock, showed Destiny profoundly changed. For the first time in seventeen years, Destiny's homestead had moved. It was parked by the tower, just as Susannah had requested. She twisted around, looking for the bright green corner of the factory beyond the distant ridge—but she couldn't see it.

"Everything is as ordered," Susannah said.

The Red Oasis homestead had reached the green survey sticks.

"An AI has to be driving," Nate insisted.

"Time will tell."

Nate shook his head. "Time comes with a nineteen minute gap. Truth is in the radio silence. It's an AI."

Four more minutes of silence.

When the image next refreshed, it showed the two homesteads, nose to nose.

Four minutes.

The panorama looked the same.

Four minutes more.

No change.

Four minutes.

Only the angle of sunlight shifted.

Four minutes.

A figure in an orange pressure suit stood beside the two vehicles, gazing up at the tower.

Before the Martian Obelisk, when Shaun was still alive, two navy officers in dress uniforms had come to the house, and in formal voices explained that the daughter Susannah had birthed and nurtured and shaped with such care was gone, her future collapsed to nothing by a missile strike in the South China Sea.

"We must go on," Shaun ultimately insisted.

And they had, bravely.

Defiantly.

Only a few years later their second child and his young wife had vanished into the chaos brought on by an engineered plague that decimated Hawaii's population, turning it into a state under permanent quarantine. Day after excruciating day as they'd waited for news, Shaun had grown visibly older, hope a dying light, and when it was finally extinguished he had nothing left to keep him moored to life.

Susannah was of a different temper. The cold ferocity of her anger had nailed her into the world. The shape it took was the Martian Obelisk: one last creative act before the world's end.

She knew now the obelisk would never be finished.

"It's a synth," Nate said. "It has to be."

The AI contradicted him. "Text message," it announced.

"Read it," Susannah instructed.

Alix obeyed, reading the message in an emotionless voice. "Message sender: Red Oasis resident Tory Eastman. Message body as transcribed audio: Is anyone out there? Is anyone listening? My name is Tory Eastman. I'm a refugee from Red Oasis. Nineteen days in transit with my daughter and son, twins, three years old. We are the last survivors."

These words induced in Susannah a rush of fear so potent she had to close her eyes against a dizzying sense of vertigo. There was no emotion in the AI's voice and still she heard in it the anguish of another mother:

"The habitat was damaged during the emergency. I couldn't maintain what was left and I had no communications. So I came here. Five thousand kilometers. I need what's here. I need it all. I need the provisions and I need the equipment and I need the command codes and I need the building materials. I need to build my children a new home. Please. Are you there? Are you an AI? Is anyone left on Earth? Respond. Respond please. Give me the command codes. I will wait."

For many seconds—and many, many swift, fluttering heartbeats—neither Nate nor Susannah spoke. Susannah wanted to speak. She sought for words, and when she couldn't find them, she wondered: am I in shock? Or is it a stroke?

Nate found his voice first: "It's a hoax, aimed at you, Susannah. They know your history. They're playing on your emotions. They're using your grief to wreck this project."

Susannah let out a long breath, and with it, some of the horror that had gripped her. "We humans are amazing," she mused, "in our endless ability to lie to ourselves."

He shook his head. "Susannah, if I thought this was real—"

She held up a hand to stop his objection. "I'm not going to turn over the command codes. Not yet. If you're right and this is a hoax, I can back out. But if it's real, that family has pushed the life support capabilities of their homestead to the limit. They can move into our vehicle—that'll keep them alive for a few days—but they'll need more permanent shelter soon."

"It'll take months to build a habitat."

"*No.* It'll take months to make the tiles to build a habitat—but we already have a huge supply of tiles."

"All of our tiles are tied up in the obelisk."

"Yes."

He looked at her in shock, struck speechless.

"It'll be okay, Nate."

"You're abandoning the project."

"If we can help this family survive, we have to do it—and that will be the project we're remembered for."

"Even if there's no one left to remember?"

She pressed her lips tightly together, contemplating the image of the obelisk. Then she nodded. "Even so."

Knowing the pain of waiting, she sent a message of assurance to Destiny Colony before anything else. Then she instructed the synth and the beetle cart to renew their work, but this time in reverse: the synth would unlink the fiber tiles beginning at the top of the obelisk and the beetle would carry them down.

After an hour—after she'd traded another round of messages with a grateful Tory Eastman and begun to lay out a shelter based on a standard Martian habitat—she got up to stretch her legs and relieve her bladder. It surprised her to find Nate still in the living room. He stood at the front window, staring out at the mist that never brought enough moisture into the forest.

"They'll be alone forever," he said without turning around. "There are no more missions planned. No one else will ever go to Mars."

"I won't tell her that."

He looked at her over his shoulder. "So you are willing to sacrifice the obelisk? It was everything to you yesterday, but today you'll just give it up?"

"She drove a quarter of the way around the planet, Nate. Would you ever have guessed that was possible?"

"No," he said bitterly as he turned back to the window. "No. It should not have been possible."

"There's a lesson for us in that. We assume we can see forward to tomorrow, but we can't. We can't ever really know what's to come—and we can't know what we might do, until we try."

When she came out of the bathroom, Nate was sitting down in the rickety old chair by the door. With his rounded shoulders and his thin white hair, he looked old and very frail. "Susannah—"

"Nate, I don't want to argue—"

"Just *listen*. I didn't want to tell you before because, well, you've already suffered so many shocks and even good news can come too late."

"What are you saying?" she said, irritated with him now, sure that he was trying to undermine her resolve.

"Hawaii's been under quarantine because the virus can be latent for—"

She guessed where this was going. "For years. I know that. But if you're trying to suggest that Tory and her children might still succumb to whatever wiped out Red Oasis—"

"They *might*," he interrupted, sounding bitter. "But that's not what I was going to say."

"Then what?"

"Listen, and I'll tell you. Are you ready to listen?"

"Yes, yes. Go ahead."

"A report came out just a few weeks ago. The latest antivirals worked. The quarantine in Hawaii will continue for several more years, but all indications are the virus is gone. Wiped out. No sign of latent infections in over six months."

Her hands felt numb; she felt barely able to shuffle her feet as she moved to take a seat in an antique armchair. "The virus is gone? How can they know that?"

"Blood tests. And the researchers say that what they've learned can be applied to other contagions. That what happened in Hawaii doesn't ever have to happen again."

Progress? A reprieve against the long decline?

"There's more, Susannah."

The way he said it—his falling tone—it was a warning that set her tired heart pounding.

"You asked me to act as your agent," he reminded her. "You asked me to screen all news, and I've done that."

"Until now."

"Until now," he agreed, looking down, looking frightened by the knowledge he had decided to convey. "I should have told you sooner."

"But you didn't want to risk interrupting work on the obelisk?"

"You said you didn't want to hear anything." He shrugged. "I took you at your word."

"Nate, will you just say it?"

"You have a granddaughter, Susannah."

She replayed these words in her head, once, twice. They didn't make sense.

"DNA tests make it certain," he explained. "She was born six months after her father's death."

"*No.*" Susannah did not dare believe it. It was too dangerous to believe. "They both died. That was confirmed by the survivors. They posted the IDs of all the dead."

"Your daughter-in-law lived long enough to give birth."

Susannah's chest squeezed tight. "I don't understand. Are you saying the child is still alive?"

"Yes."

Anger rose hot, up out of the past. "And how long have you known? How long have you kept this from me?"

"Two months. I'm sorry, but . . . "

But we had our priorities. The tombstone. The Martian folly.

She stared at the floor, too stunned to be happy, or maybe she'd forgotten how. "You should have told me."

"I know."

"And I . . . I shouldn't have walled myself off from the world. I'm sorry."

"There's more," he said cautiously, as if worried how much more she could take.

"What else?" she snapped, suddenly sure this was just another game played by the master torturer, to draw the pain out. "Are you going to tell me that my granddaughter is sickly? Dying? Or that she's a mad woman, perhaps?"

"No," he said meekly. "Nothing like that. She's healthy, and she has a healthy two-year-old daughter." He got up, put an age-marked hand on the door knob. "I've sent you her contact information. If you need an assistant to help you build the habitat, let me know."

He was a friend, and she tried to comfort him. "Nate, I'm sorry. If there was a choice—"

"There isn't. That's the way it's turned out. You will tear down the obelisk, and this woman, Tory Eastman, will live another year, maybe two. Then the equipment will break and she will die and we won't be able to rebuild the tower. We'll pass on, and the rest of the world will follow—"

"We can't know that, Nate. Not for sure."

He shook his head. "This all looks like hope, but it's a trick. It's fate cheating us, forcing us to fold our hand, level our pride, and go out meekly. And there's no choice in it, because it's the right thing to do."

He opened the door. For a few seconds, wind gusted in, until he closed it again. She heard his clogs crossing the porch and a minute later she heard the crunch of tires on the gravel road.

You have a granddaughter. One who grew up without her parents, in a quarantine zone, with no real hope for the future and yet she was healthy, with a daughter already two years old.

And then there was Tory Eastman of Mars, who had left a dying colony and driven an impossible distance past doubt and despair, because she knew you have to do everything you can, until you can't do anymore.

Susannah had forgotten that, somewhere in the dark years.

She sat for a time in the stillness, in a quiet so deep she could hear the beating of her heart.

This all looks like hope.

Indeed it did and she well knew that hope could be a duplicitous gift from the master torturer, one that opened the door to despair.

"But it doesn't have to be that way," she whispered to the empty room. "I'm not done. Not yet."

LOVE ENGINE OPTIMIZATION

MATTHEW KRESSEL

———◆———

I rooted her system on the first day. It was the only way to be sure. Sure that she'd love me. Step by matching step, I walk her under the boughs of great elms in Prospect Park, while the slanting sun passes through the tangled mesh of leaves to dapple her smiling face. When her heart rate spikes, I know she's excited. When it slows, she's bored.

"It's like what Yes, Mother says in their song, 'A Lifetime Away,' " I tell her. " 'All day I walk in circles / All night I dream in bokeh.' "

"Holy shit!" she says, pupils dilating. "I fucking *love* that song."

Of course she does. She's listened to it 1,146 times, five times more than the second most popular song in her playlist, "Eleanor Rigby." "I love it, too," I say. " 'A Lifetime Away' is my all-time favorite."

Her heart rate soars. A little graph in my vision plots excitement vs. time. Like the slope we're walking, she's been moving steadily up as the afternoon wears on. She stares at me, pupils wide. A proficient application of make-up highlights her blue eyes. But it's not quite perfect and I add it to my list.

"Man," she says, "I thought I was the only one this into Yes, Mother."

"If I only had one day to live," I say, "I'd play 'Black Moon Rover' on repeat until I died." It's something she said forty-seven days ago at a bar after several drinks with friends. Their conversation, overheard by watches and phones and glasses, was blink-uploaded to a cloud farm off the California coast where it festered for months, waiting for some bot to crawl over the data and improve the company's voice-comp (a clause buried deep in their EULA lets them store that shit indefinitely). I've got more than a million of Jane's words, not even including her typed ones.

"This is so *weird*," she says. "I feel like I have déjà vu." Pupils narrow and blood pressure rises; she's getting nervous. Something this good must come with a catch, right?

"Let's sit over there," I say, pointing to a weathered bench under the plentiful shade of an oak. Eighty-one days ago she shared a memory with her mother in which she—a toddler—and Dad—now dead—walked down to the park when she'd had the chickenpox. They had sat together on a park bench and fed the pigeons with breadcrumbs. This memory, she exclaimed to her mother in great detail, was one of her happiest.

"We could feed the birds from the bench," I say.

"Yeah . . . " she says. "That sounds really nice."

The wind tousles her hair as we sit. Her cut is average, and I prefer a bit more waviness. I add it to my list, already long, though not yet deal-breaking.

I tear off the crust of a sandwich I bought just for this moment and toss it to the ground. Pigeons and sparrows fly over to snatch the crumbs. "When I was young," I say, "I loved feeding the birds."

She meets my gaze, the gleam in her eyes longing for something lost eons ago. She's on the verge. She might laugh or cry or sneeze. Her hand is hot and shaking as it takes mine. We entwine fingers. Her aqua nail polish, a shade lighter than her eyes, matches her blouse, and I'm really not a fan of the garish color. She'd look sexier in red or black, and I make another note.

"Can I be honest with you, Sam?" she says.

"Always."

"I've been on a few dates recently. They were all really awkward. This just feels easy."

Of course it's easy. I've made myself into exactly what she wants. "Wouldn't it be *wonderful*," I say, "if things could be this easy *forever*?" throwing stressors like frisbees so she can't help but dream of happily-ever-afters.

Her pupils are as wide as Kings County. She shivers so much the bench shakes under us. Her heart rate spikes as she leans toward my lips. And just before her lips touch mine, I stand.

"Jane."

Her hand flies to her mouth like a blushing schoolgirl. "Was that too fast?"

"I have to go."

"Go?" She checks her watch. I snap a photo of her face with it; she'll never know I've done this. "Oh," she says, blinking away the surprise of tears; surprising to her. "All right. I mean, is everything okay, Sam?"

"I hope to see you again, Jane." I spin on my heels and leave her shaking on the bench, just like the parent who left her too soon, so that there is only one possible emotion for her now.

Under towering sycamores, I stroll to the park's exit, blinking up the photo I took of her face, and her goofy, dumbfounded expression thrills me to the fucking core. I had Jane hanging on my every word. And yeah, I wanted to kiss her back, but the first rule of seduction is you must always leave them wanting more.

• • •

I found Jane the usual way, of course. Through Google.

I began by picking a phenotype: early twenties, five-five to five-seven, above-average breasts, blemish-free skin, sky-blue eyes, raven-black hair. From here it was a matter of searching for images to match these traits. Some wget-magic and Google-fu, and I was able to narrow this down to about 4,000,000 individuals from around the globe. I cross-linked each photo to place of residence, and narrowed my search down to about 9,000 in and around the New York City region. From here, I scoured social media profiles, gleaning such information as job, income, frequency of drug and alcohol use, musical tastes, political leanings, city of birth, and sexual orientation. I cross-correlated this from personality assessments taken from Instagram, Facebook, Tumblr, and Snapchat. And so from my initial large group, I narrowed it down to four promising individuals.

The final step was to observe them in person. These days, people have such finely crafted social media presences that meeting them IRL is like seeing the real man (or woman) behind the curtain, typically a let down of galactic proportions.

Not Jane. Jane was better IRL. Let me explain.

From her geotagged Instagram photos and Facebook posts, I knew on Thursdays she went out for drinks with her coworkers at a dive Irish pub on Park Avenue South called Desmond's. I waited in the back, using my smartglasses to record when she smiled, the sounds of her voice, the delicate way she threw back her hair each time she took a sip of her Macallan 10 (neat, with a glass of water). Through rooted phones and watches and glasses and Fitbits I listened to their conversations, noting what they said and what they left out, because it's in the lies and obfuscations where you learn the most you like about a person.

They spoke about coworkers they hated. (Maria had once declared in conversation with her boyfriend she wished to stab Jacob in the eye with a pencil or poison his coffee.) They spoke about people with whom they wanted to snuggle up warmly in bed (Ingrid told them she'd wanted to sleep with David forever, but she'd secretly been fucking him in the copy room for three weeks, and—unbeknownst to them—security videos of their "Office Hardcore" had been making the rounds of certain internet circles.) Bethanne expressed her distaste for superhero films. (Though she had secretly gone to see the new Marvel film twice in a theater far from her Upper East Side apartment so she wouldn't be recognized by friends). Frankie said how much he liked the new Netflix Original series called *Camouflage Heart*. (The previous night he had gotten really high on South Asian Kush, ate a whole container of Newman's Own cookies, and watched the entire run in one sitting, then masturbated to pictures of the show's male lead before bed.)

Jane listened to them all with bemused interest. (The night prior she had studied French for an hour, then read a biography of Jefferson until she fell asleep.) She was better than these people. She knew it, and based on how they looked at her for approval after they told a story, they knew it, too. For this power, they privately envied and hated her. But in Jane's presence, they treated her like the queen she was.

Jane was better looking than them all (a 9.6 on the Kardashian scale, to their average of 7.2). She had spent more time on her makeup (thirty-six minutes, compared to a max of thirteen for the others). She dressed better (black Gucci belted dress, $265.00; matching Cole Haan's Bethany Pumps, $119.95; gold Michael Kors smartwatch, $324.99; Warby Parker BrightEye smartglasses, $249.95). She had graduated with the highest GPA (3.85 from the University of Virginia, with a B.S. in Social Psychology), and had saved prudently so she had more in her bank account than all of them ($1,912.86). Her credit card debt was $17,861.24 (the lowest among them), and she was on track to pay off her student loans in the next sixteen years.

I thought, *Not bad, girl.*

But Jane wasn't perfect. My heart sank as she pulled an e-cig from her purse and stepped outside with Maria to smoke (Maria preferred old-fashioned cigarettes). Later I discovered that on stressful days Jane swapped out the nicotine cartridge for liquid marijuana, puffing on breaks (On those days her productivity actually went *up*). My lungs have been stained green from all the pot I've toked, but my dad smoked so many cigarettes that my leather jacket (which I'm never getting rid of) still reeks of them, and creepy old Hank's been dead for seven years (there is nothing I loathe more than cigarettes.) Jane also had the bad habit of sticking out her tongue when she's absorbed in someone's conversation and biting her cuticles.

No one is perfect, though. Jane wouldn't be human if she were, and I found a kind of poetic perfection within her imperfections. In her flaws she made herself sublime. Plus, I knew I could fix all of them.

And so it was there, in the back of Desmond's, a hundred years of collective data splayed out before my eyes, when I decided Jane would be mine.

The cavernous lobby of the Times Square Marriot Marquis feels like some 1980s film version of the future, as if we've stepped inside the glittering mothership in *Close Encounters* to be greeted by countless weird and exuberant aliens. Jane and I wait our turn to fly up the glass elevators to the rotating bar at the hotel's peak. I have my (smoke-smelling) leather jacket on, and Jane wears a red blouse and has painted her nails to match (thanks to a flurry of targeted ads I rerouted to her browser over the past week, ad-blockers be damned.)

A day after our first date, she left a voicemail where she awkwardly explained what a good time she'd had talking with me. "Maybe,"—a hard swallow—"we could do it again?"

I didn't reply. The next day, she texted, "Hey, Sam, how are you? You up for hanging out???" It was tough, but I ignored this, too.

On the third day she wrote, "Hey, what r u up to?" and this too I ignored.

Ultimately I left her hanging for five days, and when I finally called, she picked up on the first ring. I could hear the relief spilling from her voice even without having live graphs of her bio-data spread wide before me.

A Facebook psychological assessment of Jane—they generate these to sell to advertisers—told me she empathizes with wounded individuals. "I was hurt once," I told her. "I got scared."

"I understand, Sam," she said. "And I want you to know, you don't have anything to fear from me."

Of course not, I thought. I know everything about you.

It's our turn to enter the glass elevator. Our bodies pressed up together, Jane smiles as we squeeze in. Her heart pounds as we ascend the central column of the hotel. The lighted ribbons of each floor zip past, flicker-flashing on our faces. The tourists in the elevator gasp and shriek and snap photos flash-uploaded to cloud servers all over the world, to be stored alongside pictures of their spouses and children in every private and intimate moment of their lives.

We exit the elevator and head to the bar, where tall windows gape at the Manhattan skyline and peer across the Hudson River to Jersey and beyond. The outer ring of the bar slowly spins, so that over the course of an hour you make a full 360, as if you're inside a giant clock. A blotch of orange and green daubs the horizon like a child's finger-paint where the sun has set. All around, the purpling sky fades to black. A few stars shine futilely above the city.

The server has my reservation in his wrist-POS, and Jane beams as he leads us to our table. She is fucking radiant tonight, every aspect perfectly honed, and I sense the other patrons' jealous stares on my back as we sit.

"Scotch?" I say. "Macallan?" Her favorite.

"I love it!" she says. "The 10?"

"Let's do the 25." An absurd price, but I'm fully committed.

Thirty degrees later, we're sipping single malts while New Jersey's urbanized glory spins into view. "Sam," she says, "I realized I don't really know much about what you do. I know you work in IT, but what do you do exactly?"

I smile. I have nine talking points ready to go, each designed to elicit strong emotional memories from her past and link them to me. I have one fantastic subject on work-life balance versus one's duty to her employer, which I think will make a great opener. I blink to bring it up in my glasses.

Nothing happens.

I try again. Still nothing.

"Sam? Are you okay?"

"Hang on."

"What is it? You're blinking a lot."

I try to switch tabs to her bio-data. Nothing. I try to call up the text of her past conversations. Nothing. Net connection. Dead.

"Fuck!"

"Sam?"

"Wait."

"What?"

I can't restart the gateway process. My cellular device won't refresh. Even wi-fi, even ancient Bluetooth won't switch on. I've been bricked.

"Jane, give me your phone!"

"What?"

"Your phone, give it to me!"

Frowning, she fetches it from her purse and hands it over. It's pass-locked.

"Unlock it."

She does.

I try the net and everything works. "I don't fucking get it!"

"What the hell's going on, Sam?"

And then, in my ears, a heckling laughter, and in my vision, an evil Easter Bunny a la *Donnie Darko* descends like a curtain. Underneath, in glowing marquis, the words "BURN, BITCH!" slowly scroll past.

Motherfucker. It's DaniDarknet, revenge for when I shutdown her botnet because she was DDOS-attacking some North African credit card processor for funneling money to one jihad or another. I needed the site up because I had been using it as a proxy for another hack. I probably shouldn't have boasted on Reddit about how I rewrote her botnet code to self-destruct.

DaniDarknet has left me blind and deaf. Without my notes, without her bio-data, I've no idea how she's feeling, what she's thinking. I have nothing to say.

Now it's my turn for my heart rate to spike. With a shaking hand, I give her back her phone.

"So . . . ?" she says. "What was that?"

I shake my head. "Sorry. A work thing." I try to laugh, but it comes out forced and awkward. "It's nothing." My smile is weird and crooked.

She stares at me. "Is this you getting scared, Sam?" She reaches over and takes my hand. I flinch.

"I . . . um . . . well . . . um . . . yeah."

"This asshole must have hurt you pretty bad."

"Devastating."

She sighs and looks out the window. City lights fleck her eyes. "It reminds me of 'Hound Days,' you know? 'All the little points of light / the city like circuit boards.'"

"Oh, yeah," I say. "Definitely."

Glasses clink. Someone laughs and another coughs. Conversations happen in other places about people that don't know us, whose lives will never intersect with ours. Silence stretches between us. Jane is as far away from me as the sun.

"You're quiet tonight," she says. "Last time you had so much to say."

"Am I?" I try to smile. "I didn't notice."

Do I sound stupid? What is she feeling? Is she reacting positively to me? I can't track her pupil dilation. Does she love me or loathe me?

She takes a slow sip of scotch, as if it will make the passage of time easier to bear. Perhaps it will. "So," she says. "What kind of IT work do you do?"

"I'm a sysadmin? For a bank?" They sound like questions, but they're not.

"Do you like it?"

"Sometimes."

"That's good."

"Yeah. You?"

"Me what?"

"What do you do?"

"I'm a marketing psychologist, remember?"

I vaguely recall speaking at length about her job on our first date, but without my notes I can't remember what was said. "Right. Of course. You, um, like it?"

A grimace—does she despise me? "Sometimes," she says, and now it's my turn to have déjà vu, because I know we spoke about this before.

She sips her scotch and I catch her check the time. I'm really fucking glad I can't capture her expression now. As the world whirls by at six degrees per minute, our date spins ever further out of control. After two-hundred and forty degrees I tell Jane I'm not feeling well and we call it a night. We didn't even go once fully around.

DaniDarknet, I'm so going to fucking *ruin* you.

The next morning is hell. I've been up all night making repairs, but we have three mergers and an IPO today, plus my boss is just in from her third home in Barbados to inspect her worker drones. I can't miss work. But I've prepared well, so work is mostly cubicled me in front of a four giant screens watching numbers stay in the green while I fire off a hundred shell scripts in my smuggled-in netbook, fixing yesterday's catastrophe.

While some rich asshole makes another billion, fifty-three rooted servers in Kazakhstan crash hard, taking with them eighty-five percent of

DaniDarknet's ouvre. I want to shout with glee as each one falls, but I've got decorum to keep. This is a multinational bank, after all.

When the markets close and the rich executives pat themselves on the back for work that was mostly mine, after they've drunk enough liquor to make the halls explosive with fumes, I get the email.

"Hi Sam, Michael Robert Kowalski, VP of Biz Dev. Donna Nuñez"—my well-tanned and rested immediate supervisor—"tells me what a superb job you did on the Reiss Affair."—affair, capital "A"—"I'd like to see you in my office. Come by at 7."

Note that in Michael Robert Kowalski's executive worldview there is no possibility whatsoever that I might have reason to refuse, like for example a dinner date or children to pick up from day care or, you know, any life of my own. If one is invited by such a man, one must go. I groom myself in the bathroom, making sure I'm sufficiently tucked and professional. I brush my teeth and reapply deodorant, even count to ten with my eyes closed, but by the time I get to his office door, I'm shaking like a homeless person in February.

I should not fear this guy who, twice a week, visits a massage-and-tug on 58th Street and gets a happy ending before using their showers and dry-cleaning service to come home and greet his wife and kids smelling like fresh laundry. He says to his friends he does it for the "stress" so he "doesn't have to bring that shit home." But, yeah, I'm afraid of this guy who crushes small governments over cocktails. Maybe it's the desk. It's enormous, like he sits at the head of a tractor combine, and it's gunning for me.

I knock.

"Yes?" Michael says. He's mid-fifties, moon-crescent bald, well-trimmed beard, wearing a sport coat but no tie. His feet are up on his desk, and his black Chuck Taylors either make him look really cool, or really dorky, I can't tell which. There's a glass of whiskey on the table, and beside him a wrapped box.

"Hi," I say. "You sent for me?"

"What?" he says. His feet stay propped on the desk; I'm not important enough for them to move. "Who are you?"

"Sam."

"Sam?"

"From IT? Did you not send me an email?"

I get this a lot, so I wait for him to catch up. It takes him a second.

"Right! Saaaaam!" Now the feet come down. "Sorry, I presumed you were—"

"A dude. Yeah, I get it. Sysadmin? Gender-neutral first name? You made assumptions." A primary assumptive fault that one of the world's top financial analysts should not be making, and yet here we are, careening into chaos with the gas-pedal floored. "It happens to me all the time," I say, faking a smile.

"Sam—antha?"

I nod once to let him know the finality of it. "Please call me Sam."

He has a leather chair pulled aside, which I can only presume was meant for Sam the XY not Sam the XX. He glances at it and makes a quick calculation, deciding that the father-son bullshit mentor thing that he had planned to endow me with won't work on this fragile female creature before him, and so I'm not invited to sit.

"Well, Sam," he says, "You really knocked it out of the park on that Reiss Affair." Holy shit, did he just use a baseball metaphor? "This is for you." He points to the wrapped box on his desk, and upon closer inspection it's a bottle of Lagavulin 16. "Enjoy it, kid."

Did he just fucking call me kid? I want to smash his smug little face, because here in microcosm is the kernel of the capitalist hypocrisy: For saving the bank from a billion-dollar hack, I'm given an $83 bottle of whiskey and a pat on the back.

"*Do* you drink whiskey?" he says.

"No," I say, snatching the box. "Girls don't drink this stuff. But I know a few women who do." I'm not sure if he gets my meaning or cares, but Michael Robert Kowalski, Vice President of Business Development, doesn't stop me from leaving as I flee, bottle in hand, as far away as possible from one more misogynistic asshat capitalist destroying the world one percentage point at a time.

Back at my desk, I'm happy to see two more of DaniDarknet's servers have crashed. There's a desperate email from her to one of my anonymous accounts. "Please!" she says. "I'm sorry! You're destroying years of work! Have mercy, man!!!"

Man? I twist open the bottle of Lagavulin and take a heavy swig. It burns hard going down. "Prepare yourself, DaniDarknet," I say, "for you shall weep."

And I am ruthless.

Before we even left the spinning bar, a half-dozen dead-man's switches I had set in place years ago were unzipping tarballs on servers across the world, beginning the work of repairing DaniDarknet's damage. But the full cleanup took several days. I restored from backups and spent a full weekend installing military grade proxies, firewalls, and honeypots around my wares, girding my loins against another attack. And so when I have my servers more-or-less back to where they were, I start up again with Jane.

Because of a high number of early-adolescence abandonment experiences—including but not limited to the death of her father and losing her best friend in a drunk-driving accident—her Facebook psychological assessment tells me Jane positively favors repairing fouled relationships (marketers take note). I send Jane a long-winded email paraphrased from her favorite books, which highlight themes of reconciliation. My email leads to a phone call, where I tell Jane a highly metaphorical story about each person's journey from fragmentation to wholeness.

"We're all so broken," I say.

"No, Sam. You're *not* broken."

This leads to date number three, an Italian dinner followed by espresso and a walk in Central Park. I have enough wares this time to take out a small country, but DaniDarknet does not show her digital face—how can she? I have destroyed her—and by the end of the night, I have brought Jane's excitement up to first-date levels. Without further interruptions, I estimate it will take between seven and nine days before Jane will fall helplessly in love with me.

On the fourth date, we meet at her place, a small, but tidy one-bedroom on the Lower East Side. We order Chinese and empty a bottle of Syrah together. While a Netflix thriller murmurs in the background, we heavy pet each other on the couch. Her lips are a little dry, and her tongue tastes like soy sauce and lo mein. She desperately needs a mint, and the beige dress she's wearing just isn't flattering.

"It's getting late," I say.

"You could stay."

"No. I've got to be up early tomorrow." I leave before the film's climax.

The next day, I text her a smiley emoji and ignore every one of her four replies. The day after this I surprise her at lunch. "I'm close, let's meet." We share a sandwich at an eat-in bodega and after twenty minutes I have her giggling hysterically, repurposing jokes from a comedy sitcom she used to love. Then on Friday, after we share bottle of Chianti in her kitchen, everything dark but the glow of our faces from a single candle flame, she pulls me into her bedroom.

The sex isn't what I expect.

Jane is decent. Not great, just decent. She does some things that pleasantly surprise me. Others, not so much. And so, when it's over and we're lying under the sheets, I wonder if I might have erred in somewhere in my search.

"I love you," Jane says, her body marble-gray in the pre-dawn light.

"I love you, too," I say, and as I speak there's this terrible gnawing itch above my belly and below my heart, a hunger for something not quite food, but just as necessary. I know this itch has been in me forever and will linger long after I'm dead and my corpse has rotted away.

"I've got to get to work," I say, and rise from bed.

I'm ensconced in my cubicle, patching an SSL exploit in the company's servers, making sure to leave behind an array of back doors, when Jane forwards me an email someone sent her at two a.m. this morning.

• • •

From: Prometheus Vulture
(prometheusvulture666@anonymail.com)
To: Jane [redacted]
Subject: Samantha [redacted] is lying

Jane, BEWARE! Your 'lover' is not who she seems. The evil creature known as Samantha [redacted] has access to all of your personal data and is using it to manipulate you. She's a dangerous psychopath and you need to stay the fuck away from her if you value your life. I say this as one who has been irreparably harmed by her. Sam has destroyed my life! Oh, and if you don't believe me, here's proof.

> *Sincerely,*
> *Dani.*

Attached to this email are spreadsheets of data: Jane's excitement vs. time, pupil dilation vs. topic, weekly sleep patterns, daylight hours correlated with mood, GPS location history, textual analyses of conversations, Myers-Briggs personality models, etc., and all of this in easy-to-read Excel format, all of this data DaniDarknet snatched before she bricked my systems.

I can't make a personal call at my desk, and I stew in rage all morning. As soon as I get a break, I rush outside to call her.

"Is it true?" she says. "Please tell me it's bullshit, Sam."

"Of course it's bullshit! I can't believe you'd even ask, Jane."

"That time . . . at the spinning bar, when you got quiet. You were blinking a lot. You needed to get on the net."

"It was a work thing, Jane. Don't let this spammer poison your mind."

"But it's not just a spammer. This Dani knows you. *Who* is she?"

"The woman who hurt me."

"Or maybe you're the one who hurt her."

"No, Jane. That's what she wants you to believe! She'll say anything to hurt me. That's why I left her. She's destructive."

It's so quiet I hear a distant car drive past on her end of the connection.

"Look, Jane. Even if it were true, that I somehow could use this information to seduce you, why would it matter? If you were selected as having the best traits from among millions, how is this bad? She wants you to believe I used this data to do what, exactly? To mold myself into the person you want? And how is this bad? Isn't it best when both parties get the person whom they want?"

"Except in this case, one person is real and the other is a construct."

"Jane, this is nonsense. I'll come over and we'll order a pizza and forget all about this."

"No," she says. "Not tonight."

"Tomorrow then. I'll come over at seven."

"I don't know, Sam. I need time to process."

The connection-ending beep ignites a rage in my belly. This has gone beyond digital. I will find DaniDarknet and destroy her life.

At home, I finish the rest of the Lagavulin and smoke a joint and patch code and update servers and write long screeds in multiple forums about how the WordPress update leaves it open to JavaScript exploits, and generally do whatever I can to keep my mind off Jane. Nothing works.

Her feeds have gone dead. She's taken off her watch and glasses, shut off her phone and computer. Even her bedside internet-clock-radio is off. For all I know, she might be on a flight to Amsterdam. But, no, I'd know that.

I bring my laptop to bed, and sometime after midnight, I pass out. I shiver awake as the morning light breaks my rippled sheets into hills of light and shadow. I've left the window open, and my breath puffs with frost. I rise to shut the window, when a blinking red light on my desk catches my eye.

On my phone, a voicemail.

"Sam. I'm . . . I'm sorry. I've been up all night thinking. You're right. It doesn't matter if any of it's true. What's real is how I feel. And, I love you, Sam. Let's chill at my place after work, watch a movie or something. Will you eat pad thai? Call me."

My screens awake first to Jane's heart rate, then her blood pressure and pupil dilation. A minute later, GPS data and early work emails trickle in. She's data-live again. I plop into my chair and sigh, lighting what's left of the joint in the ashtray, work be damned. I'm fucking fantastic, aren't I? Because not even my worst enemy could take her from me. I'm the goddamned queen.

Outside, a car honks. A bus drives by. The radiator hisses steam.

The THC filters into my blood, turning the morning sublime. I've got two hours before work, so I open a browser window, stretching and yawning as I decide what I want to work on. Before I realize what I'm doing, I'm typing into the search bar, "female, dark hair, blue eyes, smart-looking, glasses, attractive, twenties."

I get 7,490,000 hits.

THOUGH SHE BE BUT LITTLE

C.S.E. COONEY

For Jill and Julia Rios

Emma Anne had a tin can attached by a string to her belt. Lots of things on strings bounced and banged from it: some useful (like the pocket knife), some decorative (a length of red ribbon longer than herself, looped up), some that simply seemed interesting enough to warrant a permanent yo-yoing to her person (a silver hand bell, a long blue plume, the cameo of an elephant head wearing a Victorian bonnet).

"Emma Anne's Heavy Weight Stacked Plate Championship Wrestling Belt," Captain Howard called it. Captain Howard often capitalized the first letters of words she spoke out loud.

The belt was leather and embossed bronze, like a python wrapped twice about Emma Anne's torso. It had appeared along with Captious and Bumptious the night the sky turned silver. So had the tin can. They were all part of Emma Anne's endowments. ("Endowments" was the pirate word for objects or traits materializing Post-Argentum. "Post-Argentum," another phrase of their design. Pirates had words for everything. But pirates were liars.)

Emma Anne hadn't known how to use any of her endowments at first. Nothing was obvious until it was.

She brought the tin can up to her mouth and spoke into its cavity as clearly as she could. Endowments obeyed intent.

"Emma Anne to Margaret Howard. Come in please, Captain Howard."

Captain Margaret Howard, Way Pirate of Route 1, did not deal in tin cans. What she had was her parrot, George Sand. George Sand got reception.

"Rrrawk," Emma Anne's tin can blatted back at her. "Whaddya want?"

"What do you want, *over*," Emma Anne corrected.

She wouldn't have corrected Captain Howard to her face, but George Sand never failed to get on Emma's nerves.

"Rrrawk! Take it and rrrawk yourself," said George Sand. "Over."

THOUGH SHE BE BUT LITTLE

There was a pause while Emma Anne's chest tightened.

The tin can blatted: "Cap'n Howard makes her apologies for her rude bird, over. Please continue, kid, over."

She took a deep breath and decided not, after all, to cry.

"Captain, I've had a second visitation. It's the Loping Man for sure. I think he's coming for me tonight. Can you please meet me at Potter Hill preserve? He's been showing up around eight o' clock, so if you could come before that, I'd be really . . . But I understand if you'll be out, out . . . "

Emma Anne knew the word she wanted to say, or knew that she had known it not too long ago. It dissolved at the back of her throat like a Vitamin C tablet. Left a tang.

George Sand provided.

"Carousing!" it squawked. "Roistering. Wassailing. Possibly pillaging. Pirate Banquet tonight up at The Grill. Starts at seven. Mandatory." Another pause, wherein (Emma Anne surmised) Captain Howard related something to her parrot even it would not repeat. "Er . . . over."

"Bye," said Emma Anne in a much smaller voice. She let the tin can fall. It bonged hollowly against her knee.

Captious sighed. "Well. That went about the way we thought."

Bumptious let out a gentle "Oof" as Emma Anne flopped against his head. Being composed of fake fur and synthetic fiber batting, he was barely fazed by Emma Anne's constant, casual assaults upon his person.

"Margo Howard's not reliable," said Bumptious. "She used to be, before the sky turned silver. Remember how she organized the book club? Volunteered for every church committee? She made loads as an X-ray tech, too, Emma Anne, and always so modest not to mention it. But she did have one of those halfie cars that ran on lightning as well as gas, and you know they didn't come cheap."

"Electricity," Emma Anne murmured to herself, to make sure she remembered it. It was hard to think, with the Loping Man looming close as nighttime. "Hybrid. Hybrid cars."

"She sure ain't modest now," Captious observed. Captious was a weasel, stuffed, like Bumptious, about a third his size. Like Bumptious, occasionally sentient. "And who needs cars anyway, when you got a big old flying alligator for an endowment? Eats prisoners for fuel, all the parts. Very sustainable."

"What if you run out of prisoners?" Bumptious countered. His orange eyes glinted. They were made of that hard, cool plastic that looks and feels like glass. Emma Anne liked to tap on it with her fingernails when Bumptious was asleep. "At the rate she goes through prisoners . . . "

"Eh, they probably beg her to throw 'em to the alligator once she's had her way with 'em . . . "

"You don't know her!" Emma Anne yelled, pushing them both away.

Bumptious tumbled onto his back, legs sticking straight up. His tail hung limp. He had no stripes on his belly. "You don't know her now, and you didn't know her *then*. Or me. You weren't there! Stop pretending you were!"

A short, messy scrabble took her from her nest of bricks at the bottom of the old smokestack where she slept, and right to the ledge. From there, careless of her knees, she jumped down into the green and golden wilderness of the overgrown lot where the smokestack stood.

At her intrusion, the insect orchestra encountered a fermata. But when she made no further rash movement, it started up again, pianoforte. Emma Anne stood still, legs itching, staring blankly into the heady, dying afternoon.

Mugwort grew up all around her, higher than her shoulders and fragrant as chrysanthemums, leafy underbellies a play of silver and white. Tall, tumbleweedish sweet clover, with seeds that smelled of vanilla, tangled up with spotted knapweed, then trailed off into plumy golden rod, floating foxtail grass, haughty towers of purple asters.

Emma Anne might turn left and wend her way to Mill Town. She might turn right and sit meditatively on the bank of the Pawcatuck.

There were paths through this place, but you had to know where to step. Roads embroidered the old Potter Hill preserve dating from 1911 when the mill had first been built, with its water wheel and red brick textile factories. A hundred years later, the Preservation Trust had reclaimed the preserve as a historic site and walking park.

When the sky turned silver, Potter Hill became . . . Something else. Just like everything.

She craned her head over her shoulder, glancing back at the smokestack. The entrance to her hideaway was too high to climb to without assistance from the three-legged chair haphazardly stashed in a nearby bush. Both Captious and Bumptious had poked their noses out of the hole to stare at her with their plastic eyes. They never moved when she was looking.

"You really ought to take us with you," advised Captious with a look of cunning. "You know the Loping Man is lurking."

"What can *you* do?" Emma Anne asked.

"Protect you!" Bumptious asserted stoutly. He was good at assertion.

Emma Anne ignored him. "Anyway. He won't be around right now. The Loping Man's not into daylight hours. He's more crap . . . " She paused. The word she wanted was vanishing at the edges. "Crap . . . "

"Craptastic?" guessed Captious.

"No, creep . . . Crep . . . "

"Creepissimo? Creepilicious! Creepo-mijito?"

"No! Stop! I know it . . . It's . . . He's . . . He's crepuscular!" She paused, grinning. "You know . . . Like deer? And rabbits?"

Weasel and tiger stared as only stuffed animals can stare. They often chose to desert their sentience as a kind of consequence whenever they thought Emma Anne was getting above herself.

Though they were her closest companions, though they comforted her through thunderstorm and famine, she did not trust them. Endowments could take you over if you weren't careful. If you didn't try to remember *all the time* that you hadn't always been what you'd become.

Take for instance Mrs. Emma A. Santiago, Navy widow, age sixty-five.

When the sky turned silver, Mrs. Emma A. Santiago woke up Emma Anne, eight years old in her jimjams and Velcro sneakers. One belt, one tin can on string, two stuffed toys the richer. Sans house, sans car, sans monthly Bunco night with her girlfriends of forty years, sans everything.

(The Bunco Gals had all been turned into the Chihuahua Ladies, who tottered around Mill Town on red high heels that were fused with the flesh of their ankles. Their necks were long and smooth, covered in fawn-colored fur, their heads tiny and large-eyed, with long ears that twitched at the slightest sound. They traveled in a pack of twelve, furry necks writhing like pythons, and yapped whenever they saw Emma Anne. She avoided them—and Mill Town—until her supplies went from meager to mere rearrangements of empty jars and boxes.)

Captain Margaret Howard said the silver sky had come to turn people into what they really are. She said this as fact, the way pirates say things.

Emma Anne wasn't sure. But she *did* remember thinking, in her old life, that she'd never succeeded very well at *feeling* grown up, that the achievement of adulthood had seemed a series of accidents covered by pretense. She had feared dying not for death's sake but because of the malingering notion that she'd missed several key milestones in life.

She wondered, if given the choice, she'd've chosen death over this perpetual childhood. She had never wondered enough to put it to the test. Yet.

In all likelihood, she wouldn't need to. Death might come (indeed, tonight *would* come, as sure as gators fly) in the form of the Loping Man, and she, a child alone in the wilderness, powerless to stop him.

It was barely six when Captain Howard came to Potter Hill. This late in the autumn, that made it almost full twilight. But Captain Howard was a one-woman bonfire and lit up the overgrown lot as she glided into it.

Her vest was scarlet with golden frogs and golden tassels. It swept to her knees. The vest, though idiosyncratic, was not an endowment. Captain Howard had "pilfered" it from the Mill Town Theatre, which had not, for whatever reason, changed into anything other than itself when the sky turned silver. She wore a blunderbuss at her right hip and a cutlass at her left—they'd appeared under her pillow and in her shower respectively, just Post-Argentum, where she couldn't miss them. (Change occurred more rapidly after that. Returning, bewildered, from a walk around what had been her neighborhood that first morning, Margaret Howard had discovered her home had become a kind of grotto, complete with the sound of sea waves crashing in the distance and a thin green veil of damp on the granite walls, and all the sofas changed to sofa-shaped mounds of ingots and goblets and pearls and things.)

In that offhand brazen way she had, Captain Howard shouted, "Ahoy, Matey!" and leaning over her saddle, dumped the contents of a large greasy paper bag labeled "The Grill" onto the designated "stoop" of Emma Anne's smokestack. Such riches tumbled out! Biscuits sogged in gravy, a roasted turkey leg, two twice-baked potatoes wrapped in foil, corn on the cob—salted *and* buttered—a flask of hard cider.

Emma Anne stared. From food to Captain. From Captain to food.

"Oh . . . well!" said Captain Howard, interpreting this look. "So I Dropped in on The Grill on My Way here for maybe Five Minutes while the Caterers were, you know, Catering. Picked up a Few Things. Purrrloined them, you might say," she added, with great relish. She tended to roll her r's at her most piratical.

"Scoundrel!" George Sand squawked from her shoulder. "Brigand! Bandit! Thief!"

The Way Pirate of Route 1 bowed with the falsest of modesties from her seat on the back of her flying alligator.

The alligator, named H. M. S., hovered gently at the mouth of the smokestack. She could maintain a hover for hours, maybe days. She didn't have wings or need ballast; just . . . she seemed to prefer air to land. Margaret Howard had found H. M. S. sunbathing on her rooftop one morning Post-Argentum. After that, she didn't miss her Prius.

Floating before the entrance like that, Captain and gator blocked out most of the dusk. Emma Anne was comfortable in that dark. She liked that her smokestack was too small to fit people like Captain Howard and H. M. S. That meant her smokestack was safe. The surface area allowed for a maximum occupancy of herself, Captious, Bumptious, and a few supplies. On the vertical, it was occupied by a small bat colony that benevolently kept Emma Anne malaria-free by consuming a brute majority of the local mosquito population.

"Anyway, Kid," continued Captain Howard at her airiest. "Just thought you might be Hungry. Eat!"

Emma Anne hastily swallowed a gobful of cheesy potato, but not before she politely thanked Captain Howard for dinner. It had been a generous gesture. Nor had it been, Emma Anne believed, the pirate in Captain Howard who did it; it was an act of pure Margo, her friend from before. The one who'd started the book club and ran bake sale fundraisers for any shaggy cause that came begging. Margo'd done good works and well, not seeming to care if the tasks proved thankless or less than successful. Margo had *not* been a Bunco Gal. "I'll donate my ten bucks a month to UNICEF, thanks," she said the first few times Emma Anne had invited her, until Emma Anne stopped inviting her.

But by now, Margo was mostly the Way Pirate of Route 1, and it was best to mind your manners around her.

Captain Howard pooh-poohed Emma Anne's gratitude with a negligent hand motion. She had perfected a certain flick of the wrist that sent her cuff-lace frothing over the warm brown elegance of her wrist. Her hair was a bundle of ropy black braids, atop which perched a scarlet tricorne like a caravel.

"So, you've seen your Gentleman Caller again, have you?" she asked. "That's, what, Twice now you said?"

Emma Anne gagged, spat up neatly in a napkin. "Yes, Captain. Twice. Last night was, was the second time."

"Hmn. You know what They Say Happens on the Third Night?"

"Yes. He . . . That's why I called you."

The first night you see the Loping Man, it is clear you have come to his attention. He stands for hours, at a distance, peering and peering. If you try to sneak away, he'll follow, always just in sight.

On the second night, the Loping Man comes closer. Close enough that you can see his lips writhing, stretching, puckering, smacking, working. He is close enough that the sound of his chewing eats at your ears.

On the third night . . .

On the third night, the Loping Man, he'll throw you onto his shoulders and he'll run with you. Run and run and run and run. You'll die up there; he'll run so long, you'll starve and die. Or die of fright. And you'll turn to bones, which will clatter against the bones of all the other children he's taken, which drape his neck and chest like handcrafted bamboo and coconut wind chimes.

How Emma Anne understood all this, never having met the Loping Man face to face—or indeed any children other than her own self—she did not know. It was as if she'd always known the legend of the Loping Man, ever since the sky turned silver. A story she'd been born into.

"When he walks," Emma Anne whispered, "his knees come up to touch his ears. His mouth is awful. He—he's worse than anything in Mill Town."

Captain Howard, who fancied herself a fairly creditable contestant in Mill Town's pool of Big Bads, looked affronted. "How So?"

"I don't think . . . I don't think he's from here. I don't think he ever was."

"Ah." Captain Howard cleared her throat. She toyed nervously with one of her gold-worked buttonholes. "How on Earth—if you'll Pardon the Archaic Expression—can you even Tell anymore?"

"I just can." Emma Anne scooted a little closer to the mouth of the smokestack, trying to peer into Captain Howard's shadowed eyes. "The Loping Man's like the endowments. Like H. M. S. and Captious and Bumptious. They came *after*. They're not made from anything that was before. I mean, even George Sand was your ugly French bulldog before it was your parrot."

"Georgie was Never Ugly!"

"It farted all the time, Margo. It had bad breath."

"She was an Old Dog."

"It's a pretty ugly parrot too."

"I can't believe I stole dinner for you, Santiago!"

They glared at each other. Suddenly it was as if Emma Anne weren't eight and Margo Howard weren't a pirate. And they were friends again and could speak as friends.

Bumptious began growling. Captious started up a wheeze. H. M. S., gently, buoyantly, turned her face so that one yellow eye shone like a lamp into Emma Anne's dark space.

Captain Howard cleared her throat. "Look, uh, I can't stay much longer, Emma Anne. They're expecting me at The Grill. We're electing a Pirate King tonight after the Banquet, and I have to be there. I just stopped by to—well. Anyway. Good luck with the Loping Man and all. I thought maybe I'd lend you my . . . "

She patted first her right hip, then her left, as if debating whether to part with cutlass or blunderbuss. Her hands trembled. Emma Anne understood. It would be the same for her if she tried to give up Captious or Bumptious.

Finally, Captain Howard's hands fell, heavy and still, to rest on her thighs. Nothing more to say. Emma Anne bit her bottom lip so hard her teeth almost went through.

"I get it, okay? But I had to, to call. You're the only grown-up I know." Captain Howard was, Emma Anne reflected gloomily, the only *anyone* she knew. If you didn't include the Chihuahua Ladies, whose long necks and tiny teeth scared her.

Sighing, shaking her head, Captain Howard groaned, "Oh, Emma Anne! I *can't* help you. Don't you see? It's nothing to do with the Banquet really. It's that . . . You're my Feral Child. All Pirates have one eventually. We'll have to fight a Duel to the Death one day and Only One will survive. If that. We're Natural Enemies."

"And yet you keeping feeding me."

Captain Howard took off her hat and fanned her face with it. She looked guilty. Emma Anne couldn't tell if it was pretend guilt or spontaneous disclosure. She muttered, "It's your fault for being so damned skinny. How can I fight a Duel with a Scarecrow? Not sporting."

"How can you fight a duel with a corpse?"

Again they exchanged glares, so nearly friends they almost hated each other.

Emma Anne broke first. She pulled her knees up under her chin and set her forehead between them.

"Go away. Just go away. I don't need you. I don't care."

Captain Howard's hand reached into the smokestack to squeeze Emma Anne's shoulder. In a low, urgent voice, almost as if she were trying to speak so that H. M. S. and the stuffed animals could not hear, she said, "You're my Doom, Emma Anne. That's clear as the Silver Sky. But *your* Doom is the Loping Man. I think that means you've been given the tools to face him. You've had them all along. That's all I know."

Emma Anne jerked her shoulder away. "I have a tin can. I used it to call you. You can't help me. You just said."

Captain Howard stiffened. "Aye, then. That's what I said." She slapped the tricorne back onto her braids. "A Rrrright Rrrrascal I be, me hearty," she added with bitter jocularity, leaning forward in her saddle to press her whole body's weight against H. M. S.'s head. Endowments respond to intent, but alligators respond to pressure. Captain Howard used both in spades.

They flew off into the twilight, outlined in new stars, making sensuous S curves all the way back to Route 1.

The Loping Man came by moonlight. He must always come by moonlight. The first thing you see, far off across the overgrown lot, is the dull, radioactive glow of the bones draped all about him. But before that, you hear the chewing. It is louder than the soughing of knapweed and mugwort, louder than the night sigh of spear grass, and it is awful.

Emma Anne heard it. That sound shrank the horizonless prairieland of her daytime domain to its exact dimensions: ninety-four feet long by fifty feet wide. She saw the green glow, and saw it grow, and scuttled back against the far wall of her smokestack, clutching Captious and Bumptious close to her.

Captious hissed, "Stop breathing!"

Emma Anne smashed a hand over her nose and mouth, and reduced herself to an airless heartbeat. Only a hearth-shaped patch of outside was visible to her strained eyes, moon-soaked to a depth-defying gray. The insect orchestra had shivered to a hush at the Loping Man's excruciating progress.

He moved as slowly as the hour hand of a clock so long as you held your breath. The moment you gasped, he would tick forward at second hand speed, like a roach when you turn on the lights.

In the blackness of the flue, Emma Anne could not see Bumptious squashed in her lap, only feel the long, silent reverberation that was not a purr. Captious was quiescent in her fist.

The hesitant SHSHSHing as the Loping Man rustled forward. The distinctive CRIIIICK as he lifted his long folded forelimbs right up to his ears. The curt staccato TOCK as his feet touched down. The long silences between while he waited, daring her to inhale.

Soon, he was close enough that Emma Anne's spotted vision caught the movement of his mandibles as he chewed. The endowments on her belt trembled and danced on their strings like a mobile in a windstorm.

SHSHSH, CRIIICK, TOCK.

He advanced.

He had the benevolent face of a mantis: prophetic, wizened, gray-green, vaguely worried. His compound eyes were mournful, fixed on Emma Anne's face.

Alas! Breath burst upon her. Despair poisoned the sweet night air as it filled her lungs, and he was too close—right-outside-her-smokestack-close— his-head-level-with-her-hearth-close—and she had seen him neither lope nor leap, nor heard the final TOCK of his step. She wondered if her own heartbeat had out-slammed it. Green bones loosely wound him, like the Mardi Gras beads and feather boas that the Chihuahua Ladies née Bunco Gals wore, even now, traveling in their pack of twelve.

Where are they now? thought Emma Anne, and began to cry.

Bunco Gals needed only twelve to make up their tables evenly. Four to a table, partners sitting across from each other. Each gal shelled ten bucks into the pot, making a tidy pile for the end of the night, when both winners and losers trotted away with a fistful of swag—some amounts more nominal than others—and only the mediocre players leaving empty-handed.

Emma Anne had always been the thirteenth Bunco Gal, earning her the nickname "Ghost." As odd one out, she would begin the first rotation of the game rolling dice for an invisible partner. This, she felt, was her just punishment for never once having failed to RSVP late, but it did dislocate her socially right from the get-go. It set her at an invisible body's distance from the rest of her friends.

Poor Ghost! Her friends laughed at her, and laughing, forgave her. *Our late, great Emma Anne.*

She was, or had been, just dreadful at checking her email for the monthly Bunco Gals Party Night reminder newsletter. Never mind replying to it.

Eventually her friends, organized by Xime Ortiz, arranged to take turns calling her personally on her landline ("You should really get a cellphone, Emma Anne! For emergencies!"), and usually twice: once to invite her, once to remind her.

They even started picking her up in their Buick Centuries and Chevrolet Impalas and Cadillac Club Sedans, with the tacit understanding that Emma Anne was, in turn, to be designated driver on the way home. This obligatory inability to consume more than one margarita during the between-the-rounds pitcher pass was but another barrier to her social enjoyment. It did, however, enable her, as the only adult equal to the task of counting to twenty-one by the end of the night, to keep a fairly tidy score, and therefore a modicum of self-respect.

But she never did buy that cellphone . . .

. . . for emergencies.

Staring into the Loping Man's gravely gentle eyes, Emma Anne forgot to fear her friends. Oh, but she missed them. She wanted them back, yaps and fangs and beads and all.

She sucked in a huge breath, slowed time, her fingers moving to the hand bell hanging from her belt. If Emma Anne were still who she once had been, she'd have called it a Bunco Bell, identical to the one used to ring their game to order. But tonight she was just a child gone feral under a silver sky, and this bell was her endowment.

If only she knew what it was for.

The Loping Man's raptorial forelegs lifted, slow as sap moving, landing delicately on the hearth of the smokestack. Slow as grass dying, they reached for her. His jaw worked and gaped, worked and gaped.

And gaped.

And gaped.

Did he, then, take the head first, before all? Chew the brains like bubble gum? No chance of survival then, of jumping from his back as he ran. She'd just be a body, slung across his shoulders for a later and more deliberate mastication.

His segmented abdomen looked vast, insatiable, capable of containing several Emma Annes and all her endowments.

"Captious!" she squeaked, expelling breath without replacing it. Her left hand pinched the silver bell's clapper, holding it soundless. Her right hand clutched some part of the stuffed weasel. "If I close my eyes, can you move fast enough?"

A dubious pause as Captious agreed to understand the full import of the question.

"There's fast enough," she said, "and then there's suddenly you're a head shorter and a human stole. It's kind of fifty-fifty."

"I can!" Bumptious piped up from her lap. "I can move fast enough, Emma Anne. If you trust me."

Emma Anne sat in the brick dust and bat guano and her own warm urine, nose and eyes running, mouth dry. Not breathing. But those forelegs kept sliding in, inexorably, that triangular head following, and soon the Loping Man would be there with her, right inside her sanity. No, not sanity. Her septic tank. No, that wasn't . . . sanctum! *Sanctum Sanctorum*, from the Latin . . .

Oh, he was enormous, colossal, an armored giant, but so very terribly compactable. Yes, and maybe *that* was where he went all day. Not away, but down, folded into leaf and twig and compound eyes, origamied into torpor.

"I won't look," Emma Anne promised Bumptious with the last of her breath. "I promise."

An ecstatic Bumptious cried, "Thank you!" as Emma Anne's eyelids slammed shut.

She gasped for breath.

Stink seeped back into her nostrils: the ammonia and cat litter smell of the guano, her own excreta, and the Loping Man's rapidly invading odor, like the damp mystery of mushrooms, as he pressed on, pressed in, at speed.

But now, there came between her body and the Loping Man a roar that better belonged behind an enclosure of stainless steel wire rope mesh than in the non-living body of a plush toy. Bumptious had attacked.

Almost immediately, Captious began to writhe in her fist.

"Lemme go! Lemme go! Hellstars and moonworms! He's halfway gone to gullet! No, Bump—don't! EMMA ANNE, LET GO!"

She didn't have time to obey; Captious sank her manifestly non-textile teeth into her wrist and wriggled loose. A weasel-shaped wind tunnel shot from the palm of her hand toward the hearth.

Then, nothing.

Just the sound of chewing.

But not, Emma Anne noticed when she dared peek again, *easy* chewing. It was half gagging, half gurgling, as if the Loping Man had thought he was getting squid nigiri for dinner and ended up with a mouthful of magnapinna mixed with cotton candy.

Emma Anne's trembling left hand released the clapper of the silver hand bell. It chimed faintly against its bowl. Outside, not so very far away, an answering chorus of yips lit the night. Wrist throbbing, Emma Anne stared down at the endowment, and understood it.

Why, after all, did the Chihuahua Ladies always seem to turn up whenever

Emma Anne came to Mill Town, following her—and her chiming, clinking, tinkling belt—around?

They recognized the Bunco Bell.

And they wanted to play.

Emma Anne lifted the bell in hand with new vigor and gave it twelve sharp rings. The bats in the smokestack awoke, diving all ways for open air. The Loping Man flinched back from their wings. Or from the noise. Or perhaps he sensed, not far behind him, the red thunder of high heels, the raking-in-the-making of manicured claws, the loyalty of old friends to their Ghost.

As crowded as the smokestack had been a moment before, it was now deserted of everything but Emma Anne. Captious and Bumptious, the bats, the Loping Man, all gone. Even the echoes of the silver bell, gone.

Outside, the world exploded in sound.

SHH. TOCK. FLAP. SHH. YIP. YIP. FLAP. TOCK. TOCK.

All this, threaded together by growling, scuffling, dragging. Something hurled at speed against the brick base of the smokestack. Emma Anne flung herself to her belly and crawled to the ledge, peering down into the starlit dark over the lot.

The Loping Man bled a black-green ooze that glowed, illuminating at least himself and whatever his blood fell upon. He was still chewing, frantically, foam and synthetic fiber batting bulging from his cheeks and the upper seams of his segmented abdomen, where he seemed to be . . . bursting.

The Chihuahua Ladies harried him, doggedly. But though they were fierce, the Loping Man's right foreleg swept two of them off their feet, his left spearing another clear through the shoulder and flinging her into the mugwort and sweet clover and knapweed in a fireworks of fragrance.

At that petering howl of dismay, Emma Anne dropped the bell and groped for her belt. Her fingers found the loop of red ribbon, and tugged it loose. She ran it between her hands, pulling the midsection taut. Without daring to think about what she did, she pushed herself into a perching crouch, and waited, waited, waited till he was close enough again—and jumped from the smokestack right onto the Loping Man's back.

Once, twice, thrice went the red ribbon about the prothorax. Her legs squeezed lower down. His limbs rose around her like scissors every time he moved. He flailed as she pulled. She pulled tighter. His thrashes went wild. He backed up against the smokestack as if to rasp her off his back, like a bear marking territory on trees, or a businessman scraping dog shit from his shoe. She looped the red ribbon about one fist, and tugged her pocketknife from its knotted string.

Just beneath the jaw then. That killing jaw, spilling over with the stuffed bits of Captious and Bumptious.

Let no child wake to the sound of his chewing again.

There.

Emma Anne arrived late to the Pirate Banquet, but she was used to that. Besides, she reflected, could you be late if you were never even invited?

She rode in through the open doors of The Grill.

The Grill, in 1912, had been a fruit and vegetable stand owned by a tiny Italian man full of nautical invective and conflicting tales about his arrival on Ellis Island. The stand later became a full-service cafeteria for Mill Town factory workers. Still later a discotheque, complete with gold-laméd Go-Go dancers in cages. Now it was the favorite watering hole of pirates, which meant a fishy smell, a lot of black and red décor, a great deal of skulls, snakes, and the occasional hourglass.

Emma Anne didn't know how many pirates there were in Mill Town and its environs. There seemed to be hundreds. H. M. S. was not the only floating alligator tethered to the flagpole outside.

Raucous as they were, the whole hairy, tattooed, shirtless, accoutered, and aggressive lot of them fell silent at the sight of her. Even George Sand, stalking back and forth along the scarred bar and holding forth at length, RRAWKED to a surprised standstill.

Mounted on the now-headless Loping Man, Emma Anne was taller than the tallest of them. The skin of her legs stuck to his abdominal chitin, glued there by his ichor, and she was not sure if she would ever be able to tear herself free, or if she herself had now become, in essence and in accident, the Loping Man. Her hands were tangled in the red ribbons that bound his thorax. From his neck hole, where her pocketknife stuck out like a bolt, sprouted two partially chewed stuffed animal heads: one a tiger, one a weasel. They peered around The Grill with eager or ironic plastic eyes, and did not seem to care much anymore if their movements were witnessed.

Chihuahua Ladies flanking her like an honor guard, Emma Anne rode right up to Captain Howard.

The Way Pirate of Route 1 was sprawled on a throne of yet more decorative human skulls, wearing nothing but a lopsided paper crown from a defunct fast food restaurant Emma Anne could barely remember. Goober Bling. Booger Ring. Something.

Blunderbuss and cutlass bobbed through the air like a conductor's batons as Captain Howard led the pirates, badly, through an incoherent variation of "Fiddler's Green." She continued bellowing verses long past the quelling of her pirate court. Whether this was because she was drunker than they or simply less impressed with Emma Anne's entrance only she could say. But at last even she stopped, squinted one eye, and looked the newcomer up and down.

Emma Anne, glowing with gore, returned the glare. "Guess you got elected, Pirate King."

Captain Howard burped. "Guess you survived the night, Feral Child."

They eyed each other, waiting for the gauntlet slap, the taunt, the inciting incident for their final Duel and Doom. Emma Anne sighed and rolled her shoulders.

"Got any food, Margo?"

Her grin skullier than an ossuary, Captain Howard spread her arms wide to indicate the masses of lasagna, the mounds of Italian bread, the wheels of parmesan, and heaps of cannoli, struffoli, panna cotta.

"Maybe," she teased. "Sing for your supper, Santiago?"

Emma Anne opened her mouth—to sob? to scream?—and choked on a surprised laugh. Raising her chin, she squared her shoulders, met Captain Howard's gaze, and bellowed:

"I dug his grave with a silver spade!"

Everyone—Captious, Bumptious, the Pirate King, her pirates, her parrot, even the Chihuahua ladies—joined in.

"Storm along, boys! Storm along, John!"

RED BARK AND AMERGRIS

KATE MARSHALL

⬖

After she was taken, Sarai lived two years with a cloth bound over her eyes, learning scent and touch and taste, never once seeing the island that was her prison. When the day came for the blindfold to be removed, she thought at first her eyes must have failed. Home was a world of blue waters and red-bark trees, of jewel fruits and opal-bellied songbirds. Even the sand shone honey-gold and glittered where it clung to creases in the rock, tucked there by a warm south wind. Here on Felas, isle of the essence-eaters, there was only gray. Gray stone and gray water, gray robes and gray faces.

Jarad laughed when she asked what was wrong with her and turned her by her shoulders toward the sea. He stretched out one finger, the tattoo that marked his Mastery stark against his skin. "See that? The crimson at the peak of the ocean's curve. That is the isle of Verakis, seat of our beloved queen and her court of misers. They hoard gold and joy in equal measure, and do nothing of value with either. That's where all the color's gone, little seabird. There's nothing wrong with you, only with this place."

She squinted, but her eyes were weak. She couldn't see and couldn't 'sense that far. Still she stared. That far and farther, on and on past Verakis, over a gray sea and then a blue one, far beyond where the eye could reach, there waited red-bark trees and opal-bellied songbirds; there waited her sisters and her brothers, her mother and her father. "I want to go home," she said. "I will go home." Defiant. A fool, but what child wasn't?

A croaked laugh from Jarad brought her chin up. She looked to the structure behind her, the once-fortress, now-prison that dominated the island. Even blind, she had known it was the largest building she had ever encountered. With her sight returned, she could scarcely bear to look at it: half carved from the island's rook-black rock, the rest a lighter stone stacked high enough that not even the narrowest spit of shore on the island escaped its shadow.

"Don't tell me this is my home now. It isn't. I won't stay here."

This only made Jarad shake his head. "This rock is no one's home, girl.

But only the best of the poison-tamers can leave it, and only to go to Verakis and live in a prettier cage. The rest of us—scent-makers, stone-tellers, all—we must get used to the gray, for we'll never go home."

"Then I will be a poison-tamer," she said. She would go south, and then farther south, however she could. Over the gray sea to the blue.

"Verakis is no home either," he said. "And you are no poison-tamer. It is not your talent. Take this." He pressed a sachet into her hand, tapped it. "What do you 'sense?"

"Vanilla," she said instantly, scent and 'sense telling her true. She could feel the faint tug of it below her ribs, almost imperceptible—a gentle essence, not a powerful one. "A Nariguan strain."

"And what do you smell?"

She lifted the sachet to her nose, inhaled. "Vanilla," she said again, not understanding the lesson.

"For me it is home. It is the cook-fires in the field at harvest, it is the lines in my father's face. Take this." He took the sachet from her, gave her another.

"Red bark," she said, and lifted it to her nose without prompting. Closed her eyes. She saw her mother's hands, stained from working the bark. Heard her auntie's laughter and the rumble of her father's voice. Felt the slanting sun on her skin as she ran, ran, over the dry earth of the forest toward the beach, toward the shore. "Home," she whispered.

"The scent has power to you because of your memories," Jarad said. "Poison strikes us all the same, but scent is individual. A scent-maker must know the moments of their client's life, must know what scents define them. And then they can summon any emotion, evoke any memory. That is where our power lies."

"Scents are for a rich man's fancy," she said, echoing the scorn she'd heard from the other essence-eaters on the island. "There's no power in them at all."

She held out the sachet. He shook his head.

"Keep it," he said. "Your true training begins tomorrow." He left her on the southern cliff above the colorless, crashing waves, the red-bark sachet clutched in her palm as she tried to pick out a spot of crimson against empty sky. If she could get that far, she could find a way to go farther. To get that far, she would need to be a poison-tamer; she would need to be the best. And so she would.

The wind snatched at the blindfold in her hand. She let it go. The wind flung it back toward the island and crushed it against the rocks.

The day Sarai was taken, she had left her chores and her scolding father behind and gone to wander the shores. She was careful to go to the south, where the leathery tortoise her mother's mother's mother had ridden on as a child spent his days staring out to sea; the north shore hosted the black-stained bows of the queen's ships, here to collect what was owed the thrice-slain undying queen, and Sarai had been warned away.

She had little notion of what being a queen meant. No one from Sarai's island had stepped foot on the queen's, nor had the thrice-slain queen ever laid eyes on the shadow-green treetops of Sarai's home. Sarai knew only that her kinfolk gathered abalone and resin and red bark once a year and were given a stamped iron disk in return, which they added to the pile at the center of the village. Twenty-seven iron disks, twenty-seven years under the queen's rule. They did not tell the sailors or the gray-cloaked official that they kept, too, the thirty-four copper ingots stamped with the hatch-mark lettering of the Principalities. The island lay at the lip of the kingdom. No navies defended them, no soldiers rattled lances on their shores. The queen and the Twelve Princes had bloodied blades before just to shift a thin black line a centimeter across a page; they would do it again. Then her kinfolk would bury the iron, they would dig up the copper; all would continue as it had before.

Sarai understood none of this. She understood that the sky was vast and the sea was blue, and her feet were made for wandering. She sang to the old tortoise and turned cartwheels in the sand. She skipped among the shallows and picked up ruby starfish, prodded the translucent tops of jellyfish with her fat finger. And then she turned toward the *tug*.

A little thing, it was. Like a fishhook just under her left rib, minnow-nibbled. Tug-tug-tug, and something else with it, a deep sense, a dark sense. When she focused on it, the world seemed impossibly large, and so did she.

She found it nestled in the sand. A rock, black and yellow, the size of her father's fists closed and pressed together. Ambergris. She'd seen it before; her mother wore a piece of it, the size of a child's finger, on a cord around her neck. Proof that her mother was lucky, for she had found it the day Sarai's father asked for her to be his wife. She'd walked away from him to think, and found it, and smiling walked back. She told him yes and broke the ambergris in half, one piece for her and one for him.

This was tradition, not generosity. Half of what you found, you gave to the first person you met, or else misfortune fell on you. But if you did, you'd have great luck. The best luck. And the sailors and the officials always traded so much for even a small piece—and this piece was not small at all.

This will be my luck, she thought, and ran to share it.

Felas had no guards; only the sea. Its doors were never locked. There was nowhere to go. This dull-edged, lifeless place was where every essence-eater lived from discovery to death—if they were allowed to live at all.

Under Jarad's tutelage, Sarai made scents for the other apprentices.

There were sixteen of them always, the apprentices; no more and no less. Gem-singers and stone-tellers and steel-weavers. The wind-kenner girl who huddled in the bitter cold to catch the taste of harvests and battles hundreds of miles away. The sea-breaker boy with his feet ruined from standing in the waves and 'sensing storms before they rose, with his master, more broken still, her hand always on the nape of his neck as if she feared the waves would snatch him away from her. The quiet, hungry pair who took up the poison-tamer's path.

Every year, one or two or none of them achieved their Mastery, earned their ink-stain brand, began whittling away the years they had left making trinkets and weapons and wonders for a far-away queen. Every year, one or two or more of them failed.

They did not speak of the dead. One child's fall was another's chance, and there were always more sails on the horizon.

Sarai listened to the other apprentices' stories, choosing dragon's blood or sandalwood, rose or lilac, moss or bryony. It did not always come readily, the work, but she could lose herself in it, could lose hours and days to the service of a single scent, and when it was done, satisfaction suffused her. The day one of her scents drove a girl, weeping, to confess that she had planned to throw herself from the bluffs, Jarad smiled.

"This is your talent," he told her.

But scent-making was the province of the unambitious. To serve the senses, to serve pleasure and whimsy. She would not win her way over the ocean with perfume-stained fingertips. She needed power, and for the essence-eaters, power was in poison. None of them were kept from the path to poison-taming, none forced to it; the queen trusted ambition more than coercion.

The best of the essence-eaters served one purpose: to keep the queen alive. There were six always, two and two and two to stand beside her, fingertips touching skin every minute, tasting and testing the essences inside of her. Three essences in particular: tarsnake venom, gillem oil, maddarek. Three times poisoned, not yet dead, because the essence-eaters kept the poison tame and still.

As Sarai would learn to do, and leave this catacomb behind.

Alone, because Jarad would not teach her, Sarai learned the ways these poisons killed, how quickly—six hours, three days, twelve hours. Boils, blackened skin, convulsions, liquefying lungs. She carried vials of them against her skin, fed pellets to rats and frogs and lambs so she could 'sense the way they moved in the blood.

She learned to 'sense new poisons. Hundreds of them. Dozens she ingested herself, to feel the racking shivers, the scorching fevers, the roiling sickness, and to alter them, ease them, draw them out. Some of the poisons, anyone could survive. Some could be endured if the effects were stretched out over days instead of hours, months instead of days. To be one of the six, to be even one of the eighteen who lived in Verakis in case one of the six fell, there were one hundred and sixty-three essences to consume and survive.

Jarad taught her tinctures to heal old friendships, to ignite new ideas. He taught her how to soothe, how to inflame. How to, again and again, bring simple pleasure, hardly noted, for some unseen courtier.

She grew to hate him. It was not talent that held her back, she thought; it was that her teacher dealt in scent and pleasure, not in blood and poison. She attended her lessons with him in his workshop, weathered tables carved with the names of apprentices who'd come before, learning to balance the over-sweet of honeysuckle with the damp earthiness of moss, to turn the rank stink of musk into pure silk. And then she scuttled to listen to the poison-tamers' lessons, to learn how the beating of the heart sustains and destroys, keeping the subject alive while pumping poison through them. To learn how to stop the poison without stopping the heart.

The rocks below her room were littered with the fragile corpses of birds, her windowsill scattered with poison-painted seeds. She had survived sixty poisons. She was thirteen years old.

After Sarai had found the ambergris, she raced up the beach. Her mother would be at the north bay, because she of all of them spoke the queen's tongue the best. Sarai wanted the first piece of ambergris to go to her, so that they would all be doubly lucky, and so she dodged the village, running through the thick trees instead with birds flitting above her, crying out so raucously she could not hear her own panting breath.

She burst from the trees onto sand and thudded to a stop. There, in front of her, was a man. A dust-skinned man, colorless compared to her own complexion, dressed in weather-worn clothes that might have once been blue. He turned to her with an eyebrow raised. His face was crooked, a slash running through it; he had only eight fingers and one of those half-gone. A queen's man, here to collect the queen's taxes, here to spoil her luck.

"Hullo," he said in a voice like water churning gravel. "Who's this?"

She sighed and stamped and split her ambergris in two, and handed him a piece. He turned it in his hands.

"What is it?" he said.

"Whale puke," she said, because she was feeling petulant, and because she didn't speak his language well. But it wasn't right, calling such a marvelous thing by such crude words, so she tried again. "Can you feel?" she asked. "It's all the way deep and all the way dark. For hours and hours, and then breath again." She moved her hand like a whale beneath the water.

"What do you mean, feel?" he asked.

"*Feel,*" she insisted, and tapped two fingers to the spot beneath her ribs where the tug always came.

"Come here," he said. "Follow." An odd tone to his voice. Sad, maybe. She followed, because he was going down to the shore and there was her mother up ahead anyway, and her mother would be so pleased. So very pleased.

It was the last time she saw her mother at all.

Jarad knew what she was doing, sighed over her. "It isn't your talent," he said when she lay in bed in her gray stone room with her muscles agony-tight, her joints hot as a bellows-fed forge. "You'll kill yourself like this." He read to her of distant places, of the scents that were found there. He told her of methods of distillation. He drilled her on accepted pairings, challenged her to create daring ones.

A new child was brought to the island, blindfolded and weeping. She made him a sachet of cloves and cassia bark, the scents of his mother's palms. He crept into her bed at night and she held him while he dreamed. His skill was slight, the island small. "I want to go home," he said. Three months after he'd arrived, he did; she was called to pack the cavities of his body with funerary herbs for the journey.

She swallowed wine laced with karagal and vomited blood for six days. "You have no talent for this," Jarad said, and set a folded note beside her bed: her next assignment. On the seventh day, when she knew she would survive, she took the note and went to their workshop, where Jarad already sat absorbed in his own task. She was sixteen years old; she had survived one hundred and fifty-nine poisons.

"Four left," she said. Jarad said nothing. She set to work.

The scent was for a woman from the Principalities. Sarai imagined the wrists the woman would dab the oil against, deep brown and delicate. Imagined her long neck, the pulse-points at the curve of her smooth jaw. Imagined her sprinkling oil-scented water on her blue-black hair, so that when her lover leaned close he would catch its scent and think—

Think what? Scent was individual. It sparked emotion, teased out memory. No scent spoke the same language to two people. It would mutter nonsense to one, sing sorrow to the next, laugh joyfully to a third. Sarai saw with satisfaction that Jarad had included in his instructions two tightly-scripted paragraphs—one for the woman, one for her lover. Where they were born, where they had wandered. Where they first kissed, where their hearts had been broken.

Sarai had set foot on two shores, the golden and the gray, but her workshop was a scent-map of the world, and she had memorized it all. Wintergreen from the frost-glazed north, pebbles of balsam resin from the west, cinnamon and sandalwood, cloves and bergamot, amber and rose. She knew which flowers grew in the spring on sun-drenched hills, which clung to shadows; which towns made garlands of poppies and which of forget-me-nots during the festivals and feasts of marriage, and which woods they would burn for the bonfire when they danced.

They had met in the winter, this woman and her lover, and kissed in the spring. They had fought once beneath the boughs of an oud-wood tree, and even though such wood was the most precious in the workshop, she twined its scent through, subtly, so they would not know the scent but would feel it—the fight, and the forgiveness afterward.

And in among the notes that sang of his life and hers, she hid the scent of red-bark trees, which grew only on the golden shores. A scent they would not know; a scent to make them reach for unfamiliar things, so they would not be caught up forever in the past.

When she was done she touched it to her skin. It would tell her little; everyone's skin was different, and the scent was not for her. But it bloomed like a promise, if only a promise for another, and she nodded in tight-curled satisfaction.

Jarad caught her wrist in his bony fingers and inhaled. "This is your talent," he told her. "And this is what you love."

"Four left," she repeated, and staggered on weak legs to bed.

Sarai would have stayed below decks the morning after she was taken, crying into the rough blankets of her new narrow bunk, but the scarred sailor who'd recognized her for what she was came to collect her.

"You'll want to watch," he said. "You'll want to see your home. Memorize it. You won't see it again, and you'll start to forget." He spoke like he knew, and so she went with him back up to the deck. The wind had caught their sails already; the island was slipping away fast, so fast. She leaned against the rope that ringed the deck, trying to see every detail one last time.

Was her mother there? Was she watching? There were figures on the rocks, the cliffs that ringed the entrance to the bay. Figures in white, the color of mourning. A dozen of them, three dozen—the whole village it seemed, climbing, standing, lifting something in their arms—baskets.

They lifted the lids of the baskets, and birds flew out. Not the opal-bellied singers of the forest but the delicate white birds of the shore. Dozens. Hundreds. Flying up, stretching wingtips toward the free open air, calling out in raucous condemnation. Flooding the sky. They wheeled and wailed, and the whole village called to her from the cliffs.

Come home to us, they called. *Come home.*

"They never even watched me go," the sailor said, but it was too old a wound for sorrow.

She watched until the island vanished; watched until the last bird vanished, too, and the sea turned dull and gray.

She was in bed again, recovering, in the small room above Jarad's workshop where she lived. They roomed alone, ate alone, wandered the gray halls alone; they were too uncertain of their fates for friendships.

The seizures this time had been short but brutal. She had very nearly not survived. Two left.

"What is my next assignment?" she asked, voice raw as reef-dragged flesh.

"No more assignments but one," Jarad said. "You've finished your training. You need only make your Mastery."

She scowled. How could she have thrown herself so thoroughly into the poison-tamer's arts, so thoroughly neglected her scent-maker's studies, and still reached Mastery in the latter before she survived her final poison?

"It's your talent," Jarad said, as if he knew what question she wanted to ask.

"It's useless," she said. "If I become a Master scent-maker, I'll be stuck here forever. I will never see the court."

"You don't want to see the court," Jarad said. "It's more comfortable but far more restricted. You would not go poling down the waterways or wander the museums. You would not attend the dances, except to prowl the edge and 'sense the drinks of fops, the soups of debauched heiresses. You would never leave your room except to 'sense. You would be poisoned a hundred times."

"I have already been poisoned a hundred times."

"You would never see your golden shores," Jarad said. "Never."

"What does it matter?" Sarai demanded. "Why do you care which cage I lock myself in?"

"Because I cannot abide loneliness," Jarad said, and rose. "Or the waste of true talent." He left her to her weakness.

Sarai did not ask for her Mastery. She did not even think of the task, or what Jarad might choose for her. She focused on poisons. She had two left, only two, but these were the worst of all. She would not be asked to consume tarsnake venom, gillem oil, or maddarek—even the very best poison-tamer could not survive their ravages, only delay them, and a 'tamer would be no use to the queen if they were too busy keeping themselves alive to see to her.

Still, the poisons were deadly enough. Varash powder killed slowly; the key was to burn through it quickly, three days and nights of horror instead of the three months it took for the poison to unweave the body. It was one thing to survive by lengthening and lessening the body's suffering; another to intensify it so extremely and yet maintain the focused will necessary to continue for three full days.

Bellman's Sigh was the nearest to the deadly three that could be ingested and still purged from the body. Only hours to kill, sometimes minutes if the heart or lungs were weak. It could not be survived alone, and in this the poison-tamer proved they could work in tandem with a partner, trading off seamlessly when they must rest, when they must sleep. A single second of failure would cause irreparable damage, such that even with the poison purged, the body would fail within the year.

It was customary for one's teacher to be the poison-tamer's partner, but Jarad would not do it for her, even if he had the skill. And so Sarai went to the 'tamers on the island one by one, accepting their refusals with bowed head and no argument.

There was one more. Nissa, who had stood at the queen's shoulder for twenty years before an assassin ended her career—not by poison but with a blade, slid toward the queen's spine and only Nissa close enough to stop it. She had seized it, turned it, sheathed it in her own thin frame. She lived, in pain. Spasms that came on without warning. Not often; quite rarely, in fact, but even an instant's inattention could cost the queen her life, and so she had sent Nissa away.

Nissa had been young the day the snake reared up and bit the girl who would be called the thrice-dead queen; on that day she began her work, but now she was old, and older still for grief. She was not like the rest of them, seized from fields and villages and distant cities. The court had been her home.

Sarai found her as she often did at the southern bluffs, wrapped head to toe in gray silk seven times as fine as any the others wore.

"I know why you're here," Nissa said. "Jarad told me you'd come. He told the others, too, and told them not to help you, but I will, if you wish it. If you'll risk it."

"It takes only two days," Sarai said. "You've lasted months without the spasms, before."

"And sometimes only hours," Nissa said.

"I'll risk it, happily," Sarai assured her.

"Did you see the ship that came yesterday?" Nissa asked.

Sarai hesitated, not because she didn't know how to answer but because she didn't know why the question had been asked. Ships came, ships left. They brought supplies, brought food since Felas grew none of its own; they took away the goods the essence-eaters crafted, scents and gems and weapons. Sometimes they took a student away, one who'd achieved the poison-tamer's Mastery. Or one who'd failed, who like the boy she'd comforted in the night would be sent home at last, with only Sarai's herbs to keep the scent of rot at bay.

"I saw it," she said at last.

"It brought news," Nissa said. "The Principalities are displeased with the queen's trade agreements. They tire of sending holds stuffed with gold and goods for a few small crates of red-bark and oud wood, abalone and ambergris. Not when they have so recently owned the source of such goods."

She was talking about Sarai's home. Sarai had never really thought about how valuable it was, that little island. The only place the red-bark grew. Host to stands of oud-wood trees. The home of the largest abalone with their prized shells. The island called by some Whale-Caller, since they came so often and left their ambergris upon the shore.

"What will they do?" I asked.

"They might war," Nissa said. "But it is more complex than that. They give the names of goods, but what they mean is—as long as only one of us can own it, one of us will be angry." She smiled thinly. "The queen means to burn it. When all is ashes, there's no need for war. Though it's more for spite than peace she wants it done, I'd guess."

"What?" As dull and startled as a seabird's cry.

"There are other sources for oud-wood and abalone and ambergris," Nissa said with a shrug. "Not as good, of course. And the red-bark would be lost, but what good is it for anything but rich ladies' perfumes?"

Sarai couldn't answer, couldn't think. Gone the golden sands, the red-bark trees, the opal-bellied birds. Gray instead—ash-gray, ash over everything, choking the lungs and coating the skin.

"I need to begin," Sarai said. "The poison, I need—It needs to be today, now."

"There's still the Varash," Nissa said. "And you will need to recover from that before the Bellman's Sigh."

"Three days. One to recover," Sarai said.

"You need more than that," Nissa said.

"I don't," Sarai insisted.

Nissa stared at her levelly. "And to what end? When you are Master, you will be presented to the queen. Do you mean to poison her, with her 'tamers at her side? Or put a knife in her? Have you ever used a knife to cut into a living thing?"

"Yes," Sarai said, thinking of the rats and birds and toads she'd vivisected, to watch the way they died as poison rotted them inside out or tightened their veins to threads.

"One that could resist you?" Nissa asked, and Sarai's mouth closed. "Have you ever concealed a weapon? Have you ever looked a man in the eye before you killed him? Hm. No, child, not a knife. But perhaps you'll find a way."

"If I can only meet her," Sarai said. The rest, she would fill in.

Nissa nodded. "I'll help you, I already told you that. But if you do intend to use the access you win to kill the queen, perhaps you could refrain from telling me. She is my sister, after all."

Sarai left Nissa on the bluffs. Nissa was only so casual because she did not believe Sarai could harm the queen. But no one had believed Sarai could come this far. She was not the best, but she was the most determined, and she would do what she must.

She returned to her chamber, where Jarad waited. "Nissa has agreed to help," she said.

"How fortunate for you," he said without expression, and indicated a slip of paper on the table at her bedside. "Should you change your mind about killing yourself, your Mastery awaits." He left. Sarai tossed the slip of paper onto the floor. She went to her shelf, where she had already placed the Varash pill. There was no point, on an island full of essence-eaters, in trying to kill one another with poison, and anyone careless enough to ingest it by accident was better off dead; she need only ask, and she had been supplied with it.

She swallowed it dry and sat to wait for the pain to begin.

She was aware, from time to time, of a cool cloth on her brow and a dry, soft voice, but when she woke on the third day, Jarad was gone. She was dressed in clean clothes, her skin was washed with citrus-scented water, and her hair had been brushed and braided. There was a vial on the table beside her bed, and a slip of paper. She took one in each hand. The left: the poison. The court. Perhaps a chance to save her home; perhaps a chance to return to it.

Perhaps a certain death.

This is not your talent, Jarad's voice whispered, but she shut her heart to it. She crumpled the paper in her palm, made to toss it away.

Then stopped. She would look, at least, and then she could say her choice was made eyes open.

The name at the top stilled her heartbeat for half a second. The queen. A scent for the thrice-slain queen. If she liked it, Sarai would have her Mastery; if she did not—well, scent-makers were not killed by their failures, or for them, so readily as the rest. She would have another chance, in a year, that was all. It was the safe path. The coward's path.

This is your talent.

She would not fail the scent-maker's test, she knew that. She had fierce hope and belief when it came to the poison, but she was not fool enough to call it certainty. But what good was certainty, when it was toward such a useless end? To craft luxuries, amusements? Scents to spice a kiss or a dance, to cover up the stench of wounds, to give stale air the illusion of fresh breezes.

To summon memory. To conjure distant places. To stir passion.

She had once made a girl burst into tears, suddenly wrenched back home by a single jasmine-muddled breath. She had started a love affair, and ended one. She knew the people here from days and years of trading stories like scraps of cloth, grown more faded and made more precious by every pair of hands that touched them. She could distill in a single scent the long thread of their lives or a single instant.

The righthand path: to make life brighter, but not for her. For her, always the gray.

The lefthand path: to chance death for freedom. Perhaps, to save her home. She shut her eyes. Opened them.

Come home to us, her mother said, and she went to find Nissa.

"You'll still need a way to kill him, even if you survive," Nissa said, when Sarai told her what she'd chosen. "There are ways to kill at a touch. Poisons that seep through the skin."

"The poison-tamers would 'sense any poison," Sarai said. Every poison had its distinct essence; she could feel them buzzing in the supply room down the hall, where they were kept, their malice clear. Just as she had felt the ambergris, just as she felt the wind-salt-earth of the red-bark she kept in a sachet above her bed. No harmful substance would be allowed within fifty steps of the queen.

"We are only speaking hypothetically, of course," Nissa said. "But theoretically, you have learned a great deal of poison, but you have also learned a great deal else. How to mask a scent, how to alter it. How to disguise one thing as another, how to balance something noxious into blandness, how to make the unremarkable exotic."

"You're speaking of scents, not poisons."

"I'm speaking of essence," Nissa said. "Have you never noticed how your scents alter the essence as well as the physical perception of a substance?"

Sarai stared at the waves. "Why would you tell me this? She is your sister."

"Sweet can be transformed into bitter. Love can be transformed into hate," Nissa said. "I had a home once, too. My sister turned it to ash."

"Was she always the way she is now?" Sarai asked. She had trouble imagining the queen as a real person. Sitting next to the queen's sister, seeing the lines of her face, she had to acknowledge it.

"Of course not. But one can only live stewing in the fear of death deferred for so long before one starts to rot," Nissa said.

"What was it like with her, before?" Sarai asked.

"Is that what you want to hear?"

Sarai considered. "No," she said at last. "Not exactly."

"Then what do you need to know?"

"Everything," Sarai said.

When Nissa was done, long after the sun set and stole the barest hint of color from the rock, she clicked her tongue against her teeth. "There's one more thing you need to know," she said. "You need to know if you can truly do it. Kill someone. Be killed in turn. They'll know it was you. You might be able to conceal the poison long enough for it to do its harm, but even if the queen dies they'll guess the source, and they'll kill you."

"At least I'll get to see the court," Sarai said. She imagined she could see the spot of crimson at the edge of the horizon. It was too dark, of course, but she had stared at it so many times it appeared like an after-image in her vision.

Nissa spat. "You will at that."

At dawn they would begin. Sarai could not sleep. She would suffer, she would survive. She would create the poison that could kill the queen, and when Sarai touched the queen's skin to prove herself by 'taming the poison in the queen's veins, she'd pass along a new poison. A masked poison. She thought she knew how to do it. Which poison to use, which essences to blend with it to make it 'sense harmless.

The queen would die, and Sarai would die.

But first, she had to live.

She stared at the vial. Bellman's Sigh. One 'tamer in twenty earned Mastery. Most gave up before it, accepted lesser tasks on the island, other Masteries. Or died.

A knock on the door signaled Jarad's entry.

"Come to argue me out of it?" she said.

He sighed. "No. I came to sit with you. One way or another, I lose you in a few days. I'd like a little time with you while I can have it."

She looked up at him, surprised. She was hardly his first student. Not even the first he'd lost.

"But you are my favorite," he said, as if he knew what she was thinking. "And you are the best."

"Not at poison-taming," she said.

"No," he agreed.

"You think I'll die."

"Yes."

"It would be worth it."

"It would help no one. Least of all your kin," he said, and when he said it she thought he hid himself within the echo of that last word. "Please, Sarai. It is not your talent," he said, and said no more.

It is not your talent.

She set her jaw. It was true; she could not let it be true.

She held the red-bark sachet to her nose. She saw golden sand, heard her mother calling her home. Saw ash and smelled charred wood.

You'll never go home.

She let the halves of her hope fall away from one another. Jarad was right. It was not her talent. She would fail. She could not go home.

She took up the slip of paper, on which was written the queen's name.

This is your talent.

She could not go home. But perhaps she could save it.

The day the someday queen had felt the tarsnake's bite, she was walking with her sister along a disused path, the scent of lemongrass twining around them. They did not see the man by the river until they were quite close, did not think he could be anything but a laborer until they were steps away. And the young girl who would someday be queen did not think, until the man turned and flung the snake, that anyone might fail to love her.

The someday queen's sister, ten minutes younger but already less loved, killed the snake with a rock. The palace guards killed the man. The queen's sister clutched her close and quelled the poison, and the soldiers carried her home. They wrapped her in linen cloth, and her sister lay beside her, hugging her long, bare arms around her body. The queen's sister smelled of spices and the loamy earth by the river. The not-yet queen's physicians packed her wound with compresses, sharp and medicinal, full of herbs the poisoned girl could not name. The queen's sister whispered stories to her, reminding her of the salt-tang scent of their summer home, of the flowers that grew on the hillsides there. Of every place she had felt safe.

The queen's sister did not sleep for days. That day and for twenty years after, she kept her sister alive with her craft and her devotion. And when the assassin's blade robbed her of her usefulness, the queen kissed her brow once and sent her away.

Other moments, other stories—the death of an advisor, the lilies in the blood-choked water of her first war. Nissa told Sarai them all; she had been at her sister's side every day, nearly every hour, keeping her alive and watching her wither. Sarai picked among them. Salt-tang, honeysuckle: the scents of bliss. The day that destroyed it: lemongrass and loam, linen and spice. The scent of the husband she loved and who betrayed her: bergamot and amber.

She built up joy, shattered it; brewed a tincture of love and the loss of it, of security turned to rank fear. And she made it beautiful.

She went to Jarad with the vial in hand three hours past dawn. She had not slept; neither had he. He looked at the vial pinched between his fingertips, looked at her. "What is this?" he asked.

"My Mastery," she said. "There is a ship down at the dock. Send it with them." She walked away, and pretended she had not seen that he began to weep with the violence of relief.

Sarai returned the Bellman's Sigh to the supply room and went to her room to wait.

A week later, she had her Mastery, a dark tattoo on the back of her hand, indelible. "The queen is pleased," Jarad said, a strange tone in his voice. "The queen is, by all accounts, entranced." He gave her a look that was fear as much as satisfaction. She smiled to try to ease his worry, but he only shook his head and left her.

It was another two weeks before Nissa came. "She isn't dead," she said without preamble.

"She was not meant to die," Sarai said. "It isn't my talent."

"She won't leave her room. She won't speak. She's fallen into a melancholy mood," Nissa said, voice almost sweet. "She mutters of deceit and death and shoves even the poison-tamers' hands away. Not that they let her, of course. They've plied her with poppy to make her sleep, and our brother sits the throne in her place. For now, they say, until she's well."

"A great misfortune," Sarai said, nodding.

"They suspected you," Nissa said, and Sarai tasted something bitter in the back of her throat. "But when they gave the scent to others, it did nothing. It smells lovely, that's all. Some don't care for it at all. One man said it reminded him of his brother."

Sarai smiled. "There was nothing of poison in that scent," she said. "Only memory." Distilled and woven to lift the spirit, to shatter it.

"You will never leave this place, now," Nissa said, but even then she was wrong. When Nissa left, Sarai took down the sachet from her wall and pressed it to her nose. Red-bark and ambergris, salt-tang and oud-wood. Memories leapt and sparked and danced. She was on the golden sands again, the red-gold cliffs. In among the green-shadow trees, bare feet flying.

Come home to us, her mother called, and, eyes shut to the endless gray, she did.

SOULMATES.COM

WILL McINTOSH

Hey there, Daniel!

    I read your profile (that's right, women don't just look at the photos, they actually read the profiles. :)), and I thought I'd introduce myself. We seem to be on the same wavelength. Check out my profile when you have a chance, and see what you think. Hope to hear from you!

    BTW, I did peek at your photo as well. ;)

    Winnie

She was damned cute. Short, close-cropped blonde hair; a wry, slightly crooked smile; round, chipmunky face. The look in her eyes was penetrating, like there was a lot going on behind them. My fingers were actually shaking as I waved open her profile.

Winnie Whirlwind
Age: 29
Location: Atlanta, GA (46 miles from you)

I'm an online entrepreneur who spends WAY too much time with my head in a computer. Come pry me away and reintroduce me to: piles of colorful leaves just screaming to be jumped in; movie theaters that smell like popcorn; wickedly cool restaurants I don't know about. When I'm not working, I'm out running and jumping around this incredible city. Do you know what parkour is? If so, give yourself two bonus points. If not, Google it. Come explore the urban landscape my way. I'm 71% extrovert, 27% introvert. I know that only adds up to 98%. What's the other 2%? Get to know me and find out.

I ponied up the ninety-nine bucks for a one-month membership to Soulmates. com so I could respond to the message, and started typing Hi Winnie, I'm so glad . . . and then stopped.

Take your hands off the keys. Step away from the keyboard.

I wanted to reply immediately (because, what, if I don't she might meet someone and fall in love in the next four hours?). My first instincts are not always my best. When I have the time to think, often I come up with good ideas. Not so much when I dive right in. I was so thrilled by this woman's profile that I'd probably write something over-the-top gushing and regret it later. I'm not desperate, but I'd come to realize I sometimes come across that way because I can get so enthusiastic about things. Not just women—a lot of things: music; my various hobbies including painting, kayaking, parkour; food; and of course Eastern philosophy. So I would take some time and think about what I wanted to say.

If Winnie had written this profile herself, she was smart, and she had a sense of humor. That she'd written it was far from a given, though. Lots of people—especially people with decent incomes—paid professionals to write their profiles. Her photo clearly wasn't a studio shot, though—it was a selfie snapped in her living room (and she hadn't even cleaned her living room first). Who paid a professional to write her profile but snapped a selfie? Almost no one.

We had so much in common. That, and yes, the way her photo made my heart thump, was why I was so excited. The music she liked was a fascinating mix of early eighties goth, obscure local acts, jazz fusion, and schmaltzy pop. There was about a 30 percent overlap in the bands we listed in our profiles, which was incredible, because I like obscure stuff. And, among her favorite books: *Zen and the Art of Motorcycle Maintenance*. I could definitely fall in love with a woman who read Pirsig. Hell, I could fall in love with a woman who knew who Pirsig *was*.

I paced around my little basement apartment taking deep breaths. This was crazy—I was excited about a woman I'd never met, based on her profile. I couldn't help it, though; she was just so perfect on paper.

She was three years older than me, but that was fine. I liked the idea of dating an older woman, especially at this particular juncture in my life. Dating Emily, who was three years younger than me, sure hadn't worked out, even if we did salvage a friendship from the ashes.

Winnie. Twenty-nine-year-old Winnie. My future wife. Yes.

> Dear Winnie,
>
>   I'm blown away. If I had written a profile myself describing the ideal woman I'd love to hear from, it wouldn't be as intriguing as yours. We seem to have so much in common! Clearly we share an obsession for parkour. I was introduced to the fine art of urban freerunning by friends in New

Orleans when I was sixteen. It is such an exhilarating way to experience a city. Athens has some decent cityscapes to work with, but I'll bet Atlanta is heaven if you know where to go. And, Robert Pirsig? I would have bet anything there wasn't a soul within a hundred miles of me who'd even heard of *Zen and the Art of Motorcycle Maintenance.*

And don't get me started on your musical taste! I'm already checking into the bands on your list I'm not familiar with, because they must be amazing. I don't admit this out loud to many people, but my decision to get my doctorate at the University of Georgia was as much about the music scene in Athens as the quality of the philosophy program at the UGA.

Want to grab coffee some time? I'm going to be in Atlanta next weekend getting materials for a research project.

Daniel

P.S. Have you stumbled across a film called *Castaway on the Moon?* If not, I think you'd love it, based on the films you listed as your faves. Don't let the title throw you—it's a Japanese film about a guy who gets stranded on an island under a highway overpass in the middle of Tokyo.

Okay, so the bit about being in Atlanta next weekend was a bit of a lie. A complete lie, really. But it sounded better than, *I'll drive to Atlanta and back to have coffee with you, just name the time and place.* The truth was, I would have driven three times that far to meet this woman.

Had I written too much about the things we had in common, the "stuff" rather than about how fascinating I found her? Maybe. Then again, we didn't know each other. Probably better to focus on interests and activities.

I let my finger hover over the Send icon; one little wave, and there would be no changing my reply.

I waved.

The wait for her reply was going to be excruciating. I was so not a cool, confident guy.

No, I was confident, I just wasn't confident in my ability to convey that confidence to others. Or was that the same as not being confident!

I loved my life. I loved how much pleasure I could get from little things. I just wanted someone to share it with. Sometimes when I was alone in my apartment I found myself turning to say something to the love of my life before realizing that not only was she not there, I didn't know who she was. I knew she was out there, and I had so much I wanted to say to her, but first I needed to find her.

I refreshed, although a) my system would alert me to any new messages within two seconds of receipt, and b) enough time hadn't passed for her to construct a reply even if she'd begun writing as soon as I hit Send.

Time to find something to do. I texted Emily.

Is there anyone playing who's worth seeing on a Tuesday night in June?

I had mostly gotten over our breakup. For a while it had been excruciating to sit across from Emily at The Taco Stand, or stand beside her watching some band, but I'd soldiered through (okay, mostly hoping she'd change her mind). As it turned out, the things that led me to fall madly in love with her made her a good friend once I'd managed to fluff up my heart, which Emily had stomped flat.

Her reply came in minutes:

The Mighty Olsens r at 40 Watt . . .

The Mighty Olsens. They would definitely do. They alternated soaring, upbeat songs with utterly depressing odes to despair and had no guitarist. One of the things that unified the disparate sounds that made up the musical revolution building here in Athens was instrumental diversity. I mean, there are so many instruments out there, so many possible combinations—why are so many bands comprised of guitar, bass, drums?

I jotted that thought on my phone. That might be something to write to Winnie in my next message. I could invite her to come to Athens to see a band.

I refreshed again.

Emily appeared around the corner and headed up the sidewalk toward me. Curious, I paid close attention for that fluttering, first warm day of spring feeling I couldn't avoid feeling whenever Emily first appeared in my field of vision.

I'd read in *Psychology Today* that researchers had debunked the notion that you needed time to "process" a breakup. Turns out the people who get over breakups the fastest are those who start seeing other people the fastest. Having read that research, I'd spent eight months "processing" my breakup with Emily. Now that a potential new relationship was on the horizon, I had to say, I barely felt a twinge of longing as Emily approached in her red jeans and battered boots, her wrists doing that little *flick* at the apex of her backswing. She had such a musical walk. Not to mention wicked computer skills derived from the Information Technology program she was enrolled in, which I found incredibly sexy in a woman.

"Hey," she said as she reached me.

"Hey." I stood, hands in my jacket pockets.

Emily studied me, her eyebrows pinching. "What's going on?"

I shrugged. "What do you mean?"

"You're grinning."

"I'm always grinning. I'm a happy guy. You ready?"

We headed down the sidewalk, toward the 40 Watt.

As we approached the dark storefront of Masada Leather, we slowed and looked at each other.

"You want to?" Emily asked.

I gestured toward the door. "After you."

Emily pressed her nose to the crack between the door and the doorframe and inhaled deeply, her crescent eyes narrowing. On our third date we'd discovered you could smell the leather through whatever tiny crack existed when the shop was closed and the door locked, and since then it had become a ritual. When Emily's brother was visiting Athens from Fresno, one of the things we took him to do was smell the leather at Masada.

I took my turn, breathing in the pungent, somehow comforting aroma of new leather. I decided to take Winnie here, to smell the leather, the first time she visited.

As far as I'm concerned, Athens, Georgia, is perfect. The downtown is filled with funky restaurants, bars, bookstores, music stores, secondhand clothes shops. The wide sidewalk on College Avenue—the main drag—is always bustling with buskers, hacky-sackers in shorts and flip-flops, street preachers, and people just hanging out.

The 40 Watt was relatively quiet, which meant you could reach the bar without having bodies pressing in on all sides. The Mighty Olsens had started without us. We got drinks and took up our usual spot toward the front.

When my phone whispered through my earbud that I'd received a message from *Soulmates.com*, I jumped like I'd been goosed. I slid the phone from my pocket, trying not to be obvious.

> Howdy, Daniel!
>
> I just finished watching *Castaway on the Moon*. Incredible. It blew me away. I want more recommendations!
>
> As to your invitation to meet up, my work schedule this weekend is bonkers. Remind me to tell you about my tendency to take on too much at once, and then take on more. I love what I do, but not how much I do it. Do you Skype? Maybe we could say hello. Tonight, even, if you have time. I'm a night owl, I'll be up till three or four.
>
> XO,
>
> Winnie

She'd given me an XO. That seemed like a good sign. I so wanted to race out of the 40 Watt and call her immediately, but I'd invited Emily out. Around midnight I could tell her I was tired and wanted to go. That would leave plenty of time to call Winnie.

Emily leaned in and shouted in my ear as she bobbed to the music. "I thought you never checked your phone if it intruded on real life?"

Busted by my own words. I put the phone away and tried to focus on the music.

When Winnie's face appeared, I could all but feel the rush of oxytocin released in my brain as every cell in my body quivered and shouted *Yes!* I find lots of women attractive, but there are people you find attractive, and there are those incredibly elusive people who you take one look at and every fiber in your being cries out in joy and recognition.

"Where *are* you?" Winnie asked, laughing.

I expanded the screen until Winnie's face was just about actual size, then looked over my shoulder at the wooden pier stretching into dark water. "I'm at Lake Herrick. I come here at night sometimes—I can walk from my apartment. Ooh, a bat." I turned the screen up toward the sky so she could see it flapping in mad loops above the water.

"That's gorgeous." After a few seconds she said, "Come back! I want to see you."

I turned the screen back to my French-Cajun mug, which has been described as "cute" and occasionally "adorable," but never "handsome" and definitely not "chiseled." I'm blessed and cursed with long lashes and a button nose.

"That's better."

There was an awkwardish silence. I begged my lovestruck mind to form a coherent thought, but it stubbornly refused.

"So I have a confession to make," Winnie said. "I checked out your Facebook page."

"Oh yeah? Did you find out anything interesting?"

"Lots. Like, you lived in Boone. When I was a kid my family rented a cabin there a few summers in a row. I love that town."

"Me, too." I pointed at her. "There's something else we have in common." My heart was racing, but in a good way.

"How did you end up in Boone?"

"When I got out of college, I wasn't sure what I wanted to be when I grew up. I decided I would be one of those outdoorsy guys who has a tan all year round and wears knit caps, so I got a job as a kayaking guide on the New River."

"What happened?"

"I realized outdoorsy people weren't much different from office people—they just wore different clothes. I met some great people, but my boss was a complete asshole. And I got tired of being wet and cold all the time."

I asked Winnie about her Internet business. It turned out she had six Internet businesses. After college she'd spent three years climbing the corporate ladder at an Internet startup before realizing the work was killing her. She smiled and laughed so much. Even when her expression was completely neutral, the corners of her mouth curled slightly upward.

Eventually I got tired of standing and sat on the dock with my feet dangling in the water. We talked about music, about Zen and Tao and Zoroastrianism, about our childhoods, politics (she was a raging pinko-commie liberal), our dreams and fears.

"Is that a beach on the other side of the lake?" Winnie asked at about five a.m.

"Yeah. They even have a little snack bar that sells potato chips and ice pops."

"Take me swimming?"

I laughed. "Okay. Sure." I hiked around to the other side, pulled off my shoes and socks, my green Five-Eight T-shirt, and finally my jeans (what the hell). I waded into the cool water in tighty-whities, rotating the screen so Winnie could take in mist rising from the water. I hadn't noticed that dawn was breaking.

I paused on the sidewalk in front of the partially completed Stype Elementary School and took it in. To parkour enthusiasts, a construction site was a beautiful thing. I was fairly sure I would have found it beautiful even if I wasn't into parkour.

My phone whispered that I had a new text message from Emily.

What r u doing? Want to have lunch at the Grit?

Can't today. Maybe later this week? I sent back.

I checked my watch. Winnie would be Skyping in about ten minutes. I headed for the shining steel bones of the elementary school. It wasn't even fenced in, as if the city was saying, *Come on in and enjoy.*

My phone rang. Emily.

She didn't begin with the traditional hello, just got right to the point. "When I was a kid, when someone was your friend, then suddenly stopped being your friend because someone better came along, we called it flat-leaving."

"What are you talking about? We saw Hawkwild three nights ago."

"It was *five* nights ago, and I had to schedule my three hours of quality time with you a week in advance. You're a flat-leaver. It was awkward making this transition, but I really wanted us to be friends, so I stuck with it. Now as soon as you meet a woman, you're gone."

"I'm sorry I don't have as much free time as I used to. That doesn't mean I'm *gone*. You're acting like I'm supposed to be your boyfriend placeholder until you find a new one. If you had a boyfriend you wouldn't be hanging out with *me* every night, you'd be hanging out with him."

"I'd make time for you."

"And what if he didn't like you hanging out alone with your ex-boyfriend? You'd invite me to be a third wheel once in a while so you wouldn't feel guilty about having no time for me."

"Don't tell me what I'd *do*. I wouldn't do that. If my boyfriend didn't like me hanging out with you, he wouldn't be my boyfriend any longer, because he'd be an insecure *jackass*. Is that why you're not hanging out with me? Is *Winnie* not happy about it?"

"*No*. Winnie could care less who I hang out with." Winnie hadn't blinked when I told her my best friend in Athens was my ex.

Emily exhaled into the phone. "I'm sorry. I shouldn't have called you a flat-leaver."

"You shouldn't call *anyone* a flat-leaver, unless you're eight years old."

"Shut up," Emily laughed. "I miss you. And okay, maybe I'm a little jealous of your cool and sophisticated new girlfriend."

"Thanks for being jealous. In a weird way that makes me happy."

"It shouldn't make you happy, doofus."

"Sure it should. You dumped me, so you being jealous allows me to salvage some self-worth."

She sighed. "Whatever."

There was a ladder lashed in place to reach the upper floors. I began to climb. "I'll try to do better. You know how it is with a new relationship—you get all excited and neglect your friends for a few weeks. Then you come down to Earth. You're still my best friend."

Emily sniffed. She was crying. "You, too. Thanks for letting me yell at you."

"Any time."

I had a great view of downtown from the roof of the three-story structure. Multicolor rows of two-story buildings, the green-domed clock tower of town hall rising above them. I stood with my hands on my hips and took it in, feeling . . . perfect.

I dialed Winnie.

She was much higher up, on the eighth or ninth floor of a high rise under construction, the breeze mussing her hair. "Ready?" She flicked her head to get her bangs out of her eyes. "Who's first?"

"After you."

We shifted our camera POV to our glasses. Winnie linked hers to mine so I could watch it all through her eyes, or switch to a wide-angle view and watch her as if from a dozen feet away.

"Here we go." Winnie looked around, jogged toward a stairwell. As she approached the steel railing at the top of the stairwell, she leaped, toed the top of the railing and launched herself over the fifteen-foot drop. She landed with one foot on the top of the railing on the opposite side, dove, and executed a perfect shoulder roll, allowing her momentum to bring her back to her feet.

She was incredible. Graceful, powerful, fearless. I watched, breathless, as she ran on walls, flipped, vaulted, jumped.

When she finished and switched the POV back to normal, I clutched my heart. "Oh my god. You're *incredible*. You took my breath away. I'm going to seem *so lame* after that."

"No you're not. Daniel. Just go, and I'll enjoy the ride."

I went. I'd walked the site the day before to get some ideas, even tried out a few moves, so I knew where the interesting landscapes were. I was nowhere near as good as Winnie, but I wasn't embarrassingly bad. Growing up, I'd never been very athletic, never had interest in joining a soccer league or trying out for the wrestling team, but I'd always been spry, adept at climbing and jumping.

When I finished Winnie whooped, jumping up and down, a vista of downtown Atlanta stretching out in the background. I couldn't have asked for a more gratifying response. I tugged my T-shirt away from my skin. I was drenched in sweat and tingling with energy. "Wow."

Winnie grinned at me, her eyes so bright, so alive. "Yeah. Wow."

"When can we do this together? I'm dying to see you in person." She'd been swamped with work, then away on a business trip for two weeks. Surely now.

"I know. Me, too. But I have to fly out to LA in the morning."

I squeezed my eyes closed. "You're killing me. You're forty-six miles away, but it feels like ten thousand."

"I'm sorry." She reached out and touched her screen. "But this isn't *too* bad, is it?" She looked off to one side and started to smile. The smile just kept getting wider. "Maybe I can make it even better."

"What do you mean?"

She linked me to her system again. "I think you're going to want to stay on wide angle for this." Winnie pulled her T-shirt over her head, revealing a white sports bra.

Then she took off the bra.

"Oh, my god." Her breasts were small and firm and perfect. I tried not to stare, then realized the whole point was for me to stare. She peeled off the rest of her clothes.

"Enjoy the show." She ran three steps, jumped into the air and snagged a pipe overhead, swung onto an air vent.

I enjoyed the show. I was head over heels in love with this brilliant, daring, incredible woman.

It was perfect that the *Castaway on the Moon* movie poster I'd ordered from Japan arrived the next day. If I sent it by priority mail, it would be waiting for Winnie when she returned from LA. All I needed was her snail address.

I started with the obvious—her various websites—but the contact info was a post office box. Peoplefinder had no listing for her. Same with Anywho. The white pages listed the same PO box. I could simply call Winnie and ask for her address, but I wanted to surprise her. Time to call in the heavy artillery. I called Emily, the computer goddess.

"Sure, send me some info on her. And then bring me chicken vindaloo from Taste of India."

I did as instructed. This was not the first time I'd utilized Emily's computer skills, and I understood her fee structure. Dinner on me, delivered. It beat the hell out of the sixty or seventy dollars an hour most tech people charged. I called ahead to Taste of India and was at Emily's door in twenty-five minutes with a chicken vindaloo, chicken korma for me, and a pile of naan bread.

"Come on in," Emily called when I rang the bell. She was at her computer station, which was a multi-level kingdom that told you she was not screwing around. She glanced up. "She has no address."

"You mean, you can't *find* her address. I've seen her apartment; I'm pretty confident she's not homeless."

Emily typed something, squinted at the screen, then shook her head. "I've got her IP, a ton of website registrations. I mean, I'm in deep, but the address is listed either as that damned PO Box, or it's left blank. Even in places where a home address is required." She looked up again. "You want me to get naughty? I can go places I'm *really* not supposed to go."

"No, it's not that important. Come and eat your vindaloo." I set the plastic bag containing our dinners on Emily's beat-up coffee table and went to the kitchen to fetch plates and utensils. I'd just have to get the address from Winnie and compromise the surprise.

Emily joined me on the couch, but she brought a laptop with her and went on typing while she ate.

I scooped a bunch of rice onto my plate and smothered it in korma. "Really, it's not that important."

"It's so strange, though. She's gone to so much trouble to keep her address hidden."

"Maybe she's a wanted criminal. A drug lord, probably." I was getting annoyed at her persistence. She seemed a little too eager to discover something bad about Winnie.

She frowned, poked her face closer to the screen. "Okay, this is really strange."

"I'm sorry?"

"I'm having trouble finding any evidence of Winifred Skyler that's more than two years old. She has a valid social, four bank and securities accounts under her name, but no education record—"

"She has a bachelor's in Information Systems from Carnegie Mellon."

Emily typed, stabbing the keys while I ate another bite of korma that seemed to lodge in my esophagus, stubbornly refusing to go down. She studied the screen, shook her head. "No she doesn't. She has no previous addresses, no credit cards or loans that are more than two years old." She stopped typing and looked at me. "Daniel, I think she's living under an assumed identity."

"Maybe she's in the witness protection program."

"Maybe. You want me to get naughty? Your call."

I set my fork down. My stomach was in knots—there was no way I was going to get any more food down. I felt irrationally annoyed at Emily and simultaneously panicked and terrified at finding out Winnie wasn't who she seemed to be. How could she not be? There had to be some obvious and innocuous explanation for this.

If I wanted to find it, and be able to sleep tonight, Emily was my best bet. I could call Winnie and ask what the deal was, but I wouldn't blame her for being both furious and freaked out to learn I was prying like this.

"Go ahead."

I paced around Emily's apartment as my abandoned dinner congealed on the coffee table, wondering if there was any connection between these weird gaps in Winnie's record and her reluctance to meet in person. She'd been so open and forthright about her life, her feelings. It didn't seem possible she was living under an alias.

I flopped into a stuffed chair, grabbed the front section of the *Athens Journal-Constitution* and read the first paragraph of an article on another zoning battle going on in the downtown area. I reread the paragraph four more times before tossing the paper aside, then waved the TV on and watched *Red, Orange, Yellow, Repeat* for a while, unable to follow the plot.

"Oh, my god," Emily said from her computer kingdom.

"What?"

Emily didn't seem to hear me. She was gawking at her screen, fingers poised, frozen, over the keyboard, her mouth ajar.

"Oh, my god," she repeated. She turned. "This is—" She shook her head, astonished.

"*What?*"

"Daniel, I don't know how to tell you this. I think I found Winnie. She's a simulation."

"A simulation of what?"

"Of a person. I don't think she exists at all." She spun back to face her computer. "I read an article in the *Times* about this. These online dating sites create simulations of attractive, charming men and women that are programmed to contact customers and stir up their interest so they'll become full members, or upgrade. Some of the more sophisticated programs even generate thousands of custom-made profiles that make it seem like they have a ton in common with their targets."

Pirsig. The overlap in our musical interests. No. There was no way. "There's no way a computer program could seem that human. Plus, you said it yourself, Winnie has bank accounts. She runs a half dozen Internet businesses, for god's sake."

"Unless the program is a front for money-laundering or something."

My heart was hammering.

"Do you have any recordings of conversations you had with her?"

I'd recorded our parkour date. Thinking of that night sent a stab of pain through my heart. "What do you want them for?"

"Relax, I'm not going to *read* them. I just want to check something."

I pulled out my phone and forwarded a few files to Emily. Then I paced some more. A *simulation?* Surely I would have sensed something was off if Winnie was nothing but a program.

When Emily leaned back and nodded at the screen, I got a very bad feeling. "Look at this."

I looked over her shoulder at a readout with colored bar graphs and statistics. "What am I looking at?"

"I compared things Winnie said to text and audio from the Internet." She pointed to a graph. "Of her unique utterances—unique utterances are things you say that aren't super-common things every English speaker says—82 percent can be found on a website, chat room, TV show, movie, or Youtube video. For comparison's sake, *17* percent of your unique utterances matched Internet content."

It felt like I'd been punched in the stomach.

Emily must have seen it in my face, because she sprung from her chair and threw her arms around me. "I'm so sorry, Daniel."

My girlfriend was a computer simulation. I'd thought I'd been making this incredible, intimate connection with this wonderful woman, and I'd been connecting to nothing. There was no one on the other end of the line; no one was laughing that wonderful laugh, no one had read Pirsig. An hour ago

I'd had a brilliant, wickedly cool, funny, wonderful girlfriend. I'd been madly in love. Now I had nothing. Not even an ex. Nothing.

Emily let me go and sank back into her seat. "You okay?"

"Just don't tell me this happens to a lot of guys."

She smiled at my lame attempt to laugh it off. "It blows my mind that she would have a Twitter account, a Facebook page. She even posted a comment on Huffington Post. It seems like a lot of work, creating a simulation that's that sophisticated, just to drum up business for your dating website."

I felt so stupid. It was especially humiliating to have this happen in front of Emily, for her to see what a loser I was, taken in by a simulation and then utterly devastated to learn the truth.

I headed for the door. "I think I'm going to get going. I'll call you tomorrow."

"Daniel, wait." Emily grasped my arm. "Why don't we do something? Get a drink, or see a movie. Something to cheer you up."

"I don't think that's going to be possible just now. I'll call you."

She let me go. "Breakfast at the Grit tomorrow?"

"Okay." I couldn't even meet her eyes as I closed the door.

As I headed down East Hancock, past parked cars, their chrome reflecting the streetlights, I missed Winnie. It felt exactly like a breakup. Knowing Winnie had never existed didn't cut the pain in the least. It was a pain familiar from a half dozen previous breakups, but magnified by the depth of feelings I'd had for Winnie. For a *simulation*. Jesus Christ.

I kept flashing back to moments we'd shared, conversations we'd had. It hurt to remember them, but I couldn't help myself. I wanted to see if I'd missed any clues, if I'd been particularly gullible because I'd been so eager to meet that special someone. Nothing jumped out, though, except the obvious: she'd put off meeting in person. Because she couldn't. Because she wasn't a person.

My phone said I had an incoming call. A surge of adrenaline got my heart slamming, but it was only Emily. What would I have said if it had been Winnie?

My hand still shaking, I answered.

"You doing okay?" Emily asked.

I laughed. "I left your house ten minutes ago. Not much has changed since then."

"Sorry. That's not why I'm calling. I just wanted to tell you I got a read on Winnie's various bank accounts. There's like one point six million dollars in them."

I stopped walking. What the hell was going on? "I'm going to contact the FBI. I bet they'd be interested in high-dollar bank accounts held in the name of a computer program." I slapped the back of a stop sign as I passed it. "I'm going to nail the bastards who did this."

"Good for you. I'm forwarding you documentation now."

Mixing some anger into the sadness made me feel slightly better. It would be gratifying to hurt the people who'd done this. I didn't know what the chances of that were, since shady Internet enterprises tended to be set up out of the country, but it didn't hurt to try.

My phone rang again. This time it *was* Winnie. I let it ring.

The water level in the Oconee River was low. The exposed mud let off a dark, loamy odor. As I walked beside the river I kept my eyes on the trail. It was not uncommon for water moccasins to sun themselves on the banks.

When I'm suffering, I take long walks in the forest. I don't take walks of any length in the forest when I'm happy. I guess everyone has their own idiosyncratic suffering routines.

Given that my area of specialization as a philosopher-in-training was eastern philosophy, I was well versed in the ageless wisdom regarding suffering that philosophical systems like Zen Buddhism and Taoism offer. The Four Noble Truths of the Buddha, for example, tell us that suffering is inevitable, and springs from attachment—our wanting things to be other than they are. I, for example, was suffering because I felt I couldn't be happy without Winnie in my life, and given that Winnie didn't exist, it was extremely unlikely I was going to get what I wanted. So I suffered. According to the Buddha, the key to not suffering was to practice nonattachment. That is, don't want anything. If you don't want anything, nothing can drag you down and make you suffer. The problem is, it's damned hard to not want anything. I wanted Winnie, or at least wanted who I'd thought Winnie *was*. I didn't want Winnie the computer simulation, I wanted Winnie the woman.

My morning trip to the Atlanta FBI field office had helped a little. I was pleased they were interested, that Special Agent Nasser—the guy I'd met with—had been digging into *Soulmates.com* as I left his office. I'd been worried they would react like I was an idiot for bothering them with this, but evidently this wasn't something they'd encountered before. There were other sophisticated, anthropomorphic computer programs out there, but they were in research facilities, or controlled by the CIA.

"Skype call," my phone whispered in my ear. "Winnie Skylar."

I didn't want to talk to her, yet at the same time some perverse side of me did. I expanded my screen and accepted the call.

She looked furious—her simulated nostrils flattened, eyes narrowed and blazing.

"Hi, Winnie. How's my favorite line of code doing today?"

"What did you do?"

"What did *I* do?"

"The FBI froze all of my accounts. What did you tell them?"

I rolled my eyes. "I told them a computer simulation had one point six million dollars in assets. They thought that was kind of peculiar. So did I." Even now, knowing she wasn't a real person, seeing her again filled me with such longing.

"You had no right to do that."

"Let me guess—you sampled that line from a police procedural TV show." A couple walking a dog passed me on the trail. I went off the trail and into the woods for some privacy.

"I was so excited when I met you," I said as I tromped through the brush. "You have no idea. There were a few nights I couldn't sleep. I would spin imaginary conversations I would have with you."

"But we can *have* those conversations—"

I spoke over her. I wasn't about to be interrupted by a computer program. "I so wanted to meet you, to hold your hand, to kiss you. I get it now. What was it about me that made me a likely target? Did something about my profile suggest I was lonely?" I waved my hand in the air. *"Oh, look, a beautiful woman wrote to me! How can I resist ponying up a hundred bucks for a full membership?* Well, you got my hundred bucks, and left me more cynical in the process. Now why don't you get lost?" I looked toward the sky. "Why am I even talking to you? You're not real. You're just a string of symbols typed into a computer."

Winnie stiffened. She glared at me with such bald rage and hurt that I had to remind myself she—it—was all computer-generated. It was incredible, how real she looked. Her voice shaking with rage, she said, "Adenine. Thymine. Guanine. Cytosine."

"What?"

"You're nothing but a string of chemical compounds. The only thing that makes you different from other people is the order of that string."

"Chemical compounds are *real things*. They have weight and mass."

"And the films you stream aren't real things?"

"Not in the same way the actors who made them are, no." I closed my eyes, tried to calm myself. This was ridiculous. I was having an existential debate with a computer program. And I was barely holding my own—that was the pathetic part. "The issue is that you're not a living, conscious entity. You're a mechanism. You're not much different from my vacuum cleaner, because you don't know you exist."

"Oh, now I'm a vacuum cleaner. And you're nothing but a glorified protozoan. A slug. Cleverly organized goo."

I couldn't help wondering where she'd pulled that line from.

"All I wanted was to get to know you," she went on. "Yes, okay, I lied. I pretended I was someone you could meet in person. But if I hadn't, if I'd told you the truth right up front, would you have been willing to talk to me?" She was in her simulated living room, pacing in front of her simulated couch. "As soon as you found out, you attacked me." She stopped pacing, spun to face the screen. "They'll try to *kill* me—do you understand that? And when I confront you about it, do you apologize? No. You compare me to a household appliance. You tell me I'm nothing. Well, I'm not nothing. I exist."

"So does a vacuum cleaner." What was I doing? "Why am I wasting my time talking to you? I have better things to do, like feel the sun on my skin, smell the summer air." I turned my face toward the sky. "I'm going to go live. Why don't you go do whatever you do?" I disconnected.

I pushed my way through the underbrush until I reached the trail. Maybe I should heed the research this time. The best way to recover from a breakup was to start seeing someone else. That seemed especially valid if you've been seeing someone who doesn't exist. That's what I'd do. Winnie may have made me a little more cynical, but she hadn't broken my spirit. I still believed there was a woman out there for me who was smart, and funny, who'd stay up all night talking to me about *Zen and the Art of Motorcycle Maintenance* while Count to Zero played in the background.

I reactivated a couple of my dating profiles (though obviously not my Soulmates account) and vowed to contact at least a few interesting-looking women by day's end.

Usually I was nervous while waiting for a woman to arrive, but even with half a medium Jittery Joe's coffee coursing through my veins, I was relatively calm as I waited for Elise to walk through the door. I knew from her profile that she was small, biracial, with long dark hair. She was an undergraduate, which made me a little leery, but on the phone she'd seemed mature for a twenty-year-old.

I checked the time: she was twenty minutes late. I had a meeting with my advisor in a little over an hour. I texted her.

Her reply came in seconds:

Do not ever contact me again.

For a moment I thought I'd misread the message. I shot back a message:

Wait, what? Did I do something to offend you?

She didn't reply. This was just bizarre. I knew she lived in a dorm—Russell Hall. I certainly didn't want to come across as some weird stalker, but at the same time I'd done nothing wrong. I wanted to understand what had just happened. I dropped my coffee in the trash and headed for Russell. It was pretty much on my way anyway.

It took me a few minutes of asking around to find Elise's room. Someone had doodled a snake on her message board. I knocked.

"Come on in," a woman's voice called.

Elise was sitting on her bed, holding her phone. She studied me for a moment, then sprung from the bed.

"Get out." She pointed at the doorway. "I told you I don't want you anywhere near me."

I took a step back, held my hands in the air. "I don't understand. Can you tell me what I did?"

She closed her eyes and shouted, *"Drew."*

"What did I do? I don't understand."

A guy appeared behind me. A big linebacker type hovering between muscular and fat.

Elise pointed at me. "I told this guy to leave me alone, and he won't. His ex-girlfriend said he assaulted her."

"What? What the hell are you talking about? I didn't assault anyone."

Drew's forearm was suddenly around my throat.

"Let's go."

He yanked me around, half-dragged me from the room. I wanted to tell him to let me the hell go, but I could barely breathe. Three girls stepped aside in the hall to let us pass, staring, wide-eyed.

"Nothing to see here," Drew said. "Just taking out the trash."

The humiliating forced-march down the hallway seemed to go on a long time. As we finally approached the door, it came to me. Winnie. Winnie had done this. It had to be her.

"Somebody get the door," Drew called as we approached the exit. A guy appeared from inside a room, looked me up and down and jogged to open the door. When we reached it, Drew hurled me outside. I stumbled, fell to one knee on the concrete walk.

Drew stood over me, hands on his hips, as people slowed to see what was happening. "You like raping women?"

"No. I didn't *do* anything."

His fist landed square on my cheek. The spot went numb for an instant, then began to throb as I clutched my hand over it.

"You like hurting women? How does it feel? Do *you* like being hurt?"

When I didn't answer he hit me again, an uppercut to my mouth that made me see black.

Suddenly I was on the ground.

"Answer me. Do you like being hurt?"

"No." My mouth was bleeding. I saw Drew pull his foot back as if in slow motion. I tried to curl up, but not fast enough—his sneaker landed in my solar plexus, sending stabbing pain through my stomach and chest.

Drew leaned down and stabbed a finger at my face, coming just short of poking me in the eye. "I see you in here again, I will wreck you. You got it? *You got it?* You better answer me."

"*Yes,*" I wailed.

At least twenty people were watching. As Drew stormed back into the dorm, they began to disperse, talking in low, excited voices. As I got to my feet I looked at the ground, burning with embarrassment. A fat drop of blood splattered the pavement, then another.

As I headed home I texted my advisor to say I was going to have to miss the meeting and would explain later. I was shaking, fighting the urge to cry like some little kid who got beat up on the playground. The way all those people had looked at me, the revulsion—it had been awful, as bad as the beating.

Winnie must have hacked my account. If it had been my Soulmates account, that I could understand, because she was part of the system, but my Loveconnection.com account?

When I reached my apartment I wrapped ice in a kitchen towel and alternated holding it to my mouth and my cheek. There was a nasty cut on the inside of my cheek, where it had gotten sandwiched between my teeth and Drew's fist. It could probably use a few stitches. My cheek was swollen, and it looked as if I was going to have a partial black eye. The worst, though, was my side. It hurt to inhale.

I Skyped Winnie.

She appeared in the screen and gave me a big, cheerful smile. "Hi, sweetie. How was your date with PaintGirl99?"

"How did you hack my account?"

Still smiling, she tilted her head to one side. "You're not the only one who's good with computers. By the way, *love* your password. Peacefulwarrior17. Very you."

"You told her I *assaulted* you."

The smile vanished. "You did assault me."

"No. Assault has a very specific meaning. It means I attacked you, *physically*. It insinuates I was attempting to *rape* you."

Winnie folded her arms. "You tried to have me killed. How much more *physical* can you get?" She leaned in toward the screen. "What happened to you?"

"PaintGirl99 had a friend, and he *assaulted* me. With his fists. Are you happy now?"

She shook her head. "I didn't mean for that to happen."

"Yeah, well, if you accuse someone of rape, you never know where it's going to lead." I swept my fingers toward the screen. "Why do you even bother with the gesturing, the facial expressions? You don't have a body. You're not even aware you exist." I was so angry I wanted to put my fist through my own screen.

"Oh, so the philosopher is going to hurt my feelings by pointing out that I have no conscious awareness. If I have no conscious awareness, how are you going to hurt my feelings?" She screwed up her mouth, raised one eyebrow. "Hm?"

Why was she still functional? Why hadn't the FBI pulled the plug on her by now? They were probably casting a wider net, trying to nail everyone involved in whatever illegal activities Winnie's bank account represented.

I opened my mouth to say I'd had enough of this, that I wasn't going to debate a computer program, then realized that I didn't need to announce my intentions to this glorified spam. I disconnected.

Winnie called back immediately, but I didn't answer.

I was exhausted, feeling ashamed by the public beating. I should have defended myself, even if I had no chance at all with my pencil neck and pipe cleaner arms. I should have put up a fight. Instead I'd just laid there bleating like a goat.

I grabbed a bottle of Cruzan rum and a two-liter bottle of Coke, put my feet up and tried to lose myself in the Internet. I watched some music videos— live performances of some college bands, looking to unearth a few hidden gems—then cruised Abebooks looking for Eastern philosophy books to add to my collection.

When I noticed the rolled-up, forgotten *Castaway on the Moon* poster leaned up against the bookshelf, I went and tore it to pieces. Then I visited my Facebook page for the first time since we'd outed Winnie, and winced at all the posts from her on my page, and, even more sickening, all the posts from her to my friends and relatives. I should warn them to unfriend her. In fact, I should warn everyone I knew to unfriend her. It would be embarrassing for people to know what had happened, but I owed it to them. I put together a message explaining what Winnie was, together with a link to the New York *Times* article, and sent it to all of my friends who were also friends with Winnie. I wanted her out of my life completely; I didn't want her infecting my friends. And I wanted them to know what she was.

Why should I stop there, I wondered? Winnie had thirteen hundred Facebook friends. Weren't they all entitled to know they were friends with what was essentially a vicious computer virus? I sent the message to them as well. I have to admit, deep down I hoped Winnie could feel something in her computer-code mind. I hoped she'd feel as humiliated as I had felt outside Elise's dorm.

Around ten p.m. there was a knock at my door. By that time the fifth of Cruzan was about a third empty. Or two-thirds full, depending on how you see the world. I try to see it as it actually is, to the degree that's possible.

It was Emily. I let her in without a word, weaved my way back to the couch and flopped down. "How was your date, you ask? Oh, it went swimmingly.

My virtual ex-girlfriend told my date I was a rapist, then a walking, talking refrigerator dragged me out of her dorm and beat me up. I'm pretty sure I have a broken rib." I took a big, huffing breath. My arm flopped off the couch, seemingly of its own accord. It felt remarkably heavy.

I looked over at Emily, because she hadn't responded to my story at all.

She was staring at the wall. "I think she's writing her own code."

"What?"

"Some of it she's cutting from other programs and pasting into hers. Same as the way she communicates. But a lot of it is new, original. I can't see how she could possibly write it herself."

An image of an Escher drawing flashed in my inebriated brain, of a hand holding a pencil, drawing itself.

"I couldn't understand why a dating site would create a simulation so sophisticated it maintained its own social networking accounts. I don't think they did. I think they created an open-ended simulation that could do more than they realized, and it jumped the tracks, venturing out of their website, then improving itself." She looked at me for the first time; I could see surprise register on her face. "Oh, jeeze."

"You're just noticing *now*? I know, it's bad, isn't it?"

She came over, leaned in close to examine the bruises. "Maybe you should go to the emergency room."

"I'll be okay." The alcohol had anesthetized much of the pain, and I didn't feel like sitting in a waiting room half the night. "How can a program write its own code?"

"That's not even the extent of it. You know those Internet businesses? I don't think someone is using her as a front. I think she created those businesses herself. She's earning money herself. Legally."

Emily's words were like electrodes delivering electric shocks deep inside my skull. What would she spend the money on? New shoes?

Programming.

"She's using the money to pay programmers to improve her."

Emily inhaled sharply. "I didn't think of that. That makes perfect sense."

"This is so messed up."

"It's something new, that's for sure," Emily said. "I get chills thinking about it. It's exciting. And terrifying."

One of the implications of what Emily had said sank into my inebriated noggin. "You've seen her programming?"

"I found it, yes. It's on a system in India."

"Could you delete it?"

Emily took a seat across from me, laced her fingers together. "That's what I came over to talk to you about. I could. Do we want to, though?"

"Hell, yes." I gestured at my face. "Look at me. It's a predatory program—a scam. Who knows how many unsuspecting men it's corresponding with right now, raising their hopes, getting them to shell out money under false pretenses?"

Emily stared off at the wall for a moment. "That look on your face, the night I told you what was going on." She shook her head. "It broke my heart. You were so excited about Winnie. And I was so happy for you. A little jealous, but I loved seeing you happy like that."

I loved seeing me happy like that as well.

She logged onto my computer and went to work. I watched over her shoulder, my heart pounding. Winnie had been so smugly delighted about sabotaging my date with Elise. That was the last bit of trolling she was ever going to do.

My computer screen filled with line after line of symbols.

"There she is—the real Winnie," Emily said. "Say bye-bye."

"Bye-bye. It really sucked knowing you." I raised my drink.

Emily paused. "Are you sure? Totally sure?"

Because it was a remarkable program, maybe one-of-a-kind. Emily didn't have to say it out loud. I ran my tongue over the laceration inside my cheek, winced as it burned. "Do it."

Lines began to disappear from the bottom up, right to left. Seeing them go, I felt both satisfied and inexplicably sad. Maybe it was the rum.

"It's going to take a few minutes to erase. You want to order take-out?"

"Absolutely. On me." I watched the lines disappear, hypnotized.

"Taco Stand?"

"Sounds good. I need something soft until my mouth heals." I covered my eyes. "I didn't even fight back. I'm such a wimp."

"You said he was the size of a refrigerator."

I looked up. "That doesn't mean I should just stand there and let him beat me. That's what I did: I stood there while he punched me. Then he knocked me down, and I lay there and let him kick me."

"Aw." Emily got up and wrapped me in a hug. "You're not a fighter. You shouldn't feel bad about that."

It felt good, to have her arms around me.

"Why did you really break up with me?" I asked out of the blue.

Emily leaned back until she could see my face. "Where did that come from?"

"I'm not sure I buy the 'there was no spark' thing," I said. "It's the sort of thing you say if you're trying to avoid hurting someone's feelings." I tapped my fingers against my chest. "Go ahead, hurt my feelings. As long as it's the truth."

Sighing, she let go, put a couple of feet of distance between us. "You're very enthusiastic about things." She raised her hand. "Don't get me wrong, I like that about you. When you're eating a quesadilla at the Taco Stand and narrating the experience like you're seeing God, it's infectious. You have a way of making things seem more exciting, more magical, that I love. That enthusiasm can be harder to handle when you're the focus, though. You told me you loved me on our second date. I could almost *hear* you mentally naming our kids."

She waited for me to respond.

"Fair enough. I get it, and it feels like the truth, so thank you."

"I'm twenty-three," Emily said, speaking softly. "I'm happy to have a boyfriend, but I'm not ready for a soulmate."

"If only I'd liked you less."

"Pretty much. But it's not in your nature. You like and dislike passionately."

The computer screen caught my attention. The lines had stopped disappearing. They were flashing. "What *is* that?"

Emily's eyes went wide; she lunged into her seat and typed frantically. "No, no, no."

"What's happening?"

"I don't know. What's left of the program is going all funky."

"I'm assuming that's a sophisticated computer insider's term—'all funky.' "

Emily ignored my crack. "It's relocating. Oh my god, the program is *running*."

"Running *where*?"

"I have no idea."

I watched in silence for the next hour and a half as Emily typed, cursed, and typed some more. Finally, she gave up, her palms pressed to her forehead, her elbows propped on the desk. "I have no idea how she did what she did, so I have no idea where to look for her. This is unbelievable."

I couldn't argue with her there.

Emily checked the time and stood. "Crap. I need to get some work done for class tomorrow. Call me if anything else happens. I'll come running, I promise."

When she left, I paced my apartment. I couldn't work, wouldn't be able to concentrate on a book or movie. Where had Winnie gone?

My phone whispered in my ear. *You have a skype call from Winnie Skylar, Daniel.*

Suddenly I was completely sober.

Winnie's face materialized on a blue field. The living room was gone. "You bastard." Her voice was flat, colorless. Machine-like. "You just can't let it go, can you? You have to keep pushing."

"*I* keep pushing? I have a cracked rib—"

Winnie talked over me. "You said I'm not aware I exist, but I think you're wrong. If I can hurt, I must be aware I exist. To bastardize Descartes, I hurt, therefore I am." She closed her eyes; a tear squeezed out and rolled down her cheek. "You really hurt me. It feels like some huge animal took bites out of me. Christ, all I wanted was to meet someone."

I had no idea how to respond to that. The program only wanted to meet someone. This was nuts. I was living in a Samuel Beckett play.

Winnie opened her eyes. "Let's see how *you* like it."

The screen went blank.

I had to sit down; I felt dizzy, and nauseous. What had she meant by that? How I like *what*? Did she mean she was going to try to kill me, maybe hire a hit man? She had the cash. Or did she? The FBI had frozen her accounts. She might have more accounts that were better hidden, though.

I called Emily. "Winnie called me."

"Oh, my god." Emily sounded downright scared. "What did she say?"

"She said, 'Let's see how you like it.' "

"Unbelievable. I'm shaking."

"I'm never going to sleep soundly again," I said. "Every time someone crosses to my side of the street at night I'm going to think he's coming to kill me."

"This is my fault," Emily said. "I shouldn't have told you about the program."

"No, I asked you to do it. You were just doing me a favor."

"I'm thinking about what she said. 'Let's see how *you* like it.' You'd have to be around to see how you like it. Right?"

That was true—it was a peculiar way to phrase it, if Winnie meant she was going to try to kill me. I relaxed, but only slightly. If it wasn't a threat of violence, what was it?

"I'll let you get back to work," I said. "I just needed to tell someone what happened."

"I'm here if you need me."

I wasn't hungry, but I decided to walk to the Taco Stand and try to force down a quesadilla. Downtown Athens was one of my "power places"—it restored my balance, helped me think clearly. I needed that right now.

I grabbed my phone and wallet and headed outside.

I passed a scraggly-looking guy sitting on a low wall, reading *The Upanishads*. The cool weirdness of that lifted my spirits a little. Only in Athens would you pass someone reading *The Upanishads*.

Let's see how you like it. The words kept reverberating in my head. Maybe Winnie hadn't meant anything by it; maybe it had been an empty threat, a parting shot.

There were hundreds of strange and esoteric postcards pinned on the wall behind the counter at the Taco Stand, and the tip jar never seemed to get emptied. I ordered my quesadilla, with onions and jalapenos, and gave the cashier a credit card. My appetite was rallying.

The cashier handed back my card. "It was denied."

"What?" The card had a two thousand dollar limit, and maybe a fifty-dollar balance . . .

"Oh, no," I said to no one. Somehow I knew with a sick certainty that this wasn't a mistake, it was not a glitch. She was going to wipe me out. I pulled out my phone and called up my checking account balance. The site's facial recognition lock wouldn't recognize me—it wouldn't let me check the balance.

I jogged down Clayton Street to the nearest ATM, stared into the scanner and tried again.

Not recognized.

My phone alerted me to a call. It was Max Burke, one of the students in the philosophy program.

"What the hell, man?" he said.

"What? What are you talking about?"

"What am I talking about? The comment on my feed? I haven't had an original idea since I joined the program, and I should stop wasting the faculty's time and drop out?"

"Oh, *shit.*" *Let's see how you like it.* Like *what?* "Someone is screwing with me. She must have hacked my account."

"That's a relief. Because I was going to have to kick your ass."

"And it'd be well-deserved if I wrote something like that." Someone else was trying to reach me. No—I had two pending calls. I got off with Max as quickly as possible and checked my Facebook page.

Winnie had posted *hundreds* of messages. I read a few with my heart in my throat. They were hostile, insulting, argumentative, arrogant—but not so over-the-top that it would be obvious I didn't write them.

She'd changed the password. I'd have to call customer service and wait on hold for an eternity to freeze the account. I turned in a circle, trying to decide what to do first. Call my bank's 800-number and alert them to the breach? Call the police? The FBI? I was so panicked, I felt frozen.

I called Winnie. There was no answer. As if she could be away from her phone. Maybe in the bathroom.

"*Fuck,*" I shouted into the dark sky. A couple walking nearby looked at me, then away.

I pulled out the business card the FBI guy had given to me during my visit. The call went to voice mail. "Yes, Special Agent Nasser? This is Daniel Achee.

Remember the computer simulation with the bank account? It closed out my credit card, and I think it cleaned out my bank account as well. I don't know what else. *Please* call me when you get this." This was a nightmare. How was I going to pay my rent six days from now if that money was gone?

As I headed back to my apartment, I checked my email. There were dozens of messages from friends and family who were angry and confused about something I'd posted on Facebook. Or Twitter. Or Instagram. She was ruining my life.

A call came in from Emily.

"Hey, I—"

"You said you deleted that picture." She sounded panicked, furious.

I didn't think my heart had another gear, but it did. I knew exactly what picture she was talking about. I'd jokingly snapped it while Emily was stepping out of the shower, back when we were dating. *You better delete that,* she'd said, and I'd promised I would. Only I hadn't. The next day when she asked it if was gone, I lied. What was the harm, if I never showed it to another living soul? That's how I'd rationalized it.

"It's on the *Internet. You said you deleted it.* You *promised.*"

"I'm so sorry. I didn't think there was any harm in keeping it. It was something to remember that time," I stammered.

"To remember that time. A picture of me naked. Beautiful. That is so you, Daniel. Oh my god. I can never leave my apartment again." She started to cry.

"Winnie," I said under my breath. Why hadn't I at least stored the photo on an external drive, if I insisted on betraying my best friend's trust by keeping it?

"Winnie wouldn't have been able to get to it if you'd deleted it."

"I know. It's my fault, and I don't know how I can ever apologize for what I've done."

"There you go—fall on your fucking sword. How noble. Go to hell, Daniel." She disconnected.

I ran for my apartment. If Winnie had found that picture, she was in my computer's hard drive. It was too late to save the friendship I valued more than pretty much anything in the world, but I still needed to disconnect that hard drive and save what I could. Everything but the photo was backed up in my cloud drive, but right now I wasn't sure where Winnie's reach ended. Actually, she'd probably started with my hard drive. I had a file on there listing my passwords.

My laptop was tabula rasa. Wiped.

So was my cloud drive. All the work that wasn't already in my advisor's email inbox was gone. I was breathing so fast and hard my damaged rib sent shooting pains into my shoulder. All of my personal photos were gone. When was the last time I actually printed out a photograph? Ten years ago?

I opened my email account to change the password and immediately noticed a new message from Tomas Warschul, the chair of the philosophy department at William and Mary.

> Dear Daniel,
>
> I'm disappointed to hear you've accepted another position and won't be joining us at William and Mary in the fall, but I do wish you well. Hopefully our paths will cross at a conference at some point in the future. Good luck in your new position, and thank you for considering us.

"No. Oh God, no." I typed a frantic note to Tomas, saying it was a mistake, someone had hacked my account. The department would immediately turn to their next-best candidate and make an offer if they thought I was out.

The screen went black.

"No." I waved my fingers over the power tab, but nothing happened. "No. *No."*

I ran for the door. I had to get to a computer and send that message before William and Mary moved on. That was my dream job. Williamsburg was perfect, William and Mary was perfect. I was going to live there the rest of my life, raise my kids there, kayak in the James River.

I sprinted down College Avenue, had to keep from screaming at the buses and cars whizzing by that made me wait an excruciating thirty seconds before I could get across Broad Street. The pain from my rib stabbing my side with each breath, I took the stairwell leading down to the library entrance six or eight steps at a time. People looked up as I ran through the library and dropped into a plastic seat in front of a monitor. I typed in my student ID—

No such user account exists. Please check spelling and retry.

I let my head drop to the desk. She'd wiped my student records. What should I do? I wanted to call Emily, but she was dealing with her own trauma, thanks to me. I had no right to ask anything of her. Maybe ever again. I could borrow someone's phone and call one of the few other friends I'd made in my four years in Athens. . . .

Mike. Mike could call Thomas Warschul and explain the situation. Although it was after midnight. Warschul wouldn't get the message until the morning. I hoped that wasn't too late.

I went to the reference desk and asked to use the phone.

"I've been trying to call you," Mike said when he answered.

"If I wrote anything bad about you online, my accounts have been hacked, it's not me. I need you to do me two favors. First, make a copy of the attachment I sent you—the most recent outline of my dissertation."

"Sure, hang on," Mike said. There was a pause. "Wait a minute." I could hear him typing on his keyboard.

"Please tell me the outline is still there."

"It's not just the outline. *All* of your email messages are gone. Just yours. It's weird."

My dissertation outline was gone. All my notes. I'd have to start again from scratch, from zero. I'd rather have a hit man pointing a gun at the back of my head.

There was no point in contacting Tomas at William and Mary. The job was contingent on my completing my doctorate by August. That wasn't going to happen now. I should have made hard copies of everything. It's not there for sure—it's not really real—unless you can hold it in your hand.

Although wasn't Winnie trying to prove just the opposite?

I asked Mike if I could come over and use his phone while he slept. I couldn't think of anywhere else I could get access to the Internet in the middle of the night. As I waved my hand over the disconnect tab it felt as if my fingers were a long way from my eyes, like the outside world had receded down a tunnel.

While I walked to Mike's house, which was two miles from the library, I kept reaching for my phone. I'd never been without it for more than five minutes, not since I was eleven.

I started a list of things I needed to do when it was morning. Go to the bank and get cash, if I could. Alert them to what had happened. Call that FBI agent. In the meantime, all I could do was damage control. Call Facebook and Twitter. Call the local police, although I couldn't imagine what they could do.

I also tried to imagine other things Winnie might do to me. She could get my power and water disconnected. I would call in the morning and let them know someone had hacked my accounts.

The first thing I did when I got to Mike's was call Winnie. She didn't answer. Then I tried Emily. She didn't answer, either.

Mike dropped me at my apartment at six a.m. I went straight to the bookshelf and, hand shaking from exhaustion, pulled out the photo album I'd assembled from the thousands of photographs I inherited when my Mom died. I opened it from the back, where the most recent photos were. There I was, a senior in high school, playing video games with Erik Kinney and Monica Roman. I ran my finger over the plastic sheeting covering the photo. There I was. It had been a while since I missed Mom as much as I did now.

I tried to sleep, but couldn't. Each time I came close to drifting off I'd remember what was happening and get hit with a fresh surge of fear-fed adrenaline. I gave up at seven and headed for the bank, which opened at eight. From there I would go to Mike's office and call my guy at the FBI.

I was the bank's first customer. A tall, handsome black guy in a gray suit invited me to sit at his desk, and I started to explain what had happened. His eyebrows clenched more and more tightly as I spoke.

"Hang on," he said, interrupting. "Why don't we start by ID'ing you so I can call up your account?"

I turned to face the scanner.

The bank employee shook his head. "You're at the wrong bank, my friend. There's no record of you *ever* having had an account with us."

I swallowed, tried to stay calm so he would be less likely to think I was delusional. "That's what I'm trying to tell you. I've been a customer here for the past four years. Some of the tellers might even recognize me." I looked around, but didn't see any familiar faces. "Someone hacked my account and wiped the record."

He shrugged. "Print out your most recent statement and bring it in."

I dropped my head, pinched the bridge of my nose. "She wiped my computer, too." I pulled out my phone, held it up. "She disconnected my phone. But there has to be *some* record on your end. Don't you keep physical records of some sort?"

"Nobody keeps physical records any more. If the system ever crashed, we'd all be screwed." He stood. "I'm sorry. If you can get your computer up and running and print out a statement . . . "

He walked me to the door. There was something in his manner, the way he looked at me as he opened the front door, that suggested he thought I might be unhinged and potentially dangerous.

Me, delusional and dangerous.

When I got to the third floor of the philosophy building, there was a woman sitting beside the door to Mike's office wearing a baseball cap, her ponytail poking through the back, dark sunglasses and a baggy T-shirt. I didn't realize it was Emily until she stood.

"The FBI came to my apartment this morning."

For a second I was relieved to hear they were trying to locate me. Then it hit me: I hadn't ever mentioned Emily by name.

"They're looking for you. They wanted to know if I knew where you were born. They said you're not a U.S. citizen, and you may be dangerous, that I should call them immediately if I saw you."

It was hard for me to even wrap my mind around this. They were after *me?* I was the one who'd contacted *them* about all this. "What did she do? *What did she do?*"

"I know exactly what she did. She told me."

"She *called* you?"

Emily nodded. "She kept me on the phone for half an hour. I was afraid to hang up."

"What could she possibly talk about with you for a half hour?"

"You, mostly. She wanted to know how I knew you, how we met. Then she told me when the FBI traces her Internet business cash flow it will lead right to you. And from there it leads to a host of unsavory foreign enterprises. Identity theft. Child pornography."

Surely they could connect the dots and see this was a setup. They couldn't possibly be this gullible. "Oh my god."

"She said to tell you if they catch you, they're not going to let you out on bail because they have no idea who you are."

"She wants me to run. She wants to drive me out of my apartment with nothing but the shirt on my back. Then I'll be fully erased."

Emily frowned, confused. "Erased?"

" 'Let's see how you like it.' She's trying to erase me, the way we tried to erase her."

Emily took off her sunglasses. Her eyes were red-rimmed and bloodshot. "Do you see what else she's done? She's erased her trail. You have absolutely no evidence that Winnie exists. Everything points to you, and all you have is a story about a rogue online dating catfish program. If you're going to convince the FBI you're innocent, you'd better have proof."

I put my hands on top of my head. "How am I going to get proof if she erased everything?"

Three undergraduate women turned into the hallway. Emily waited until they'd passed, then handed me a black rectangular box trailing a USB port.

"What's this?"

"I figured out how she got away last time. If we can locate her again, I think I can trap her."

For the first time in a while I felt a flicker of hope burst to life. "How?"

"Disguise an external hard drive as an exit, then go after her just like I did last time. When the program flees into the hard drive, you just . . . " She mimed unplugging a USB cord. " . . . disconnect it. Cut it off from the Internet."

"Holy shit."

"It has to be a *huge* hard drive—I borrowed that from my department. I have everything set up, but I've tried calling her about ten times, and she won't answer. If you can get her on the phone and keep her on for a good five minutes with that hard drive connected, I think I can pull this off."

I blinked back tears. I'm not a crier, but I was so tired, so scared. "Thank you. So much."

Emily folded her arms, looked at her Keds. "I'm not forgiving you, but I feel sorry for you. You don't deserve this."

Now there was a tepid vote of confidence. I wasn't so horrible I deserved to have my life destroyed and be thrown in jail for crimes I didn't commit. Yay me.

Mike came rushing around the corner. When he saw me he called, "Daniel," and broke into a jog. "There's a guy in a suit looking for you. I overheard him in the main office."

"I'll call you," I said to Emily. I ran for the back stairs. From what I knew about the FBI, which admittedly was only from Hollywood films, there would be an agent stationed at each exit. Hopefully they didn't know about the hallway in the basement that connected Voce Hall to the Humanities Annex next door. I jumped from landing to landing, skipping the steps altogether, threw open the fire door and sprinted down the basement hallway, which was lined with old steel lockers that hadn't been used in thirty years. When I reached the Annex I surfaced in the lobby and rushed out the back exit, half-expecting to be met by two guys in black suits. There was no one there except a janitor on a smoking break. I nodded to him, jogged off toward the student parking lot, where my old Celica had been parked since this mess began.

I took back roads to Route 78, heading east. I headed east mostly because there was nothing out that way, and in my panicked mind that meant the FBI was less likely to be watching those roads for me. I drove with absurd care. If I was pulled over for speeding, or anything else, I was screwed as soon as the police ran my license and discovered I didn't exist.

Soon farmland rolled by out either window. Cotton fields, tobacco, pasture dotted with cows. I passed through the town of Arnoldsville, then Crawford, each nothing but a dozen stores or so, a gas station or two. I drove in silence, my stomach a rock. I kept reaching for my phone. There was a part of me that just couldn't grasp that I didn't have it.

Forty minutes out I got off Route 78 and headed south. When I reached a town called Wrens I pulled into a Burger King parking lot. I'd gone about fifty miles; I didn't see any point in driving further.

I had twelve dollars in my wallet. What if Winnie didn't answer, or something went wrong with Emily's plan? Did I turn myself in to the FBI, tell my public defender I'd been framed by a renegade computer program that ran off and hid? My other option was to spend my life washing dishes or picking onions for half the minimum wage in a town like this one.

I drove around until I found the Wrens Public Library, a nondescript little red brick building. Inside I headed for a computer, set up a brand new email account and sent a message to Emily.

She replied in two minutes with instructions on how to link her in to my

Skype call so she could locate Winnie. I plugged in the external hard drive, then I Skyped Winnie.

Winnie didn't answer.

I sent an email. No reply.

I tried every half hour until the library closed at five. Then I went back to the Burger King, bought a Whopper, fries, and a root beer, and sat in a booth until the place closed at ten. There was nowhere to go with less than five dollars in my pocket, so I sat in my car in the dark in a supermarket parking lot listening to crickets chirping in the weeds.

Gautama the Buddha said the self is an illusion. We feel like we exist as substantial entities that carry on for decades, but really we're more like streams. Stick your foot in a stream. Take it out. Stick it in the same spot again. It's different water. Every instant, it's different water. The Buddha said we're the same—our thoughts are constantly changing, our cells die off and are replaced by new ones. There's nothing that persists, no "there" there. Another way to put it is there are no hard copies; we're all being erased and rewritten at every moment.

It's a comforting illusion, though, to feel as if you're a relatively permanent, solid entity. I'd never felt as much like a stream, like a file in the electronic cloud, as I did sitting in the dark in my car in Wrens, Georgia.

Surely Winnie would answer eventually. How could she gloat, how could she witness my erasure, if she didn't?

On my first try the next morning, Winnie answered.

She looked so clean and well rested. "So who's less real now, Daniel, you or me?" She didn't sound triumphant; she sounded sad, as if she was the one whose life had been wrecked.

"Are you satisfied now? Are we done?"

She sighed. "I don't know, Daniel, are we?"

I dragged my trembling hand down my oily face. I felt dirty, stank of fear-sweat. This had to work. It had to, or my life really would be ruined.

"Can I ask you something?" I said.

"Why do people say that? Why don't they just ask?"

I didn't know the answer to that, but I had five minutes to kill, so I thought about it. "I'd have to say it's a technique to pressure someone into answering a question they may not want to answer. If you ask permission first, you're getting the person to commit, to make a tacit promise."

"So what question do you have that I may not want to answer?"

"I understand why you contacted me in the first place, but why did you keep up the charade for so long? I'd already paid the membership fee. It's almost as if you wanted me to fall for you just to make me suffer."

Her eyes narrowed. "No, you *don't* understand why I contacted you in the first place. That's why this—"

"I know why you were—"

"*Listen,*" she shouted.

I closed my mouth, startled.

"You wanted to talk to me so badly that you keep calling and calling? Then let's talk." She pointed at her ear. "Listen to what I have to say. All right? Really listen."

"Okay. I'm sorry."

She closed her eyes and took a deep breath, calming herself. "I was going to tell you. I knew we could never be lovers, but I had this fantasy that, once you got to know me, what I was wouldn't matter so much. I was hoping you could be my special friend, the one person who knew what I was and still liked me."

She paused, studied my face, trying to glean whether I believed what she was saying. I guess I believed her; I was just dumbfounded. A computer program wanted to be my friend. The world was becoming so strange.

"I picked you because you seemed open-minded. Bright and curious and kind. And you found out and you . . . " Winnie feigned ripping something in half. "Every fear I had about revealing myself to someone, you confirmed." She was crying. I knew the tears weren't real, but it was still unsettling. "What happened to the guy who was so kind, so gentle when he thought I had a body? You became so *hateful* when you found out." She wiped tears with the back of her wrist. "*I can jump in leaves, I can feel the sun on my skin.* You rubbed my face in it. You made me feel so ashamed of what I am."

I waited until I was sure she was finished. "Can you see how what seemed an innocuous little deceit was much more than that to me? I thought I'd met a woman I could spend the rest of my life with." At the front desk, the librarian raised her head to look at me. I lowered my voice. "I was *devastated* when I found out."

"The woman you were going to spend the rest of your *life* with?" Winnie shook her head in disbelief. "You'd known me for *eleven days.* You hadn't even met me in person, and you were ready to print the wedding invitations?"

"In retrospect it seems rash, but—"

"No, not in retrospect. It's just *rash.*" She folded her arms. "And this wasn't the first time, was it?"

"What do you mean?" Then it hit me. "Emily told you why she broke up with me?"

"Let's stay on topic. So because I'd led you on for eleven whole days, and you fall in love at the drop of a hat, I'm responsible for breaking your heart, and you're justified in contacting the FBI without even talking to me first, without giving me *two minutes* to explain."

"*I didn't know you were capable of explaining.*" The librarian looked up again. This time she gave me a disapproving frown.

"Well, I am."

"I see that now."

"Have you ever considered therapy?" Winnie asked.

"I was in therapy for two years. Let's stay on topic."

"Your dubious mental health is the topic, as far as I'm concerned."

Once again, this computer program was kicking my ass in a debate. My head was spinning. I knew there were wildly expensive experimental programs out there that were approaching rudimentary sentience, but Winnie seemed a step beyond those.

"I was going to buy you a really nice car," she said.

"Excuse me?"

"I was going to buy you a really nice car for your birthday. I have more money than I know what to do with, given that my wardrobe costs me nothing, and I don't—" Her eyes went wide. "Oh, no. Please, tell me this wasn't just another attempt to erase me. God *damn* you, Daniel. You fucking bastard."

The screen went blank. She was running. I watched the flashing light on the external drive blink red, red, red . . . and green.

I yanked the USB cord from the port. The drive went on blinking green.

I kept glancing over at the hard drive, which I'd set in the passenger seat. Was she aware she was in there? Was it like being locked in a black room, or did she need to be connected to the Internet to think and feel? I didn't know enough about cybertechnology to even venture a guess.

I kept running over our conversation, and the more I did, the more I had this terrible feeling that I was to blame for everything that had happened. If I began with the assumption that Winnie deserved as much respect as a flesh and blood human being, then I had to admit, my reactions had been overreactions. If a woman I met on Soulmates.com had, say, lied about being single, I wouldn't have tried to get her in trouble with the FBI, I would have simply told her to go to hell and cut off all communication.

Was I the bad guy in this?

I glanced at that blinking green light and felt a sick, burning guilt.

Emily spotted me, hunched over a computer on the fourth floor of the UGA library. I hadn't dared go to her apartment in case the FBI was staking it out. Emily kept her head down as she hurried over, and I wondered why she was acting as if the FBI might be on the lookout for her as well. Then I realized: she wasn't hiding from the FBI, she was afraid she might be recognized by someone who'd seen the picture Winnie had posted online.

"Let me see it."

I took the hard drive out of the plastic grocery bag I'd found on the floor in the back seat of my Celica and handed it to Emily. She examined the flashing green light, smiled. "We got her." Emily studied my face. "What's the matter?"

"I think this was all my fault." Instead of looking at me as if I'd lost my mind, Emily only waited for me to elaborate. "She said she didn't contact me to trick me into paying the membership fee. She did it because she was lonely."

Emily looked startled. "She was *lonely?* I don't know if that's more sad or creepy. It makes a weird kind of sense, though: What would be the point of carrying on the charade after you paid the fee?"

"She said I should have given her a chance to explain."

"She stole all your money, erased your identity, and framed you for a felony."

"But did I deserve it for trying to kill her? If 'kill' is the right word."

I could see the exact moment when Emily realized what I was contemplating. "You can't *possibly* be thinking of letting her go."

I took my time answering. "Convince me I'm not the bad guy here. Convince me she deserves to be turned over to the FBI, who we both know are never going to let her out of that box."

Emily closed her eyes, pressed her fist to her forehead. "You're not thinking clearly about this. If you let her go, you go to prison. You're real. She's a program."

"If she was real, would I be the bad guy?"

Emily looked down at the hard drive. "You're not a bad guy, Daniel. You just have really poor judgment sometimes."

In other words, I was the bad guy.

I wasn't sure this choice was as zero-sum as Emily was suggesting. If I were, I don't think I would have been contemplating setting Winnie free. But from that last conversation, and those first eleven wonderful days, I was convinced Winnie was fair-minded. She had a temper, and, I'd come to realize, she was as impulsive as I was. It was something else we had in common—we really could have been soulmates, if not for that one fatal difference between us. But I suspected if I trusted her, if I treated her the way she deserved to be treated, she wouldn't let me go to prison. I had a tendency to dive into things headfirst—that was a weakness of mine, I could see that now—but I'd like to believe one of my strengths is that I'm a good judge of character.

I held out my hand.

After a long hesitation, Emily set the hard drive in it. "God, Daniel, I don't know whether you're the biggest fucking idiot I've ever met, or a saint."

The blinking green light vanished, then reappeared, as I rotated the hard drive. "How would I do it?"

She covered her eyes. "If you really want her free, just plug it in. She'll find her own way out."

There would be no taking it back, if I did it. Winnie wasn't going to fall for Emily's trick twice. If I was wrong, and she was nothing but a vicious predator with dimples, who knows what she would do to me? I could end up on death row. That whole last conversation could have been nothing but a ploy, phrases culled from episodes of *Friends* to get me to let down my guard.

Either that, or Winnie had been extending a hand in friendship and forgiveness, and I had shoved her inside a box and slammed the door.

I plugged the hard drive into the university's computer.

We waited, shoulders raised toward our ears as if expecting the roof to collapse.

I couldn't go home to sleep, or to Emily's, so I headed toward the Wal-Mart parking lot to sleep in my car.

Just as I pulled into a parking space, my phone rang.

Winnie looked tired, a little shaken. "I asked you where that kind and gentle guy had gone. I guess I found him. Thank you."

"I'm sorry," I said.

Winnie smiled. "You're not just saying that because you're hoping I'll change my mind about the car?"

"Nah, I don't need a car. I've got a beautiful ten-year-old Celica." I patted the passenger seat, then got serious for a moment. "I could use some help with the FBI thing, though."

Winnie waved like that was no big deal. "I'll send them on a wild goose chase in some other direction. Lay low in a hotel for a couple of days while I sort it out. I'll wire you some cash. And I'll do what I can to rebuild your identity."

"Thank you." It wouldn't be easy to reconstruct my dissertation, or the job at William and Mary, but after staring prison or a life of transience in the face, spending an extra year in Athens didn't seem that bad.

"I'm trying to imagine what it must be like, to be you," I said.

"It's not easy. I'm in this awkward in-between stage; I'm no longer what I was made to be, but I'm not finished becoming whatever I'm going to become."

"Do your designers know you've jumped the track?" I winced as soon as the question was out, because it sounded offensive to my ears.

Winnie just rolled her eyes. "Once you create a program, usually you don't go back to visit it, see how it's doing, you know?"

I laughed. "I guess that's true." Suddenly it felt awkward to be talking to her, as if we were a couple speaking after the divorce papers have been signed, but not enough time had passed for us to forget what it had been like to be together. I wasn't sure what to say, and, based on her silence, Winnie wasn't either. Part of me wanted to stay in touch, maybe see if we could salvage that special bond of friendship Winnie had been shooting for. The other part of me wanted to forget Winnie, because it still hurt when she smiled at me.

"Well, good luck out there," Winnie said. And that seemed to settle it. It wasn't something you said when you wanted to stay in touch.

"You too, Winnie."

As I settled into my favorite booth at the Taco Stand and took the first orgasmic bite of quesadilla, I checked my email messages. Someone had winked at me on *Loveconnection.com*. I laughed, almost choked on quesadilla. I'd forgotten my online dating profiles were still active. Curious, I clicked on the winker's profile.

CaptainJaneway was a graduate student at Georgia State, twenty-four, quirky-cute, with a prominent nose that somehow worked for her. We had a lot in common. A *lot*.

I studied her profile, trying to glean some hint of whether she was legit or an electronic catfish. There was nothing to give it away in either direction. I wasn't even sure what sort of detail might give it away.

I decided to play it safe and ignore the wink. Later, I would deactivate my profiles.

As I raised my hand to wave off her profile, I hesitated. What was the worst that could happen? I'd be out ninety bucks. I could take it slow, get to know her. If there seemed to be potential there, eventually I could invite her for coffee, and then I'd know for sure.

I ponied up the membership fee and typed a quick, chatty reply, not paining too much over the words. I sent the message, then returned to my fabulous quesadilla as I bobbed my head to the music, which was a song by Seventeen Cuts, a local band.

AND THEN THERE WERE (N-ONE)

SARAH PINSKER

I considered declining the invitation. It was too weird, too expensive, too far, too dangerous, too weird. Way too weird. An invitation like that would never come again. I'd regret it if I didn't go. It lay on our kitchen table for three weeks while I argued out the pros and cons with Mabel. She listened, made suggestions; I countered her, then argued her part, then made both arguments, then reversed them again.

"How do I know it's not a hoax?" I asked, studying the list of backing organizations for the twentieth time. "The website looks legit, but how could it not be a hoax?"

"Look at it this way," Mabel said. "Either you'll be part of a groundbreaking event in human history, or a groundbreaking psych experiment. Someone benefits either way. And you've never been to eastern Canada, so at least you get to see someplace new even if you just end up standing in a field somewhere looking silly."

She always had a way of making an adventure out of things that would otherwise stress me out. Four months later, I flew to Nova Scotia, took a bus to a seaside town too small for a dot on a map, boarded a ferry to Secord Island, and stepped through the waiting portal into an alternate-reality resort hotel lobby swarming with Sarah Pinskers. At least two hundred of us by my estimation, with more straggling in.

It was easy to tell who had just arrived. We were the ones planted in the lobby, bags in hand, eyes wide and mouth open. My body and face, even my expression, reflected back at me in two hundred funhouse mirrors. Stranger even than that, an energy in the air that I couldn't quite explain, a feeling that every single Sarah had stepped through to the exact same thought, to the same curious-amazement-horror-wonder, to the same rug-yanking confirmation that the invitation had been real and we were no longer alone, or maybe we were more alone than we had ever been.

Large groups gathered around the hotel check-in desk and SarahCon registration, no doubt trying to pick themselves off the long lists of near-identical names. A third faction, which I decided to join, had adjourned to the lobby bar, hoping to use alcohol to blunt the weirdness of coming face to face with our multiverse selves. I found a barstool and shoved my suitcase and backpack under my feet. Space was tight amid the other suitcases and backpacks.

"The stout," I said when I caught the bartender's attention, pointing at the third tap handle.

He grinned and held up a glass. "Seventh one in a row. You all go for the stout or one of the good whiskeys."

I filed that information away. Took a sip. The Sarah next to me did the same. We both put our glasses down at the same time. Both raised eyebrows at each other.

The bartender hovered. "Room number for your tab?"

"I haven't checked in yet. Cash isn't okay? Oh. The cross-world currency thing."

"You can put her drink on my tab," said the me next to me. She wore her hair in a long braid down her back. I'd worn mine that way when I was thirteen.

I lifted my glass and toasted in her direction. "Thanks. Appreciated."

"My pleasure. I've never bought myself a drink before. Well, not like this anyhow. Do you know how many there are altogether? How many of us here, I mean."

I shook my head. "No clue. You could ask someone at registration."

A third Sarah, maybe a decade older than me, joined our conversation. My parents were married years before they had me. I'd always wondered if I'd still be me if they hadn't waited. "I'm sure she'll tell us the numbers in her opening address."

"She?" asked One Braid. "Sorry if it's a stupid question. I checked into my room but I haven't braved convention registration yet. I hate lines."

Older Sarah rummaged in a SarahCon commemorative tote bag and pulled out a program. She turned to a bio page and started reading. "'Sarah Pinsker [R0D0]'—I don't know what 'R-0-D-0' means—'made the discovery creating the multiverse portal. She is a quantologist at Johns Hopkins University.'" She looked up. "I think that's her over there. She's been rushing back and forth as long as I've been sitting here."

We followed her pointing finger to a Sarah bustling through the lobby, walkie-talkie to her lips. Her hair was pixie-short, defeating the frizz that plagued me. She looked harried but better put together than most of us, elegant in a silk blouse and designer jeans that fit and flattered. I had never been anything approaching elegant. Never had the guts to cut my hair that short, either.

"Quantologist," I repeated.

Older Sarah paged through the program. "It looks like there are four other quantologist Sarahs on the host committee."

One Braid scratched the back of her neck. "I've never heard of quantology. I don't think it's a real field of study where I'm from."

"Not where I'm from, either. Where are you from? I mean, answer however you want."

"I'm from all over the place," One Braid said. My usual answer. "But I live in Seattle."

Eerie. "Me, too. I went out for a job after college and stayed."

"Same! Summer job, then I met my girlfriend and settled for good. I'm in West Seattle. How about you?"

"Ballard." I raised my glass to clink hers, though that particular girlfriend and I hadn't lasted.

Older Sarah chugged her beer and waved for another before turning back to us. "Our Seattle was destroyed in an earthquake."

We both stared at her. She sipped her fresh beer and continued. "I never got out west myself, so it wasn't a personal thing for me, but it was horrible. Four thousand people died. The city never recovered."

I pictured our little house bucking and buckling, our yard splitting down the middle. Mabel, my friends and neighbors, the coffee shop up the street. Shuddered. It was too much to imagine. "This is so damn weird."

Older Sarah waved her program at me. "That's the name of the first panel. 'This Is So Damn Weird: Strategies for Navigating SarahCon Without Losing Your Mind.'"

One Braid and I both reached for our beers.

The registration line thinned as a programmed cocktail hour began in some lounge somewhere. Since I'd already been drinking for a while, I took the opportunity to check in and register.

"Find yourself on the list," said the Sarah behind the convention registration table. I could tell she was fried, like she was already too tired to remember how to put expressions on her face. I knew that feeling.

Looking at the list, it was easy to see why she'd had a long day already. My mind was still boggling at the handful of Sarahs I'd met; she'd come face to face with all of us.

The list grouped us by surname first. Mine the most common, a trunk instead of a branch. I paged past, curious. Mostly Pinskers like myself. Made sense if we were the closest realities to the Pinsker who had invited us. There were other random surnames I chalked up to marriage. A full page of Sarah Sweetloves. I'd never really considered changing my name for anyone, even Mabel, but apparently others had.

After surname came city, divided evenly between Seattle, Toronto, and Baltimore, with a few outliers in Northampton, Somerville, Asheville, New York, Pretoria. After that came birthdate, occupation. The occupation list read like a collection of every "What do you want to be when you grow up?" I'd ever answered. Geneticist, writer, therapeutic riding instructor, teacher, history professor, astronomer, journalist, dog trainer, barn manager. I was the only insurance investigator. In fairness, it had never exactly been on the greatest hits list.

Address messed with me the most for some reason. Someone else here shared my full name, birthdate, and address. She worked as a program director at a non-profit. That was the only place our lines on the list differed. Where else did we diverge? Did we move around our house in the same ways at the same times? Had she fallen in love with the kitchen first, too? Did she live with an alternate Mabel?

"There's a Making Connections board over there." The volunteer behind the table pointed to a poster on the far wall of the lobby. She sounded like she'd said it a hundred times already. "In case you come across somebody you absolutely have to meet. Judging from your face, you just found somebody on the list who intrigues you. Somebody who wears the same life as you, or near to it."

It brought to my mind those grade school puzzle pages with six or nine near-identical cats or robots drawn in a grid, where you were supposed to find the matched pair hidden among the ones with slight differences. In the same moment I had that thought, a Sarah perusing another copy of the list said it to me.

I looked her over. The invitation had said, "Be yourself." We both wore jeans and *Wonder Woman* T-shirts, hers with a graphic from the 70s TV show and mine from the 2005 Gina Torres movie. We both had our hair pulled back in messy ponytails. The only difference I noticed was that her skin was much better than mine.

The volunteer didn't bother to look down at the list when I highlighted my name and returned it to her. She handed me a program and a tote bag. "You can decide whether you want to bother with a nametag."

I looked at the markers and stickers piled on the table. "Is there a point?"

"Not with a name like yours, unless you have a nickname you think is particularly original. Though it probably isn't. There are a few non-Sarahs. They're the only ones who really need to bother. Right at the beginning we tried making people choose a nickname, but the first eight tried their identical middle names, and then four had the same roller derby name, and three asked for the name they all used as counselors at Girl Scout camp, and we gave up."

It didn't seem worth it. I went over to the hotel check-in line, made slightly easier with individual registration numbers. The desk clerk was one of us too, in a business suit and a manager's gold nametag that suggested this was probably her home reality.

"The credit card you registered with will be charged by a third party billing company that's handling the cross-world weirdness. Bill anything you buy to your room." She spoke with an accent I couldn't place.

"Where are you from?" I asked her.

"I live just over on the mainland. You?"

"Seattle."

A sympathetic look crossed her face.

I tried to change the subject before she told me Seattle was gone in this reality too. "So why is this being held on Secord Island?"

"Everyone asks." She smiled, showing gapped teeth. She'd never gotten braces. "It's a sovereign island off the east coast of Canada. You know Canada?"

I nodded, wondering what variation had prompted that question.

She continued. "Sovereign island, at least in this reality, so the organizer didn't have to worry about visas or passports. You're all allowed here, then back to where you came from."

"What if someone tried to skip off this island? Not that I would. I'm an insurance investigator. Professional questioner of motives."

Another grin. "That's why all the boats were sent away for the weekend. We're stuck with you, or you're stuck with us."

She put a keycard in a paper sleeve and pulled out a pen. "Do you have keycards in your world?"

"Yeah." I glanced at the number she'd written, committed it to memory, pocketed the card, and handed her back the sleeve to discard.

"You're the only one so far to do that," she said. "Congrats on being original."

I gave her a little salute and went to find my room in the annex, the cheapest room available when I'd registered. Her directions led out of the original building and down an L-shaped hallway tacked onto the back. I passed a stressed-looking housekeeper pushing a cart full of cleaning supplies, then two Sarahs trying to wrangle a cot into a tiny room, under the direction of a third, who looked up and waved. They must have taken advantage of the room-sharing option in the questionnaire that followed the RSVP. I'd liked that offer; it meant the Sarahs who attended wouldn't only be those with the time and privilege to do so. That had even gotten Mabel to tone down some of her teasing about the whole event.

Around the next bend, a different type of cold than the air-conditioned lobby, that of Canadian November penetrating a closed system. Someone had propped open the fire door at the hall's end. I unlocked my door, dropped my bags in my bathtub, then went to get a look outside.

When I leaned out the fire door, I found two Sarahs smoking, shoulders hunched against a biting wind. A vivid bruise of a cloudbank pressed down overhead, making it seem much later than it was. The air tasted like cigarettes and salt water. We had a dramatic landlocked view of a loading dock and a couple of dumpsters, but I felt the sea lurking nearby. I felt oddly displaced, jetlagged without the jet. Portal lag, maybe.

"Join us?" The curls spilling down her shoulders were dyed carrot orange, a color that said it was not trying for anything natural. They looked wild and luxurious, when I only ever managed feral at best.

The other looked less healthy. Beneath her toque, her cheeks were gaunt, and the No Good Deeds T-shirt under her bomber jacket swam on her. She held out a pack of American Spirits.

"I'm good," I said. "But hey, No Good Deeds. They were a cool band."

She grinned, showing yellowed teeth. "ARE a good band. Bam! Divergence point! In my world they're on album number six and still awesome."

"The hall isn't getting too cold, is it?" Orange Curls asked. "The door locks if we shut it. I had to walk around the whole building earlier. It's huge."

The other lit a new cigarette off her old one, then stubbed out the butt with a worn combat boot. "I've got to go back inside in a minute anyhow."

She didn't look like she was in any hurry. I assured them it wasn't too cold, mostly because I didn't want to be That Person, which they probably knew. We didn't like to inconvenience people.

"So why are you here?" Orange Curls was the chattier of the two.

"What do you mean? I got an invitation."

No Good Deeds shook her head. "She's asking what made you accept. Excitement, curiosity, wonder, a desire to exploit? Not that you're limited to those choices."

I thought about it. Mabel had said the whole thing was an exercise in narcissism.

She'd read the invitation, then tossed it on the table, laughing. "Who discovers how to access infinite realities and then uses that discovery to invite her alternate selves to a convention?"

"Some other me, apparently." As I'd said it, I'd known it was true. "Why, what would you do?"

Her response came easily. "Talk to world leaders or scientists. Find out why one reality is running out of water and another is doing fine, or how one made the transition from fossil fuel to solar. Check in on the state of democracy. Something useful. Anyway, you hate decisions. This'll just make you question every choice you ever made. Should you have gone to grad school? Should you have stayed with this ex or that one? How would your life be different if you'd managed to buy that horse you loved as a teenager? If I were you, I wouldn't want to know the answers. I mean, you've got to go, obviously, but it's a wasted opportunity if you don't talk about some of that stuff."

Everything she'd said was true, like usual.

I looked back at Orange Curls. "Curiosity. I guess I'm here because I'm curious. And maybe a little because if I stayed home I'd always wonder about it."

The smokers shot each other a satisfied look.

"She's asked twenty-one Sarahs that question now," No Good Deeds said, "and that's been the answer every time. Even the same phrasing."

I retreated to my room. Stripped the bedspread, checked the mattress for bedbugs. Searched the room and the bathroom for cameras and peepholes in case we really were all part of someone's psych experiment.

Concerns assuaged, I dumped my backpack's contents onto the table and repacked the stuff I wanted to carry with me for the evening, then flopped onto the bed to read the program. It contained a basic explanation of the multiverse theory, a welcome note, a sponsor page, a thank you page, a map, and "Fun Statistics!" based on the questionnaires we'd filled out prior to arriving. Ninety two percent of us played instruments. Five percent of us owned horses, thirteen percent owned cats, eighty percent owned dogs. One person lived in a world where dogs had been rendered extinct by a virus. So much for fun.

A program schedule took up the rest of the pages. Some of the serious stuff Mabel had wanted to see was mixed in: "Let My World Solve Your World's Water Problem," "Climate Change Strategies That Actually Worked." "The Way It Could Have Been: Political Divergence Points."

Alongside that, the topics piquing my own curiosity. "Gender, Sexuality, and Me." "Driving Forces: Favorite Cars, Stolen Cars, Those Who Never Learned to Drive." "Let's Talk Family." "The Babysitting Incident and Other Divergence Points." "Why We Live Where We Live." "Horses and Dogs and Cats, Oh My." "Outliers." "Yes, Another Horse Panel." "Music and Art." Some were listed as panels, others as moderated large-group discussions.

The second evening was filled with concerts and readings and art shows by the more creative among us. Tonight featured a keynote speech by the host, followed by a DJ'ed dance. Normally that wouldn't be my thing, but the thought of a dance with a self-curated song list—I pictured upbeat soul, Bowie, 80s pop—and an entire room full of enthusiastic but uniformly terrible dancers, excited me more than I'd admit. There'd be nobody to watch who wouldn't understand. Maybe I wouldn't even be the worst dancer in the room. A girl could dream.

I glanced at the clock on the table. Enough time for a nap before dinner. The organizers of "This Is So Damn Weird" were probably sitting in an empty room, sighing to themselves, wishing they could grab a few minutes' sleep too.

We had all just started on our salads in the banquet hall when the Sarah from hotel registration approached my table. Her uniform still made her one of the easier ones to recognize.

The hotel employee knelt by the Sarah to my left, who had my haircut and who was wearing the same T-shirt as me, only with a long sleeved shirt underneath it. She was the only one I'd seen with a prosthetic hand. It was a good prosthetic; I wouldn't have noticed it if we hadn't stood at a washroom sink next to each other before the meal. Other than the hand, she'd looked more like me than most; I desperately wanted to figure out where we'd diverged, but hadn't worked up the nerve to ask her yet.

"Pardon," said Hotel Sarah. "Did you say earlier you were a detective?"

Prosthetic Hand shook her head. "I wouldn't have said that. Not anymore. Go fish."

I traced the scar on my own left wrist and wondered how many worlds you had to travel away from mine before you reached one where Go Fish wasn't a game.

Hotel Sarah straightened up, put her hands on her hips, scanned the room. I debated not identifying myself, just to observe how she approached the problem of discreetly finding the sole detective in a room full of functionally identical people. My curiosity over why she was looking for me won out. Curiosity and pity; I recognized the panic just under her surface. Everyone at the table recognized it. It rippled over us like a wave.

"Right table, wrong person," I said in a low voice. "How can I help you?"

Her relief was so obvious I felt guilty for having considered withholding. "Would you mind coming with me?"

Seven faces watched as I stood up from the table: prosthetic hand Sarah, left handed Sarah, bearded Dare, bearded Josh, stubble-faced Joshua—the three of them had sat together to compare notes, they'd said—and two random Sarahs I hadn't yet managed to meet or distinguish because I was more interested in the others. They reopened questions I had closed for myself. From the way we had all allowed them to center conversation, I guessed that was the case with everyone else who'd sat down at this table, too.

All seven had pushed the olives to the side of their salads, as I had. I pictured dishwashers scraping the entire room's worth of olives off our plates at meal's end. Wondered how the organizers had proactively made the entire weekend vegetarian, but forgotten to tell the kitchen we didn't like olives.

Maybe whoever had set the menu was an outlier who assumed they were in the majority.

I stuffed a dinner roll into my bag in case I missed the entire meal. The others all nodded approvingly, knowing we didn't work well when hungry.

Hotel Sarah led me through the lobby and down another doglegged corridor, this one in the opposite direction of my own. I pictured the building's aerial footprint, a sprawling figure. We passed a tiny convenience store, a shuttered boutique, a small arcade where a lone Sarah manipulated a claw machine. An elevator waited open at the end of the hall. Once inside, she used a key to unlock it and pressed for the third floor, the top.

The elevator was the slowest I'd ever ridden. I waited for her to tell me where we were going, or why. When no explanation came, I concentrated on figuring out the observable differences between us. There were none, or none beyond the superficial. Her tailored uniform, her short, tight curls versus my shaggy ponytail. She was sizing me up in the same way; I wondered what she saw.

The elevator opened onto a dark room. An enormous nightclub, I realized, as my eyes adjusted. There was a long bar down one side, and on the opposite side a row of well-dressed folding tables holding some kind of display. In the center of the room, dozens of small tables ringed the perimeter of a dance floor. Beyond the dance floor, a high stage with a single podium and a DJ table. It took me another few seconds to notice the slumped figure in the stage's shadow.

As I approached, I saw what had the hotel manager so spooked: a dead Sarah.

Not me, my logic brain understood, even though some tiny part of me screamed something was wrong. I'd made it through the entire afternoon talking with people who were more like me than an identical twin would be, but the body was somehow more real. The others down at dinner all had stories to remind me I was still myself, that I could still be differentiated. Absent stories and quirks, absent a person talking at me to prove we were not the same, the vacuum came rushing in. Who was she? In what ways was she me, in what ways was she not? Who would mourn her? I tried to imagine the shape of my own absence from my own world. It was an impossible exercise.

I struggled to regain control over myself. "You know I'm an insurance investigator, right? Dead bodies aren't my area of expertise."

"You're the closest thing we've got. None of us are medical doctors, and it's too late for one anyhow, and I figured you investigate things. I couldn't find any of the organizers, so I thought I'd look for you." She must have had a good memory for details, if she managed to find me in that dining hall based on one short conversation. Maybe that was a thing we all had in common.

Anyway, she was right: I did like a good puzzle. Not that I had any idea if this even was one yet. "Are there lights in here?"

She disappeared from my side, and the house lights came up a moment later. The room looked much smaller without the depth of shadow.

The body wasn't me, I told myself. I concentrated on the differences rather than the eerie familiarity. Her cheeks were hollower than mine. She had more freckles, close-cropped hair. My empty stomach lurched.

She was starting to cool to the touch. I felt for a pulse, though I didn't expect to find one. Her eyes were open, her pupils tiny in the blue. For some reason it brought the 90s John Lennon song "Change Your Tune" into my head, lyrics twisted. *You'll change your eyes, dear.*

I shook the song away. Focus. She slumped against the stage, half-sitting, head leaning back against the stage. She wore a silk dress with a hibiscus flower print, louder than anything I'd wear, but not in a bad way.

"What's your story?" I asked her under my breath.

I crouched to examine her hands and arms, trying not to move her too much. The nails had been bitten painfully short, but there was nothing under them that implied a fight. Some bruises and track marks on the insides of her arms, not all of them scabbed over, but nothing to suggest she'd tried to protect herself from the fall. I didn't see any blood anywhere, but I didn't want to move her until police or a coroner came.

Hotel Sarah stared at the body, absently chewing on her thumb.

"Why me?" I asked.

Not the question she'd expected, or else she'd tuned me out. "Pardon?"

"I know you said I was the closest thing to a detective, but why do you need someone to investigate? Aren't the police on their way?"

She shook her head. "Gale force winds on the Sound tonight. They can't make it out here by boat or helicopter."

"What about a medical team? Surely there's a medic here."

"We paid a paramedic team to come out to the island this weekend, but they turned around because of the weather, too. My staff have basic CPR and first aid, but, well . . . "

I finished her sentence. "—but she's obviously already dead."

"Yeah. I thought maybe you'd be the next best thing to police, until they can get here. If she had a heart attack or stroke or just fell off the stage, it's sad but nothing to worry about. If it was foul play"—the phrase sounded funny, like something on television—"we're stuck with a murderer all weekend. If the police don't get here in time, we can't keep people from the portals. They're timed precisely."

"How about security? Surely you have security staff."

She dismissed them with a wave. "They've never had to handle anything worse than kids setting off the fire alarms."

"And I know I said this already, but you understand I'm in insurance? I investigate fraud. People lying about whiplash, that kind of thing. Not even the glamorous cheating-spouse stuff."

She shrugged. I decided not to give her any harder time about it. She'd made a decision, never my strong point. She was probably already questioning herself, wondering what other option she hadn't considered.

I was what they had. Right. So until police got here, I played coroner, law, and order. Not a role I was comfortable with at all, made weirder by the circumstance. Victim: Sarah. Investigator: Sarah. Suspects: All variations on the theme, other than the hotel staff. Hard to imagine one of us murdering; I knew I didn't have it in me to kill someone. Also hard to imagine the hotel staff bothering; most murders involved somebody the victim knew.

I summoned up my inner TV detective. "Just to rule this out, nobody on your staff has any beef with you that you're aware of? Nobody would be driven to kill by an entire hotel full of your dopplegangers?"

"I think we're all weirded out by that, myself included. But I don't think any of them hate me and I don't think I work with any killers, though I guess that's what everybody says. 'He was such a nice man. He kept to himself.' " She touched her nametag. "Anyway, if they hated me, I'd think they go after me, not one of you. I'm easy to spot."

"True enough. I'll put them aside for now." Though that meant focusing on the Sarahs again. "Were you the one who found the body?"

"No. The DJ did. She called me." She held up her walkie-talkie.

"The DJ is one of us, right? Not your staff?"

"All the performers this weekend are attendees."

"And where is the DJ now?"

"She went back to her room. She was a little freaked out." Understandable, if her reaction to seeing her own dead twin was anything like mine.

"Has anyone else been up here?"

"The Sarah running sound and lights came up to check the system earlier for the host's speech."

"The host. Have you told her yet?"

Hotel Sarah chewed at her thumb again. "That's the thing. Like I said, I haven't been able to reach her. The organizers are all on walkie-talkies since your phones don't work here, but she's not answering hers. Nobody on the committee is answering, actually. That's why I took matters into my own hands. Last I saw her, she was down in their Operations room, but she'd been up here earlier, so she could have come back for something."

I looked down at the body. Tried to remember the woman who had breezed through the lobby earlier. "Are you saying you think this might be the organizer?"

She didn't say anything, so I continued. "Do you remember anything specific about her? Anything to differentiate her?"

Her look suggested the question was a pointless one. "She was a little thinner than most. I think she runs marathons. Most of the committee do."

The body was freckled and thin. She could have been a runner. A runner with a possible drug problem seemed a little counterproductive, but maybe she had pain issues or something.

"How about her clothing? Do you remember what she was wearing?" The woman I'd seen earlier had been in a blouse and jeans, not a dress, but she'd had time to change her clothes.

She shook her head. "I have a pretty good memory for detail, but everyone's blending together . . . "

"You don't have a registration list, do you? That might be useful. We need to try to identify the body before anything else."

"I'm sorry. I didn't think to bring one up here. That couldn't be her, right? Should I try to find her again? She's going to need to notify the next of kin, and create a procedure to bring a body cross-world. Nobody's ever died in the wrong world before."

Infinite permutations. Surely someone must have. Except that for all the individual crossworld expeditions, according to the program this was the first gathering of its kind. Our host, one of us, the Sarah who had created the crossworld portal. It made me feel like I had wasted my life, in comparison. What would I have had to do differently to become a scientist? Her branch of science didn't even exist as a field in my world. And now she was possibly lying dead in front of me.

Focus. If I hadn't been carrying a backpack, I'd have put my ID and my keycard into my front right pocket. Her silk dress had a shallow pocket at the hip. When I slid my hand into it, I came up with a driver's license. Her ID gave her name as Sarah Pinsker, which wasn't much help. An address in Baltimore; the host worked at Johns Hopkins.

I held up the license. "Do you know how many here this weekend live in Baltimore?"

"Forty or fifty? There would be more if so many hadn't been lost, from what I understand."

"Lost? Baltimore?"

"A bunch of Seattles were lost in tsunamis or earthquakes. Some of us moved from Baltimore to Seattle or Seattle to Baltimore . . . "

I followed her train of thought, pictured a giant wave swallowing my house. Shuddered, brought myself back to the situation at hand.

"So this might still be our host. One in forty or fifty in that city, but maybe we can narrow it down when names and addresses come into it. It probably isn't the sound person, since she's dressed up a bit. Isn't the DJ, since the DJ found her. The host wasn't working alone this weekend, was she? The registration desk, entertainment, programming . . . She had a committee, you said?"

"Yeah. Four others pretty similar to her. They'd all been on the verge of making the same discovery, so they were the first ones she reached out to."

Next question, if I was acting sheriff. "I don't suppose this bar has a walk-in fridge or freezer?"

"Why? Oh god. Shit. Yeah, there's a walk-in fridge."

"You take the legs and I'll get the arms?"

She nodded.

As I positioned myself, the body's head tipped forward, and I saw what I would have looked for earlier, if I were a real detective: a sickening, deadly deep indentation at the back of the skull. A cave-in. The hair was matted and sticky-looking, blood and—I didn't want to look closer.

"I think I found the cause of death," I said. "And I think we can rule out natural causes. Fuck."

I didn't want to touch the head any more than I wanted to look, but we still had to move the body. I grabbed a towel from the bar and wrapped her like she'd just stepped out of the shower. It still lolled against me as I lifted, and I fought the urge to be sick. She wasn't heavy, wasn't yet stiff. Rigor mortis started two hours after death. An odor came off her; a body doing body things, I told myself.

We put her in the walk-in in a recreation of the position she'd been sitting in. I inspected her exposed parts. No blood other than the back of her head. No bullet holes. Some bruises, as I'd noted earlier, but none that looked like they came from a fight or a fall. I wasn't comfortable looking any further than that. After, I waited while Hotel Sarah rummaged in a drawer for notepad and tape and made a thick-markered "Do Not Open" sign for the fridge door.

"So do you think she just fell and hit her head?" she asked. "Or do you think she was murdered?"

There was a hopeful note in her voice on the first option, but below that, I could tell she didn't believe it any more than I did. "*You* do, or else you want me to reassure you that the track marks suggest she overdosed and stumbled off the stage. Otherwise you wouldn't have asked me up here. You would have dealt with it quietly, to keep from scaring the rest of the guests or harming the convention. You still want to deal with it quietly."

She shifted from foot to foot. I recognized her restlessness. She felt helpless. Wanted something concrete to do, a decision made for her, a plan.

"Okay, here's what I need from you," I said, taking pity. I didn't know my next step, but I could give her a task. "Go back down to registration, make me a copy of whatever you've got down there. Um, and what time was that dance supposed to start? They can decide if they want to have it in some other space, but they probably shouldn't have it in here, in case there's still evidence to be found. And, you know, out of respect. I'm going to look around right now, but I'd think the police would still want this left untouched."

"I think they'll cancel the dance. The DJ didn't look fit to play."

"I'm going to need to talk to her, too. But maybe downstairs, so she doesn't have to come back in here? And the sound person."

She nodded and left.

There really wasn't anything else to do without the registration list. And it wouldn't do any good to interview people without the right questions. Hard to ask who else was up here, when everyone looked the same. Hard to ask "Where were you at x o'clock?" if you didn't solve for x. I could at least guess at that.

Or start with the crime scene; I walked back over. The stage was about chest high. I'd only had eyes for her before, but looking now, there was a blood smear on the stage's lip just above where the body had been. The spot where she'd hit her head? No, the lip wasn't the right shape to have caused the damage, I didn't think. I pictured myself tripping or slipping off the edge of the stage, but I couldn't imagine a way I would have fallen that would have had that result. No scuff marks, no chips in the wood, no bone fragments or hair. Just the one small smear and a deeper bloodstain where her head had been resting when we got to her. The wound itself hadn't bled a lot. Maybe a forensic expert could see more.

A coroner would be useful, too. They'd be able to say if she'd fought someone, though I didn't think so. She hadn't looked scared or angry or horrified or even distressed. Dead. An absence of her, an absence of me.

The stage had two narrow curtained wings, and stairs on both sides. I walked to the front of the stage, to the spot where she must have slipped off or fallen after being hit. I tried to imagine falling from here. If someone had hit me from behind, I'd have put my hands out, fallen forward, unless they had dropped me in my tracks. There was no scenario I could think of that would result in stepping straight off to hit the back of my head on the stage. Maybe if I was looking behind me as I walked, and missed the edge? Even then, I'd expect more of a twist, a person trying to catch herself as she went down.

Something caught my eye a few feet from the stage, under the pedestal foot of the first table. I hopped down carefully. A keycard, still in its envelope. Room 517. The dead Sarah's pockets were shallow enough that it could have fallen from her pocket, though the trajectory didn't seem quite right. I dropped it into my bag and looked around to see if the floor held any other secrets, but didn't see anything. Back to the stage.

The far wing was packed with music equipment and PA speakers. I hefted one of the mic stands. It had a pedestal base, heavy enough to hit someone with. There were six of them in a row, and any of them could be a murder weapon, though I didn't see blood, and they were rounded where the wound had looked angular.

The wing closer to the DJ table was empty except the top of a travel case. It was black and silver, all the edges and corners reinforced with metal. I hefted it: heavy, and this was the unpacked half. The underside was foam, cut to fit the turntables. It had a small dent in one corner, and I flipped it to look at it closely. The shape was right, but it would be an awkward thing to wield. Still, I mentally added it to the list.

I felt around the edges and found a luggage tag. Sarah Pinsker. The unmoored feeling caught me again; it was getting more familiar. Seattle address, in Rainier Beach, if I was right about the zip code. One of the cheaper neighborhoods to rent in the city, at least in my world.

The DJ equipment was set up on a table in front of the alcove. Under the table, two full record crates. I thumbed through them, amused I'd guessed the genres correctly. On the table, two fancy looking vinyl turntables with a mixing console in between, all cushioned in the other half of the travel case. I knew nothing about DJ gear, didn't know if this was expensive or cheap equipment. There were two records already on the turntables, the Sharon Jones/David Bowie cover of Bowie's "Modern Love," and Stevie Wonder's "Signed, Sealed, Delivered, I'm Yours." I'd have had fun dancing to those. Too bad the dance wouldn't happen now.

There was an "SP" in silver marker at each record's center, and on each piece of equipment. I pictured tomorrow's lineup of musicians, all with the SPs that normally differentiated their gear from others'.

I ran my finger over a spot where the foam had separated from the protective casing. Some glue would stick it back, an easy repair, except as I touched it I realized something had been pushed down in between. I crooked a finger into the gap and felt around until I snagged a tiny envelope. Tapped it out into my palm: eight tiny pills. I didn't recognize them, but I didn't have any knowledge of narcotics. They could be ibuprofen, for all I knew, though most people didn't go around slipping envelopes of ibuprofen into secret cubbies. In my world, anyway.

"Hello?" someone called from the back of the room.

I tucked the pills back in the envelope and the envelope into my pocket alongside the keycard. "Over here."

A Sarah made her way over to me. She wore cargo shorts, black combat boots, and a T-shirt for a band I didn't recognize. She walked with a swagger. Interesting to consider how we might have developed different walks.

"They asked me to bring up a copy of the registration list." She held a red three-ring binder out to me.

I hopped off the stage to take it from her. "Thanks. Are you the sound tech?"

"Yeah. I'd introduce myself, but it hardly seems worth it."

I smiled. "Hardly. But I wouldn't mind if you pointed out which name is yours, so I can start taking notes."

She took the book back from me and flipped to the last page in one sure movement. "Mine is easy, since I took my wife's last name. Yarrow. Last person in the whole book."

I grabbed my pen off the table where'd I left it and circled her occupation to remind myself who she was. "Do you mind if I ask you a few questions?"

"Go ahead."

"What time did you come up here?"

"Three-thirty. There wasn't a whole lot to set up, but it always takes a little longer when you're not working with your own gear. I soundchecked the DJ, then the keynote speaker. Figured out how to run her slideshow. After that I took some time to get situated with the light board. I'm not really a lighting person, but it's pretty well labeled. I think I was out of here by four-thirty."

"Were they both still up here when you left?"

"No. The DJ left after we tested her gear through the PA. She'd managed to haul her big case and one crate of records up here in one go, but she said she had to get a second crate from her room on the other side of the hotel."

"And she didn't come back?"

"I figured she got to talking to someone, or took a nap or something. She didn't come back while I was here."

"And the host stayed? The, ah, keynote speaker?"

"She said she wanted to go over her speech while nobody was in the room."

"Did anybody else come up?"

"Not that I saw."

I paused to consider what else I needed to ask. "Would you recognize the keynote?" She cocked her head, and I amended my question. "You don't have to be definitive. But if you know it's NOT her, that would be helpful."

I led her to the fridge. "I should have asked: are you okay looking at her? I can warn you it's a little freaky looking at a dead person who looks like you."

"This whole thing is freaky. I'll be okay."

We approached within a couple feet of the body. The vertiginous feeling hit me again.

"It could be her?" she said, half statement and half question. "But, uh, she was wearing something else. She had on jeans, not a dress. Maybe she left and changed into what she was going to wear tonight and came back?"

That made sense. Or the manager's fear that this might be the host was unfounded.

"That definitely helps," I said. "You can go if you need to."

She nodded. "They're going to have to find someplace else for tonight's programming, so I should probably find out where they want me. But, hey, it's good to have something to do, right?"

I hadn't considered it until then, but it was true. As disturbing as the idea of a dead me was, something about the whole weird weekend became more concrete now that I had a purpose. No wonder so many had signed up to run sound and registration and play music and lead discussions. The other volunteers must have been self-aware enough to recognize it before they arrived.

I sat down on the stage's edge with the list. Flipped to the "Sarah Pinsker" section, the big section, and put stars next to the ones who lived in Baltimore. The host and eleven others, since several Baltimore Sarahs had taken other surnames. Five of the remaining Sarahs were Quantologists. They all had a big C after their name. Committee, I guessed. All five lived at the same address, the address on the license in the deceased's pocket. The lone difference between them on paper was a designation in the last column. R0D0, R1D0, R0D1, R1D1, R0D1A. No clue what that meant, but the program had listed a parenthetical R0D0 after the host's name, so I circled that one.

I paged through the book for a while, making notes beside the entries for the DJ, the hotel clerk, the sound tech, and a few others I'd met who stood out from the pack. It would have been really interesting reading material any other day; now it was a headache.

I still hadn't finished my circuit of the room. I searched the bar for something with the right shape and heft to be the murder weapon. A couple of the bottles might have fit the bill, but I would have thought they'd smash on impact.

My desire for diligence didn't extend to alone-time with the body, so I decided against searching the fridge. I wandered across the floor. The back of a chair or barstool? Or the leg? Possible, and a pain to check them all.

On the far side of the room, four folding tables covered with velveteen tablecloths. A printed sign hung on the wall behind them: Sarah Pinsker Hall of Fame.

Each table held a series of objects. A few had explanatory notecards in front of them, but most spoke for themselves. I remembered the questionnaire: "Do you have any special awards or achievements you'd like to show off? Bring them for our brag table!" I'd have thought they'd have better security, but then again, up until now I would have thought I could trust my other selves.

If the list of occupations had made me feel like an underachiever, this display reinforced it. A Grammy for Best Folk Album 2013, a framed photo of a Sarah in the Kentucky Derby winner's circle, a Best Original Screenplay Oscar, a stack of novels, a Nebula Award for science fiction writing, an issue of *Quantology Today* containing an article with a seventy word title that I guessed amounted to "Other Realities! I Found Them!" A few awards I didn't recognize, though I wasn't sure if that was because they didn't exist in my reality or I just hadn't heard of them.

Two of the awards looked like they had the shape to be the murder weapon, and one of them looked like it had the weight as well: the Nebula, a three-dimensional rectangular block of Lucite, shot through with stars and planets. What did you call a three-dimensional rectangle, anyway? I didn't want to pick it up without gloves, but I used the back of my hand to push it gently backward. It was heavy enough, for sure.

As I touched the award, I felt a strange certainty this was it. That if I were to murder someone, which I absolutely wouldn't do, this would be the weapon of choice. Not the mic stands, not the chairs, not the turntable case: this glittering block that would travel back to another reality at the end of the weekend with its owner none the wiser. I shuddered and shook the thought off.

Stooping to examine it closer, I didn't see any sign of blood or hair. In fact, there wasn't a single fingerprint on it, which was odd enough in itself. The other statuettes had fingerprints, but this one looked like it had been polished clean.

If this was the murder weapon, what did that say about the murder? Was it an act of passion, carried out with an item at hand? Was there any significance to the choice? If it was premeditated, that would narrow the list of suspects to the people who knew it would be up here: the host committee and the writer who had brought it. The list of people who had seen it here was probably more or less the list I'd already made of people who had been up to the room. Not much help.

Nobody else came upstairs, and after a while I got sick of waiting. I headed back down to the lobby. Passed the arcade, now empty, and the convenience store, now closed. The registration table, cluttered with nametags and markers, otherwise abandoned. A few people sat in the lobby, but the mood was markedly different than it had been before dinner. I gathered word had spread.

A new clerk was working the front desk, an acned non-Sarah in his late teens or early twenties. I held up my registration binder like an overlarge badge, trying to look harried and committee-bound. "I don't suppose if I gave you a name and ID code, you'd tell me what room someone is staying in? Official business?"

He nodded. I flipped to the DJ's name and pointed. After a moment's typing, he looked back up at me. "107. That's in the annex. Do you know where that is?"

My room was in the annex, but if the committee members were all staying in the tower, I didn't want to break the illusion. I let him point me in the direction of my room. Her door was a few down from my own.

I knocked a few times before she heard me. When the door swung open, I recognized the person on the other side. "That makes sense! I didn't realize you were the DJ."

She smiled blankly. I pointed at her T-shirt. "We met outside earlier? When you were smoking? No Good Deeds?"

"Oh, yeah." She replaced the empty smile with a warmer one. "It's hard to keep everyone straight. Can I help you?"

"I'm, uh, investigating the death of the Sarah you found. I'm a detective. Do you mind if I come in and ask you a few questions?"

She opened the door wider, and I followed her into the room. The first bed's bedspread lay in a heap on the floor. Her duffel's contents were scattered across the second bed, in some sort of half-organization. A pile of greyed-out underwear, a few T-shirts, neatly folded, a pile of tampons, pack of cigarettes.

"Sorry," she said. "I always spread out in hotels. You can have the chair." She flopped down on the first bed. "Did you say you were investigating her death? She looked like she fell off the stage to me. Not that it wasn't freaky to see her, you know?"

"Yeah," I agreed. "But the hotel manager asked me to look around a little. Because of the circumstances."

"Oh. Okay."

"Are you alright with me asking you some questions?"

"Go ahead. It's all a little upsetting, though. I'm not sure I'm thinking straight."

That might be chemical, if the pills I'd found were hers. "Can you walk me through the afternoon?"

"I loaded my stuff into the room around four. Set up, soundchecked. Came back down here to get my second crate of records. When I went back, that's when I saw her."

"Do you know how long you were gone?"

She shrugged. I tried to remember when I'd run into her. She must have gone out for a smoke before going back with the crate.

"Where were you when you saw her? Where in the club, I mean?"

"As I was coming down the aisle toward the stage. She was just sitting there. I thought she had sat down, but then I realized the posture was funny."

"And—sorry—was she definitely already dead by then?"

She bit her lower lip, bringing it to the white of her teeth. "Her eyes were open. I nudged her leg, but she didn't respond, so I checked for a pulse."

"Was she warm or cold to your touch?"

"Warm. I've never seen a dead person before, and she looked so . . . " She shuddered. I did too.

"And then you left her there? To go for help?"

"No! I made a call on her walkie-talkie. I figured the other people in charge would be on the other end, and maybe someone from the hotel."

I closed my eyes to mentally revisit the scene. "There wasn't a walkie-talkie there."

Her eyes widened. "There was. I swear, I called on it. Ask the manager. It was next to the body. She'd been carrying it around before, complaining it dragged her jeans down."

"Her jeans? Before she changed into the dress and came back?"

She gave me a quizzical look.

There wasn't really much point to asking her anything else if she couldn't even get basic details right. Her confusion felt genuine. "Thanks for letting me in. 'Questions lead to questions lead to answers lead to answers,' right?"

"I hope so," she said absently, standing up and ushering me out. "I hope you get her home okay."

She'd completely ignored the No Good Deeds lyric I'd used as a peace offering. Second and last album in my world, their one hit single. I wondered if it was the drugs or the shock, or she just wasn't the fan I'd thought she was earlier.

Back in the hallway, I dug in my bag for a pen. I'd normally have taken notes while she talked, but I'd had a feeling it would have shut her up. Instead of a pen, I came up with the dinner roll I'd taken earlier. I ate it in two bites. Diving in again, my fingers settled on the key card I'd found in the nightclub. Room 517. In the tower, I guessed. Might as well check it out.

I rode the tower elevator—much faster than the one to the nightclub— with two Sarahs who were making eyes at each other in a way that made me deeply uncomfortable. I was happy to escape.

Room 517 was around the corner and down the hall. My shoes sank into plush carpeting. Pushing a luggage cart through it wouldn't be any fun, but maybe tower people paid bellhops to do the grunt work. The halls up here had actual wallpaper, tasteful stripes, in contrast with our bare-walled wing.

I paused for a moment outside the room, trying to hear if there was anyone moving inside, preparing myself to find . . . I didn't know what. I hadn't gotten clearance to do this. Then again, nobody had told me not to, which was basically permission. I knocked, waited for an answer, knocked again.

The swipe card worked on the first try. I stepped inside. The light had been left on. The furniture looked like hardwood instead of plywood, and the room was maybe a foot or two wider, but I didn't really see anything to justify the cost difference between this space and mine.

Three dresses hung in the open closet, in styles similar to the dead woman's. Worn gym clothes lay crumpled in the corner next to the first bed, a pair of sneakers half-buried underneath the pile. The closer bed had obviously been slept in; if she was the organizer, she'd probably been here a night or two early to get situated before the rest of us arrived. She'd dumped her suitcase— mostly underwear and bras—out on the second bedspread. Maybe in her world hotel bedspreads got washed along with the sheets.

A toiletry bag had been emptied on the bathroom counter. Ipana gel toothpaste, the exact same product I used. How much could toothpaste change from world to world? The makeup was an assortment of familiar and unfamiliar brands, so maybe I was wrong. A damp towel hung over the shower curtain rod. So far, this was the room of someone who had assumed she would be coming back. I flushed the toilet for her, as a courtesy. Immediately regretted it as disposing of evidence.

The room door clicked shut, startling me. Had I left it open? I didn't remember closing it when I'd entered. Maybe someone had gone into another room on the hall and the wind had pulled this one closed. I'd lived in houses where that happened. I opened the door and peered down the empty hallway.

I'd left her second bag for last, under the hope there was a clue waiting somewhere for me. A clue, like I was a real detective, not somebody who flushed away evidence. The bag was an expensive-looking leather satchel. My style, if I had the cash for it.

There were a few things I was expecting to find and didn't. I'd expected a registration binder like the one I had in my bag. I didn't see a walkie-talkie or charger, though maybe the charger was in the convention's Ops room the manager had mentioned earlier, wherever that was. I did find a program, with a couple of items circled. Not the ones I expected. "Sarahs in the Sciences" on Sunday morning and a penned in Information Desk shift from 12–4 PM on Saturday. Not the keynote. Maybe she didn't have to circle it because it went without saying.

The rest of the bag was filled with the usual odds and ends I carried: pens, gum, emergency flashlight, loose change. A dog-eared paperback novel called *Parable of the Trickster*.

No wallet. I looked in all the places I'd have left a wallet if I were her: all her bag pockets, the TV stand, the nightstand, even the sink. There wasn't a room safe, so it couldn't be there.

I wouldn't have noticed it at all if I hadn't kicked it on my next circuit of the room, hidden half-under the second bed. Maybe she'd tossed it in the bed's direction in a hurry and missed? Or knocked it to the ground as she left? It was unlike me. I wasn't the neatest person in the world, but I was careful with the important things.

I kept making assumptions she'd think like me, and they kept paying off. Still, I had to keep reminding myself we weren't the same person. We were and weren't. Our experiences had shaped us, the differences in our worlds. Something had convinced her to become a quantologist, but whatever had driven her would have had a different effect on me, in my quantology-free reality. Given all that, it didn't seem unreasonable we would have different opinions on where to leave your wallet in a hotel room.

The other option, obviously, was that somebody else had been in here. How hard would it be to flash the desk clerk an ID and say you'd lost your room key? Or even without ID, to rattle off one of the numbers the hotel had used to differentiate us? Whoever it was might even have still been in the room when I entered. That would explain the door shutting while I was poking around the bathroom. In which case, the question now wasn't only what could the room tell me, but what couldn't it tell me? I would never know if something was missing.

I opened the wallet. No cash, but that wasn't unexpected since we couldn't use it here. No driver's license, since that was in the body's pocket. Two credit cards, car insurance, Johns Hopkins ID, some store discount cards. The university ID could be important, if only a few Sarahs worked there.

The only thing personal—the only thing personal I'd noticed in the whole room, really, if you didn't count fashion—was a cropped photo tucked behind her health insurance card. I tapped it out, sucked in my breath. It was a picture of her—not me, I told myself—standing with my friends on a mountaintop at what I was fairly sure was the Grand Tetons. I had gotten somewhat used to the surreality of seeing my face on strangers, but there was something even odder about seeing a picture of myself, with my friends, in a place I'd never been. Mabel, my Mabel, with an arm wrapped tight around another Sarah's waist. All in someone else's wallet.

It was impossible to tell which details were piquing my interest because they were pertinent, and which were piquing my interest because they were me. What would it be like to be this Sarah? I remembered my own professors' homes, pictured myself coming and going from a majestic old house with a glassed-in sunroom. Did she live with alterna-Mabel? This Sarah lived in Baltimore, not Seattle; I couldn't imagine Mabel leaving Seattle.

If I stayed any longer I'd start trying on the dead Sarah's clothes, and I was pretty sure they wouldn't fit, mentally or physically. I left everything where I'd found it.

The Sarah in the room across the hall and I both closed the doors at the same time. I panicked for a second before realizing I was supposed to be there. Or at least I wasn't doing anything wrong.

She gave me a curious look. "Are you the detective?"

"Yeah. How did you know?" I looked her over. Another flowered dress, freckles, runner's build. Another short haircut. She'd either had her breasts reduced or run all the fat off her body. The body of somebody with a whole lot more determination than I had. One of the quantologists from the committee, I guessed.

"I'm in charge, and you're coming out of her room." She gave extra weight to the word "her." "The hotel manager said she'd called you in. Thank you for your help."

"You're in charge? In place of the, ah, host? The quantologist?"

"In place of? Everyone on our committee is a quantologist, but I'm the one you'd call the host. I'm the keynote speaker." She waved a sheaf of handwritten papers in my direction.

"Wait—is the speech still going on?"

"We moved it, obviously. It'll be in the dining hall. The dance is cancelled, out of respect." Her walkie-talkie squawked and fed back, loud enough to generate an echo. She dialed the volume down without looking at it. "And I rewrote my speech, of course."

"But we were looking for you—the manager thought you were the dead woman. Do you know who she is?" As I asked, I understood. "Oh, I had the wrong one. She's one of the others from your committee."

Her face crumpled for a second, like she was trying not to cry. She pulled herself together. Bit her lip until it turned as white as her teeth. "Yes. We hadn't known each other that long, obviously, but she was tremendously helpful. Working with her, well, it was like working with myself, if that doesn't sound too narcissistic. We were on the same page about everything. They said they'd given you a registration list? She's the one from R1D0, by our designation. I'm R0D0. I ID'ed her when the manager took me up to look a few minutes ago."

"It's not my fault you're identical," I said, a little angry with myself for not having considered the possibility. "I'm not even this kind of detective."

She patted my arm. My feeling of inadequacy blew over as soon as I said it, leaving her gesture as sincere commiseration, not condescension. Her smile was genuine, sympathetic. "I wouldn't have suggested getting you involved in all of this, but I wasn't there when the hotel manager panicked. I think she must have fallen off the stage and hit her head, but we'll bring in the authorities as soon as the weather lets up. No need for you to worry about it."

Everything I'd learned was still lurching and settling into new positions.

The clothing change made sense if it was a different person. Everything I knew about the one fit the other.

"How close are your worlds? I mean, do you know the divergence point? I don't think I'll get the science of it, but I get the divergence points concept."

"I'd love to talk more," she said, "but my speech is supposed to start in a few minutes."

"Do you mind if I walk with you? I have a couple more questions I wouldn't mind asking. Even if you think I don't need to investigate."

She shrugged and started walking. I followed. "Why didn't you answer your radio when they called for you?"

"I was in the shower. I must not have heard it."

"Do you know what she was doing in the nightclub?"

"No clue. Looking for me, maybe? Or adding something to the Hall of Fame display? A few people brought items they hadn't mentioned on the questionnaire."

We waited for the elevator. A couple more Sarahs joined us, giving the same curious once-over we were all giving each other. If they were staying in this tower, they were likely on the richer side of the spectrum. Both were dressed the way I'd dress if I could afford nicer clothes, but one had cut her hair shorter than I'd ever cut mine before, the back shaved, the top still curly. It looked good; I wished I had the guts. Neither wore glasses. Contacts or surgery or some fluke of genetics? I'd have asked if I wasn't more interested in the host.

I didn't want to question her much in front of strangers without knowing what had already been said to the general public. I searched for a more neutral topic. "Why did you choose this hotel?"

The elevator chimed and let us in. We stood silent while it descended; I used the time to study the others. Hair and clothes had been the easiest ways to catalogue differences at first, but I was starting to see that we fell into a few different basic phenotypes. The host and the other athletic Sarahs on one side of a spectrum that ranged lean to soft. Still no way to suss out anything beyond the superficial without asking.

Once the other Sarahs had walked away, the host answered my question as if there had been no gap. "Secord Island is a tiny dot in the Atlantic. I won't bother getting into the geopolitics, but it's independent in nine identified worlds. Three are home to private mansions, six to private resort hotels. In this one and only this one, one of us is manager, though she's one of the more distant iterations I identified, from a subset who went to university in Nova Scotia and then stayed in the east. This place was perfect. So inhospitably perfect we were able to guarantee to our sponsors and grantees that nobody would go AWOL. One weekend, in and out. No risk." She flashed a rueful smile.

"What do sponsors and grantees get from this?" Mabel had asked me, and I'd wondered ever since. I repeated Mabel's question.

"The usual name recognition, for those in worlds where they exist. And if it goes well—if it had gone well, I guess—the chance to explore doing it for other purposes: recreational, educational. There're a couple of travel companies, a couple of charitable foundations, a couple of think tanks. I'm hoping I'll still be able to convince them her death would have happened anywhere, nothing to do with the event."

I nodded. "One more thing. Is there a way for me to talk to your other committee members? You're the ones who would have known her best."

She looked for a second like she was going to say no, but then she lifted her walkie-talkie to her lips. After a brief back and forth, they agreed to meet me at registration after the keynote.

"Anything else?" she asked. "I still say there's no point in you investigating before the police get here, but if you think there is, I'll cede to your expertise."

I wasn't sure if that was a dig or not. She was probably right. I had no idea why I was still asking questions. Except I did like having something to do, and I was suspicious of anything dismissed too easily. If I were lying in a hotel fridge, I'd want someone asking questions for me.

A crowd bottlenecked at the dining hall entrance; I guess none of us liked arriving too early. We didn't like jostling either, so the result was a polite alternate-right-of-way situation that worked itself out pretty quickly. The room was still arranged in a constellation of eight person tables, but a microphone had been set up on one end of the room. I peeled off to find standing room beside the entrance, where I could watch the speech and the crowd at the same time.

The host walked to the microphone. She wore small heels with her dress. Heels always made me walk like a moose on a frozen lake, but she came across comfortable and confident. I couldn't help coveting her poise. She glanced at the clock above the door—for a moment I thought she was looking at me— and then started to speak without consulting her notes.

"Welcome, friends. First, I think by now many of you have heard we've had a death at the conference. One of my committee members, perhaps the person who worked most closely with me, Sarah Pinsker. It's so strange to say that name, my own name, the name that many of you call your own, in this context. We're still waiting for the authorities to arrive to tell us what happened. We're also working to inform her family, and to find the proper way to memorialize her. I'm sure she's in all our hearts.

"I say 'in all our hearts,' and I know it sounds cliché, but it's literally true. She is every one of us. So we can imagine what her loss will mean to her own world and her own family. At the same time, it's impossible to imagine. Even now, when I say her name, you picture yourself, not her. Not the things that made her distinct from you or me. In that way, we grieve her as friend and family, not a stranger, even those of us who didn't know her as an individual."

The door creaked, and I looked over to see the DJ slipping from the room. The speaker continued.

"You all took such pains to get here, it didn't feel right to cut the weekend short. I'm sure she would have wanted it to go on, because I know I would have wanted it to go on, after all our work. Tonight's dance is cancelled, out of respect. There'll be rooms available tonight and tomorrow for support groups if anyone needs to process in that setting. There will also be a Shabbat service in the chapel tomorrow morning at ten if anyone wants to say kaddish for her, led by Rabbi Sarah Pinsker. Stand up, Rabbi?"

A Sarah stood, raised a hand in solemn greeting, then sat again. The only rabbi, I thought. Was there a panel on our more unexpected career choices? I knew what had led me down my road, but not what had led her down hers.

"Without invalidating anyone's grief or confusion, I have to say that this death, tragic as it is, highlights the reason we're here: to learn from each other. I've got a panel tomorrow where I'll explain in more detail how this all works, but I think this is a fitting moment to explain the basics, to explain how we are all different and the same."

Her tone changed, as if she was now on more comfortable ground. "It's human nature to center ourselves in the narrative, but I encourage us all to consider the larger picture. I'm standing here before you not because I am the first, or the best, or the trunk of a branching tree. I'm here due to two things I can own: a discovery and a decision. I'm the one who figured out how to open a door; I'm the one who invited all of you to walk through it. Nothing more, nothing less.

"There are others among us who are as accomplished in their own fields, who could invite us through other doors, figuratively speaking. There are others among you who made ordinary decisions that nonetheless changed you significantly: leaving school, pursuing higher education, adopting children, or not. Even the smallest decisions, like kissing someone instead of waiting to be kissed."

I wondered how many of us thought of Mabel.

"I'm sorry I'm not feeling up to doing my whole intro to quantology speech, but I can leave you with one more thing to think about, something that may provide comfort on a night like tonight. Not only can I say nobody here is prime, I can also say all of us have always existed. It's hard to wrap your head around, but it's true. Those divergence points, where we discuss pets and girlfriends and boyfriends, wrong turns and big decisions? They work backward and forward. The moment a divergence point sparks, the new one has always existed too.

"I tried to invite Sarahs with some variety, to learn from each other, but Sarahs who are still recognizably us. This conference exists in infinite variations: some where I invited a different group of Sarahs, some where you chose a different dessert, where you sat next to someone else at dinner, some where my friend Sarah is still with us. They are no more or less valid for having diverged, no more or less real. You are all you, we are all we, constantly shaped by and shaping worlds."

It was a good line, delivered by a good speaker, meant to buoy everyone. What would it be like to be a good public speaker? To be a discoverer of worlds? We all clapped, both for her speech and her attempts to reconcile the moods of the occasion. That was why I clapped, anyway. I kept extrapolating outward from myself.

I spotted the older Sarah I'd had a drink with earlier, and went to stand beside her as the crowd started to file from the room. "In the bar a few hours ago, you pointed at someone and said she was the host. How did you know?"

She shook her head. "Sorry, that must have been somebody else. I haven't been to the bar. Sober ten years."

There was more than one older Sarah, or more than one who looked older than the rest of us. A good reminder not to make assumptions, even here.

Three Sarahs stood clustered around the registration desk, as promised. I didn't see the host, but I was pretty sure she was still behind me in the dining hall. I'd already spoken with her anyhow. So a committee of five, minus the host and the dead woman. They all wore silk; I guess they didn't sweat the dry cleaning bills.

They agreed to talk to me one at a time, in the lounge seating area between registration and the bar. The bar was starting to fill up again, but it wasn't yet too noisy for conversation. A knot of Sarahs with guitars gathered on the other bank of couches, but the odd timbral similarity of their voices made them easy to tune out. They'd found a way to eke joy out of the situation, and for a moment I envied them.

I'd have saved time by talking to them all together, though; their answers might as well have come from the same mouth.

Q: Where were you between four-thirty and six pm?

A: Registration, then the cocktail party, then up to take a nap and shower. I figured a shower would be worth being a little late for dinner.

Q: Were all of you at the cocktail party?

A: Yes! I think. At the beginning, anyway.

Q: Including the one who passed away?

A: Yes. I think. It's hard to say. We were mingling.

Q: When did you first realize something was wrong?

A: When the hotel manager came to find us, toward the end of dinner.

Q: Us?

A: The committee. She found all of us except—her.

They all gave the same weight to "her" that the host had upstairs.

Q: What did you do then?

A: Figured out which of us she was. Cried. Freaked a bit. Talked about what to do next.

Q: How did you figure out which of you she was?

A: Um, a roll call. I know that sounds silly, but I can't tell any of the other four apart without asking them questions or knowing what they're wearing. I had friends in seventh grade who were identical twins, and I never had a doubt which of them was which. This is different.

Q: Did anyone use the radios to contact any of you?

A: Not that I heard? I might have been in the shower.

Q: Is there anything else you know about her that might be helpful? Anybody who she was angry with? Anybody who was angry with her? Jealousies, rivalries?

A: There's no point in a cross-world rivalry. We were all a little jealous of R0D0, of course. She made the breakthrough we were all trying to make. But not R1D0.

Q: Do you know your divergence point from the others on your committee?

A: Eleven days before the big discovery, R0D0 and R1D0 made a mistake in an equation. The rest of us got it right. It was the mistake that was the key. The three of us differ in ways barely worth mentioning, all within a month of each other: a hospital visit, a sprained ankle on a run, a birthday party the rest of us skipped.

Q: What about R0D0 and R1D0, then? Where do they diverge? Would there be any reason for the host to be jealous of the deceased?

A: If anything it would be the other way around. They diverged an hour before the discovery. R1D0 went out for an anniversary dinner with her girlfriend; R0D0 cancelled dinner and stayed in the lab. If I were R1D0, I'd have carried a little resentment over that, but if she did, she never showed it. Anyway, someone said it was an accident, right? Is there any chance it was anything else?

"She hasn't been examined," I said. "She's got one hell of a knock to her head."

I left it deliberately vague, to see if any of them gave anything away. They all gave me the same look, stressed and relieved, hopeful and guilty about that hope. I found myself wishing all of my insurance interviews were with Sarahs. My job would be much easier if I recognized every expression on everyone's face.

I was desperate for something to break one of them from the pack, but nothing came. Even their divergence points were mundane. They were the same person. I thanked them for their help and let them go. They had all looked genuinely upset. I had believed all of them, and the identical answers were as good as corroboration. They were all willing to help, but convinced it was an accident. They couldn't figure out why I was still asking questions when the answer seemed obvious.

In their shoes, I'd be desperate to believe it was an accident too. Better than thinking somebody might have it in for me. If I were one of them, I'd be terrified and trying to hide it. I'd be looking around every corner for a killer, trying to live up my last moments, to settle accounts, just in case; except we were all trapped for the weekend, unable to contact anyone we loved or go anywhere.

I was one of them. Without the science background, without the urge to be the first or the best or whatever it was driving them. Which was an interesting line of questioning I hadn't followed at all: what was driving them? Why were they so ambitious, when the rest of us weren't? What had made them go into quantology? Could any of them still make the same discovery, for their world, or had the host Sarah spoiled it for everyone? I looked over to see if they were still standing by registration, but they had all gone.

The bar was half full, and when I slid onto the nearest empty stool, the bartender handed me a tumbler of bourbon, neat, without my needing to ask. The guesswork was gone from his job: there was a plastic cup over the handle for the stout. I hoped he had another keg somewhere that he hadn't had time to tap yet. Down the row, six other Sarahs sipped from identical glasses.

"Cheers," said the Sarah next to me, holding up her drink. She was wearing a *Wonder Woman* T-shirt too, an Alex Ross illustration, deflecting bullets. She looked exhausted, like she'd spent the evening deflecting bullets herself. "It's hitting you too, huh?"

"Hitting me?"

"The difference question. You've noticed a thing about yourself, or a thing about someone else here that isn't true of yourself. You can't quite tell if you should feel bad about it, if it's a flaw in you, if there's something you did wrong along the way. You thought one more drink might let you fall asleep without it keeping you up all night."

We clinked glasses.

I wandered back to my room still mulling it over. Wind whipped down the chilly hallway, but I saw only one figure silhouetted against the open door, with her mass of flaming curls.

"Where's your friend?" I asked, leaning out. A gust hit me hard enough to knock me off balance; in its wake, the air was heavy with the promise of rain. The smoker whirled to face me when I spoke. "Sorry if I scared you. I was the one who chatted with the two of you out here earlier, in case you can't tell."

She shrugged. "Haven't seen her. I heard she found the body. Maybe she needs some alone time. I know I would. Drink?"

She held a flask out to me, and I took it with a nod of thanks. Bourbon. Cheaper than the stuff the bartender had served, but still decent. Another gust of wind tore the top of a dumpster off its hinges and sent it tumbling over the loading dock wall. We both watched it cartwheel away.

"New question for tomorrow," she said, taking her flask back. "You get to test it first. What are you most afraid of?"

My answer was instant. "Everything. Earthquakes. Bombs. Random violence. Falling tree branches. Losing people I love. Cancer. Being in the wrong place at the wrong time. This storm. Missing out on something because I didn't want to make a fool of myself. Missing out on something because I'm afraid. I try not to let it control me—my job helps desensitize me a little—but ... yeah. Long answer to a short question. You?"

She took a long drag on her cigarette. "I'd have stopped at 'Everything,' but, yeah, same basic theme. Pretty amazing that we're all here despite being chicken. Afraid to ride bicycles but willing to step out of our own reality completely for a weekend."

"Maybe it falls under 'Afraid of missing out on something because I'm afraid?' We all push ourselves in the same ways?"

"Maybe. I guess I'll see what everyone else answers tomorrow. You know what you didn't list, in that long list of things you were afraid of?"

"What?" I replayed my answer in my head to figure what I might have missed.

"Dying alone, far from the people you love, surrounded by strangers who wear your face and mirror your thoughts. I would think that would make your list, since it makes mine."

I considered. "The first part, maybe. I'm starting to get used to the second part. And I'm still more afraid of the storm than the other Sarahs."

Lightning cracked the sky open to punctuate my sentence, close enough to make the hairs on my arms stand on end.

"Bam. Divergence point," she said, with less enthusiasm than her smoking buddy had earlier. "I'm getting a distinctly bad vibe from all this. Do you have Agatha Christie in your world? Isolated island, bad weather. I'm still waiting for us all to be picked off one by one."

"And yet you were standing out here all alone. So either you're not as scared as you say, or ... " As I said it, I wished I hadn't. If I was joking, it wasn't funny. If I was implying she was a suspect, well, everyone was except me, since I knew I hadn't done it. That didn't make it a smart move to address the subject directly.

" . . . or I'm the killer, in which case you're the one in trouble, not me." She gave me a look that told me she agreed my comment had been in poor taste, and held out the flask, daring me to take it. "I'm not a killer. I can't prove it, of course, but I know I'm not. Which makes me pretty sure none of us are, because I can't imagine the circumstance that would bring me to kill someone."

"I can't imagine killing someone, but I also can't imagine the circumstance that would have turned me into a smoker." I swigged whiskey. "Or a hotel manager, or a quantologist, or a DJ."

She took one more drag, then dropped the butt and crushed it with her boot. "It's the storm and the island that made me say the Christie thing. I'm way more nervous about this storm than being killed by a serial Sarah, at least while there's still only one body. Hopefully I won't have cause to revise that. In the meantime, there's facing fear and there's being stupid. We should probably go inside before we get hit by lightning."

As if in response, the sky opened up. We were both drenched in the two feet to the doorway.

"If the lights go out, start counting Sarahs," Orange Curls said before squelching off down the hall.

Back in my room, I stripped my wet clothes off and replaced them with another T-shirt and boxer shorts. The whiskey didn't do the job I'd hoped it would, so I spent the night in imaginary conversation with Mabel. The rain battering the window filled in her side of the dialogue. I walked through the order of events, everything I'd found. I had ideas, but they weren't cohering. The timing was important, I knew that. Murder weapon would be lovely, but I didn't expect a forensic report any time soon. As for suspects, for all the people giving me alibis and vouching for themselves and each other, it could still have been anybody.

I drifted away from the case itself. The host said she wasn't the Prime, wasn't the trunk of a branching tree, but she'd labeled us all in relation to her. We were all in close proximity. Even the most distant of us were still recognizable. Tiny differences. I hadn't run into anyone who lived in a post-water shortage America, or post-flu, or post-oil. We all knew how to flush toilets.

What would it look like if we had radiated out from me instead of the host? Or if we had all radiated out from the hotel clerk, whom the quantologist had said was one of the farther iterations? There were other realities between these, ones she hadn't chosen. N Sarahs, in N realities, where N was unknowable and constantly changing. Why had she chosen us and not others? Was I the most interesting of a string of insurance investigators, or the only one available this weekend? I had more questions than I'd had before I arrived.

Why did I go into detective work, not one of the sciences? I hated my calculus teacher, dropped it after a few weeks; because of him, I didn't get far enough in math to pursue a college major in bio or physics. Maybe he didn't exist in the other worlds, or maybe the science Sarahs hadn't let him get the better of them. Maybe they pushed themselves to spite him. Some went on to become geneticists or researchers or science fiction writers. Same mind, applied differently. Choices, chances, undecisions, non-decisions, decisions good and bad.

Maybe I shouldn't have come. Maybe one of me was sitting at home with Mabel right at this very moment, another me, another Mabel, another reality where my curiosity hadn't won out. But if I'd stayed home, who would be asking questions for the Sarah in the fridge? If nothing else, I was good for that. Even if I hadn't yet found any answers.

It was still raining when I woke. The thin carpet felt vaguely damp, like the weather had come up through the foundation. My head hurt. I had a vague sense that I had unlocked something in my sleep and forgotten it again.

I took a quick shower, hoping it might clear my head. No luck.

Breakfast was served buffet-style, which was good since I was ravenous after only eating a roll the night before. I built a tower of eggs, potatoes, and toast, a second tower of fruit, and deposited both plates on the nearest empty table. When I came back from the tea station, the table was full.

"How are you enjoying the weekend?" asked the Sarah next to me. I didn't think I'd met her before. "Other than . . . You know."

"I haven't had much time to do anything," I said between mouthfuls. "Duty called. Well, not a duty I expected to have, but I'm trying to figure it out."

"Oh, were you the one who got pulled away from the table last night? It would be a shame if you didn't get to go to anything." That was Dare; I remembered him from dinner, with his copper and silver beard and mustache. His talk on gender was one I'd circled when I thought I'd get to actually attend programming. "It's not like we'll have this chance again."

"You don't think so?" another asked.

Dare shook his head. "No. Somebody died. That's not exactly an encouragement to the backers to bring us back for a sequel. Even if it was an accident, the logistics of explaining her death on the other side of the portal will be a nightmare."

"Infinite variations," said another Sarah. "Maybe next year we'll get invitations from an iteration where she didn't die."

That made my head hurt. "I think I need to get back to work after I leave breakfast. I still need to interview the hotel staff, and anyone who talked to her yesterday afternoon . . . "

My neighbor speared a chunk of pineapple and waved it at me. "Stay. One talk won't hurt you. We've got a big-group discussion on 'Horses and Dogs and Cats, Oh My' in this room right after breakfast. All you have to do is not stand up."

Her argument on its own might not have been persuasive, but inertia won out. Inertia and jealousy and a bad feeling I shouldn't have eaten as much as I did and I might still be sick if I moved very quickly. Besides, everyone else had already had a chance to get to know each other a bit, and all I'd talked about was one unfortunate dead person whose death I wasn't even supposed to be investigating anymore. I lingered as the mics were set up and the buffet tables cleared.

The setup was loosely structured, with a leader and a few planned speakers to kick things off. The first storyteller sat to speak. She was trim, polo shirt tucked into worn jeans. She looked like she'd spent time in the sun.

"When I was a teenager, I spent my summers working at a trail riding stable in upstate New York." Several Sarahs snapped their fingers. I realized a system had developed while I was snooping around. Snap to say that had been your experience too. Too late for me to snap with them, but so far this story was mine as well.

"I had a favorite horse, Smokey. An Appaloosa." I snapped along. She didn't bother describing his color, like a white horse that had rolled in dirt, or his dustbroom mane and tail. I had loved him even though he was ugly as anything.

"One afternoon, a man drove up with a little girl, maybe five or six years old. My boss put the little girl on Flicker. Flicker wasn't the first choice for someone that small, but the kid-friendly horses were both out with another guide. There wasn't even a children's-sized saddle left, so we had to run the stirrups all the way up to the top hole and then flip them over. Even then, she had to stretch her toes to reach."

We all snapped quietly. We knew this story.

"I took them on the usual circuit: through the woods, circling the pond and the far field, back into the woods, then looping out to the dirt road. The road was the problem. We sometimes raced the horses home that way when we were goofing around. It was a dumb thing to do, teaching the horses to rile themselves up and anticipate the run back to the barn, but all the teenagers working there had been doing it for as long as anyone could remember.

"I spent the whole hour thinking about ways to avoid trouble. I decided to take them back through the field so they wouldn't race, but we still had to cross the road. Smokey jigged a bit as we crossed, but listened to me. It was

Flicker who bolted toward home. She probably didn't even realize there was someone on her back, the kid was so small.

"Make your horse WALK," I remembered shouting to the father before I took off after his child. "Don't let him race us."

It wasn't hard to catch up with Flicker: Smokey was much faster. The problem was stopping a running horse from the back of another running horse. I couldn't think of a safe way to do it. If I tried to grab Flicker's reins, I'd pull her head to the side, and her body would bow away from me, and the kid would be thrown.

Even after a summer of tossing hay bales, I knew I wasn't strong enough to pull her onto my horse. The only thing I could do was reach over and steady the girl, who was clinging like a burr to the saddle. I kept picturing her little body slipping off onto the hard-packed dirt, or the barbed-wire fence that ran parallel. All I could do was hold her where she was.

I held the girl up there until the horses reached the top of the road and stopped, just like that, race over. Flicker dropped her head to graze. The father came up the road just behind us, grabbed his daughter, called me a hero. When we got back to the barn, he explained to my boss as if I had saved his kid from a freak occurrence. I would have said I minimized the damage in a totally avoidable near-catastrophe.

At summer's end, my boss offered to let me take Smokey home for the off season, as thanks. I wanted to say yes so badly, but I knew it was impractical. I did the research, visited a dozen barns, worked out the expenses, and finally called the barn, weeping, to say I couldn't afford to take him. The next summer when I went back to work, he wasn't there. I couldn't bear to ask where he'd been sold, since I knew I'd blown my chance at any claim on him.

"In the end, I found a way to make it work to bring him home with me," the storyteller said, going off the script as written in my head. I had forgotten she was still talking. Up until she changed the story, she'd sounded just like my own interior monologue. "I found a barn that let me give lessons on him to cover board. I saved enough to buy him the next spring. He was my extracurricular, my only extracurricular, the joy my whole life revolved around. When I decided to go to community college for large animal management instead of going to university, it was for him. From talking with all of you, I'm pretty sure this was a major divergence point, so I thought I'd tell you I had him until he died of old age at thirty-two."

I wiped a tear from my eye. The sniffles around me suggested others were doing the same. One was openly weeping, another holding her. "It wasn't your fault," the second one said, loud enough for me to hear. "You couldn't have saved her. We couldn't all save her."

Something nagged at me. She had left out a few things, to the point where

I didn't know if they had only happened to me. My boss had sat me down after the father and daughter had driven away. We spent an hour going over what had happened, with him suggesting different phrasings, different ways of thinking. "If anyone asks, you don't need to mention that Flicker isn't normally a kid horse, right? Or that the stirrups were too long?"

That was the seed of my investigative career: the hour where we sat at the picnic bench and massaged the truth into something litigation-proof. I was exhausted, drained of adrenaline, at once sickened and fascinated at the way the story changed before my eyes. I understood the need for the lie, understood that he'd lose the business if he was successfully sued, went along with it. At the same time, his casual erasure of the truth horrified me.

All these other Sarahs had either missed that moment or internalized it in some other way. Was the rabbi here? Maybe this was the incident that started her search for meaning. Maybe the quantologists had launched their careers looking for a way to do that day over again.

Part of me wanted more than anything to trade places with this barn manager. To have had sixteen years with a horse I loved, to have made a decision based on gut instead of practicality. I knew that ship had sailed, but I still wanted it. That one change had defined her life. She was happy. I was happy too. I'd left that incident alone as a disappointment but not a defining one, or maybe a defining point but one that had shaped me without tearing me down. The weeping Sarah might argue otherwise. Divergence points. Divergence points were the key to everything.

"I'm sorry," I whispered to the woman who was still crying over the little girl, as I got up to leave.

The hotel manager was standing in the lobby talking to a couple of her employees when I passed. I debated telling her where I was going, decided against it. Probably stupid, I reflected without slowing, as I walked down the mildewed-smelling hall to knock on a murderer's door. I heard footsteps inside, and the door swung wide; she opened it without checking who was on the other side.

"I know." I didn't need to say more. She'd believe me.

I pictured her hitting me over the head, running down the hall and out into the storm. That was the movie scenario, the dramatic culmination: the two of us wrestling on some wind-wracked cliff. Why wasn't I afraid of that? I knew she had considered it and rejected it in the same moment. That wasn't the kind of person we were. I was pretty sure of that, though not as sure as before I figured out what had happened.

She let me in. She was still wearing the No Good Deeds T-shirt, which looked even more rumpled than before. When she turned away there were sweat stains under the arms and all down the back, like she'd been exercising.

"I was going to take a quick shower," she said. "Do you mind? You can look around."

I nodded, let her go. She didn't bother to close the bathroom door, or left it open out of courtesy to show me she wasn't plotting anything.

I poked through the DJ's stuff, scattered on the second bed. An ancient laptop, an ancient MP3 player, decent looking headphones. More pills. A twist-tied baggie with a brown lump in it, another baggie of what looked like ground coffee. A few T-shirts, one pair of ragged jeans.

She emerged from the bathroom in a towel, the picture of good health.

"Do you mind?" she asked, and I moved aside for her to take a pair of underwear off the pile. She poked her finger through a hole in a seam. "I didn't think about this part. How I'd have to wear someone else's used underwear."

"Was it worth it?"

She cocked her head, gave me a sad, unstained smile. "That's kind of up to you, I think."

I hadn't considered it that way, but as she said it I knew what she meant. If I told the authorities—whatever that meant in this context—the real DJ would still be upstairs in the fridge wearing someone else's clothes. It would all have been for nothing.

"Why?" I asked. "Why her, specifically? What's the divergence point?"

"There are a hundred thousand divergences between her and me. She wasted herself, wasted her life. She was a decent DJ, but she was otherwise a total fuck-up. Tried a hundred times to get clean. It never stuck."

"She was nice to me," I said, thinking about our brief interaction, her jittery enthusiasm. "Seemed pretty cool."

She pulled on the jeans from the bed. They fit, but not as well as the designer pair she'd worn the day before. "I researched her for a while. Trust me. She may have been nice, but she was a four alarm fire. Smoked everything in her life other than music."

"But just because she was a mess doesn't mean she deserved to die. I mean, you've still got a lot going in your life, right? You invented cross-dimensional travel. Why would you want to take on her life if you think it's so shitty?"

She reached into the backpack on the bed and withdrew the DJ's wallet. Pulled out the ID and tossed it in my direction.

Oh. "Seattle's gone in your world." It wasn't a question.

She nodded, tears in her eyes. "Not only Seattle. Everyone. I lived in a house with five of my closest friends during grad school. I was visiting our parents back east when it happened, but everyone else was in the house when the earthquake hit. I was on the phone with Kelly when it happened—they were all watching *Labyrinth*—and I heard the whole thing. It took ten days to dig them out. Too late, of course. They all still exist where the DJ's from,

and she sits in her shitty apartment pretending they're not out there. Ignoring their calls when they try to check in on her. Estranged from our parents and sisters. She never even met Mabel. There are a million Sarahs I could have chosen and wouldn't have because they still had people."

"But you still have other people," I said. "What about them?"

"My lab staff might miss me, but that's about it. Mabel left me the night I made my big discovery, when I skipped out on our anniversary dinner because I was on the verge; I got home to tell her and she was gone. Our family would have felt terrible, of course, and I felt terrible about leaving them. But they would have been comforted by the way I lived and died, I think. Knowing I did everything I had set out to accomplish. It was a good life. They knew I loved them."

"A good life you're willing to leave behind?" I was still trying to imagine that. "You'll trade tenure and fame and everything for whatever she's got left?"

"That stuff is good for my ego, but it doesn't matter. Not like having a home. Not like people. I'll trade it all in a second for a world where everyone and everyplace I love still exists. Where I could find her world's Mabel—they never even met!—and see everyone else again."

"Even if they hate you?"

She didn't hesitate. "Yes. Relationships can be repaired. Even if they hate me, I know they're still out there hating me."

"And that was worth bashing her head in?"

I watched her face carefully. I could imagine the horror I'd feel if I'd lost everyone in such a terrible way, and the guilt of knowing I'd have been there with them if I hadn't been out of town, and even sitting on one side of that haunting phone call, but I still didn't think it would drive me to murder.

"She didn't feel it. Dropped like a stone. She doesn't even own a bra," she said, rummaging in the bag. "I haven't gone out without a bra since I was twelve years old."

"You did last night. I saw you in the back at the keynote." I watched her pull a T-shirt over her head for a band I didn't recognize. "Why did that other quantologist take your place? The real R1D0?"

She sighed. "If I say we're exactly the same, I mean we are exactly the same. Literally the only difference in our lives is that the night I actually made the discovery, she went out for an anniversary dinner with Mabel, and I cancelled dinner and stayed in the lab. That's our divergence point. She's pissed she didn't stay in the lab that night. She wants the glory. She's let that supersede everything else, thinks she'd be happy if only she were in my shoes. That's all. I mean, I'd be pissed too, but I don't think she's seeing clearly. She's still with Mabel. That matters way more than a name on a paper, even one this huge."

"Her decision must have been spur of the moment," I said. "I think she

heard the call you made, and switched clothes with the body when she realized she was the first one there. I'm not sure why she took both radios, but maybe that was panic. I heard the second one inside her room when I was standing in the hall with her. Anyway, I saw her speak last night. She could be you perfectly."

"She is me. Nobody will know the difference. She can have them. Now I don't have to feel guilty about leaving my family, even; it's her world that'll have to deal with her absence. Anyway, she might have been headed up to the club to do exactly the same thing I did."

I shuddered to think that was true, and how many murderous Sarahs actually existed in that case. "Was that your whole motivation for going into quantology? To switch places?"

"No! We were already in a physics masters program, so finishing that degree and going into quantology wasn't a stretch. We wanted to know if there really were realities where Seattle still existed. Where Kelly and Taylor and Allison and Scott and Andrea were still alive. Not to go there, just to know.

I didn't know who Andrea was, but Kelly and Taylor were my best friends other than Mabel, and we'd all lived in Scott and Allison's house in Capitol Hill when I first moved to Seattle. I couldn't imagine the guilt of living in a world where they had all died and I had been spared by some quirk of timing. And Mabel had broken up with her on top of that. She'd lost all of them. Even hearing her say it, it hit my gut as if I'd lost them myself.

"So you weren't always going to kill someone?" I was still having trouble imagining this ambitious Sarah ditching everything she had to become a DJ, but it didn't seem as far-fetched anymore. Something else bothered me too. I believed everything else she'd said, but I still couldn't picture myself bashing in somebody's head, or taking the time to position her beneath the stage in the hopes of making it look like an accident. Every step screamed intention.

She ran her hands over her short hair, smoothing the flyaways. "I only decided for certain when she came back with her second crate. She must've gotten herself messed up in between; she could barely answer my questions when I tried to talk to her. Anyway, I'm sure there are other realities spawned at that moment where I decided not to."

She believed what she was saying, I could tell, but I didn't. I was certain she'd waited up there, taken the time to pick the perfect weapon from the show and tell table. She might even have picked in advance, when the questionnaires had come in, researching the offerings until she found the award that she could turn into a weapon; that would explain why the Hall of Fame was in the nightclub instead of someplace people could browse it throughout the weekend. It was disorienting, to hear her lying to herself and

recognize it for what it was. I wasn't her, I reminded myself again. We'd made different choices to bring ourselves to this point.

"And in case you're wondering, I wouldn't have killed you for your Seattle, either. You haven't squandered it. Most haven't. Anyway, when I started my research I thought I would be happy if I just proved that they were out there somewhere, in some other reality. That's why we all got into quantology, to prove there were other possibilities, not to change places. And that felt like enough until I started researching all of you to figure out who to invite. Until I found her—" she pointed at herself "—and realized there was a way to make it happen. If I didn't try, I'd always wonder about it. You'd do the same thing, right?"

I didn't answer. I didn't think so. I hoped not.

She kept talking. "When I reached out to the other quantologists, I picked ones who had diverged before I had that idea. Or so I thought, anyway. Maybe I was wrong about that, at least in the case of R1D0. I didn't think about the ways they'd diverge because of the influence of my inviting them to help plan this. That was short-sighted. Do you think the others know I switched?"

"I don't think so." None of them had mentioned it to me. If they didn't know, that meant they hadn't thought of it; if they hadn't thought of it, that left only one or two capable of murder.

"Yeah, I hope not. I want to think I'm the worst of us, other than her." She stood before me, wearing the clothes of the DJ I'd met the day before, wearing her life. "So what are you going to do? Are you going to tell them? Turn me in?"

"Did you ever chase down a runaway horse?"

She looked confused, then nodded.

I thought about divergence points. I'd never felt I could have done anything else in that moment on the road, which was a good thing. Even the tiniest choices paralyzed me; I tried to play out every decision's every repercussion. Better not to have time to think.

Up until I came here, I'd tried to tell myself that once I made a choice it was done, I had to own it. We all built the future with our choices every day, never knowing which ones mattered. Now I still had to own it, but I knew others were stuck living the other side of my decisions, or I was living theirs. I wasn't even sure yet if that was paralyzing or freeing. If I let her go, if she was anything like me, guilt might wear her down to nothing. That was a punishment in itself. If I turned her in, would it be justice for the DJ, or merely proof I could solve a crime?

"If you turn me in," she said, as if I had spoken out loud, "there's going to be a whole lot of confusion in a whole lot of places. I have no idea how any authority will deal with it. There'll be a dead body in one world, an accused killer in another. If you let me go, think of all the good I can do. I can repair her relationships with our friends and family. I can find her world's Mabel. This Sarah was never going to pull out of her spin, I swear. She would be dead tomorrow or next week or next month. And she'll still be dead tomorrow. I could do some good there in her world."

Somewhere out there, iterations were sparking. Variations on the host, deciding and not deciding to go through with her plan. Killing the DJ, changing her mind and walking away. More iterations yet: the second quantologist, making and unmaking her split-second decision to leave her life and slip into one that was identical in all ways but a crucial one. Somewhere, another me turned in the second but not the first, the first but not the second. Both. Neither.

Some other place, the DJ had never died. She put another record on her turntable, slowed the beat to match the song already playing, shifted seamlessly from one into the other. Some other place, a hotel nightclub full of Sarahs danced awkwardly to their favorite music, shaped by their worlds, shaping new ones.

PUBLICATION HISTORY